HANDLING SIN

HANDLING SIN

A NOVEL

by *Michael Malone*

LITTLE, BROWN AND COMPANY

BOSTON   TORONTO

FIRST EDITION

Excerpt from "I Can't Give You Anything But Love" used with
permission of Belwin-Mills Publishing Corporation, Aldi Music Company
and Ireneadele Music Publishing Company. Copyright © 1928 by Mills
Music, Inc. Copyright renewed. All Rights Reserved.

Library of Congress Cataloging-in-Publication Data

Malone, Michael.
    Handling sin.

    I. Title.
PS3563.A43244H3   1986   813'.54   85-24041
ISBN 0-316-54455-8

BP

Published simultaneously in Canada
by Little, Brown & Company (Canada) Limited

PRINTED IN THE UNITED STATES OF AMERICA

For my father
Thank you for the gift

This book is cald Handlyng Synne. It contains Tales and Marvels.

> Handyl hem at onys euerychone
> Noght one by hym self alone
> Handyl so to ryse from alle,
> That none make the eft falle
> With shryfte of mouthe, & wyl of herte,
> And a party, with penaunce smerte;
> Thys ys a skyl that hyt may be tolde
> Handlyng synne many a folde.

> Robert of Brunne, 1303

Contents

THE RETURN

Acknowledgments

I'D LIKE TO THANK some friends who made *Handling Sin* easier.

I'm grateful to Roger Donald at Little, Brown for his faith, for his insight, and for the pleasure of his charming company.

It was warm and heartening to feel Phil Pochoda's trust in the beginning and his exuberance at the end of this long trip.

It was a comfort to rely on my agent Peter Matson's decency and daring. It was important to have Malcolm Cowley's postscripts always grousing at me, "Keep writing, keep writing." It was a blessing to be able to borrow Marilyn French's quiet house in the country for a few weeks and to feel free to burn up her woodpile. It was a delight to know that Twentieth Century–Fox wants to put Raleigh and Mingo in the movies, and for that I thank Sara Colleton, Scott Rudin, and Larry Gordon.

Handling Sin took considerably longer than I foolishly figured. I appreciate everybody's patience. My thanks to them all — in particular, Peter Schifter. And as always, for everything, thank you, Maureen and Meg.

The character Victoria Anna Hayes first appeared in "Get Up and Go," *Southern Humanities Review*, Vol. XVI, Spring 1982. The character Flonnie Rogers first appeared in *Viva*. I'm indebted to John G. Barrett's *Sherman's*

March Through the Carolinas (Chapel Hill: University of North Carolina, 1956, 1983) for the Civil War song.

There are three people without whose friendship, nudges, winks, and wise teaching, I never could have written *Handling Sin*. They are Miguel Cervantes, Henry Fielding, and Charles Dickens. I owe them more than I can say, and a lot of what I've said.

Prologue

THERE LIVED IN THE PIEDMONT of North Carolina a decent citizen and responsible family man named Raleigh Whittier Hayes, who obeyed the law and tried to do the right thing. He had a wife and two daughters, and he owned his own house, his own business, two oceanfront rental properties, two automobiles, his own retirement plan, and a large number of Treasury bonds. Thus was he well established in the middle class. Also he took care to be a member of the Civitans, the Chamber of Commerce, the Baptist Church, the Neighborhood Association, and the United Fund. Everyone who knew him called him reliable Raleigh, hardworking Raleigh, fair-and-square Raleigh, and, in general, respectable, smart, steady, honest, punctual, decent Raleigh Hayes.

The day came when the members of the court of Heaven took their places in the presence of the Lord.

THE CALL

ONE STOP CONSTRUCTION CORP.

2090 - 7TH AVE.
NEW YORK, NY 10027
(212) 662-5101

CHAPTER

1

In Which the Hero Is Introduced and Receives a Blow

ON THE IDES OF MARCH, in his forty-fifth year, the neutral if not cooperative world turned on Mr. Raleigh W. Hayes as sharply as if it had stabbed
him with a knife. Like Caesar, Mr. Hayes was surprised by the blow, and
responded sarcastically. Within a week his eyes were saying narrowly to
everything they saw, *Et tu, Brute?* The world looked right back at the life
insurance salesman; either blinked or winked, and spun backward on an
antipodean whim, flinging him off with a shrug. This outrage happened
first in his little hometown, which was Thermopylae, North Carolina, and,
soon thereafter, all over the South, where Mr. Hayes was forced to wander
to save his inheritance from a father who'd, again, run ostentatiously berserk.

Of course, there were warnings. Like Caesar, Hayes ignored them. A lunatic had gotten into the fortune cookies at the Lotus House, the only
Oriental restaurant in town. Suddenly, along with their checks, patrons
began receiving, coiled like paper snakes, harsh predictions or dreadful instructions: "You will die of cancer." "Someone close will betray you."
"Sell all your stocks at once!" Either the manufacturer had unwittingly
hired a sadistic sloganeer, or here in the Lotus House kitchen the Shionos
themselves (ingrates despite decades of Thermopylae's hospitality) were
tweezering out the old bland fortunes and slipping inside the cookies these

warped prognostications. The Japanese restaurateurs were already suspected of holding a grudge about the war, of catching stray cats and serving them to unknowledgeable palates as Cantonese chicken, of meaning
by "C. Chow Mein" on their menus, "Cat."

The Thermopylae Civitans met at the Lotus House anyhow, because it
served liquor without resembling a bar, and the Civitans didn't think of
themselves as the sort of people who would eat lunch in a bar. As Raleigh
Hayes did not drink, and as he found disturbing the mingling of foods
customary in Oriental cuisine — so many vegetables, meats, and noodles
heaped communally together violated his sense of privacy — he never
would have eaten a meal in the Lotus House had he not been a member of
the Civitans Fund Drive Committee. Had he not reached for a fortune
cookie to give his hand something to do other than twitch to choke to
death the committee chairman for wasting his time, Hayes never would
have pulled from the shell of stale pastry the strip of fortune that read,
"You will go completely to pieces by the end of the month." Obviously,
nothing could be more preposterous. Mr. Hayes knew himself to be an ir-
revocably sane man; nor was this conclusion reached in a vacuum: He had
a great many blood relations who were not in one piece, and he could see
the difference. Folding the nonsensical strip, he put it absentmindedly in
his pocket.

Next to Hayes, less imperturbable, fat Mingo Sheffield curled up his
paper fortune and set it on fire with his cigarette without telling the other
Civitans what it said. It said, "Your spouse is having an affair with your
best friend. Solly."

"Who's suh . . . Solly?" asked Sheffield as nonchalantly as he could.

Nemours Kettell, the chairman and a veteran, took it on himself to explain. "It's Jap for sorry." He picked at a sharp fragment of cookie stuck in
his receding gums, a public display of his mouth that irritated Hayes, who
also disliked Kettell for abbreviating words, although he'd never been able
to decide why this verbal habit so incensed him. Kettell shook his own
fortune. "Somebody's pulling our you-knows here. You may think it's
funny, Wayne." Wayne Sparks was Kettell's son-in-law across the table,
now giggling because he'd just read his slip, "See a doctor. You have the
clap," and he was thinking about making a joke in mimicry of his wife's
father, by saying "clap" was Oriental for "crap." On the other hand, it was
quite possible he did have a venereal disease, so he rolled the paper into a
spitball and stuck it under his plate like gum. Kettell was still nodding.
"But I don't happen to think there's a lot to ha-ha about when I see this
kind of anti-American blasphemy." He passed his fortune around the

table. It said, "Jesus is a bag lady. He saves trash." Nobody thought it was funny but Wayne.

Nemours Kettell now banged his fork on the cymbal-shaped cover over the last of the pepper steak. "I want some info on this cookie business. This could be like pins in the Snickers bars, remember that? I hate to believe the way the world's turning to dirt, poisoning aspirins and shooting at the President over some girl you never even met."

"What the hell did we drop the bomb for, really, you know, if we have to put up with this kind of Jap backtalk?" threw in Wayne facetiously. A neo-hippie who'd had the bad luck not to be born until 1962, he was in line to inherit Kettell Concrete Company, and liked to take these risks with his future.

Raleigh Hayes kept calm by polishing his unused knife with his napkin while Kettell rapped on the dish cover until finally the tiny Shiono grandmother looked up from her Japanese newspaper. Like a pigeon through snow, she shuffled across the empty room of white tablecloths toward them. When the Civitans waved their fortunes at her, she bowed with a smile; when they pointed at the messages, she smiled and pointed at her newspaper.

"Doesn't speak the lingo," suggested Kettell's son-in-law.

Mrs. Shiono smiled. "Check? Quit it, Claude."

"Credit card," Kettell translated. "Look here, Miz Showno, you want our business, you won't ask us to come in here and read this kind of garbage." He snapped a cookie in two; nothing was in it.

"Oh, for God's sake," said Hayes who had two prospective clients to see on the way back to his office. But not until Nemours Kettell was satisfied personally by the Shiono grandson, Butch, that they would complain to their fortune-cookie supplier in Newport News, would he let the Civitans adjourn. They had already voted to host a fish fry in June and donate the proceeds to diabetes research. That's what they'd voted to do for the last ten years. Kettell's wife had diabetes. So did most of Raleigh Hayes's relatives; if it weren't for his sensible diet, no doubt he'd have it himself.

Outside their restaurant, the Shionos had grown a dogwood tree in a box on the sidewalk. Raleigh Hayes, preoccupied, started to snap off a blossom. He was stopped by a sweat coming all the way back from Sunday school, where he'd been taught it was against the law to mutilate a dogwood because Christ had died on a dogwood cross and the rust on the petal tips was His blood. The flower dangled bent, and Hayes propped it up on a neighboring branch. "Back to work, Mingo," he told his next-door neighbor.

"What for?" Mingo Sheffield sighed at Thermopylae, the rolls of his neck billowing out above his yellow short-sleeved button-down shirt. "I tell you what. Downtown is starting to look like that old movie, *On the Beach*. Did you see it on TV last night? The whole world was dead from fallout, not a soul on the streets. They thought somebody survived, but it was just a Coca-Cola bottle."

"Gas has dropped," said Hayes. "That's why."

"Just a Coca-Cola bottle clinking on a telegraph key."

"Everybody's back on the beltway headed for the mall again."

Sheffield looked forlornly across Bath Street at the stone facade of Knox-Bury's Clothing Store, whose menswear manager he was. "They're sure not here," he said.

"How's Vera doing?" asked Hayes by way of initiating his departure.

Pouches of flesh slid up over Mingo's eyes as he recalled the fortune cookie's warning about his wife Vera's being an adulteress. It occurred to him that Raleigh Hayes was his best friend. At least — except for Vera — he didn't have any other close friends, and hadn't had since high school, and hadn't had very many then, being fat, timid, and furtive. "What do you mean?" he asked with a hard look. He certainly didn't want to find out that his cookie had told the truth and that he had lost his wife, and his only friend, the only neighbor who had accepted his fortieth-birthday dinner invitation, the next-door neighbor who could be relied upon to recharge a battery, explain a 1040 form, call the police if robbers started packing up his house.

"How's she doing?" Hayes repeated.

"What do you mu . . . mu . . . mean, doing?" Sheffield stalled, hanging on to innocence.

Hayes grew impatient. "What do you mean, what do I mean?"

"You mean her diet?"

"She's dieting?" Hayes didn't even much like Vera Sheffield. She had too many things going on at once; she was a religious maniac and a lewd joker at the same time. She was altogether gluttonous. She was almost as fat as Mingo, as fat as Hayes's dead relatives, and not-yet-dead relatives, most of whom had ballooned off the top of his Mutual Life healthy-weight charts. She was a fat, born-again loudmouth.

"She's lost forty-two pounds," Sheffield was saying.

"She *has?*"

"She had her teeth wired together. You know how they do."

"She *did?*"

Mingo Sheffield relaxed with a heave at the sight of his neighbor's unmistakable amazement. Surely, if Raleigh and Vera were having an affair, it wouldn't have escaped his notice that her mouth was wired shut and forty pounds of her were missing. Now, Mingo said proudly, "It was a last resort and my hat's off to her, that's for sure. She's been through all get-out." Sheffield never dieted himself, but slenderized vicariously through his wife's suffering. She'd been losing weight for a quarter of a century, but always with a backlash. Two years ago she'd had Mingo put a lock and chain on the refrigerator door, but then had gone crazy and sawed it off while he was out at Chip 'n Putt. She'd even eaten the bread that had turned blue. Last year, after not missing a single Gloria Stevens exercise class for eight months, she'd tried for first prize in the Civitans' Christmas fruitcake fund-raiser by buying the ones she couldn't sell and eating them herself. "She's doing it for Jesus," explained her husband. "Forty-two pounds!"

"Well, I hope He appreciates it," Hayes offered in parting.

"She's not in such a hot mood," Sheffield called after him, and then walked across the silent street to look at the family of picnicking mannequins he had himself arranged in Knox-Bury's display window. Sharp-creased summer clothes stuck out stiffly from their arms and legs, and new shoes hung off their toeless feet. The mannequin mother was taking a rubber pie from an ice chest and the mannequin father was looking fixedly at his tennis racket as if he were wondering why he'd brought it along on a picnic when there were no courts in sight and nobody to play with. Lonesomeness fell on Mingo Sheffield; there wouldn't be soul to talk to in the empty store, and at home his wife's teeth were wired together. He felt like climbing in the display window and sitting with the mannequins on the plastic grass and staring with them into the aluminum-foil lake on whose surface the boy mannequin's fishing line lay tangled, as if he'd tossed it onto an ice lake without bothering to drill a hole. Mingo looked back down the sidewalk but Raleigh Hayes had disappeared. His friend was a fast walker, thought the pensive floor manager; a man with somewhere to go.

Raleigh Hayes always walked fast, even if he was only walking to the bathroom, even if he was only walking along the beach. He hurried because forty-five years had already gotten away from him, because life was always two uncatchable steps in front of him, running away like a burglar with satchels full of all the things that should have belonged to Raleigh Hayes — like money, position, a home in which nothing was unrepaired, and, in general, a future, and, mostly, his just deserts. What our hero didn't know as he hurried back to business was that the burglar was just

now getting ready to wheel around and scare him to death by flinging the
satchels at his head. That, at any rate, was his father's plan, if a man like his
father could be said to have formulated anything that could reasonably call
itself a plan, which Raleigh would have denied.

On the surface, Raleigh Whittier Hayes looked like his father, (ex)
Reverend Earley Hayes, but the resemblance hadn't soaked in. For that,
the son was grateful. Indeed, he resented even the physical likeness. The
blueness of Raleigh's eyes, the high color of his cheek, the corkiness of his
sand-colored hair and soft loose fullness of his mouth had, all his life, led
people (even those who hadn't known the father) to expect of the son a
Rabelaisian insouciance he neither possessed nor approved. He was continually a disappointment to those who assumed he would live up to his
looks, and they were a disappointment to him. By forty-five, he'd done
what he could to bring his surface into conformity with what was inside:
he'd put his eyes behind glasses, fretted away a third of his hair, and tightened his mouth. Raleigh'd grown tall and lean and pale, so that he'd come
to look like Earley Hayes stretched on the rack and, consequently, bitter in
the face.

What was on the inside of the son belonged to the mother, second of
Earley's three (so far) wives, and the only one with any money. A great
deal of money (well, not a great deal, but enough for a reasonable man),
money that Raleigh Hayes was to inherit as soon as his father died, which
should have happened a long time ago. Not that Raleigh wanted it to
happen at all. In fact, he and his single sane aunt had spent the past six
months persuading the seventy-year-old gadabout to enter the local hospital for the tests he was now having for his blackout spells. It was just that
Hayeses rarely lived into their seventies. Most of the foolhardy gene pool
had died laughing of one carelessly aggravated congenital malady or another, years and years younger than Earley Hayes was now. Somehow, Earley kept bouncing up and down on the tip of the diving board without
ever slipping in. His son, Raleigh, considered himself fortunate that he'd
been bequeathed only the father's looks, for the majority of those with any
Hayes blood shared a dangerously blithe character as well, and they'd
horsed around as if life were child's play until they'd toppled (uninsured)
into early graves.

As a life insurance agent, Raleigh was appalled by the fact that he'd
never been able to sell his relatives a single policy. They were too cavalier
to insure themselves and too sentimentally superstitious to insure anyone
else. But they were glad to let him take out his own small policies on

them, although it seemed to them a terribly dull use of money. Because of their calamitous genealogy, the premiums were exorbitant. He sank the returns into land; it lasted longer than the creatures who lay under it. He now owned two beach houses near Wilmington, and he rented them out to vacationers, and lent them to his relatives. They loved the beach.

On the twelfth floor of the Forbes Building at the Crossways (as the center of downtown Thermopylae was called), Raleigh Hayes overlooked his reflection in the glass door that bore his name and title. INSURANCE AGENT, MUTUAL LIFE. The phone was ringing while he was opening the door. He couldn't imagine why Bonnie Ellen didn't answer it. She was his new secretary, and the reason she didn't answer the phone was she was at home arguing with her husband about whether or not they should move to California. But Hayes wasn't to find out why Bonnie Ellen had let the phone keep ringing until much later, because when Chief Hood came to his house to ask him if he'd killed her, he'd already left town.

Raleigh snatched up his own receiver and announced himself.

"It's me," said his wife, out of breath. Her name was Aura, and as a result, her sensible, if somewhat cryptic, remarks struck others as having a mystical elusiveness.

"What's the matter?"

"Your daddy's gone!"

"He's dead. Dear God."

But Aura blew a puff of air into the phone. "Oh, Raleigh, no. He ran off from the hospital before they could finish his heart tests. When they brought in his lunch tray, there was nothing on his bed but his suitcase! Honey, I hate to say I told you so." She didn't explain what she had told him, but it certainly hadn't been that his father was going to skip out of the hospital, undetected, and vanish.

Hayes sat down without even looking for his chair. His tailbone hit the corner of the armrest and shot pain up his spine like a dart. "Why wasn't I informed?" he asked, as if he were already talking to the hospital officials, which, in his mind, he was. "Why has all this time been lost?"

"Honey, don't take it out on me, if you don't mind. The nurse thought he was down getting X-rayed."

"All morning?" he asked her picture on his desk.

"Well."

"I'll go to the hospital. You hold down the fort."

She said, "Fascinating how these macho metaphors hang on."

"Aura, good-bye." But as soon as Hayes hung up and yelled, "Bonnie Ellen," the phone started ringing again, and a man laughed in his ear. "Whatcha say, Ral pal?"

"Who is this?"

"Well, don't chew up my face. It's one of your cousins."

It was Jimmy Clay, son of Raleigh's father's sister Lovie, and a salesman at Carolina Cadillacs on the beltway. He said, "Just saying muchas grassy to a fellow Civitan."

"What for?" Hayes was pulling the phone cord over toward the door as if he could hang up sooner if he got closer.

"For Big Ellie."

"I don't even know what you're talking about, Jimmy." Raleigh's cousin was a conversational obscurantist, and always had been. At six, he would telephone Raleigh after school and talk nonstop in his own gobble-degook language, saying things like "Oomauchow laow laow tingo fringo agaknockah." At fourteen, he'd goose Raleigh from behind, shouting, "Hotchahotcha gotcha!"

"Jimmy, I'm a little pressed for —"

"Your daddy," said Clay. "He bought Big Ellie. First thing this morn-ing. Said he did it for you. Oogah boogah, press the pedal through the metal and tear up the roads, boy!"

"Just a minute." A sour Oriental taste was coming into Hayes's throat. "Are you telling me my father just bought a car from you?"

Jimmy Clay snickered. *"A car?* She's just the biggest, purtiest, custom-built yellow El Dorado Cadillac convertible we ever had sitting for two years on the lot! Why, I myself would call that baby a Lookie, nookie catcher. I sure wouldn't pay $11,395.77 for something I just wanted to *drive!"*

Raleigh's heart socked his chest so hard he could feel his shirt jump. "Paid how?" he whispered.

"Hunh?"

"Paid how?"

"Cash on the dash. Lootierootie-scootiebootie-boolucha!" In his enthusi-asm, Jimmy Clay had lapsed back to his childhood lingo.

"Cash!"

"A check. Why, is it gonna bounce? Plus, traded in his old Chevy."

Raleigh leaned against the wall, then sank down it to the floor. He hadn't sat on a floor in twenty years. His father, who had indifferently driven the same green Chevrolet for a decade, had just spent $11,395 of *his* money for a car, for four wheels and a motor and yellow paint and not even a top on it. Raleigh could have remodeled his basement, he could have paid off his daughters' orthodontist, he could have bought more beach land, he could have *saved* it.

"You there, Raleigh?"

"He said he bought it for me?"

"I said to him, 'Uncle Earley, you sure? Kind of hard to picture old fussbudget Raleigh behind *this* wheel.' Told me, 'Said I was buying it *for* him, didn't say I was giving it *to* him.' You know how your daddy is!"

"No, I don't."

The insurance agent taped a note to his door that said, "Be back soon." This proved to be a lie, but he couldn't be expected to know that now. As he hurried down the hall, somebody invisible ran beside him and tried to screw a bolt through his temple. He stopped to bang his head once against the door to the supplies closet. Behind it, the janitor, Bill Jenkins, almost dropped his brandy bottle.

Half an hour later, Ned Ware at Carolina Bank and Trust shamelessly admitted that he had not only transferred thirty thousand dollars from Earley Hayes's savings account into checking, not only sold the man five thousand dollars in traveler's checks, not only promised to have ready the cash from ten thousand dollars in negotiable bonds in an hour; he had done all this from the drive-in teller's window! To Raleigh, that fact added unbearable insult to injuries already doing damage to every one of his vital organs.

"Why I did it is your daddy didn't feel like he ought to come inside," said Ned Ware, a high-school halfback now (like Hayes) forty-five, who'd gotten his manager's job at the bank from the same Thermopylae Rotarians who'd sent him to college.

"Why couldn't he come inside?" His face wild, Raleigh bent his knees to keep from falling down in the middle of the bank, and stuck his hands under his arms to keep them from shaking. He looked as if he were about to start a Cossack dance.

"I guess, because he was in his pajamas. Plaid ones."

The more distraught Raleigh Hayes felt, the more polysyllabic his language, the more sarcastic his tone; it was a way to ward off howling. Now he said, "You conducted financial transactions of that magnitude with a seventy-year-old man in his pajamas in a drive-in window!"

"Well, first, I figured he had on a kind of a beach outfit. So I said, 'Headed for the beach, Mr. Hayes?' So he said, 'Not hot enough yet to drive to the beach in pajamas.' He had the top down, though."

"I presume he was in a yellow convertible?" If Hayes had known the Latin word for *yellow,* he would have used it.

Ned Ware whistled through the gap in his front teeth. "I wish I was with him; God, don't I?" He began to swing both arms fast from one side to the other. Papers blew off his desk. "Spring hits, I can't sit still. I'd kill for a car like that on a day like this."

Raleigh stooped to pick the papers up off the orange carpeting, just to have something to do as he snarled, "I can't believe you gave him that much money that fast, when even a baboon could have deduced that my father was not behaving exactly *normally,* without informing me first. I goddamn can't believe it!"

Ware nodded. "Your daddy said you'd say that. But don't call me a baboon, hear?" He puffed up. "It's his money and unless you can prove he's gone non compost mennis, that's the name of the game, and I know you're upset, but watch your mouth, Raleigh. We've got women in this bank."

Hayes looked around the lobby. A big swatch of orange over brown paint shot in a straight line around the walls near the ceiling. It looked like a highway to him, as if, defying gravity, his father had zoomed sideways in his yellow Cadillac right around the room, then sped out the doors, and out of town with money that was his only by accident, and belonged by right, by blood, by character, to the sole son of Sarah Ainsworth Hayes, now deceased.

Ned Ware confessed to having not the slightest idea where Earley Hayes was headed. "All he said was, tell you when you showed up that he was taking a little trip and not to worry."

Raleigh's laugh was the strangest he'd ever produced. "All right, Ned. Just don't spread this around, will you do me that favor?" Not that Raleigh couldn't see from the smirks on the tellers' faces that they already knew everything. "Just don't talk about it."

"You mean about the teenage colored girl?"

Dear God, thought Hayes, let this witless blabbermouth suddenly have developed a sadistic sense of humor. Let this all be a joke at my expense.

But the old halfback's wide face was crumpling into solicitude. "I know. It must have been awful hard to swallow. 'Course, I figured she was a nurse or something at first, 'cause she had on, looked like a white uniform, even if she was sitting up there in the front seat, brown-bagging it in broad daylight. But when I tried to, you know, ask him about her, and your daddy told me he was planning on getting married, I swear my heart went out to you, Raleigh. I can't help it, I mean, I'm no racist, but this little number, that blond wig and purple eyeshadow and all, well, hell, she looked like a hooker to me. She sure didn't look like somebody *I'd* want for a stepmother. Bob Lane said he'd bet a dollar she's not more than sixteen at the most. She didn't even count those traveler's checks, just dumped them in her overnight case."

Ned Ware was still talking in this vein as Raleigh Hayes turned around as if summoned by a hypnotist, and walked out of the bank. He walked down the precise middle of the sidewalk three blocks to the Lotus House, and anyone who didn't move, he bumped against without even noticing.

There wasn't anyone in the Lotus House except the Shiono grandmother behind the counter, adding up on a little brass abacus the money in the cash register. Hayes pulled a shiny red menu out of the rack, found the word *cocktails,* and pointed to the first name under it. It was Singapore Sling. He ordered three by holding up his fingers. They came in fish bowls. As he drank the first one, he took from his pocket his fingernail clipper, and cut his nails to the quick. Putting it back, he felt the wrinkled slip of paper that had come out of his fortune cookie less than two hours ago. He read it again. "You will go completely to pieces by the end of the month." The anonymous soothsayer had hedged his bet much too cautiously.

When Mrs. Shiono brought Hayes his bill, there was a fortune cookie on top. He crunched it to bits with a slap of his palm, and took out the coiled slip.

"Quit it, Claude?" she asked him. He gave her his Visa.

Raleigh Hayes didn't read his new fortune until he had staggered outside, astonished that balance too had deserted him, entirely drunk for the first time since his wedding reception twenty years ago. By excruciating will, he brought into focus the little sliver of print. It said, "This is your lucky day."

CHAPTER

2

Which Treats of the Strange Message the Hero's Father Sent Him

IN SASHAYING CURVES, Raleigh Hayes's Ford Fiesta swirled down First Street like a square dancer's skirt. The more the intoxicated man tried to make the car go straight, the more gaily it danced. His arms pushed so tightly on the wheel that a charley horse twisted through his left biceps, and he had to steer with his right hand while in a frenzy of pain he shook the other one out the window. Behind Hayes, the teenaged driver of a Triumph sportscar pounded his falsetto horn, downshifted, and as he passed the Fiesta, yelled, "You old drunk asshole, get off the fucking road!" This unprecedented verbal assault so stunned Hayes that he slammed on the brakes, bumped the curb, and stopped. Without knowing why, he walked to the rear of the car to stare at his license plate — a vanity plate given him by his wife for Christmas to serve as a business ad, a reminder to tailgaters to purchase MUTUAL LIFE INSURANCE. But the state had only allowed Aura enough letters to spell out MUT LIFE. Hayes had left it on to prove his indifference to wisecracks, including his wife's.

He rubbed the plate. It was inescapably his own; that obscene adolescent had undeniably shouted at *him,* at Raleigh Hayes, father of teenaged female twins who might even know the lout, who might even have sat in his Triumph's passenger seat, cheering him on with shrieks and giggles as he rampaged through Thermopylae.

At the far end of First Street was Raleigh's father's little white stucco house where he'd lived with his third wife after Raleigh's mother had divorced him. Now two women and a man were standing in the yard, among so many dandelions that the fidgety threesome looked to him as if they were up to their ankles in bees. They were all pointing at the roof, but as far as Hayes could tell, his father wasn't on it. Then they hurried into a station wagon at the curb and drove away before he could even find his key, which was in his left hand and not in the ignition, where he futilely kept attempting to turn it.

Once the insurance man was close enough to read the sign in front of which the trio of strangers had apparently been standing, he simply took off his glasses, dropped them in his lap, and drove on. He drove on past the house, eyes locked to the fore, foot firm on the accelerator. But there was no use pretending he hadn't been able to read the FOR SALE sign staked through his father's unmown lawn.

"Mama, he's crazy," said Raleigh Hayes on the way to the hospital. Then he said, "Ha ha." But there was no use pretending he believed he could communicate with his deceased mother, nor any reason to suppose this appraisal of her former spouse's sanity would be any news. Unlike most of his relatives, Raleigh never conversed with the dead, or the Deity. He found offensive the way, for example, his aunt Lovie in a poker game would call for aid upon her deceased brother Hackney (a semiprofessional gambler who'd died chasing a fly ball in a semiprofessional baseball game). "Come on, now, Hackney, just give me one more jack, that's all!" Lovie would yell to the ceiling, as if above, among the empyreal seraphim, Hackney Hayes crouched over a cloud's edge, mesmerized by a few middle-aged hicktown women in a nickel game of seven-card poker in which not only were threes and nines wild, but extra cards were handed out to anyone with a four.

Raleigh found outrageous his kinfolks' assumption that an Omnipotent Being had nothing better to do than arrange reality into parables for their personal benefit: In 1933, God had closed the banks to keep his great-aunt Mab from squandering her savings on a bigamist from Chicago. His uncle Furbus (now dead of lung cancer from smoking three packs of Lucky Strikes a day) had married Emily Shay because she'd fallen out of the bleachers at a Thermopylae High School basketball game, landed on top of him, and broken his clavicle. "I don't see how God could have said it any plainer, how Little Em was meant for me," said Furbus, year after year.

Now when our hero had asked God please to assure him that He'd precipitously transformed the banker Ned Ware into a malevolent comedian, he certainly didn't think God was anywhere in the vicinity listening to what he said. He did believe in God, but, frankly, he didn't trust Him, and saw no reason in the world why he should. If God's idea of salvation was Jesus Christ, God was too eccentric to rely on. Mr. Hayes was a church-goer (indeed, a deacon), but he considered his religion a civic duty, a moral discipline, a social obligation, and (he was honest) a business asset. That's why as an adult he attended not the small Episcopal church where his father had once been rector, but the large Baptist church across the street, where most of his clients went. Hayes was a Christian, but if the truth be known, Christ irritated him to death. With the army in Freiburg, Germany, in 1959, he'd read the Gospels while cooped up in the infirmary, and he'd argued by pencil in the margins against the Savior. In his personal opinion, Christ's advice sounded like civic sabotage, moral lunacy, social anarchy, and business disaster. Hayes had been a serious young man; and he still believed in virtue, which he suspected Christ of ridiculing by gleefully making up stories in which decent people were cheated by wastrels and the deserving blithely passed over in favor of bums, like Raleigh's own younger half-brother Gates, who'd actually served time in jail, and now, thank goodness, had disappeared.

Hayes believed in virtues like fortitude. Consequently, he was able to keep calm when at the hospital the doctor (half his age) showed not the slightest remorse at having lost his father; when, shrugging, this adolescent physician yawned that if Earley Hayes didn't want them to evaluate his heart, it was a free country. He kept calm when this . . . *kid* threw in some unwanted advice: *He,* Raleigh Hayes, should cut back on the booze, with his kind of blood pressure! The rage to keep calm burned all the alcohol out of Raleigh's blood and left him with only a massive brain tumor throbbing against his eyes and ears. Palm pressed on one eye socket, he stood with his father's abandoned tan suitcase in the hospital gift shop, where he had to buy a Get Well card because the cashier wouldn't change his dollar so he could use a dime to call his wife. The cashier, a flagrantly sadistic woman with a deceptive grandmotherish look, deliberately gave him a quarter and two cents in change.

"Come on home," said Aura. "Earley left a message on the doorstep. I've got to go back out right away. Where'd you go?"

"What do you mean? Where is he?"

"Can't you find him? It was just sitting on the welcome mat."

"What was? Why didn't you hold on to him, Aura, for Pete's sake?"

"Well, I guess because I never saw him. He must have sneaked by while I was over painting signs at Barbara Kettell's."

"Message?" Raleigh hauled shut the phone booth door. Two doctors stood in the hall, comparing their clipboards and laughing loudly. Hayes bared his teeth at them.

"On a package. It says, 'Raleigh, play this. Love, Daddy.'"

"Aura, what are you talking about? Play what?"

"I didn't open it, of course. You know how you can't stand anybody opening your mail. It says, *'Raleigh,* play this.' It doesn't say, 'Aura,' or even 'Raleigh *and* Aura, play —'"

"Could I intrude on your busy schedule, Aura, to ask if you'd mind opening it now!" Hayes bit the hairs off his forefinger while he waited.

"Well," said his wife, "it's funny. It's one of those tape recorder tapes, and Earley wrote 'Message For Raleigh' on the side. Did you try his house? Maybe he's just not answering his phone."

"Aura." Hayes moved the phone to his other ear while decompressing with a long sigh. "Aura, Daddy took thirty thousand dollars out of the bank and bought a yellow Cadillac convertible from Jimmy Clay and ran off with a colored teenage girl. And his house is for sale."

Raleigh's intimate companion for twenty years monstrously revealed herself as a total stranger. She laughed.

"Is that all you can say?" he asked, although she hadn't actually said anything.

"Who was she?"

"She was wearing a white dress. According to Ned Ware, Daddy's planning to marry her."

"Maybe that's why they picked half the daffodils out of your greenhouse. For a wedding corsage. Your daddy!"

"Aura, good-bye. I'm coming . . ." He couldn't bring himself to say "home" to this bizarre woman. He said, ". . . to the house," and hung up.

Mr. Hayes returned to the gift shop to purchase extra-strength aspirin, four of which, to the consternation of the cashier, he chewed right up like mints. This feat humanized her, and she asked, "Don't those taste bitter?"

"Not at all," said Hayes.

"You forgot this." She gave him the Get Well card he'd bought without seeing. It showed Jesus, wide-armed, smiling out of the sky, ready to hug anybody He saw. Across the rainbow in quotation marks was written, "I am with you always," and inside was a poem.

When days are dark and full of care,
When rain clouds come, the Lord is there.
Just call His Name, just say a prayer.
The rainbow proves, the Lord is there.

This promise was followed by the command "Get well soon," and by assurances that not one tree had been destroyed to produce the card. Raleigh was flexing his wrist to pitch it in a waste bin, when beyond the glass door he saw Victoria Anna Hayes, his sane eldest aunt, go by, pushing her sister Reba in a wheelchair toward the elevator. Hurrying out, he told them, "Don't go up, Daddy's disappeared." Then he realized that his aunt Reba had on a hospital gown.

"What happened?" He asked the question of Victoria Anna, a blue-eyed unmarried woman of seventy-two. She was a semiretired traveling saleslady for a missionary supplies company, and burned still with a ruthless energy. She was the only Hayes, other than himself, whom Raleigh considered entirely rational. "What happened to Reba?"

"Raleigh, why bother to ask," Victoria Anna reminded her favorite nephew with a twitch of her watch-spring curls.

Reba, gray in the face and fatter than ever, answered, "Honey, they took my other one."

"Leg," said Vicky Anna.

Raleigh looked down. Indeed, both his aunt's bedroom slippers were fastened to wooden feet. "Diabetes?" he whispered.

Reba nodded. "Just like Papa."

Her elder sister made a spitting noise. "Please don't say it like you're glad to see y'all had something in common."

"Vicky Anna, our papa was a wonderful man."

"That's right, Reba, and he's lying out in the Hayes plot next to his legs, and now *your* legs, under a mountain of six thousand dollars' worth of marble saying how much everybody loved him, not that it crossed y'alls' minds to hide those Coca-Colas somewhere he couldn't get at in his wheelchair."

Reba told Raleigh, "It was the fried eggs and peanut brittle with me, Dr. McConors said."

Spinning Reba's wheelchair to face the elevator doors, Victoria addressed her nephew. "You say Earley's discharged?"

"Just left, without asking a soul, went on a spending spree and is presumably intending to marry a young Negro woman."

Victoria stared at her nephew. "Says who?"

"Ned Ware at the bank."

"He's a fool."

"Ned? Or Daddy?"

Miss Hayes didn't answer this. "I just got home a few hours back. I want you to know it takes more traveling time to go on a Trailways bus to Texas than fly to Singapore." Once she had covered the Far East territory, but World Missions now confined her to the Deep South. She was the only Hayes who'd gone places.

Reba said to the wall, "Earley was hiding in my bathroom when I got back from trying on my leg. He said he didn't have time to stay in the hospital but don't tell Vicky Anna because he didn't want you to get your feelings hurt that he didn't keep his promise. He was real upset about you, Vicky. I mean about his promise."

Raleigh spun his aunt's chair around. "Where was he going?"

"To go do something for you. 'I've got to do something for my little fellow, poor old Raleigh, let me borrow your raincoat,' is what he said, word for word."

Hayes looked anxiously at his watch to justify his immediate departure. "Aura just told me he left a message. I better go get it. Would y'all excuse me, please?" He handed his aunt Reba the unsigned Get Well card, and hurried out to the wide flat sea of parked cars, where dizzily he searched for his hatchback, mildly surprised to find it had not been stolen.

He drove home on the new Thermopylae beltway, which had taken Kettell Concrete Company twelve years to pave and had sent all five of Nemours Kettell's daughters to college, each in a new Mustang — for even the one who'd had no more brains than to marry the giggling Wayne Sparks had attended Boggs County State until they'd both flunked out. Raleigh had already set aside enough money to buy higher educations for his twin girls. When he thought of how many hundreds of jaw-aching hours of smiles he'd had to spend to accumulate that money, how many stomach-twisting words in praise of life insurance he'd had to wheedle past the slow negative mumbles of the mindless who didn't want to hear they were ever going to die, or couldn't care less about the consequences to their loved ones of that inevitability; when he thought of how he'd endured decades of these indignities not for the athletic, presidential son he'd been unjustly denied, but for daughters — whom he might anyhow be throwing into the collegiate arms of a Wayne Sparks — even supposing Holly and Caroline could raise their averages sufficiently to be accepted by even Boggs State; even supposing Caroline, in response to his inquiring about her educational plans, had not lifted her creamy shoulders into a shrug and mugged with her peachy face the look of one who'd sucked on a rancid lemon; even supposing Holly (in conjunction with her request that he advance her eighteen thousand dollars from her college funds so she could purchase used from a Pepsi Challenge pit crew a Grand Nationals modified white Ford with crash net) had not announced her intention to become a lady stock car racer and to repay him with future winnings; when Raleigh Hayes's thoughts sped — as they often did as he drove down the Kettell-enriching highway — toward this cul-de-sac of his paternal aspirations, he performed a spiritual exercise. By quickly calling to mind any randomly chosen half-dozen cataclysmic disasters so far *not* inflicted on him, he was able to stiffen his will so as to bounce despair off it. At least his twins were not Siamese twins. At least they were not cocaine-snorting hookers in Times Square. They were not helpless pawns of Communist aggression. They had not been stolen by the Moonies. At least Nemours Kettell had *five* daughters.

Raleigh rushed through these hypotheses like rosary beads now as he wound around the Drives, Lanes, and Courts of Starry Haven, Thermopylae's first, and now second-best, subdivision, where he owned a three-bedroom Colonial home with a bas-relief fluted column on either side of the green welcome mat on which his father had left some ridiculous message.

"Okay," said Hayes to the sight that greeted him.

On his rolled, seeded, fertilized, edged lawn where in precious leisure time he had crawled on hands and knees to tear out clumps of crabgrass, he saw leaping — her blond ponytail in the air like a deer's tail, her legs spread perpendicular, so that he could see her panties beneath a skirt as short and ruffled as a tutu — his sixteen-year-old daughter Caroline. At first he thought she was shaking over her head two fat boughs of his lilac blossoms, but as he drove closer he identified the objects as two blue pompoms. Caroline was apparently a cheerleader, despite his strictures on extracurricular activities unless her grades improved. He had no time to prepare any interrogation, for blood flooded his eye sockets as, turning past his rhododendrons, he saw backed into his driveway the red Triumph sportscar that had run him off the road an hour ago. The hood was up, and projecting from its crimson maw was the bottom half of his blue-jeaned daughter Holly, buttock to buttock with the longer, leaner jeans of, no doubt, the Triumph's foul-tongued driver. The father's paranoiac ironies had turned prophetic on him.

Hayes swung wide, skittering into Mingo Sheffield's gravel, which abutted his own paved driveway. As soon as he flung open his door — which instantly swung back shut on his shin — he was jolted by a bloodcurdling shriek from Caroline. "YAHHHHH!" She leaped in a split while shouting to the snap of her pompoms:

Tomahawks! Tomahawks! Kill, kill, kill!
If Kevin can't do the job, BOOGER WILL!
YAHHHHHHHH!

"Caroline, stop stomping on the grass," called Raleigh, stumbling over the bricks that bordered his property from Sheffield's gravel. He was temporarily blinded in the afternoon sun by the glitter of his daughter's glossy sunglasses, gold chains, sequined T-shirt, and the metal box attached to her waist. "Caroline, I'd appreciate it if you'd —"

Toma Toma Tomahawks. Here comes the hatchet!
LOOK OUT, Huskies! You're gonna CATCH it!
YAHHHHHHHH!

Undoubtedly she was a cheerleader for the Thermopylae High basketball team, named the Tomahawks by a long-dead coach under the erroneous assumption that the ancient Thermopyleans had been a tribe of American Indians.

"Caroline!" Hayes tapped one of the little blue earphones on her head.

She screamed, *"Ew,* Daddy, you toedully terrified me, rilly! You're not supposed to be here!"

"Obviously. Were you just smoking a cigarette?"

"No, sir." She lied with astonishing candor, and would probably someday get off scot-free in a murder trial. Her father crushed out the smoldering butt in the grass beside her, and moved it back and forth in front of her sunglasses. She pouted, "Oh, you always blame everything on me. Like *everything!"* Since babyhood, Caroline had inevitably become overwhelmed with self-pity when caught red-handed.

In Hayes's peripheral vision, the blue jeans wriggled. "Exactly who is that in our driveway?"

"Holly."

"Yes, I realize it's Holly. Who *else* is it?"

On one knee, Caroline began solemnly to shake the pompoms from side to side as if landing a plane approaching from somewhere above and behind her father. "Oh, him. Booger."

"Booger?"

From across the lawn came, "Yeah? Oh, hi there, Mr. Hayes."

Raleigh turned toward the male voice. By God, the brazen hood appeared to have absolutely no recollection of their encounter on First Street.

Uncoiled now to a height of approximately six and a half feet, he was grinning affably.

"Hi ya, Dad, lose your job?" called his only other child, Holly, waving a wrench. There appeared to be a beer can at her feet. Was this the life they really lived while he was away? Hayes suddenly noticed that Aura's station wagon was not in the drive.

"GooooooOOOOO, THERMOPYLAE!"

"Caroline! Where's your mother?"

Caroline arched her shoulders, leaving them raised until Raleigh turned to stride into the house.

At least all the furniture was still there. The cobbler's bench coffee table. The cabbage-rose-skirted couch. The untuned spinet that nobody but Mingo Sheffield ever played. From room to room, calling "Aura?," Hayes trotted over the light-green wall-to-wall carpeting, and received an ugly electric shock from accumulated static when turning the metal doorknob to the downstairs bathroom, where the sink was smeared with large black handmarks and the toilet seat had been left up. Back in the kitchen he smelled a horrible odor and snatched a pan of burning spaghetti sauce off the stove. Stuck with a bobby pin through the straw shade of the swag light was a note on the back of a perfectly good bank deposit slip. "Gone to belly dance class after M.F.P. Stir sauce." Below was the noseless smiling becurled cartoon face Aura had for some reason always used as a familial signature though it bore not the slightest resemblance to her. Perhaps it was to be taken as a sign of the covenant of her continued goodwill toward the family, despite her increasingly frequent absences, hitherto charitable or civic, now presumably in pursuit of a career in belly dancing.

Below the light on the butcher block counter sat a cassette tape. "Okay," said Raleigh as he turned it over and over in both hands. Outside, a motor roared, stopped, roared, stopped. "All *right!*" shouted the boy named Booger. "Ex!" Holly shouted in reply. "Hey, Car, want a ride?"

"With you greasers? I'm shurr!" (Caroline)

"Kiss my tuna!" (Holly)

"Go bag your face, zods!" (Caroline)

They were as verbally berserk as Jimmy Clay, with whom perhaps the mysterious Aura had long ago betrayed her marriage vows.

Hayes heard the hideous falsetto horn as the Triumph screeched out of his driveway, carrying away his child. The front door slammed. The house shuddered as someone clumped upstairs and hurled shut another door. Raleigh followed, knocked at Caroline's sticker-plastered door, interpreted the sound "Yo" to mean "Come in," and did so, clawing his way through the wind chimes that hung everywhere from the ceiling, and stepping over Tab cans, wet towels, and mounds of clothes heaped like flashy October leaves in the yard.

"Don't say anything about my room, 'cause, okay, rilly?" insisted Caroline who lay on an unmade bed among what looked like a mass of small massacred animals, but were actually the dilapidated stuffed bears, rabbits, dogs, cats, pigs, and seals of her childhood. Caroline possessed everything she'd ever owned, and had as a consequence very little living space left to her. Beside her stereo she kept a crib jammed with limbless dolls. The bookcase leaned threateningly forward with the weight of coloring books. She had a poster of Mickey Mouse beside a poster of a guitar-wielding young black man wearing ruffles and mascara. She had broken crayons jumbled together in baskets with more cosmetics than she could possibly use in a lifetime even if she joined the circus.

Hayes picked up from her bed the Walkman cassette player now detached from her waist. "May I borrow this thing for a moment?"

Surprised into letting deflate the globe of pink gum that obscured her face, Caroline said, "Shurr. You like Toto?"

"Who?"

"They're okay, too."

"Caroline, just tell me when your mother will be back."

"How should I know?"

"Well, do you happen to know what M.F.P. means?"

She wrinkled her nose, and crossed her eyes trying to look at it. "Oh, rilly, Daddy! You know. Mothers for Peace."

"Ah, of course." Hayes bit down on his lower lip. "Please clean up this room before I come in here with a blowtorch and do it myself."

"Jeez, you ever hear of child abuse?" From Caroline's rosy mouth blew a pink cartoon balloon that popped as Hayes highstepped out of the debris, kicking off the cord of a blow dryer.

Down in what was with naïve nostalgia called the family room, in his button-tufted Naugahyde recliner rocker, Raleigh Hayes took off his tie, toyed with the notion of hanging himself, placed the strange little foam knobs on his ears, ejected a tape labeled *Toto,* inserted his own, and punched Play. He heard nothing for five minutes but an actually rather soothing hum. Turning the tape to side B, finally he was listening to his father's voice. Naturally, Earley Hayes was laughing, in that loose-throated way he had. Then he spoke. "Well, now, anyhow. Don't take this hard. I know you love me, even if you don't think so, and you know I love you,

Raleigh. You're my son, and you're a good man, but time to time you get your ass screwed on backwards."

Hitting Stop hard, Hayes rewound the tape. The voice began again, a soft reedy drawl, sounding on the recording somehow frailer, if no less exasperatingly merry or offensively profane. "Raleigh? Raleigh? This is a test, one, two, three, and ah one. Just a second, I want to see how this gizmo works." Clicks and thunks followed. "Okeedoke. Christ sakes, I sure don't sound like Earley Hayes to me. Sound like *Gabby* Hayes, don't I?" Laughter. "Now. Hello, Raleigh. I'm at the counter here at the Sound Center buying this doohickey, and by fuck if I didn't just look out the window and see *you* flying through the door of the Lotus House and go staggering off down the sidewalk loop-legged, like you thought you were trying to walk across one of those waterbeds!" Laughter, as jolts shot through Raleigh's arms and legs. He could have nabbed his father hours ago, if he'd only known! The Sound Center? He'd never noticed a store called the Sound Center.

"Don't believe I ever saw you lit up that way before. Illuminated!" Laughter. "Well, now, if I know you, Raleigh, you've already been to that crappy hospital. The thing is, some teenager referring to himself as a heart specialist popped into my room and stuck his foot in my trashcan and pulled over my breakfast tray. Okay, Lord, I said, a word to the wise, so I left. My apologies to you and Vicky Anna, but I couldn't take the risk of staying.

"And I bet you've run over to the bank and gotten yourself in a state talking to musclehead Ned Ware and you're driving yourself crazy now about where is the senile old fuck and how can I grab him quick and maybe slip him into some peaceful nut hatch where that little pizzle Jimmy Clay can't come sell him any more of his old Cadillacs. Am I right?" Laughter, as Raleigh dug his fingernails into the rubbery Naugahyde. The outrageous injustice of the man!

"Now listen to me, Little Fellow. I'll keep this short."

"I bet," mumbled his son. Little Fellow! Scarcely still an appropriate salutation when the father was half a foot shorter than the son.

"I would have called, but I didn't want you getting your ballocks in a twist arguing with me, because I don't have the time. I've got some loose ends I need to get knitted up."

"Loose screws," mumbled Raleigh.

"I know how worried you are, son, but I don't need my heart tested. I've always had a just fine heart." Laughter. "Could be my damn *brain* needed a little work." Raleigh nodded vigorously. "Howsoever, Specs, the ticker and I are about to kiss and part."

What was that supposed to mean? The muscles of Raleigh's own heart jumped. He would sue that crappy hospital for every dime they had!

"So I want to settle some affairs, and I need your help." There was a long pause. Was that it? Hayes turned the sound up, pressed the plugs tighter in his ears. Then he heard a twangy young voice saying, "Yes, sir, and this model's $189.95 plus tax. So altogether that makes, hold on, $334.76. Cash?" My God, what was his father buying now?

"Why thank you, sweetheart . . . Excuse me, I'm back, Raleigh. Now, listen, if you don't want to help, 'course that's all up to you, but you're gonna have to take the chance of my blowing out the old wazoo every nickel of all this loot of mine you're planning on adding to that stash of yours." Insufferable laughter. "But if you *do* help, and, naturally, you've got to piss and vinegar *succeed,* too, you'll inherit every blessed thing I've got. And by nature of an inducement, I'll tell you a secret, Specs. You don't even know the half of what I own. You don't know the tenth! I'm a rich man, and when I say so, I'm not yanking your wank!" Sophomoric chuckle. Hayes could just see his father, standing merrily at the Sound Center counter (in plaid pajamas and Aunt Reba's raincoat?); his father, seventy years old, white-haired, with the round pink cheeks, round blue eyes, and filthy vocabulary of a twelve-year-old. "You do what I say, and I'll tell where that loot is. Deal?" The tape whirred on. "So here it is. First thing I want you to do is . . . I'm not going to tell you everything all at once 'cause I don't want you to get discouraged . . ."

Hayes swayed; he realized he hadn't been breathing.

"Is, locate Jubal Rogers for me. Give him five thousand dollars and ask him to come with you to New Orleans.

"Second thing is, find that fuck-up of ours, your brother Gates, and bring him too.

"Third thing is, bring me Grandma Tiny's trunk, and the family Bible. Find out for me if you would, son, who Goodrich Hale Hayes's wife was and see if she's got any descendants besides Hayeses. That's the kind of thing Vicky may know. Oh, don't tell Vicky you're looking for Jubal. And, Raleigh, buy me that little cabin up on Knoll Pond from Pierce Jimson. That's where I want you to bury me. Don't tell Pierce that, the pompous tight-ass. Also while you're at it, I want you to steal me that crappy little bust of PeeWee Jimson his wife stuck up in the library, and bring it along. Bring my trumpet.

"And bring a gun.

"Talk to you soon. Well, now, anyhow. Don't take this hard. I know you love me, even if you don't think so, and you know I love you, Raleigh. You're my son, and you're a good man, but time to time you get your ass screwed on backwards. I want you to enjoy yourself for once, Specs. I want you to think of this as a holy adventure, by God. And if that doesn't do it, just remember how rich you're going to be, believe it or not. Over and out, roger. Isn't this thing fun?"

In the television screen beside the chair, Raleigh Hayes saw the face of a dead test pilot, eyes glazed, mouth fallen open, headphones askew. It was himself.

"It's a joke," he whispered. "It's okay. It's just one of his stupid jokes, like when he claimed he'd come over here last Halloween in a hobo mask and I didn't even recognize him and gave him an Almond Joy. It's a joke."

Someone was leaning on the front door bell. From Caroline's room, Hayes heard howls; her stereo, he hoped. He hurried through the house, his brain furious: You can't just bury somebody anywhere you feel like it. Steal from a public library?

"Yes?" On the step was a black teenager holding a brown paper bag.

"Hey, man, why don't y'all answer your door?"

"Why don't you keep a civil tongue in your head?" snapped Hayes.

"Racist turkey." The young man shoved the bag at Hayes, and loped across the lawn to a van, which he drove away as Raleigh was calling, "Come back here, you've got the wrong house!"

In the bag was a bottle of whiskey and an envelope. In the envelope was ten thousand dollars in cash, clipped to a note. "I bet you thought I was joking. Five for Jubal, five for the cabin. Here, have another drink. Then you and that damn beautiful Aura run upstairs and grab a nice warm daytime fuck. Then you better get along. You've got a lot of work to do. I forgot to say, unless you hear from me, meet me, noon, the 31st, St. Louis Cathedral, Jackson Square, ole New Oreleens. Bring it all and I'll come on home. Love and hugs, Daddy."

Hayes shut the door, locked it and leaned on it. For God's sake! His father had entrusted a bagful of hundred-dollar bills to a black delivery boy! He *should* have the man committed! And besides, Pierce Jimson was never going to sell him that rotted cabin, for any price. All the Jimsons hated all the Hayeses. And where in hell was he supposed to find his half-brother Gates, who was doubtless either dead or back in jail, and had last been heard of five years ago when he'd sent a *postcard* from Winnemucca, Nevada, asking for a loan. A postcard of a motel flashing neon slot machines on its roof! And this "Jubal Rogers," Raleigh didn't know from Adam. Maybe he was related to Flonnie Rogers, the old black cleaning woman who'd lived at his grandmother's house for half a century, and must by now be long dead. Trunk? How should he know where Granny Tiny's trunk was? Why was there a big "PEACE NOW" poster on a stick in the umbrella stand? Maybe he should picket the house with it. Steal PeeWee's bust? And the suggestion about Aura, that they should . . . ! Age, far from purifying his father's nature, had distilled it into a reservoir of juvenile lewdness. Ten thousand dollars in a paper bag! Serve him right if he, Raleigh Hayes, Little Fellow, Specs, called the state asylum right this minute about committal papers!

"Ooomiiigodddd! Daddy's brown-bagging it!"

Raising his eyes to the stairs where the giggling Caroline, now wearing a Yasir Arafat costume, pointed a finger at him, Hayes noticed that his hand was in fact wrapped around a brown bag wrapped around a bottle that was inexplicably but incontrovertibly opened, for the cap was in his left hand. "Did you clean up your room?" he snapped.

"Yes, sir." A preposterous claim, as the Army Corps of Engineers could not have done the job in less than a month. "You said it was trashy to drink from bottles."

"I have an abscessed tooth." Having heard himself say this, Hayes turned the darkest shade of the proverbial beet. He had lied. Moreover, lied uselessly, for the notion of medicinal whiskey meant no more to Caroline than the notion of gaslights or the Fifth Commandment. His daughter immediately seized the advantage and resorted to blackmail, coupled with the parodic flirtatiousness of kissing noises.

"Well, I won't tell. Kiss, kiss, please, please, please, can I borrow the car for a second? It's a total necessity. If I don't get to the mall and buy a new pair of jeans, there's no way I'm going to school tomorrow."

It was only when he heard the clatter of the Sheffields' gravel hitting the street that the numb Hayes, while hiding the cash in his socks drawer, brought to full consciousness the fact that he had either absentmindedly handed his daughter the keys to his car, or that she had already made her own set from a wax impression. At any rate, she was gone; his wife was gone wherever it was that women went to belly dance in Thermopylae, and he (with so many errands to run — buying cabins, locating Negroes, robbing libraries) was stranded in Starry Haven.

Hayes looked out his kitchen sliders. Protruding from the garage next door was Vera Sheffield's old yellow Pinto. Never had Raleigh been a borrower, never had he failed to feel a mild contempt for the Sheffields' addiction to that improvident habit. Nothing could more emphatically prove that he was no longer himself than his decision (hardly a decision, for he was already squeezing through the clumps of shrubbery he'd spaced down his property line) to knock at the Sheffields' back door and ask Vera to lend him a car with a "God Is My Co-Pilot" sticker on its smashed rear end.

He hurried across their patio, past his own (rusting) gardening shears, his seed spreader, and his edge-trimmer. Glancing in a pane of the kitchen door, he pulled back the hand he had already raised in order to knock. Shock tingled through him like a shiver; fortunately by instinct his other hand closed around the bottle in the bag that he wasn't aware he was still carrying, or he would have dropped it. To the Sheffield refrigerator was glued a full-length mirror. In front of it swayed Vera. Or maybe it wasn't Vera. Maybe it was Dolly Parton. Maybe the buxom star was an old friend of Vera's, and had asked the Sheffields not to mention it because she didn't want to be bothered on vacation. No, it was Vera, wearing a platinum wig. She must have lost thirty more pounds since Mingo's noon report. She must have lost her religion too. Why else would a born-again Christian be wearing black high heels, a black vinyl bathing suit, a spiked dog collar, and swishing a riding crop at her reflection in a mirror alone in her kitchen in the middle of the day? Hayes considered Christ a loose man, but not that loose. However, what most distressed the insurance man on this Ides of March, when his whole world was conspiring to betray him, was to feel against his very own thigh the movement of revolution starting to stir.

He stepped to sneak backward away, tripped on the prong of a rake he had lent Mingo, and saw Vera turn toward him, the wires on her teeth glistening.

CHAPTER

3

Of a Misunderstanding between Our Hero and His Neighbors

THE SHEFFIELD DOOR was snatched back, and a white arm hauled Hayes inside.

"Ooo shared ee! Oo shought uh she shame shying un ee!" Vera's amazingly long and sooty lashes lifted to show eyes much more expressive of her indignation than whatever it was she'd hissed at him through her wired teeth. (It was, "You scared me! You ought to be ashamed, spying on me!")

Shaking, wordless, the two stared at each other, both breathing through their mouths. Having to speak with her lips so widely stretched open had given Vera a viciously carnal look that matched her outfit, and had turned Raleigh to stone. He figured he'd have to stand there forever, like somebody from Pompeii. Strenuously he tried to move one arm; wetness sloshed his hand. It was the whiskey.

Finally, Vera's head began to shake. "Shesheshesheshesheshe." She was giggling. The riding crop flicked against his arm, then whacked the bagged bottle. "Oh! Ouer zhinking!"

"No, I am *not* drinking, I assure you, I, I, Vera, I didn't mean to startle you, listen, pardon me, I just came over here to inquire if I could borrow your automobile." The spell was half broken; if not move, he could at least talk. In fact, he had the feeling he was babbling. "Sort of a little bit of an emergency. Caroline took off with mine, and Aura's gone to a . . . to a class."

The riding crop kept twitching against his arm. Vera kept giggling, no doubt on the verge of an hysterical mania. Evangelism and dieting had utterly addled her wits. He had to make her think there was nothing implausible in her appearance; cajole her, then flee. Somehow he produced a chuckling noise. "Well, I guess I know who's going to be the hit of the new show, hunh?" Raleigh swatted the sweat from his forehead, relieved. In fact, probably that *was* the explanation. Wasn't Vera always in the church Easter play? Last year, in her heavy days, hadn't she hopped into the Sunday-school class dressed up as a huge purple rabbit carrying a basket of colored eggs in her paws? Yes, that was it. The church must be doing some modernistic show this year. She must be playing Sin or Mary Magdalene or something like that. "Well, Vera, never mind about the car, I'll just get on back; Aura ought to be —"

Clearly deranged by the trauma of her mortification, Vera continued to giggle, or to hiss, as her little whip nervously smacked harder and harder against his arm. Raleigh jerked up his elbow abruptly; the crop spun out of her hand and fell between his feet, where she squatted to retrieve it. Hayes was staring unavoidably down at two swelling creamy orbs overflowing their black vinyl confinement. This time his rebellious privates lunged desperately in frantic efforts to escape his control. In trying to jump backward, he jostled the rising Mrs. Sheffield, unsteadily balanced on her high heels, and she lurched against his thigh, throwing her arms around his buttocks. Her face nuzzled between his legs. She was kissing him there! Inches below his now rioting genitals. Hayes pulled back. Her face followed! Her warm lips moved urgently against his trousers as barbaric whimpers came from her throat. He shook his leg roughly, flinging her head back and forth with it and gouging his skin with the spikes on her collar. *"Shop! I'm shuck!"* she shrieked.

With both hands Hayes grabbed at her clustered blonde ringlets. The bottle crashed to the floor. He yanked and the hair came terrifyingly loose from her head and hung tangled from his fingers, revealing Vera's customary black bobbed curls below.

Raleigh was screaming too. *"What?"* He looked down; the cloth of his good gray slacks, wet from drool, stretched out into Vera's mouth. He was stuck to a loop of her teeth wire.

Just then the insurance man heard two sounds simultaneously: One was the familiar rattle of a door opening. The other resembled the records Caroline played at top volume in her room. A bloodcurdling moan crescendoed in high-pitched yawps of the sort a dog might emit if the end of a piano landed on its tail. Raleigh twisted his upper torso, hauling Vera with him, and saw fat Mingo Sheffield at the door attempting to stuff both his fists in his mouth.

"Mingo," Raleigh began solemnly.

". . . ingo!" squeaked Vera.

But, eyes averted, Mingo ran with dainty fat-man swiftness right past them and into the front of the house.

"*Now,* look!" growled Raleigh, and tried to rip his pants loose despite Vera's clawing at his leg.

"*Shop, shhop!*" she hissed. The despicable wire had corkscrewed its way through the fabric. Hayes was not sufficiently abandoned to yield to his impulse to rip her teeth out of her head, so he stood there in a shower of sweat as she pulled down his pants. Mingo ran back into the kitchen pucker-faced and burst into a wail of tears at the sight of his wife groveling at his barelegged best friend's feet. In Sheffield's fat hand was a gun.

"*For God's sake, Mingo, listen to reason!*" stuttered Raleigh, whose sex organs, so recently reckless, had scurried into hiding with a craven celerity. He tugged his blue-striped shirttail down over his boxer shorts as he hopped free of his pants.

"Y'all didn't even stop!" pouted Mingo. But instead of shooting them, as at least Raleigh expected, he trotted jiggling with sobs out the kitchen door, across his crowded patio in a light-footed weave, and disappeared over the slope at the yard edge.

"Shave him!" begged Vera, Raleigh's trousers dangling from her mouth as if she'd devoured the contents. She started a longer sentence, abandoned the effort, and resorted to charades: cocking her thumb and pointing her forefinger at her temple. Then she shoved Hayes with such force out the door that he broad-jumped the back steps entirely, galloped headlong over the lawn, and slid down the brambly incline. In Raleigh's backyard, wedged in the little double chair on the twin's old swing set, Mingo Sheffield sat wistfully, one hand pulling and pushing on the rusted metal bar from which the chair hung, one hand on the gun in his lap. *Screak, screak. Screak, screak,* sighed the old brown deserted swing.

"Now excuse me, Mingo, you have the wrong impression," began Raleigh as he scrambled to his feet, noticing while doing so that in his slide his shorts had come unsnapped, and — as his cousin Jimmy Clay had once taunted him in front of a girl — his barn door was open. Fortunately, Mingo, lost in a pensive reverie, hadn't noticed.

"Mingo, I insist that you not jump to false conclusions. I came over to borrow Vera's car and her teeth got caught in my pants."

Sheffield stared stolidly ahead. "I guess I'm the last to know."

"There's nothing *to* know," Raleigh persisted, and pressed his hand to his heart. "I have *no* idea why your wife's in that getup, but as far as I'm concerned, I swear on —"

"I guess I'm just the town clown all over town." Mingo wiped his nose with his gun hand. "I had to hear about it from a Chinese cookie." Now he glanced shyly over at Raleigh, then looked away. "Y'all thought I went straight to Tuesday choir practice like usual, I bet. Well, they canceled it!"

"Mingo, I didn't know you went to choir practice at all!" The issue of whether choirs practiced had never entered his mind; although surely, after bellowing the same half-dozen hymns for three decades, his neighbor ought to know them by heart. "You practice every Tuesday?"

"Mama warned me! And I was out at a bowling alley the night she died! I was drinking beer while she was spitting up blood." Tears ran sideways around the fat of Sheffield's cheeks.

By now, Hayes (incensed against his father, on whom he put the entire blame for his present predicament) had decided that both the Sheffields were psychotic. Moreover, he simply could no longer bear the rusty screaking rhythm of the swing. With a pounce, he grabbed the metal bar, and then the gun. "Now, you give me this!" he shouted, although the big boneless hand had made no effort to hold on to the weapon.

"Just go on and shoot," Mingo sighed. "I'm too chicken to pull the trigger. I guess that's why she's leaving me. She hates a chicken."

Hayes shook the bar as hard as he could. "For Pete's sake, will you get it through your fat skull that she hasn't left you! There's nothing between Vera and me! *Tell him!*" Vera was now making her way, in bathing suit and heels, down the slope, Raleigh's gray pants over one arm. "Tell him he's got it all wrong, Vera!"

"Oh, honey," she hissed, and threw her arms around her spouse. "Ooo didn't eally shrink *at?* Ee an Raleigh? Raleigh? Oh, honey!" She tossed the pants at the negligible Hayes, who was hurt to see himself so mentally unbraced that he was *insulted* by how hilarious she found Mingo's accusation. As he watched in horror, the vicious woman wiggled onto Sheffield's lap (for some reason the whole swing set did not collapse), and nuzzled among his chins. "Why, oo sheet ole shack of sugah. Ouer jhealous!" She kept on in this vein with remarks which her husband appeared to follow better than Hayes could, until Mingo was actually starting to smile with a furtive tremor. By the time Raleigh had pulled on his trousers, the couple were kissing. Astonishingly enough, no explanation was asked for or offered regarding Vera's pornographic apparel. Perhaps it was no surprise to the blubbering crybaby.

"Well, I'm glad that's all cleared up," said Hayes somewhat snappishly. His neighbors appeared to have no intention of apologizing for what they'd just put him through. Indeed, they were ignoring him completely. "So if y'all will excuse me!" He stormed back up the slope away from the screaks and coos below, enraged by a memory of having chosen the eight-year-old Mingo *first* for his side in a softball game, bravely in the face of Ned Ware's groans of *"Whaletail?"* He was enraged by a memory of having in the fifth grade denied the rumor that Mingo would eat leaves and dirt to get attention, when he himself had seen the pig doing it a hundred times.

Safe in his own home, Raleigh Hayes flung himself down on the living-room couch, pulled a ruffled pillow over his head, and fell asleep.

"Why, Raleigh, this isn't like you. I didn't know you were in here. Are you sick?" Aura's voice was above him, but he'd lost his sight. No, it was dark.

"Have I been asleep?"

"What a funny question. Don't *you* know? I hate to say it, but we've already eaten."

"Who's we? Where are the girls, did they come home?"

"From the game? They just left. It's seven-thirty. Raleigh, are you coming down with something?"

It was strange talking with Aura in the dark from the living-room couch. It was strangely pleasant, this disembodied conversation with so calm and affectionate a voice. Like a voice one recognizes coming out of the past over the telephone. A voice so unlike Vera Sheffield's.

"Aura, the Sheffields have turned into psychos. I want you to keep away from them."

"Really? Vera was just over here, borrowing a cucumber. I didn't notice."

"A cucumber! What was she wearing?"

"I don't think I noticed. Would you like some supper?"

"Turn on that light! What are *you* wearing?"

But Aura did not sport the sheer harem pants and cymbal-tinkling fingers Raleigh feared. Her honey hair in a loose twist, she was dressed trimly in a green cotton skirt and a white polo blouse.

"Why do you want to know what Vera and I are wearing? Did you want to go *out* to eat?" Hayes's wife eyed seriously his grass-stained shirt and ripped trousers. Then she knelt beside the couch, sniffing him as if they were a couple of chimpanzees.

He slid away. "For Pete's sake!"

"Yep. Caroline and Vera both mentioned you were hitting the bottle."

Hitting the bottle? Where had she acquired these hard-nosed expressions? He pulled himself wearily to his feet. "Don't be preposterous. I don't know what Vera told you, but this was an accident, and entirely her fault. I've got to go out."

She opened a bobby pin with her teeth and used it to catch up a loose strand of hair. "Oh," she said, with Caroline's sly smile, "are you going to a bar? Mind if I come along?"

"Aura, really. How old are you?"

She winked. "What have you got in mind?"

"You've known me long enough to realize that I do not frequent bars."

She turned off the lamplight, moved toward the hall. "We met in a bar. Have you ever thought how your whole life could have been different if we hadn't?"

"That was a bierhaus."

"Well." Now she shrugged, making progressively apparent where Caroline had acquired mannerisms Hayes had always thought the product of today's inarticulate times.

Stuffing his shirt in his pants, Raleigh sat back down exhausted. "I won't even tell you half the things I've got to do. You just go listen to that tape on my chair in the family room. Daddy has gone completely insane."

She looked sympathetic. "Like the Sheffields."

"I trust you aren't being facetious." Maybe he *was* talking to Caroline. The light was quite dim. "Did you say seven-thirty?" Hayes remembered that he hadn't yet jogged the two miles it was his invariable habit to run each evening before dinner. "Where's the flashlight? I'm going jogging before I leave."

Aura now wiggled the fingers of both hands tip-to-tip at eye level, undulating her elbows. "You know," she said as she thoughtfully watched her hands, "I read an article at the checkout counter about a man like you."

Hayes did not pause on his way upstairs to hear what kind of man the increasingly elliptical Aura might consider him to be. He changed into the white jogging suit he was now sorry he'd purchased from Mingo Sheffield; he rifled the kitchen drawers for his flashlight, glanced in disgust at the open pizza box on the table, and ran out briskly into the night. Naturally, the batteries died before he left his own yard; nor did he wear his glasses, useless this late anyhow. As he ran, a peculiar ease seized him. Hayes did not jog for pleasure, but to outrun his paternal genes, to seek reassurance through each strained sinew and slender bone that life was pain, and the race to the sternly stoical. But there was a peacefulness to running after dark. He was not jolted with massive surges of adrenaline at the sounds of unleashed dogs and the horn blasts of drivers warning him of their superior size. Children did not shoot out of their driveways on plastic motorcycles. Only the moon ran with him now, and the moon was quiet. Ordinarily, nothing more distressed Hayes than trying to compel his eyes to make sharp distinctions without the aid of their glasses. Tonight the world was a comfortable blur. From ranch house, Cape, contemporary, and Colonial, flicked through piny lawns only the silent blue rays of television sets.

Hayes's course took him along Heritage Drive, around Strawberry Patch Court, up Red Mill Lane to the pool and tennis courts communally owned by residents of Starry Haven. He was himself Treasurer of the Association, although he never used the pool or the courts. But Caroline and Holly wasted their summers there, greasing and frying their almost entirely exposed bodies. Trotting beside the chain-link fence, Hayes was startled by the high white wooden lifeguard's chair, looking, moonlit, like the seat of some ghostly giant.

He jogged suddenly backward. Yes, the gate was unlocked. Teenagers. Copulating. No, he heard splashes. Teenagers, swimming, without lights, when the pool was officially closed. Splashes, and incoherent shrieks. Was someone drowning?

"Hey!" he shouted. "Hey! Who's there?" He couldn't see a thing as he ran. "Need help?" The rubber-capped toe of his left jogging shoe caught on the aluminum leg of a lounging chair that was supposed to be stacked in the shower room, and he plunged headfirst into the eye-poppingly cold water.

"Jesus!" shouted a man's voice. Then Hayes was in a tangle of arms and legs, held under by a huge girth of naked squishy flesh.

"*Jesus!*" shouted Hayes too, when he finally pummeled his way to the surface for an instant.

Coming up again, he heard, "EEshus!" Yes! It was Vera Sheffield. And
the white jiggling blob wrestling him was his neighbor Mingo.

"Let me loose!" Hayes gasped.

"Raleigh!" Mingo backkicked, swinging Vera behind him. *"Leave her
alone, can't you!"*

Unless his weak eyes deceived him, the paddling Vera was . . . yes, she
was definitely bare-breasted. Hayes trod water backward. "What are y'all
doing here?"

"Ush?" spluttered Vera. "Ud boud oo?"

All three circled in a dog paddle, Mingo careful to block Vera from Raleigh's view.

"Mingo, y'all are breaking the rules. You know the pool's closed."

"Tough titties," incredibly replied the man Hayes had befriended since
boyhood, against all inclination *and* social advantage.

"Yesh, shuf shiddies!" Vera spat a spout of water in air, arched and
plummeted, exposing as she dived the moony globes of her posterior.
They were skinny-dipping. At their age! They must be on drugs.

"Okay," said Raleigh. "Okay." He swam to the ladder rung, where he
fought to pull his sodden suit and shoes free of the weight of the water.

"Are you going to t . . . tell?" called Mingo. Always his old sissy childhood question.

Hayes didn't answer. In the aluminum chair, he saw stacks of clothes
that he considered taking with him, but why sink to their level? Behind
him he heard Mingo whisper, "He won't tell. That's one thing you *can* say
about Raleigh." Burning through Hayes was a fire of memories. True, he
didn't tell. He had not told the fearsome den father that it was Mingo
who'd eaten all the marshmallows meant for the campfire roast. He had
not told the gym teacher that it was Mingo who had vomited from terror
all over the locker room. He had not told the world that Mingo Sheffield
had wet his pants, cheated on algebra tests, denied that he'd run over his
own dog backing up in his father's truck which he'd been forbidden to
drive, lied to the IRS, and now, presumably, was a sadomasochistic pervert
probably addicted to illegal narcotics.

Hayes took off his shirt, squeezed what water he could from his pants,
shook his feet, jogged rapidly home, rang the doorbell.

His wife appeared, disguised as Holly in jeans and sweatshirt, and
smiled. "Yes, can I help you?"

He snarled sarcastically. "Who am I, Aura?"

She leaned in contemplation against the fluted column. "Lately, you've gotten in the habit, you know, of asking a lot of strange and obvious questions. I wonder why."

"Please don't. Would you excuse me?" Raleigh squished past her, marking his path to the upstairs bath with puddles. He was naked, wringing out his socks in the tub, when she stuck her head in the door, which he had not taken the time to close.

"Was that sweat? Because it's not raining. Raleigh, I've read you can overdo this exercise business. Especially on top of so much alcohol." She was looking him over with an appraising gaze. Hayes blushed and, holding the socks in front of him, sucked in his stomach surreptitiously. He doubted he had ever stood before her naked, under a bright light, in casual conversation. She nodded. "You look pretty good. You've got a nice body."

He heard himself reply, "Thank you," and blushed.

They stood there, both pink-faced, then she went on her tiptoes to whisper in his ear, "Say, how about a roll in the hay?"

"What?" Roll in the hay? Hit the bottle? What kind of magazines was she reading? "Good Lord, Aura, it's eight-fifteen."

"Is that too early? Or too late?" She began pulling bobby pins from her hair. "You're not leaving for New Orleans tonight, are you?"

"Oh. You read Daddy's note. Did you listen to the tape?"

"Your daddy!" She laughed. Why had she always found his father so amusing?

Hayes thought he had an explanation for what was now happening. "Okay, I see. His note. That's where you got this idea."

She shook her hair loose. "Listen, Adam and Eve had this idea."

Raleigh was letting her lead him out of the bathroom. "That's right. Look what happened to them."

"Oh, they had this idea before the snake even spotted the tree. Besides, your father was a minister." Meaning what? That Earley Hayes, who had been *fired* by his church for betraying Raleigh's mother with Roxanne Digges, was an authority on the chronology of the Fall? "I hope he's okay, you know how much I love him," Aura added.

"Who doesn't, except anybody that has to live in the world."

"What? Oh, don't change the subject." She prodded him down the hall.

"From what?"

"Aren't you going to jump my bones?"

She must have heard that on cable television. "Aura, I don't even know what you're talking about."

She was closing the bedroom door. "Come on, I bet it's just like riding a bicycle. It'll all come back." Now she was pulling off her clothes.

"Aura, let's be serious for a second. This isn't like us. You're acting like you used to back in Germany when we first met."

"What do you mean? We didn't sleep together in Germany. Or did we?"

"Of course we didn't. You were only there two weeks. Jesus!"

She lay rosy on the bed, stretching. "Ah, two wonderful weeks. Remember?"

It was true that the Hayeses had met in a bierhaus, in 1960, in Freiburg, where Raleigh was stationed, and where Aura, abroad seeking an Existential Life with the two other bohemians in her class at Mary Baldwin College for Women, was sightseeing, after they'd gotten off the train there to take a shower. At that bierhaus, Aura had told Raleigh that she'd agreed to date him because he was the only GI she'd met in Freiburg who hadn't claimed to be a bunkmate of Elvis Presley. Three years later, back in North Carolina, where Aura was enrolled in nursing school, they'd become engaged on a chartered bus going to John F. Kennedy's funeral.

"What I mean," Hayes explained, "is you were kind of crazy. You know, with your sandals and your mandolin and Simone de Beauvoir."

She rubbed against his side. "You sure know a lot of crazy people."

Vanquished, Raleigh Hayes shook his head. "Well, it's true. Something funny's happening here."

Aura rolled him over against her. She said, "So I see."

CHAPTER

4

How Raleigh Received His Name

IN 1938, during the second term of Franklin Roosevelt and on the day that Adolf Hitler seized Austria, our hero, innocent of the strength of these world shakers to rattle his own minuscule life, was, by his father, splashed in the face with cold water, told he'd just been made an inheritor of the Kingdom of Heaven, and christened by oil in the arms of his sponsors (who were recklessly making all sorts of promises in his new name): RALEIGH WHITTIER HAYES. This shocking and undignified assault the infant Raleigh greeted with the same roving malevolent silent glare with which, forty-five years later, he habitually was to look at all this world's irrational affronts. Aghast to hear his blithe sponsors vow to send him immediately off to war against Sin and the Devil, the swaddled Raleigh did emit one squeal of indignation, but he did not cry, and for his stoicism was praised by the smiling looming face of his mother, who'd stood at the ready with a pacifier.

At the baptism party, in the rectory of Thermopylae's tiny Episcopal church, his father gave him a small sip of muscatel wine, and his seventeen-year-old godfather, his uncle Whittier Hayes, gave him a small copy of *The Poetry of John Keats,* which he didn't want either. Four years later, both Raleigh's father and his godfather had moved out of his life, commissioned by Franklin Roosevelt to fly overseas and stop Hitler from tak-

ing countries that didn't belong to him. Thus our hero, Raleigh Whittier
Hayes, bore the names of two soldiers who wrote poetry and died violently, for like Sir Walter Raleigh, Whittier Hayes — blown up in a tank
near Bizerte, North Africa, shortly before his twenty-second birthday —
had been a poet. He had written not only "Valedictory Ode" ("Ring out
the old! We go to climb the sky!/ So, Thermopylae High, good-bye.
Good-bye."), which was still recited at commencements, but he was the
author as well of six love sonnets mailed from Africa in 1943 to, and until
this day cherished by, Betty Morrow (now the widowed Mrs. Perry
Hemans) and SueAnn McClung (now Mrs. William Swain), neither of
whom suspected the other possessed six identical thin worn sheets of fading ink, both beginning

> *When I have fears that death may capture me*
> *Before my eyes once more have seen your face,*
> *That face that means my home, safe, lost, and free,*
> *Soft summer love far from this hard hot place . . .*

And both ending with proposals of marriage.

Raleigh could not remember his uncle Whittier except as a photograph
on his grandmother's dresser; it sat on a white doily before a small jelly jar
in which there was always a dahlia or narcissus or ivy sprig, at which the
thin soldier was always smiling.

Of the other warrior poet whose name he carried, Raleigh could recall
no more from an oral report he'd been forced to present in the seventh
grade than that the glamorous Sir Walter, spending every shilling he possessed on a suit of silver clothes, had come to London to fling his cloak
down over a mud puddle for Queen Elizabeth I to walk across; that, in
thanks for this (as it seemed to Raleigh Hayes even at twelve) profligate
swaggering, the Virgin Queen had given Sir Walter the ships to defeat the
Spanish Armada and to send the Lost Colony to North Carolina — which
he had called Virginia, in honor of his monarch's chastity. Someone had
chopped off the first Raleigh's head; who, or with what justice, Hayes
could not now resurrect; possibly he'd lost his head for losing the Lost
Colony, or possibly it was for flirting, or atheism. What Hayes recalled
most about this oral report was his embarrassment at the sniggering response of his pubescent classmates to his mention of the word *virginity*. He
could still hear those sniggers, and the moronic joke devised on the spot
by his cousin Jimmy Clay, and repeated by him, with accompanying
shoves, in the halls, cafeteria, and playground, whenever he saw Raleigh.

"How long was Queen Elizabeth's period? About as long as all the other girls'. Hotcha, hotcha, haw, haw, haw."

Hayes's memories of his nominal ancestor were therefore not very pleasant ones. In later years he felt no impulse to learn more about the old extravagant Elizabethan; certainly he had no more urge to read the man's poems than he'd had at his baptism to thumb through Keats (although, in fact, he would have discovered, in Sir Walter's cynical contempt for the folly and rot of the world, a concise echo of his own views). Instead, Hayes resented the imposition of so flamboyant a past on his identity, just as he felt burdened by the inheritance of his father's cavalier good looks; and he didn't correct people who assumed (however ridiculously) that he'd been named for the capital of the state in which he lived.

And in which state (sometimes in the city, Raleigh, and occasionally named Whittier), the Hayes family had lived for several centuries. Of his heritage, our hero was largely and unreluctantly ignorant. He had no time for all the living Hayeses — and rarely saw them except at funerals — much less leisure to get to know the long-expired. Raleigh had no idea who this Goodrich Hale Hayes (whose wife's descendants he was now instructed to trace) might have been. He was a dead Hayes, that's all. North Carolina was filled with them. As might be expected of a man in the business of insuring the future, Raleigh had primarily a predictive interest in the past. It was, for example, important to remember that five years ago when his father had begun playing bingo with a self-described cocktail waitress he'd met at a church social, it had been possible (if time-consuming) to discover that this woman had deserted, but not divorced, her husband in Greensboro, had served time for forging a check and was still on parole, had lost her job at the I-85 Lounge for lewd solicitation, *and* had cheated nightly at bingo. It had been possible for his aunt Victoria to persuade this woman (in the church's ladies room) to stay away from Earley Hayes. It was important to remember that similar vulnerabilities could doubtless be unearthed about the young black girl off in that yellow Cadillac now, and similar pressures brought to bear.

The past was to Raleigh this kind of warning device, easily read by anyone with eyes. Anyone knowing the diet of his aunt Big Em Hayes Leacock (so designated not so much for her obesity — which was manifest — but to distinguish her from her brother Furbus's wife, Little Emily Shay, a petite woman who had to buy her shoes in the children's department, and could never find the styles she wanted: "Ho, ho," laughed Furbus, year after year. "It had been *Big* Em fell on me in the bleachers, she'd of squashed more'n my collarbone, right, Big Em?" "That's right, you'd of been pancakes!" laughed Big Em, year after year) — anyone knowing that this 260-pound diabetic could not or would not deny herself pecan pies and semisolid pitchers of iced tea containing three cups of sugar might have easily predicted that what happened to Big Em (death) was going to happen. That, furthermore, the same fate was soon likely to overtake more of her younger sister Reba than simply her legs.

Such statistical records of the past were worth keeping. But for the past *as* past, Hayes harbored no nostalgia. Perhaps by a trait inherited from his Philadelphia mother, he was immune to the Southern homesickness for yesterday. Raleigh didn't know that Henry Ford had said, "History is bunk," but he wouldn't have argued with so successful a man. With America, he was willing to encapsulate decades and forget them, willing to leave behind. Of course, he still lived in Thermopylae, but his presence there, initially accidental, was ultimately irrelevant. Thermopylae would do. Of course, he could have migrated, and so escaped all his relatives, but he had never required space in order to lose touch.

No, Raleigh made no claims on the past. Of his maternal ancestry, he'd heard not a single story: Sarah Ainsworth had appeared in Thermopylae one summer day in 1936 to visit a friend. Unprecedented and unencumbered, the only child of a deceased, kinless, well-off widower, she'd promptly given herself away to Earley Hayes. She'd mentioned no relationships but one to her bank trustee in Philadelphia, and before Raleigh had thought to press her for details, she had died. On his paternal side, he'd heard nothing but details. Whole lives lost to chatter. He'd forgotten most of these stories, and could scarcely remember the old storytellers, including his great-grandmother (nicknamed Tiny), who'd often tried to bribe him to go buy her peppermint sticks at Woolworth's by promising to betray family secrets. He didn't recall the secrets. He didn't know, and suspected he wouldn't enjoy learning, who all his predecessors were.

This indifference distinguished Raleigh from most of his Thermopylean neighbors, who would tell him with straight faces that their forebears had invented Coca-Cola, written "White Christmas," set fire to a million dollars in Confederate money to boil turnips by, stopped a bullet destined for Andrew Jackson, slept with Mary Queen of Scots. Nemours Kettell had wasted God knows how large a fortune trying to prove himself illegitimately descended from Napoleon's emigrating general, Marshal Ney, Duc d'Elchingen. Hayes had only taken off his glasses and rubbed his eyes when obliged to listen to Kettell at Civitan luncheons attempt to persuade *him* to hire a genealogist who might be able to trace him back to Sir

Walter Raleigh, or at least to the poet John Greenleaf Whittier (part of whose interminable poem "Snowbound" Hayes had been forced to memorize and recite in that same seventh-grade class). The subject of genealogies was made more distressing to our hero by the fact that his half-brother Gates had been arrested for selling fake family trees and forged Confederate holographs to unsuspecting women passionate for antebellum glamour. No, Hayes saw no cause to claim the past.

Until today. On this awful Ides of March, as he had jogged home sopping wet from his immersion in Starry Haven Community Pool, it had occurred to Raleigh Whittier Hayes that perhaps his perspective on his injuries had been insufficiently far-reaching. To blame the imbecilic Ned Ware, the infantile Mingo Sheffield, the gibble-gabbling Jimmy Clay, and boorish Booger, or even to blame his impossible father, was not only somehow unsatisfying, it was intellectually puny. As he ran, it had occurred to Hayes to stretch indignation back to the very headspring of his genesis; not, that is, as far as Adam, but all the way back to the original Raleigh, whose name now entered his mind for the first time in many years. Yes, he would blame the fact that he was jogging home soaked from a near drowning at the hands of a fat naked deviant . . . on Sir Walter! He would lay it all at the no doubt jeweled feet of that roving, vaulting, sleek and spangled, open-handed, bee-headed, moon-mad, lecherous clothes-horse, Walter Raleigh! Had this grabby fool never shipped hapless Englishmen over to Roanoke to slap sweaty-palmed at mosquitoes, dodge arrows, and poke grit-grimed in the sand for gold, until they managed to get themselves lost, or eaten, maybe the long string of simpletons who'd followed them over the ocean, in a line that led straight to the first Carolina Hayes, never would have gotten the idea that they could skip off to a New World every time the Old one rubbed them wrong. Maybe they would have stuck with their sheep back in Sussex, as Raleigh Hayes himself would sensibly have done. (Wasn't he still in Thermopylae where fate had randomly dropped him?) If Sir Walter had kept his cloak on his back where it belonged, Raleigh Hayes could have grown up in England, where people's cousins didn't sell people's fathers yellow Cadillacs, and people's neighbors didn't wear spiked collars or go skinny-dipping an hour after failing to commit suicide. Hayeses wouldn't have trooped to America in that stream of harebrained optimists leading to his cousin Kenny Leacock (son of Big Em), who'd moved his wife in a Winnebago to Los Angeles, where they'd spent years trying to get on *The Price Is Right,* disguised as papier-mâché salt and pepper shakers.

It's unfortunate our hero was so in the dark. He would have derived a wry satisfaction from the knowledge that the first American Hayes (baptized Obed in 1632 by a Cheapside evangelical Separatist who was subsequently hanged for his violent views on altar cloths) had been just such a harebrained optimist. Duped by a ship company's placard posted on Bishopsgate Street, London (having failed to read the fine print), Obed Hayes had discovered only in the middle of the Atlantic Ocean that in exchange for his free passage to Cape Fear, he had bound himself to five years' indentured servitude bent over a fermenting vat on a Carolina indigo plantation. Once there, Obed had learned that he'd been duped by the Cape Fear ship company's *large* print, for it had outrageously vouched for "The Healthfulness of the Air" in that Indian-infested swamp, and for "The Fertility of the Earth and Waters, and the great Pleasure and Profit to accrue to those that shall go thither to enjoy the Same." Raleigh's first native forefather had lost his hair to scarlet fever and his arm to a tomahawk and, after five years stirring blue dye, for the rest of his life would never own anything blue (in fact, could scarcely bear to look at the sky). But somehow, Obed had survived to begin, with a New Bern printer's daughter, a Hayes family tree, whose newest branch, our hero Raleigh, had never traced himself back to a bough, much less the trunk called HAYES; who had no idea he actually was — by a tenuous collateral limb — remotely related to John Greenleaf Whittier, from whom, perhaps, his soldier-uncle Whittier had inherited the gene of his poetic nature. Who hadn't a clue that his great-great-grandfather, Major General Goodrich Hale Hayes, C.S.A., had been in charge of a mule-drawn, false-bottomed wagon retreating from Sherman's relentless advance through North Carolina, and that this wagon had gotten itself as lost as Sir Walter's colony, and that the mules had balked at every red muddy hill on the Piedmont road to Thermopylae, because the false bottom was lined with gold bars, and — as Raleigh Whittier Hayes did know — gold is heavy.

CHAPTER

5

In Which Raleigh Blackmails an Enemy and Frightens the Kaiser

RALEIGH AWAKENED disoriented with a face warmly snuggled in his bare shoulder, and, like a traveler studying a strange motel room, he squinted warily at his surroundings. He was, however, in the "Mediterranean Modern" bed where he always slept, beside the person who always slept beside him. On the other hand, neither he nor Aura was wearing the pajamas they always wore; the alarm clock was not singing, the sky was the wrong color, it was only five-thirty in the morning.

In the bathroom, Hayes stepped with a shudder on the cold soggy heap of his jogging suit. He looked shyly in the mirror at his flushed sleepy face and rumpled hair. A former Raleigh Hayes about thirty-five years old tentatively smiled back. Not wanting to wake his wife (even at their normal hour not an eager riser, but one who would punch Doze every ten minutes until, defeated, the system shut itself off), not wanting to wake his girls (a superfluous concern), the head of the family dressed, and tiptoed in socks down the carpeted stairs. Beneath the couch he found the cordovan wingtips that had carried him over yesterday's dreadful journey. Sitting to lace them, he felt between the slipcovers the tiny black pistol he'd obviously dropped there, having, so it seemed, carried it away with him after disarming Mingo Sheffield. "Kill himself!" Hayes snorted when he opened the gun and found it unloaded. Nevertheless, Mingo in his present volatile state was certainly not to be trusted with a deadly weapon, nor could Raleigh leave it in the house with unwakable women. He put it in the pocket of his blue seersucker jacket; he was surprised at the heavy way it pulled on the cloth. He also had safety-pinned there in his jacket two sealed envelopes containing five thousand dollars each, which he intended to deposit as soon as the bank opened.

For breakfast, it was Raleigh's habit to have fresh fruit for digestion, whole-grain cereal for roughage, and coffee for speed. But belly dancing or M.F.P. had no doubt taken Aura's mind off her shopping, for the only fresh fruit he could find in the crowded kitchen were three hard limes in a basket with the nubbly stem of an otherwise missing bunch of grapes. The only cereal was all bright green and pink and cut in the shapes of cartoon characters, and while there was ample coffee, there were no filters. Hungry as he was (and he'd had nothing to eat since the orange slices in yesterday's three Singapore Slings), Hayes would not breakfast on pink puffed comic strips, nor would he drink frozen orange juice, not since once reading of a lady who'd opened a can and found it entirely filled with a frozen mouse. Nor would he use, as Aura seemed to, a paper napkin with a flower design as a coffee filter.

"Didn't wake you. Gone out on this business of Daddy's. Will catch a bite to eat. No filters." Pen twitching in hand, Raleigh studied this note to his wife, then unclipped it from the coffee machine and added, "Love, Raleigh."

Out in his little greenhouse — where a third of his daffodils had indeed been snipped off — Raleigh extravagantly cut ten more, which he arranged in a water glass on the kitchen table. He dropped an aspirin in the glass, believing that they prolonged plant life, and suspecting that unless roused by the frenetic radio announcer on station WACK, Aura would sleep past the petals' prime.

Outdoors, the silent streets of Starry Haven had at dawn a lush pastoral look, as if God, dissatisfied, had erased the world and started over. While the Fiesta had been returned to the driveway, undented, the seats were dewy because its hatchback had been left open. Moreover, the ashtray was half closed on a cigar butt. Hayes could not decide which was worse: that Caroline and Holly now smoked cigars, or that they gave lifts to strangers who did so, or that there was a nocturnal smoking joyrider loose in the subdivision. But, he thought as he fished for his keys, at least the tires had not been slashed, at least Vera Sheffield was not lying naked in the back seat, ready to flick him with her vicious riding crop.

At six A.M., as Raleigh drove out of Starry Haven, in the driveways of

Capes and Colonials and ranch houses still sat his neighbors' cars, patiently waiting to take their owners to wherever day after day their owners drove to do something to pay for them. He saw not a soul, heard not a song but the musical comedy of the local bluejays, who were as big as pigeons and as bad tempered as gulls.

What had happened — come to think of it, now that his friend, the World, had proven so noticeably fickle — what had happened to the nice old noises of early morning? The bell of the vegetable truck with its swinging brass scale, the milkman's chinkling rattle, the newsboy's thunk? Where had everybody gone? Where was the man who came offering to sharpen scissors and lawnmower blades, the man who came with the saddle pony to see if anyone wanted a photograph of their child taken, the man who took away the knotted bunches of soiled laundry left on porches? Where were the eager pastor, the sleep-slouched doctor, the men wanting yardwork to do, having brushes to sell, white-papered meat to deliver? Where were the Mormons, the vendors, the carolers, the candidates? When had the world stopped coming to the door?

These uncustomary reflections on the past occupied Hayes as he sped along the beltway toward downtown Thermopylae and the 1927 Forbes Building — the town's only skyscraper, with twelve floors (a third of them empty), on the highest of which Hayes had his office. In the building's cavernous gilded lobby, across from the defunct tobacco and shoe-shine stand, was Forbes Corner Coffee Shop. This establishment, Hayes, who never ate breakfast out, now entered. He recognized from the rear, their haunches hanging over the stools, the row of downtown businessmen flanked with their newspapers along the counter. They were the coffee shop regulars and preferred this side-by-side linear arrangement (as if they were still on the bench of the Thermopylae High football field) to any of the perpetually empty Formica-topped tables behind them.

Hayes knew them all, Nemours Kettell and Wayne Sparks, Pierce Jimson, Ned Ware, Mingo, and the rest; knew they rose early so they could come here to talk sports and money together, to vaunt together, shifting indiscriminately between boasts of success and boasts of failure.

"I tell you what, I one time lost fifty dollars on a six-point spread I had on the Cowboys," Mingo smugly whined (and lied — for Raleigh knew it was only five dollars he'd lost) to Boyd Joyner, the best-looking Civitan.

"Yeah, well, you gotta know what you're doing. I'm seven hundred ahead this month. You think I'm gonna tell the wife?" Joyner wrung his own neck.

"Hey, Boyd, I bet you sure didn't tell her what you dropped in Atlantic City, right? You'dah got grounded for sure, right? Ball and chain!"

Boyd Joyner socked Nemours Kettell in agreement. "You know it. Eight ball and chain gang. *Your* wife 'ould *kill* you!"

They enjoyed pretending they were afraid of their wives. They enjoyed pretending they were flirting with the two middle-aged waitresses, Doris and Lucinda (thick-shouldered and raw-handed from years of lugging and washing dishes), who worked the counter and wearily grinned at invitations to shut off the grill and run away to lives of illicit passion.

As Hayes sat down at one of the empty tables, the pharmacist, Tommy Whitefield, was shouting along the row to Ned Ware, "Says here South Savings and Loan is gonna give you an Atari computer if you take out a mortgage. Better watch out, Ned, South Savings's giving away Ataris."

Nemours Kettell shot a hand over his flattop like a jet leaving a carrier, and answered for the ex-halfback, Ned, who was not quick at this repartee. "Trick is, you find a guy in this town with the dough-re-mi to plunk down on a mortgage in the first place that's going to give it to a colored-run business like South Savings just for some Atari. Right, Ned?"

"I guess so."

"You tell 'em, Ned," said Kettell's son-in-law, the closet hippie, Wayne Sparks.

"I sure would like one of those Ataris," said Ned, doing one-arm curls with the napkin dispenser as a dumbbell.

Raleigh Hayes was standing to wave his fork at the waitress, when Boyd Joyner (who, with olive skin, black mustache, and salmon loafers, looked like the Italian owner of a Miami nightspot, but was actually a Scots-descended native Carolinean building contractor) grabbed the woman's hand and said, "Hey, Doris, come on, let's make a fast run over to a bed at Holiday Inn. You too, Lucinda. Y'all need to get off your feet."

The elder of the women, Doris, tugged up with her thumb on the bra strap that had worn a gorge across her shoulder, visible through the sleeveless nylon sweater. "I don't know, Boyd," she drawled speculatively. "It's a little early in the day for me, do anything fast." All the men laughed. Although she was not nearly as attractive as Lucinda, Doris was more popular, because Lucinda made the men nervous; she never wisecracked or called them by name, only smiled, and sometimes didn't even do that. The regulars much preferred Doris, in whose retorts, particularly if insulting, they all delighted.

"Two eggs, no juice, how much I owe you?" politely inquired Joyner now, all kidding aside. He left a tip half the size of his check, pulled on his sunglasses, announced, "Well, boys and girls, another day," and left.

Nemours Kettell, who'd spun around on his stool to sock Joyner good-bye, saw Raleigh, fork-raised in the corner, which was more than the waitress had done. "Look who's here! Aura kick you out or what?" Kettell's wide hand smacked the unfortunately empty stool beside him in invitation. "This place's been integrated for years, Raleigh, come on over. Pour him a cup of cof, hon. Hey, Ral, get over here."

Raleigh knew that Kettell was thinking that he'd sat across the room because he'd seen his family enemy Pierce Jimson seated at the counter. Everybody knew that Pierce's father, PeeWee Jimson, had once clerked for Raleigh's grandfather, Clayton Hayes, then had somehow ended up sole owner of both Hayes Market and Hayes Furniture Store. Everyone knew that the Jimsons had stayed hostile to the Hayeses ever since; it was hard to be nice to people you'd gypped. Actually, while Raleigh didn't much like Pierce, he didn't hold the slightest grudge about the past. What he couldn't stand was eating with people squeezed in on his sides, reaching across him for ketchup to splatter on scrambled eggs, fluttering their newspapers over his bare arms, and talking with their mouths full of grizzled ham about who should have thrown what ball where.

Said Tommy Whitefield, "Soon as I got rid of my hook — hi, there, Raleigh — I lost my putt. On the green in three, and my putt goes to hell."

Raleigh greeted everyone, including Pierce Jimson, who only nodded and studied his *Wall Street Journal* while sucking in coffee with his ant-eaterish upper lip. "I'm on the run," Hayes apologized. "Excuse me, miss, do you have anything to go? Leaving, Mingo? Nice seeing you." Sheffield waddled off with a sheepish wave.

"Danish, honeybun, jelly, glazed." Doris fluffed out her beehive hair as she nodded at five sticky lumps of dough under a plastic cover. "What's your pleasure?"

"Say, hey, Doris, 'what's his pleasure'? You just met the guy. Matter of fact, he's into B and D." Wayne Sparks guffawed at his own remark, unaccompanied. He failed to understand why no one laughed at his jokes, which were much funnier than, say, Boyd Joyner's innuendos. Well, probably no one at the counter knew what B and D meant, being more accustomed to alimentary than erotic abbreviations. Wayne sighed and thought of leaving town to join a commune, but sank back down on the stool as if handcuffed to his father-in-law.

"So, Ral, how's Mut Life?" smirked Kettell.

"Pretty good, Nemours, how's concrete? Yes, thank you, I'll take those five. And black coffee, thank you."

Ned Ware leaned around Sparks. "You find your daddy yet, Raleigh?"

Doris flapped open a bag. "You want all five of them?"

"Yes, all right, fine, thank you."

"Five?"

"Earley lost or something?" Kettell asked.

"No, just gone on a trip for a few days." Raleigh glared at Ned. "So," he added quickly, "Boyd's looking okay. Contracting business finally picked up?"

Wayne took another risk and said, "Only thing picking up in Thermopylae is people picking up and moving out. Right, Mr. K?"

"This town doesn't need your negativity, Wayne," said Mr. Kettell.

"Sorry." Sparks raised eyes and hands to an Attendant Spirit hovering above, who presumably sympathized.

"Boyd's going to lose his house," Ned Ware announced with somber sympathy. "I feel real sorry for Boyd."

"Gosh, I thought he was a big shot," Doris sighed.

"Overextended," explained Nemours Kettell, who had specialized in highway graft and done very well. "Built three condos, couldn't sell them, didn't even finish the last one. I drove by there, saw the bulldozer just sitting in the hole for the pool."

Pierce Jimson, without raising his eyes from his paper, spoke for the first time. "Lizzie Joyner came in the store and asked me for a job."

Kettell stuck his little finger in his mouth to rub his gums. "That's pitiful. I can't believe America's gotten to the point where a man like Boyd Joyner has to let his wife go out and earn a living."

Uncharacteristically, the younger waitress, Lucinda, a short blonde with large breasts on a thin frame, made a remark. She said, "America got to that point about fifteen years ago as far as I'm concerned."

Only Wayne laughed.

"Anyhow," said Tommy Whitefield, the druggist, "I heard Boyd's wife was running around."

"I heard that too."

"Somebody ought to tell him."

Everyone nodded solemnly, except Raleigh, who didn't gossip, and Pierce Jimson, who was having an affair with Mrs. Joyner.

By now, Raleigh had paid for his greasy bag of pastries. "I've got to run." He showed them his watch. It surprised him by announcing that it was only 6:50 A.M. "Ned," he said to the banker, "keep in mind our talk

yesterday, will you?" Ware looked at him blankly, then smiled. In the exasperating certainty that, under the guise of troubled solicitude, Ned
Ware was going to blab the whole story of Earley Hayes's current antics
with the young black woman and the convertible Cadillac, Raleigh decided on the spur of the moment to lure Pierce Jimson away before he
heard it. He only then realized he was going to try to negotiate with Pierce
to purchase the cabin at Knoll Pond. "Pierce, talk to you a second?" he
asked, hand poised (with that precise Southern sensitivity to social nu-
ance, lacking which Raleigh's Philadelphia mother had often been accused
of being both too friendly and too frosty) exactly three inches above Jimson's right shoulder.

Tommy Whitefield was bragging to Jimson at the time, "Look, my wife
tried any funny business like Boyd's on me, I'd kill them both, wouldn't
you? Look, I heard on TV where all these guys in Brazil are getting off free
as a bird for shooting their wives right through the head for having affairs
and getting jobs and even just wearing short skirts, I'm not kidding. It's a,
you know, a question of honor. In Brazil, I heard juries let them just walk
away right and left."

Pierce Jimson shook his check at Doris, who asked him, "Wasn't Desi
Arnez from Brazil? Desi sure never tried to pull anything like that on Lucy
when she got her divorce. In real life, Lucy was the brains, anyhow."

"Cuba," said Wayne Sparks. "Aiii yi yi yi! Desi was from Cuba!"

"Cuba!" snapped Kettell, as if Wayne had personally arranged that island's revolution. "Okay, listen, boys, I want everybody to show at this do
I'm throwing for Charlie Lukes tonight, you hear? Send him back to Congress, he'll take care of places like Cuba. Let's get behind him now."
Everybody nodded, but none really shared Kettell's passion for political
fund-raising, and besides they were too busy watching the unprecedented
sight of a Hayes and a Jimson chatting as they strolled into the lobby together. For Jimson, to their surprise (but then they didn't know how
eager he was to escape further discussion of Mrs. Joyner's infidelity), had
announced in his sonorous voice, "Walk me out, Raleigh," and Hayes had
answered, "Sure thing."

At fifty, Pierce Jimson was a balding, freckled man of unprepossessing
looks, average in height and narrow-shouldered, with a long upper lip
above a pronounced overbite. At twelve, he had acquired one good fea-
ture — the strong, mellifluous baritone voice he had since then assiduously trained in debating clubs and choral singing. This voice was so rich
and commanded such authority that everybody in Thermopylae had come
to assume that the man behind it was large and rich and powerful,

too. Consequently, he'd become so, and, over the years, had himself, like his neighbors, lost any realistic perspective on his appearance. When Pierce Jimson looked in a mirror, he saw his voice. A stranger, comparing the homely Jimson and the handsome Boyd Joyner, might have puzzled at Mrs. Joyner's infatuation with the former, but a Thermopylean would have been surprised only because Jimson's voice didn't mess around like that. That voice, calling the roll at town council meetings or leading the choir in "God of Our Fathers," was the voice of their own moral rectitude, of order in the home and in the state — not conceivably the voice of covert phone conversations and disheveled motel rooms. In fact, Lizzie Joyner was not enamored of the power of the voice; she was enamored of the overwhelming passion for her that, to Pierce's bewilderment, had set upon the heretofore contentedly married man six months ago. They were both addicts of his passion.

Of course, Raleigh Hayes didn't know any of this. He kept talking about Boyd Joyner after they reached the lobby, only because he was nervous, and didn't want to open immediately with the topic of Knoll Pond. "I'd hate for Boyd to hear those rumors about his wife, wouldn't you? I mean, on top of his business worries. Boy, I remember when he came home from Korea with all those decorations. Big Marine hero, so young. Everybody thought he was really going places. Damn shame."

"Economy ought to pick up." Jimson was thinking that Raleigh Hayes never gossiped about people, never *talked* about people, rarely ever talked to *him*. What was going on?

"Boyd's a nice fellow, too. Aura took judo lessons from him at the Y. She liked him a lot. Nice fellow. Terrible temper, though. I'd hate to think what would happen if he found out anything like that about Lizzie. Well, listen, by the way, Pierce, any likelihood you'd be interested in letting go of that old rotted cabin up near Knoll Pond? Somebody mentioned they heard you were thinking of trying to get rid of it. I used to do a bit of fishing up there. Might be willing to take it off your hands."

"What?"

"Fishing's my love affair. Every man's got to have one, right?"

Raleigh was blushing at his speech, hastily prepared on the way to the lobby. First of all, he was blushing because he always did when he lied, and, second, he expected Jimson to laugh at him and then reply, "No." In fact, he looked forward to the rejection; it would mean that he had failed to carry out one of his father's outrageous instructions, and so, having failed, need try no more. When Jimson, wiggling his long upper lip, turned without a word, walked to the abandoned shoeshine stand, climbed into one of its high seats, and put his feet on the iron shoerests, Raleigh assumed the merchant had found his proposal so great a social breach of their families' long-lived antagonism that he wasn't even going to respond to it. He was certainly staring at Hayes with a disgusted, astonished look. The look intensified when Raleigh, blushing hotter, went on. "Matter of fact, it was Boyd Joyner I used to do a lot of fishing with, you know, back when we were kids. I haven't done as much lately as I'd like." (Indeed, Hayes hadn't gone fishing once in the last five years.) "Just haven't found the time, what with work and family." He now tried a little humor of the Civitans sort in hopes of changing the terrible look on Jimson's face. "What I can't figure out, Pierce, is how these damn adulterers find the *time*." As Jimson still sat there glowering, Raleigh decided to leave. "Well, think it over."

"Just a minute." Even lowered, the baritone reverberated in the big empty space. "Look here."

Hayes turned back. "Sorry if I offended you, bringing this up, Pierce, but I figured you and I were adult enough not to be stopped by a bunch of foolish family emotion. I don't pay any attention to my family in things like this, and naturally I assumed you felt the same. This was strictly a business deal."

Jimson was staggered. He was shocked speechless by the certainty that a man like Raleigh Hayes (a Civitan, a church deacon, a former president of the Better Business Bureau) was blatantly blackmailing him with threats of exposing to her husband his illicit affair with Mrs. Joyner. That this was what was meant by all the veiled references not only to love affairs but to Boyd's deadly martial skills, Jimson did not for a moment doubt. He was so obsessed with his infidelity that he assumed everyone else was too. What he wasn't certain of were the blackmail terms. Hayes appeared to be selling his silence for a broken-backed shack near a weed-clotted pond, un-cleared miles away from the old Hillston Road. Jimson wasn't even sure exactly where. Annually he paid taxes on a thin strip leading on an un-farmable rise from the road to the knoll, having inherited the land from his father, who'd gotten it in some entangled financial fallout (he seemed to recall) with Raleigh's grandfather. "Bunch of foolish family emotion?" he faltered.

Hayes nodded. "Far as I'm concerned. Why should we hang on to that old nonsense? They need never know."

Jimson was awestruck by the until now utterly unsuspected depths of

Raleigh Hayes's jaded cynicism. The sanctity of marriage was old nonsense, foolish family emotion? Clearly, no appeals to the pain that knowledge would cause the innocent Mrs. Jimson and Mr. Joyner were likely to
mean a thing to him. The man was a monster; he had to be placated. "Raleigh, you want to fish out there, you go right ahead. Be my guest. You
don't have to buy it."

"Gosh, Pierce, that's really very nice of you. I appreciate it. But the fact
is, I *want* to buy that old cabin. It has, well, a sentimental significance of a
nostalgic aspect." Hayes could hear Aura saying, "Raleigh, you're upset,
aren't you? You're getting polysyllabic." He took off his glasses so he
wouldn't have to see Jimson's response to this latest fabrication. "It means
a lot to me. Don't you ever wish you could get back to feeling, well, innocent like you used to be?" Raleigh blushed brighter, as it all of a sudden
struck him that he wasn't lying; he actually had, long ago at the pond, felt,
what? At ease. He actually could feel wriggling somewhere distant inside
him an urge to feel that way again.

Jimson, however, interpreted Hayes's remark about innocence as sadistic
irony. He lifted his head from his arms and studied the blackmailer as if he
were some horrific sideshow exhibit. "You really want to buy it? It's not
worth anything."

Raleigh tried a companionable, shrewd chuckle. "Then I won't pay
much. But I will pay cash."

Warily, Jimson climbed out of the shoeshine seat, so bringing himself
physically down to Raleigh's level. He felt defeated, but oddly relieved:
Everybody was immoral, sinners in league to protect their sins. Wouldn't it
have been worse if Hayes, in pure disinterest, had counseled him to *stop*
seeing Lizzie? He became crafty and businesslike. "That's it? That's all you
want? You're sure? You just want that old cabin?"

"Well, and the land it's on." Hayes repeated the chuckle. For Pete's
sake, was Jimson really going to sell him that property, and if so, for whatever reason in the world? He merrily patted the merchant's arm. "Don't
worry. I swear nobody's discovered any oil out there, honest."

That very thought had just crossed Jimson's mind, but clearly a Machia-
velli like Hayes would never have brought up the subject if such were the
case. It was more probable that Hayes wanted a hideaway for some of his
other nefarious enterprises. Something he didn't want traced; why else
offer cash? Heaven knows what the man was capable of. "Okay, Raleigh,
you win. What do you want to pay for it?"

"Well, what are you asking?" stumbled Hayes.

Jimson put his hand in his pocket. His fingers touched the packet of new ribbed condoms he'd bought in Charlotte. Lizzie would be at the furniture warehouse in an hour. If he only had time to figure out what Raleigh was really up to, but he didn't dare wait, not with the bubble of his reputation on the lips of so heartless a man. "How about three thousand, then?"

"Three thousand?" Excited, Hayes shifted his bag of pastries from one hand to the other. "*Three?* Are you kidding?" (He had hoped for six, and expected to hear seven or eight.)

"All right! Twenty-five hundred."

"Sold!" cried Hayes, and set the bag down on the shoeshine stand to shake on the deal, but Jimson was already walking away. "Do we need, Pierce, do we need a lawyer?" he called after him. Jimson shook his head emphatically no. Raleigh turned his back, reached inside one of the buttoned pockets where he'd safety-pinned the envelopes of money, undid one, and ran after the merchant. "Hey, hold up, Pierce. Might as well take it now."

Jimson stared as Hayes fastidiously removed twenty-five new one-hundred-dollar bills from a white envelope. He stared as Hayes scribbled in a small notebook: "Received of R.W. Hayes, $2500.00 cash, in full payment for all property now owned by me in the area known as Knoll Pond, said property to include the remains of the cabin there, and the access lane from Hillston Road." Hayes looked this over, then tore out the page. "No time like the present, Pierce. Sorry to rush you, but I may need to leave town, and I'd like to settle this. If you'll just sign now, then your lawyer can fix it up legally."

Jimson kept staring. "I don't believe in hurrying business this way. . . . Maybe we should . . ." He backed away.

Hayes closed Jimson's fingers around the pen. "Pierce, you can't afford not to do this. Can you? You don't know what might happen. I might come to my senses. Am I right?" He laughed, but couldn't manage to sound even remotely sincere.

And with a long sigh, the adulterer signed, and crammed the money deep in his pocket beside the condoms.

"Oh, Pierce, by the way, now we're doing business, do you have a life insurance policy?"

Jimson wheeled around. "I'm already fully insured."

"Good. You should be."

"Meaning what?!"

"Everybody should be. Give my best to your wife."

"Just don't push too far, Raleigh, goddammit."

"Pardon?" What a strange fellow, thought Hayes, as the lobby doors slammed on his question. Absolutely unpredictable.

And still shaking his head from time to time, Hayes rode the rattling elevator up to his office, where he found his note "Be Back Soon" still taped to the door. Bonnie Ellen! He'd forgotten to call her last night. Why hadn't she called him? Why hadn't she removed his note? And wasn't she usually a little bit neater? For Hayes now noticed details in the anteroom where she had her desk, details that yesterday, in his distress about his father, he'd failed to see. (Not that he was ever, according to Aura, particularly observant where Bonnie Ellen Dellwood was concerned: Aura had told him her silly theory that Bonnie Ellen had a crush on him, adding, "I don't blame her." And when Raleigh'd dismissed this as preposterous, she'd further explained, "You probably subconsciously find her sexually attractive too — who wouldn't, with those breasts and outfits — so you *have* to ignore her. You don't notice her out of loyalty to me, but, honey, you don't have to be *blind* to be faithful." Raleigh'd replied, "Aura, please don't tell me who I am and I don't know it.") However, he admittedly had ignored the fact that Bonnie Ellen was as untidy as her desk now appeared to indicate. White circles tracked the path of a paper Coke cup. Flies were crawling on a tangle of french fries. A crimson paperback titled *Flame of Castle Fury* sat with its spine cracked atop the typewriter; beside it, Hayes saw three letters he thought had been mailed a week ago. They were sprinkled with dirt from an overturned knobby cactus plant that lay on its back, roots up, like a crab. Dust balls had gathered on the floor, a spider had spun at leisure a substantial web in a window ledge. Maybe Bonnie Ellen (who periodically called in with bouts of flu — perhaps too periodically for a healthy young woman of twenty-three) had been taken ill while at the office and had gone home in a hurry. Still, she might have left a note, or had her husband call (if he was her husband — which Aura doubted). Admittedly, Hayes knew very little about Mrs. Dellwood, whom he'd hired as a temporary replacement six months ago, when Betty Morrow Hemans, his secretary for twenty years, had abruptly retired to devote herself exclusively to the novel she'd been writing since he'd met her. Had he, in fact, hired Bonnie Ellen *for* — and not in spite of — her flashy looks? What a horrible discovery, if true, which it wasn't, of course, thought Hayes.

Seated behind his own meticulous desk, Raleigh took out his lukewarm coffee and his huge, clammy glazed pastries. Made reckless by hunger, he gluttonously devoured all five as he worked. He recalled having eaten such things for breakfast long ago, back in college, when obviously his stomach had been impervious to assault. Now horrible pains seized him. He was squeezing his sides when the phone rang. It was not Bonnie Ellen, but Aura.

"Where'd you go?" she said. "What about the afterglow?"

"What? Aura, it's seven-o-five."

"I'm sure you're right. Sweetheart, have you by any chance bought a new watch lately? You keep wanting to tell me the time. Thanks for the flowers, by the way. What in the world are you doing? Are you kissing me through the phone? I find this new you absolutely fascinating."

Hayes was licking from his fingers the glazed sugar that had webbed them together. "Don't be silly. Did Bonnie Ellen call?"

"I see. Now you've had *me*, you're after her."

"I don't know where she is."

"In the sack with her boyfriend, probably. It's only, let me guess, seven-o-six."

"Aura, do you mind? And I wish you wouldn't say things like 'in the sack' at your age."

"You want me to wait till I'm older?"

"Ha ha. What are you doing up? You never wake up by seven."

"Mothers for Peace, remember? Today's a big day for me. Besides, the phone woke me. Aunt Vicky wants you to come over right away. About your daddy."

Hayes took his fingers from his mouth so quickly his cheek popped. *"She's got him?"*

"No, no, he just called. Long distance. You know," Aura yawned, "you're starting to get like that guy in Victor Hugo."

Raleigh stood. "I don't have time to wonder what you could possibly mean."

"You know."

"Really?" he asked her smiling photograph.

"I mean, *obsessed,* like the detective after the man who killed his wife, in that TV series they stole from *Les Misérables.*"

"Aura, good-bye."

"Yes, you better hang up. It's probably seven-o-eight. But aren't you going to ask me what I'm wearing? You were so into women's clothing yesterday."

"For God's sake, I was not!"

"I'm *au naturel.* My, I'm in a French mood today, aren't I? Well, *bon* whatever the word for morning is. Oh, *matin*. Listen, the girls won't be home for supper and I may be late, but there're plenty of leftovers. Wish us luck."

"Aura, what are you talking about?"

"Really, Raleigh! M.F.P.! But let's get to bed early. Ummmm."

She'd hung up. Perhaps Aura had precipitously entered a midlife crisis. Perhaps for women they took this distinctively carnal cast. Look at Vera Sheffield. And, apparently, Lizzie Joyner. Perhaps in addition to their politicking against nuclear war, they'd all joined some local consciousness-raising group that encouraged this aggressive kind of sexual behavior. Hayes, soliloquizing, prepared his own mail. Then he telephoned Bonnie Ellen's apartment. The woman who answered the phone said her name was Mrs. Hannah Pruck. She said, "I rent them my upstairs and it's a mess. I'm up here now. I'm as disgusted as I can be."

"I'm sorry. This is Mrs. Dellwood's employer, Raleigh W. Hayes? I'm sorry to disturb you so early."

"I can't sleep nights," the woman told him proudly. "I've been up since the crack of dawn for ten years."

"I'm sorry to hear that. Is Bonnie Ellen sick or something? She left work yesterday without saying anything."

"You don't know? Well, that takes the cake. Young people don't have the manners of a hog. They went to California, and didn't tell you, me, or the lamppost. Never even mind the holes in my walls."

"I beg your pardon?" Raleigh began to monitor his pulse with his thumb. "California?"

"Her husband — that's a laugh, between me and you — stuck a note on the door. With a *nail!*" added Mrs. Pruck. "About how a job had come up in California and they both had to leave right away and they'd be in touch, according to this note, but don't make me laugh."

"I don't believe it." Hayes could find no pulse on either wrist.

"You wouldn't put it past them you took a good look at this room. My husband died in this room, and look at the way they've treated it. First of the month, every bit of theirs goes in the trash. I'd be ashamed to take it to Goodwill, and so would you."

Hayes hung up and said to someone, "Ha ha. Thanks a lot." Now, he would have to beg Betty Hemans to set aside her novel and return to work until he could find a new secretary. A flood of anger against Chinese food lifted Raleigh from his chair and swept him to the door. He had the unassailable feeling (simultaneously discounted as absurd) that had he never opened that fortune cookie at the Lotus House yesterday, Fortune would never have gotten loose to play these kinds of tricks on him, like a genii on a rampage — out of her bottle after a million years.

But Fortune, unbound by the human limits of even the most dyspeptic irony, knew tricks Hayes was certainly not imagining as he hurried down the hall past the supplies closet, in a corner of which Bonnie Ellen Dellwood had been lying unconscious for an hour. If Hayes had only left the coffee shop five minutes sooner, he would have seen Eddie Dellwood rush panicked through the lobby, convinced that he'd accidentally murdered his young wife. If Hayes had only opened his office door twenty minutes earlier, he would have heard Bonnie Ellen yell at Eddie that she wasn't even sure she wanted to go to California, that she refused to clear out her office without even writing a note to Mr. Hayes, who had treated her so decently, and that she "sure as shit" was not about to tell Eddie the combination to Mr. Hayes's safe. At which point Hayes would have heard a scuffle, followed by a thunk, followed by a crash, as Mrs. Dellwood was shaken by her husband, slipped, hit her head against the corner of her desk, and fell to the floor.

But Hayes was twelve floors below, ordering pastries, and, therefore, he concluded that Bonnie Ellen was a very thoughtless, irresponsible young woman, and he never should have allowed Betty Hemans to persuade him to hire her. That's the kind of trick of which Fortune is capable.

At the elevator, Hayes took from his seersucker jacket Mingo Sheffield's little black .22 pistol. Its solidity was strangely comforting. He pressed the barrel first against his head, then against his heart — not in any serious way, just theoretically. Then he aimed at the elevator doors, and mentally shot them for not opening. At that moment, they did. Behind the old-fashioned sliding iron grille was a big pushcart crammed with buckets, mops, and brooms. Behind the cart was the Forbes Building janitor, Bill Jenkins, a heavyset black man. He wore a white mustache of Teutonic flavor and had one withered hand. For those two reasons he had been nicknamed "Kaiser Bill" by some now long dead Thermopylae wag.

Staring at Hayes, Bill was motionless as an overweight rabbit with no hope of successful flight, his huge brown eyes on the gun, his large ears twitching as he more and more rapidly chewed on a cheekful of gum.

"Are you coming out or going down?" Raleigh finally asked impatiently.

"Whichever you say, Mister Hayes. Bill's not studying to get in your way at *all*." (As if inspired by his imperial alias, the janitor always referred to himself in the third person.)

"What's the matter with you? Come on out." Absentmindedly return-ing the gun to his pocket, Hayes slammed back the grille with a loud clank. "Is there a problem?"

"No, sir!" Jenkins, chewing even faster, sidled behind his cart and bumped it out of the elevator, without ever taking his eyes from Hayes's pocket. "Just you don't give the old Kaiser one more thought, you hear? He's gone. Here he goes. He's gone."

"Wait!" called Hayes. "Stop!"

"God Almighty!" Halfway down the hall, Jenkins froze, and spun the cart between himself and the insurance man.

Hayes threw his weight against the elevator door, which was shoving back at him in abrupt heaves. "Bill, listen, Bill, do me a favor? My office really needs a good cleaning. Can you take care of it for me?"

"Sure can."

"Tell you what, I'll give you twenty dollars extra. Really clean it out. That enough?"

"Sure is."

"Listen, I'm sorry I kind of snapped at you. I'm in a big hurry."

"Um hm."

"Well, you have a good day, Bill."

"Sure will."

As soon as the elevator door rammed shut, Kaiser Bill abandoned his cart and sprinted to the supplies closet for a restorative sip of the cherry brandy he kept hidden behind stacks of toilet paper. He felt for the light cord. The bulb was a dim one, but bright enough for him to see Bonnie Ellen Dellwood wedged in the corner where her husband had just propped her.

Bill Jenkins's arm, momentarily arrested, now continued on to the shelf, found his bottle, and unscrewed the cap. His eyes on Mrs. Dellwood, he contemplatively drank for a while, screwing and unscrewing the cap be-tween each sip. Bill had been told (and told by four generations — by his parents, his wife, his children, and his grandchildren) that he was (as he was the first to admit to them all) "slow in the head." Intelligence he did not consider one of the higher-ranking human assets anyhow, having en-countered in his long life so vast a crowd of smart stupid people. He pre-ferred to rely entirely on the outside advice of the Man Upstairs, whom he consulted regularly and with perfect satisfaction. "Bill," he now said, "the Lord's going to pull you through this like a duck on ice. Don't you fret your mind. You just listen to what He say."

Sip by sip, the message came: Mr. Hayes had just shot his secretary. No one would want to believe this. They would prefer to believe that Kaiser Bill had shot her. That's why she'd been put in his closet. Mr. Hayes expected Bill to, as he'd said, "take care of it." For this he would pay twenty dollars, which was certainly cheap, considering; but on the other hand, better than going to the gas chamber at Bill's age. That much was clear when the Kaiser rehid the bottle and locked the closet. Means and method came as he began to vacuum the Oriental rug in the dentist's office down the hall.

Ten minutes later, with a thick carpet roll slung over his shoulder, Mr. Jenkins rode down the elevator, strolled out of the Forbes Building and into a dented, rusted, dilapidated station wagon that, twenty years earlier, had been the pride of a Starry Haven suburban wife and mother. She never would have dreamed, as she'd unloaded groceries and shubbery and children and bags and bags and boxes and boxes of newer and newer things to buy in the halcyon spring of 1963, that one day a Negro janitor, his name and phone number painted on the side of her car, would ease into its rear door a stolen Oriental rug containing a presumably murdered secretary who hadn't even been born until 1960.

During these manuveurs, no one stopped or even stared at Kaiser Bill. The carpet trick worked as well for him as it had for Cleopatra when she'd slipped in, similarly rolled, to meet Caesar. The Kaiser had a naturally imperial imagination.

Following a further signal from the Man Upstairs, Jenkins gently lowered Mrs. Dellwood into the pit excavated by Joyner Construction Company for the condominium pool they had run out of money to complete. In fact, Bonnie Ellen's husband had helped dig the hole. It was only after Boyd Joyner had laid Eddie Dellwood off that the dream of starting over in California had gripped the young man in such a terrible clasp.

CHAPTER

6

Of the Advice Given Raleigh by His Only Sane Aunt

THERMOPYLAE, in the red clay Piedmont of North Carolina, east of the capital and south of Hillston, was a very small town. It was even smaller than it used to be. In the 1950s, the Civitans, led by a youthful Nemours Kettell, had mailed letters all over the country inviting businesses to "Come Help Us Grow." No one had even bothered to RSVP. Thermopylae had bad luck. Before her born-again days, Vera Sheffield had been a spiritualist and had lectured at the "Take a Book to Lunch" Club on "Thermopylae and the Amityville Horror: Are We Jinxed?" She reminded the club that Indians had massacred the area's first white settlers, and scared off all followers until 1774, when the Indians were themselves decimated by a smallpox epidemic that had spread from the filched frock coat of a scalped minister. According to Mrs. Sheffield, the ghosts of these Indians had jinxed the town.

It was true that the town's unlucky founder, Waverley Sheppard, Esq., a runaway Loyalist, was in 1776 hanged by a gang of marauding revolutionaries who called themselves the Independence Boys. (Among them was the grandson of Obed, that first Carolina Hayes, who'd risen from the indigo vats to partnership in a New Bern printer's shop and whose son had run away into the wilderness that was then Thermopylae.) The boys had lynched Sheppard only two years after he'd named the town, on the run, as it were, from creditors in Williamsburg. He'd called it Thermopylae for the natural hot springs into which, galloping past, he'd been pitched by his horse and broken his leg. Those hot springs might have made Thermopylae's fortune, but they were entirely ignored for the next century. The man who finally rediscovered and bought them was Goodrich Hale Hayes. He had no luck either. In 1860, he sank all he had into building on the spot a resort hotel for affluent invalids from the North. Scarcely was his paint dry, when his springs were too, sucked entirely away as if by the ghosts of malevolent Indians thirsty for revenge.

A few years later, a large group of Northern visitors did arrive in town, and they did stay at the Hayes Hotel, but not as paying guests. When these soldiers left, they stole everything they could carry off, from cut-glass doorknobs to a garnet locket containing strands of Mrs. Hayes's hair, which one of Sherman's sergeants took home to his fiancée in Rochester. They razed the garden, killed the livestock, and burned down the building. They also shot two teenaged Confederate stragglers who'd imprudently fired on them out the loft window of the smokehouse. On their way out of town, they set fire to every house on Main Street except Mrs. Agatha Kettell's, where Sherman had lunched. Her neighbors cut her dead for the next two years.

Yes, Thermopylae was unlucky. After the War, while other towns were stuffing cured tobacco into little pouches and selling them to the Yankees, Thermopyleans rebuilt their charred homes and entered the crockery business. They used the mud that the old springs had left behind. It became clear over subsequent decades that Yankees would buy a great many more cigarettes than red clay pitchers. Carolina crockery had never entered the club of fortune where tobacco sat puffing in a rich leather chair. The century turned, and, a wallflower, Thermopylae was lost in the American shuffle, and sat out that long fast dance called Progress.

According to Vera Sheffield, the town's only flurry of hope for Success had perished in 1929 when the Indian demons had shoved the great businessman Zebulon Forbes out the top window of his new skyscraper. (In fact, out the window of what was now Raleigh Hayes's office.) Forbes's building had soared on one side of the Crossways, and a new courthouse had risen to face it, business and government seeing eye to eye, and winking at each other, as they were all over the country in those rich Coolidge days. The Crossways had quickly become the heart of the town, a hub from which six streets spoked off, three on either side, like a spider with two missing legs. In the Roaring Twenties, Zeb Forbes's commercial cathedral inspired Thermopylae with enthusiasm. Nemours Kettell's fa-

ther slapped asphalt over Main Street (until then, brick) and over Church
Street (until then, dirt), and Mr. Knox built a big department store with
Mr. Bury on Bath Street, and on Sheppard Street a man from Delaware
opened a hotel with a ballroom. Clayton Hayes, a grocer and butcher,
branched out into furniture, at his wife's urging, and hired PeeWee Jimson as his clerk. Everybody thought that the twenties would sow money
like dragon's teeth and that up and down those six streets, tall, rich buildings would grow overnight. Everybody thought this was just the beginning for Thermopylae. But, said Vera Sheffield to her small but attentive
audience, "How wrong they were. They forgot the hex moaning up from
the graves." The market crashed, Mr. Forbes jumped (or rather was pushed
by poltergeists), and that was that.

In the 1950s (when the Civitans found out that "Loyalist" meant someone *opposed* to American Independence, pulled down the statue of Waverley Sheppard, and changed Sheppard Street to Dulles Boulevard), there
was even talk of changing the name of the town as well. There was nothing progressive or upbeat about an ancient Greek mountain pass, everyone
of whose three hundred Spartan defenders had been annihilated by Asiat-
ics. Maybe the name Thermopylae was itself a jinx. But the weight of tra-
dition proved too heavy for the Civitans to throw off, and Thermopylae
the town remained, and downtown remained only three blocks long and
three blocks wide, and Time zoomed past on the Interstate, chasing
Progress.

Raleigh's eldest aunt, Victoria Anna, commenting on the unrelieved in-
significance of her hometown, liked to say that she could crack an egg in
the frying pan, walk from one end of Thermopylae to the other, and get
back in time to serve it over easy. At seventy-two, Miss Hayes continued to
take such brisk strolls, but in this custom she was now almost unique. To
her disgust, people used their cars to get from one block to the next. The
cause most often ascribed to the disuse and decay of "Downtown" was in-
adequate parking. Everyone had lost the habit of walking, and they could
no more recover the instinct than their primordial ancestors could return
to tree-swinging. Everybody could buy cars, and so everybody drove cars
everywhere they went. It did not, for example, occur to Raleigh Hayes this
morning (determined as he was to prolong his life by strong doses of exercise) to walk the three-quarters of a mile between his office in the Forbes
Building at the Crossways and his aunt's house at the eastern end of Old
Main.

He drove. He drove without thinking down blocks he'd seen too long
to see anymore, seen first from his baby stroller, then from skates, then

bikes, seen for years on the way to school and to the family furniture store (now Pierce Jimson's) and to the library (now guarding PeeWee Jimson's bust) and to pay restless calls with his mother on neighbors and relatives now dead. Furious at Bonnie Ellen Dellwood for running off to California, and at his father for running off to wherever in the world he was, Raleigh drove to the end of the street and parked in front of the white-framed, green-shuttered, three-storied Carpenter Gothic structure that he still thought of as Grandpa's House. Raleigh's father and all his aunts and uncles had grown up in those seventeen rooms. Years ago, they'd given the house as a surprise present to their only unmarried sibling, Victoria Anna, when World Missions Supplies had forced her into semi-retirement. They had made her swear then not to sell the house and divide the profits, as she'd expected them to do. She'd sold the side yard anyhow. It was now a paved parking lot for a new Baptist church that looked like a brick motel and even had a neon sign on its roof. JESUS IS THE WAY, it said. Across the street was a new discount drugstore, and on the other corner was a new funeral home. The Hayes house had been raised by time into a commercial property. Raleigh expected to inherit it from his aunt.

Victoria Anna sat on the porch in one of the old green rockers. She poked a pencil impatiently through her tight iron-colored curls as she studied a folded newspaper held arm's length away. She was, Raleigh knew, analyzing the stock market. He was always too timid to take her advice, and was usually sorry. Since his childhood, Raleigh and Victoria Anna had shared a special relationship, based on their baffled disapproval of and careful estrangement from the rest of the Hayes family. The two talked together daily, like colonialists at their club in Bombay, like doctors in a lunatic asylum, like Puritans at a Roman carnival, to reassure one another that they were separate from their surroundings, and that the world in which they found themselves was not the world as it was meant to be. Raleigh considered Victoria the only ambitious Hayes. Fifty years ago she had committed herself to a life that had narrowed to two quantitative and verifiable goals. The first was to set foot in more different towns and cities than any other Thermopylean, man or woman. In so doing, she was not traveling for enlightenment or pleasure or wealth. She was traveling to cover the ground. In her trunk, she kept a notebook of every site she'd ever visited; her list had more names in it than the Thermopylae phone book, and despite her company's pleas that she resign, her list was still growing. "Which is," she said to Raleigh, "the complete opposite of the case with Thermopylae, since there's about nothing at all left here but a bunch of Hayeses playing softball on empty streets, and those left over sitting in the stands to cheer them on."

Victoria's other goal had become to possess the immense bronze plaque topped with a relief of Dürer's *Praying Hands* that was awarded to any World Missions Supplies representative who reached a total of one million dollars in sales. Year by year, hymnal by communion cup by portable altar kit, trading with Adventist and Catholic alike, she had so far credited to her account $917,332. Her only fear of death was finally that it should come one commission too soon, rob her of her plaque and so nullify her life. On six previous occasions, she had already won a smaller plaque given annually to the top salesperson. Long ago, running the child Raleigh's fingers over the name *Victoria Anna Hayes* indented there, she'd told him, "I fully expect that's the only bronze the name of Hayes is set to. Besides a dented baby cup to start off with and a big slab of tombstone nobody can afford, to finish." (On that occasion she had just flown home for her father's funeral to find him already buried beneath, as she put it, "the Rock of Gibraltar," which in the profligacy of their grief her siblings had *charged* at Living Monuments, Inc. in Charlotte.) "You remember, Raleigh," she said, pressing his hand into the Braille of her achievement, "they gave me the dinkiest assignments in the book, that no *man* up on the ladder would touch, and I came right out of the jungle with the orders in my purse. I have earned my way through the world to where I could have my name carved into something special. And do you think a single soul in this house has got the sense even to understand me? They wouldn't leave Thermopylae if the sky fell in on it."

Raleigh did understand Victoria Anna, and admired and envied her her courage and ruthless stamina and determined self-esteem. He was also, still, a little afraid of her. "Aunt Victoria," he called from the sidewalk now. "Where's Daddy? Did you find out where he went?"

"Tell the world about it," she replied, then waited, lips pinched, until her nephew climbed the wide wooden stoop and sat down in the rocker beside her. Finally she said, "I expect you want some coffee."

"Actually, could I have some aspirin?" Yesterday's headache was drilling into his temple again.

"Never touch them," replied Victoria. "I've traveled far and wide for fifty years despite being told a woman couldn't bear up, and never touched an aspirin, not even in Istanbul, Turkey, where they stole what they hadn't managed to beg, including my samples case." She set her rocker in rapid motion. "Earley called me at six A.M. this morning."

"Yes, Aura said —"

"Don't ask me from where, but I could hear a jukebox."

"Did he mention getting married?"

"Talked nonstop gibberish, which I hope you'll have the decency to explain. How he'd sent you a message."

"Well, Aunt Vicky, yesterday —"

"Asked me, didn't I have Tiny Hackney's trunk in the basement? Said, tell you he just remembered he gave his . . ." Victoria crossed her arms tightly. ". . . his trumpet to Roxanne Digges."

"Oh, great!" Raleigh flung back and had to catch himself on his aunt's armrest. Roxanne Digges, Earley's third wife, the woman with whom he'd had the affair that had cost him his church, was the mother of Raleigh's ne'er-do-well half-brother, Gates, and not someone Raleigh Hayes wished ever to have to see again; nor had he ever expected to, since she'd left Earley thirty years ago. "Did you happen to ask Daddy what in the world he thinks he's up to?"

Miss Hayes rubbed both earlobes as if she'd just removed some uncomfortable jewelry. "Raleigh, I would not ask that man the simple time of day. I *told* him I had telephoned his doctor and his doctor said he could drop dead in a second and have nobody but himself to blame if he didn't get back in that hospital bed." She rocked more strenuously, and Raleigh found himself keeping pace.

"Aunt Vicky, did I tell you it looks like Daddy put his house on the market?"

"No. I found out on my own. You didn't tell me much of anything." She swatted his arm with the folded newspaper. "I don't know why you didn't bother getting back in touch with me last night, Raleigh, since you and I have always taken care of this Earley business together, unless you think I'm too old . . ."

"No, of course —"

"But Aura explained you had to go to bed early. I'm surprised you could sleep."

Raleigh blushed. "I meant to call you, but this latest has just worn me out."

"If I'd gone to bed early in the rain forests of Molucca, I'd like to know where I'd be now."

"Aura said —"

"Aura said she was too sleepy to explain about this, what she called, 'quest' your nincompoop father's sending you on. 'I'm not a morning person,' is what Aura said."

And so Raleigh paraphrased, without the profanity, and, for now, omitting, as his father had requested, any mention of Jubal Rogers, the tape recording and the note that yesterday had been thrust upon him like a ransom demand. Victoria took her bifocals from the pocket of her baggy gray cardigan sweater and carefully threaded the stems through her watchspring curls. "Why New Orleans?" she inquired when he finished.

"Why?" Raleigh's glasses flashed right back at hers. "Ha ha."

She nodded. "All right.... Now, maybe he picked these particular things out for a reason. But don't count on it." Taking the pencil from her hair and pulling a small spiral notebook, like the one Raleigh carried, from her pocket, she waved them at him. "If you're going to do a thing, do it. Are you?"

"I can't even stand to think about it." Raleigh pushed up out of the rocker and hugged the nearest porch column. "Couldn't we get the police looking for him, couldn't they find him before he gets to New Orleans, and bring him on home?"

Miss Hayes began writing in the pad. "They might find him. I doubt it. But they can't force him to come home. Now, he says he'll come back to the hospital if you go get him. Plus, Raleigh." She looked at him over her glasses. "He told me to say, if you do what he asked, he's going to leave you a lot of money, and if you don't, he's going to cut you right out of his will. Of course, he laughed when he said it."

"I don't care about the stupid money."

"Don't be ridiculous. Well, I'd like to know how that man keeps finding so much to laugh at, unless he's unhinged. One thing that's always burned me is how happy crazy people can be. Raleigh, stand still or sit down."

"Hayeses laugh," said Raleigh.

"It's no credit to them. Right here in this house, joking and talking away their years of golden opportunity. Driving down to the beach, stopping for a treat every fifteen miles. And playing, they didn't care what, cards, baseball, you name it."

"Trumpets," sighed Raleigh. "Daddy and Furbus and Hackney in that combo, remember? Why in the world did that man ever go into the ministry? Obviously it was not the right calling. By a long shot!"

Victoria tightened her mouth angrily. "The less said about that combo the better."

"Whatever happened to it? I can't really remember...."

"Nothing...." She pulled a Kleenex from her pocket and twisted her nose with it. "They never had the get up and go to do anything with it, except drive the neighbors off of their porches in the heat of July, they played so loud and late."

Suddenly — in her frayed sweater and garden-soiled cotton print dress and wound gray curls — she turned into Raleigh's grandmother Ida, who'd sighed over Hayeses all her life. Inside Raleigh, time spun around, and he saw the porch crowded with his relatives. Aunts and uncles and cousins were in the swings and rockers, they sprawled on the stoop and perched atop the wood rail, feet looped between the slats. Men in high belts and felt hats and bright ties; women in checked and dotted and flowered dresses, and their soft summer white polished shoes.

He could hear the baseball game on the radio, the piano playing "Heart and Soul," and Hayeses talking, joking, playing. He was five years old, running back toward those safe sounds from the dusky wooded side yard, where, behind the high dahlias and hollyhocks, his older cousin Paschal, and Bobbie, the girl from next door, both with their underpants around their ankles, stood with their hands on their private parts. Shocked, Raleigh had run back to the porch swing, and his father had leaned down to him, bobbing hello with the glittering gold trumpet.

The past whirred off and Victoria Anna was saying, "Joked away a fortune in land before Papa's time, then Papa sat down talking while PeeWee Jimson stole the meat store out from under his nose. Not that Papa had any business in the butcher business anyhow. One time he asked your daddy to hold a calf while he hit it with an axe, and your daddy pure and simple let the thing go. And it bolted down the street till I could catch it while Earley and Papa sat right out there on the back steps crying and laughing till tears raced down their faces. The only surprising thing is, it took PeeWee till Papa died to get control of the furniture store, too. No, the only one with any get up and go was me. I was the only one that got up and went, too."

"You had natural push," Raleigh agreed, as he always did. "God knows where you got it."

Her mouth pulled stiff with pride. "Even if I was a girl, I wasn't about to sit around Thermopylae and watch the gate rust off its hinges and fall into the road. All the rest of them built as close to Mama and Papa as anybody could without adding on to the roof. You could have swung a chicken and slapped them all in the face with it."

Despite Victoria's contempt for her family's garrulousness, she had increasingly become, Raleigh noticed, quite a gabber herself, particularly on the subject of her own character. He interrupted. "Daddy left his suitcase on the bed to fool the nurse. I supose I ought to go back to the hospital and see if I can't find out who this girl he ran off with is."

Victoria pushed up her frayed sweater sleeves. "A vagrant. I already found that much out. One of those poor stunned no-names the police pick up loitering at the bus station without a cent to their names." Raleigh's aunt acknowledged his surprise with another vigorous shove at her sleeves. "They took her over to the hospital for some observation and Earley slapped a blond wig on her head that he stole out of Reba's bathroom and waltzed off with her before they found out a thing."

"That's just great," said Raleigh and rubbed his head along the square wood column he hugged for comfort.

"Raleigh, you want to know, you've got to ask. You want to do, you've got to do."

"That's true."

"Of course it's true. You don't know how true it is unless you've had a donkey keel over and die out from under you in the jungles of Borneo." As she talked, Victoria Anna kept writing in the spiral notepad, pressing so firmly that the paper curled. "No," she concluded, with a tap of her pencil, "if there's rhyme or reason to this so called by Aura 'quest' your daddy's put you up to, it's by me. You're supposed to meet him in New Orleans on the thirty-first. This is the sixteenth." She checked her newspaper for confirmation. "And bring, one . . ." She circled the "1" on her list. ". . . his trumpet. Where does Roxanne Digges live?"

"I haven't the foggiest idea and could care less."

"Two, PeeWee's bust. Well, we know where that is. And, three, Gates."

Raleigh pressed his head hard into the column. "I haven't heard from Gates in five years."

"I bet Lovie has. Four — pay attention, Raleigh — Tiny's trunk. I already looked in the basement. It's down there, rusted shut. And Lovie's got the family Bible. She came over here a few years back and dug it out and took it with her to the hospital for luck."

"Luck? Seems like she lost her breast that time."

"That's right." The two realists nodded at one another over the inefficacy of talismans. "Now. You know who Goodrich Hale Hayes was?"

Raleigh shrugged. "Some old Hayes."

"He had get up and go. I bet there's where I got mine. He built a kind of hotel spa used to be out on Hillston Road near Knoll Pond. The Yankees burned it down. When I made my plans to join the Daughters of the Confederacy . . ."

"You?"

Victoria snorted. "You don't have to believe the nonsense, but if you're in sales, you have to join the clubs; you know that, Raleigh; I've taught you that. But naturally not a soul I asked could recollect who any of our ancestors were. 'Course, if Gates had just been born back then, I could have asked him to forge me up a family tree, but as it was I had to look things up for myself, and Goodrich Hayes was a major at Vicksburg and a colonel at Atlanta, and made it all the way back up here to North Carolina, and ended up getting shot the last week of the war. By then he was a general. I found this all out in nineteen thirty-five, and I'll go over the papers for you this afternoon."

"You still have them?" asked Raleigh. Aura couldn't find her coffee cup if she put it down to answer the phone.

"Raleigh, I have got my entire life in three steamer trunks. I can put my hand on any item you could name in the dark." She made a vigorous circle on her note paper. "Of course, there's one thing that's never going to happen in this world, and that's Pierce Jimson selling you that old cabin on Hillston Road, or any old anything, once he knows anybody named Hayes wants it."

Raleigh could not resist his body's urge to swing out by one arm around the porch column. "I bought it this morning," he announced.

"You bought it?"

He could not resist a grin. "I bought it."

"Knoll Pond?"

"From Pierce. For only twenty-five hundred dollars." Raleigh changed arms and swung back the other way. "This morning."

Aunt Victoria snapped open the silver watch chained to her dress belt. "It's only seven fifty."

He kept grinning. "I guess you're not the only one with a little get up and go."

"Well, good for you, Raleigh." She snapped her watch shut and spun it like a globe, nodding as if she were ticking off her travels as it turned. "Though I don't know why you didn't bother to say so right off."

Raleigh's elation slid away as he admitted, "Well, it just sort of happened when I happened to run into Pierce and . . ." As it was impossible to conceive, and so explain, why Jimson had agreed to sell the cabin, Raleigh ended his sentence by leaning over the porch to break irregular shoots off the top of the bordering hedge. "Anyhow, the whole thing's entirely preposterous. Does Daddy honestly believe I intend to acquire a gun . . ." A chilly horror rushed over Hayes like ice water as he remembered, as he *felt*

at this minute, Mingo's pistol in his jacket pocket. He stuttered quickly
on, "And *steal* public property from the public library, and even if I
wanted to, you think nobody's going to see me carting off a big plaster
bust right past them? For Pete's sake!"

With a decisive rock forward, Victoria propelled herself to her feet, and
briskly pinched at her dress front. She said matter-of-factly, "PeeWee Jimson was a conniver, a thief, and a fat-faced false-hearted ugly-mouthed
hog."

"I didn't really know him."

"My papa was a fool," she added as she jammed the notepad in her
pocket. "You come back over here when you finish, and we'll haul that
little trunk out. This afternoon, we'll drive to Cowstream and see Lovie.
Maybe by then she can locate that Bible under those two or three months
of unironed clothes piled on the couches with chicken bones and poker
chips."

"Finish?" Raleigh stared at her. "You mean, you think I *should* —"

Victoria jerked up her big watch again and opened it in her nephew's
face. "Library opens at nine thirty." From the stoop she took a waiting pair
of cotton gloves and long shears. Starting at the sidewalk corner, she
whacked ruthlessly at her shrubs while she quizzed Raleigh. "What's
across the street from that library?"

"Elementary school."

"Other side."

"Grandpa's old store." He moved behind her along the hedge, dodging
the bristly hedge-tops as they flew out of the shears. "Why?"

"You ever go down in the gully at the end of the parking lot, see where
the old culvert used to come out? Old water pipes from way back?"

Raleigh shook his head.

"Big old round tunnel went under Garden Street. Earley and the rest
used to play hideout in that tunnel. They didn't want me, but I said I'd
tell, so they had to let me along."

Raleigh now recalled that he had run with Jimmy Clay and Mingo
through this same abandoned water pipe once, that Mingo had collapsed
in claustrophobic paralysis when Jimmy turned off his flashlight and began
to howl, "GHOOOOOSTS!!! VAAAAMPIRES!!! BLOOOOOOOD!!!"
He brushed a branch out of his hair and adjusted his glasses. "Aunt Victoria, what are you talking about?"

She kept clipping. "That tunnel branches. There's a fork to your left,
just inside, look up, you'll see a lid cover."

Had, in her old age, congenital insanity caught up even with her? Snap, went the shears. Greenery like epaulets gave her sweater a military look. "That cover opens up in the library basement. It's got a throw rug over it. I'm on the book-binding committee, and I was asking just a while ago, when I was down pasting spines and I stubbed my toe on that lid, why nobody ever sealed it up. They used to say how folks hid slaves down there, but I don't believe it. I do know it was voted back in the fifties, when everybody got in such a snit about the Communists, to turn it into a fallout shelter, but nobody ever got around to it. Earley and the boys used to sneak through there at night into the library and moon over any book they could find with a naked woman in it." She gave a last quick set of whacks to the hedge and shook out her shears. "They'd have been with me in Fiji, they could have seen enough bosoms to last a lifetime." Victoria crossed to the far side of the shrubs without a look at her nephew, who stared, large-mouthed, at her straight back, until her elbows again started their energetic scissoring. "Get going," she told him. "Don't dawdle."

"Aunt Vicky, are you seriously suggesting that I crawl through an abandoned *sewer,* even supposing it's not filled in, even supposing the cover's not rusted shut —"

"It's not." The blades sparkled like scimitars in the green branches.

"And *rob* the library, of which you are a board member, and haul Pee-Wee's bust all the way down to New Orleans? Are you, a religious woman like yourself, seriously intending to make that suggestion?"

Victoria pulled her glasses down on her sharp nose, exposing the undiminished blue ruthlessness of her eyes. "Raleigh, let me tell you something. I'm no more religious than you are. My family put me down for the religious one without bothering to ask, since they'd decided Big Em was a good homemaker and Lovie was a clown and Serene was sweet and Reba was pretty. That just left religion for me, is the way they figured it, I guess. Every last one of them is satisfied I signed up with the World Missions Company just the way you'd sign up for a nun in a convent." She wrestled a twig stuck between her blades. "I wanted to get out of this town and I became a traveler. That's the short and simple of it. Missionaries see a good part of the world. I saw it right behind them. I've got no use for Christianity. Love's not enough and never was, and if any Hayes had ever looked up from a piano in Thermopylae, they'd know better than to think so. Now I believe your daddy truly is religious, and that ought to give you some notion of my views on that subject. So." She snapped off a glove. "Do you want Earley — and don't think he's not crazy enough, because I've known him a lot longer than you have — to give your entire inheritance away to every poor, begging mental patient he happens to meet on the road?"

Raleigh had to admit that he didn't.

"Have you ever even been to New Orleans?"

Raleigh confessed that he hadn't.

Victoria shook her glove in her heir's face, as if she planned to challenge him to a duel, as in fact she did. "Well, Raleigh, then get up and go."

CHAPTER

7

In Which the Hero Commits a Crime

WITH AUNT VICTORIA'S OLD CHROME FLASHLIGHT and older huge canvas knapsack on the seat beside him, Raleigh Hayes drove in low gears down Main. He kept the slow pace of the child Raleigh, whom he could now see pulling hard at a wagon heaped with dozens upon dozens of empty Coca-Cola bottles; these he had once collected, to sell for two cents each, from the sugar-greedy Hayes house, where there was even a separate refrigerator on the back porch with nothing in it but soft drinks and beer, and maybe on the bottom shelf a few cantaloupes and half a watermelon. His aunts and uncles called all soft drinks that weren't orange, "Cokes," and they drank them straight out of the ice-frosted small green bottles. On a summer night, scrunched in a corner of the big porch, Raleigh would watch the dark liquid vanish in their great loud long-throated swallows. They drank them from morning till bedtime. Uncle Hackney, who liked to freeze his Cokes, so that he had to pound on the bottle with his fist to pop out the chunks of crystallized caramel, once drank eighteen on a single evening. As soon as he finished a bottle, he'd wave it in the air, and call, "Raleigh, two cents!," and laugh a long singing laugh, and pull a cigarette out from behind his ear, and pick back up his ukulele to strum "Love, oh love, oh careless love. . . ."

Careless love, for certain. And careless life, and sooner or later (mostly sooner) careless death. Who but a careless lover like Hackney (three hundred pounds of potato salad, pork ribs, and lager ale; cigarettes wedged against his skull by his fat ears; one lung punctured by the fishing knife of a sore loser in a five-card-draw game at Wrightsville Beach; and a heart that had already warned him twice to quit it), who but a careless Hayes like Hackney would chase a fly ball on a Carolina July noon, with the sun as big and round and hot as he was, chasing after him? Careless, uninsured death.

What had been so funny about selling the empty bottles anyhow? Driving now, Raleigh could see himself pulling that wagon; he could hear the pant legs of his baggy, tight-belted corduroys brushing each other; he could feel the wind swooping into the short sleeves of the red plaid shirt that flapped against his thin chest and arms. An odd, hot, thick pity for that boy — frail, earnest, hurrying along the sidewalk — swelled in Raleigh's throat. Why pity? Why not pride? Hadn't he purchased his own bicycle (a black Raleigh bicycle, as if custom-made) with that bottle money? Hadn't he kept that bicycle in such good repair he was able to sell it four years later for scarcely less than it had cost him? And the extravagant bicycle that his father, then living in adultery with Roxanne Digges, had brought on Christmas to the house where Raleigh lived alone with his mother, hadn't he spurned it with a proud and righteous "No, thank you"? Why not pride?

The adult Hayes, thinking about the child, had already neared the intersection where the stern windows of Carnegie Library squinted across Main Street at the elementary-school playground, squinted in disdain at the ancient but freshly painted seesaws and swings as if outraged by the gaudy lures of her old rival for the hearts of the young. The library hardly bothered to look at all at Jimson Furniture Store to its right, despite the bold invitation painted in huge white letters along the brick side: STOP, SHOP, SAVE.

According to Raleigh's digital watch, which daunted doubt, it was 8:32:37. School, thank God, had started. Yard, steps, jungle gym, all were deserted. There was no one in sight. Except for . . . except for the mammoth bulk squatted at the top of the tall three-bump slide. The bulk moved, and the tie sparkled on its yellow shirt. It had to be — and it was — Mingo Sheffield. Instead of heading from the coffee shop over to open Knox-Bury's Clothing Store, as he must have unfailingly done for twenty years, Mingo had picked today of all days to come amuse himself at the elementary school for old time's sake. The man was demented. He'd

regressed entirely to an infancy he'd never successfully escaped. First Holly
and Caroline's swingset, then skinny-dipping, now the slide. Moreover,
Mingo had obviously spotted the Fiesta at the stop sign, for he was wailing, "Raleigh!" at the top of his gargantuan lungs.

He was probably stuck up there between the ladder rails. Or he had
chickened out — just as he'd always done in third grade, on that very same
slide, panicking at the sight of the steep slope below, and so forcing the
whole disgusted line behind him to back down the ladder or be trampled
by his retreat. Hayes cursed: Sheffield had to be dealt with quickly, if he
was going to rob the library before it opened. Resisting the impulse to ram
backward into his neighbor's brand-new Chevrolet, he parked, stomped
across the playground, kicking up dirt with quick angry steps as he went.
He walked so fast he had reached the base of the tall slide before he noticed the immense long-nosed flat-handled gray pistol his fellow Civitan
was pointing at him.

"All right," called Hayes, furious. "Where'd you get that?"

"It's mine," Mingo sniffled.

"No, it isn't. I've got yours." Raleigh pulled the tiny .22 from his jacket
pocket.

"That's Vera's."

Hayes looked at the pistol in his hand, then at the larger one gleaming
dully down on him from twenty feet above. For God's sake, he was living
next door to a heavily armed loony bin. In silence, the two businessmen
aimed at each other, then Raleigh slowly sighed. "Mingo, will you please
stop this trying to shoot me? I'm really busy, I really am."

"Oh, stop bragging about how busy you are." Hayes's fat friend's
face crumpled like an old pumpkin, as he began to cry. "Maybe other
people aren't as busy as you are, but you don't have to be so mean
about it."

"Me, mean? You're the one with the gun!" Raleigh dropped his
own back in his pocket. "You're the one trying to kill an innocent
person."

Tears dripped down on Mingo's starched yellow shirt. "I don't want to
kill you at all. I just want to kill me, okay, if I ever could."

"For Christ's sake, Mingo! Over me and Vera? That wasn't even true! I
thought y'all worked that out last night." Hadn't they been splashing
about, festive as seals, in the Starry Haven pool only eight hours ago? A
spasm pinched Raleigh's neck, which he'd been craning straight up. "Slide
down, Mingo. Let's talk this out. Is that gun loaded?"

Sheffield shook his head over and over. "I'm sc . . . ared," he stuttered. "I came up here to think and then I got sc . . . ared and now I can't get down and I don't want to ssh . . . ssh . . . shoot myself . . ." The vast shoulders jiggled with grief. ". . . where all the k . . . kids will see me at recess." Abruptly he let out a loud wail of sorrow and with both hands pressed the gun into his stomach as if he'd already been wounded there.

Terror froze Raleigh's scalp and fingers so fast they tingled. Maybe Sheffield actually was insane enough to commit suicide. He looked to see if there were any children watching from the classroom windows, or a teacher who might call the police, but spring-leaved maple trees blocked the view. "Mingo. MINGO! Stop crying. Hold on, I'll get you down. What's the problem? Mingo? Don't worry, listen."

Sheffield kept shaking his head. "I've been up here thinking and thinking."

"Really? Why don't you tell me about it?" With a nonchalant sidestep, Raleigh edged toward the slide's ladder.

"I can't stop thinking about that movie on TV. *On the Bub Bub Beach.* I kept on hoping there was somebody alive in San Francisco but then Gregory Peck opened the door and it was a kuk, kuh, Coca-Cola bottle! And so, and so," burbled the fat man, "what's the use at all, at all?"

By now Raleigh was halfway up the ladder rungs and could see the back of Sheffield's bobbing head. Memory rushed off with him to the sound of a whooping siren over the school loudspeakers and the sight of Mingo at thirteen, pudgy arms over his head, crouched beneath his desk during a civil defense air raid drill. In those days the Thermopylae schools had practiced for the Bomb seriously; students wore dogtags so their charred remains could be claimed by . . . whomever, and everyone donated canned goods to the school fallout shelter, which had progressed further than had apparently the one in the library basement. The Bomb, good Lord. Why was everybody talking about the Bomb again all of a sudden? He certainly never would have thought Mingo Sheffield capable of a *philosophical* suicide over an abstraction like nuclear holocaust! By now Raleigh had his hands on the top rail. "Is that what's depressed you, *On the Beach?*" Hayes made a profound effort to sound sympathetic. "Here, why don't you let me hold on to that gun for a second and I'll help you get down."

Slick as butter, Sheffield twisted his shoulders around, pointed the pistol in Raleigh's face, and with a wide macabre grin, whispered, "I lost my job."

Hayes had swung so far away from the mouth of the gun, he'd almost lost his grip on the rail. Now, he lunged forward with such desperate intensity, he shoved Mingo down the slide's incline. The gray automatic flew away in the air. Mingo, his buttocks riding not on the seat, but creased in the sides of the guard bumpers, shot bouncing downward, legs flailing, and landed with a vibrant thud in the loose dirt below. He still sat there, his mouth and eyes circles of surprise, when Raleigh (after running to retrieve and pocket the gun) reached him, and said, "What do you mean, you lost your job? How could you lose your job already?"

Mingo didn't move a muscle but his lips. "You tricked me. You know I'm scared of that slide."

"You did fine. It was an accident. You mean Billy Knox fired you? What in the world for?"

"I went right down that slide, didn't I? I never did that before!"

"Yes, fine, fine."

"That's the first time!"

"For God's sake, will you forget the slide, Mingo! There're more important things here. You tell me you've been intending to commit suicide and you tell me you've just been discharged! And I've got to go! *What happened?*"

Sheffield stretched his round legs out straight in front of him and sorrowfully stared at them. "They're closing Knox-Bury's because there's no use in it. Nobody comes."

"What?"

"I went in early to change my window and Billy said they're moving to Colony Mall in Hillston this summer. And . . ."

"And? *And?*"

"And they don't even want me to come even if I wanted to which I wouldn't if they paid me. Billy said they already got somebody new with a manager degree, and all I got was two weeks' notice. He said they were going for a new image and everything." Sheffield picked up scoopfuls of dirt in both big fists. Hayes half-expected him to start eating it as he'd often done under stress as a boy. But instead the fat man only watched while the soft earth sifted down through his fingers. "I guess they don't want me," he added.

Hayes took off his glasses to rub his eyes. "Well, gosh. Mingo. Gosh, I don't know what to say."

Mingo scooped up more dirt to watch it fall. "I had my wuh . . . window all figured out. I was going to show the whole family in some nice Easter outfits. They were going to be on their way to church. The mother and daughter were going to have on blue straw hats and the daddy and the little boy were going to have blue bow ties. I had a b . . . b . . . blue sky, and the church in the background, and I had two baskets of lilies. I had some good ideas." The fist of dirt was drawing perilously near the fat, quivering mouth. "What was wrong with that, Raleigh? You know?"

"Nothing." On the pretext of clasping his neighbor's hand, Raleigh shook the dirt out. Then with the authoritative deliberation that so rarely worked on his daughters anymore, he said, "Now, listen, Mingo, you've got to think of Vera. I want you to go back to work now. We'll figure something out. A man of your experience is going to have no difficulty obtaining employment. I promise you." After a serious pause, Hayes heaved Sheffield to his feet and dusted him off.

"You promise me," Mingo echoed.

"Absolutely." And silently fretting — where in Christ's name was he supposed to find a job for Mingo Sheffield? — Hayes added, "Now, you aren't going to try any more funny business, are you, because I'm going to call Vera if you don't give me your word."

Sheffield smiled with the relief of a punished five-year-old. "Okay," he vowed. As Raleigh led him to the car, the insurance man kept up his rash assurances that among Mingo's many friends (and the man was so gullible he immediately believed himself buttressed by a broad circle of supportive pals, whereas only yesterday he'd lamented the lack of a single real friend but Raleigh himself), that among these friends was a lead to an even better line of work than straightening stacks of sweaters in an empty store. Sheffield was actually smiling when he drove away. He was extraordinarily (in fact, annoyingly) quick to take heart. It was only 8:48:14. Unfortunately, there was still time to rob the library.

Soon thereafter the Fiesta was hidden behind a dumpster at the edge of the Jimson Furniture Store parking lot, and Raleigh W. Hayes had crawled down through high undergrowth into a gully, where hidden by blackberry brambles, kudzu vines, and, he suspected, sumac, and further obscured by a high dank wall of rotted leaves stacked by years of winds, the culvert opening revealed itself by a curved glint of concrete. After beating himself an entrance with a long stick, Hayes waited for the flock of bats and stampede of rats he was prepared to see rush from the dark hole. Nothing came. No red eyes glittered back at his flashlight. Nothing answered when he banged the stick or swirled it around the tunnel, gathering egg-clotted spiderwebs like cotton candy. The worst he could expect then was sudden death from the bite of a black widow spider. He stooped and crawled inside.

Tunnels themselves did not bother Hayes. He was not claustrophobic; why should one so capable of holding himself by the bounds of character in such circumscribed inertia that he had survived the last two days without ripping out his hair, why should such a man fear caves and tunnels? He hadn't minded the closed tanks that had started some of his army companions hyperventilating. He wasn't subject to the vertigo that had caused Mingo Sheffield to *faint* in the head of the Statue of Liberty with two hundred North Carolina sixth-grade Safety Patrols spiraling up the steps right behind him. Hayes's phobias had nothing to do with space, which he had found generally reliable. Hayes feared the quick, erratic, and unreasonable. He feared madness, fire, death, rodents, and insects. For the last reason, he grew increasingly certain as he straddle-stepped, crook-necked, through the chilled, slimy, smelly black cylinder, that a spider was at that moment loosening its grip on its spun thread and dropping into his hair. Continual ruffling of his hair with the sides of his flashlight did not calm him, and finally he tied knots in the corners of his pocket handkerchief and fit it on his head. Then, limbs stretched like a four-pointed starfish, he hurried on, knapsack flapping loosely on his back.

Doubtless his daily jogging had served him well, for no sooner had his thigh muscles seriously spasmed when the light bounced across the fork in the culvert described by his aunt. He hopped to the left, looked up, saw the metal lid, gripped his flashlight under his chin, and shoved up with both arms. To his surprise, the lid moved. He shoved again. The lid moved again. Bracing his shoulder beneath it, he looked like a medieval illustration of Atlas supporting a flat world.

Soon, under the blue-checked knotted cap the mud-smeared face of Raleigh Hayes was peeking around the door at the top of the basement steps. At the end of a double phalanx of tall card-catalogue cabinets stood the fortress of the library's square mahogany circulation desk, where long ago he had been obliged to reach above his head to return books for his mother, and more recently been obliged to pay large fines to return books wantonly checked out by Aura, sometimes ten at a swoop. For the first time, there wasn't a soul in the musty room, except all the made-up ones living inside the books. It occurred to Hayes that he had stopped reading books — at least stopped reading what his mother had called "real books." He hadn't noticed, but he must have stopped decades ago. Somewhere along the line he'd grown too busy, too old, too serious, for stories. He hadn't had time for the people he actually knew, much less fictional ones. Only women and children had time for fiction. Oh, he still read magazines and newspapers and an occasional book of advice, to keep up with the times, to see where the world was headed in what until this week he would have called its "course." But he realized now that over the years whenever he'd thought (not that he'd thought it often), "Didn't there used to be more people in my life, more *interesting* people than, say, the Kettells or the Sheffields?," when there seemed to be somewhere in the back of his head a dim recollection of his having himself led a more interesting life; that perhaps what he was remembering was not his own life (and certainly not the "former lives" Vera Sheffield had claimed in her reincarnation phase), but, instead, the lives he'd met in books. It occurred to Hayes, with a peculiar ache of loss and even betrayal, that many of the wise friends he'd forgotten, and the women whose enchantment he could only vaguely recall, lived still shelved in this waiting room, and had long ago given themselves to others.

"For Pete's sake," Hayes muttered impatiently, "I'm starting to think like Aura." And so, he marched without a look past shelves of those lost acquaintances, and hurried over to the corner by the dictionary stand. There, inside a glass cabinet, mounted squirrels, raccoons, and chipmunks craned forward as if trying to look up a word. On top of the cabinet, the plaster porcine face of PeeWee Jimson, stub-nosed and lopsidedly jowled, grinned at him with insufferable smugness. The indignity to which the library benefactor (if imposing stuffed rodents on the reading public could be called beneficent) was now briskly subjected by Hayes did not wipe away this smug smile. Jimson's plaster eyes, however, were popped open, and he was stark white as a ghost, as if, feeling the hands of the grandson of his dead, outmaneuvered boss, the hands of a *Hayes,* squeeze around his neck, he had dropped immediately dead himself from shock.

Lifting the statue, Raleigh received his own shock. A penciled note was taped to the back of the thick neck. It was not the artist's signature; everybody knew that Mrs. PeeWee Jimson herself had sculpted the bust at home during a Ladies Art Club class more than thirty years ago. This note was much more recent. It said, "I'm proud of you. Love, Daddy."

Hayes said, "You son of a bitch," which was not an expression he was in the habit of using.

The bust could not be forced past its neck into Victoria's big knapsack; it continued to stare in outraged indignation at its abductor's back as it was whisked away, lowered into a hole, heaved against shoulder blades, and jostled through a black culvert. As for the thief, he felt, as he confessed, a pure fool, and was convinced that the light at the end of the tunnel would be shuttered by the blue legs of a Thermopylae policeman. But there was no one in the gully except a fat-chested robin, who disappointedly spat out a berry and flew away. There was no one in the parking lot either, as far as Hayes could see when he crawled to the ridge and peered around, with PeeWee Jimson's broad white chin gouging into his shoulder. In order to make a run for his car, Hayes took off the blue-checked handkerchief to shove down over the statue's glistening bald head.

Meanwhile, at the other end of the long lot, at the crack in the furniture store's warehouse door, Pierce Jimson's anteaterish profile slowly emerged. The adulterer wanted to be sure the coast was clear, as he always said to Lizzie, before he let her sneak out to her car (or rather Boyd Joyner's car, for Lizzie owned nothing in her own name, not even — as her husband reminded her — her clothes). As Pierce Jimson's universe had imploded to a single planet (Venus, patroness of illicit passion), his first impression of the distant movement that caught his eye was that two lovers were embracing down in the gully. Then, more specifically, and horribly, that a pale, plump woman, wearing a blue-checked scarf with an Aunt Jemima look, was rubbing herself all over the infamous Raleigh Hayes, who was proving himself a rogue of consummate vice, not to mention daring. Then, as Hayes raised up to scan the lot, Jimson, devastated, came to a more alarming conclusion: Hayes had a huge video camera strapped to his back. He had followed Jimson here this morning. He was hiding, waiting to film Lizzie as she left the warehouse. Or, worse, Hayes had somehow slipped inside, and had already filmed him and Lizzie on the box springs! Was that possible? No, it couldn't be possible. They would have heard him. Would they? And Pierce turned the chalk color of his sculpted father — now lying heaving on Raleigh Hayes's back.

Jimson shut the warehouse door. Lizzie would have to leave by the front door. He could tell his clerks that she'd come back again to ask for work, and wasn't it a shame he couldn't help her. Times were bad. And the infamous Hayes? He'd see that Hayes got his deed to the cabin, and the pond, before noon! But the fiend would have to understand that any further attempts — any further *suggestion* — of blackmail, and he'd find himself, pronto, in jail. A man could bear only so much. Of course, he, Pierce, couldn't really go to the police, and so lose Lizzie. Lose Lizzie? He couldn't breathe without her.

Smacking the tops of stacked dinette sets as he walked back through the warehouse, Pierce Jimson called, "Lizzie!" Only a whisper came hoarsely from his throat. His Voice! Was Raleigh Hayes going to rob him of his *voice?* It was intolerably unfair. Why couldn't God afflict Raleigh Hayes with something awful like Love, and see how *he* liked it, to know what you were missing if you had to give it up.

CHAPTER

8

And Is Nearly Arrested

THIEF! He was a common thief! Well, stealing public statuary could not really be called "common." Not that removing Mrs. PeeWee Jimson's rendition of her spouse from atop a cabinet of chipmunks was exactly in a league with scratching up the *Pietà*. Still, crime was crime, and now he was a criminal. He who had never stolen a thing in his life. No, Hayes instantly admitted, that wasn't true. He had stolen on at least half a dozen previous occasions, each of which, when remembered, seared his mind like a brand. He had twice stolen change carelessly chucked about the house by his father. He had several times stolen (in the sense that he had eaten them while Aura dawdled among the aisles) a bag of smoked almonds from the supermarket. Worse, once he had stolen and hidden in the trashcan a jack-in-the-box belonging to his little brother Gates; first, because he couldn't stand to listen to "Pop Goes the Weasel" anymore, and perhaps, too, horribly enough, because he knew how much Gates liked it. But childhood pranks and grocery munching were ordinary crimes, and everyone Hayes knew had committed them, far, far more often than he. Why, Jimmy Clay had stolen a *car* right out of the church parking lot and driven it to Myrtle Beach.

So Raleigh Hayes conversed with himself as he drove toward home. His burning need to get rid of PeeWee's bust was as physical and as miserable as a long-repressed urgency to, as he called it, use the facilities, when doing so was impossible because he was in a church pew or on a bus or in the tiny stuffed living room of an elderly lady client who wanted to know why he was opposed to making her cat her beneficiary instead of the daughter who didn't even like her *or* the cat. Hayes couldn't have felt more anxious if Jimson's head, now on the floor of his Fiesta hatchback, had been not plaster, but as fleshy as the bloody head of John the Baptist, and he, Hayes, were as guilty of murder as Herod.

Almost on the beltway, Raleigh abruptly decided that nothing could be more idiotic than trying to hide PeeWee's bust at home, in a house where three women were always frantically searching wherever they liked for something to wear, where next door his neighbors were armed psychotics with no sense of privacy. Wheeling around, Hayes headed back toward the Crossways and his office. Since his secretary had deserted him, he could safely hide the head there.

From behind, a sharp mechanical shriek scared him witless. In the rear window, he saw the waxy orange glob of Halloween candy that meant a patrol car. Thermopylae had only three. Naturally, one of them was following him. A momentary twitch of his toes on the accelerator was Raleigh's only gesture of rebellion before he slowed to a stop beside an excavated lot behind a steel-mesh fence labeled Joyner Construction Co. Quickly he slid out of the car and hurried over to the sidewalk to keep the policeman (policeboy, rather, for the officer looked to be about the age of Holly's friend Booger; in fact, he looked very much like Booger) away from his car. Suddenly, Raleigh felt two lead weights in his jacket pockets. His hands gripping the guns, he helplessly smiled. Great! Here he was with two concealed weapons, wads of hundred-dollar bills, and a stolen statue! *Dear God, do something!*

Instantly, the policeman turned around to walk back to his car. Hayes, quicker than thought (indeed, entirely irrationally), hurled both Mingo's automatic and Vera's .22 over the fence into the red clay pit. His arms were casually crossed by the time the policeman managed to get the siren turned off, and looked back at him.

"Good morning, what's the problem, officer?" said Hayes, trying to sound cooperative, self-assured, and puzzled.

"Can I see your license, please?"

As Hayes reached to his back pocket, he followed the man's glance from his best seersucker suit, now smeared with dirt and beaded with prickly burrs, down to his mud-caked shoes. One pants leg was ripped open at the knee. He was a filthy shambles. The lanky patrolman, gadgets hanging from his midriff in glossy precision, looked studiously back and forth from the neat, tight-lipped photo on Hayes's driver's license to the black-faced grubby man on the sidewalk. Raleigh combed his fingers through his hair. "I was assisting my elderly aunt to retrieve a, a trunk up out of her basement. It was, ha, sort of a pigsty. I was going home to change. But I'd left my office unlocked, important papers . . ." Hearing himself babbling, he wiped his hand over his mouth to shut it, then removed his glasses. The white skin around his eyes gave his face a thievish raccoon look.

The officer handed back the license, which Raleigh also examined, sadly, as if heartbroken to see how respectable he had once appeared to the world. "Mr. Hayes, you made an illegal U-turn."

Mr. Hayes apologized.

"I'm going to let you go with a warning."

Hayes thanked the pompous teenager through gritted teeth.

"People get in a hurry, that's when accidents happen," added this insufferably sanctimonious youngster, whose wolverine face was horribly familiar.

"Absolutely true, officer. Look," said Hayes, "do you happen to know anybody named Booger?"

The policeman went instantly from a deadpan to a grin, sparkling his thin long teeth. "Sure thing. He's my kid brother. You go to the games?" He shot an invisible basketball into an invisible net.

Hayes nodded. In fact, he hadn't been to a basketball game in twenty years, although ages ago he himself had played left guard for Thermopylae High. "I think," he added mournfully, "I think Booger's a friend of my daughter Holly."

"Could be," agreed Booger's brother. "Yeah, he likes the girls and vice versa. He's wild. You'd better watch her."

Well, at least Booger's brother hadn't said, "Yeah, I hear they're getting married," or "Yeah, I hear they *have* to get married." Or . . .

"Okay, take it easy, Mr. Hayes." The law tapped the insurance agent on the shoulder, then sauntered back to the orange car, and waited there until Hayes drove at a crawl away.

What if trespassing children found that (possibly loaded) pistol? Hayes circled the block but stopped at the intersection when he saw the patrol car still parked by the unfinished condominium. Why was that loafer sitting there, on taxpayers' money? He backed into a filling station, where he used a pay phone to call Police Emergency. When they finally answered, he held his nose. "There're two guns in a construction hole, corner of Broad and Elliot."

"Come again? Who is this?"

Raleigh repeated his sentence slowly and hung up.

The sadistic fates otherwise occupied for the moment in ruining somebody else's life, our hero was able to slip the knapsack through the Forbes lobby and up the elevator and into his office unobserved. There he found Kaiser Bill emptying the trashcans into a big plastic bag on the side of his cart. With a nod, hugging Jimson to his chest, he walked past the Kaiser to his inner office. The bust would not fit into his file cabinet. When he returned to the anteroom, the big black man still held the trashcan raised at a tilt. He appraised its contents thoughtfully as he said, "Mister Hayes, it's took care of."

"Yes, thanks." Hayes glanced around the room. "Look, do you have an extra one of those trash bags I could borrow?"

"Sure do."

Raleigh groaned as he leaned to take the folded bag; he must have twisted his back in that tunnel.

"You okay, Mr. Hayes?"

"Frankly, no. Has anybody been around here looking for me?"

"Not yet." The Kaiser was experiencing a feeling that he interpreted, as he did all things, as instructions from the Man Upstairs. He felt himself moving from an intrigued dread of this muddy, disheveled creature toward something akin to pity and protectiveness. God wanted Hayes watched over. The poor soul had messed up badly — first killing his secretary and now fixing to stick what looked like a petrified white man with no arms and legs into a plastic trash bag. Having helped Hayes once, noblesse oblige compelled the Kaiser to keep on forever. "You hurt bad? Can Bill get you something?"

"Pardon?" Raleigh was reaching in his wallet for the twenty dollars he remembered he owed Jenkins; promptness in paying his debts was a source of pride. "What do you mean?" His wallet was almost empty; all he had was a ten. He took out one of the envelopes; there was nothing but hundreds in it. He therefore turned to the bookshelf where he kept a twenty for emergencies inside *The Home Companion to Medical Symptoms.* "What do you mean, 'hurt bad'?"

"Beat up," the Kaiser explained. "Bad," he added.

Hayes was offended. "I fell in a ditch," he snapped.

The custodian (who had now concluded that Hayes was robbing banks as well as killing people) stroked his white mustache, twice on one side, twice on the other. "You want to listen to Bill, you don't want to mess with trouble this way."

"I'm sorry, I don't know what you're talking about. Could you just finish up here, okay? Here, much obliged, okay?" Hayes pushed the money at Bill's hand; it was, however, the withered one, and the bill fell to the floor. As Hayes, embarrassed, stooped to pick up the money, the smell of the mop in the pushcart reminded him that he had to find this Jubal Rogers. For the mop made him think of his grandmother's porch, washed every Saturday by Flonnie Rogers, a small, bad-tempered black woman who'd lived at the house more than half a century. Slapping her wet mop side to side across the wide planks, she'd often threatened to cut off Raleigh's head with an axe if he walked on her floor before it dried. Raleigh wondered now whether he should ask his aunt Victoria why his father had said he was not supposed to mention Jubal Rogers to her, and ask her whether she knew what kin Jubal was to Flonnie and why in the world his father should owe this man five thousand dollars.

That there was some connection between blacks of the same surname, he did not doubt. Thermopylae was half black, and half of Thermopylae was too little, and too ingrown, and that particular half too circumscribed, to have room for strangers. All the local blacks lived at the south end of Church Street in an area called so matter-of-factly "Darktown," when Raleigh was a boy, that not until he was ten did the meaning of that name penetrate; it was a word, like Thermopylae itself, untranslated and without connotation.

Nobody called the area Darktown anymore, but most of the blacks still lived there. Flonnie'd had a sister who lived there. Maybe Jubal Rogers lived there too.

Thinking of Flonnie, Hayes kept kneeling, until he was shocked by the weight of the custodian's broad hand on his head. "You got troubles, Mr. Hayes?"

Raleigh stood up fast with the money. "I told you, I fell in a ditch. What's the matter with you? Here. Thank you."

"Nothing." Jenkins accepted the twenty dollars, and looked politely at the portrait of Andrew Jackson, as Hayes walked out of the room, then immediately returned.

"Bill, let me ask you something? Do you know anyone called Flonnie Rogers?"

Bill spoke to President Jackson rather than Hayes. "Mean old lady, never got married? Used to live way back with some white family?"

"Mine."

"That so? They was yours?"

"She was employed by my grandparents."

"That so? She whipped me once."

"Me too."

"Uh hunh." Jenkins rubbed President Jackson's face with his big thumb. "She dead?"

"I have no idea."

" 'Spect so. My mama knew Flonnie Rogers at church and my mama died old. Passed away of an early evening, listening to the radio, just like this." Jenkins tilted his head and rested his cheek in the palm of his hand. Then he gave a quiet sigh.

"Well, ah, that sounds, ah, peaceful," said Hayes uncomfortably. "I'm glad she didn't suffer."

The Kaiser did not bother to correct this innocent opinion, except obliquely. "No suffering Up Above," he said. "What you want about Flonnie Rogers?"

"Actually it's *Jubal* Rogers I want."

"Jubal! He's gone from here. Long time. Could be he's dead, too. Jubal got something to do with your troubles?" Jenkins moved behind Bonnie Ellen's desk and settled himself into the chair, leaving Hayes, already disconcerted by the janitor's presumption of a relationship that certainly had never existed between them before, with the awkward feeling that he was a visitor in his own office.

"Bill, I just wonder if he was kin to Flonnie Rogers."

Meditatively lighting a pipe, the Kaiser told Hayes in a much too leisurely way that Jubal Rogers was, perhaps, Flonnie's nephew, or near to. Was approximately Jenkins's own age (somewhere near sixty-five), or near to. Had grown up in Darktown, played the clarinet, or some such, gotten drafted and been sent to fight the Germans, or thereabouts. After the war, had moved up North to join a radio band, or something like. Had probably gotten himself killed over one of a large number of vices (women, liquor, dice games, and Communist talk among them). If dead, he had assuredly gone Down Below, for he'd given nothing but sass and grief to the Man Above. "He were good-looking, he dressed good-looking and he act good-looking and he throwed his money around and his mouth too. The ladies they act like he was Christmas candy, and —"

"All I need to know is his whereabouts," Hayes said.

Jenkins had no idea of his whereabouts.

"Well, thank you. Excuse me." On the pretense of needing to get something from Bonnie Ellen's desk, Hayes forced Jenkins up out of the chair so he could open the drawer. In it he saw wrappers from Snickers bars, uncapped felt-tip pens, a *Glamour* magazine, and two letters addressed to him. These he took, and excusing himself again, confessed that he needed to get to work.

"Don't mix yourself up with Jubal Rogers's kind. Things bad enough already." And Jenkins astounded the insurance agent with another pat on the head as he left.

Hayes stuffed PeeWee Jimson into a plastic bag, which he hid in the closet. Then he sat down with a moan at his tidy desk. "One step at a time," he told himself sternly.

His office was an austere and symmetrical place, a raft of sanity in a foaming sea. In the exact middle of each wall were two framed objects. South: his college diploma and his "Thermopylae Civitan of the Year — 1978" plaque. East: Aura's oil painting of "Day Lilies in Red Clay Pitcher," and her charcoal drawing, "Twins Asleep, Thank God." North: the windows (out of which Mr. Forbes had jumped). West, facing any prospective purchasers of life insurance, a calendar and a print of "The Sinking of the Titanic" — as if to remind them that time flies, and life's uncertain. Dead center on the brown rug, equidistant from two file cabinets and two chairs, sat the desk. At it sat Raleigh telephoning Betty Hemans, who, at sixty-three, suddenly had abandoned him to go home and write novels full-time; who had picked as her replacement Bonnie Ellen Dellwood! So much for her feel for character.

"Hello. This is the residence of Betty Morrow Hemans. I can't come to the phone right now but if you wouldn't mind leaving your name and your number and around the time you called and your message and . . ."

It was a recording. The first home-answering service he'd ever heard. Why should a retired widow. . . ?

"At the sound of the beep. I'll call you right back. Be sure you wait for the beep. It's loud, now."

It was very loud. Scared, Hayes rushed into words at a tumble. "Betty? This is Raleigh W. Hayes? That girl you got me, Bonnie Ellen? She's departed for California without a day's notice; I presume, permanently, and left a mess behind. My daddy's not well, he's disappeared, and can I prevail on you to do me a favor and come back to —" *Beep!* He must have run out of time. Hayes hung up and dialed again. The line was busy. He slammed down the receiver. It rang.

"Raleigh. This is Betty. Bonnie went to California?"

"I thought you weren't there."

"That's my machine."

"Why?"

"My professor said a writer needs to keep her concentration going without disturbance," Mrs. Hemans explained. "Peace and quiet is a pure necessity. I even had to give my gerbil Boots away. He made so much racket doing that exercise wheel."

Raleigh, offended that Mrs. Hemans had obviously stood right beside her phone listening to him make a fool of himself into her machine, refrained from asking how she could concentrate while eavesdropping on recorded messages. Instead, he removed his glasses to press his palm against his eye socket, and he threw himself on her mercy. "So, I'm just desperate," he finally concluded. "I've got to go find Daddy. It'd only be a week or so, really, and maybe you could write a little here at the office like you used to."

Mrs. Hemans had a warm spot in her heart for Raleigh Whittier Hayes, who knew nothing about it. The shape of his ear and the sandy hair curling behind it were the flint that struck against her memories and produced this spark. She liked Raleigh for looking like his uncle Whittier, that dead poet warrior with whom, forty years ago, she had been so passionately in love, and whose sonnets she still kept in the false bottom of her jewelry box. Her novel, *Remember Me,* was, in fact, their own tragic story of romance and young death — though, of course, she'd changed all the details. She told Raleigh that if he'd come pick her up, she'd return to work until she could find a replacement.

"Oh, Betty, I swear I'll never forget this!" said Hayes. It was exactly what Whittier had said to her on a June night in 1941 in the backseat of her father's new Oldsmobile; in Chapter 32 of *Remember Me,* she'd transferred the line to a bombed church in a London blackout.

For the next hour, Raleigh tried to leave his office, but his phone kept ringing. A fellow Civitan had decided to cancel his life insurance policy. "In my opinion you're going to regret it," predicted Hayes. "When your worries are over, your wife's will be just beginning."

"Good," the man said.

Hayes was distracted and spoke more bluntly than was best for business. "Fine. It's your funeral. So long."

Hayes was distracted because he'd opened one of the letters that Bonnie Ellen had forgotten to give him. Postmarked Midway, South Carolina, it was written in shaky pencil on a memo pad with two big eyeballs at the top. It was from Roxanne Digges, his father's third wife, who'd left behind Earley and their child Gates for a long-distance trucker named Fred Zane. The letter was a month old.

Dear Raleigh,

I guess it looks funny me writing to you like this because underneath it was no secret we never had much use for each other.

But have you seen Gates or heard from him at all? I know you kept up with him in prison and then about five years back he needed some money in Nevada, which I didn't have, but maybe he got in touch with you?

I'd as soon not pester Earley — no love lost there, what with Fred, and anyhow he lost track of Gates way back. The problem is and I'm not one to tell my troubles, but they don't give me too long here. Because of cancer getting into my liver. Otherwise I wouldn't bother you. But it'd mean something to me if I could get in touch with Gates, if he's around. I guess it's real funny, me asking you where my own son is, considering the past, *etc.* But I'd appreciate it a lot if you felt like you could drop me a line c/o address above. I hope everything's fine with you and yours. P.S. Fred died on Sept. 5, 1977.

Sinc., Roxanne

As Raleigh left the office, something remorseless grabbed each end of his stomach and gave a hard twist; spastic colon, he thought, doubled over. It certainly didn't occur to him that news of Roxanne Digges's imminent death could cause him pain. Like everybody else, Hayes felt more than he knew, and was better and worse than he believed. Bent over, he noticed an envelope that had been shoved under his door. Inside was an official bill of sale for Knoll Pond, its cabin and lot, clipped to a lawyer's card. Also attached was a peculiar note, presumably from Pierce Jimson.

Take it and leave us alone. If you try something else or fail to keep your end of the bargain, I swear I'll go to the police.

That Hayes was snared in the deep toils of a nightmare, he could no longer doubt. He was dreaming, and that was why even people like Pierce Jimson talked nonsense; why the world, utterly off its axis, chased him down alleys like a bowling ball; why he could not get on with his real life. In his real life, it was three days ago. He was really asleep, dreaming a horrible dream about his father, who was really in the hospital having his heart checked. "Ha ha," said Hayes as he turned into Starry Haven and saw the crowd. Since it was all a dream, it made perfect sense for him to be seeing, as plain as day, an angry mob of women all over his front lawn,

women waving placards in the face of the same juvenile policeman who
had almost arrested him this morning.

Hayes had to park his car around the corner of the block, where, as in a
dream, he thought he saw Mingo's new Chevrolet. He had to park so far
away from his own driveway because there were no empty spaces any
nearer his house.

CHAPTER

9

The First Sally Takes a Strange Turn

ACCORDING to their placards, these women were adamantly opposed to nuclear war and to Congressman Charlie Lukes, Republican representative from Thermopylae's district and a fervent defender of bombs for defense. Lukes had never said he was specifically in *favor* of nuclear war, but he had often announced that he wasn't afraid of it. Raleigh now remembered that this very evening he and Aura had been invited to attend a reception for Congressman Lukes that Nemours Kettell was hosting at the golf club. He had forgotten about it. Obviously, so had Aura, here dressed in one of her old RN uniforms, with black armbands, waving a poster, like a flag, inches from the blandly officious face of Booger's brother. On the poster a deadly mushroom cloud puffed up out of the congressman's head. Had these women gathered to practice marching across the golf course and storming the Club Room reception line? In which case, perhaps Raleigh's duty as a Republican and a Civitan was to warn Nemours Kettell, particularly since he was now close enough to distinguish in the moil *Mrs.* Nemours Kettell, unfurling, with her daughter Mrs. Wayne Sparks, a long banner painted, "THERMOPYLAE MOTHERS FOR PEACE. NO MORE NUKES. NO MORE LUKES."

All the women were arguing with Booger Sr., who kept throwing both hands in the air, in exasperation, or surrender, as Aura was saying, "Don't we still have the right to free assembly in this country, Mr. Blair, or correct me if I'm in Russia by mistake."

"*Yahooo!*" Young Mrs. Sparks, wearing a Halloween skeleton suit, gave the Rebel yell.

"Ma'am," the policeman tried, "I'm not even here about —"

"And the right to protest, and the right to march —"

"Well, I think you need a permit to march, but —"

Raleigh elbowed his way nervously into the press of hostile females, and scrunched down behind someone busty wrapped head to foot in bloody bandages, who shook a sign, "THOU SHALT NOT KILL!" Hayes feared being seen by this officer Blair, who had either changed his mind and come to arrest him because of his U-turn, or to arrest him because Pierce Jimson had "gone to the police," as threatened (but how could Pierce have already found out about Raleigh's stealing his father's statue out of the library?). Or Booger's brother had come to arrest *Aura* (apparently a left-wing radical, as well as a belly dancer and God knows what else). Somebody's sign smacked Raleigh on the back of the head; he lurched forward into the buttocks of the bandaged protestor. "Sorry," he murmured. The woman squeezed around, saw him, and gasped, "Oh! You!" White gauze covered everything but the mouth and the scalloped-lashed violet eyes that indisputably belonged to Vera Sheffield. Beyond doubt, she would use any excuse to deck herself out in some outlandish costume.

Vera's eyes narrowed with accusations. She whispered, "What do you want? Do you want Aura to see you stumbling around drunk in those clothes?"

Raleigh glanced at his ripped, mud-caked rag of a suit. "I fell in a ditch," he whispered back. How dare someone wrapped in catsup-spattered shredded sheets criticize *his* clothes! A fact suddenly registered. "Wait a minute, Vera! Your teeth. Your wires are gone!"

"No thanks to you," she muttered darkly.

From the commotion's hub, Aura's voice rose brightly. "Well, officer, if you wanted the Sheffields' house, why didn't you say so in the first place? Naturally, we thought you came to arrest *us.*"

"Naturally," nodded Mrs. Kettell, disappointed.

The hapless policeman tugged up his gun belt. "Listen, ladies . . ."

Aura pushed through the placards. "Where are you, Vera? It's your house he wants. Why, *Raleigh,* what happened to you?"

"I fell in a ditch. Excuse us for just a second. Could I speak to you a moment, Aura?"

Abruptly, as if they'd rehearsed, the crowd of women backstepped into a circle; some watched Vera hopping slowly with the patrolman across her driveway; some watched Raleigh Hayes, in filthy tatters, turn purple. With clamped teeth, he led his wife away from them to the front steps.

"You know," Aura mused. "The way you look, maybe you'd like to march with us."

"I'm not marching anywhere, and I hope you aren't either."

Her smile was brazen.

"Aura! Are you smoking?"

From her lips a stream of smoke French-curled up into her nostrils. She nodded without much remorse.

"Oh, Aura, I'm really pretty shocked, I'm sorry to say. I'll tell you this, I feel betrayed. I was under the impression that we gave up cigarettes ten years ago!"

"Every once in a while, I slip up. I hope you can forgive me."

"Did you know Caroline is smoking too, and possibly even Holly? They may even be smoking cigars?"

"Raleigh, is that what you came home to talk to me about, smoking? Because, darling, as you see," she pointed at the massed women behind them, "I'm in the middle of something right this minute."

Hayes nodded wildly. "Umhum. Umhum. I can see you are. What's going on! I thought Mothers for Peace was a *discussion* group! Why are you dressed like that?"

She raised an eyebrow. "I might ask you the same."

"Don't change the subject."

"From what?"

"From this." Raleigh snapped his head at the "Peace NOW" sign.

Adjusting her snowy nurse's cap, Aura explained, "We're against Congressman Lukes."

"That much I have deduced. Did you happen to realize that we were supposed to be attending a cocktail party in the man's honor this very evening?"

"Maybe you were." Aura blew three consecutive smoke rings, each inside the one before, a feat that Hayes suspected required extensive practice.

From across the yard, Barbara Kettell was yodeling. In her orange fringed poncho, she looked like a large teepee. "Aura, EXCUSE ME, AURA!, if we're going to get there before he starts talking, don't you think we better get going right away?"

Raleigh grabbed his wife's starched sleeve. *"Where is 'there'?"*

"The VFW post on Dulles. . . . I'M COMING, BARBARA! LOAD UP THE CARS! LET'S MOVE!"

God, she sounded like a cowboy movie. Hayes brought his face very close to his wife's, and stared first into one eye, then the other. He spoke with profound gravity. "This is possibly and probably the worst crisis of my life. All right? My father has disappeared with my entire future and is endeavoring to coerce me into a wild goose chase and illegal shenanigans. Some of which," his voice fell to an ominous whisper, *"I have already committed.* My secretary has vanished. I am receiving strange mail, including a psychotic note from Pierce Jimson. . . ."

Aura pulled her head back and gave her cigarette a long puff. "Pierce, psychotic, too?"

"I come home, and here you are, staging a goddamn peace rally in our yard, right when I need you the most!"

With a sigh, Aura stubbed out her cigarette on the step. "Raleigh, I'm ashamed of you. I see you're upset, and I'm sorry. Maybe you ought to just go lie down. But, be honest, what's more important in the long run, your 'crisis,' or world crisis?"

"Mine," Hayes defiantly snarled.

"Do you know why I married you?"

Hayes sat down on the steps. "I have no idea."

His wife scanned the sky, seeking the past there. "You cared about right and wrong, that's why. About fairness and peace. Do you remember that person? You cared about stupidity, and if you ask me, there's nothing you can possibly think of that's stupider than nuclear war."

Hayes pulled himself back up by the doorknob. "Aura, did you and Mingo by any chance watch *On the Beach* together on the late show recently?"

"Cynical humor isn't the answer, Raleigh. Talk about feeling betrayed. When I met you, you were a *Democrat!* You cared about something besides money."

"I didn't have any money to care about."

"That's why you were a Democrat? I wish F.D.R. could hear you."

"Oh, for God's sake!" Hayes jerked open the door. "I'll see you later." He ripped off his jacket and flung it into the hall closet. "Unless, of course, the world's destroyed by Charlie Lukes, which, frankly, would be an immense relief."

Aura laughed, despite her just professed animadversion to humor. "Oh, Raleigh, go take a long bath and lie down."

Upstairs, Raleigh threw himself with a bounce on his bed. He didn't even scream when Mingo Sheffield proved to be hiding behind it. He simply closed his eyes, laced his fingers beneath his head, and shuffled his shoes off with his toes. Quietly, he remarked, "Get out of my dream, Mingo. I don't need but one nightmare at a time."

"Have they gone?"

Hayes didn't answer.

"Raleigh, you promised you'd help me. Have they gone?"

Hayes leaned on an elbow and stared a long while over the top of his glasses at the fat man's head floating wobbily above the blue horizon of the coverlet. Finally he said, "Yes."

More of Mingo heaved into view. "You saw the police leave?"

"Ah. The police. No, I thought you were inquiring about the yardful of Mothers Against Charlie Lukes. They've gone." Hayes lay back down.

"The police are after me, Raleigh! Don't go to sleep!" Mingo lurched onto the bed, tilting Hayes into a slide that he could halt only by grabbing the mattress edge. "I saw them coming, so I sneaked in your back door, and Vera's supposed to say as far as she knows I'm still at Knox-Bury."

Hayes snuggled his head into his pillow. His voice had the distant calm of a psychiatrist talking through a megaphone to a mad killer on a rooftop. "And why *aren't* you at Knox-Bury's? I thought you were given two weeks' notice."

"I guess . . . I guess . . ." Mingo began pulling at the tufted threads that patterned the coverlet. "I guess I went a little bit to pieces when I got back to the store, thinking about how Billy just didn't even want me anymore. I guess I wanted to show them what it feels like."

Hayes opened one eye. "Excuse me, Mingo, would you mind not pulling the threads out of my covers? Thank you."

Sheffield grabbed one fat fist with the other, and shoved both between his thighs. "I guess I yanked a lot of Better Menswear off the racks and threw it in a pile."

"Um hum."

"I guess maybe my Easter paint got poured all over it." Mingo flipped himself supine beside his neighbor. "Nobody saw me."

"Well, that's good."

"But I think maybe they suspect me, you know? Raleigh, are you listening?" Rolling onto his side, Sheffield poked at his friend's arm. "My mama would die if I had to end up in prison."

Hands behind his head, Hayes studied the spackled ceiling. "Your mama did die, Mingo, several years ago. So don't worry about that."

Hurt shuddered through the mammoth body. "Raleigh, why do you always have to be so mean?"

Before Hayes could carry out his impulse to laugh maniacally, "You don't know what *mean* is," then to clamp a pillow over Sheffield's face and sit on it for an hour — the phone beside the bed rang. Through the wire's crackle, Hayes heard the high-pitched, slow-paced merry slur of an unmistakable voice. "Hello, Little Fellow, it's Daddy. Whatcha up to?"

Ravishing irony, peaceful as Christ, descended upon Raleigh and allowed him to escape a massive coronary. "Oh, hi, Daddy. Nothing much. I'm just lying here on my bed with my neighbor Mingo Sheffield, shooting the breeze about the police being after him either for vandalizing Knox-Bury's Clothing Store, or for constantly attempting to commit suicide. Excuse me a second." To Sheffield, flailing with arched back in protest, Hayes whispered, 'Oh, don't worry. My father won't tell on you. He doesn't care a thing about law and order. . . . So, where are you, Daddy? You certainly have kept us guessing, ha, ha! 'Bout ready to come on home?"

His father chuckled. "You get my message?"

"Yes, several, um hum." Raleigh amazed himself. His limbs were not rigid; his veins were not bulging; his heart had not cracked his sternum in two. "Oh, yes, got your messages. Everything's moving right along. Pee-Wee's bust, Pierce's cabin, Tiny's trunk. *Goddammit, where are you, Daddy?"*

"Raleigh, listen. I was talking to an old friend, and I hear Roxanne's not feeling too well."

"I know. She wrote me."

"She did? Humm. . . . Anyhow, she's gone to the hospital outside Midway."

Is that where Earley was? Briefly, Hayes wondered if he could get Mingo to run back home and ask the operator to trace this call. A glance at his neighbor (crawling across the rug to peek his head over the windowsill) convinced him of the futility of bothering to ask.

"Son, maybe it'd be a good idea to try to get Gates up there to see her."

"Up there." Ah, so the man was somewhere south of the middle of South Carolina. That certainly narrowed things down. "Raleigh? Have you found Gates?"

The first vein popped. "Strangely enough, I haven't, Daddy. I realize he's only been missing for five years and I have had a whole day to work on the problem in my spare time from robbing the library."

Guffaws. "Oh, I remember when you were little, I'd say to Sarah, 'Go on, let the little fellow talk back. Sarcasm's like Pepto-Bismol on his system.' So, did I hear you say you got that fuck Pierce to sell you the cabin?"

"I'm sorry, I don't recall that I was in the habit of 'talking back' to my mother."

More, more laughter. "And supercilious! That was always your other trick. Oh, I love you, Specs!"

Standing now, Hayes wrung the receiver's neck. "Listen to me! Where are you? Daddy, do you realize that your doctor says you are seriously jeopardizing your health by leaving the hospital?"

"Try to get hold of Jubal, if you can. I've got a surprise for him. And if you can find Gates, just take him to Midway. Take him to her first, not me."

Calm cracked like ice in a frost heave. "How should *I* know where Gates is! When his own parents don't! He hasn't even kept in touch with his own mother!"

"Ask Lovie. She's the one he cares about. And just keep on doing your best, son. I'm proud of you. Ooops. Okay. I've got to go now. I'll be in touch. Everything's going to be fine."

"Don't you dare hang up!" Hayes was hyperventilating. "Did you marry a . . . colored . . . mental patient you . . . abducted from . . . the hospital?"

Laughter poured into Raleigh's ear like boiling oil. "Specs, you're such a worrywart." A click was followed by the long howl of the dial tone.

"Your daddy married a colored mental patient?" asked Mingo, on his knees by the window.

Raleigh stared at the telephone receiver as if its purpose escaped him. "Of course not. That's just an old family joke." Hayes tried to call the operator quickly, but didn't get her for some time. Then she either would not, or didn't know how to, trace the call. On the other hand, she was able to tell him that Earley Hayes's phone service on First Street had been disconnected; so his father wasn't charging these calls to his home phone. Where was he?!

"Raleigh, listen . . ."

"No. Pardon me, Mingo, but I'd like to take a bath." Hayes removed his pants and yanked out the belt; having emptied the pockets, he crammed the trousers into the wastebasket. "Mingo, I said —"

"Oh, sure, go ahead. . . . VERA! VERA, UP HERE!" Sheffield wedged up the window screen with his shoulder, and stuck half his bulk outside. By holding to the bedpost, Hayes was able to stop himself from charging the elephantine rear and slamming it through the opening.

As it was, by the time he had helped haul Sheffield back inside, Mrs.

Sheffield, still heavily bandaged, had whirled into his bedroom. Paying no attention to Hayes, she rushed as quickly as she could under the circumstances over to her squatting husband and began violently to shake him by the ears. "Why did you do it? Why! I can't believe it, I can't! Lord Jesus, be with me now in my darkest days."

Raleigh, in shirt and shorts, loudly and pleasurably sighed. "Vera," he said, "I know it looks bad, but honest to God, Mingo and I are not having an affair."

Ignoring this, Vera was now swaying Sheffield side to side by the shoulders. "Tell me I haven't lived with a man twenty-five years and didn't know I was married to a murderer?!"

As Mingo, mouth open, could not answer Vera's extraordinary request, Raleigh shouted at her, "What the hell are you talking about? Who's been murdered? The police are here about a murder? They think Mingo murdered somebody?"

"YES. Some *woman*. All they found is her shoe, and blood in an Oriental rug over in some construction site. And they won't say why, but they're looking for Mingo!"

There was a very hard thump. Mingo had fainted.

Hayes was not a heartless man. He did not simply step over the pile of bodies — Sheffield's prone; Vera's swaddled, atop him — on his way to a bath. Instead, he looked out the window. "The policeman's gone."

Vera wailed, "I know! He said he'd try again later. Oh, it was awful. Mingo just ran out the back and told me, just like that, 'Say you don't know where I am.' " She slapped her husband a half-dozen pats. "So I did, but lying gives me hives, it really does. It was awful."

"Well, obviously, Vera, it can't be too serious or the police would *wait*, for Pete's sake. If they really thought Mingo was a murderer! This is some misunderstanding. Or a joke. So, you just call Chief Hood and get it sorted out. All right? Now calm down." Raleigh took a glass of stale water from the night table, knelt down and tossed it in Mingo's face. "The police are only after Mingo for pouring paint on the menswear after Billy Knox fired him."

Sheffield spluttering to life, heard his wife shriek, "FIRED him?," and rolled back over, huddled up like a hippopotamus fetus.

"Look, y'all will excuse me," said Hayes. "You've got a lot to talk about, and I'm going to take my shower. I'm supposed to be in two different places right now. I'm leaving town, Vera, so you'll have to handle this. I've got to drive all the way to Cowstream, and possibly New Orleans." As

Raleigh moved about his bedroom, collecting clean underwear, noticing that someone (Aura, Holly, and/or Caroline) had been borrowing his socks again and hadn't even bothered to do so surreptitiously, as his top drawer was a shambles. It was clearly not the best hiding place for the thousands of dollars that he had never had a moment to take to the bank; not with Holly so desperate for Grand Nationals modified Fords, and Caroline so capable of spending every cent of it on cosmetics, and Aura so eager to stop the arms race, whatever the cost. Hayes put the money in the pockets of his blue gabardine (his only other spring suit — his *only* spring suit, now that his seersucker was ripped to shreds).

As Raleigh chose his wardrobe, he sidestepped the Sheffields, who continued to lie on the rug in tears. "Pardon me," he remarked each time he passed them. He found enormously satisfying this new style of serene irony.

"Why does everything have to always happen to me?" Mingo was sniffling. "I never killed a fly."

Hayes spoke pleasantly as he chose a tie. "What about your dog you ran over and wouldn't even admit it?"

Vera was calling on her Savior to kill Billy Knox immediately for discharging on two weeks' notice the sweetest man who ever lived.

"Thou shalt not kill," smiled Hayes. "Good-bye now. Make yourselves at home."

The shower's hard heat was an immense comfort to the insurance man's sore body. While under the spray for the longest stay of his life, he began to let himself hope that he could beat back Chaos by organizing it. He would take Betty Hemans to the office. And take Jimson's bust out of it. He would take his aunt Victoria to his aunt Lovie Clay's, fifty miles east in Cowstream. He would pick up the trunk and the Bible. He would . . . well, beyond today, he would not risk thinking. As for Aura's politics, if she went to jail, the twins could drive out for pizza with Booger Blair in his sports car. As for Mingo's crimes, let Mingo take care of himself; Raleigh had acquired enough crimes of his own. Anyhow, it wasn't feasible that Mingo had killed anyone so soon. Even psychoses took a little time to grow. You couldn't progress from slopping paint on clothes to murdering women overnight. Even madness was bound to keep a schedule.

Despite the lessons of the past few days, Raleigh Hayes was still far from following those who teach that Chaos reigns over a universe of random black holes. He'd always known Chaos was out there lurking, and he could see now how vast the abyss was, but he still clung by his nails to an edge of the cliff of reason, in the uncrumbled faith that the cliff was there. Nor had recent events led Hayes to consider even the most tangential chance that he himself could be, by the frailest link, involved in this suspected murder — no more than he would ever have thought, reading in the papers of a homicide, that the police would soon come rapping on his door to ask him about it. The police would rap on the doors of the sort of people who did that sort of thing. That he was not the sort so defined Hayes, so constituted the language of his self, nothing in his recent conversations with Pierce Jimson and Kaiser Bill suggested to him that the former thought him a blackmailer; the latter, a killer. This same failure of the imagination kept Hayes from even hearing Vera say that the supposed murder happened in a construction site, much less connecting the news with the fact that he had himself recently tossed two guns of Mingo Sheffield's into just such a place.

Nor did it once cross Hayes's mind that because his secretary Bonnie Ellen Dellwood had disappeared, she might be this unknown victim of foul play; whereas he had no trouble assuming that Bonnie Ellen and her so-called husband were inconsiderate enough to move to California without a moment's notice. In other words, Hayes was a skeptical man, not a believer. The paranoid sensibility with its faith in the connectedness of outside forces irritated him profoundly — whether in books (he couldn't stand the espionage novels Aura loved), or in life (he couldn't stand the way, whenever Mingo was an hour late home from work, Vera came over to predict that he'd died in a crackup on the beltway, and to ask had Raleigh noticed any flaming wrecks off the road). Raleigh's commitment to the managerial power of the will was such that it was far easier for him to believe people would *do* idiotic things on purpose than that idiotic things could be, without purpose, done to them. Were this not true, sanity would be a useless skill, was probably a handicap. Therefore, his aunts and uncles were dead because they chose to smoke Lucky Strikes and swill Coca-Colas. He was alive because he chose to jog and fasten his seat belt. He was alive because he insured life against accidents.

While dressing in the steamy bathroom, Hayes did give the matter of the "murder" some thought. He concluded that the bloodstained carpet and the lady's shoe were most likely litter dumped by some uncivic slob. It was even conceivable that they were the abandoned evidence of some virgin's deflowering. These were more reasonable theories than murder.

But, in *fact* (as Aura always said when he sneered at her taste for spy novels), stranger things have happened. In fact, the Oriental carpet belonged to Dr. Jasper Kilby, a dentist in the Forbes Building, who'd made enough money to quit working on Wednesdays, so hadn't yet discovered his rug was gone. The shoe belonged to Bonnie Ellen Dellwood. As much as it would have shocked Hayes to hear that Bonnie Ellen had been rolled in Dr. Kilby's rug and dropped in Boyd Joyner's excavation lot, exactly where Hayes had thrown the guns, it would have shocked Kaiser Bill (who'd put her there) just as much to hear that she'd gotten up and walked away, after Mingo's pistol struck her in the side of the head and jarred her back to consciousness — though not self-consciousness — for she'd wandered off, bruised and groggy, with no memory of what had happened to her. Who, in any case, would care to remember that her husband had even accidentally almost killed her; who would care to discover that the Forbes janitor (thinking her employer had shot her) had rolled her in a carpet and left her in a construction pit; who would want to know that the Thermopylae police, like frantic princes, were searching all over town for the foot to fit her slipper?

When Raleigh Hayes, combed, shaved, starched, and in control, finally strode back into his bedroom, he was pleased to find the Sheffields gone. When he walked outside, he was less pleased to find his car gone as well.

"Aura took it," called Vera, as Raleigh stomped back around the corner. She stood barefoot in her driveway, wearing a man's raincoat and looking suspiciously naked beneath it. "She had to use the Fiesta to take my Nukes group, and Barbara Kettell drove Aura's wagon. She thought you were going to take a nap. But, Raleigh, you're welcome to the Pinto." Key shook glittering in the sun. Already backed to the curbside was the garish yellow vehicle with "God Is My Co-Pilot" on its smashed rear fender, and KISSY PU on its license plate.

A seizure, strong as, and otherwise resembling, electrocution, shot Hayes racing toward his house with a vague notion of smashing his body into the siding. But he came to his senses before he even crossed the lawn, took a slow breath, walked back, and accepted his neighbor's offer. Yes, he was still in control.

"Keep it just as long as you like." Vera smiled in her husband's shy, furtive way. "There's a bunch of clothes for the Salvation Army in the back. Don't mind them."

"Thank you, Vera. Could I impose on you to tell Aura . . ." Tell her what? To go into analysis? Move to Moscow? "Tell Aura I'll call her. I'll be back late tonight."

"BACK? I thought you said you had to go to New Orleans?"

"Not tonight." For Pete's sake, what business was it of hers? Hayes slid into the front seat, which, like the steering wheel, was covered by a nappy sheep pelt. He turned on the ignition; the key chain was a cube of Lucite with a St. Christopher's medal in it. Atop the dashboard, a little plastic statue of Jesus was flanked by two roly-poly black Buddhas whose heads jiggled "yes" on springs.

In parting, Hayes said, in his close-to-howling style, "Vera, in the hypothetical eventuality that my wife is apprehended this afternoon by the Federal Bureau of Investigation, would you mind looking in on the twins, when and if they drop by our house after school? Thank you very much. And speaking of spouses and prison, where's Mingo?"

"I couldn't tell you," Vera vaguely replied. "Well, I guess this is goodbye. Have a safe trip. God bless you, Raleigh." To his amazement, she leaned into the car (she *was* naked beneath the raincoat), and kissed him on the cheek. "The Lord's with you, Raleigh. He's with you every step of the way. Bye-bye."

"Vera, I'll be back tonight!"

But Mrs. Sheffield guessed better than Raleigh. He did not return from Cowstream that evening. He did not see Thermopylae again for two weeks, not until Easter, not until after his world was rearranged in ways he wouldn't have imagined a few short days ago.

Of course, Vera had inside information. No sooner had Hayes driven her rattling Pinto onto the beltway than he heard, behind him, *"Tschoo! Tschoo! TSCHOOO!"*

No sooner had he cursed a rear tire for blowing out than he felt, at the back of his neck, the cold muzzle of a pistol, and heard the voice that had grated on his nerves for forty years.

"Raleigh, don't turn around. I've got a gun on you. It's me. Mingo."

"Oh, really?" Hayes turned around anyhow. "Jesus Christ! How many goddamn guns do you own?"

Tented by the crinolines of Vera's pink taffeta evening gown, Sheffield raised up from the backseat floor, revolver in hand. His eyes were all pupil; his voice, a hoarse lunatic whine. "Raleigh, they're not going to get me. I'm not waiting around to be strapped in the gas chamber."

"Mingo! You scared me to death! What did you say! Good God, don't tell me you actually killed somebody?"

"You think being innocent's going to save me? Didn't you see *Birdman of Alcatraz?*"

"Put that goddamn gun away!"

"You better shut up!" The muzzle poked at Raleigh's now distended neck. "You're going to take me with you to New Orleans, so I can get a freighter to South America. You hear? Slow down! You're going to get us pulled over!"

"Mingo, are you crazy? The only place I'm going is Cowstream. You think I'm going to New Orleans in Vera's Pinto?!"

"It was her idea."

"Without a suitcase! This is real life! This isn't some goddamn movie of yours! Are you crazy?"

Maniacal giggles pierced Raleigh's right eardrum. "I *am* crazy." The round loony face leaned into Raleigh's peripheral vision. "That's exactly right. I am crazy. That's why if you don't take me to New Orleans, hee hee hee, I'm going to blow your brains out, hee hee hee, and then I'm going to blow out mine! What do you think of that? Wouldn't you call that crazy?"

Hayes tried to see Mingo and the highway at the same time. He shouted, "Why drag me into this? Mingo, this is a bad time for me, it couldn't be worse. I've got fifty different things I've *got* to do today."

"It sure could be worse. I could kill you!"

"I don't believe this. I goddamn don't believe it!" Hayes beat his head and hands against the sheepskin steering wheel, slammed on the brakes, and skidded to a stop on the beltway shoulder. "Get out of this car, you blubber-headed son of a bitch!"

The gun moved slowly up through Raleigh's hair, then the hammer clicked, sharp as the rattle of a snake. He heard a whisper that didn't sound at all like Mingo. "I guess you thought I was just kidding. Well, I'm not. Do you believe in God?"

"Wh . . . at?" Hayes was, now, seriously frightened.

"Just ask Him if I'm kidding. Go ahead, you don't believe me, ask Him. He'll tell you."

Hayes started to move his head, felt the point of the gun slide through his hair, and froze. He opened his eyes and was looking straight at the little white plastic statue of Christ taped to the dashboard. As crisp as the unclouded sky above him, as palpable as his own hand, as inescapable as Mingo's rushed breath in his ear, Raleigh Hayes heard coming from the tiny sealed plastic mouth of that cheap trinket the words "Take him with you. He's not kidding." On either side of Christ, the ebony Buddhas shook their heads, "yes yes yes."

And with a gasp, the insurance salesman felt the cliff of reason tremble, felt his fingers loosen in the crumbling stone, and then he was tumbling, still scrabbling for a hold, off the edge of the only world he thought there was. "Don't believe it, Raleigh," he called to the falling man. "Hang on."

The Buddhas laughed like fools, as if Christ had just told them a big joke, at Raleigh's expense.

CHAPTER

10

How Raleigh Was Confirmed in His View of the World

As a baby, like all his peers — for there are no agnostics in the cradle — Raleigh Whittier Hayes had been a believer; the world contagious with magic, he the center and circumference, his the mana to summon Titans to his bedside, set birds flying, move clouds with a stare, scare waves away. Maturation immunized him by slow infection. His powers weakened. By five, he could no longer change a traffic light from red to green, had no idea what dogs and cats were talking about, and was considering the possibility that he might be mortal. At six, he declined to join Jimmy Clay in leaping from a high tree bough with a towel safety-pinned round his neck and "KAZAAM!" on his T-shirt. That shattering his scrawny arm did not dent Jimmy's belief in his omnipotence struck young Raleigh as another crowding example of faith's folly and self-conceit. That Mingo Sheffield (a little boy so fat he had neither wrists nor ankles, and couldn't even buckle the sandals he wore over droopy socks), that Mingo sobbed, "You're a liar!" and butted the soft bristles of his crew cut into his pillow, when told by Raleigh that Santa Claus, the Tooth Fairy, and the Easter Bunny were only parents, struck the seven-year-old with the rich sense of superiority to his neighbor that was never to leave him.

When Raleigh's father warned him that if he spit at a star, he'd blind an angel, he didn't believe it. Not because he already discredited angels, but because he more modestly appraised his own powers. And so, like stars blinking out, Raleigh's world faded from the sacred to the profane, pausing along the way in an elaborate totemic system of supplication and avoidance, based on the hope that while he might be powerless, he would still be able, by unswerving ritual, to appease whatever, or whoever, the Powers were. The first star seen at night remained to be wished on; crossed fingers, four-leaf clovers, a ring made from a quarter luckily found in the curb, clothes worn inside out — these *might* mediate for mortals. Whereas, years earlier, he would not eat snap beans because he heard them beg so piteously to be spared, now he ate them with numerological exactitude: three beans followed by five corn nubbins followed by two bites of pork chop would propitiate the Powers. Miscalculations, on the other hand, could conceivably enrage them into the sort of spitefulness with which they were known to respond to some hapless soul's breaking a mirror, walking under a ladder, opening an umbrella indoors, or even getting out of the bed on the wrong side. The sidewalk itself was mined terrain: a stepped-on crack and his mother's back would be broken; passing other children on the sidewalk could spell disaster — "Two's company, three's a crowd, four on the sidewalk isn't allowed."

In this church of spells and curses (to which all his Hayes relatives belonged — seeing no conflict between their chucking salt over their left shoulders, snapping wishbones, or rubbing rusty horseshoes, on the one hand, and their Christianity on the other), Flonnie Rogers was high priestess. Under her, his grandmother's ancient black maid, Raleigh served his novitiate, for Flonnie's boasted victories over Satan, and her own scathing disposition convinced the boy that, of all his acquaintance, her conjurations were likely to have the most impact on the Powers. Personal witness soon confirmed this opinion.

In the old Hayes house, at the end of the upstairs hall, Flonnie slept in a cubicle curtained off by two blue quilts hung on a rod. Blue kept witches away. Beneath her loose-springed bed with its swallowing mattress (goose feathers sucked away lightning), she kept a tin trunk, whose secrets she would never reveal to him, except to say they might be rattlesnakes and they might be ghosts. From her trunk came a potion which she said would remove the warts that had grown on Raleigh's hands when he was six. (It was at this time that he had first heard adults whispering that his father was "seeing" Roxanne Digges.) Even had Flonnie known about his family troubles — and she probably did — her diagnosis would have been the same. She did not believe in psychosomatic responses: *Action* caused reaction. Personal offense alone brought down punishments like warts. Raleigh had warts either because he had killed a toad-frog, had sat in a chair backward on the Sabbath, had failed to reverse nine steps after being crossed by a black cat, *or,* and most likely, he had warts because he had aggravated the peace of mind of someone cherished by the Powers, namely herself.

These dreadful possibilities she listed on the cold, black, lonesome night when a bad dream chased Raleigh down the hall of empty bedrooms to her cubicle. It was one of the rare times when his grandparents' house was not crowded with some assortment of aunts, uncles, and cousins, for (according to Victoria Anna) no Hayes could ever face the notion of growing up and leaving home for good; on this occasion (in February!) most of them were at the beach for George Washington's Birthday. "Pack of fools," said Flonnie Rogers. This cold, scary night, Flonnie had begrudgingly allowed Raleigh the safety of her company, *if* he allowed her to take care of his warts first. From her trunk she took a jar of paste, spat into it, stirred it with her finger, and smeared it roughly on his knuckles where the warts grew. The paste smelled like lard, rotten eggs, and tobacco, and stung like hot peppers.

"I bet a million dollars it won't work," sniffled the six-year-old Raleigh.

"The Lord hates a betting boy, much as a boy who wiggles and whines. I won't truck with the fidgets." Flonnie Rogers was old, but not much taller or larger than Raleigh. Her long nightgown, like her sheets, was starched cotton, sharply creased, and cold and white as ice. Her hair was white too; it always astonished the boy when she took off the knotted handkerchief with his grandfather's initials sewn into it that she wore under a baseball cap, and unwove dozens of braids, until the hair stood stiffly out around her dark face like a halo of icicles. Astonishing too the way she reached inside her mouth with a funny grin, pulled out her teeth, then dropped them in a glass of water on the table beside her kerosene lamp. Raleigh stared at those teeth while, on his knees, her thin hand clinched round the back of his neck, he waited shivering as she prayed with intrepid bossiness to the Lord. Afterward, she sang Raleigh a lullaby that scared him to death.

> *Way down yonder, in the meadow,*
> *Lies a poor little baby.*
> *Gnats and flies, picking out his eyes.*
> *Poor little thing is crying, "Mammy!"*

Teeth chattering as he lay in the cold cotton, Raleigh whispered, "Did his mama save him?"

"No, she never did. You want to know why she left her own little baby boy out there with his eyes all eaten up and bobcats gnawing off his toes?"

Raleigh both did and did not want to know.

"Because that self-same day that boy had tromped all over her fresh-mopped floor. Now you hush and stop that wiggling."

Raleigh tried desperately to keep still, holding his penis to pacify himself.

"You got to pee?"

"No, ma'am."

"You get out of this bed and get downstairs and go to the bathroom. I'm not fixing to have you mess up my sheets in the middle of the night. And don't you go in there and wake up your grandma either."

Her accusation of incontinence mortified Raleigh. As he crept through the downstairs rooms, he cried. The bathroom was dark miles and miles away, along a black corridor past the kitchen. The cracking linoleum on that corridor was like frozen snow under his bare feet. Feet that bobcats crouched in wait for.

The next evening, Raleigh's warts had begun to dry up; a week later they were gone.

And so Flonnie Rogers held a compelling fascination for the young boy. Whereas all his cousins kept carefully away from the sharp-tempered old woman, he followed her secretly about the house to study her magic. Indeed, it could be said that she, along with his aunt Victoria Anna, formed his wary view of the world. Under their uncooperative tutelage (for the two women couldn't abide each other), Raleigh was confirmed in his opinion that you had to grasp life sternly in order to shake any sense out of it, and that most people had so little power and get up and go that they let life flop and flail them about like sheets in the wind.

During the first months that Raleigh hovered in the shadow of Flonnie's potent protection, she shooed him away with that indiscriminate wrath she appeared to feel toward all children. "None of your nevermind how old I am. You, Bassie, get out from under my feet 'fore I toss you in the fire and fry you quicker'n you can say 'Jack Robinson.' "

"I'm not Bassie. He's my uncle. I'm Raleigh Whittier Hayes."

"You think I'm studying what you calling yourself? I never come across *any* boy wasn't a fool and aggravation to start with, and growed into worst, if the law didn't catch him and throw a rope around his neck first."

"Why would they throw a rope around his neck?"

"To choke him till his tongue stuck out all swollen and his eyes bulged loose from his head."

"Why?"

"For pestering folks."

But one day, after twisting a knuckle into his scalp for messing with her flour sifter, Flonnie suddenly thrust into Raleigh's hand the lace pattern of dough left over from the pan of biscuits she made daily, whether there were two or twenty to eat them. He wadded it into a tight ball and kept it in his pocket until it was so dirty only Mingo Sheffield would have eaten it. Another day, as he hid among the green cornstalks, spying on her from the garden that stretched for half a block behind the house, she called him over to the wood stump to hold her axe while she caught a chicken. In a sweat of horrible excitement, he watched her twist the poor hen's neck, whip it in a feather-flying arc over her head, and, grabbing the axe, slap it shrieking on the stump, and whack its head off. With grim satisfaction she watched the short mad scramble of the headless body to flee what had already happened. She turned to Raleigh and said, "You see this axe? When I was a little slave girl, I took it and stove in my master's head. I couldn't abide his hatefulness one more minute. He was a mean man, had a big old sugar plantation right down the road from here and he starved everybody to death and beat us to death and sold us to anybody had a dollar in his pocket. One day I took and sharpened this axe and sliced him in two different pieces. They jumped up and tried to walk off in two different places, then they both dropped down dead as doornails at my feet."

Heart pounding, Raleigh watched her as she cupped her apron to wipe onto it the blood from the blade. He stood speechless as she grabbed up the dead chicken by its feet and started toward the back steps. "Now, go scuffle and pick me some collards 'fore I pack you in a crate, put you on the train with a note says deliver you to that old master, and he'll have you cutting cane sunup to sundown till your fingers bleeds and your bones crook. Till you're knee-bent and body-bowed. Then he put you on the block and make you look spry, he lay it on and then rub pepper in your sores, and stick you in the calaboose where the sun burn you up alive."

Raleigh faltered. "No, he won't. I'm just a child."

"He's worse on a child. Tie you to a tree all day in the fields so the plow won't cut off your toes. Make you hoe, make you eat slops from a hog trough, and you try to get a little learning, he pokes out your eyes."

These horrors defeated Raleigh. He squatted on the ground to think. Finally, he ran over to the steps. "How can he? You said you chopped him up!"

Brown feathers leaped from Flonnie's fingers. "I did chop him. He grew back."

Years later, after Raleigh knew that there had never been a sugar plantation in the red clay country around Thermopylae, and that, old as she was, Flonnie was not old enough to have wielded an axe in the 1860s, he nevertheless knew her story to be true. As true as the other unsensible stories he was starting to hear adults tell at that time. Stories about terrible Nazis and barbarous Japs and brand-new bombs that could erase whole cities in a wink of an eye. And stories that his aunt Victoria brought home about what had happened in China to some of her missionary customers in particular, and what had happened in general around the world since the world began. "Getting loved by Jesus will not buy you rice," Aunt Victoria took him aside to say at a Hayes family reunion where his cousins were singing, "Jesus loves me, this I know," atop a picnic table.

"No, Jesus never gave me much indication of loving everybody equal, and if you care to come back with me to Malaya, little boy, you'll see what I mean."

At seven, Raleigh was already concluding that Life was not the bowl of cherries his uncle Hackney kept strumming about on his ukulele. Life was a race, a test, a fight, and God didn't care who won, or how. Hadn't Ned Ware outraced Raleigh by jumping the teacher's whistle? Hadn't Judy McClung outspelled him because she'd gotten "house" and he'd gotten "ocean"? Hadn't Jimmy Clay outfought him by sticking his fingers in his eye? Either God didn't care, or God had His favorites. "You're my favorite, Little Fellow! My favorite thing in the whole wide world," Raleigh's father would shout, tossing him in air as if he thought he could fly. But Raleigh had heard his father make the same profligate vow to a dozen other people, and it only made him angry.

Raleigh was suspicious, too, of the way God chose His favorites, if Flonnie was right that Elwood Bragg was one of the Chosen.

The day Flonnie told him about the slave master, while she was on the back steps, plucking the still bleeding bird, she abruptly yelled at the boy, "Run quick cross the street, tell Miz Cawthorne to get out back, Elwood's robbing her clothesline again."

"No. I'm scared of him," Raleigh told her.

For Elwood, flat-haired and gap-toothed with a wide, pasty imbecile face, and always wearing the same old Eisenhower jacket and bright red tennis shoes, did not make sense, and irrationality was as disturbing to the child Raleigh as it was to the adult. A man in his thirties, Elwood, for reasons Raleigh could not comprehend, coveted the voluminous undergarments that an elderly widow hung out on a line in her backyard. Whenever Mrs. Cawthorne saw him snatch one of her three-sectioned pink girdles off the line and hook it on over his baggy jeans, she'd tear out of her porch door and chase him down the sidewalk, waving at him the wire fly swatter the funeral home gave away as advertisements. Raleigh's older cousin Paschal delighted in this scene and would hide behind the hedge to watch, but Raleigh was terrified of Elwood's sudden dancing steps and loud inexplicable laughter.

"I won't go!" he shouted, so Flonnie ran herself to the street curb, cupped her hands and yelled, "YOU, Elwood Bragg! You put Miz Cawthorne's drawers back on the line like they belong! I'd be shamed to be a growed-up white man and act like a fool the way you do!"

Stunned, the large pudgy man burst into awful tears, dropped the underwear as if it were burning, and hopped clumsily backward around the side of the Cawthorne house.

"He's crazy," whispered Raleigh. "I wish they'd put him in jail for good!"

Instantly, he felt Flonnie's hand, dry and thin as paper, slap his cheek. "Those touched in the head belongs to the Lord. They His special chosen. If I catch you and Paschal teasing him, I'm going to whale the stuffing out of you. That's trash, acting that way. Like teasing your poor old grandpa, sneaking up and spinning his wheelchair every whichway."

"I didn't do that!"

"You watched. I don't truck with trash."

Raleigh, who'd heard Flonnie condemning things as "trash" since he'd met her, asked her now what trash was.

"It's most white folks. And most colored folks, too. And it's anybody pops his gum out loud the way you do. Spit it out in the wrapper. I need you to go up to the corner and get me a can of Tuberose. Sciatica's got my legs so bad I can't walk it. And you can have a nickel." From the pocket of her bloody apron she took a dollar bill folded to the size of a button. Carefully, she smoothed it out. "Don't you dare to waste time looking in the Five and Dime. The police chief's hiding in there just waiting to catch little white boys and throw them in the jailhouse where you so quick to lock poor old Elwood up for good."

Raleigh took the dollar. "I don't care, I heard they do have places they put crazy people."

Flonnie was stuffing Raleigh's striped T-shirt into his corduroys, turning him roughly in a circle. "That's right. They put anybody in there they feel like. Chain them to walls and never turn them loose till they nothing but bones, and you can see the marks where they dug their fingernails in the stones trying so hard to get free."

Raleigh's teeth bit down on his tongue. "Did you see the marks?"

"Go get me a can of Tuberose snuff, and don't walk under that ladder where they're painting the bank. And don't you dare to drop my change. I got to pay Mr. Overton on my burial insurance today."

"What's your burial insurance mean?"

"The way you always telling how you already know everything there is to know, how come you don't know that?" She took a green broken-toothed comb from her pocket and yanked it through Raleigh's hair. "I been taking care of myself my whole life long and I 'spect to go on doing it after I'm dead. I pay in to the insurance man, and when I'm gone, he pays all my bills so I get a decent burial beholden to nobody. I don't count on nobody but me."

"Ouch!"

"Hold still. I don't count on the Lord and He knows He don't have to take up His time worrying over me."

"Does He only like crazy people?"

"Now go on. And keep that hair out of your eyes 'fore they cross they-selves and you can't get them unstuck."

And so, apprenticed to Flonnie Rogers, Raleigh was learning not only such tricks as how to keep ghosts out of the house with St. John's wort, such facts as that if he saw an egg sweat blood by firelight, he'd meet his sweetheart in the morning, but, more usefully, the trick of insurance against the fact of a world of trash and folly. In Flonnie's superstitions, and his own, however, he eventually lost faith: A sidewalk crack had no effect on his mother's back, peas didn't care in what order they were eaten, it was as silly to carry around a rabbit's foot as a crow's claw or a goat's hoof. Eventually he forgot about his warts. He forgot, too, about Flonnie's notion that God had "chosen" the moronic Elwood Bragg. He remembered only her warning not to rely on the Deity, but get insurance instead.

Nearly a year after the day of the chicken-slaying, Raleigh was again visiting his grandparents alone, for his mother had gone away by herself to "think" about her marriage, and his father had been called away by the archdiocese to answer charges brought by his parishioners that he was morally unfit to be their pastor. The first night at supper, Raleigh sat by himself in the immense shadowy dining room at the end of a table meant for twenty. His feet rested on the rung of the dark, high-backed, cane-bottomed chair; from his neck billowed a huge cloth white napkin. Circled around him sat small plates of sausage patties, sliced cantaloupes, hard strips of country ham, butter beans, stewed corn, stringy okra (which he hated), snap beans with fatback, cold biscuits, and cold chicken — all left-overs from lunch. He hoped he wasn't expected to eat everything. Flonnie and his grandmother (one on a black iron wood-burner, one on a white metal gas stove) went on cooking for the family that had moved out, but kept dropping in.

Raleigh ate alone while his grandmother fed Grandpa Hayes from a tray in their bedroom. Clayton Hayes had already lost both legs from diabetes and now was partially paralyzed by a stroke. He even had to wear diapers. He passed his time in his hospital-style bed or his big wooden wheelchair, conversing with family and neighbors who came to visit, or listening to radio shows, laughing night and day at programs like *The Jack Benny Show* and *Fibber McGee and Molly*. To Raleigh's ears, his grandfather's laughter closely resembled the idiot Elwood Bragg's, and was similarly terrifying; his incoherent imitations of language made the boy so uneasy that he always pretended not to hear the invalid calling him over for a hug or a back scratch or a game of checkers. The old man's motor control was so poor, anyhow, that more often than not he'd upset the checkerboard and they'd have to start all over. Whenever Raleigh saw his father or an aunt or an uncle sit by that metal bed, carefully combing Grandpa Hayes's thin hair, or bathing his white useless arms with cloths dipped in rubbing alcohol, the boy would wonder if *he* would ever have to do such awful, intimate things to his own father, and he would vow never to grow old and help-less himself and subjected to the ministrations of others.

While Raleigh ate alone that first night, Flonnie sat on a high stool be-side the black mahogany floor-to-ceiling china cabinet, where she was pol-ishing silver napkin rings initialed *H*. (Napkin rings that the adult Raleigh would have liked to own, but nobody could remember what had happened to them.) While Flonnie scrubbed at the tarnish, she muttered angrily one of the songs she sang when she worked.

> *I don't want no (huh!)*
> *Cornbread, no molasses (huh!)*
> *They hurts my pride (huh!)*
> *They hurts my pride.*

To the child, she looked like a gnome from a fairy tale, bent over her treasure hoard of silvery rings.

After another verse, about "cold iron shackles," Raleigh said, "Excuse me, Flonnie. I want to get insurance. You could give my money to that man that comes to get yours for your burial."

Apparently unsurprised by his continuing a conversation begun the previous summer, the old woman scratched at her head through her knotted handkerchief, and replied, "Chillen can't get it."

"Can just colored people?"

She spat at a ring and rubbed it. "I could tell you some white folks right close by that ought to have got it and they wouldn't be so hard up now."

"Who?"

"Never mind. Don't you spill that milk. I got to go see my sister this evening. You can come if you don't act up."

Raleigh was astonished. "I didn't know you had a sister! I didn't know you had anybody but us."

"Us!" Flonnie dropped a ring onto each bony finger and held her hand up to the overhead light. "You think I belong to *you?* Huh? I don't got to stay here one minute past I want to. You think you going to boss me like that sugarcane master and haul me up on the block? Huh!"

"No! Honest." Raleigh had conflated the "block" to which Flonnie kept mysteriously referring and the stump on which he'd seen her decapitating chickens, and he feared she suspected him of plotting her murder. "I didn't mean that. I was only asking about your family. I was just wondering if you were married."

"Hush." She shook her hand into the cabinet's open drawer. The silver slid sparkling down. "I'm not studying to marry no aggravating fool and raise no pack of wild shirttail niggers to drive me crazy with the police knocking on the door."

Raleigh swallowed too large a lump of cantaloupe, which squeezed its way coldly down his throat. "Is that what your sister did?"

"Never mind."

"My daddy had another wife but she died before I was born. Her name was Grace Louise, did you know her? She got dip-something. I hope my mama doesn't get it."

"Diphtheria. Eat that okra."

"I'm full."

"You don't eat right I'll be laying you out the way I did your daddy's little wife." Flonnie began roughly stacking dishes on a wide wood tray. "Here. Help me clear this table, you want to come."

"Does lay her out mean put her in a coffin?" With plate and glass, Raleigh followed Flonnie into the kitchen. "Flonnie? Did you put her in the coffin?"

Covering food with wax paper, Flonnie told him that laying-out meant dressing the dead in nice clothes and arranging them attractively in the parlor for visitors to see. "When Grace Louise passed, it was the day but one your poor old grandma lost her twins."

"You mean my uncles?" Raleigh had heard stories of the sudden deaths, at four, of his grandmother's "babies," the twins Thaddeus and Gayle. And he had seriously studied, for clues to their fates, the photograph in which they were seated together in a wicker armchair, both wearing sailor shirts, with their hair parted in the middle and wet-combed. They looked exactly alike, except one was squinting.

"I laid the boys out in the front parlor and I had to put Grace Louise in the back. She wasn't more than a child herself. Earley carried on so, they thought he'd lost his mind for good. Here, take this rag and dry those plates off, and don't drop them."

"Do you know why people die, Flonnie?"

"You getting ready to tell me you got it all figured out? They die when it's time."

"That doesn't make any sense."

Flonnie shook her hands in the scalding water, dried them on Raleigh's cloth, and put a pinch of snuff in her mouth. "You think God Almighty cares what you think about it, a skinny little six-year-old boy?

"I'm already seven. I don't think it's fair for God to fix it so He's the only one that doesn't have to die."

"Don't poison your stomach with so much chewing gum and you won't have to either."

Raleigh's grandmother now entered the kitchen, making the low clucking noise of a worried pigeon that always announced her presence. "Flonnie, don't you be talking to Raleigh about dying. He'll be having nightmares again."

"Yes'm, Miz Hayes," muttered the old, tiny woman, and she said not another word until she and Raleigh climbed up into the bus to ride to Darktown to visit her sister — who was actually the widow of Flonnie's brother. Having dropped in the dimes she'd been tightly holding in her fist, Flonnie walked Raleigh to the first seat, sat him down, and said, "Stay put."

He clutched at her hand. "Where are you going?" There were no other passengers near him.

"Back here."

"Why can't I come? I'm scared up here."

"I thought I heard you bragging how you could read."

Trembling, Raleigh shook his head yes. Flonnie lifted her hand with its shopping bag toward a sign above the driver's head. "WHITES SEAT FROM FRONT. COLOREDS SEAT FROM REAR." By the time Raleigh had deciphered, though not understood, this notice, Flonnie had gone to the crowded back section, where she was poking furiously with her patent-leather shoe (which was no larger than a child's) at the foot of a seated young black man, three times her size. "Get up out of there, 'fore I take hold of your hair and pull you up. Where's your manners, trash, you sitting like you can't even see me!"

His ears fiery, Raleigh watched horrified to see if the young man was going to pick Flonnie up and snap her like a twig, or if the bus driver was going to go back there and have her put in jail for acting up. But the black man only grinned, murmuring, "Now, granny, now, granny," and stretched up out of the seat, and let her take it. All though the trip, Raleigh craned his neck back, whenever the bus stopped, to make sure Flonnie didn't get off at the rear door and leave him alone in an alien world. But the straw hat, red as a revolutionary flag, never moved.

Thirty-eight years later (while driving to Betty Hemans's house with Mingo's gun to his head), the memory of that first trip to Darktown suddenly flashed as fully in Raleigh's mind as if he still stood shyly beside Flonnie in the small, dim room, walled with magazine pictures, while she kept shouting at her sister-in-law, an overweight, tearful woman who wore a nubbed bathrobe over her clothes. Suddenly, he could remember the room, the church calendar on the wall beside the hat and coat, the steel drum of water by the sink, the blanket thrown over an old couch and tucked into the corners. Suddenly, thirty-eight years later, he could again see the woman sobbing, could again hear Flonnie saying things about the woman's son. He could hear them call the son "Jubal." Yes, Flonnie was saying that Jubal was always sassing and wild with his music-playing and his socializing with trash in bars and his fast talk about what was wrong with America; and he was too full of himself and too good-looking for his own good. She was saying that Jubal's going up North had just made it worse, and that going to war probably hadn't helped either, because war was full of fools just like him. She was saying that the last thing Jubal needed to do was come home to Thermopylae, where it was as true now as it had been back when he first took up with "her" that nobody was going to put up with a colored boy messing with a white woman. Saying, besides, "she" was never coming home either, and had gone all the way to the other side of the world, and Jubal had better get it out of his mind once and for all. Saying maybe a prison camp in Germany was as good a place as any for Jubal to figure out how to use his head.

This memory curled over Raleigh like a wave, completely enveloping him. Then it receded as quickly as it had come, carrying all the small bits of words and pictures back into the past. On the narrow wood shelf beside Flonnie's sister's rocking chair had been a white plaster statue of Christ, which the sobbing woman had picked up and hugged to her bosom, talking to it softly as she swayed in the chair. No doubt, it was the plastic Christ on Vera's dashboard that had brought this scene so vividly back to Raleigh Hayes. For he was keeping his eye fixed on the little figure as he drove, as if it might pass him a warning, if necessary, that Mingo (who'd allowed him to run his errands as long as he remembered his "life was on the line") was about to go entirely berserk and shoot him. Hayes kept checking back on Christ through the horrible endless hour it took him to move into his office his old secretary, Betty Hemans, with her grocery box filled with coffeepot, bedroom slippers, cigarette cartons, Thesaurus, and the 900-page manuscript of *Remember Me;* the horrible endless time it took to carry PeeWee Jimson's bust back down through the lobby and into the Pinto's trunk. He kept glancing in on Christ as he strapped to the Pinto's luggage rack his great-grandmother Tiny's little black trunk, as he tried to explain to his suspicious Aunt Victoria why Mingo Sheffield was following them from room to room through the lonely old house. Raleigh Hayes kept his skeptical eye on Christ, who smiled back, the whole while he drove out of town, past the Civitans sign that he himself had taken charge of installing, back in the days when he'd been silly enough to believe the world made sense, back when he would never have thought the words on that sign could apply to him:

YOU ARE NOW LEAVING THERMOPYLAE. WE HOPE YOU'LL COME BACK.

THE QUEST

CHAPTER

11

In Which Our Hero Attends a Surprise Party

THE PINE-LINED, unshouldered two-lane highway to Cowstream had a bad reputation. The curves were cheaply banked, the hills steep and sudden, the yellow line faded. Over the years in the night, hundreds of Carolinean drivers (as Nemours Kettell annually reminded the state highway commission, when encouraging them to give him a contract to rebuild Old 52), hundreds, or at least dozens, of drivers had flown off into darkness and sometimes death. Night or day, the hazard was impatience. Imperturbable tractors would creep onto the road out of a scraggly soybean or cotton field. Behind the tractor, six furious cars would weave for a passing view, until somebody, horn in a rage, would slam out into the other lane, meet an eighteen-wheeler coming the opposite way at seventy miles an hour, and would sail over a red clay gully into a pine barren or a tobacco crop or a roadside shack selling tomatoes.

Raleigh Hayes had now been trapped behind a log truck for five miles. On the downgrades, this sadistic vehicle barreled away, straddling the middle of the road; on the upgrades, it slowed to a crawl, and half its pile of twenty-foot logs began jiggling loosely, convincing Raleigh that one of them was going to slide off, shoot through the windshield, and remove his head. Aunt Victoria snapped, "Pass him, pass him! We'll be here all day!"

and Mingo squealed, "Don't do it, Raleigh, Vera's got no acceleration at all."

An hour earlier, when Raleigh had found his aunt pacing her porch with her pocketbook under her arm and her overnight case already on the steps beside her, he'd tried to explain that Aura had borrowed his Fiesta and that therefore he had borrowed Mingo's Pinto, and that coincidentally Mingo would be coming along, on affairs of his own. "And I'm sorry, Aunt Vicky, but I'm going to head straight on down to New Orleans on this business of Daddy's, so do you think you could get Lovie to bring you back home from Cowstream? I really apologize." Raleigh grimaced, the gun jabbing at his spine.

Victoria had opened her saddlebag of a purse and carefully counted the bills in a wallet leather-tooled with coconut trees. She snapped it shut. "I guess if I could get a Bugis smuggler to take me, along with forty illegal elephant tusks and three live panthers, across the Sarawak River into Kuching, I can get my own sister to drive me fifty miles over a paved road back to Thermopylae. Though the fact Senior Clay ever got Lovie to move out that far in the first place is a miracle."

"Excuse me, Aunt Vicky —"

"Hayeses never move. None of them would ever leave off jabbering in Papa's dining room to look out the window at an eight-car crackup. Granny Tiny herself lying propped up in the goosedown bed right in the room where people had to see her while they were eating, scared she'd miss something, licking on peppermint sticks, day in, day out, until one Sunday she was dead. What Earley wants with Granny's trunk, we'll never —"

"Excuse me, Aunt Vicky —"

"Don't dawdle, Raleigh. It's down in the cellar. Go get it."

So deep ran the strain of Hayes garrulity in Raleigh's eldest aunt, even when her theme was her relentless dissatisfaction with the rest of the family for "gabbing their lives away," that once the three travelers finally got on the road, Mingo (who'd become strangely eager to talk about matters that he had just threatened to shoot Raleigh for revealing) could scarcely get in a word of confession.

"Are you going to New Orleans on business or pleasure, Mr. Sheffield?" the old saleswoman had finally asked, at the end of a prolonged monologue on the poor habits and consequential poor health of her grandmother, her father, her brothers, and her sisters; by the end of which catalogue, Raleigh had already turned off the beltway, leaving behind the little six-spoked skyline of Thermopylae, with the Forbes Building at the Crossways glistening high above the rest. "Maybe you're attending a convention?" Victoria suggested to Mingo, as the fat man appeared to be at a loss for words.

"Will she tell?" Mingo whispered in Raleigh's ear.

"Tell what?" She turned to the backseat. "It's none of my business."

"I'm going to South America."

"Whereabouts?" She waved away his smoke with her white-gloved hand.

Disappointed that the announcement itself had not fazed her, Sheffield admitted, "I don't know."

"Well, you better find out before you get there." The elderly woman prodded Raleigh in the ribs, raised her eyebrows at him, and murmured *sotto voce,* "You don't have to hang from a tree to be a nut."

"What was that?" Mingo lurched forward.

"I said it's a lot bigger than Thermopylae. I never covered that territory myself, but I've met folks that wouldn't go back to South America if you paid them."

"Where's a good place to get a job there?" Sheffield asked her.

"Depends on what you do. If you shoot people for a living, you ought to try Chile or Nicaragua or maybe just go straight to El Salvador."

Eyelids narrowed, Sheffield leaned, panting, halfway over the front seat. "Why'd you say that? Did Raleigh tell you I shoot people? That's a lie. Just 'cause I lost my job . . ."

Raleigh flung out his arm and shoved Sheffield back. "Mingo, she was just joking. Now be quiet."

But Victoria was curious. "What *did* you do for a living, Mr. Sheffield? And could I ask you to please stop dropping your ashes in my hairdo?"

The fat man sighed as he unpeeled a banana. He had a whole shopping bag of food that Vera had obviously slipped into the car along with her husband and her cast-off clothes. For ten long miles, Sheffield smoked and ate as he outlined his lost career at Knox-Bury's Clothing Store, highlighted by detailed descriptions of his most successful window displays. "Can you believe Billy Knox wouldn't want me at the mall, when the *Charlotte Observer* came and took a picture of my Christmas window for their Sunday supplement? I had all the reindeer in the new style sweaters at a disco, and Santa Claus wearing a double-breasted London Fog with a zip-in liner, and . . ."

Raleigh, whose eyes were tearing from the smoke (if not his life), rolled down his window, and stared morosely at the tractor-drawn plow in front of him, whose driver looked to be taking a nap.

The next ten miles went to Victoria Anna's rendition of how, half a century ago, her father had lost control of both his furniture store and his butcher business. "Well, Mr. Sheffield, that hog PeeWee Jimson had bought up Papa's loans behind his back and next thing we knew, the Hayes name was chiseled right off the building where it'd been since eighteen eighty-five. After he was told he was sick, and kept on living as he pleased, lost one leg, and still kept on — six or more Coca-Colas every day of his life — and lost the other leg too before they wired me to come home — after Papa was gone, I got all his account books out of the cellar where they were gathering nothing but mold in an ice chest, and I totaled up $53,540 in uncollected bills over the years. Time's expired on them now, and it's money we'll never see. Everybody in Thermopylae owed him, and I remember plain as yesterday how he'd cross over the street to keep from reminding them of that fact. Raleigh, pass that tractor before I lose my mind!"

"Don't do it, Raleigh!"

"Mama couldn't do a thing with him. I remember she'd say, 'Mr. Hayes, I don't believe the neighbors are all that ashamed of not paying their debts as you keep worrying they are.' Poor Mama."

"My mama's dead," said Mingo. "She died two years ago February."

"I'm sorry to hear that, Mr. Sheffield, but you are sticking that lollipop right on my suit jacket. I don't believe I ever knew an adult who ate as much candy as you do, except a Hayes. It always amazed me how any of them had a single tooth left to show up in their high-school graduation photos. Well, we're almost there."

"Thank God," said Raleigh sincerely.

"Last time I came out to Lovie's, I was flying home for Big Em's funeral. No, it was Furbus's. Came from Kuala Lumpur."

Sheffield laughed. "That's the funniest name I ever heard."

"Not to them."

"Boy, you sure have been a lot of places, and had a lot of adventures, Miss Hayes. I wish I could have had your life instead of mine, except of course for Vera and all. But I guess I would have been too chicken. I'd be scared of live panthers. You must be pretty brave."

Now, Mingo Sheffield had just happened upon the key to the door to Victoria Hayes's heart. She acknowledged his compliment by turning all the way around, and propping an elbow on the seat back, as she continued her interrupted story. "Well, the whole family came out to the airport waving 'Welcome Home' signs in my face and yelling like the natives I left behind. Take this first right, Raleigh."

"I know."

"Bassie slammed his hand on the horn the whole way down this road and the children were screaming, 'She's here!' in case the rest of the county was interested. Reba came out, she was on a cane. That's the first I knew she'd lost one of her legs. Now it's two. Those kids threw my bags open on the floor and pawed through them like Arabs in a bazaar."

"One time for my window I did pajamas in an Arabian Nights motif? Billy Knox *said* he loved it." The lollipop stick and cigarette that hung from Sheffield's mouth quivered like tusks. "Y'all got a lot of family. I wish I did."

"A lot!" Victoria gave her nose a sharp twist. "Mingo, you are all too right." She had by now entirely thawed toward Sheffield, who, however peculiar, was at least conversational, whereas her nephew was glum as a clam. "Yes, Mingo, there's probably hundreds of Hayeses wandering the countryside within a fifty-mile radius. There were *thirteen* of us children. Papa called us his baker's dozen. If he'd been a baker, he'd have been better off. It's hard to get ahead as a butcher if you can't stand killing animals."

"Thirteen! That's sure a lot. But it's an unlucky number."

"You don't know the half of it. Reba's in the hospital, and Raleigh's daddy ought to be. A.A. ran off to the North and never bothered to keep in touch. And why it was the two of them that got to go to college and not me is a question for the Women's Liberation Movement that didn't bother to get going till it was too late to do me any good. Well, diphtheria took the twins. Poor Whittier was killed in the war." Victoria ticked off her siblings' necrology with stern indignation. "It was cancer with Furbus and Serene, then Hackney had his heart attack on the ballfield, the fool, then Big Em succumbed to diabetes. . . ."

Mingo leaped in. "My daddy died overnight; he didn't think there was a thing wrong with him. I've got two sisters but they don't even send me a birthday card from one year to the next."

Raleigh Hayes drove through the single sad block of Cowstream, a town of aging storefronts, a movie house with FOR RENT on its marquee, a beauty shop with pictures in the windows of hairstyles nobody had worn since Lyndon Johnson was President, and a thriving McDonald's on the corner. He pondered extreme alternatives. He could leap from the car and hide out for the rest of his life in the abandoned movie theater, peacefully staring at the empty screen. He could puncture his eardrums and never have to listen to another word anybody said. He could forfeit his inheritance, let Mingo and Victoria jabber their way to New Orleans by themselves, while he sold his house and beach property, and, investing his profits in canned goods, move to the Knoll Pond cabin to await the approaching nuclear holocaust with Aura and the twins; he'd fish, and Aura would teach the girls to belly dance.

"Raleigh, right here! Turn! The brick ranch house with all the cars in the driveway. Back up. That's it."

Raleigh had missed the house because his mind was, as usual, elsewhere, and not because he didn't recognize it. He had spent many weeks of many summers in this house, built in the mid-fifties by his aunt Lovie's optimistic husband, William "Senior" Clay, as the model for a suburban dream that never woke up. "There's no city to be a suburb *to,*" sneered Raleigh, the caustic sixteen-year-old. "You can't build something called Paradise Homes on a bunch of red dirt outside Cowstream, North Carolina! Your daddy's nuts," he'd told the first of Senior's five sons, Jimmy Clay. "Fung gu!" Jimmy had rebutted, and added, "Wanna see a gorilla, look in the mirror." "I don't care," Raleigh had persisted. "He's going to lose his shirt."

Senior Clay had lost his shirt, and had returned — his pleasant faith in American capitalism inexplicably undiminished — to selling ice cream products for a dairy syndicate. Now, thirty years later, there were only four other ranch houses on Paradise Street, huddled together like covered wagons on the Western plains; their kitchen sliders looked on stubby forests and their picture windows on gullied fields. In the Clay's side yard was still the fair-sized pond that Senior had always intended to drain and replace with a swimming pool. An oak tree leaned out into the water, but the rope from which the boys had once swung was frayed to a nub of ravel.

On the long, flat lawn stood the same white plaster birdbath with a midget St. Francis praying beside it, waiting for birds to come dive off his hands into the basin. There was the same flagpole embedded in a concrete slab crusted with flecks of colored glass. In the driveway were four big new cars that announced that they'd been bought at Carolina Cadillacs in Thermopylae. All was the same.

"Don't forget, Raleigh," Mingo whispered. "Okay?" The two men had been left behind by the fast-walking Victoria Anna, who'd already reached the Clays' front door. It was decorated with a glittered shamrock and cutouts of an Irish girl jigging and an Irish boy swinging a knobby stick. "Even if you do get away from me, Raleigh, and maybe you will —"

"You're goddamn right," Hayes whispered savagely. "I'm not about to spend my life in a toilet with you, the way you eat!"

Mingo grabbed his arm. "Maybe you will, and then I'll just blow out *my* brains and you'll never forgive yourself."

"Don't count on it. Besides, I don't believe you could kill yourself if your life depended on it."

Mingo started his crazed giggling again, as he snatched the Lucite-cube key chain out of Raleigh's hand.

Victoria Anna was opening the door. "They can't hear us. Probably got three TV sets going, nobody watching any of them."

In the empty living room a color television the size of a sideboard was in fact tuned to a game show. From elsewhere came laughter and the tune "Roll Out the Barrel," being played on a honky-tonk piano. The same inexpensive modern couches and mock Louis XIV armchairs were filled with the same windbreakers, magazines, and overweight cats. Copies of Gainsborough's *Blue Boy* and Reynolds's *Pinkie* still stood on opposite walls, staring in sweet private reverie past each other. In the middle of the imitation Chinese rug sat a card table covered with an almost finished jigsaw puzzle of a moose knee-deep in an autumn lake. Under the table the biggest of the cats was eating potato chips.

Victoria sighed. "I stepped on a plate of deviled eggs the last time I was here."

The three intruders followed the laughter; a sign shaped like an arm pointed them down some stairs to "The Wreck Room." This space, once the basement, ran the whole length of the house, and was still crowded. Against a wall of sports trophies, photographs of dead Hayeses, and a textured print of Trumbull's *Battle of Bunker Hill* was a player piano, whose chords were bouncing up and down as if set upon by a saloon ghost. Above the piano, green balloons and green streamers were taped to the cork ceiling. At the far end of the long room, in the light of a lamp made of a drunk clown hanging on to a lamppost, a collection of live Hayeses leaned laughing around a red vinyl bar. The center of the cluster was Raleigh's aunt Lovie Clay, a tall, big-boned woman who had changed little since he'd seen her last, except that her bouffant hair was now perfectly white. She wore purple toreador pants and a sleeveless blouse and silver sandals. Her arms bent strangely, her face twisted, she was rolling her head and talking gibberish out of the side of her mouth. Then she banged herself sharply on the side of the head. " 'Wut dom wod, Llub bey?' So then he reaches right over and takes Reverend Coldon's ballpoint, to, you know how he does, draw it, and he says, 'Mind I steal your dom penis?'! That poor minister turned the color of my pants! Oh Lord!"

The group around her was laughing so loudly, some kicking at the bar rail, that they hadn't yet noticed their visitors in the far doorway. Shaking her head, Victoria Anna whispered to Raleigh, "Lovie always got a lot of attention for being a clown." She added for Mingo's benefit, "She tapped, too, and wanted to go into the movies. 'Course, she never got up and did anything about it."

Now someone sped toward them in a wheelchair. "VICKY ANNA! Why, and Raleigh! This is a treat!"

"Reba!" Victoria was surprised to see her sister. "What are you doing here? What in the world are you doing out of the hospital?"

"Jimmy brought me. I had my last fitting this morning." Reba patted her new leg. "I'm doing real fine."

"You mean you've still got your arms?" Victoria muttered darkly.

"Why you know I wouldn't miss Lovie's sixtieth birthday. Your phone didn't answer. Hattie! Swan! LOVIE! SURPRISE! VICKY ANNA'S HERE! AND GUESS WHO?"

The crowd swarmed over. Wheat hair and strawberry hair and honey hair and white hair and bald heads. Glasses and hearing aids and molar bridges and neck braces and finger splints and plastic aortas and portable catheters and wooden legs and all. Greetings and hugs rushed around the circle, in the midst of which was hurled Mingo, whom many of them had met, and whose bathing trunks Lovie instantly claimed to have seen fall off thirty years ago when he'd belly-flopped at Forbes Pool. "Don't mind me, honey, I'm a kidder," she added, and proved by introducing "the stranger" Raleigh to his own relatives as her young lover from Winston-Salem.

In fact, Raleigh felt a stranger. He confused a grandson of his dead aunt Serene with one belonging to his dead uncle Hackney. He mistook an ancient palsied creature, who claimed to be his grandfather's spinster baby sister Hattie, for Little Em, his uncle Furbus's widow. Raleigh didn't spend much time with his relatives.

While Lovie took Mingo over to introduce him to someone wrapped up on the couch, Victoria asked Reba, "What was Lovie doing, banging on her head like that?"

"Imitating Bassie. She's so good, she oughta be in the movies. Get her to do Lucille Ball for you tonight, Raleigh."

"Tell you the truth, Aunt Reba, I expect I'm going to have to leave be-fore —"

Victoria pushed in front of him. "Imitating Bassie? What's the matter with Bascomb?"

Reba's hand flew to her mouth. "Didn't anybody tell you? I thought I told you in the hospital. You were in Texas so long."

"Told me what! Nobody tells me a thing."

Reba took Raleigh's hand. "Poor Bassie, bless his heart, had a stroke out on the fairway, on the sixteenth hole. We thought we were going to lose him, but God pulled him on through."

The old missionary traveler leaned against the wall and crossed her arms. "Has anything else happened lately, Reba? Y'all are so forgetful, I'd hate to find out a few more of my relations had died and were buried, and y'all neglected to bring it to my attention."

Reba took her hand, too. "No, we're all doing fine."

"Except Bassie had a stroke. Why, he's only fifty, he's the baby!"

"Honey, he woke up a blessed baby, that's for sure. Couldn't talk better'n one, had to wear diapers too, just like Papa. Couldn't read, couldn't think of the word for something as simple as a chicken leg. Called them um-brellas! But everybody's been working with him. The kids just had the best time; they taught him to read all over from scratch with Golden Books. And Lovie's so sweet. She went out and bought him one of those toy pianos to play on with two fingers. You know how Bassie loved the piano."

Victoria took off her glasses to scrub at the bridge of her nose. "You think Bassie'd think Lovie was so sweet if he saw her making fun of him like that?"

Reba spun around, swirling them both with her. "Why, he's right over there on the couch, see?, having the best time in the world. Come on and give him a big hug."

Propped up on the couch, Bascomb Hayes (until recently a golf pro) was now as badly off as Lovie's imitation had implied. Beside him sat Big Em's busty daughter Tildy Harmon, a frequent divorcée with platinum hair and skimpy clothes, who had given to her cousin Raleigh, at twelve, what she'd called a "free demonstration" of an open-mouth kiss. She sat on the couch to hold her uncle's drink so he could slurp it through a straw. It looked like a lime snow-cone, but was actually a frozen daiquiri for St. Patrick's Day. They were all drinking them.

"Doesn't Bassie sound just like Papa?" whispered Reba to her sister Victoria, who snarled, "Exactly." Bascomb also had the strange sharp laugh that had so frightened Raleigh when it had burst from his grandfather long ago. "Excuse me, need some air," he said, and hurried to the stairs.

As he passed the ghostly piano, speeding along through "Swanee," Hayes suddenly saw his dead uncle Furbus wriggling along its bench, as in the old days, his tobacco-stained fingers feathering higher and higher notes. Beside him leaned Hackney, furiously strumming his little ukulele. These hallucinations from the past were unnerving Raleigh. He had to get outside and breathe. But on the back porch he found himself automatically stopping to look in the old ice cream freezer to see if among the dozens of cartons, there were any Fudgsicles (once his favorite). His head hit the lid when he was crudely goosed from behind.

"Gotcha molotcha, Ral pal. Hey, hey, stealing Fudgsicles again, hunh? What'd you think of Uncle Earley's car? I bet you loved it. You just don't see too many like that anymore. Move over. Any orange in there?"

CHAPTER

12

Raleigh Escapes

LOVIE'S SON, JIMMY CLAY of Carolina Cadillacs, reached into the freezer for an orange Popsicle. He wore a pink bow tie and slacks a Doublemint gum-wrapper green. At forty-four, he had the same long, loose-limbed look, the same jug ears, the same loafers, and even the same habit of sucking on the stone in his huge class ring that he'd had in high school. The only thing missing was his hair. It was amazing that someone so juvenile could be so bald. Clay's tongue danced around the orange ice. " 'Member how I used to get my tongue stuck on these things? The stucky yuckies. 'Member?"

"No."

"Seriously, Ral. I appreciate you coming all the way out to help Mama enjoy her big six-o. Guess what I got her? A poker table, real felt, the workaloopas. What'd you get her?"

Raleigh, who'd had not the slightest inkling that March 16 was his aunt's sixtieth birthday, said, "Wait and see," and walked outdoors, where smoke from two rusty charcoal grills streamed across the lonely fields.

Clay loped after him. "Whatcho doing in that old Pinto with the KISSY PU plate? Didn't you drive an 'eighty-two Fiesta?"

"It's Mingo Sheffield's."

"Oh yeah. I thought I saw old Whaletail downstairs. Nice of him to come." Clay was now stroking the fender of a new white Cadillac. "A demo," he explained, licking the sugared ice caught under his ring and dripping down his wrist. "Look in there, Ral. Air, tape, cruise control, message center. Out-Japs the Japs. Stars and Stripes on wheels." He turned to point at the American flag atop his father's flagpole in the front yard. "Hey, why, listen, ride with me to pick up some more rum, and check this beautaroot out. I'll give you a great deal on it if you're interested."

"I'm not." Hayes opened and savagely shut the door of the gleaming car. "You already gave my daddy one of your family specials. Thanks a lot. He's taken that convertible to New Orleans when he's supposed to be under a physician's care. Now *I* have to go all the way down there and bring him back." Hayes walked briskly away to the edge of the pond. Frogs, with a frightful suddenness, kept leaping ahead of him into the rusty water.

"To New Orleans? Land of dreams do bop de babaroom?" Clay skimmed a popsicle stick into the pond. "Listen, you'll have a ball. Bourbon Street is *hot!* Some of those shows, I swear, people are *doing* it. Food's great too." Then the car salesman was solemn. "You know, Ral, Ned Ware's telling folks Uncle Earley bought that El Dorado for some little black —"

"Yes!" hissed Hayes. "I know he is, damn him."

"Good golly, Miss Molly! It's not true. Is it? What's he want with a hooker for at his age? You think we'll be able to get it up at his age? Seriously?"

"Jimmy, for God's sake, would you just go on to the goddamn liquor store."

But Clay had started the same nervous cough he had so annoyingly used as a signal decades ago when passing notes to Raleigh during geometry tests, notes scribbled "What's the ans. to #6?" "Ur ur ur. Something bugging you or something, Ral? Ur ur. I need to ask you some advice. You've got a head on your shoulders." And in demonstration, Clay grabbed it in an affectionate arm lock until Raleigh wrestled free. "Here's the thing, ur ur. You think I ought to marry Tildy Harmon? Or not?"

"Not."

"Seriously, Raleigh."

"I'm serious."

"I'm tearing my guts out over this thing. I'm all over the map." His face swollen with earnestness, Clay pulled his reluctant cousin farther away from the house, to the edge of the weedy orange pond. "Let's keep this under our hatracks, okay? Here's the thing."

"Yes? . . . Jimmy?"

Clay plunged into words. "I'm in touch with my feelings in a much more growing way, now I'm going to group."

"Group?"

Clay crossed his arms one way, then the other, then put his hands in his pockets. "And I'm man enough to lay it out. . . . I've got a problem with a little bit of impotency."

"Please don't lay it out, Jimmy."

"But I'm not totally to the stage of self-acceptance where it wouldn't, ur, bother me if Tildy knew. . . ."

"Better her than me," muttered Hayes and kicked at a wedged rock.

"About my, well, it's just when I tense up. But the thing is, I'm always pretty tensed up round Tildy, due to being in love since I was fourteen. You 'member that."

"Vaguely." Hayes pulled out his handkerchief to polish his glasses.

"Well, come on, what's the answer? Do you think I should? Or not? I need your help here."

"What does your 'group' think?"

"It's a support group. We're not allowed to make suggestions. That's a rule."

"Ah." Hayes took a long breath and blew on his glasses. "Shall I be honest?"

"As the day is long." Clay sucked noisily on his class ring, as if it were a pacifier.

"Jimmy, the day is long. In fact, the day is just about done. You have been asking me for a quarter of a century whether you should marry Tildy. Apparently, you have never gotten around to asking *her*."

"The thing is —"

"You could have grown children and your own home by now. Instead, what have you got?" Hayes unfolded his fingers one by one, a mannerism of his Aunt Victoria's that he'd always admired. "You've got a dinky little apartment with no bathtub, and your old model train on the dining-room table. You've got a dozen different-colored bowling balls. A bunch of X-rated video tapes you try to force people to come over and watch with you. And a tank of stupid fish you're always having to flush down the goddamn toilet. And that's it. That's what you've got. Well, you asked me to be honest."

Jimmy Clay, his eyes wide open, had sucked his entire ring finger into his mouth.

"Meanwhile." Hayes looped his glasses around his ears, which were fiery hot. "Tildy Harmon is your cousin. Meanwhile, she's already been divorced, *three times,* and I say this in all sincerity, Jimmy, everybody in the county but you knows *why* she got divorced. Meanwhile, Tildy had already slept with at least two guys I could personally name back in high school when you started all this 'should I marry her?' in the first place!"

With a baleful stare, Jimmy Clay put his hands on the back of his hips, then on the sides. He stepped back and then rushed forward and slammed his cousin in the stomach with his head.

"Ooofff . . ." said Raleigh as he landed in the muddy grass, with one sleeve in the water. He caught his breath, shook his arm, listened to his watch, and yelled after the tall green figure stomping off. "In other words, no! In case I didn't make it clear, Jimmy, *no,* I *don't* think you should marry Tildy! How's that! That's my advice!"

"Who asked you?" yelled Clay. The white Cadillac shot backward out of the crowded driveway.

Alone, Raleigh began prying large rocks out of the mudbank and heaving them into the pond. Their loud splashing thunk was as satisfying as if each rock had been a Hayes. During a boyhood visit, he had idly loosened one of these rocks with his bare toes, to find himself stared at by a large yellow-eyed snake that lay coiled beneath in a circle tight as malice. Nothing had ever before looked at him with so contemptuous an indifference, and from then on he was ready to believe that snakes had once been God's rivals in heaven. Clearly, they had, in Flonnie Rogers's phrase, the Power. Clearly, they'd held a grudge. God might have changed their shapes, but not their eyes. God's eyes probably looked just the same, only worse. After all, God had won. Had won — thought Hayes now — and had sat back and kept those eyes of His on His old enemies while they were having a great time torturing fools like Jimmy Clay.

"Okay," said Raleigh as he stood to brush mud off the seat of his pants. "One step at a time." Now to find his aunt Lovie a birthday present so he could ask her a few questions. The gift was necessary. Among Hayeses, present-giving was both incessant and evanescent; mounds of gifts were exchanged on every known ceremonial occasion, and it had long been clear to Raleigh that the contents mattered less than the ritual of (sloppily) wrapping and (rapidly) unwrapping as many little surprise packages as possible. His daughters, genetically infected, were always disappointed when on their birthday he presented each of them with "one really nice thing." In the continual family potlatch, merchandise rotated, season to season, Hayes to Hayes, without memory, as handy objects lying about junk-jammed houses were offered up, with bright paper slapped round them, as "little surprises." For Valentine's Day, Reba was likely to give Lovie the same brass figurine of an elf under a toadstool that Little Em had given Reba for passing her realtor's exam. There was no true Hayes who would not rather open a surprise grabbag of junk than dollar bills wrapped in wax paper. (This was how Big Em's son — disguised as the pepper shaker on *Let's Make a Deal,* had ended up with the three goats behind the curtain instead of the $3,000 he'd had in his hand.)

Raleigh plowed through Vera Sheffield's old clothes in the backseat of the Pinto. He found a fur stole made up of three foxes, each with its tail in the next one's mouth. He found a huge black acetate scarf with orange poppies all over it. He rolled the fur stole up inside the scarf and tied the ends together into a bow. Then he went back inside the house and tried to call Aura; no one was home. No one was home at the Sheffields' either. Aura and Vera were probably in jail by now. Peeking down from the door of the Wreck Room, Raleigh saw his relatives singing "I'm Alabama Bound," accompanied by the player piano, while Mingo Sheffield spun jiggling to a jitterbug with Tildy Harmon, who should have been wearing a brassiere. Both dancers gasped for air.

"Up here, Raleigh!" His aunt Victoria was at the end of the hall with Reba, conversing with Lovie through the open door of a small bathroom. "Your arm's wet . . . Lovie's in there."

He said, "Excuse me."

"Honey, stay." Lovie coughed. "I'm just smoking. I've got to do it in here where it goes up the ventilator fan. Then I spray with Lysol."

"Ah," Raleigh murmured, wondering if perhaps Aura did the same.

From her wheelchair, Reba tugged up at his sleeve. "Senior would die if he knew Lovie'd kept on smoking after the doctors told her she better quit because of her heart."

"Her heart?"

Victoria pursed, then stretched her lips with a click. "Yes, Raleigh. I thought it was cancer too, but turns out it was both."

"Called it coronary thrombosis. Just like Hackney," Reba explained.

Lovie nodded. "I had my attack selling chrysanthemums at the State–Wake Forest game for the Elks."

Raleigh whispered, "A bad one?," and Lovie's laugh shook her earrings of dangling purple beads. "Well, darling, what's a *good* one?" Her hand reached out the door and twisted his shirt-front into a tight ball. Her fingers were crowded with inexpensive rings and her broken nails were painted the color of her earrings. "This one," she whispered dramatically, "was kind of like an elephant squatting on your chest and wiggling around."

Victoria pushed her arm past Raleigh, jerked the lipstick-glossy Pall Mall out of her sister's mouth, and threw it in the toilet. "Mind if I ask you why you don't quit smoking before you have another attack! And please go locate that Bible so Raleigh can take it to Earley before that idiot drops dead, too." Giving Raleigh's convenient arm a sharp twist of exasperation, Victoria spun the wheelchair around, banging it against the walls. "Come on, Reba, I want those chickens on the grill. I don't intend eating supper at midnight again."

Reba leaned her head back to smile upside down at her sister. "Don't you love it when we have a big crowd like this?"

As Victoria marched away, she snorted. "Reba, you don't know what a big crowd is unless you've sailed steerage from Rangoon to Singapore with a rooster on your head and a leper lying across your legs."

Lovie finally found the Hayes family Bible in a dresser drawer under her old tap shoes, her wedding-night lingerie, and an envelope containing all her sons' first teeth and first-cut hair. She confessed she had no idea whose were whose.

"Here's a little surprise," explained Raleigh when he reached out his hand for the Bible and saw he was still holding the poppy-wrapped foxes. "From us, and, ah, the Sheffields."

"Why, that Mingo is the sweetest thing! I'll put this on the pile. Did you see my new poker table Jimmy gave me? Let's play some Mexican Sweat tonight, deuces wild. I feel lucky today."

"Well, actually, Aunt Lovie, I need to press on, I've got to —"

"Honey, I know. Vicky Anna said you're going to take Buddy-Gates to patch things up with Earley. That's just wonderful."

Raleigh sat down on her bed, shoving aside the feet of an old Shirley Temple doll already reclining there. "Yeah. I'm supposed to find somebody called Jubal Rogers, too."

Lovie dropped her unlit cigarette. "Does Vicky know?"

"Who is this guy? Do y'all know him? Is he Flonnie Rogers's kin?"

Nodding, Lovie sat down on the bed beside him. "You know, I bet Earley's *right!*" She patted Raleigh's knee. "Go get him. But I wonder if he's dead."

"Daddy?!"

"Jubal. Wonder if Flonnie knows."

"Maybe she's dead."

Lovie laughed. "Good gracious no. She's too mean to die." Now his aunt shook her head sadly; like her son Jimmy's, her face could slide from glee to grief and back in seconds. "No, Flonnie's gone to one of those nursing homes, spite of all of us begging her to move in. This place is just for colored people. It's about halfway between Goldsboro and Mount Olive and they don't even have but one TV set in the whole place and it's not on the cable."

While Lovie located an addressed package of little surprises she'd been meaning to mail to Flonnie, Raleigh turned the stiff mottled pages of his family's Bible. The corners of the leather covers had crumbled away and the smell of age rose from the paper. A pressed rose, thin and brittle, fell apart as it dropped from a page of the Gospels, a page in which Christ was supposedly waltzing on the waters while His petrified disciples turned green back in their seasick boat. Raleigh flipped to the Old Testament, vaguely looking for the Book of Job. He couldn't find it. Maybe one of the Hayeses had removed the whole chapter as out-of-keeping with their preposterous sanguinity.

"*You will meet, but you will miss me!*" Lovie had returned and was singing. "*There will be an empty chair.* I remember how Papa sang that song the night he died, trying to get everybody to laugh, but nobody would. And then he told Earley to go get that very Bible, and 'Read me on out, son. Read me the good parts of the Song of Songs.'" Lovie's imitation of Raleigh's grandfather's stroke-garbled speech was eerily accurate. "And Earley read on all through the night till Papa was gone." She began crying, then slapped her ringed fingers against her purple pants, and laughed. "Earley said later on, he'd peed right there in his pants 'cause he didn't have the heart to take a break." To Raleigh's embarrassment, Lovie now reached inside her blouse and pulled out what had appeared to be her right breast, but was in fact a large round wad of Kleenex. She unwound a few tissues, and returned the others. "It evens me out," she explained, and blotted her tears. Then she announced she'd come to a decision. "I wasn't going to tell you where Buddy was, 'cause I promised him I wouldn't tell a soul." ("Buddy" had been the nickname the Clays had given Gates, when Earley and the small boy had moved in with Lovie for the first year after Roxanne left them.)

"You know where he is?"

"He's my boy, Raleigh, and I'm going to stay in touch, even if nobody else will, and even if Senior swears he'll file for divorce if I send that poor child, my own nephew and my own godson, another red cent, but I say if we can't help out those we love, we might as well all climb over the Iron Curtain and settle down in Russia alone."

Raleigh did not care to pursue politics, or even to argue with her description of his thirty-five-year-old brother, a compulsive gambler, unsuccessful con artist, relentless liar, and probable parole violator, as a "poor child." Instead, he told her, "Gates's mother may be dying. I'm going to take him to see her."

Lovie squeezed his hand. "That's just like you, honey. After what Roxanne did to Buddy, I don't know if I could get my lips to say a decent word to her face. But you're just forgiving and forgetting. It's a lesson to us all. . . . Raleigh, Buddy's hiding out in your rental cottage at Kure Beach."

Indignation carried Hayes to the other side of the room. "Why wasn't I told? Who told him he could break into 'Peace and Quiet'?!" Raleigh himself had painted the name "Peace and Quiet" above the porch gable of his first beachfront property, a little wood house on the Cape Fear side of a spur poking into the Atlantic. It sat there in wonderful seclusion, unbothered by neighbors, undisturbed by even a phone. Every August he went there to spend his own vacation repairing ravages inflicted by his renters. The doors were bolted shut now! "I don't believe this! Why didn't Seabreeze Realty stop him? Who told you this?"

"Raleigh, now don't take on." His aunt spun him around as he rushed past her, thumping the Bible like an evangelist in a frenzy. "Aura had a feeling this would rub you the wrong way."

Raleigh slowly pulled back. "Aura? Aura Godwin Hayes to whom I am married?"

"Well, honey, she said the realtor didn't have a thing lined up for that cottage till the first of May, and here was poor little Buddy-Gates with no place to turn and needing to be on the ocean for a few weeks anyhow. Besides, I couldn't keep hiding him out at the Elks Club because they only turn the heat on on Wednesdays and weekends, so this looked like a godsend, and Aura agreed. So there he is, and you have this wonderful idea about helping Buddy go make up with Roxanne and Earley, and now you don't even have to look for him! Now, let me see a big smile. Come on, can't you do any better than that?"

Raleigh, in fact, was not even attempting to smile. He was biting the inside skin of his mouth and swallowing the blood with a terrible pleasure. He sat down too quickly in an armchair piled with laundry and, by the feel of it, a sharp rake (it was, in fact, a set of electric curlers). "Aunt Lovie," he began softly. "Forgive my inquisitiveness if I attempt to clarify certain factors here? Do you mind? One, why does Gates 'need' to be at the ocean?"

"He needed to run an errand."

"Two, why does he 'need' to be anywhere except in prison, to which I presume he's now been sent again, and escaped."

"He did not. He's paroled." Lovie had taken a string of red and white popbeads from her jewelry box; when she opened the lid, a ballerina began twirling to the tune "Fascination." "It was all a misunderstanding anyhow."

Hayes snorted. "Taking a great deal of money from foolish women to trace their genealogies so they can get in the Daughters of the Confederacy and then *making up* the charts? Selling them *forged* letters from Robert E. Lee? That's a misunderstanding?"

"Well, I sure don't think they ought to put you in jail for it! Not after you served in Vietnam!"

"Lovie, if he finished his parole, why were you hiding him at the Elks Club?"

Lovie had now found some old Christmas wrapping paper which she was twisting around the popbeads. "I don't know, but he said it didn't have a thing to do with the police."

"I bet."

"He said he had to deliver something important to a friend at the beach, and a bunch of gangsters were trying to stop him for no good reason." She lowered her voice dramatically. "Because he knew too much. He was on a train with a gangster who talked in his sleep."

"Lovie, that is, well, I'm sorry and forgive my language, but that is typical Gates bullshit. You don't believe that."

She tied a bow around her little package. "If you won't believe your own brother, honey, you might as well go live in a cave in the middle of the ocean."

"Sounds great," said Hayes, as he stood up. "Could I use your phone again, Aunt Lovie?"

But, of course, Aura was still not home, and besides, why should he ever go see her, whoever she was, again. It occurred to Hayes that maybe he *wouldn't* go back home now; maybe he would go straight to the beach and throw his brother out of "Peace and Quiet"; maybe he would go straight to find his father so he could throw Gates in his face; maybe . . . But he certainly wasn't going to do any of this accompanied by Mingo Sheffield; not that, after those first terrifying minutes, he really thought Mingo would shoot him, or even (probably) shoot himself; on the other hand, he did think Mingo capable of serious irrationality, so maybe he *would* start shooting. Raleigh's inability to understand unreason made him feel very vulnerable; he was incapable of predicting the path of the erratic, and what he couldn't predict, he couldn't cope with. He *had* to get away from Sheffield, who nevertheless had the keys to the Pinto in his jacket pocket.

Hayes wandered brooding through the house, past the dining room where the same bowl of faded wax fruit sat on the table, where the baby shoes of all Lovie's sons still hung in dusty bronze on the wall. He wandered down the steps to the Wreck Room, past gilt-framed photographs: Lovie, with baton, high-hatted, raising a bare leg in white-tasseled boot. Lovie, at seventeen, holding the year-old Jimmy in one arm and his new baby brother Junior in the other, while Senior, her dazed teenaged husband, stared down at his two-toned shoes. Lovie and Reba, handsome and festive, Red Cross volunteers, thrusting up magazines at soldiers, who leaned out, grinning, glad to see girls, three to a window in a transport train. Lovie and the five-year-old Gates, both in hobo costumes, holding hands, set to go out trick-or-treating. Jimmy, all arms and legs and ears, leaping — twenty years ago — with a basketball in one splayed palm.

Jimmy! An idea came to Raleigh, as he caught a glimpse of Mingo now slow-dancing with Tildy Harmon, dips, spins, and all, while everyone else in the Wreck Room was singing "That Old Black Magic" around the piano, or throwing cards and chips all over the new poker table that still had an enormous red plastic bow tied around a leg. Mingo was dancing in his sweat-soaked shirtsleeves, and his madras jacket (with the key in its pocket) was thrown over the couch. Perhaps on top of Uncle Bassie, who wasn't visible.

Quickly, Raleigh ran back up to the kitchen. "Jimmy back?"

His aunts Vicky, Reba, and Lovie said no. They were rolling and patting high stacks of hamburger patties. Reba (now wearing as a little surprise Lovie's red-and-white popbeads) was crying. So was Lovie. He assumed it was onions.

"Well, Vicky," Lovie sniffed. "I guess you want me to go trotting up and down the sidewalk, eating germs. That's what yogurt is, you know, *germs.* But if I can't go on with what I call living, I'll just drive on over to the cemetery and lie down with Mama and Papa and Serene and —"

Victoria pinched her nose, both ears, still wasn't relieved, and burst out: "That's exactly right. You'll die!"

Reba cried louder. "Oh, Lovie, don't listen to her. You're not going to die. Don't think it!"

Lovie abruptly started to tap dance and sing, her silver sandals tapping in time to the hamburger patty she smacked between her hands. *"O dem golden slippers, o dem golden slippers, gwine to put on dem golden shoes, climb de golden stairs."*

Victoria shook Reba's wheelchair as she shouted, "Y'all don't seem to care if you die or not, so why should I! Reba! Stop bawling!"

"When I gets to Heaben, gonna put on my shoes, dance all over God's Heaben, Heaben, Heaben . . ."

"Y'all seem to think Mama and Papa and everybody's up there in the sky still eating fried chicken and listening to *The Lone Ranger.* LOVIE, PLEASE!"

Lovie stopped in midnote. "How do you know they're not? Vicky Anna, you sound like you don't even believe in Heaven. Maybe they've got angels singing on a radio up there."

"I believe Hayeses are lying in the ground, period. And precious few of them with all four limbs attached." The old missionary saleswoman had pounded her hamburger patty into pieces and had to start over.

Reba reached out to both sisters. "Of course Vicky believes in Heaven! Why, she had a calling! She gave up a chance for a personal life and carried the Lord on out to the corners of the world far and wide."

"Oh God Almighty!" snapped Victoria. "Raleigh! Come out here to the grill with me and carry this bowl."

In the yard, while Raleigh circled, choking, to turn the sputtering black chicken, he advised his aunt not to be alarmed if he left suddenly in order to escape Mingo Sheffield, who might be wanted for murder.

"Fiddlesticks. He never murdered a fly. But I don't blame you for wanting to get out of this place fast. I just want you to imagine, Raleigh, what it must have been like to have to grow up in a madhouse with all this laughing and loving when they don't even know what they're *talking about!* It just drives me insane. If they'd seen a half of what I've seen, they'd shut off that damn piano. I've seen people that would kill you for what's on this grill right now. Love is not enough, and never was. Never was. Move those drumsticks over. So, I hear we know where Gates is now. Maybe."

"Yes. Can you believe that?" He scraped charred chicken into the bowl.

"I can believe anything, Raleigh, except that Somebody with brains is in charge of this universe. Well, go on. I'd come with you if I didn't expect Reba and Bassie'd be buried before I got back. You keep in touch with me over this Earley business. And if you need help, you just remember, if I can knock a Surabaja bandit over the head with a dead pig —"

"Who's this Jubal Rogers?"

Before answering, Victoria stabbed pieces of chicken and dropped them into the bowl. ". . . Why?"

"Daddy wants him."

". . . That's your daddy's business."

"He didn't want me to ask you about this guy. You didn't like him? You don't know where he is, do you?" Raleigh heard a horn honk as Jimmy Clay pulled back into the driveway.

His aunt pulled the glasses down from the hard blue eyes, now blinking from smoke. She looked at him, then pushed the glasses back. "No, I don't know where he is," she said. "Go on if you're going."

Raleigh surprised himself, and his elderly aunt, by leaning across the warm bowl of chicken to kiss her shyly on the cheek.

"Hold down the fort!" he called, as she marched, straight-backed, across the lawn with the birthday dinner.

His plan was a success. Upon returning with the rum, Jimmy Clay was touched to find his cousin waiting in the driveway to apologize for having hurt his feelings. (As a matter of fact, Raleigh — after looking at that high-school photo, and the bronze baby shoes, and those little white nubbins of teeth and straw wisps of hair that might have been Jimmy's — really did feel meanhearted for having dragged the deluded imbecile over to look at the shallow pit of his life.) Clay was also touched by Raleigh's concern in warning him that Mingo Sheffield was down in the Wreck Room giving every appearance of making a play for Tildy Harmon. Clay threw open the front door so fast, the shamrock fell off.

Luckily for Raleigh, Sheffield and Tildy were now doing the twist buttock to buttock. Luckily, when Jimmy cut in by jabbing his elbow into the fat man's shoulder blades, Mingo lunged forward, smashing a small rocking chair, out of which Raleigh's palsied great-aunt Hattie leaped, with remarkable spryness, just in time. Quick as Hattie, Raleigh grabbed Mingo's huge madras jacket from the couch, ignored his uncle Bassie who lay there asleep or expired — a Golden Book of *Peter Cotton Tail* on his chest — and fled up the stairs. Behind him he heard Mingo's astonished wail. "WHhhhutt, wu wu what'd you push me for, Jimmy? Golleee!"

The overweight cats scattered in a flurry from the living room as Raleigh sprinted through it, Lovie's Bible and Flonnie's package under his arm like a football.

"Pick me up some Marlboros while you're at it, will you, Raleigh?" pleasantly called his cousin Paschal, from the card table where he was working on the sky of the moose jigsaw puzzle.

Raleigh cackled — it was not a laugh or a chuckle, but a cackle — as he threw Mingo's fat suitcase out onto the lawn. The Pinto spit gravel as he wheeled around all the Cadillacs. "I don't care," he said. "I don't care if I don't have my car or my clothes and I have to drive all over the country while Betty Hemans writes novels in what used to be my office. I don't care! At least, I'm, ha, ha, *alone!*"

Our hero's freedom lasted precisely one hour and twenty-three minutes. At that time he was returning with the tow truck (which he had walked four miles to find, and paid thirty dollars to hire), to the hilly highway shoulder onto which the Pinto had rolled to a stop after very loudly and very quickly and very disgustingly, unforgivably throwing a rod only seven miles east of Cowstream. As the tow truck came back over the hill, its young driver was nearly scared off the road by the sudden seizure that attacked his passenger, a hitherto stolid, tight-lipped man. For Raleigh Hayes began to bang on the dirty dash, to tear at his own hair, and to chant, "Goddammitgoddammitgoddammit."

Raleigh had gone to pieces at the sight of a white Cadillac parked behind the Pinto. For he had seen that from under the crippled car's yellow side protruded two unmistakably fat legs in baby blue slacks.

Leaping from the truck, Hayes ran straight to the Pinto's smashed rear bumper, and began to kick at the "God Is My Co-Pilot" sticker. "Get out from under there, Mingo, before I tow this trashheap right across your body! How'd you find me?! Get out!"

The young mechanic scratched his beard as he watched. "You had a friend with a Cadillac, how come you was walking?"

CHAPTER

13

Wherein Is Continued the Account of the Innumerable Troubles Endured by Our Hero

"RALEIGH! You're supposed to be my best friend, and I guess I'm beginning to wonder."

"Okay. Okay. How'd you find me, Mingo, how, how?!"

"Maybe anybody'd start to wonder, you know, after somebody stole their jacket and their car, and *broke* it!"

"Did Lovie tell you where I was going? Did she? She did!"

"And didn't even ask when they gave their aunt your wife's foxes that used to belong to your own mother!"

"Answer me, Mingo! How the hell did you sneak off with Jimmy's Cadillac, which by the way doesn't even belong to him!"

"He said I could borrow it, I sure didn't just *steal* it, that's for sure, like some people I know!"

Leaning on his truck, the young bearded mechanic pulled an apple out of his denim jacket. Decals were sewn all over it; one said, "U.S.A. #1," one advertised motor oil, and one said his name was "Jumper." He was small and sinewy and mottled with freckles. Jumper asked, "Y'all want this Pinto towed to the station? Y'all do, y'all got to take that trunk off of the top, you hear?" But the two Thermopyleans were yelling so loudly that they didn't hear.

Mingo was livid. "Plus, told lies! That's right, Mr. Better-Than-Anybody

Hayes. Lies about me wanting to marry Tildy Harmon when I *never!* When wild dogs couldn't make me trade Vera for all the gold in China and you know that!"

"I didn't tell Jimmy you wanted to *marry* Tildy Harmon."

"I guess you didn't leave me there to get sent to the gas chamber either!"

The mechanic chewed energetically on his apple.

"*If, Mingo, if* you aren't guilty, you glutinous cretin, you won't go to the goddamn gas chamber!"

Jumper joined them. "That's what you think. A colored guy used to work at the station, they said how he knifed this old lady and they fried him lickety-split and then later on it turned out he was left-handed."

"See!" shrieked Mingo.

"Mister, would you stay out of this, please?" Hayes carefully patted his hair and his heart. "Okay. All right. I apologize, Mingo. In all seriousness, I honestly didn't think much of your plan to run off to South America. I honestly thought you ought to go back to Thermopylae and talk to Chief Hood and clear this situation up."

"How, hunh? After you just ran off and left me and *stole* my car?"

"I said I was sorry I took your miserable car. Believe me, if I showed you my feet, you'd know how sorry I am. I left you because I was *sick and tired* of your poking your you-know-what into me everytime you felt like it."

Jumper choked on a chew of apple.

"That's another thing you took," spluttered Mingo. "Where is it, Raleigh?"

"Right where you left it, in your pocket, but don't think I'm about to let you get your hands on it again."

By now Jumper was edging toward his truck. "Look, y'all, if I'm not back to the station by seven, my brother in the Guards comes after me."

Hayes turned on him. "Then why are you standing there eavesdropping on matters that don't concern you, instead of hooking up that Pinto, Mr. Jumper, as you were *paid* to do?"

"Y'all are weird," commented Jumper without rancor, and set to work.

Mingo was pouting. "Well, I'm not going back, I'm just not. If you're running away, I don't see why you won't let me come too."

Raleigh stared at the gloomy sky, at the scrub pines and young maples so shaken by wind they seemed to be snickering; he stared at the disinterested highway pointing in both directions. Nothing seemed to care much one way or the other. Nothing he could *think* seemed to bulk with much reality. He couldn't hold a thought. In his way were the size of the luxurious Cadillac and the size of Mingo Sheffield with his round quivering mouth. Raleigh Hayes sighed. "If I let you come with me, will you stop acting like a fool?"

Sheffield stared solemnly back. "I swear! . . . Where are we going anyhow?"

"To a nursing home and the beach."

"Oh. . . . I thought we were going to New Orleans."

"One step at a time. Will you call Vera and try to get this mess sorted out?"

Sheffield was all earnestness. "Yes."

"All right then."

His moon face bobbing, Mingo tried to hug his friend, who ducked. "Raleigh, I knew you didn't really mean to leave me behind. I'm sorry I had to say I was going to shoot you. You knew I never would, really. But how can we go, with the Pinto like it is?"

Hayes pointed at the new Cadillac.

"But I kind of told Jimmy I'd bring it back in about an hour."

Reckless in the grasp of this powerful new fatalism, Raleigh even smiled. "Oh, Jimmy'll understand. Tell him you enjoyed driving it so much, you decided to buy it for Vera. He's trying to sell it, and, frankly, she needs a new car."

And brushing aside Sheffield's worries, Hayes placed his jacket on the plush maroon seat of the Cadillac, and took the next step. He transferred Tiny's steamer, PeeWee's bust, Vera's clothes, Lovie's Bible, Flonnie's package, and Mingo's gun from the Pinto into the capacious trunk of Jimmy Clay's big demo. He tied the trunk shut with Vera's gold lamé belt. "Okay," he said calmly. "Let's go."

With Raleigh in the tow truck and Mingo in the Cadillac, they drove back through darkening farm fields, to the crossroads where the filling station leaned against a garage, both half-strangled in kudzu leaves. There, sipping a Budweiser and gazing morosely at a disemboweled engine, was another bearded young man, labeled "Crash," who looked as if he might have resembled Jumper a few million beers back. Together they considered the case of the yellow Pinto. Finally Jumper spoke. " 'KISSY PU' here ain't in such hot shape. Take about three weeks."

"Four," said Crash with a sorrowful spit.

Mingo, speechless, couldn't cope, but Raleigh was indignant. "Four weeks of *work?*"

"Gotta order the parts," said Jumper, and his brother added, "Prob'ly won't git 'em."

Hayes asked for a written estimate; when he saw it, he laughed. "Eight hundred dollars!"

"Nine," said Crash.

Mingo whimpered.

"Okay," said Raleigh, on a different tack. "How much would you *give* him for it? Cash? We're in a hurry."

Jumper and Crash strolled around the car, sharing pensive glances and remarks.

"Looks bad."

"Not good."

"Threw a rod."

"Yeah. Cracked the block."

"Oh yeah. Head's damaged. Look here."

"Looks bad. Bent the valves."

"Oh boy. Engine's shot."

"So's the body. Oh yeah."

"Yeah. Well. Boy."

Mingo followed helplessly behind them, as hurt as if they had Vera on the operating table and didn't see much hope. "The tires are practically new," he whispered.

Jumper slammed one with a wrench. "Yeah. Well. KISSY PU's headed for the dump. Fifty dollars."

"Hunred-fifty," said Crash, who seemed compelled to overbid his brother, whatever the issue.

Forty minutes later, Mingo had signed over Vera's Pinto for $180, minus four dollars' worth of Corn Puffs, Mars Bars, and orange sodas. Raleigh sent him to make his phone calls while he cleaned out of the old car's backseat the slops from the glutton's afternoon binge; while he removed the KISSY PU plate, the Buddhas, and, with an angry squeeze, the little statue of Christ. Jumper and Crash, their faces masks of melancholy, watched him work. They nodded when he asked if they owned the station, and kept nodding when he suggested that perhaps they didn't get much business out in the middle of nowhere — except for unlucky accidents like his own.

"But better'n punching a time clock, better'n having a boss," Jumper pointed out.

"Only country left where they can't stop you from owning your own business," Crash said. They added that if things didn't pick up soon, they supposed they'd enlist in the Marines.

As Raleigh and Mingo drove away, headed for the shortcut to Mount

Olive, behind them a wide black cloud with hulking arms loomed over the hill like a giant in a nightmare.

"Your seat belt is not fastened. Thank you."

"Leave me alone, Mingo."

Sheffield, who was driving with Corn Puffs and a can of soda crushed between his enormous thighs, giggled. "I didn't say it. The car did. It's been talking to me all along. Listen, here it goes again."

"You are running low on fuel. Thank you."

"Isn't that something, Raleigh? I mean modern technology. Now you wouldn't have thought when we were little that someday there'd be a man in the dashboard to keep on telling you you're low on fuel. And he told me to shut the door and get some windshield fluid, and all sorts of things. I wish he'd tell me where the lights are. I can't exactly see the road."

Hayes turned on the signal indicator, the wipers, the tape deck (which burst on with a terrifying shriek by a woman singing that she'd been a fool too long for love); finally he found the lights. "Mingo, do you mind if I ask you why you didn't buy some gas when we were sitting at a filling station for more than an hour?"

"I forgot."

"Well, will you please stop at the next place you see?"

But there was no next place. There was nothing but scrub pine, corn stubble, burnt-over soybean fields, jungles of kudzu, and the old asphalt two-lane, so bypassed by the New South that suddenly every hundred yards, the past appeared in little panels, once red, washed pink now. Mingo read each one:

> Does your husband
> MISBEHAVE?
> Grunt & Grumble
> Rant & Rave?
> Shoot the Brute Some
> BURMA-SHAVE

There was also an old billboard still insisting they IMPEACH EARL WARREN. There was nothing else but blackness, wind, and the deep rumbling growl of the storm cloud, which had now stretched out and spread itself over the whole sky.

"You are running low on fuel. Thank you."

"Shut up," said Raleigh, craning to see the gas gauge, which disappeared below empty as he watched.

"Ohh, gollee," said Mingo. "Something's wrong. I guess we're stopping."

"I wonder why!" Hayes snapped. "Mingo! Get the damn car off the damn road! No, *on* the shoulder, on the —"

The Cadillac was rolling into a little grove of pecan trees. Raleigh knew they were pecan trees because lightning shot all over the sky and lit them up.

"I'm scared," Sheffield confessed. "Lightning scares me, I can't help it."

The insurance agent told him what he'd often told Holly and Caroline, and, indeed, assumed to be true. "A car's the safest place you could be." Why add what he was thinking? That rolling to a stop under the only cluster of trees in a flat meadow was the fatheaded act of a half-witted butterbrain? "Shut off the lights, Mingo!"

They sat there for a while in the dark.

"Mingo, please stop trying to start the car. Isn't it fairly obvious that we're out of gas? Hasn't that remote possibility crossed your mind?" Pawing through the glove compartment, Hayes was obliged silently to bless his cousin Jimmy Clay, for there was actually a flashlight in there, along with a videotape of *Debbie Does Dallas.* "Stay here. I'll flag somebody down."

"Who?"

Sheffield was right. Not a car passed. Not a truck. Not a one of the tractors whose sluggard pace Hayes had cursed that afternoon. Not a man, not a dog, and although presumably those pecans had not planted themselves, there was not a houselight in any direction.

Thunder cracked overhead, loud enough to make Hayes jump out of the coma of helplessness that had paralyzed him. As lightning seared a streak of white behind him, he heard a sizzling sound. Then rain poured out of the sky as though somebody up there had tossed it to douse the smoke now steaming from the pecan grove. Raleigh ran. And smacked into Mingo Sheffield, who tried to climb right up him, as if Raleigh were a tree.

"You said it wouldn't! It got me!"

Over the thunder, Raleigh shouted — rain splashing into his mouth. "It did not! Run back to the car! Move! . . . Jesus Christ! Why is my door locked! *These doors are locked! MINGO! Unlock the goddamn door! Look in your pants pockets then!* YOU COULDN'T HAVE! GODDAMMIT!"

But a flick of the flashlight undeniably revealed the little white bowling ball on Jimmy Clay's key chain, hanging from the ignition like a lost planet in a black galaxy. Sheffield, hopping backward, howled, "Don't kill me! It was an accident!," while Hayes, fingers out like a hawk landing, flew after him.

Murder, however, would not keep the rain off — unless he slit Mingo open and crawled inside. Moreover, Hayes had a shred of dignity left. He snatched at it, and walking, head high, to the tied-open trunk, he pulled from it the biggest article of Vera's clothing he could find. It was a floor-length peasant dress she'd bought in Acapulco when she weighed a hundred and seventy pounds. Flinging it over his head, he stomped resolutely back to the highway and headed east. He did not turn to look when he heard behind him Mingo's thudding feet and wheezing cries of "Raleigh! One little button and all the doors snap locked. Wait! Maybe you could have made the same mistake, you know, maybe. Raleigh!"

Pelted by rain, they trudged for half a mile. Raleigh in front, bent into the wind, shawled in brightly striped cotton, looked like a mistreated Old Testament prophet, down to his clenched fist and crazed wrathful eyes. Ten yards behind stumbled Mingo, tripping over Vera's pink ruffled gown, which he clutched around his neck; it gave him the bedraggled gaiety of an elephant in a rainy parade.

Finally from the west, beams of light fluttered across the rattling trees. Hayes ran into the middle of the road, wildly flapping both dress and flashlight.

The black van almost hit him, then swerved with a rubbery squeal to a stop. "Uh oh," said Hayes, as the vehicle backed toward them, revealing across its rear doors a vivid painting of Satan with his tongue out and flames leaping from his furry ears. "Oh shit!" Hayes added, uncharacteristically, when he saw *"Sympathy With The Devil"* in huge red script along the van's side, a skull-and-crossbones flying from its antenna, and a ring of spikes protruding from its hubcaps. The occupants weren't even North Carolineans. They had a Georgia plate. "Don't mention the Cadillac," he hissed at Mingo. "Just say what I say!"

The girl driving the van wore sunglasses, a skullcap with a propeller on top, and an earring, pierced through the side of her nostril. The young man beside her, with smoke trickling out of the corners of his mouth, had nothing on his torso but tattoos; his pale red hair was shaved across the crown of his head and hung to his shoulders on both sides. Yelps of music bawled so loudly from their speakers that Hayes wasn't sure exactly what the couple were saying to him, but in general he didn't care much for their tone, which was unabashedly derisive and included most of the four-letter words compounded in ways he had never heard.

"Never mind, no thank you," he replied, stepping back, only to be jostled by Mingo, who stuck his face right in the window to beg for a ride. The side door slid silently open, pale writhing arms like a Shiva reached out, and before the two astonished Thermopyleans could protest, they were face down in the dirty shag carpeting of a Hell on Wheels. That's what was written on the T-shirt of the hefty girl sitting on Raleigh's back, and that's what it was.

They were in the back of the van, which was curtained from the front; the seats had been removed, dice-shaped track lights added, and walls, windows, ceiling, and floor covered with a thick, tangled black rug like gorilla fur. Cards and hamburgers were scattered all over. The air was rank with smoke that smelled like Aura's burnt spaghetti sauce. On plastic beanbags sprawled three fiendish individuals in their underwear, one of whom had his nose in a spoon on the floor. One — fat as a sumo wrestler — was playing a guitar that wasn't there, and the one with the crew cut was female. A fourth individual (bigger than Mingo, and leaning his elbow into Mingo's neck) looked remarkably like a werewolf; a bushy beard whorled all over his face except for his eyes and the tip of his nose, and even his hands and feet were hairy. He spoke first, in a rumbling bass voice. "Helloooo, baaaabeee! Dis is de Big Bopper speakin'! Back up! Look here! We got old dorks in drag! Cruising in the midnight hour!"

The crew cut pulled her chin out of her bosom. "They're wet," she announced after a long stare. "It raining?"

The hefty girl bounced on Raleigh's back. "Rain rain go away," she sang.

"Oh zow, wow, Wendy, ride 'em!" The fat player of the imaginary guitar crawled over to tug at the pink ruffles twisted around Mingo's petrified body. "Man, this is one wet fairy!"

By bucking, Raleigh threw Wendy off. Livid, he rose to his knees. "Stop it! Let us out of this van!" He felt for his glasses and put them back on.

The long-haired creature up front stuck his head through the curtains. "We flag you, Pops? Or you flag us? Hey? Right? We're the fuckin' good Samaritans. Hey?"

The werewolf sang in agreement. "Shhboom shhboom. Yada da dada da yada dum."

Mingo said, "We just wanted a ride."

Longhair smiled; his teeth had never been brushed. "Well, this is more like a cab, hey? Hear the meter tick?"

"Tick TOCK tick TOCK," went the werewolf. "The fare's gonna be huhighh!"

They all howled, and began grabbing at the Thermopyleans' pockets. Mingo squeaked, "Please don't! All we want's to call Triple A! Isn't that right, Raleigh! Please! Give me my wallet back! I need that to go to South America!"

"Calliiinng Triple AAAEEE!" screamed the guitarist, as he fanned Mingo's money. "Jackpot!"

The crew cut had managed to raise her head again. "We playing strip poker or not?" She kicked the beanbag beside her; its occupant toppled over, his nose sliding in the spoon along the carpet.

Our hero, in whom righteous indignation had always been a stronger emotion than self-preservation, exploded. "I don't know what you filthy perverts think you're up —"

Growling, the werewolf tackled Raleigh, rolling over on him and tugging out his wallet. Hayes flailed and kicked, but ended up with the obese guitarist lying on his head, while Wendy jerked his trousers down around his ankles. She even slapped him on the rear. That instant, the most hideous in Raleigh's entire life, popped every circuit in his brain. He swelled into a monster. For a few minutes, the van was a flurry of arms and legs.

Then the driver slammed on her brakes, and everyone flung forward. "Oh easy easy," whispered the man with his nose in the spoon, and curled himself into a ball.

"Dump 'em," called the longhair from the front seat. The door shot open and Raleigh and Mingo shot out of it, landing on their hands and knees on a gravel road. The werewolf was tossing things at them, as he howled, "FRUITS! Say thanks for the lift, how 'bout? Adios! Aiiooooohhhh! Aiiooooohhhh!" The blaring music roared away.

Raleigh gasped weakly, "Get their number."

But Mingo was apparently dead, or had fainted again. The howls Raleigh kept hearing were coming not from the van, long gone, or from his friend, out cold; but from dogs. A great many large-sounding dogs, close by, and, he prayed, penned up.

Raleigh couldn't tell what was blood and what was rain, what was broken and what bruised, what was blindness and what the loss of his spectacles on a rainy night. Nevertheless, he sternly reminded himself as he struggled to pull up his shorts and trousers, all was not lost. At least, it wasn't raining quite as hard. At least, he had not been raped, castrated, shot full of drugs, and hung from a tree. Best of all, at least he had not been wearing his suit jacket, which was still locked inside the Cadillac, with not only $7,500 in cash in its pockets, but also the extra pair of glasses he always carried in case of an emergency. Not that in his worst nightmare had he ever dreamed that such an emergency as this one ever could have befallen him. No, at least he was not dead; he might yet live to track down those loathsome thugs and pour acid in their faces. With that image, Hayes consoled himself, until he heard a shuddering "Ohhhhh. Ohhhhhhh." The growls of the dogs had already subsided. This howling was human.

Groping his way over to his neighbor's body, Raleigh's hand struck the flashlight that must have hit Mingo, for the moaning fat man was clutching his head.

"You okay, Mingo?"

When the light flashed at him, Sheffield opened one puffy eye, saw his friend's bloody face, sat up, and vomited onto the gravel. Hayes rolled away until he'd finished. "Ohhhh," Mingo began again. "This is aw . . . aw . . . ful! Why'd you have to make them so mad? *They took all our money!*"

"Why did *I?* . . . Never mind. Never mind. Calm down. All right." Hayes knew he had to be careful; he knew he was on the edge of going someplace from which he wouldn't return unless jolted back with shock treatments. "I'll just look around," he said serenely. "They were throwing things." And, using the flashlight, he indeed did find both their wallets and his glasses, all of which the devil sympathizers had charitably flung out the van door on top of their victims. For some reason they'd kept Vera's dresses. One lens of his glasses was shattered, but through the other one, Hayes examined the wallets. The money was gone, but their licenses, their credit cards, all the plastic verification of their existence was still intact.

Swaying on his hands and knees, Sheffield was not consoled by this news. "What'll I do? *A hundred and eighty dollars!* Plus I had two fifties for my trip!"

Hayes forced himself to his feet, which appeared to work. "You were planning to move to South America with two fifties? Smart." He hauled Sheffield up.

"I have a hundred more in my shoes."

"Well, that's good. Don't grab my arm."

"They didn't get my shoes. I can be glad about that, I guess."

"Why not."

"They got all yours, hunh?"

In fact, Hayes had had only ten dollars in his wallet, but he thought this fact might depress Sheffield, so he merely said, "I have a little more in my jacket in the car. Where are we?" He turned slowly around. Lights were shining through the woods a few hundred yards down the gravel road. He pulled Mingo toward them.

"That was lucky," said the fat man. "And you know, Raleigh, another thing that's lucky? Suppose those Jumper brothers hadn't gypped me? Suppose they'd paid me four or five or even six hundred dollars for Vera's Pinto? Gosh, just think how I'd feel if those muggers had taken my *six* hundred dollars?! I'd shoot myself, that's for sure."

"Good thinking, Mingo. This is your lucky day, all right. I certainly envy you your ability to look on the bright side."

Now, Hayes did not at all envy his neighbor, but his sarcasm went unnoticed by Sheffield, who said, as they hobbled along in the rain, "It's true. A lot of people have told me I must have just been born on a sunny day, because I do have this optimistic personality. If you see a cloud, some people would say, 'There's a cloud,' but the other kind, and I guess I'm one of those, is the kind that says, 'If we didn't have clouds, we wouldn't have rain, and if we didn't have rain, we wouldn't have plants, and if we didn't have plants, we wouldn't have animals, and —'"

"I think I get your point, Mingo, thank you."

"Well, I guess it's hard to be my kind of person unless you were born that way."

"Undoubtedly so," said Hayes, limping on.

"Oh God, somebody's there!" Sheffield grabbed his friend's arm, pinching a nerve. "Raleigh, Raleigh, Raleigh, shine your light!"

The woods had cleared, the gravel road forked in a Y. To the left was a parking lot. To the right was a garden with brick paths and two benches. In the middle was a long low brick building. Motionless right in front of them stood a tall pale woman holding a baby. Hayes turned the flashlight on her.

"Gollee," said Mingo.

"What the hell is that doing here?" Hayes replied.

It was a life-sized plaster statue of the Virgin Mary holding her son.

Beside the door of the building one plaque said, "A.K.C. REGISTERED ST. BERNARDS." Another said, "MERCY HOUSE RETREAT CENTER." A note beside the buzzer said, "PRESS FIRMLY. WAIT PATIENTLY." It wasn't long, however, before lights came on and the thick oak door was swung open by a stocky, short, bespectacled woman about Raleigh's age, who wore a Boston University sweatshirt, baggy jeans, and sneakers.

"Dear Jayzus!" she said. "Cah crash? Any more out there?" Pulling the men inside, she slammed the door shut on the rain.

"No, just us. Hitchhiking. Muggers on the highway." Raleigh, holding his one good lens to his one open eye, mumbled, "Could we possibly prevail upon —"

She cut him off by suddenly blowing the whistle she wore around her neck. Then she peered intently at the two victims, pulling open their eyelids and feeling their pulses. "Yah poor guys. A shiner apiece. Nothing looks broken. How's it feel?"

"Broken," said Hayes.

"Heavens, Sister Joe!" Hurrying down the corridor trotted one old and another very old woman, the first wearing a nun's black habit, the second wearing a plaid bathrobe with big fluffy slippers.

"Mother, the poor souls just got mugged."

Mingo shivered, flinging rain on the rug. "And beaten up and robbed of all our money by a bunch of Hell's Angels in a van instead of motorcycles. We were on our way to New Orleans."

"I'll call the police," said the nun in the habit.

"No!" Mingo shook his head violently.

Raleigh, also shaking, added, "He means, not now. . . . If we could just . . . Please excuse us, bursting in on you." He noticed in the mirror on a large Victorian coatrack, a wet bloody man with shattered glasses, his shirt torn to pieces, his chest, face, and hands gritted with dirt and gravel. "Bursting in, like this."

"Don't be silly, young man," the nun in the habit said. "That's what we're here for." She had a thin homely face and a melodious, oddly accented voice. "I'm Sister Catherine, the Mother Superior here at Mercy House."

"The boss," said the woman in the sweatshirt. "I'm Sister Cecilia Joseph, but I hate Cecilia, so call me Joe. You sure got the dogs going good."

Mingo wiped his hand and held it out. "They just threw us right out of the van, so I guess we're lucky to run into you, all right. Nice to meet you. I'm Mingo Sheffield and this is my friend Raleigh Hayes."

"I'm Sister Anne and I'm so sorry," whispered the eldest nun, clutching her bathrobe.

Sister Joe took Mingo's arm. "Okay, guys, let's clean off the blood. I'm a nurse. Better stay the night here." Raleigh explained about the Cadillac up the road. "We'll take care of it," she said. "You came to the right place."

Mingo smiled tentatively. "Y'all are all nuns, aren't you? Catholic nuns?"

They nodded.

He stopped. "I'm a Baptist. Is that okay?"

"Okay by me," said Sister Joe.

The Thermopyleans were led through the lobby's clusters of thick stodgy armchairs and dark frayed couches. Pots of African violets lined the windowsills. Hand-stitched modernistic tapestries hung on the stucco walls: the one with doves said, "PEACE BE WITH YOU," and one with shooting stars said, "HE IS RISEN!" They passed through huge rooms arranged like auditoriums, through a vast empty cafeteria and down a hall of numbered doors.

"Y'all live in all these rooms?" asked Mingo, peeking in.

Sister Catherine told him that the Sisters of Mercy supported themselves by hosting retreats, and by selling pedigreed St. Bernards. "Only eleven of us live here but sometimes we have as many as a hundred visitors."

"We had a wild bunch last week," grinned Sister Joe.

"They were a hoot," Sister Anne whispered. "I don't mean that in a bad way. I'm sorry."

Mingo patted her back. "Well, y'all are a mercy to us, that's for sure, isn't it, Raleigh? I'd of killed myself in a few more minutes, I'm not kidding you."

"Aw, bull," Sister Joe told him, and Raleigh agreed with a snarl.

Luckily, the two men had suffered only cuts, bruises, black eyes, lacerations, a sprained wrist (Raleigh), and an egg-sized lump on the head (Mingo). After they were cleaned off, patched up, and dressed in sets of the gardener's blue overalls (which were too big for Raleigh and too small for Mingo), they were taken to the kitchen and fed bowls of hot pea soup with mugs of hot cocoa.

"You ladies are about as nice as you can be," Sheffield sighed as he slurped away a second helping. "Excuse me saying this, but I always used to think nuns were, well, kind of, well, you know, smacking you with a ruler and making you worship the Pope and sewing your pockets up and things like that. . . ."

"That comes later," said Sister Joe, who then confessed that she'd put a mild sedative in their cocoa.

"I never take drugs," Hayes protested.

"It's out of the herb garden. Would a nun hand you a bum steer? Believe me, otherwise you guys would be up all night feeling like total crud."

"I already do," he told her. "Excuse me. About the car, I'm very worried that —"

"Two of the sisters went back up the road for your car. With some gas. How many Caddys in a burnt-out pecan grove can there be in these sticks, you know?"

"But it's locked. I told you. The key's inside."

Sister Joe dunked a doughnut in her cocoa. "Sister Mary Theresa can handle it. God took her from a life of breaking into locked cars, but He left her her talent."

"It comes in so handy," whispered Sister Anne. "I only mean, I'm sorry, I'm so forgetful with keys, excuse me."

Fortune clipped Raleigh Hayes one last blow from behind as he returned from the bathroom to the small bedroom assigned him by Sister Catherine. Passing an open door from which burst shouts of "Right on, sister!" and "That's the way! No more Nukes, no more Lukes, I love it!," Hayes peeked into what appeared to be a television lounge. Half-a-dozen women in various stages of nightwear, nun's apparel, and jogging clothes sat cheering the eleven o'clock news. More specifically, they sat cheering Raleigh's wife, Aura. Backed by her placard-waving Mothers for Peace gang, she stood on the terrace of the Thermopylae Golf Club, Chief Hood on one side of her, a television reporter on the other. Aura's cheeks looked green and her lips blue, but that was probably simply poor reception out here in the wilderness. She was still indisputably Aura, and she was clearly enjoying herself. She was in what her husband called her high moral-thrill mood. Sheepishly, Chief Hood tried to take her arm, but she raised it right in front of the camera, and kept talking. "I say, when a man tells us we shouldn't be afraid of nuclear arms, then we should be afraid of *him!* I say, men like Lukes must go, before we *all* go!"

A very young nun on the floor yelled, "Give peace a chance!," and then the screen showed the news show anchorman, who said, "Aura Hayes of Thermopylae, organizer of Mothers for Peace, will join our guest, Congressman Charlie Lukes, on Channel Seven's *Woman Alive!* tomorrow morning at eleven. And now, a flaming inferno on Highway Three-forty-five. Todd Brace is live on the scene."

Raleigh's knees were rubbery and his eyes half-closed by the time he'd returned to his room, after asking the Mother Superior if he might make a collect call. He could hear Mingo next door already snoring. When he found the old cord-pull lamp by the single bed, he saw beside it a missal, and on the wall above it, a wooden crucifix with a twisted Christ. "I know how you feel," muttered Hayes.

"Mothers for Peace."

"Collect to anyone from Raleigh W. Hayes. Will you accept?"

"Uh, gee, my mom's in the tub."

"Will you accept the charges?"

"Holly! Excuse me, operator. Holly, accept the charges."

"Oh, okay, gee, sure."

"Go ahead, please."

Raleigh breathed slowly. "Holly, would you mind —"

"Sorry, Dad, but Mom. . . . Oh, ex! It's you! You okay? This is great! Mom's freaked up the wall. . . . MOM! DAD'S CALLING! . . . You coming home?"

"Eventually."

"You didn't leave Mom?"

"Don't be absurd. I'm trying to find Grandpa Earley. What are you doing up at this hour?"

"Phew! What a relief. I said to Car, he's split. You see it on TV all the time. Rat race gets to these middle-age guys, and they're gone! I said to Car, that's the ball game, 'cause she said you were already into her rock tapes."

"Holly, get your mother!"

"MOM! DAD! EVERYTHING'S COOL. . . . She's getting a towel. Hey, guess what? Mom was on the news! She was great!"

"Yes, I saw her. Listen to me, Holly, I have to be away awhile on this Grandpa business. I want you to hold down the fort. And by the way, while I'm gone, I don't want you dating your friend Booger anymore."

"We're not 'dating'!"

"His brother gave me reason to believe Booger's a little too wild and fast with girls. You're only sixteen."

"Seventeen." Holly laughed, remarkably like her mother. "Gene Blair is *so* hung up, God! Dad, Booger's gay!"

"Gay? You mean homosexual? The basketball player at our house? Are you sure?"

"Well, gee, I never personally caught his action, but he's been telling me so since seventh grade; I don't see why he'd make it up. And now he's trying to come out, but it's really not that easy a life, you know, Dad, give him a break. Here's Mom. Take it easy. See yah."

Hayes heard them whispering phrases like "spaced out" and "in jail?"

"Raleigh? Raleigh? Oh God, thank God you called!"

"What's the matter?! Aura, have you been arrested?"

"Me? Have you? Are you in jail? I've been worried sick about you, Raleigh! Whatever possessed you not to *call* me? Where are you?"

Hayes sat down on his narrow bed. "I attempted on many occasions to telephone you, but as I have just had the pleasure of catching you on the local news, I gather you've had a busy day. Why aren't *you* in jail?"

"Mothers for Peace? Oh honey, it's so wonderful what's happening. I just wish you could be here. They backed right down! Well, they weren't about to put the mayor's sister in the slammer at eighty-six! Isn't that fantastic? They didn't know what hit them. But where are you, sweetheart?"

"In a convent east of Goldsboro," replied her husband with tightened teeth. "Didn't Vera explain to you where I was?"

"Raleigh, we don't know where *Vera* is! Their house is all locked up and both cars are gone. Did you say a convent? Oh, honey, I don't think the police honor that thing about sanctuary anymore. But I guess it's a good try."

"Aura, why do you keep mentioning the police and jail? You haven't involved me in your antiwar movement, have you? Because —"

"Where's Mingo? And why are y'all stealing all these cars? I mean you steal his, and then he steals Jimmy's. Really, Raleigh!"

Hayes took a pencil from the bedside table and began to chew its eraser off. "Jimmy told you Mingo stole his car? When did he say this?"

"He just hung up about half an hour ago from Cowstream."

"That damn Mingo! He told me he'd called Jimmy! Did Jimmy call the police?"

"No, not yet. I talked him out of it. Don't think it was easy."

"Well, Aura, don't think I don't appreciate it."

"I don't know why you're being sarcastic with *me*. Actually, Raleigh, I had to tell him we'd *buy* the Cadillac. It's not exactly my style, God knows, but the wagon *is* on its last legs. So give poor Mingo back his Pinto, which, frankly, honey, I wonder why you stole that piece of junk in the first place. If you couldn't wait for me to get back with the Fiesta, why didn't you call Hertz or somebody?"

Having bitten off the eraser, Raleigh chewed on the wood. "Given a chance, I would explain this situation."

"Fire away. This isn't a bit like you. I'm all ears."

Hayes spoke directly to the crucifix. "One. I'm trying to find my father before he has another stroke."

"I know you are, dear."

"Two. I'm trying to honor his asinine instructions."

"Don't pretend you don't love him, Raleigh."

"Do me a favor, Aura, try not to analyze me. Three, I bought Knoll Pond from Pierce Jimson and stole his father's bust out of the library. After that, Mingo forced me at gunpoint to drive him to Aunt Lovie's. . . ."

"Whatever for?"

"I mean, he wanted to go to South America, but I . . . never mind. I got away from him in the Pinto, but it fell apart so we had to sell it. Mingo locked us out of Jimmy's Cadillac in a lightning storm. We were hijacked by a van of devil-worshipping thugs who robbed and beat and *humiliated* us, and then threw us out on the road at this convent. I just want you to know that my pants were ripped off and a girl in a 'Hell on Wheels' T-shirt—hell on wheels, Aura, a girl no older than Holly — struck me on my bare buttocks. That's what the world has come to! Forget Mothers for Peace. Take the twins and run!"

There was a pause, then Aura cleared her throat. "I feel very guilty. The way you kept saying everyone *else* was psychotic. That was a cry for help and I wasn't listening. Where are you, Raleigh? Is there somebody responsible I could talk to? Oh, sweetheart!"

Hayes spit out pieces of wood and lead. "Aura, you know I'd appreciate it at this moment if you wouldn't imply that I'm insane. By some hideous miracle, I am not. All I want to know from you is why you allowed Gates to hide out in 'Peace and Quiet.' "

"He's your brother, isn't he? But what's that —"

"And I am slightly curious about why you think the police are after me. Then I'm going to bed. The nuns put drugs in my cocoa and I'm woozy."

And so our hero learned from his wife that the Thermopylae police were still searching for an unidentified body that might belong to the shoe found beside the bloody Oriental rug in Joyner Construction Company's excavation at the corner of Broad and Elliot. He learned that the police had been looking for Mingo Sheffield because an anonymous phone call had led them to the site, and there they'd found two guns that proved to be registered in his name.

"Oh shit," muttered Hayes. His eyes fluttered wide open. "I threw those guns there."

"Honey, I'm not sure you should admit it. Of course, I can't be forced to testify. But that's what they already think. Booger's brother said he'd pulled you over right there at the scene. And they found one of your Mutual Life ballpoints in the rug. And, you might as well know, your fingerprints were all over the guns. They had you on file from the Police Safety Booth at the Civitan Fair last summer."

"Those shits." Then despite the news that he was wanted for murder, Hayes yawned.

"Raleigh, you do not sound like your old self. I'm very concerned about you. I know you didn't kill anyone —"

"Thanks." Hayes lay down on the bed and pulled the covers up. "You're right. I didn't. Neither did Mingo, who is the only person I *might* kill. I don't even know who they think *has* been murdered, if anybody, and I'm so tired I don't really care. This has probably been the worst day of my life. I'll sort everything out in the morning. And I'll call you. . . . And Jimmmm. . . ." Hayes yawned again. "Good night, Aura."

"I could jump in the car."

"Just hold down the fort. I'm okay, Mingo's okay, I'll find Daddy, don't worry, everything's okay."

"You know, Raleigh Hayes, I really do love you an awful lot."

"Thaz nice. 'Night."

"Call me."

" 'Night."

The small room was still and peacefully spare and blessedly quiet. The sheets were as crisp and clean as Hayes had once been certain he could keep his life. They were cool white sheets. They felt safe. They felt, thought the insurance man, sinking to sleep, like the sheets on Flonnie Rogers's bed, behind the blue quilted curtain that kept witches away.

CHAPTER

14

Sudden Impulses Overwhelm Our Hero

AT DAWN, Raleigh Hayes, achy all over, awakened to music, to glad voices singing a tuneful hymn. He lay there while other awakenings tumbled through time. He was at home, in bed beside Aura on a Sunday morning, reaching to turn off the radio alarm. He was a boy, shaking off sleep during services in the church that had once been his father's. He was a child, cuddled by Hayeses on the long porch swing, drowsy with their harmonies and the summer heat. Then his eyes opened on the white narrow room, the white metal bedstead. Had he been hospitalized? He saw above a little desk a tinted print of Christ leaning on a shepherd's hook, gazing contentedly at a solitary sheep, while the whole rest of the flock was escaping over the horizon. Mercy House. That's where he was. And the singers were Sisters.

In the hall outside his door lay a neat stack of his clothing, cleaned and pressed, even the shredded shirt. In one shoe was Jimmy Clay's bowling ball key chain. Hayes was in a hurry to find the Cadillac, especially as Aura had offered to buy it, and even more particularly as all his money was lying in his jacket on the front seat. Could an ex-criminal, even if now a nun, really be trusted to withstand such temptation? An unusually imaginative paranoia gripped Hayes. Had he really been drugged because the nuns wanted to rifle his car? What had they done with Mingo? Were these women really even nuns? Were they perhaps a covey of Lesbian racketeers, or feminist guerrillas infiltrating such pockets of conservatism as the rural Carolina lowlands? Were they cheering Aura because they *knew* her? And Sister Joe telling him those dogs he'd heard were the pedigreed St. Bernards that Mercy House sold to supplement their income. Might they not be training a canine attack squad for who knows what leftist cause?

Despite these odd forebodings, Hayes found the long white Cadillac parked right outside the front door. His jacket was there, the money was in it. The steamer trunk was there, and PeeWee's bust and Mingo's gun. The only thing changed was that the dealer plate was in the trunk, and the KISSY PU plate was on the car. The only thing missing was the radio; there was now a hole in the dashboard.

Hayes was trying to find his way back in the kitchen, in hopes that nuns were allowed to drink coffee, when he passed a glass-walled room where a crucifix, looking so human it scared him, hung suspended from the cathedral ceiling. Below it, a very young priest with a scanty mustache and loafers sticking out at the foot of his cassock stood at an altar draping black cloths over little objects. In a circle around him were all the nuns. Between Sister Anne and Sister Joe, and sharing their sheet music, was Mingo Sheffield, in one of his Hawaiian shirts, singing so hard that veins pulsed in his neck.

> *I bind this day to me forever,*
> *By power of faith, Christ's incarnation. . . .*

Mingo's ebullient baritone reveled with the sopranos like one of their St. Bernards rolling in flowers. Clearly his neighbor had made himself at home.

> *The whiteness of the morn at ev'en,*
> *The flashing of the lightning free,*
> *The whirling wind's tempestuous shocks,*
> *The stable earth, the deep salt sea.*

Yes, here was Mingo, a Gargantuan cherubim, merrily celebrating the same bolts of lightning that had scared him witless and caused all the disasters of last night. Here was Mingo, who had once informed Raleigh that the Vatican performed forced castrations on promiscuous priests and kept spies in the White House, here was this born-again-and-again Southern Baptist genuflecting and crossing himself and imitating everything else the nuns were doing, and no doubt, if no one stopped him, ready to jump in line for a Roman communion wafer as well.

The song the Sisters were ending, "St. Patrick's Breastplate," they sang in honor of the day, March 17, the Feast of Ireland's patron saint. And for the occasion, Sister Joe, announcing she was glad to say her parents came from Galway, read a tenth-century prayer by St. Brigid of Kildaire, which ended, shockingly, as far as Raleigh was concerned:

> *I would like a great lake of beer*
> *For the King of Kings.*
> *I would like to be watching Heaven's family*
> *Drinking it through all Eternity.*

Apparently, St. Brigid had been another one of those ne'er-do-well good-time Charlies, whose company the Savior preferred to that of decent men and women. Perhaps if Earley Hayes had been a tenth-century Irish Catholic instead of a Southern American Episcopal minister, a thousand years later, he too could have become a saint, instead of losing his job. Depicting Heaven as one big beer-blast in the sky was just the sort of sermon that (compounded with Roxanne Digges, and attempts to integrate his congregation) had led to Raleigh's father's dismissal.

In the cafeteria, Sister Anne, the smallest, oldest nun, gave Raleigh and Mingo some toast. "I'm so sorry but we haven't any eggs and bacon because we gave them up for Lent. But . . ." She paused, too meek either to talk or to leave, and silently hovered there, moving the jam jars first to the left, then to the right.

Mingo said, "I don't believe Baptists celebrate Lent, but I sure would hate to give up eggs."

Raleigh whispered, "Mingo, somebody took out the car radio."

"Oh, yeah, I gave it to the Sisters for their truck. They just love music and we don't really need it."

Hayes's gulp of coffee scalded his throat. Trying to censor himself in front of the benignly smiling nun, he started to splutter. "Ah, pardon me, but, ah, in fact, well, that's nice, but, do you recall a phone call you promised me you'd already made yesterday regarding that car, and *repeated* to me your pleasant conversation with Jimmy Clay?"

Sheffield's mouth turned sheepish. "I know, Raleigh. I made it up. I was too shy to call him."

"Too shy. Ah."

"And besides, I don't have enough money to buy that car, and besides, I don't want the police to know where I am." To Raleigh's horror, Mingo patted the nun's hand and told her, "The police are after me, Sister Anne, for a murder I didn't commit."

Desperately chuckling, Hayes shook his head. "For heaven's sake, don't exaggerate! He's joking, ha ha. Of course the police aren't after you. Could you excuse us for a minute, ma'am?" And prodding the fat man brusquely toward the coffee machine, Hayes poked him in the sternum with his finger. "I swear I don't know how much more of you I can take."

"Ouch! What did I do?"

Sheffield's outrageously unfeigned surprise was so exasperating, Hayes had to close his eyes as he said, "Do you realize *Jimmy* almost called the police on us, if Aura hadn't stopped him, and now *I* have to buy that Cadillac? No! Don't say a word. Did you even bother to call Vera? Do you realize that she's missing?"

A furtive mask froze Mingo's features. "She's in hiding. Leave her out of this."

"In hiding? Hiding from what? Never mind, don't tell me. I don't want to know. Now, look, as long as they don't have a body, they can't charge either of us with a crime. They have to demonstrate there was a death caused by murder."

"You're right! Habeas corpus. Raleigh, I always said you were smart."

Hayes sighed. "Corpus delicti, Mingo. Anyhow, I thought it all over last night, and I've decided we shouldn't get in touch with Chief Hood after all, because if we don't *know* they're looking for us, then we're not failing to comply, understand? So, remember, we know *nothing.*"

A thought began slowly to move the flesh around Sheffield's mouth. "Wait, you mean they think *you* did it too?"

Jolted, Raleigh blushed. Where was his brain? No one had told Sheffield why he was under suspicion; he didn't know the police had his guns because Raleigh had thrown them in that cursed hole. Given the facts, Sheffield might, in all fairness (and Hayes considered himself the fairest man he'd ever met), *blame* Raleigh for making him a wanted man. On further reflection, the awful truth was that if Raleigh hadn't taken those idiotic guns, and dumped them in a panic, he wouldn't now be stuck with Mingo at all. The realization that he'd flung this fat albatross around his own neck jarred the insurance agent so strongly, his body literally spasmed. He took a breath; embarrassing as it was to admit his folly to a fool (although, parenthetically, on the other hand, if the idiot hadn't claimed twice in one day to be trying to commit suicide, he, Raleigh, wouldn't have been forced to take responsibility for those guns), humiliating as it was, still it was only fair to say, "Mingo, I threw your pistols in the excavation where they found the rug and shoes. They have my fingerprints. At this juncture, they're far more likely to be 'after' me than you."

Sheffield squeezed both his friend's hands, sending a jolt of agony through the sprained wrist. "Raleigh! I'll never let them get you. If they try, they'll have to climb over my dead body. As God is my witness," and here he actually raised his right hand, "I swear, you can count on me. I know you're innocent and I'll tell that to every court in the land."

This was not the response Hayes would have made, and therefore not the response he expected; now he was even more embarrassed. Imbecilic as his neighbor's vow might be, there was nevertheless something touching about it that Hayes wanted to balance. "Let me explain about why I threw your guns away."

Sheffield squeezed him again. "I know why. You're my friend. Trying to save me from my darkest impulses, and I won't forget that, Raleigh, till the day I die. Old buddy."

Hayes, speechless, shook his head and returned to the breakfast table. With a punch of the swinging door, Sister Joe came into the room, pushing ahead of her an alarmingly emaciated, barefoot young woman with very short platinum hair in which very black roots were visible. This nun wore a coarse white robe, a rough-hewn cross, and had deep bruised circles under her eyes, as well as a scar across her cheekbone. She was introduced as the novice Mary Theresa, who'd broken into the Cadillac. To Raleigh's expression of gratitude and his offer to pay for the gasoline, she bowed, solemnly crossing her hands over her chest. To Sister Anne's request that she eat just one small piece of toast, she shook her head and backed slowly out of the room. Sister Joe explained that Mary Theresa was keeping a Lenten silent fast; all she would imbibe were juices and nuts — perhaps hypothesizing that even the Savior, wandering forty days in the desert, picked up in the occasional oasis the rare orange or almond.

"I noticed her bare feet," Mingo said. "It's like in *The Nun's Story.* When Audrey Hepburn was getting initiated, she couldn't even talk to her best friend and she had to lie on a stone floor all night. Finally, she just got married instead, or became a scientist, I forget which. I guess getting into the nunhood is about as hard as pro football."

"About," said Sister Joe.

Mingo poured another bowl of cereal. "Do you get to choose what you give up for Lent? I mean, does it have to be eggs, or dessert, like that?"

"Oh, it can be much worse," Sister Joe told him. "Me, I'm trying to give up thinking I could run the world better than the people in charge."

Raleigh, who shared this opinion, shook his head. "But what if you're right, why shouldn't you think so? That's false humility."

"Certainly is," she agreed. "That's why giving up eggs is a breeze, compared; why do you think pride is the worst sin in Hell, Mr. Hayes? Believe me, gluttony, lust, sloth, they're dog poop compared to pride."

Sister Anne shuffled quickly in her bedroom slippers to the door, as she invited Mingo Sheffield to follow her and "take a tour."

"Show him the puppies," called Sister Joe.

"I love puppies," Mingo said.

"Here's a thought, Mr. Hayes," Sister Joe went on, busily washing dishes. "We're both in the life insurance business. Ever think of that?"

No, Hayes had never thought he and the Church were in the same business; he assumed that the nun was talking about how, by piety, one could insure a place in Heaven, as opposed to Hell. Not believing in either as a destination, he had no more faith in that kind of insurance than his relatives (who gave every impression of not much believing in death — despite continual evidence to the contrary) had any interest in buying his kind of life insurance. His reply was therefore noncommittal. "I suppose so, in a sense."

Scraping more plates, the sweatshirted nun pursued her analogy. "Our premiums are higher, but then so's the payoff."

"Eternal life?" Hayes regretted his sarcasm as soon as he heard it; no need to sound ungrateful, given their hospitality.

But she grinned. "You bet. Anyhow, don't get me talking shop. I told you, I gave up advice for Lent. Otherwise, believe it, I'd be a real buttinski on your case, Hayes."

Affronted, Raleigh reached in his jacket for his spare spectacles. "I don't follow you," he said coldly as he blew on the glass.

Sister Joe rested her crossed arms on her athletically plump bosom. "Anything we can do to help? Cops? Lawyer?"

"No, thanks." Raleigh Hayes was not interested in sharing his problems; he never had been. He would drive for an hour searching for an address before he'd stop to ask directions. Of course, it rankled that circumstances prohibited his going immediately to the Mount Olive police station to file charges against those hoodlums. He, who'd never called on the police in his life; now, when he wanted them, they wanted him, for a capital crime. It simply wasn't fair. Of course, Hayes could have filed a complaint anyhow, returned home, sorted out with Chief Hood (a moron but a fellow Civitan) the misunderstanding over Mingo's guns, and so settled in again to his upright life. But the fact was, he didn't want to. Having once set out (however inadvertently, however irrationally), having once undertaken this idiotic quest, all of his will, the whole generative drive of his soul was now concentrated on its fulfillment. Nothing could keep him from completing, to the dot of the letter of the law, every task set him as a precondition to his father's return. His life was set aside, blinkered. He could see nothing but this goal and his unyielding resolve to reach it. Not because it was worthy, but because he had bent his character, his *self* to the task, and, for that cause, no one and nothing could stop him.

Before the Thermopyleans said good-bye to the Sisters of Mercy, Raleigh (now breezy in one of Mingo's mammoth Hawaiian shirts) borrowed the Mother Superior's office to telephone Aura. In his own room, a surly nun was already stripping the sheets for the next spiritual conference — some school guidance counselors on retreat from teenagers. The sour curve of this nun's mouth was reassuring to Hayes. All that good cheer and matter-of-fact kindness prominent in her ten companions had unsettled him. Why should God succeed in tricking nuns into happiness?

As it appeared that Aura had already left to "make up" at a television studio, he spoke only to Caroline, and to her only briefly, because Kevin was waiting.

"Waiting for what? Who is Kevin?"

"Oh, rilly, Daddy, you know, *Kevin.* Like *Kevin,* you know. Oh, Daddy, please please please don't sell the wagon, give it to me! We *need* three cars."

Hayes recalled with a groan that he'd bought a Cadillac. "You're too young," he said.

"I mean, it's toedully unfair. You and Mom are never home, like you aren't even interested in my whole life, and I don't have any clean clothes to wear, and then you treat me like a baby!"

"Caroline, I assure you I don't have any clean clothes to wear either, if that makes you feel any better."

Hayes was spared further comparisons of injustices committed against himself and his daughter, by her abrupt screech, "Ohmigod! Kevin's blowing up. Mommy said, tell you, call back this afternoon. Bye, Daddy, kiss kiss kiss."

Looking up from the buzzing receiver to the desk across the room, Hayes saw Sister Catherine, her plain intelligent face swathed in a white wimple, pulling the handle of an adding machine with the resigned look of a regular customer at a one-armed bandit in Atlantic City. She announced in her peaceful accent, "If the Church hadn't enjoined us to poverty, these bills certainly would. Thank God for the dogs."

Here was a subject with which Raleigh could genuinely sympathize. "Your mortgage must be horrendous, a place this big."

"Oh, heavens, Mr. Hayes, we could never afford to *buy* Mercy House; it's all we can do to keep our small charities going, the unemployment in this area is so bad, and the farms in such trouble. When I first came here, I could not believe the farms, how small they were, and poor."

"Are you from . . ." He was going to say "somewhere in Europe," but she had already said, "Wisconsin. Swedish."

"What are you doing in North Carolina?" he asked her.

"I was sent here."

"But why?"

She smiled. "One always wonders that, don't we?"

"I mean, there can't be many Catholics around here."

"Precious few," she admitted. "But we're not missionaries, Mr. Hayes. We're here because of Mercy House. It was bequeathed to us by a local gentleman." She pointed at a disgruntled photograph on the wall. "Poor man. He converted to Catholicism, and his family renounced him. And so he left his entire estate to us, but with the condition that we build on his land here in Mount Olive. I'm terribly afraid he did it for the express purpose of spiting his relations."

Raleigh, who was then searching his appointment book for the number of one of his own relatives, accidentally said what he was thinking. "Perhaps you should have refused to be a party to such a motive."

Sister Catherine looked at him. "What a foolish thought, young man."

Raleigh did not consider himself either foolish or young, and would have been pressed to say which accusation was more offensive. He walked back to the phone, and, reaching his cousin Jimmy Clay on the first ring, apologized for awakening him. He then hurried into an involved, although abridged explanation of why the Cadillac hadn't been returned, followed by queries about the car's cost and the station wagon's trade-in value. "Ned Ware can draw up the loan with Aura, Jimmy. Jimmy? Are you awake? What? Stop whispering. I can't hear you."

Muffled grunts replied. "Ungh, trying to sneak out of, ungh, cord's caught, damn, out of here, hold on, lemme shut, door here, one sec, damn, cord's too short, there!" Hayes then heard the click of a door closing and, immediately afterward, a startling whispered outburst from his cousin. "Raleigh! Guess what! You're looking at the happiest man alive! She's in there. She is, no kidding. Sweet yamakadamas, can you believe this, Raleigh? I did it! I did it, old Ral, twice! A big two! Listen, I can't talk now, got to get back before she wakes up. But I just want to thank you sincerely, okay, from the bottom of my heart. Sincerely."

Now Hayes was whispering as well. "Jimmy, what are you talking about? Thank me for what?"

"Oh, my group's gonna go wild about this! They were *so* right. About not tensing up, and just letting my feelings show. That was it. All it was. Huhuhhhuhuhheeheehuh." Mirth overcame Clay, as Raleigh took a stab at its source.

"Tildy's there?"

"All because of you."

"Me?"

"That angel gave me a ride home? After Mingo ran off after you in my car? She said she'd never seen me so, get this, Ral, 'virile' before! Me! The thing is, if you hadn't told me off — I mean, I know you didn't mean a word of it, just trying to get me in touch with my more assertive male potentials — and boy oh boy, did it work! When Tildy saw me light into Whaletail, well, she just gets goosebumps all over. How about that! Got to go, Ral, got to wake her up and see about getting married. You think I should? Or . . . Well, *I am so happy,* I'm hanging off the roof."

Raleigh glanced at the miserable philanthropist on the wall. "Jimmy, I'm sorry — I mean, I'm glad for you, but, isn't it against the law to marry your cousin?"

"Ral, don't get negative on me. You've got that tendency. Let's don't look for problems. 'Sides, we're only second cousins."

"No, Jimmy, Big Em and Lovie were sisters. That means —"

"No problem. Tildy was adopted, she told me so."

A preposterous claim, but why on earth had she made it? Except, of course, from an understandable desire to escape so disastrous a gene pool. Then again, suppose she was adopted? As Aunt Victoria lamented, the family often neglected to mention details.

"But, Ral, listen, I owe it all to you, Brainface, and I want you to be my best man, you will, won't you? Alllll . . . righhhhhttt! Bye-bye."

"Jimmy, the car!"

"Hey, no problem. I'm giving Aura the deal of a lifetime."

Having replaced the phone, Hayes walked to the window and muttered, "Deal of a lifetime."

"Were you speaking to me?" asked Sister Catherine, her hand still on the adding machine lever.

"No, ma'am." Raleigh said his farewells. Then on a sudden impulse he did something he instantly regretted. He took two hundred-dollar bills from his envelope of cash, and placed them quickly on her desk. Stiff-mouthed, he mumbled, "I'd like to offer a contribution, a payment, your hospitality, appreciate it."

The elderly nun looked at the money, then at the donor. He didn't smile and neither did she. Finally, she opened a drawer. "As payment, it's too much. As a gift . . ." She took out a pad. ". . . It's lovely of you, and it's tax deductible. I'll give you a receipt."

Hayes was still blushing when he left. Blushing because he had thrown away two hundred dollars on Catholic nuns when he only gave ten dollars a week to his own church, on whose records his contributions were publicly acknowledged, and privately compared: if he were going to throw away money, he should have at least done it where he'd get the credit for it. Blushing, too, because he felt it might have been more honorable had he left the money anonymously behind at Mercy House, or at least not so eagerly accepted the tax receipt. His scruples were ethical; they had nothing to do with Christianity; as he'd explained to Sister Joe, he was not interested in insuring his immortality. Eternity was too much to get through. Life was hard enough.

His own ethics did interest our hero, and these he kept considering even after Mingo and he were back on the road. He was bothered by Sister Joe's notion that pride should fling someone into Hell's lowest depths. Why in the world should pride — reasonable, legitimate pride, now; not unjustified conceit (as if he thought himself as bright as Einstein), or deluded vanity (as if he imagined every woman he met desired him) — but why should a proper, appropriate pride in authentic virtues (for who could deny that Raleigh Hayes was a decent, responsible, intelligent citizen, a faithful husband and a good provider), why should pride like his be a sin worse than hoggish gluttony, worse than bestial lust, worse than improvidence! It was utterly infuriating that he should be made to feel guilty for feeling a little proud that within the puny borders of his admittedly insignificant life, he had done nothing to disgrace himself or injure others.

Our hero harbored no aspirations for glory or grandeur, even moral grandeur. Naturally he hoped that *if* Life, hurling together its great chronicle, should fling him for a conspicuous instant forward into singularity, then he would acquit himself as well as the next man. He liked to think he would have hidden Anne Frank in his attic. But not since high school had he been absurd enough to believe Life had any grandiose plans for him at all. He was not going to lead a nation, an army, a cause, nor cure cancer, not paint masterpieces, nor sail the farthest, run the fastest, build any fortune or following or *any* better mousetap to bring America running to his doorstep — not even so fast-forgotten a mouse trap as the hoola hoop. Not only had no heroic role been written for Raleigh W. Hayes, he was the most minor of minor characters in the epic of his age; in all likelihood, he would never be noticed beyond the limits of Thermopylae, and, except possibly by his descendants, would soon be only a vague memory there.

This modest appraisal caused Mr. Hayes no grief. If he was not to be even a footnote in history's book — and over the centuries, how many thousands, now nameless, had scrabbled to get there — what difference, in the last analysis, had even the greatest heroes made? The Caesars and Christs? In the last analysis, the world tumbled on, wobbling through millennia, a speck on an infinitesimal granule of space, a drop in the bucket of chaos. So what? He could still, he *would* still, take pride that among the microscopic scintillas called man, he, Raleigh W. Hayes, was a virtuous specimen.

As the insurance man silently conversed with himself in this way, beside him in the Cadillac, Mingo Sheffield (the lump poking from the center of his forehead making him look as if he were about to turn into a unicorn) smoked and babbled. "I guess you couldn't ask for a nicer bunch of nuns anywhere, hunh, Raleigh?"

"Um hum."

"Poor old Sister Anne. I forgot what she called her leg disease. Wasn't she sweet? I told her I was going to come see her again, and take one of their marriage retreats. Vera'll love it there. And that poor little Mary Theresa, you wouldn't believe the life she's had. You didn't get a chance to talk to her, but I swear. Before she met Jesus, she was in women's prison three different times, and even tried to stab her own daddy with a fork. Then she fell in with a bad crowd. Her girl friend gave her that scar while she was sleeping! But she ought to eat more. I want Vera to sit down and talk to her about how dieting can be pretty damn dangerous if you don't have the right information. Hey, did you see that? 'Eat at Chill's. Where the Bill Won't Kill.' That's cute! One mile. Let's stop, okay? I've got to have some eggs or I'm nothing all day."

Raleigh had between his legs the map Sister Joe had drawn him to the Woodrow Wilson Nursing Home; he was glancing from that to the rattling truck in front of the Cadillac, an old truck heaped with swaying crates of noisy, crowded chickens. White feathers whirled out in a trail, as if the birds were frantically attempting to lead some rescuer down the route of their kidnappers. Raleigh said, "We just ate. I thought that novice was supposed to be keeping a silent vigil. How come she was out there telling you her entire life story?"

"I guess she forgot while we were fixing the car. Listen, Raleigh, lucky Mary Theresa noticed we had dealer plates. She says cops will pull you right over if you're using them at night. She showed me a lot of tricks, too, to get away from the highway patrol. So, I start telling her about the first time Vera and I were born again right after my mama died, and I was having the worst spell of those dark impulses, you know, to just shoot myself or something, and so Mary Theresa starts telling me about this priest that taught the poetry class at her prison, and so we start exchanging our lives, you know how it is. 'FIVE HUNDRED YARDS TO CHILL'S CHILIDOGS.' "

Oh, yes, Raleigh remembered the Sheffields' summer of salvation; he'd been the one forced by the Starry Haven Residents Rules Committee to call upon his neighbors and make clear to them that their evangelistic assaults on the subdivision had to stop. They were ringing doorbells at dinnertime, pretending to borrow a cup of sugar or a pint of milk, and then, once in the kitchen, pulling out their Bibles on unsuspecting acquaintances, whom they attempted to redeem then and there. Raleigh remembered how they would even bring their Bibles to the Starry Haven pool, and how as soon as they were spotted in their bright gigantic beach robes, the whole crowd would duck under water and frog-kick furiously to the far end.

"Raleigh, you're passing Chill's. Oh, well, it's gone out of business anyhow, poor thing."

Hayes caught a peripheral glimpse of stained stucco, smashed windows, and dangling sideways from the roof a washed-out sign in the shape of a hotdog with human arms and legs. "What a world of trash," sighed Raleigh Hayes, who had no idea that he was repeating a phrase he had often heard in childhood, when he had already begun, young as he was, to share with the old black woman washing his grandmother's porch her contempt for folly and her intolerance of what she called — although Flonnie Rogers had never read Nietzsche — "God's first mess-up, this old world of trash."

In Which Is Continued a Conversation
Begun Thirty Years Ago

NOT EVEN RALEIGH'S FATHER could remember a time when Flonnie Rogers had not lived in the old sprawling house on East Main. She'd simply shown up one day in 1906, a short, wiry, sharp-tongued young woman, to begin a job no one had quite realized they were offering her, had moved into her cubicle at the back of the stairs, hung up her blue quilts and her string of red pepper charms, and had stayed, terrifying generations of Hayes children with her tales of bogeymen and bobcats and monstrous slave masters. Raleigh's first frightened memory of Flonnie was watching her throw aside her mop, haul his cousin Paschal up the porch steps by his hair, push him down beside her on the stoop, and shockingly force the boy's hand to close around her big toe. Paschal had been choosing "It" in a Kick-the-Can game by the old rhyme,

> *Eenie meenie meinie moe*
> *Catch a nigger by his toe.*
> *If he hollers, let him go.*
> *Eenie meenie meinie moe.*

Flonnie gripped Paschal's hand. "You hear *me* holler? *You* the one hollering now. Now, you cotch my toe, and now I let you go right over my knee, I hear you say that again!"

Paschal had run, and Raleigh had run after his older cousin into the side yard, where he found Paschal kicking in a rage at the trunk of the crabapple tree, and cursing, "Damn stupid old nigger, damn her, stupid old, stupid old nigger." That evening Raleigh's father had instructed them to change the rhyme word to "tiger." He said Flonnie had raised him and all Raleigh's aunts and uncles, and if the two of them couldn't see what was wrong with their game song in general, remember in particular that Flonnie was a member of their family.

Flonnie often said that the new generation of Hayeses was an even worse batch than the first had been, more evidence that the world was racing to its trashy conclusion. She had no use for the new. As late as the 1950s, she'd kept her chickens in the backyard, and her chamber pot under her bed, would not eat canned vegetables unless she'd "put them up" herself, and would not cook on an electric stove. She was a Tory and a moral aristocrat, she would have no truck with loud-mouthing trash, white or black, George Wallace or Little Richard. She was a reactionary and a radical.

The young child Raleigh had thought that Flonnie's refusals to drink from a particular water cooler or eat at a particular lunch counter were her own idiosyncratic, ornery rules, imposed for the incomprehensible reasons that all adults gave whenever they said, "No." Soon enough, his father made it clear to him that the rules were idiosyncrasies of the town, of the South, and of the nation, and that Flonnie's pride lay in her *choosing* to go into the rest room for "Women" not "Ladies," so that she never gave the world a chance to make her acknowledge that she had no choice but to obey their rules. As a young teenager, Raleigh had tried once to let her know that he understood her stance and wished to congratulate her on her contempt for the South. She called him trash for bad-mouthing his homeland.

By then, not only had Raleigh's grandfather Clayton died, but several of Clayton's many children had died too, and the rest had started their own homes, so that no one lived in the big house but Raleigh's grandmother, Ida, and Flonnie Rogers. In the end, the two women were closer to each other than to anyone else. They tormented one another as only the intimate can. On visits, Raleigh would sit with them in the back parlor at night, close to the kerosene stove whose long twisting pipe disappeared into blue flowers on the wallpaper. Every night, Flonnie would slowly place on her nose the gold-framed spectacles that were looped by a piece of twine to the thin plastic belt on her dress. Slowly, she'd unfold the *Thermopylae Evening Star,* and begin silently to read, the paper held in front of

her face. "My my my," she'd mutter in a loud whisper. And, "That's pitiful." And, "What's happening to this world?"

Flonnie could read, and Ida Hayes could not. Raleigh had often been
told that his grandmother had never had the opportunity for the education he was (supposedly) enjoying, that she'd worked on the line at the
textiles factory from the time she was eight until the day his grandfather
(a Thermopylae college boy and a dandy) had seen her, at sixteen, walking
with a friend along the industrial railroad tracks, and, then and there, had
told his brother, "I'm going to marry that girl with the ribbon in her
braid." That was the family story. As to how Flonnie Rogers had learned
to read, no one knew; she'd said it was none of Raleigh's business when
he'd asked her.

On visits to the old house, lying on the hook rug, reading his own
book, Raleigh would listen to the metallic tick of the brass-bell clock, and
the rustle of the paper bag on his grandmother's lap as she shelled butter
beans, and the flurried shake of Flonnie's newspaper as she deliberately rattled in the other woman's face a mysterious world of printed pathos and
catastrophe. "Good Lord amercy!" Flonnie would gasp, as if she'd just read
that Mars was going to crash into downtown Thermopylae in the morning.

"What?" Raleigh would ask, but the tiny black woman would shake her
head. The sound of the clock would come back until in a while a low
snuffling sound seemed to escape Flonnie against her will.

"What's so funny?" Raleigh would ask.

"Nothing funny," she'd reply, the whites of her eyes elaborate with a
pretense of innocence.

And Ida Hayes just as ostentatiously pretended to be oblivious of the
turning pages. She took her revenge by changing the radio stations to soap
operas or news programs while Flonnie was listening to one of her baseball
games, a love of which sport she shared with (or had acquired from) the
rest of the Hayeses, some of whom had played semiprofessionally, one of
whom (Hackney) had died in the outfield during the eighth inning of a
hot summer's game. That radio's lethargic litany of balls called, strikes
swung on and missed, was the sound that the Hayes house always made in
Raleigh's memory. "It's a long drive ... up ... up ... up ... Willie Mays
is going *over,* he's back ... He's ... GOT IT! An unbelievable catch!"
During such rising static of activity, Ida Hayes would reach out and turn
the dial. Flonnie never looked up, but soon the newspaper would start to
flutter again, and its reader to sigh or chuckle or mutter, "Well, I never!"

* * *

On the "sun porch" of the Woodrow Wilson Nursing Home, at the far end of a small rectangular slab of dirty gray concrete, Flonnie Rogers sat in a wheelchair, reading a newspaper.

"I'm sure you won't recognize me, Flonnie, but I'm Raleigh Hayes. Hayes? My grandfather was —"

"Don't you shout at me, Earley. It aggravates through my ear machine like a pig squealing."

"Earley's my father, Flonnie."

"You bring me some snuff?"

"I'm *Raleigh,* Earley's son."

"Humph. You look just like Earley, but not so good."

In Hayes's opinion, Flonnie Rogers did not look so good either. She'd faded to a sooty gray, skin, lips, and nails; her feet and hands were gray gnarled little roots. Her white icicle hair had thinned to limp gray wisps; her snarl had thinned to a whine. Everything had shrunk except the bright false teeth. Nevertheless, Raleigh had known the minute the nurse opened the glass door to the sun porch who that shriveled creature was, hunched over in the metal wheelchair. Magnified now by enormously thick lenses, her eyes were as angry as ever. The eyes and the stooped hump of her shoulders gave her the look of a small old hawk.

"Who's that fat grinning man behind the window?" she asked Hayes testily. "That Furbus? Why y'all wearing those ugly shirts? You back in that band?"

"No. Furbus is dead, I'm afraid. That's my neighbor, Mr. Sheffield. We wanted to see how you were doing."

The look of contempt with which the old woman greeted this bit of politesse set Raleigh's ears on fire, while he stammered on, "And to bring you this package from Aunt Lovie."

"I had a squirrel cross my path first thing this morning. That's a bad sign. Looked up, saw a flock of sparrows head by. That's a good sign. Now which brings you? You was a little boy, you didn't believe in my signs. You worried at me all the time how you had the answer for everything smarter than me."

"I didn't think you'd remember me, Flonnie."

"'Member how you pestered. Let me see your hands." Hers were crooked, rough, light as bird bones. Then, before Hayes could pull away, she spit into her palm, rubbed her saliva over his swollen wrist and over his knuckles (still cut from last night's fight with the Hell's Angels).

Raleigh stammered, "What are you doing?"

"No warts. You get you a piece of liver on that eye."

Staring appalled at his sticky hands, Hayes said, "How are *you* doing, Flonnie? Everything okay?"

"I'm a hundred and one."

"That's just amazing. How do you feel?"

"How you think? Axe yourself how you feel when you get this old. It's all hurt and it's nuthin' works. Cain't do nuthin' no more." She leaned to look out at a yard of small sparse garden plots, two-foot squares of a few weedy flowers, a few limp vegetable seedlings.

"I'm sorry to hear that," said Hayes. He thought of Flonnie's old garden, behind the big house, stretching on forever down the block, great green trees of tomatoes and corn, great leaves like fans shading squash too heavy to carry, high nets hung with long peas and fat cucumbers, and all the dark brown earth magically full of carrots and radishes, onions and yams. He thought of the big mahogany table in the dining room, crowded with butter beans and okra and turnips and melons. "I'm sorry," he said again.

"I'm on my way and cain't turn back, spite of all the world. I'm waiting for the word." Frowning, Flonnie shifted her slight weight in the wheelchair. Despite the warm morning sun, she was heavily padded round with thin, cheap blankets, and her arms trembled when she tried to undo all the tape haphazardly wound about Lovie's gift. Raleigh helped her tear it open. Cans of Tuberose snuff rolled out. A red, marked-down heart-shaped box of Valentine candy was there, with three pairs of white socks, a comb, a boy's cardigan sweater with with the letter "C" sewn on it, and two tabloid newspapers like the one Flonnie already had in her lap: the sort that told of the seventy-year-old Liverpool woman who'd been raped by Satan and given birth to triplets with hooves; of the Iowa man who'd buried twenty-eight bodies in his backyard without his neighbors noticing; of the Brooklyn wife who'd had her husband's ashes (at his request) made into an egg timer; of the night of shame Liz Taylor could never forget; and in general, of the world of trash Flonnie Rogers knew she'd been obliged to live in.

The old woman held up a gaudy bottle of inexpensive cologne. "What's that fool Lovie think I want with this? She think I'm fixing to jump up and go someplace I need to smell like this? I wisht she'd send me a radio, that be something I could use."

Raleigh picked up the snuff cans that had fallen to the floor. "Lovie wants you to come home, Flonnie, and live with them. This place . . ." Hayes shook his head at the Woodrow Wilson Nursing Home. It was grimy and dim and cheap and mean. The furniture was spare and graceless;

so was the building, so was the staff. In the lounge he had seen two very old ill black men sitting side by side on a cracked vinyl couch. Their hands rested loosely in their laps. Their heads never moved, their eyes were glazed and patient, except when a doctor walked by. Then they flinched, hands tightening, eyes widening, until the white person had passed them. "Lovie really —"

Flonnie opened a snuff can. "Lovie don't own me. Y'all not my home. I'm beholden to nobody."

"Well, gosh, Flonnie, you lived at Grandpa's more than fifty years."

"I earned my pay." She pushed snuff up in her gums. "Miz Hayes had her day's work."

"That's not what I mean. I meant the family naturally feels —"

"I laid Miz Hayes out in her rose-print dress. That was her particular favorite. With her white earbobs belonged to Serene 'fore she passed. Reba come in and ask me, 'Which you think Mama looks best in?' Her rose-print's what I said, 'cause I knew how it was her favorite. Vicky Anna didn't know, been gone so long, couldn't tell her own mama from a dead catfish in a mudhole. I tole her and tole her, 'Miz Hayes, don't you try to rake in those leaves, you stay in that bed.' "

Flonnie Rogers had hired her own limousine to ride to Ida Hayes's funeral. She'd sat alone in the backseat of the long black Cadillac, her head just visible in the rear window, her red straw hat a flag of mourning and defiance. Then, she'd moved without explanation out of the Hayes house before Victoria Anna moved in, abruptly left as mysteriously as she'd arrived, taking with her the tin trunk she'd kept half a century under her goosedown mattress.

"Aunt Vicky says hello," Hayes lied.

"Humph."

"And, well, the truth is, Flonnie, I'm looking for Jubal Rogers."

She looked at him sharply. "For her?"

"Her?" Raleigh took a breath and looked up at the sky. "Daddy's sick, Flonnie. My daddy, Earley. He wants to see Jubal Rogers, and he wants me to find him and give him some money, and bring him to New Orleans. I don't know, I mean, were they friends or something? He's your relative, isn't he?"

Flonnie spat out a dark squirt of snuff.

"The point is, Flonnie, Daddy is seriously endangering his health by checking out of the hospital and leaving town, and what he wants is for me to bring him this person named Jubal Rogers. . . . Well, Lovie said to ask you."

Flonnie leaned over with a painful slowness and spat again into the scraggly grass. "Where's Hackney?"

"You mean Bassie? Hackney died a long time ago, Flonnie. Remember? Before Grandma died."

"I laid her out."

"Yes. I know. Bassie's not well, he had a stroke."

"Miz Hayes sent me out to the woods with his suitcase. She said, tell him, quit those cards and come home with me, or she be gone when he get back. I set that suitcase down in the middle of all those white men. Pack of fools. I set it down right smack on top of the cards. Back he come laughing, swinging that bag."

"Are you talking about Grandpa?"

"You're Earley's boy."

"That's right. Flonnie, you took me once to meet your sister? Was she Jubal's mother?"

Her eyes squinted hard behind the thick lenses. "You're Raleigh. All the time pestering me 'bout my burial 'surance. Your mama died of the diphtheria. Nothing but a child."

"No, that was my father's first wife. Grace Louise. My mother was Sarah. Somebody told me Jubal might have moved to Chicago?"

"I'm not studying Jubal. You the police?"

"No, I'm in insurance. I'm trying to find Jubal to give him some money."

"I'm all paid up, my funeral's paid in full."

"That's good." Hayes tried to smile. "But you don't look like you'll be needing a funeral any time soon."

The old look withered him. "I don't truck with a lie. I'm going over Jordan. Sooner the better. This world and me don't get on and never did. It's not worth nuthin'."

Raleigh was stung by her retort about his polite lie, stung into honesty. "You're right. It's not. So what does that make of the Lord you were always snapping at me to respect more? You think it's 'smart' to respect whoever made such a shabby mess?"

"You bring me some snuff?"

To Raleigh's astonishment, the salt of tears stung his eyes. He couldn't see the woman in the wheelchair. He saw forty years back, the woman with her hoe, angrily stabbing weeds and flinging them over her shoulder out of her careful garden. That woman, her thin strong arms bright in the summer heat, was saying, "You think God Almighty cares how much you respect Him, a skinny little boy like you? He don't care what the President thinks."

"Well, I don't care about Him either. I think He's stupid," said the small boy behind her, the wicker basket so laden with soft red tomatoes, he had to loop both elbows under the handle.

The woman spun around, clinched his chin in her dark hand, and jerked his head straight up at the hot, unclouded sky. "You make you one of *those*," she snapped. "You fixing to try it, you so smart? Or one of *these*." She yanked a long crooked carrot sliding out of the earth. "See this little finger? Look here! You see this little nail on it?" she clicked the tiny nail, clogged with dirt, rough-edged, on her small moving finger. "That's just a little ugly thing. It ain't nuthin'. Well, little boy, you make me one, and bring it on here to me, and then maybe I listen to you telling me how you just as smart as the Almighty Lord."

The glass door to the sun porch of the Woodrow Wilson Nursing Home shuddered open, startling Raleigh Hayes, and he kept blinking until the past went away. An overweight nurse in a dingy uniform called, "Ten-thirty. She's got to go to P.T. now." Flonnie growled as the woman came closer.

What, at this point, physical therapy was supposed to do for Flonnie Rogers except cause her discomfort, Hayes couldn't imagine. He stopped the wheelchair with his hand. "Okay. Just one second. Flonnie, please, I'd really appreciate it if you'd help me find Jubal. I'm scared Daddy is going to, I'm scared he may die before I can get there, and do this for him, I guess." Stooping down, Hayes rewrapped the package in her lap, and slid one of the snuff cans into her bathrobe pocket. "Please. Do you know where Jubal is? Flonnie?"

Flonnie put her thin dry finger to his mouth. "Hush," she whispered. "Don't you tell anybody, you hear me? Jubal's still down in Charleston, Earley. Still working at the Bayou Lounge. But don't mess with him. Leave it lie. Just leave it lie."

"Pardon?" Raleigh's legs were cramping as he stayed bent down beside her.

"Hold still," she told him. She roughly brushed his hair back with her fingers. "I don't want to catch y'all down in Darktown again, messing with those jugband niggers. They going no place but Hell. The Lord's got His special mark on you, Earley. I can feel it. I got the power to feel it. He's chose you. If the law don't hang you first."

Raleigh lost his footing when the impatient nurse nudged the wheel-

chair forward. "Poor old thing," she said briskly. "She doesn't know where
she is, nine days out of ten."

"I hope that's true," he replied.

So disturbed was Hayes by the old woman's confusing him with his father — as if he'd intruded on the most intimate moments in the man's life,
and so gained knowledge he shouldn't have, and didn't want — so shaken
was he by Flonnie's strange elision of all the past and all the people in it,
that he walked right past Mingo Sheffield in the lobby. Sheffield was trying to bring in the picture on an ancient television set by twisting the aluminum foil atop its rabbit ears. The two old men, still seated together on
the vinyl couch, watched him.

"Hey, Raleigh, where're you going? Raleigh, wait! . . . Well, so long,
you two. I can't fix it any better. Y'all sure could use a new set. Bye-bye.
RALEIGH! Wait up! Where're we going? You find that colored mental
patient your daddy wants to marry? That wasn't her in the wheelchair, was
it?"

Mingo kept talking as Hayes drove angrily back to the intersection of
stores he'd noticed coming in, the huddled cluster of McDonald's, K
marts and Pizza Huts that were now nourished by even the small Southern hamlets. "Everybody in that place," Mingo was saying, "was so old
it was sad, wasn't it? Didn't you think so? If my mama hadn't died,
I sure wouldn't put her in a place like that, and neither would Vera.
I don't mean 'cause they were Negroes. I wouldn't put her in there if it
was white. Ned Ware did. Put his mother in one. Just because she
wrapped up the garbage in Christmas paper. Do you think that's fair?
And she got killed, too, because they didn't have a rubber mat in the
bathtub."

"Stay in the car, Mingo, I'll be right back."

But when Raleigh returned with his package from the discount appliance store, Sheffield had disappeared. Finally Hayes found the fat man in
line at the counter of Kentucky Fried Chicken, where he was ordering biscuits, corn on the cob, and a bucket of Extra Crispy.

"Mingo, for God's sake! It's not even eleven-thirty!"

Eleven-thirty! Aura! Wasn't she supposed to be on television at eleven?
"Mingo, quick, I've got to go back to the appliance store. Quick. Pay."

Flushed, Sheffield turned around to whisper, "Can you lend me twelve
dollars? I just remembered they took my money, the drug gang."

"They took mine, too," snapped Hayes. "You've got money in your
shoes."

"That's for emergencies."

"Look, you've got fifties, Mingo. All I've got is hundreds. Use your damn shoes. Come on!"

The teenagers serving Sheffield were now staring openly at the two men, one thin, one fat, both in flowered Hawaiian shirts, both with black eyes, the fat one groaning as he squatted to remove his wide suede oxford and shake a folded bill from its toe.

It was 11:23 when Hayes made it back to the double row of television sets lining the back wall of the appliance store, a cavernous, nearly deserted place.

"Gollee! Raleigh, it's AURA! Isn't it? That's Aura! Look at her, she's all over. Here. And here. There must be fifteen of her. She's on every set! Aura! She's famous!" Sheffield, with a red-and-white bag of food under each huge arm, bobbed his head joyfully at the long row of televisions, where, indeed, Aura Hayes smiled in all shades of color and focus. She smiled, in full close-up, and said, "Let me answer your question this way. What Congressman Lukes doesn't seem to understand is, we already have enough nuclear weapons to blow up the *entire* world thirty times over. Do we really want to spend trillions of our taxpayers' dollars so we can blow it up thirty *times* thirty? If we're all floating on a sea of gasoline, do we really want to play macho games about who can stockpile the most matches?" Applause rattled the sets.

Raleigh's heart was thudding. Here was his wife, sounding so poised, looking so crisp in a blue blouse and beige suit he didn't think he'd ever seen. He was angry and proud and mesmerized.

"It's Mothers for Peace!" shouted Mingo. "Hot damn!"

"Shut up, I can't hear."

Congressman Lukes was saying something about wanting to shove the Russians back to the line, hold them there, and when we fight, fight to win. Aura was saying, "That sounds like teenaged locker-room talk to me. This country is not a football game. We don't need a coach trying to prove his masculinity by shooting off bigger and bigger rockets. We need a congressman trying to help us save the human race."

"Oh shit," Raleigh groaned. "Aura, you're going to get us sued!"

Shouts of "NO MORE LUKES. NO MORE NUKES" had burst out, and the screens switched to the poster-waving studio audience. It was mostly female, mostly shouting, and some of it was familiar. "Mingo, there's VERA. Good God, there's Barbara Kettell and Wayne Sparks and NEMOURS!"

Sheffield pulled the chicken leg out of his open mouth to shout, "VERA! You're supposed to be in hiding!"

The hostess of *Woman Alive!*, a young handsome woman with tawny streaked hair, paced the aisles with her microphone. "Please, ladies, let's keep it down, and try to get in one more question!"

Barbara Kettell leaped to her feet, swatting at her livid husband's flattop beside her as he grabbed at her poncho in an effort to pull her down. "Yes," she panted nervously. "I have a question for Mr. Lukes. Yes. Well, it's this. He says he wants to get the government off our backs and out of our lives, and I agree, and then he says it ought to be against the law for any woman to have an abortion even if she's raped because it's the same as murder. So that's my question."

"*What's* your question?" asked the hostess. But Mrs. Kettell had abruptly disappeared from the screen, presumably jerked back into her seat by her spouse, the apoplectic president of the Civitans Club and chairman of the Re-Elect Charlie Lukes Committee.

As the camera turned back to Aura, she was seated in a swivel chair across a coffee table from the congressman. "Perhaps," she smiled (and the smile made Raleigh whisper, "Uh oh"), "perhaps, Mrs. Kettell's question is to ask Mr. Lukes whether he's ever been raped."

"Now, hold on, Mrs. Hayes." Charlie Lukes held up a hand. He was a thickset, jowly man in his late fifties, whose fluffy hair looked like a wig and whose gray polyester suit looked too tight. He gave Aura a smile as specious as her own. "I may not be a murderer or a murder victim, but I sure as shooting can make the judgment that murder's a crime." The Lukes faction clapped.

Aura leaned forward. "Why is abortion murder, and the deaths of those millions and millions of innocent men, women, and children, those 'acceptable losses' killed in your 'winnable' nuclear war not murder?" She sat back to applause from her faction.

Lukes held the hand up again. "I know Barbara Kettell personally," he told the camera. "Known and admired her for years. I know she's a fine mother and a fine wife and just a darn sweet gal, and I'm certain her friend here, Mrs. Hayes, is just the same. So I don't mind taking the time to come try to shed some light on these vital issues with the public and with these ladies, whose interests couldn't be more sincere I don't have a doubt in the world. But, ladies, pardon me, the topic here today is our struggle to rebuild our military strength in order to insure a lasting peace and honor throughout the globe, and I'll be danged if I see what that's got to do with abortion, which is a profound and sacred issue too, but as these ladies are not lawyers or doctors —"

Aura snapped, "First, Mr. Lukes, how dare you assume we aren't! Second, *you* are not, and never have been, a doctor, a lawyer, or for that matter, a professional anything except a professional bigot and a warmonger, whose only political experience prior to your *regrettable* election to Congress was using the Thermopylae zoning board to keep blacks out of decent housing!"

"WHY DON'T YOU GO HOME WHERE YOU BELONG?" yelled a male voice, and claques of "*Yeahs!*" and "*Boos!*" fought through the television speakers.

"Was that Nemours yelled that?" whispered Mingo, the chicken leg still poised at his mouth.

"Sir, no food allowed in this store!" A prissy salesman pushed himself between the Thermopyleans and the televisions. "You'll have to take that outside. We have a rule that —"

"Will you please be quiet!" Hayes shouted at him. "I'm trying to watch this!" He craned to see around the man. Aura, Lukes, the audience, and the hostess all seemed to be talking at once.

"You can't shout at me like that, sir." The clerk now started turning off all the sets. "And you two can't stand around watching TV for free either."

"Free?" Hayes, losing his temper, thrust a stapled bag in the salesman's prunish face. "I just bought a $49.95 radio in here not ten minutes ago! And frankly, there's not another goddamn soul in your whole goddamn stupid store, so what's it to you?!"

"That's true," said Mingo wistfully. "It's just like Knox-Bury's. I'm glad I'm gone."

The clerk, still clicking off sets as fast as he could, asked Hayes to take his profanity elsewhere, and asked Sheffield to just take a look at the chicken litter all over the floor. And, as *Woman Alive!* appeared to be off the air, and the few remaining screens were now filled with cats doing the mambo, the Civitans didn't argue with the seething clerk, but left.

"If I'd known a radio meant so much to you, Raleigh, I wouldn't have given ours to the nuns. Can you believe that was Aura?"

"Frankly no."

"She's real photogenic. Didn't you think she was as good as Ingrid Bergman, when she talks back to her judges in *Joan of Arc?*"

Raleigh passed two cars at once. "That seems to me an ominous, if not a prescient, comparison."

"What?"

"Never mind. Mingo, since Vera is obviously not in hiding, perhaps you wouldn't mind telling me why you thought she was?"

Sheffield nibbled his corn on the cob, sometimes rotating the ear, sometimes shooting his teeth down the cob like a typewriter return. "Well, she can't tell a lie."

"Oh?"

"So we decided she ought to go to her sister's." The teeth gnawed to the end of a row, and reversed. "If the police had really gotten to her, it'd have been all over for me."

Raleigh swung the white Cadillac into the driveway that led to Woodrow Wilson Nursing Home. "Please try to remember, Mingo, you didn't murder anybody. You aren't guilty. There's nothing *to* hide. Except throwing all that paint on Knox-Bury's merchandise." He parked the car.

"I wouldn't go back to work for Billy Knox for love or money."

"I doubt he's going to offer you much of either. Excuse me a minute."

"Where are you going? Hey, we just left here. Raleigh? Raleigh!"

When Hayes asked to speak to Flonnie Rogers, he was told that she was still in physical therapy and couldn't be disturbed. And so he left the radio for her at the reception desk. He wrote her a note, which he pinned to the bag.

> Dear Flonnie.
> Enjoy the games. Take care of yourself.
> Yours, Raleigh (Earley's son)

He straightened the piece of paper, wondering again, for the first time in more than thirty years, how Flonnie Rogers — who claimed she'd never been to school — had learned to read; wondering, for the first time, why his grandmother — in those decades of evenings alone together with the black woman — had been too proud to ask Flonnie to teach her.

16

In Which Raleigh and Mingo Fall into a Swamp

OUR TRAVELERS headed away from Mount Olive and the high tangled cliffs of the Neuse River, headed deeper into Carolina's flat coastal plain. In Calypso, they stopped for Mingo to buy a liter of Pepsi-Lite and use the bathroom. Raleigh called Aura. No answer. He called the realtor who managed "Peace and Quiet," his Kure Beach cottage, but she didn't answer either. There was no phone in the cottage; there was no choice but to drive there. It would be infuriating if his half-brother Gates really were hiding out (and from what?) in Raleigh's property. It would also be infuriating if he had disappeared. Since first grade, when he'd stolen Raleigh's meticulous model airplanes and sold them at recess for a quarter apiece, Gates had never done anything but cause trouble.

In Warsaw, they stopped for Mingo to use the bathroom and buy some cigarettes. Raleigh continued making phone calls while the fat man charged to his Visa card two cartons of Viceroys, a box of peanut brittle, a cream container with a cow muzzle spout, and a souvenir Confederate cap.

Oddly enough, the insurance man's temporary secretary actually answered his office phone. "Raleigh W. Hayes. Mutual Life. Would you hold please?" Hayes then found himself listening to Frank Sinatra warbling, *"Lauraaaa . . . is the face in the misty light. Footsteps . . ."* Had Betty

Hemans rigged Musak to his telephone? " *'And you see Lauraaaa. . . .'* Thank you for waiting. How may I help you please?"

"Betty? It's Raleigh Hayes. Where's that music coming from?"

"Why, hello, Raleigh! I'm sorry I put you on hold."

"That's okay. Where's that —"

"I was just this minute where Lady Evelyn gets the telegram that Gordon's plane's been shot down, and first I thought she ought to faint but then I decided, no, she puts that telegram in her pocket and goes right on dancing with the first GI that asks her."

"Betty, I'm afraid I don't know what you're talking about."

"Remember Me. My novel! Didn't I tell you I changed Evelyn from an American girl to British nobility? 'Course, now I have to go back and fiddle with the first five hundred pages."

"Betty, what's that music?"

"My record player? Oh, I brought it in to keep me in the forties mood. I'm a mood writer. I took a course at the university, and that's what the teacher said. I write from mood. Did you find your father?"

"Not yet." Hayes sighed. "Betty, you know how much I appreciate your coming in, and all, so please don't think I'm not grateful, but, what with your novel keeping you so busy, don't you think we ought to get somebody else to, well, maybe talk to any clients that might call?"

"Raleigh. I sat here for twenty years. I could run this office blindfold. Heaven's sakes. You've got two renewals, one increased coverage, and a new premium package."

"I have? Since yesterday?"

"But I want to apologize right here and now for hiring Bonnie Dellwood. This place was a pigsty. I really owe you an apology. To look at your files, I don't believe that girl was familiar with the alphabet. All I can say is the personal items she left behind lead me to suspect California is exactly where she belongs."

"How could she just go to California? She was due for a paycheck Friday."

"Life, Raleigh, is an odd affair." Mrs. Hemans was quoting her heroine, Lady Evelyn, who'd made just that remark to her aristocratic fiancé, when asked why she was leaving him for an American flyer she'd met five days earlier. The novelist added that odd affairs were occurring right here in the Forbes Building. The janitor Bill Jenkins kept dropping in every few hours to ask how Raleigh was doing, and to request that the following message be passed to him: "Keep laying low." This morning the dentist had run down the hall shouting that someone had stolen his best Oriental rug off the floor of his waiting room. When the police arrived, they'd taken the dentist away with them to the station for questioning. The police, she said, were absolutely in a fret. They were scared that a maniac was loose in town, or a conspiracy. Obscene fortune cookies had been passed out at the Lotus House, Knox-Bury's had been vandalized with blue paint. The memorial bust of PeeWee Jimson had been stolen out of the library. A pile of cannonballs on the Confederate Memorial at the Crossways had been pried loose and removed.

"Good God," Hayes exclaimed. "Who would do that?"

"Well, Chief Hood's so flummoxed, he's practically rabid. In fact," Mrs. Hemans coughed apologetically, "he was in here looking for you with a very nasty attitude. I told him you'd been called out of town on a serious family emergency and weren't reachable."

"Oh, Betty, thank you. And you didn't say anything that wasn't true. Believe me."

She gave a warm contented sigh. Raleigh Hayes sounded so much like his long-dead uncle Whittier, that warrior poet with whom, once again, because of her novel, she was so passionately in love.

After an extremely long lunch at an empty motel restaurant that was not prepared to make Mingo breaded veal cutlets on the spur of the moment, and not equipped (or inspired) to prepare his pork chops in less than forty-five minutes, Sheffield took the wheel of the Cadillac. Beside him, Hayes began making in his appointments book detailed notations of all expenses so far incurred on his trip. His father would be handed an exact reckoning. "Fifty to Seventeen," said Raleigh without looking up.

"I guess I've been driving to the beach all my life," Mingo mumbled, crunching Cheesos. "I guess I know the way."

"Fine." And Raleigh went back to his calculations. Outside Beulaville, he looked up and asked Mingo what they were doing outside Beulaville, since it was not on the way to Kure Beach. Sheffield explained that he was avoiding a notorious speed-trap about which Sister Mary Theresa had warned him.

"Fine." A curious and comfortable lethargy overcame the habitually vigorous insurance man. Nestling his head in the Cadillac's plush red velour, he fell asleep, and did not wake up till nightfall. As soon as he opened his eyes, it was clear to him that they were lost. It was clear that if not actually in a swamp, they were closer to swampish elements than major roads are likely to be built, even by the most conscienceless contractors. Even Nemours Kettell, as ruthless a capitalist as the state capitol allowed, would never have had the audacity to construct a highway in such slop and ooze, such boggy weeds and twisted stumps, such marshy sloughs and mangles of trees, as the Thermopyleans now found themselves.

"Mingo! This isn't Route Fifty. Route Fifty is a highway. Highways are *paved!*"

But the driver protested that he had followed three separate signs announcing, "Topsail straight ahead," and since Topsail was on the ocean, and Kure Beach was on the ocean, one was bound to lead to the other. "Look there!" he pointed. "There's another one. 'Topsail, one mile.' I told you."

When the brights flicked over the faded sign, Raleigh let out so anguished a wail that his neighbor slammed on the brakes, sending the Buddhas on the dashboard into a jigging dance. "You numbskull, Mingo! You ass-brained stupid idiot. That sign says, *'Topsoil!'* Not *sail, soil!*"

"Really?" said Mingo.

Minutes later, they glimpsed a deserted shack surrounded by huge heaps of sandy dirt that loomed up like dunes by the road sign, "TOPSOIL 4 SALE." "Turn around," Hayes commanded.

"Oh, Raleigh, I can't stand turning back. This road is bound to go someplace."

"There's no road, Mingo! We're in a goddamn SWAMP! What's that hitting the car?" Cypresses, up to their knees in brackish water, stood on the tips of their roots and leaned plaintively out to the road; Spanish moss, hanging like ratty boas from their branches, brushed the roof of the Cadillac. "Dammit, Mingo! *Turn around.*"

"Oh! Look what you made me do, yelling!" The front tire hit something, rolled over it, and then the wheels were spinning uselessly in a boggy rut.

"STOP!" Grabbing the flashlight, Hayes leaped out, sinking instantly to his ankles down in a sponge of molasses. Ahead, behind, and around him was nothing but dismal, Stygian . . . swamp. They were caught on a rotted knotty tree stump, at which Hayes, crouched in the muck, was peering when Sheffield suddenly accelerated, spraying black gook all over his companion's face. Hayes stood up and shouted "Fuck!" for one of the few times in his life. He smeared as much mud off his glasses as he could.

"Sorry, my foot slipped." Mingo opened the door to explain.

"Would you mind?" Raleigh hurled the fat man out of the car, then snatched the ignition key. "You dug us in deeper. Okay. Let me think." Hayes thought of several ideas. None of them worked. It was impossible to go forward or backward, or to lift the front of the car. Meanwhile Sheffield bounced with sucking pops of noise from one enormous foot to the other. "Oh, yuck, this feels like a swamp," he groaned. "Uh oh, what was that!"

Hayes listened, glaring into the moonlit shadows of the quagmire. "Owls," he said, "That 'whooo'? That's just owls."

"Do they bite? I'm scared. JESUS!" A low whooshing sound burst with terrifying quickness from a tree overhead, as an immense bird, its wings as long as Raleigh's arms, flapped out of the dark and crossed the road.

Mingo ran for the car, but Raleigh stopped him. "No you don't. We've got to unload the trunk and get the jack." They could hear scurrying rustles all around them as they worked. Hayes, not immune himself to an urban dread of the primeval, kept reassuring them both that alligators and bobcats never migrated from the Okefenokee to more northern swamps, but when something unmistakably alive slithered past his shoe, fear buckled his knees and he staggered. In silent undulation, the snake slid away. "Just a black snake," he whispered, hoping that was in fact true.

"Snakes?" howled Mingo, and with a furious abandon, singlehandedly threw the steamer trunk out onto the side of the road beside the plaster bust. When the jack wouldn't hold, Raleigh ruthlessly wedged Sheffield's suitcase under it. When the stump wouldn't budge, he wedged two pairs of Vera's voluminous Bermuda shorts under the rear wheels. "Now," he panted, "the idea is, listen to me, Mingo. . . ."

"I hear something. I hear voices."

"The idea is, we give a good shove, and we, more or less, *fling* the car back off the jack and over the stump. That's all we have to — Let go of me!"

Sheffield was hiding behind his friend, whispering in his ear. "Listen! Raleigh, Raleigh, Raleigh, it's spooky. It's like ghosts or werewolves or something. Isn't it?"

"No." But now he could hear it too. A grunting noise.

". . . Huh Ouu. Huh Ouu. Huh Ouu."

Hayes pried the other man's finger out of his shoulder. "There's no such thing as ghosts." On the other hand, the chant rumbling nearer and nearer did not have a particularly benign sound. Whoever the voices were, they were male, they spoke English, and there were a lot of them. Out of the black stagnant woods, their rhythmic shouts grew louder and sharper, punctuated by clanking rattles, until Raleigh — frozen as a squirrel — distinctly heard the words of a grunted choral song.

Huh Ouu Huh Ouu Huh Ouu.
I screwed a gal in Carolina.
She had warts in her vagina.
Huh Ouu Huh Ouu Huh Ouu.

"My God," Hayes murmured. In the moonlight, he could dimly see large bulky shapes swaying toward them down the road. At least a dozen men trotting triple file, and all apparently wearing large backpacks and a great deal of loose metal.

Huh Ouu Huh Ouu Huh Ouu.
We can lick the U.S. Navy.
We eat raw meat, and piss out gravy.
Who you gonna call?
Maaaariiines!
Who you gonna call?
Maaaariiines!

Mingo leaped out from behind his neighbor. "It's the Marines!"

"Great," Hayes replied, as a big beam of light hit him in the face.

"Halt!" shouted the man marching in front. "I said, HALT, you dumb fucks!" With thuds and rattles, his followers stopped.

"Excuse me," began Hayes, but was yelled down by another "Halt!" as he and the Marine met in the road and blinked into each other's flashlights.

"It's a coon!" snickered a young voice in the crowd.

"A raccoon or t'other kind?" another voice guffawed.

The leader wheeled on them. He was, Hayes could now tell from the three curved stripes above crossed rifles on his sleeve, a sergeant, an extremely young sergeant, lanky but well muscled, with a big nose and narrow-set eyes. He pointed his spotlight at the troop. "Who said that?" No one moved. "Who's the asshole comedian?" No one spoke. "All right." He walked back to them. "All of you. Hit the ground. I said, DOWN. Flat! Right down! That's it. Now get those faces in it. Rub 'em in it." To the amazement of the Thermopyleans, the entire file of Marines fell to their knees and then to their chests in the black boggy mud, where they rolled their faces fervently from side to side while the sergeant paced among them, periodically shoving his foot down on someone's shoulder blades. Finally he commanded, "UP!" and they rose, dripping muck and spitting. "All right. Big joke. Now you *all* look like coons. Am I right? I said, am I right?"

"YES SIR!" they shouted.

"Whaddah you look like?"

"COONS, SIR!"

"What else are you?"

"MARINES, SIR!" they stumbled hopefully.

"No, you're not. You're assholes. You're garbage. You're losers. That's why you're out here tonight. And last night. And tomorrow night. Till you stop being assholes, which is what you are. What are you?"

"ASSHOLES, SIR!"

By now, Hayes, realizing that the original remark about "coons" must have been a racial slur on the black mud all over his face, was scrubbing away at himself with his shirt. "Excuse me," he began again.

The sergeant came within inches of his nose. "What are you jokers doing out here?"

"Where are we?" Hayes asked.

Laughter from the shuffling file died instantly when the sergeant waved his light over the front row.

Mingo bobbed forward with his hand out. "We're lost. We accidentally took a wrong turn, I guess. I'm Mingo Sheffield of Thermopylae. What's your name?"

The Marine did not offer to shake hands, but instead flashed his beam directly in their eyes. "I didn't ask you who you were. I asked you what you were doing here. You're trespassing on U.S. government property. This property belongs to Camp LeJeune. This is a United States Marine base, no unauthorized personnel allowed. I suppose you're gonna tell me you didn't know that."

"Absolutely not," Hayes nodded.

"I'm Field Sergeant David Stein. I'm gonna ask you for some identification."

"Absolutely, of course," Hayes agreed. Holding out his driver's license, he attempted to make clear the innocence of their predicament, while Mingo, despite all efforts to silence him, kept trying to start a conversation, with remarks like, "I guess you thought we were spies. Do you have a lot of trouble out here with spies, and terrorists, and things like that?"

Sergeant Stein looked carefully at the two men, at their car and its KISSY PU license plate, at the bust of PeeWee Jimson lying in the mud, at Vera's flowery bermuda shorts under the wheels, and at the rotted tree stump that had snagged them. He took off his helmet to pull on his wiry matted hair. "Dumb," he said, and Raleigh sadly nodded. "Okay, garbage heads," Stein yelled at his men. "Fall out and move this car."

"YES, SIR!" The pack of teenagers uncoiled with a gleeful energy, and stormed yelling forward as the Thermopyleans sprang away, startled, into the bog. Shoving together against the front bumper, and seizing this brief opportunity to break loose from the constrictions that chafed them at boot camp, the Marines howled at the top of their lungs, raised the Cadillac off the jack, and pushed it at a run fifty yards back before Sergeant Stein's "HALT!" harnessed their romp. "Now pick up all this junk and put it back in the car," he ordered; so at least the travelers did not have to lug the bust and trunk down the road in pursuit of their Cadillac.

"Thank you," Hayes said.

"Go a mile, take a left, go two, take a right. I oughta turn you jokers in, but fuck it. Just get out of here before somebody shoots first and checks you out later."

"Thank you," Hayes grimly repeated.

To his disgust, his obese neighbor now slapped his fat thighs together and saluted. "God bless you. If it hadn't been for y'all showing up . . . well, you saved our fannies, I guess. I want you to know, I love the Marines. Honest. I mean, I was never in the Marines. But I always wanted to be when I was little. I saw *The Halls of Montezuma* at least five or six times. With Richard Widmark. And I think Jack Palance was in it, too. Anyhow, if you ask me, you're doing a great job defending the world, and I don't care what anybody says."

"Thanks. Why don't you get back in your car," advised Stein.

"I just want you to know how I feel. I'm really sorry about your friends getting killed in Lebanon. You try to help people, and then they let a terrorist do something awful like that. It makes you wonder."

"Mingo, let's go." Hayes pulled his friend back from the young sergeant, who was scrutinizing him in an unpleasant way, perhaps trying to decide if these idiotic remarks were facetious — whereas, of course, the babbling Sheffield was entirely incapable of irony.

With Hayes at the wheel, the Thermopyleans backed slowly down the road, while Mingo waved good-bye out the window to the small file of soldiers, now marching once more through the dark mud, chanting their adolescent obscenities.

So rattled were both men by their misadventures that as soon as they found the highway, they looked for a place to have a drink; Raleigh himself suggested it. The place they found was further evidence that, although not yet at their destination, they were indeed in the vicinity of an ocean. It was a roadside seafood spot called Captain Nemo's, and it was crowded indiscriminately with every variety of fish, from tiny crappies to a hammerhead shark painted bright blue, all mounted and labeled on the walls, and suspended by wires from the ceiling, and caught in dangling nets over the heads of the customers. There was a plastic octopus drooping almost into Raleigh's hair as he stood at the bar. "Yeah?" said the proprietor, on whose T-shirt a man with a wooden leg stood grinning in a whale's mouth that was held gaping open by a giant whiskey bottle wedged in its jaws. The shirt was printed, "I had a Whale of a time at Captain Nemo's."

"Whiskey sour on the rocks," Mingo told him. "And have you got good french-fried onion rings?"

"A beer," said Hayes. "And a scotch. And a telephone."

"You want me to mix 'em?" the bartender asked loudly for the benefit of three young men standing around a beeping video game. They laughed.

In the bathroom, Raleigh hung his Hawaiian shirt on an oar while he scrubbed off as much of the black mud as he could with no soap and no towel but toilet paper. Then he telephoned collect to his wife. A strange woman answered, "Mothers for Peace. Starry Haven office," and gave the operator another number where Mrs. Hayes might be reached. Raleigh recognized the digits as his own Forbes Building office number.

"Mutual Life and Mothers for Peace," said Aura. "Accept the charges from Raleigh W. Hayes? I'd be absolutely thrilled."

"Don't overdo it, Aura," snarled Hayes.

"Hello, sweetheart. Where are you now? Are you in New Orleans?"

"How could I be in New Orleans, dammit? I'm in a bar near Camp Le-Jeune. What are you doing in my office?"

"I don't know why you keep telling me you don't frequent bars, Raleigh. It's obvious you have a whole secret life. I wonder for how long?"

"You're in no position to bring up the subject of secret lives," he said, wringing water from the bottom of his shirt. "You're the one all of a sudden turning into Jane Fonda."

"Oh, I wouldn't say it was all of a sudden," Aura serenely replied.

"You mean you admit it?"

" 'Admit'?"

"Did I tell you Mothers for Peace could use my office? Did I?"

"Oh, Raleigh, really! What about one flesh and one blood? Honey, I've got some news for you from the police. That rug belonged to Jasper Kilby down the hall, and it looks like somebody wrapped up Bonnie Ellen in it. Those were her shoes."

"Oh my God! Oh, Aura, no!" Hayes staggered back against the wall.

"Honey, no, no. I'm sorry. Calm down. She's alive. A friend from her aerobics class saw her wandering around downtown bloody and barefoot in a daze, and took her to the hospital. She's covered with bumps and bruises and she can't remember what happened to her, but she did recognize her shoes. I went over to see her. Poor girl. Eddie's gone, cleared out their apartment and vanished. So now the police think they must have had a fight at your office and Eddie knocked her out, panicked, and put her in the rug. It's absolutely horrible, but at least nobody's dead. She doesn't remember a thing between sitting here at this desk, and then walking downtown wondering how she'd lost her shoes."

In his shock, it took Hayes a while to assimilate all the details of Aura's story. She had to keep repeating things. "No, I told you, she's fine. She's staying with her friend, but I told her she could count on us to help. Thank heavens, you'd gotten her that insurance. But that's you, Raleigh. Always taking care of everybody else. So, how are you, honey? Everything okay?"

"Very funny. Aura, how do you think my clients are going to feel when they hear I'm sharing an office with Mothers for Peace?"

"We had to have more lines. You wouldn't believe the calls coming in today. It's incredible. Volunteers. Contributions. But, don't worry, they promised to get our phones in downstairs tomorrow." Aura went briskly on to explain that Mothers for Peace had rented one of the empty rooms on the fifth floor of the Forbes Building.

"This is insane, Aura. I'm out of town for two days, and you open an office! Where are our children?"

"Downstairs helping paint. And Holly and Booger are putting in some shelves."

"I guess you know that according to your daughter, her friend Booger is a homosexual."

"She told you? Now, that's interesting, Raleigh. I'm glad to hear that. She must feel that you're loosening up a little, and she can share things with you without the old fireworks."

"I don't know what you mean by the old fireworks, but I'll tell you this, things are getting out of hand. I think you ought to take a moment and reconsider your priorities. You're a mother."

Aura snorted in a strange way. "A mother shouldn't run Mothers for Peace? A mother shouldn't do what she can to see that the planet's still around for her children to enjoy? A mother —"

"Aura, I already heard your speech on TV this morning."

"You did? Oh, Raleigh, that's sweet of you. What'd you think? How'd I come across? Did I sound squeaky? Vera thinks I ought to lower my voice."

"Vera?" Hayes peered through the hanging lobster pots and fat-lipped grouper fish to the far end of the room where Mingo Sheffield, visible in blinks of electronic light, watched two Marines bombing the solar system on a noisy video game. "Vera? Where *is* Vera? According to Mingo, she was supposed to be in hiding, whatever that means."

"Oh, you know Vera."

"No, I don't. I don't know anyone anymore. I don't even think I know me, and I apparently don't know you, Mrs. Hayes, or should I say Ms. Godwin?"

She laughed. "Of course you do, and I know you, and I love every inch of you, and I'd love to see a few, one of these days. When are you coming home?"

"Aura!" Raleigh blushed.

"Vera went to get her portable TV. We think we may make the news on Channel Seven. Is there a set in that bar you could watch? And what are you doing at Camp LeJeune? I wish you had some of our flyers with you to distribute there. But I thought you were going straight to Kure?"

"Don't ask. Are the police still after Mingo and me? Can you believe I'm actually in a position to have to ask that question? Now he's found Bonnie Ellen, does Hood still want me about those guns?"

"Not really. I mean, he's blustering around, calling up and so on. The fact is, he's after me, and he's trying to take it out on you, too. He actually came up with this preposterous notion about how Mothers for Peace was staging anti-male crimes all over Thermopylae to get publicity. I mean, really! Are we going to waste our time throwing paint on men's sports clothes and stealing stupid PeeWee Jimson's bust out of the library or chiseling off cannonballs? It's hilarious. Anyhow, I just refer everything to Dan. He can handle Hood."

"Dan Andrews?" This was Raleigh's lawyer, his neighbor, and his old college roommate.

"How many Dans do we know?"

"Well, Aura, I thought perhaps you were referring to Dan Rather on CBS, or maybe Daniel Schorr."

"Raleigh, am I picking up some subliminal hostility? What were you really trying to say when you started in on that little-woman-get-back-to-the-kitchen grunting that you don't even believe deep down."

"Every man believes it deep down."

She sighed. "Sweetheart, sad to say, that's probably true. It's not going to be an easy fight."

"I'm not fighting."

"I'm not talking about you. I'm talking about the whole kit and ca-
boodle."

"Fine. Fight on. Up the revolution!"

"It's not funny, Raleigh."

A thin boy in a Marine uniform, his hair shaved to a nub, his pimples
scrubbed to a flame, was now fidgeting behind Raleigh, slapping his dime
loudly from palm to palm. "Somebody's waiting for the phone, Aura. I'll
call you as soon as I get hold of Gates and know what I'm doing. I don't
suppose you've heard any more from Daddy?"

"No. Not a word, and neither has Vicky Anna. She lent us three chairs
and a desk. By the way, I'm supposed to tell you that, let's see, Grandpa
Clayton's grandfather married an orphan, a girl from the state home."

"Frankly, Aura, I don't care if he married Abraham Lincoln's widow."

"Well, Vicky said you asked her to look it up."

"Oh. Are you talking about that general? Goodrich Hale Hayes?"

"Darling, they're *your* family. That damn little Earley! I hope he realizes
what he's put you through. Did you see Flonnie Rogers? Did she know
where this man Jubal is?"

"She said Charleston, but she's a hundred and one, and she thought I
was Daddy. Aura. Tell me, am I crazy? What am I doing?"

"Trying to do the right thing by everybody. Like always. Now, don't
worry. We're fine here, and Betty can run the office as long as you need
her. You know how much she loves you. But tell me the truth. Do you
want some help?"

"No, thank you. I'm okay. Bye."

After a little silence, she said, "Bye."

"Aura? Aura? You still there?"

"Raleigh?"

"Listen." Hayes moved the receiver to his other ear. "I was proud of you
on TV. Bye."

"Raleigh Hayes!" He heard her laugh. "That's what I was waiting for!
That's the man I married! Bye-bye, honey. I love you too."

"Too? Did I say I loved you? All I said was I was proud."

"Oh, Raleigh, where have we been all these years? I feel like I'm twenty
years old, don't you?"

"Considering that's around the time I was in Germany, digging latrines
in the snow, yes, that's pretty much what I feel like."

Yielding the phone to the young Marine, who said loudly, "Thank you,
sir," dropped his dime, and scowled with embarrassment, Raleigh Hayes,

feeling oddly elated, returned to the bar and drank his scotch. Four more people had joined Mingo in the high vinyl chairs; two were soldiers, two were a couple nuzzling one another with a defiant self-consciousness. The man was burly and wore a wine-colored shirt open over a cream polyester sports coat. The woman was tiny and wore designer jeans with a ruffled blouse. The young Marines over by the video games eyed her wistfully.

Sheffield had taken it upon himself to order two Captain's Platters, saying, "It's already dark, we might as well eat here as there." The food was brought to them in a booth looped with little hammocks holding starfish, sand dollars, and tropical shells that no one had ever found on a Carolina beach. Their dinners were jumbled piles of greasy fried dough in which tidbits of seafood could be faintly detected. "If you don't want yours, give it to me," Mingo mumbled, trying to chew a leathery clam neck. "You sure are picky, Raleigh."

The insurance man handed over his plate, and continued to update his neighbor on the Thermopylae news. "So, so much for your wife's disappearance. Vera and Aura are in this Mothers for Peace thing together. Mingo, I honestly think you ought to go home. Now that the police know nobody's been murdered, all you have to do is apologize to Billy Knox. Maybe you could get your old job back. Can't hurt to try. You've got to think of the future."

Sheffield rubbed a napkin in circles around his mouth. "Are you trying to get rid of me? Because you promised I could come." Tears welled in his round eyes. "I've never even seen Charleston, or gotten to go hardly anywhere at all. Ever since the *tenth* grade I've had a job, and nobody ever fired me before. Not once. I mean, that's not a lie, is it, Raleigh? And now all I want to do is go on this little trip and try to be some help, and you keep making these insinuations. I'm not the one that got to go to college and join ROTC and get to see Germany and everything."

"That was not exactly a vacation. And please don't misunderstand me." Hayes took off his glasses, because the sight of Sheffield's tears was making his own eyes water. "I told you you could come along, and you can. But I don't want to waste your time. The point is: I need to look for my father. You need to look for a job. You have obligations."

The fat man licked away a tear. "Well, don't worry about us. Vera and I are working on a plan."

"A new business venture?"

"I don't want to talk about it right now."

"All right." Raleigh was familiar with previous forays by the Sheffields into private enterprise. While the Hayeses had bought Tupperware, Amway, Avon, magazines, plant hangers, and vegetable slicers from them, not enough other people had. "Care for some coffee?"

"I'm coming with you?"

"Oh, Mingo. Okay, fine."

Mingo grinned as wide as the moon.

At seven, Raleigh persuaded the bartender to turn on the television perched on a shelf in the corner. Twenty minutes later, the two travelers were in a fistfight with half the customers at Captain Nemo's. It started when the smirking anchorman on the screen announced that earlier that morning a Thermopylae couple had been charged with creating a public disorder right there in the Channel Seven studio, following the taping of *Woman Alive!* They'd been fined fifty dollars each, and released with a warning. "The outburst began during a heated question-and-answer period between the studio audience and *Woman Alive!* guests, Congressman Charlie Lukes, up for reelection in this summer's primary, and Mrs. Aura Hayes, president of Mothers for Peace." A clip came on, at the sight of which Mingo gasped. "Gollee, that must of happened after that mean guy turned our sets off in the store! Gollee!" Half the studio audience were not only on their feet, they were swinging their arms, apparently trying to separate Nemours Kettell and his wife, Barbara, who had each other by the shoulders and were shaking and jerking each other so furiously that people around them screamed as toes were tromped and elbows flew into abdomens. Wayne Sparks, beatifically smiling, looked on. "Mr. and Mrs. Nemours Kettell apparently fell into a political argument over the discussion between the congressman and Mrs. Hayes," blandly noted the voice-over. "Kettell is a successful businessman and the Thermopylae chairman of the Re-Elect Charlie Lukes Committee. Mrs. Kettell is vice-president of Mothers for Peace." In the next clip, two policemen were dragging out the backdoor of the studio Barbara Kettell, who appeared to be either practicing the old style of passive resistance by going entirely limp or had passed out; behind them came Wayne Sparks, fingers raised in the peace sign. After him hurried somebody with his jacket pulled over his head. "That's Nemours," Mingo pointed. "I sold him that jacket at the Washington's Birthday Sale."

The voice-over continued as a new clip showed Aura and Lukes glaring at each other from their swivel chairs on the dais. "The disturbance broke out in the final minutes of today's program." Aura was in midsentence. Her eyes were glittery and her voice icy. "No, I am not 'proud' that we sent the Marines in to invade that tiny little Caribbean island, in complete violation of every international law. I think it happened two days after the deaths in Lebanon *because* of that tragic bungling. And comparing it to the invasion of Normandy? That's too ridiculous and too pitiful for words."

"Well, *I'm* proud," said Lukes vehemently. "It gave America something to feel good about again."

"Killing a few dozen Caribbeans, including hospital patients, not to mention the deaths of young American men, makes you 'feel good,' Congressman?"

"I'm losing my patience here." Lukes savagely gripped his hefty thighs. "You're doing nothing but revealing your ignorance of very complicated issues."

At Captain Nemo's bar, the man in the wine-colored shirt suddenly shouted, "You're damn right. He's damn right. Get her off of there! Send her back where she came from." The woman in the frilly blouse and designer jeans beside him nodded too. "He's right." Lined up in front of the couple were at least eight imported beer bottles. Seconds later, the man shouted again, "I *hate* those damn bitch feminists. All they're interested in is queers and abortions."

"He's right," nodded the woman, shaking four gold chains out from under her blouse. "A real woman's got no use for them."

It was when the man repeated, "Damn bitch," for the third time that Raleigh Hayes flung back his chair and stood up. "Okay," he shouted across the room. "Excuse me. *Excuse me!* I'm going to ask you to refrain from making any further comments about my wife."

In complete silence, everybody in the place tuned to stare at him. Then the three young Marines started nudging each other and chortling. Then the couple at the bar began to giggle. "He's a nut," the woman told the bartender.

"That *your* wife?" the man asked.

"Yes," Hayes said, coming toward him. "Even if she weren't, your remarks are uncalled for."

"On TV? Sure. Sure." The grinning drunk looked Hayes up and down, from his damp dirty Hawaiian shirt to his mud-caked shoes. "Well, why don't you tell her to wash your clothes, you bullshit." He elbowed his girlfriend and she laughed loudly.

Beyond reason now, Hayes snarled, "I told you to keep filthy comments to yourself." At this, the burly man leaned out from the high chair and shoved our hero, who skidded backward onto the floor, sprang up before he even stopped sliding, and hurled himself at his assailant. In seconds they were grappling in zigzags across the room, while the woman hopped up and down shrieking, "Kill him, Daryl!," and the bartender yelled, "Quit that! Quit that! Hey! Watch out!" A few seconds more, the man was on top of Hayes, banging his head against the floorboards. With whoops, the three Marines piled on, striking out indiscriminately at both combatants and at each other. Down at the bottom of this churning mound lay poor Raleigh, a knee crushing his face and a chin digging into his ankle bone. Suddenly, he heard a long loud hollering, like a sonic boom, coming closer; then bodies began to fly away from him. His attacker shot backward with an astonished look. The same look opened Hayes's mouth when he saw the big man spinning in air on the Gargantuan shoulders of a twirling Mingo Sheffield, whose amazing uninterrupted bellow was vibrating the glasses on the bar shelves. The flailing man above him squealed, "Stop! I'm gonna puke. Stop!" Mingo looked up in surprise, as if baffled to find a stranger flopped around his neck, and stopped with a jolt, heaving off the body of the drunk, who rolled over and quickly lurched toward the hall where the bathrooms were. His girlfriend stumbled after him in high heels. After trying to rebutton his torn shirt, Sheffield brushed back his hair, which he wore with a deep careful side part to cover his bald spot. "Well, gollee, I'm sorry," he said to the Marines and the bartender, all of whom crouched behind furniture at the alert. "But four on one isn't fair."

Hayes was feeling under the tables for his glasses, which he found fortunately unbroken, just bent. The two Thermopyleans quickly paid their bill, and left Captain Nemo's. The news wasn't even over yet. The weather girl was slapping black magnetic clouds all over her map of coastal North Carolina. Walking to the Cadillac, Hayes coughed twice, then stuck out his hand and shook his friend's. "Thank you, Mingo."

"I didn't even know what I was doing. I guess I never would have done it if I'd ever known what I was doing. Did you see that! Did you see what I did! Oh, damn, I wish Vera could have seen me. You'll tell her, won't you, Raleigh? And Tommy and Boyd and everybody? They're never going to believe me, so you say it's true." Sheffield's postbattle exhilaration continued unabated as Raleigh drove straight to the highway, never taking his foot from the accelerator until he saw the sign for Kure Beach.

Sand drifted over Surf Street, and on either side, cottages sat in the dark, their windows boarded. But far at the end of the road, Hayes could see the lights beckoning from "Peace and Quiet," and as he pulled into his hand-paved driveway, he could hear blasts of a Dixieland blues record. Sneaking around to the porch and crouching there at the window, he watched his half-brother Gates weaving mournfully in front of a full-length mirror propped against the wall; his head was thrown back, his black curls glistening, as he pretended to play a bright gold trumpet pointed at the sky.

CHAPTER

17

Raleigh's Confession

RALEIGH HAYES was nine years older than his half-brother Gates, who had been born approximately two weeks after Raleigh's father married Roxanne Digges. This gulf of time (Gates had been only nine when our hero left town to go to college, only thirteen when the army sent Raleigh to Germany) was not only deepened by the rift of divorce, it was made unbridgeable by the most profound differences of character. No two men, bound by blood, tied by upbringing, could be more dissimilar. They had nothing in common but a father, blue eyes, and curly hair. They shared nothing but the past. Gates had stopped worshipping Raleigh at four, stopped admiring him at seven, and started hating him at twelve, when his older sibling became to him simply a churlish, niggardly, self-righteous, pompous square object to be manuevered; a dull, smug beaver to be weaseled into a begrudging loan. For his part, Raleigh had resented Gates at birth, struggled to tolerate him as a toddler, tried to reform him as a teenager, and given him up soon thereafter as an irresponsible, destructive, dishonest, shameless embarrassment; a profligate otter, tumbling avalanches in his careless path. First of all, Gates had always been careless with private property, including Raleigh's — scratching his records, tearing his books, losing his basketball, breaking his camera, denting his car, stealing his change, his socks, his anything and everything that Gates felt a momentary fancy to own or sell or, most often, wreck and forget. He always said he was sorry, he even added tears to his apologies. "I was just trying to wind up your watch for you, Raleigh, and then it stopped ticking all of a sudden. I guess it wasn't a very good one. I'm sorry. Okay, I'm sorry," he would say time after time. And time after time, Raleigh would say, "What good is sorry? Would you please just leave my things alone? Would you please just use your brain?"

Gates was all that Raleigh wasn't, and didn't like. Raleigh couldn't stand surprises, Gates couldn't bear familiarity. Raleigh was a saver, Gates a discarder; Raleigh was a husbander, Gates a pirate, looting life and moving on. "Oh, that job. I quit. Man, I was bored out of my gourd, the sameo sameo crud, Jesus, forget it. I'm a flyer, Raleigh; stick me on the slow train, it's loony toons, you know what I mean?" He had always been that way. "Oh, that girl. Oh, that school. Oh, that toy." Contemptuous of learning, impatient with routine, he started endless grand schemes and great relationships, got frustrated and lost interest, moved on. Everyone ageed that Gates was exceptional; he was most assuredly exceptionally good-looking, but also exceptionally bright, exceptionally talented. Everyone said he took after his aunt Lovie (who had more or less tried to raise him), sharing her theatrical flair and her gift for mimicry. But even Earley Hayes — in Raleigh's opinion, no rock of stability, no temple of moderation himself — urged Gates, in vain, to settle down, to slow up, to take hold. And Raleigh's own advice as well fell on deaf ears. Raleigh's advice never changed. It was, "Think."

"You just want me to be like you. Well, I'm not," said Gates.

"God knows," said Raleigh.

"Why should I be?"

"Because I'm not the one that got arrested for shoplifting, I'm not the one that rolled Daddy's car and broke my leg, I'm not the one that got thrown out of college my sophomore year."

"Well, big whup for you, Raleigh, okay."

"I'm not the one standing here in *your* office trying to borrow money from you to get some girl an illegal abortion, goddammit, am I?"

"What do you want me to say, hunh, what? I'm sorry? I screwed up? I'm a shit? I never do anything right, and you never do anything wrong? Okay? How's that? You're perfect, Raleigh. You're so perfect, you're going to lend me this money because rotten as I am, I'm still your brother and you've got to come through for me. That's what it's going to cost you to keep on being good old perfect old Raleigh. Listen, at least I'm trying to get her an abortion. I could have just told her to get lost. Really, a lot of guys would. Doesn't that give you a glimmer of hope, Raleigh? Okay, want me to say I'm sorry? Okay, I'm sorry."

And Raleigh, red with anger, would snarl, "I just want you to *think!* I want you to use your head for once in your life. I just want you to sit down and talk to yourself and ask yourself why you keep acting this way."

"Why should I talk to myself? I've got you and Daddy and everybody else talking to me every other minute! Why don't you talk to yourself? Why don't you go sit down and ask yourself why you don't get off my back?"

"I talk to myself all the time, Gates. I think before I act. That's one difference between us."

"Well, hooray for you," Gates would say and slam the door.

It was true. Most of our hero's waking time was spent in conversation with himself, and — analysts would have us believe — at night, his dreams simply made an allegory of the day's internal monologue. He was never not thinking. As he ate, bathed, ran, drove, worked, even as he listened to the conversations of others, he was carrying on, within, a critical commentary whose purpose was to query, clarify, and otherwise explicate that soliloquy entitled Raleigh W. Hayes. This continual checking of his mental temperature so preoccupied Hayes that he had been known to walk past friends without a word, to hang up phones without good-bye, to overlook clothes, food, holidays, and weather; the very seasons wheeled above, dropping leaves or snows or showers on his busy, disinterested head. And while he lived inside himself with the blinds drawn, Life walked noisily by the windows, unheard. Had Hayes been allowed to tell his own story, this would have been a very different narrative indeed, and, doubtless, a much more modern one, with scarcely any characters and very little plot. It would have been one long stream of consciousness. It would have been, in other words, a confession.

Now, in its common usage, the word *confession* did not at all appeal to our hero. It had the suggestive prurient sound of priests and Catholic adolescents hidden in high shadowed concupiscent corners, titillating each other through musty curtains with graphic whisperings about forbidden sex. More personally, the word *confession* implied an admission of fault, and, as we know, Raleigh with good reason considered himself (comparatively) unflawed. Try as he might during church services, he honestly could not think of any manifold sins and wickednesses that he needed to repent. He honestly did not see why, in all fairness, *he* should have provoked God's wrath and indignation when there were so many really provoking people (like his father, like Gates) out there getting off scot-free; nor did he see why he should feel guilty and responsible and worried and all the things he had to confess he did feel, when the truly guilty appeared not to have a care in the world; nor did he see why he should keep begging God for mercy, when all he wanted, from God and everybody else, was justice, if he could ever get it, which he couldn't, so wretchedly unfair were the blithe, if not downright cynical, ways of the Creator.

By the time Raleigh was old enough to understand the drift of the General Confession, stumbled through together by the small congregation of Thermopylae's Episcopalians, his father had already been dismissed by his parish, left by his wife, and was living across town in a little stucco house with the pregnant Roxanne Digges. While the bishop had not defrocked Earley Hayes, he had declined to give him another church, and so, a priest without a pulpit, Earley (to everyone's astonishment) took a teaching position at a small Negro college in the nearby textile town of Hillston. He taught (of all things, thought Raleigh) the history of religion and moral philosophy. And as if this weren't embarrassing enough, he eventually became the director of the college's marching band, actually appearing — to the horrified disgust of many of his former parishioners — every Fourth of July on the streets of Thermopylae at the head of a procession of high-stepping young blacks in gold and red uniforms. Raleigh resigned his position as first trumpet of the Thermopylae Junior High School band. "I don't have time to practice, not if I'm going to play basketball," he explained, but everyone assumed that he was simply too mortified to march past crowds gawking at his father as he paraded through town with Negroes. "At least," said Mrs. PeeWee Jimson, "Earley has the decency never to set foot inside our church again!"

Raleigh's mother, the divorced Sarah Ainsworth Hayes, continued, however, to attend St. Thomas's, to chair the vestry, to arrange the altar flowers, and to advise the new rector, a vague, mumbling bachelor who typed out perfect copies of sermons on such unenthusiastic topics as the Synod of Whitby or the Hebrew etymology of *anointed,* and then read them to the drowsy pews in a stammer of shyness. The former Mrs. Hayes, dressed in black, like a young widowed dowager, continued to sit in the first pew on the right, from which vantage she led everyone behind her in the liturgical ballet of standing, kneeling, bowing, and responding that served to keep the faithful awake. In a succession of blue suits and clip-on bow ties, Raleigh sat for years beside her. He memorized creeds and prayers in the cool rhythm of her Northern voice. But during the Confession, Mrs. Hayes said not a word aloud, except an occasional phrase like "the burden of them is intolerable." To the son, glancing up at her clear, motionless profile behind the net of her hat, her dark eyes seemed to be looking into some remote place that made her either sad or angry, he could never decide which. What he did decide was that the Confession was too easy a way out for people like his father who *had* committed grievous offenses. Was it enough for them to say they were heartily sorry, if they then danced off, forgiven, into that newness of life the rector handed out with an embarrassed wave of his hand? No, it wasn't enough. The sorrow of the offender was no satisfaction at all. "I'm real sorry you're hurting, Little Fellow," his father kept saying. "I'm sorry I've caused you even a minute of hurt." But what good was that? Absolutely none. It didn't change the past. Not even God could wave His hand and wipe away the past.

For seven years following the divorce, Raleigh lived alone with his mother in the large brick house near St. Thomas Church, the house out of which his father had suddenly one day moved his clothes, his records, and his rumpled easy chair. When he left, Earley Hayes had taken with him, too, all the noise; for while the Hayes family refused to give Sarah up — persisting until she left Thermopylae in unannounced visits and undeterred party invitations — and while Sarah insisted that Raleigh spend time not only with his father but with his father's family, still, things were naturally never the same, and as Raleigh grew older, the handsome house seemed to shrink and to fade and to grow quieter and quieter. Raleigh and his mother ate breakfast together in the meticulous kitchen and ate dinner together in the formal dining room, and while on those occasions they chatted together comfortably and bantered mild sarcasms with a quiet affection, they otherwise went their own ways, off to their own work and their own rooms. They each had two private rooms, a bedroom and a study. Neither entered the other's without knocking, and only then for a significant reason. Raleigh spent a great deal of those seven years in the room he called his workroom.

He was a serious boy; he took his schoolwork seriously and was a diligent student, copying his homework into thick neat notebooks with colored dividers. He took his responsibilities seriously, and not only proudly did more chores around the house than his mother thought to request, but sought odd jobs around the town (cutting lawns, delivering papers, bagging groceries, loading crates at Carolina Pottery) in order to earn himself the pocket money his mother would have given him had he asked, so that he could buy what he would not accept from his father as a gift. He took his hobbies seriously, and labored hour after hour alone in his workroom, painstakingly bolting together erector sets and gluing together model airplanes, and scrutinizing with a magnifying glass the foreign stamps Aunt Victoria sent him, and dutifully practicing his trumpet, and carefully labeling his posterboards of minerals, butterflies, arrowheads, classic fishing flies. The years went by, unnoticed, while the boy with a frowning absorption built, from kits he'd bought himself, a crystal radio, an ant farm, a darkroom, a stereo system.

The years went by, while his arms and legs pushed out like flower stalks from the cuffs of pants and shirts, while he scrubbed at his face and lifted barbells and struggled with his voice, his moods, his appetite, his desires. The years went by, while, at his mother's request (and only, he insisted, at her request), he spent his summers and his holidays in the small noisy stucco house with his father, Roxanne, and Gates, and a crowd of Hayes family and Hayes friends. Sometimes (especially in the years after Roxanne had abruptly left Thermopylae, leaving the five-year-old Gates behind), sometimes, at a picnic playing baseball or over at Lovie's house listening to everybody singing around the piano, Raleigh would forget to be angry at the injustice done his mother; he'd forget that he disapproved of his father and didn't like spending time with him. Then guilt would rush over him and send him sullen off by himself. And later he'd ask permission to return home early to the quiet brick house. He'd say he was worried about his mother. "There's nothing to worry about, Raleigh," she'd tell him when he hurried up the stairs to her room. "I'm absolutely fine." And that seemed to be true.

Sarah Hayes was as serious as her son. She read thoughtfully, she gardened assiduously, she volunteered a reasonable amount of her time to the church and to town services, she drove daily to the state capital to work as a bookkeeper for the Bureau of Taxes — not because she needed the income, but because it seemed appropriate to her that a healthy, intelligent woman should have a job. In the evenings, she sat by the radio or her record player, listening to music, while she worked at her hobby: she made flowers from glass, fusing with a flame small colored fragments into beautiful, botanically perfect replicas; these she gave away as Christmas presents, although Raleigh often advised her to keep the collection together and offer it to a museum. "I just like to make them," she'd say. "I don't want to keep them."

As for her personal life, Sarah Hayes neither avoided company nor particularly sought it out, neither insisted that acquaintances stop trying to find "a new man" for her, nor ever involved herself with any of the men they found. She appeared to require little of life. In her dress, in her conversation, in her habits, in her relations, she was consistent and reasonable and temperate, and to the Thermopyleans who puzzled about her, the un-answered mystery of Sarah Ainsworth Hayes was why in the world she had ever married — and married so precipitously, and stayed married to for nine years — an immoderate, impractical, improvident fool like Earley Hayes. Once, when he was in high school, Raleigh asked her why. She answered, "I loved him."

"But you don't still. After what he did, I don't see why you make me go over there, why I have to spend the whole stupid summer over there. After what he did to you."

She answered, "There were mitigating circumstances."

"I don't know what you mean." And Raleigh, one arm through the sleeve of his basketball jacket, one hand fiddling with the strap that held on his glasses, added, "See you later, Mama, I'm late," and left. In fact, although he wouldn't have thought so, he didn't want there to be any mitigating circumstances.

Years went by; Raleigh carefully packed up his childhood to store in the attic, and, leaving his room neatly arranged, he drove away to college. There he made a schedule of the courses he would take over four years. He took the courses, he graduated, he flew to Germany, and at the army's request diligently practiced driving a tank around the countryside. He kept his tank as orderly as his stamp collection, as neat as his college desk. One day Raleigh was called to the overseas operator and told by his father's faint crackling voice that his mother had suddenly, surprisingly, died of a cerebral hemorrhage. "I don't believe it," said Raleigh. "It doesn't make any sense."

All his life, he'd clung to reason like a parachute. What didn't make sense couldn't be true. Had he heard that another Hayes had died, that would have been different. Hayeses died. And grandparents died, aunts and uncles died. But Sarah Ainsworth, who wasn't very old and didn't smoke or drink or stuff herself with gallons of sugary tea and platters of fried chicken, how could she be dead?

And then the second shock. How could Sarah Ainsworth, who, humiliated by betrayal, had more than a decade ago asked her husband to leave their home, who had often said to and of that husband that he appeared to be constitutionally incapable of understanding the value of money — how could Sarah Ainsworth, a bookkeeper, even had she been foolish enough ever to make a will leaving $60,000 to Earley Hayes in the first place, *how* could she have forgotten to change that will after the divorce?! It wasn't the money. Raleigh, of course, had inherited the bulk of the estate: the house, the insurance settlement, and $60,000 of his own. No, it wasn't the money. It was the principle. Earley didn't deserve a cent, as even he had admitted himself, right there in the lawyer's office, the afternoon before Raleigh flew bewildered back to Germany.

His first night of leave after his return, he walked fifteen miles in snow from the Freiburg base to a little Rhine village, turned around and walked back in worse snow. He spent the next month in the army infirmary, fevered with bronchitis, and then pneumonia. Most of the time he slept, the rest of the time he criticized Christ in the hospital's bedside Bible — a liberty for which he was taken to task by a nurse, who ordered him to erase his marginalia. And all this while, and quite despite his lifelong habit of talking to himself and thinking about himself, Raleigh did not realize that the shock of an unreasonable, unacceptable loss, the perplexity of all these now unanswerable mysteries about his mother — all the now irretrievable loose ends: why the money, why the love, why the mitigating circumstances? — had made him not only dangerously ill, but so furious with God that he'd challenged His Son to a debate; challenged Him, and in Raleigh's opinion, settled things once and for all to his own satisfaction. God was a bastard, and Christ was a fool.

And so he got on with his life. He returned to his schedule. He chose a career, he chose a wife, they bought a house, they brought home children. Hayes took the past to the attic, stored in cartons, neatly labeled. Dust settled silently over them. Until now. And now this week, this awful endless senseless week, it was as if all that past — forgotten words, dead people, lost times — had burst through those boxes in the attic and rushed downstairs, crashed through windows, stormed into the quiet house of Raleigh W. Hayes and were noisily tumbling it to a shambles.

Memories leaped around Hayes as he crouched on the porch of the little single-story cottage "Peace and Quiet," and looked in at the old-fashioned furniture he'd brought there after closing his mother's house, as he looked in at his brother Gates pretending to play a trumpet (accompanied by the stereo Raleigh had himself built from a kit years ago). Hayes sighed and said aloud, "The remembrance of them is grievous unto us. The burden of them is intolerable."

"What?" whispered Mingo.

"Nothing."

"What did you say?"

"Nothing."

"Is that Gates? Gollee, he looks kind of like a movie star now. He sure is a good trumpet player."

"For Pete's sake, Mingo, can't you tell that's a recording? You know, I really wonder about you."

The jazz blues — horns, drums, piano, clarinet, and bass all talking at once — was so loud the windows rattled. As a result, Gates had not noticed the Thermopyleans, but when Raleigh stood and, finding the door locked, shook the handle, the mock-musician reacted dramatically. He fell instantly to the floor, crawled to the wall, and pulled the lamp plug.

"Gates! Open the door! It's Raleigh!"

The porch light came on, and was instantly assaulted by bugs that must have been lying in wait. Then the door opened the width of a chain that Raleigh did not recall having put there. He saw one immensely blue, long-lashed eye, the tip of a sharp nose, and part of a thin black mustache.

"Shit! It *is* you. Who's that with you?" was Gates's greeting to a brother he hadn't seen for five years.

"Open the goddamn door. It's Mingo Sheffield. What's going on here?" was Raleigh's return greeting.

The door swung open and the two men stared at each other. Gates was handsomely built and beautifully dressed in odd white fabrics of a space-age Japanese cut; Raleigh was smeared with mud and blood, and was looking fairly frail inside the billowing rags of Sheffield's Hawaiian shirt.

"Fuck. They got you!" said Gates. "Jesus! Are they still out there? Get in!"

"Is that my trumpet?" said Raleigh simultaneously. "What gives you the right to waltz in here and make yourself at home!"

"Where'd they go? How many were there? Did one of them have an ivory cane? Shit!" said Gates, wedging a chair against the door. "Get away from the windows!"

"It happened at Captain Nemo's," said Mingo. "Whole bunch of guys started beating Raleigh up, but I practically pulverized them. Didn't I, Raleigh? I didn't know what I was doing. All of a sudden —"

"Captain Nemo's?"

"A restaurant type of a bar."

"Where's that? That's not around here. Who are you?"

"Mingo. You remember me. I'm Raleigh's best friend."

"Okay," said Raleigh. "Who is 'they'? Who's AFTER YOU?" Gates had switched off the phonograph, and Raleigh's shout bounced around the room. He lowered his voice and stroked his face. "Okay. Okay. Let's everybody calm down. Nobody followed us here. Whatever your problem is, Gates, it's got nothing to do with the people that beat us up."

"We beat them up, Raleigh! Gollee!"

"Mingo, please! All right, Gates, would you be good enough to explain what you're doing here in 'Peace and Quiet'? Gates, would you please . . ." Raleigh's brother was sidling along the walls from window to window, living room to kitchen to bedrooms, peering out, nervously fingering the trumpet he still held. "Hey, right, great, sure, fine, hey," he said as he went. Finally — apparently satisfied that they were alone — he returned to the couch where Sheffield had flopped, and at the arm of which Raleigh was glowering; there were a number of round black holes burned into it.

"Fantastic." Gates now smiled. "You guys like a drink?"

"I'd like an explanation," his older brother said.

"I'd like a rum and Coke," said Mingo cheerfully, "or maybe a screw-driver, or a whiskey sour's fine too. Can I have this piece of pizza on the coffee table? I don't mind if it's cold. This is a nice place, Raleigh. I wish I'd known it was this nice. I'm going to bring Vera here next summer. Listen, Gates, how have you been? Gosh, I haven't seen you in ages. I was real sorry to hear you had to go to prison like that. I know what it feels like; the police are after me for murder; well, they're really after Raleigh, but we're as innocent as you are."

"How 'bout a beer?" smiled Gates, behind the couch, spinning his finger round his temple in the old icon of madness, then crooking the finger at Raleigh, who followed him to the kitchen. "Is that porker loose from the nuthouse or what?" he whispered to his brother.

"Yes," said Raleigh. "Forget him."

"Fine. He's your pal." Gates took beers from a refrigerator fuming with sour milk and moldy leftovers of junk food. "So. Who'd you kill, Specs? Daddy?"

"Don't call me Specs. And Daddy's killing himself. He ran off from the hospital, and God knows what he's up to. I'm trying to find him."

"What a pisser." Gates laughed.

"Gates, what are you doing in my house? You have no right."

"So, what can I say? I'm sorry. It was Lovie's idea. She checked it out with your wife. How's Aura doing? How're the girls? Have a beer."

Hayes pushed the bottle away. "You are unbelievable."

Gates smiled, shrugging, strangely reminding Raleigh of Caroline; they had the same eyelashes and the same impenetrable nonchalance. "Is that my trumpet?" Hayes pointed back at the living room.

Rubbing the beer bottle slowly against his cheek, Gates stared at his older brother. "Man, you've gone kind of freaky, you know that? I don't think I can handle it, Raleigh. You show up here in a tacky Hawaiian shirt, wasted, the middle of the night, twinned up with a fat nut talking about bar fights and murders, and it sounds like you drove here for a fucking trumpet. I definitely can't handle it. I'm under a lot of pressure, I don't need this." He walked back into the living room, where Mingo had astonishingly already fallen asleep, snoring, stretched on the couch, his huge, fat suede oxfords dangling over the end. "Anyhow, it's not your trumpet, okay. It was Daddy's."

"Well, he wants it. So give it back."

"Sure. Take it easy. Hey, I do remember this guy. Mingo. Right. His trunks fell off at Forbes Pool. Used to eat whole loaves of Wonder Bread, squishing the pieces into balls." Gates made gobbling noises.

"Gates, listen to me. Lovie said you were hiding out. Are the police looking for you again? You haven't been selling any more of those forged genealogies, have you?"

"Oh, that. Are you kidding?"

"I thought you told me when I sent you that money to Nevada that you'd finished your parole."

"Sure, I did. I've got no problems with the South Carolina cops, if that's what's worrying you. I'm clean as a baby."

"You told me you needed that money to get married."

"Oh, her. That didn't exactly pan out. I get the feeling I'm not meant for the picket fence. It's sad, you know what I mean. But, what can you do? You're stuck with who you are. I'm a flyer, Raleigh. Listen, I'm in a new line of business, big stuff."

"I bet."

"Thanks a lot for the love and support."

"What are you up to, Gates? One, you were clearly under the impression that somebody followed us here. Two, you were frankly scared out of your wits. Three, Lovie distinctly said something to me about gangsters. Now, I admit Lovie has a tendency to dramatize things but —"

"Good old Lovie. She's the only one that ever really cared about me. I mean even Daddy got on my case." Gates slumped with ostentatious self-pity into the armchair that had once been Raleigh's mother's. "How's Lovie doing, anyhow?"

"Fine. . . . Well, actually, I'm afraid she has cancer." Blushing, Hayes took off his glasses and pulled on the bent stem. How was he going to tell Gates that his mother also had cancer, was dying of it? He sat down across from him.

"Yeah, I knew about that. That's fucking life, isn't it? A pisser. I love that lady." Gates sighed, then bounced to his feet. "Listen, Raleigh, you just passing through, looking for a trumpet, or what?"

Hayes, suddenly so weary his arms slid from the chair rests into his lap, glanced up at the handsome man now stretching his body into slow-motion karate positions. "Gates. Gates. Daddy asked me to find you. Your mother's, well, she's pretty ill. She didn't know how to get in touch with you. She wrote to me. She wants to see you. I'm taking you to Midway."

"Roxanne?" The loose white sleeves continued to float out in slow arcs.

"What do you mean, 'Roxanne'? Yes, Roxanne. Your mother. Your mother's pretty ill. She's very ill."

"Too bad," said Gates, bending, stretching one leg.

"She wants to see you."

"She should have thought about that when she ran off."

Raleigh crossed his arms tightly. "I'm not getting into the past with you, Gates. I'm just telling you I'm taking you to see her. It's not my responsibility —"

"Right." The left leg suddenly shot out in air, swinging over the couch where Mingo slept peacefully oblivious, little bubbles on his fat lips.

"But I'm going to do it." Hayes stood. "I'm not going to leave without you."

Gates spun around, then tapped his brother on the chin. "Sameo sameo Raleigh. You're not even kidding, are you?"

Hayes didn't move.

"Listen." Gates frowned. "I'm sorry about Roxanne. Okay? I mean, you know, we weren't exactly up there in a league with Oedipus Rex. I haven't even laid eyes on her since, shit, who knows when."

"I thought she came to see you in prison?"

"Big whup. Once. And she didn't bring a file in a birthday cake either. But okay. I'm sorry."

"I'm glad to hear it. Just ask yourself how you'd feel if she should, well, die, and you hadn't taken this, this opportunity."

"Right. Fine. I don't mind going, but I've got to meet a friend first. I promised I'd pick up some stuff of his tomorrow night and take it to Myrtle Beach. Old Vietnam pal. You always said, keep your promises, right?" Gates went to the wall mirror and watched himself move his arms in what Hayes assumed were more karate gestures. "So you just go on. I'll catch you in Midway. Boy, what a boonie town. And Fred! The boonie boozer trucker. Boy oh boy."

"Fred died."

"Right. Who doesn't."

"Don't be offended, Gates, but I think I would prefer to stay with you until we get to Midway. So I'll go with you while you run this 'errand,'

and then we'll leave. And first thing tomorrow, you call Roxanne and tell her we're coming."

"Awwh. He doesn't trust me to go see my own sick mother. That hurts, Raleigh. Awwh." And the two men stared at each other in the mirror until Gates said, "You want to come with me to run this errand?"

"No. I don't want to do a great many of the things I am obliged to do. But I do them. That's one of the differences between us."

Gates turned, strangely smiling. "All right, big brother. It's a deal. You come with me, I come with you. Now. All settled. How 'bout a beer? Family reunion. Happy St. Patrick's Day and all that jazz."

And so it was that twenty-four hours later, midnight on Friday, Raleigh Hayes, drenched and terrified, found himself rolling and bucking in a black heaving sea, while he held to the wheel of a dirty, dilapidated, thirty-foot motorboat called "Easy Living"; while his brother leaned from its helm hauling in a rubber raft in which was tied a large plastic bag; while the two shadowy men in the fishing boat that had tossed the raft overboard at them screamed at Gates in a foreign language that Gates later confessed he didn't understand.

CHAPTER

18

How Mingo Fared Alone at Myrtle Beach

WHEN MINGO SHEFFIELD ROLLED OFF THE COUCH at nine in the morning, he woke up, cramped, sore, and scared to find himself suddenly on the floor of a strange beach cottage, but relieved to be no longer chased by Billy Knox in the Hell's Angels' van — which was what he'd been dreaming. In one bedroom Raleigh lay sleeping with his arms crossed over his face; in the other, Gates lay curled in a ball in the corner of the bed. They were still asleep after Mingo showered, studied his scrapes and bruises, dressed in a fresh pink polo shirt and checked pants, and (finding in the kitchen no food that wasn't green with fungus) drove the Cadillac back to the center of Kure Beach to a grocery store where he spent some more of one of his shoe fifties to buy a week's worth of food, plus some souvenir saltwater taffy. When he returned to the beach cottage, there was a telegram wedged in the door, addressed to Raleigh Hayes. Mingo's heart was thudding. Somebody must be dead! Should he wake up Raleigh right now? What a terrible way to get bad news! On a piece of paper! Maybe he should find out what it said, and he could help Raleigh prepare himself; make him take a big drink, or lie down, or something like that. Mingo held the envelope against the kitchen light, but he couldn't see inside. There was nothing to do but try what they did in the movies. And so, having boiled a pan of water, Sheffield steamed open the telegram, and, his fat fingers trembling, read: LOVIE SAID YOU GOING TO KURE. YOU'RE DOING JUST FINE, LITTLE FELLOW. LOVE, DADDY. The telegram had come all the way from Memphis, Tennessee.

Mingo was so relieved, he had to sit down while he pounded the wrinkled envelope closed. Maybe he wouldn't mention that he'd opened it.

The two Hayeses weren't awakened even by the noise he made accidentally-on-purpose by dropping pans while he cooked himself breakfast; they slept on while he ate three fried eggs and (gradually, without intending to) nibbled away every piece of fried bacon. Had Raleigh not been twitching and Gates snoring whenever Mingo sneaked in to check on them, he would have been certain that his fears had been realized, and they were the ones who were dead.

After breakfast, Sheffield sat on the porch with an old *Time* magazine. It was full of last summer's urgent news that nobody cared about anymore. He rolled it into a telescope, and stared through it across the Atlantic Ocean. If he only had magic eyes, he'd be able to see right onto the beach in England or France or Spain or wherever was straight across from exactly here. Maybe some foreigner was on that beach right this minute staring at him. Maybe the two of them were looking right into each other's eyes and didn't even know it. "Well," said Mingo to that possible European, in the absence of anyone closer. "Here I am. Mingo Sheffield. 'Peace and Quiet.' Surf Street. Kure Beach, North Carolina. United States. North America. Planet Earth." And having made this announcement of his whereabouts in the style he had once used on his schoolbooks, he fell silent.

So little was happening in "Peace and Quiet" on this Friday morning that had Mingo been an analytical man, he would have had plenty of time to consider the foolishness of his driving around the countryside with his neighbor, Raleigh Hayes, whose behavior (had Sheffield taken a moment to think about it) was thoroughly bizarre, and whose motives (had Sheffield bothered to question them) were entirely obscure. But in fact Mingo was not an analytical man. He was, by nature, a man of faith, and it hadn't even occurred to him to worry that his neighbor had so lost his way, if not his mind, that for days he'd been leading them absolutely nowhere for no apparent reason. Mingo had always believed that Raleigh knew what he was doing, and if Raleigh didn't care to share his plans, that, too, was nothing new.

Meanwhile, the truth was, Mingo was enjoying himself immensely. Of course, he missed Vera, but other than that, life on the road was certainly more pleasant than life standing around in Knox-Bury's Clothing Store getting his feelings hurt for two more weeks, while trying to guess from

Billy Knox's face if he was suspicious about who'd thrown all that paint on the best spring selections. Yes, here he was, on the road, just like he'd always wanted to be, except he'd been too chicken. He wouldn't want to be on the road *alone,* that's for sure; but here he was with Raleigh, going to one new place after another, going to parties like the one at Raleigh's nice aunt's house, meeting nice people like Sister Joe and Anne and that poor little Mary Theresa; having adventures, just like he'd always dreamed about, but could never think of any himself, and even if he could have, he was not a very good organizer. That was the wonderful thing about Vera: she was full of new ideas, and full of energy, and had just a natural management personality. He was lucky to have Vera for a wife, and Raleigh for a friend, and if he had to lose his job and his car and get robbed and beaten up in order to go places, well, that was life, and life, when you got down to it, philosophized Mingo as he scanned the beach with his rolled-up magazine, was more interesting by a long shot than Better Menswear. So, all you had to do was keep your courage up and stick with a good organizer.

Still hearing no noise from the bedrooms, Sheffield took off his shoes. He looked at his feet for a while. It seemed to him that his second toes were getting longer. Finally, his Confederate cap on his head and his checked pants rolled as high as they would go up his enormous calves, he ambled for a long while zigzagging along the beach, where he found three only moderately broken shells, a horsecrab skeleton, and a barefoot woman with a bucket of seaweed. He trotted over to her and said, "Hi. Nice day."

"Not really," she replied, frowning. And, in fact, she was right. The sky churned with gray clouds; the ocean churned with gray swells; even the sand was gray.

"Well, it's not too hot. That's always nice. I'm Mingo Sheffield. I'm just visiting here with my neighbor, Raleigh Hayes. We're in 'Peace and Quiet.'" He pointed back at the cottage. "You collect seaweed?"

"Not really."

"You know, they say if we'd all just eat seaweed, we could feed the whole entire world and knock out starvation for good. Does it taste funny?"

"I suppose. Excuse me. Good-bye." The woman turned her back and hurried away into the surf like a sandpiper.

"Nice talking to you," called Mingo, digging his toes in the cool sand. He walked slowly back to the corner of Surf Street, where he'd noticed a pay phone. He took a chance and called Vera. She hadn't left yet for the Forbes Building to help Aura organize the new M.F.P. headquarters, and she was very happy to hear from him, particularly as it was now clear that nobody had been murdered with his guns, and there was no reason for him to flee to South America, or for her to have to keep telling lies. She was happy even though he had to confess that he'd sold her Pinto and then been robbed of the proceeds by Hell's Angels. He had a great deal more to tell her, too, including his victory at Captain Nemo's, including his decision to continue on this trip to rescue Earley Hayes, since Raleigh needed somebody to help him — as Captain's Nemo's had shown — and who but his friend should stick by him no matter what.

Vera had things to tell him as well. Billy Knox had no idea who'd thrown the paint on his clothes, but he didn't for a minute suspect Mingo, and, in fact, when she had gone in there to tell him that Mingo was so brokenhearted about getting fired that he'd seriously tried to kill himself, and was still so upset that he'd had to leave town for a rest cure, Billy Knox had himself gotten so upset that he'd promised to give Mingo an extra month's severance pay on top of the two weeks already agreed upon — and to do so whether Mingo felt well enough to return to work during that time or not. Meanwhile, Pierce Jimson was buying the Knox-Bury building, because he was expanding his furniture business, and Billy thought maybe Mingo should talk to Pierce about a job there.

Mingo didn't think he'd like furniture as much as clothes. Besides, he had great hopes for a new business idea of Vera's, which wouldn't require much venture capital — or much space either, as it would be mostly a mail-order business — and now that Vera had found out how cheaply you could rent one of the smaller empty offices in the Forbes Building, maybe her brother-in-law would lend them enough to get going, even if they hadn't quite paid him back what they'd borrowed a few years ago to start the door-to-door plant hanger company that hadn't worked out too well. Cheerfully, the Sheffields talked on and on until Vera heard Barbara Kettell's horn honk. She had only a second to share some other news: After Barbara Kettell's release by the judge, Barbara had told Nemours she'd never step back inside his house unless he apologized for his behavior at the *Woman Alive!* show. So poor Barbara was sleeping in the baby's room at her daughter's, Mrs. Wayne Sparks's. The Sheffields agreed that they were lucky, and kissed each other through the phones.

Back at "Peace and Quiet," Mingo found Raleigh, still wearing last night's disheveled Hawaiian shirt, staring in disbelief at the opened telegram. "Hey, Raleigh, you're up! That came for you, I just put it there on the table for you. I hope it's nothing serious."

"Grrrrrh," said Hayes.

"So! What are we going to do today?"

"I don't believe this," Hayes replied, now peering up at the kitchen clock. "Eleven o'clock. I never sleep till eleven o'clock. I'm a very early riser."

"Where's Gates?"

"Gates," said Hayes sadly. "He went to make a phone call, and take care of some arrangements."

"He's got a car? I didn't see it."

"A motorcycle."

"Boy, I'd be too chicken to ride one of those. Is he coming with us on our trip?"

"With us?" Hayes now shook himself. "Listen, Mingo. Gates has to go see his mother. She's dying."

"Gosh. Poor thing." Mingo sat down. "Boy, I sure know what that feels like."

Raleigh sighed. "But first, he has to run an errand for a friend, and I've agreed to go with him, and it now appears, I'm afraid, that this . . ." He sighed again. ". . . errand involves taking a boat out from Cape Fear late tonight, and getting it to Myrtle Beach. So, Mingo, I have to ask you a favor."

"A boat on the ocean? At night? Gollee! What for? Are you crazy?"

"Very possibly." Raleigh reached for one of Mingo's cigarettes on the kitchen table and lit it. "So I need you to drive the car to Myrtle Beach, and get a motel, and we'll meet you there."

"By myself?"

"Would you prefer to accompany my brother on this boat, because, frankly — " Hayes broke off, his face ruptured by a loud fit of coughing.

"Raleigh, you're smoking!"

Hayes smashed out the cigarette in his saucer. "Oh, for God's sake. I don't smoke. Are you going to do me this one little favor or not? All I'm asking you to do is drive the damn car you forced me to buy to Myrtle Beach."

"Then are we going to New Orleans?"

Hayes stood. "I don't know where we're going! Isn't that transparently clear?" Hayes began twisting the knobs on the sink faucets, which were dripping.

"Come on, Raleigh. Don't tease me," smiled Mingo. "Where are we going?"

Now Hayes had crawled under the sink and was banging at the pipes. "All right, Mingo. How's this? We're going to Myrtle Beach, then we're taking Gates to Midway to see his dying mother, then we're going to Charleston to give five thousand dollars to an old Negro friend of my father's, then we're going to row to Cuba and bump off Castro, all right? I'm really in the CIA, Mingo, I wasn't supposed to tell you. All right? Now I've got to do some work around here. This place is falling apart. Where are the car keys?"

"You're kidding about Castro." Sheffield followed his fast-moving friend outside.

Downtown at Bob's Hardware, Mingo had an idea while Raleigh was ordering, with an enviable expertise, small items like washers, bolts, nuts, and putty, that he always seemed to know what to do with. Dropping the handyman back at "Peace and Quiet," Mingo returned to town to search among the fishing tackle stands and the family surf-and-turf restaurants for a clothing shop. Finally he found a musty department store so old-fashioned the pants were folded in stacks on dark wood shelves and the shirts didn't even have plastic wrappers. The place had no style at all. The two mannequins in the window were just standing there side by side, like they had lockjaw; the woman, in a winter coat that was far too big for her, didn't even have any shoes on, and the man's Bermuda shorts hung down to his knees. Nevertheless, a sticker in the window announced the acceptance of all major credit cards.

"Hi there, how you doing? What have you got in a forty-two long lightweight suit, blue or tan?" Sheffield asked the young pregnant woman who'd been watching him shake his head as he wandered the aisles. She wore her white-blond hair in dozens of tight tiny pigtails; like the mannequins' clothes, her maternity blouse was too large and out of fashion. He put down on the counter a pair of socks, a pair of bikini jockey shorts, a baby-blue-striped shirt, and a blue-dotted tie. "And congratulations!" he added. "I see you're about to have a happy event. That's wonderful."

"Tell my folks that," she sighed, and slowly sidled from behind the counter over to a small rack where she jerked aside a few dusty suits. "You sure you wear a forty-two?"

"Me? Gollee, no, I wear a fifty-two. I'm buying this stuff for a friend. We're on a trip to Charleston and New Orleans and maybe even Cuba, and he forgot his suitcase, so I thought this would be a nice surprise, 'cause he's been wearing my old muddy shirt for days. I know all his sizes because he's bought all his clothes from me for ages and ages. I'm in Better Menswear." He smiled, bobbing his moon face. "Well, I used to be."

The girl looked awhile at Sheffield, but apparently decided that if insane, he was harmless, for she smiled back. "This is all we've got." She held up a stark white, broad-lapeled polyester three-piece suit. "It's half price."

"I guess so," said Mingo. "This isn't exactly my friend's style. It kind of looks like a disco dancer."

"I don't really work here anymore. I'm going to Atlanta soon as I get some money together."

"Is that where your husband is, Atlanta?"

"Sort of." She squished her lips together fretfully. "I just got to get out of here." She looked around, as if for an escape route. "Oh, do you want this suit?"

Mingo nodded, and found his Visa card. "Well, you're lucky to be having a baby. Vera and I, she's my wife, we tried for years, but God didn't bless us. I mean, don't get me wrong, He blessed us in lots of other ways."

Folding the white jacket, the girl all at once burst into tears.

"Oh, dear! What's wrong?"

"Nu, nu, nothing."

Distressed, Sheffield stood there, patting her on the shoulder. After a few minutes, he said, "My name's Mingo. What's yours?"

She took a long breath. "Diane. Listen, I'm sorry about this. Kind of lost it. Diane Yonge."

"Well, look here, Diane, I just got robbed by some Hell's Angels, so all I've got left is fifty in my shoe. But I could lend you that, and I bet you could get the bus to Atlanta. Listen, okay, how's that? I'd be glad to."

Diane looked up at the fat man's wide bobbing face with the little Confederate cap above it. "Are you kidding?" She looked puzzled, then skeptical, then her lips twisted into bitterness. "Sure. I get it. And what do I have to do for you?"

Mingo was struggling to bend down to untie his shoe. "For me? Well, maybe you could send me the money back if you get a chance. Here." And he wrote his address down on the fifty-dollar bill. The young woman kept staring, first at him, then the money. Finally her mouth loosened into a smile. "Boy . . ." she began, "why are you so nice?"

Sheffield grinned, rubbing his immense palms together. "Now! Diane! Let's you and me have some fun, and take your mind off your troubles. You have any construction paper or some tissue paper and maybe some paint?"

Startled back to cynicism, she shoved the shoppings bags at him. "I knew it. Okay, mister, you can just get out of here."

"Knew it? Hey, wait a minute. Wait a minute, Diane, I'm serious. Your display window's got no style. Honest. It's bad for business. Wait. I can help you fix it up. I'm not really all that busy today, and I guess maybe you're not either, and this way you won't have to sit around and miss your husband."

And so it was that when Gates Hayes bumped his motorcycle up the curb and parked it in front of Yonge Department Store, he saw in their window Mingo Sheffield crawling on his hands and knees beside a female mannequin who now lay reading a magazine in a bathing suit and jacket on a bright beach towel under a striped umbrella. Next to Mingo, a pretty pregnant girl was fitting a fishing cap on the head of a male mannequin, who stared, rod in hand, out over a blue tissue-paper sea. A sign in the yellow cloth sand said, "IN THE GOOD OLD SUMMERTIME!"

"Definitely a bimbo," said Gates, laughing, then strolled into the bank across the street, where he removed from his recently acquired safety deposit box the black leather shaving kit containing four thousand dollars in recently acquired cash. When he got back to his motorcycle, Sheffield was standing on the sidewalk hugging the girl. She waved at him as she closed the shop door.

"Hey, Mingo! Hi. You zone in fast," grinned Gates and ran his thumb over his thin black mustache. "What's your secret? Not a bad-looking babe. Just a little knocked-up maybe. So, what you got in the bags? How 'bout a beer? Let's go down the street, blow it off. Just don't get in a fight, tear up the place. I hear you're a killer! Okay?" He laughed.

Mingo smiled shyly. People in Thermopylae rarely invited him to come have drinks; especially such wild, worldly people as Gates, who wore clothes like they did in New York magazines: in his crumpled silver pullover, full of big zippers and big pockets, he looked like a space-traveling pirate.

At the best table in the Blockade Runner, the two drank beer and ate boiled shrimp. "I was sorry to hear about your mother," Mingo said. "Mine died two years ago in February, and I guess I still can't believe it." He sighed.

"Yeah." Gates called for a waitress by pointing his forefinger at her and winking. "Yeah. She's in the hospital. Just called her on the phone. Some chick at her house gave me the number. Big reconciliation scene. Boo hoo. Told her I was sorry I'd been such a pisser. 'Course, Mingo my friend, I want you to know I only laid eyes on this woman three or four times since I was a little kid, and she was soused half of those. She was not exactly gushing with maternal milk. I never could figure out why old Earley married Roxanne. Just 'cause he knocked her up, I guess. Boo hoo."

Sheffield was a little shocked by Gate's tone, but he concluded that such tough talk was typical of the exotic convict adventurer type of person that Raleigh's brother appeared to be. In the movies, these types always really did love their mothers.

"Yeah, old Raleigh made me call her, so I charged it to his phone. But I did it. He was always making me do shit." Gates shook his curls at the waitress, and zipped a few zippers on his sleeves back and forth as she took their order. "Good old do-the-right-thing Raleigh. Man, doesn't it blow you away to see a tightwad like him driving that Cadillac! Man, it blew *me* away! I mean, he can afford it. The guy's richer than Midas — you knew that, didn't you? Got a bundle from his mother, and stuck it all in the bank and let it breed like rabbits ever since. I thought he wouldn't touch it if his teeth fell out. Owns all these damn beach houses. I don't see Roxanne leaving me a wad of family jewels, do you? All she left Earley when she skipped out, was *me!* What a pisser! What a world!" Gates kept laughing.

Mingo felt he ought to explain. "I think Raleigh is maybe afraid your father might have married a teenaged Negro mental patient. I think."

"Aces!" Gates snorted. "Now that'll be hard to top!"

Mingo found Gates easy to talk to, or rather, to listen to, for all through their meal, the younger man held forth on one fascinating topic after another. He used different voices and different accents and it was just like being at the movies. He told of the noisy, gilt gambling casinos and long-legged show girls of Las Vegas, and the famous nightclub singer with the terrible voice whom he had personally slept with in her dressing room.

"Gollee!" said Mingo, his eyes round.

He told of the still, steamy terror of Vietnam jungles, and the pals he'd lost there. He told of the cramped smelly cells and hard-muscled, hard-minded convicts of the South Carolina prison, and the notorious old master criminal Simon "Weeper" Berg, whom he had personally bunked with. Weeper Berg, now seventy, who in his heyday had hobnobbed with the very popes and cardinals of organized crime, and had most recently almost gotten away with the highly publicized robbery of the Sheikh of Enbar's Hilton Head lovenest.

"I read about that!" said Mingo, his mouth round.

Gates told of rooster fights in Mexico and dog races in Florida and poker marathons in Texas that he'd personally lost his shirt at. And cycles and cars and boats that he had personally driven faster than they'd ever been driven before.

"Gosh," said Mingo. "You sure have done a lot of things. I've never really gone very many places. I mean, until now. I've mostly stayed in Thermopylae. In Better Menswear."

"Um hum," Gates said, ordering more beer and more shrimp. "You're stuck with who you are. Me, I'm a funny dude. I'm a flyer, Mingo. I like to be in motion."

"I guess so! What do you do for a living, Gates!"

"Little of this, little of that. Have some beer. I see you wearing a Confederate cap. You interested in the War Between the States?"

"Oh, yes! I love it. I've seen *Gone With the Wind* about a hundred times, I guess. And I get the Time-Life book series, I'm up to volume seven. I love everything about the Civil War. I mean, except that we lost."

"Me too," smiled Gates and cracked the pink shell of his shrimp to dip it in horseradish. "Aren't these good? While you're here at Kure, hey, you ought to go look at Fort Fisher. Ever been there? No? You'd love it. Did you know, the heaviest land-sea battle of the whole Civil War took place right there? Really. Between January thirteenth and fifteenth, Yankee ships threw two million pounds of artillery at Fort Fisher. Two million!"

"Wow! What happened?"

"We surrendered," Gates laughed. "More than the Vietnamese did, right?" He laughed some more, and Mingo joined in, delighted to be laughing with somebody, even if he didn't quite catch the joke.

"Boy, Gates, you sure know a lot about the Civil War."

"Well, in all modesty, Mingo, I used to be a bit of a scholar of that period, did a bit of work in archives, genealogical line, you know." Gates's voice, gestures, face, even his mustache (now drooping), had changed remarkably. He suddenly sounded like a dusty, preoccupied professor. "I imagine you've naturally had your family tree traced, know which ancestors fought for the South, what battles they distinguished themselves in, their acts of heroism, so forth?"

Sheffield took off his souvenir cap and looked reverently at the Stars and Bars decal. "Gee, no. I never did, I guess. You think some Sheffields were in some of those battles? Really?"

"The name does seem to ring a bell. Yes, yes. Sheffield. Was it Bull Run? Let's see. Chancellorsville?" Gates shook his head. "Well, never mind. But, really, someday, if I were you, I'd look into it. Absolutely amazing what I've been able to find out for people who didn't have any idea the famous heroes they were directly descended from!"

Mingo leaned over the beer pitcher in big-eyed wonder. "You think *you* could find out for me?"

"I might." Gates nodded for about five seconds. "Well, gotta scoot." He rubbed his mustache and looked again like a pirate. "Grab the check, will yah, my friend? Catch you later. Aces!" He was gone in a flash, as the waitress hurried over and blocked Mingo in the booth. The fat man looked at the bill, which was considerably more than the eleven dollars he had left from his last shoe fifty. "Excuse me, miss, do you take credit cards?"

Sheffield drove straight from the Blockade Runner to Fort Fisher, and although what he saw was mostly just high long mounds of grass called "Confederate Earthworks," he stood there solemnly for a long while, as he dreamed of his ancestor, some Major or Colonel Sheffield, loved by his men and known to his friends as St. Hilary George Stonewall Phillippe, or something like that, who shook his filigreed sword at all the blasting Yankee ships and shouted, "We shall never surrender, sirs, think not that we shall!" Then it started to rain, so Mingo drove back to "Peace and Quiet."

He found Raleigh on the sink counter, busy glazing the kitchen windowpanes. He was wearing army fatigues, his own old army fatigues, which he'd found in the attic. Mingo sighed. "I wish I could wear something that old. I bet I couldn't even get my leg in my old clothes. I don't know how I got so fat." Hayes turned his head to stare at his friend, who was pawing through his saltwater taffy looking for the strawberry ones. "Gates and I just had lunch at a nice place. He sure is pretty interesting. He's done just about everything you could think of."

"I know," said Hayes.

"He said maybe he'd look up my genealogy for me. Wasn't that nice? He thinks my family had some heroes in the War Between the States, and he'll research them for me."

"Forget about that," Hayes snarled, wheeling around on his knees. "He'll do no such thing."

"You mean he doesn't have time?"

"I mean that's what he went to prison for!"

"For family trees? Gollee!"

Hayes slapped more putty on the sill. "Where have you been? It's five twenty."

"Oh." Sheffield shyly held out his shopping bags. "I didn't know you had your uniform. It's just clothes." He shook out the socks, shorts, the blue shirt and dotted tie. Then he held up the white suit. "Well, it's just this. It was the only one Diane had in your size. If you don't want it, I'll take it back."

Raleigh was staring at the fat man, his face bright red. "Diane?"

"At the store. Poor little thing, she's having a baby and her husband's gone to Atlanta. I guess you don't like it, hunh? I kind of didn't think you would."

"No, it's . . ." Hayes slid down off the counter to take the glossy white wide-lapeled jacket that Sheffield still held up by both shoulders. "Well, Mingo. Well. Gosh. I don't know what to say. It's really, it's really nice of you. But you shouldn't have. Really."

Mingo happily bubbled over. "You had to have some clothes, didn't you? You couldn't keep wearing mine, could you? Here, try it on. Look at that! Perfect. Cuffs and everything. Gosh, Raleigh, stop saying I shouldn't have; what are friends for?" He retired to the bathroom, picking up on the way a book called *The Optimist's Daughter.* He took it because he considered himself an optimist, and he wanted to see if the one in the book was like him. On the flyleaf was signed in beautiful handwriting, *Aura Godwin Hayes.*

When he finally came out of the bathroom, he saw Raleigh crawling around the living room floor, squeezing wood putty in the cracks. Back on the kitchen table, he saw a long list of all the tasks the industrious life insurance salesman had or would accomplish. Judging from the bold check marks beside them, he had already taken care of the following: "Kitch. fauc. drips. Tight. pipes. Sh'wr head caulk. Hinge, frnt. dr. Gates, call Rox. Reserve Holiday Inn. Change realtor. Loose porch. Glaze. Cracks." The only items left undone were "Fert. az. bshes. Deposit Aura, Dan, deed," and "Bathroom light cord." As Sheffield had no idea what "Fert. az. bshes" meant (or, for that matter, what Hayes had in mind under "Deposit Aura"), he decided to help out his friend by taking the new brass-beaded pull lying on the table beside a screwdriver, and attaching it to the light fixture on the wall by the bathroom sink, since, as he himself had noticed, someone must have jerked the old one out. Carefully, he removed the bulb, held it up, and looked at it as if it were an idea. Then he took off the porcelain base. Then he studied the socket. He saw the hole into which the little brass beads must go. But how? Maybe he better not touch that socket with his bare hand. Sheffield reached for the washcloth on the sink. Seconds later, Raleigh stood panting in the doorway, shouting, *"What? What?"* The fat man was lying on the linoleum with his head in the shower stall, still holding in his hand a smoking cloth spotted with little brown scorched smelly nubs. "I'm on fire," he yelled. "Raleigh, Raleigh! Don't touch that! It'll electrocute you!"

"Not anymore." Hayes held up the burnt black cardboard casing. "You blew all the fuses."

Fifteen minutes later, as Raleigh was handing Mingo his suitcase, and loading into the backseat his own new clothes and his father's trumpet, and loading Mingo into the front seat, to send him, hours early, off in the rain to the motel room already reserved in Myrtle Beach, Sheffield kept repeating, "I was just trying to help, that's all. Why do I have to leave so soon?"

"The best help you can be, honestly, is to go to the Holiday Inn now, and wait, and if I'm not there by the time you wake up in the morning, call the Coast Guard, and tell Aura my last thoughts were my regrets that I never saw her belly dance."

"What?"

"Never mind."

"What do you mean, 'if I'm not there'? You're scaring me."

"I'm only kidding." Raleigh pushed his gigantic friend into the driver's seat. "And don't run out of gas!"

"But, Raleigh, I haven't got any money!"

"What about your shoe fifties?"

"I spent one on food, and I gave the other one to Diane at the department store so she could take the bus to Atlanta."

"You what?" Hayes tossed his arms up into the rain as if he were hurling them away. "For God's sake! Wait here."

Raleigh ran back, the old *Time* magazine over his head; he handed Sheffield a hundred-dollar bill. "Don't spend it all," he warned. "Good-bye. Thank you for the clothes. Be careful."

"But, Raleigh, how do I get there?"

"I thought you said you'd been to the beach a million times? Okay, just go back to Seventeen, and stay on it. It's only about seventy miles."

"What about if I took the ferry to Southport, wouldn't that be faster?"

"Fine."

"But maybe the ferry doesn't run when it's raining, because of lightning. I sure wouldn't want to get caught in another lightning —"

"Mingo, I'm getting soaked! Just get on the damn highway and stay in the damn car! A car's the safest place you can be. Good-bye!"

But Sheffield did not stay in the car; he made a number of stops. As a result he didn't arrive at the motel until four hours after he'd left "Peace and Quiet." The first place he stopped was a massage parlor. At least he thought it was a massage parlor, for although it looked like a large mobile home in a tar pine forest, there were plenty of signs saying it was a professional massage parlor, welcoming adults only. Now, Mingo had always wanted to have a professional massage, because he frequently saw people in the movies get them — people like James Bond — and it looked to him as if a professional massage really would make you feel better, especially if you'd been recently mugged by hoods, and been in a bar fight with Marines, and been shot full of electricity. But before tonight, he'd not only been too shy to go into a massage parlor, he'd never actually even seen one. In Life on the Road, however, things seemed to fall right in your lap, the way fighting roosters and chorus girls did for Gates Hayes. If he didn't go in there, right now, he'd be a chicken for the rest of his life. So, taking a deep breath to fill his Gargantuan lungs, Sheffield knocked, like opportunity, once on the door.

It was quickly opened by a thin woman in a red shortie nightgown; she was wearing, in Mingo's judgment, an awful lot of makeup. "Hey, you're big. They call you Paul Bunyan? Step up out of the rain."

"Mingo Sheffield. Nice to meet you." Sheffield ducked into the trailer's living room, where two more women sat at a card table in their nightgowns; a large pretty one was playing solitaire; an angry one was counting cash and credit card slips, which she stacked in a metal box. A very young woman, fairly fat, was stretched out on a couch, watching a rerun of *Bewitched* on the color television. She was lying there in her underwear, which was shiny purple and too small for her. All these women were wearing an awful lot of makeup. Their furniture was a little on the gaudy side too, especially the tiger face print on the rug, and the big picture on the wall of some naked women holding their breasts. He did like the mobiles made of seashells, but there were an awful lot of them, and he kept banging his head. From behind a closed door, Mingo could hear squeaking noises.

"I'm Delilah," said the thin woman.

"Really?" asked Mingo. "I never met anybody that actually had that for a name before." He'd never met anyone who had such greenish-yellow hair before either.

The pretty woman playing solitaire called over, "If we're talking 'actually,' actually her name's Mary Ella."

"Shut your f'ing mouth, Jackie, you want to? Okay, Paul Bunyan, what do you have in mind?"

"Is this where you do massages?"

"The very place." Delilah greasily smiled.

Mingo thought he heard grunts or moans from the closed door. "Excuse me," he said, ducking as he stepped around the fringed swag light. "Could you tell me how much it costs? I mean just for an ordinary one. That doesn't take too long. I'm really supposed to be going someplace."

"Aren't we all?" the woman called Jackie said.

"Jackie, will you please?" Delilah spoke briskly. "Seventy-five for a straight lay, you on top; hundred if I'm on top. One twenty-five for a head job."

Mingo looked nervously around. He heard a man's voice go, "Yeah! Yeah! Yeah!" "You massage heads?"

Jackie laughed. "Why not?"

The girl in her underwear giggled at the television. The heroine of *Bewitched,* who kept trying to be an ordinary suburban housewife even though she was in fact a powerful witch, had just accidentally turned her husband into a cocker spaniel right in the middle of a big business deal. The dog was frisking all over his client. "Boy, I've had a few of those in here," laughed the girl on the couch.

Mingo was growing suspicious that this was not the sort of professional massage parlor he'd seen in the movies. "Seventy-five *dollars?*" he asked.

"Are you pulling my leg?" Delilah was no longer smiling. "I saw that Cadillac."

Mingo ducked around the room. "Gosh, that's not mine; it's my friend's. I don't really have much money at all, and I lost my job. I got robbed by Hell's Angels and I gave what I had left in my shoes to a poor little pregnant girl. I just felt like I'd like to have a massage 'cause I never had one, but I thought it'd look more like, well, the Y, but fancier. So, I don't know, but I'd really be interested to know where y'all get your lingerie. Do you buy it in a store or order from a catalogue or —"

"Call Wylie!" yelled Delilah. "We got another nut!"

Jackie stood up beside Mingo. He could see right through her nightgown. "I like him" she said. "Tell you what. It's raining, things are slow, I'll do you for fifty." And she gave Sheffield's genitals a soft warm rub, leaving her hand there. "How's that?"

The closed door opened. A skinny, bald man hurried out through the room, not looking at anyone.

By now Mingo knew that the words "Massage Parlor" were definitely a euphemism. "Well," he stuttered, "Wu . . . wu . . . well. That feels nice." Then he sighed. "But, well, I guess maybe I don't think Vera would like it so much. And I feel like it's half her money. She's my wife." He sighed again. "But thanks anyhow."

"Suit yourself." Jackie went back to her solitaire.

Mingo couldn't help but be sorry she'd taken her hand away. Maybe Vera wouldn't have minded just a few more seconds. "Black ten on the red jack," he said, trying to stay friendly.

Twenty minutes later, Mingo had won $1.75 from Jackie, playing double solitaire at a quarter a game, and had taught her the one-handed cut.

The fat man's next stop was in Calabash, where he'd wanted to go because he'd always gotten a lump in his throat whenever Jimmy Durante had walked from one little spotlight to another, tipping his hat and shaking his head and saying, "Good night, Mrs. Calabash, wherever you are."

Then Mingo stopped for gas. Then he stopped to use the bathroom. Then he stopped under a highway overpass, because, while it wasn't raining anymore, he thought he saw lightning ahead. When he began to think the bridge was going to collapse on top of him, and inched the Cadillac back on the road, he was happy to find out that the brightness in the sky was only the lights of Myrtle Beach's boardwalk amusement park. So he stopped again, for if there was one thing Mingo Sheffield loved, it was amusement parks, except, of course, for the scary rides. It wasn't as much fun to go by yourself, but still it was better than sitting alone in a motel room waiting to find out if Raleigh had drowned.

The first thing he did was watch a woman make cotton candy; he loved the way she spun it out of nothing into pink clouds. Next, he spent ten quarters trying to get the little robot arm behind the glass case to pick up the ladies' watch and drop it through the slot to him so he could give it to Vera. But all the arm would pick up was a plastic horseshoe with a penny in it. He didn't win anything by pitching dimes at colored glass plates either — the dimes just slid right off — or by throwing darts at balloons. But at the shooting gallery, Mingo won, to the disgust of the owner, the biggest stuffed pink bear the man had, and after that he won a fluffy monkey on a stick, and then a white unicorn with a rhinestone collar, and by then a little crowd had started to gather to watch Mingo, his fat face snuggled against the rifle, his round eye squinting down the sights, shoot away one pop-up target after another, shoot them right in the center of the little bull's-eyes. Down flopped the tin cut-out bears, and Mingo picked a giant can-can doll for a little girl watching him from her father's shoulders. Down dropped the flying ducks, and Mingo chose a baseball glove for a little boy who'd wriggled to the front row beside him. Finally the man who owned the shooting gallery whispered so nastily, "That's it, bub, give somebody else a chance," that Mingo put down his rifle. He gave the unicorn to a teenaged girl who looked as if she might be sad because she was fat, and he gave the monkey to a baby in a stroller. He kept the big pink teddy bear for Vera.

Hugging the bear, Mingo bought a candy apple. He stood in the middle of the midway and watched families and teenagers scream in hysterics at having paid $1.50 to be slammed, tossed, jerked, flung, and otherwise tortured for two minutes by the Blind Bullet, the Hammer, and the Tilt-a-Whirl. Mingo even got halfway through the line to ride the Roller Coaster, but he chickened out, so it was just as well he was by himself and nobody saw. He was a little embarrassed to ride the merry-go-round without taking a child with him, but it was his favorite ride, because he liked to pretend he was in a cowboy movie; so, studiously choosing a horse that had a nice face and good reins, he heaved himself up, and holding the bear in his lap, rode two times, happily circling the glittery mirrors, and watching, whenever he went past, the cymbals clang together and the old drumstick hit the tattered drum.

Emboldened by his past success at the Thermopylae elementary school, Mingo even climbed up the giant slide, which stretched bouncing down forever and ever. And after politely allowing a dozen small children to go in front of him, he put down his mat, hugged his bear, and asked the two little boys behind him to "Shove". . . which they were happy to do. Mingo had never been so frightened. Or so thrilled. He slid twice more, then recklessly bought a ticket for the Ferris wheel. When he felt as if he might scream or vomit after his seat jerked to a swaying stop at the very top, he shut his eyes, clutched the rail and the bear, and told himself that this was Life on the Road, and all he had to do was keep his courage up. Slowly, the nausea passed. He blinked open one round eye and looked, not yet down, but straight out, over the rides, over the wooden boardwalk, where lovers strolled blindly, kissing as they walked, until crashed into by a skateboarder or a drunk. The sea was black and swelling and so immense that Mingo couldn't tell it from the starless sky. He certainly couldn't see anything on it. Certainly not his friend Raleigh Hayes.

"Poor Raleigh," whispered Mingo, then, whoosh, down he went, leaving his stomach behind, as the Ferris wheel began turning faster and faster. He liked it! It was even better than the merry-go-round! He liked looking down at the bright moving colors of the other rides. And all the little wandering people looked much tidier from above; they milled about with a kind of overall orderliness, forming pleasant patterns that they couldn't see, but he could. Maybe, thought Sheffield, that's the way God feels about the whole world, like Somebody on a universal Ferris wheel.

Too bad, they were slowing down, and riders below him were getting off. Sheffield inched along in his swaying seat, when, all at once, hideous terror struck him full in the chest. Who should be standing just below him, first on the ramp of the impatient waiting line, but four of those Hell's Angels! There they were! The two biggest of the men, the werewolf one and the sumo wrestler one who'd played the invisible guitar! Plus the girl driver with the propeller cap and the earring through the side of her nose, plus the girl with the crew cut who'd pulled down Raleigh's pants! He was looking right at them, but they couldn't see him. He'd recognized them instantly. The ones that had been wearing any clothes that night hadn't even changed them, but the sumo guitarist now had on a leather jacket with a red devil's face painted on the back. So, that's where they'd been headed! The beach! They probably had paid for those Ferris wheel tickets with his Pinto money! Mingo leaned over and yelled, *"Hey, you Hell's Angels! Hey you, give me back all my money you stole!"*

The four looked up. So did everybody else. The devil sympathizers did not, however, seem to recognize the enormous man clutching the pink teddy bear, at least not before he was whisked away up the backside of the Ferris wheel. So, the crew cut with the werewolf and the pierce-nose with the guitarist, they fell into their own seats and joined the ride. By now, throwing caution to the winds, Sheffield had turned completely around in his seat and was hanging over the back in order to shout across the spokes at the two couples rocking on the other side. *"Hey you!* Hell's Angels! You took our money and beat us up and threw us out in the rain! And you even stole Vera's pink strapless! And I want it back! Hey you!"

The werewolf slapped his head. "Shit, man, it's that fat crazy fairy!"

"Groovy," said the crew cut girl.

Round once more everyone went, with Mingo yelling that he wanted his money back, and the Hell's Angels shrugging innocently for the benefit of the crowd, and giggling to themselves. Finally, Mingo's seat was stopped, and he was bounced out, despite his protests that while he hadn't been robbed right now on this ride, he *had* been robbed a few days ago in Mount Olive, North Carolina, by those very two couples laughing at him from the top of the Ferris wheel. "Try a cop," said the frazzled attendant. But, instead, Mingo waited at the barrier, telling everybody around him how vilely he'd been mistreated in that hellish black van.

Unfortunately, when the four hoods finished their ride, they shoved into the waiting line, and ran down the up ramp together, as fast as a horde of vandals. They knocked the gate over into the crowd, then loped off down the midway, howling some rock-and-roll song. Mingo, trying to squeeze around the barrier, was knocked down and then pushed swiftly back upright by the angry people crushed beneath him. He took after the hoods in his amazingly fast-footed weave, keeping his eyes on the werewolf's hairy head and the spinning propeller atop the nose-pierced girl's cap. For a second, he lost them. Then, there they were, piling into little cars that shot them through the doors of the House of Horrors. Without pausing to think that he was terrified of darkness, not to mention darkness with cackling fluorescent witches leaping out at him, Mingo used his last ticket to squeeze himself and his bear into the next little car, and follow the chase.

As soon as the doors slammed shut behind him, chains rattled, bats screeched, and a casket flew open with a lit-up vampire in it. Mingo forgot all about the Hell's Angels, burst into an icy sweat, and started praying, "God oh God oh God oh God!" as his cart whipped along the track from ghosts to ghouls to hanged men. Ahead of him he heard the werewolf's "Yahhooo! Yahhooo!"

"Give me back my money!" he screamed, which was a bad mistake. For a second later, something huge and furry jumped into the seat behind him, fixed him with a red glowing eye, squeezed a big arm around his neck, socked him three fast sickening times in the stomach, rumbled, "Fuck off, dork. And stop calling us Hell's Angels. We ain't. Yahoooo!," and disappeared. Mingo knew none of this was part of the ride. He was vomiting over the side of his cart when he bammed out through the doors back into the noise and neon. A woman waiting in line turned around and left, pushing her children ahead of her. "Forget it!" she said. "You're not going in there if it's that bad!"

Sick at heart as well as stomach, Mingo Sheffield slumped back to the parking lot. Not only had he failed to retrieve his money, he'd been mugged all over again. On the other hand, he thought, as he drove, rubbing his bruised belly, along the luminous strip of beach motels with nice pools, and appetizing restaurants with nice specials, gosh, at least he had *chased* the Hell's Angels (or whoever they were); he hadn't been too chicken at least to try. And, really, when you thought about it, he'd been pretty lucky. They hadn't taken Raleigh's money from where he'd hidden it in his windbreaker hood. Or stolen Vera's bear. And one thing was sure: he probably wouldn't ever be scared of any ordinary House of Horrors again. And he'd ridden the Ferris wheel and slide, and seen Calabash, and been to — if not a professional massage parlor — at least a whorehouse (which he'd never been in either, having promised his mother decades earlier), and he was having adventures right and left, that's for sure.

By the time Mingo had checked into the big brand-new motel, and checked out all the interesting things in the room (including cable TV, a bed vibrator, a cute little baby refrigerator, and some very nice shoeshine paper towels), he was so enormously cheered that he ate two orders of Chicken Cacciatore in the Mermaid Room, where he fell into pleasant conversation with the night manager, who advised him to take a motel-training course, as he himself had done when he'd been laid off by his clothespin company. This fellow was so affable, he agreed to carry out Mingo's inspiration, which was to add to the motel's huge illuminated highway sign that had plenty of space left, since it only said, "FRIDAY SPECIAL, PRIME RIBS, $9.95," the hospitable greeting "WELCOME, RALEIGH & GATES HAYES!"

CHAPTER

19

In Which the Hero Finds Himself at Sea

AT "PEACE AND QUIET," Raleigh Hayes passed much of Friday in conversation with himself; he was trying to give himself the same advice he'd been annoyingly offered by sluggards all his life: "Slow down." "What's your rush, Raleigh?" "Where's the fire, Raleigh?" "Rest easy, Little Fellow." All his life, Raleigh, ignoring them, had hurried on, to get Somewhere, and if he couldn't precisely describe that elusive place, he nevertheless knew it existed, and that he had not yet succeeded in reaching it. Instead, for example, here he was now, at the beach, in *March,* which was the sort of thing that his ridiculous relatives might suddenly decide to do. Moreover, he was stuck here until it was time to run Gates's "errand," whatever asinine and probably illegal activity that would involve. He did not for an instant trust Gates to go to Midway without him, and while Raleigh was not at all fond of Roxanne Digges, he did think (even beyond the fact that he had committed himself to carrying out successfully his father's impossible instructions) it was only decent that a mother's dying wish to see her son should be honored. Even a careless mother like Roxanne, even a careless son like Gates. Indeed, there was a certain satisfaction in compelling Gates to do the right thing. There always had been. Righteous indignation, properly nourished, had its own stern pleasures. Imagining the coming hospital scene, accomplished under his personally inconvenient supervision, gave Hayes the same satisfaction as the newly hinged door and the dripless faucets that he now surveyed in "Peace and Quiet." Necessary tasks, well done.

So, he told himself, he would slow down, and endure these detours like Midway and Myrtle Beach. What else could he do? First of all, his infuriating father might be *anywhere*. The phone call had seemed to come from south of Midway; the telegram had come from Memphis. Memphis! The man might simply be, without plan or purpose, joyriding from one end of the country to the other with his young companion. The hideous image of a map of the United States with a tiny yellow convertible scooting like a bee all over it entered Raleigh's mind. Earley Hayes had given no inkling of his future whereabouts between now and the thirty-first of March, nearly two weeks away. Apart from bringing in the Bureau of Missing Persons (and, in any case, as Victoria Anna had pointed out, how were they to *force* Earley Hayes to return to the hospital?), there was absolutely nothing Raleigh could do but passively wait for further messages, which might or might not come, and might or might not completely change all previous plans. He had to wait. For two weeks.

It wasn't easy. Hayes liked to think of himself as a man of active virtues; he despised passivity, and was contemptuous of sloth, in himself and in others. Every habit encoded in his muscles kept them twitching to return to Thermopylae until the day came to fly to New Orleans and nab his errant parent, to return to take up the plow of cultivating new insurance policies, to take up the rake of combing through the confusion of his home. Every earnest fiber in his brain was convinced that, surely, without him, his clients would vanish, his family would collapse; they and he would all sink quickly into a chasm of poverty and despair, and end their days morosely cramped together in a dank debtor's prison.

It was shocking today to hear Betty Hemans tell him business was going on as usual; it was shocking to hear Aura tell him that, while of course they missed him enormously, life was going on as usual, except more dramatically now that she had rediscovered, like an old forgotten bank account, a rich world of interests she'd set aside to raise the twins. It was almost a disappointment to hear that the house had not burned down, that the twins had not crashed the cars, that order had not slid off its throne and rolled away. It was almost a blow to his self-esteem. It was almost a foretaste of death.

Yes, the first hard lesson Raleigh Hayes had to force himself to master this slow afternoon at "Peace and Quiet" was that he had to learn simply to wait, and the second lesson, even harder, was that he could stand still without the world's stopping too, and so hurling out of its orbit into Chaos. He could let go of the reins without the horses smashing the sun into one planet after another, incinerating the universe.

While, with rippled brow, Hayes thought all this through, he was not, naturally, gazing on the beach out over the eternal sea. He was busily repairing everything he could find in his rental property, busily firing his indignant realtor for failing to telephone him personally before giving Gates the key to his house, busily making collect phone calls full of instructions to Betty Hemans, and to Aura — telling her to deposit this money there, and that money here, and water the following plants, and instruct their lawyer to see Pierce's lawyer about the deed to Knoll Pond, and so forth until she said, "Raleigh, slow down." In fact, he'd set himself so many busy tasks, he'd barely finished checking the checks on his list when it was time to load up Gate's motorcycle to run their "errand."

Nothing could have been more aggravating than to hear Aura tell him to relax and consider the next two weeks a vacation. He never took vacations, except to come to the beach and do what he was doing now — repair things. He couldn't afford vacations; he didn't have the time and he didn't have the money. Now, the truth was, he did have both, and this was the third hard lesson Raleigh struggled all day to accept. The truth was, he could spare two weeks, and two weeks could spare him. The truth was, if he never worked another day in his life (and if he didn't live too long, and if he continued his careful frugality), he could live until he died on what he'd already earned, saved, inherited, and invested, and, afterward, his family could live quite nicely on his insurance. Raleigh didn't want to believe that he had time and money to spare; it rattled every plank of the foundation on which he'd built the stable scaffold of his Life's Plan. On the other hand, he had a great respect for the truth, and therefore he was struggling.

Nor did Raleigh want to believe that Aura was right when she predicted, "What fun! Oh, you'll enjoy that!" upon hearing that he was going on a nightime deep sea voyage with his brother Gates. "I doubt it," he'd said. And as it happened, Hayes proved to be terribly right.

He did not enjoy riding in the rain on a motorcycle, straddled between Gates's back and Gates's leather luggage, nor going to a sleazy marina where Gates whispered for a long time to a man whose arm and nose were broken, a man who wished them "Good luck," with nothing but hopeless calamity in his voice. Raleigh did not enjoy his first view of the motor craft called "Easy Living," or rather "Easy iving," for the *L* was worn away. Nor did closer inspection of this craft add to his pleasure, as the boat was a dirty, dangerous wreck, with rungs off its ladder, holes in its flying bridge, rusty cables thrown in its broken toilet, and ripped life jackets tossed in its sink. Its motor had to be kicked into cooperation. Its floor was a treacherous bed of nails, strewn with beer cans and stinking fish, one of which Raleigh stepped on, squishing out its malevolent eye.

No, it was not all that much fun lugging aboard not only gasoline tanks but the motorcycle itself. It was certainly not an unmitigated treat to be bossed about by his little brother and told to cast off this line and pull in that bumper and check the starboard clearance and read out the depth gauge and stay aft, and other such conceited gibberish. It was less than a thrill to discover as they spluttered under a black whirring sky, out of the sheltered Cape Fear basin to head past Corncake Inlet, that waves rose up to try to stop them, and that "Easy iving" retaliated by slapping each wave as hard as she could, so that everything loose in her (including Raleigh) was flung front to back, back to front, or, as Gates insufferably corrected him, "Fore to aft."

At the wheel, Gates, grinning like Captain Blood, looked disgustingly at home in cold black winds and deadly riptides — so thought his brother, as he spun, headfirst, down the galley steps.

"If you feel queasy, Raleigh, stay out on deck! But sit still. Stop running around. Little choppy." Yes, Gates was in his element as, louder than the motor and the sea, he yelled laughing at the sky, "Hey, J.C., where are you when we need you, man? Calm these waves for my brother here, and turn this water into wine while you're at it! Hey, J.C.! Hey Raleigh! Can you believe our old man was a minister! One of Christ's boys in the field! Man! What a pisser! Can you believe it?"

"Yes!" shouted back Raleigh, huddled shivering, despite his army jacket, against the strapped-down motorcycle. "Yes I can."

Yes, he believed Earley Hayes was precisely the kind of fool to follow a hobo like Christ over any and every hill and dale. Precisely like John and James, those two disciples who just threw down their nets and ran off as soon as they heard Him whistle, leaving their poor father Zebedee standing there in the surf wondering how he was going to keep the family fishing business together without any help. That was the annoying thing about Christ. He never bothered to think of the consequences. Like when He cast those legions of devils out of the madman and let the devils talk Him into putting them in the pigs instead. What about the poor farmer who'd owned those pigs? Imagine how that farmer'd felt when he heard his three thousand pigs had gone crazy and leaped off a precipice! Imagine how much industry in those hard times it must have taken to raise three thousand pigs! But what did Christ care?

Thus Hayes brooded on the dark slapping waves. What he didn't know (how could he?) was that along that very channel, three hundred years earlier, there had sailed, bucking and creaking through the Cape Fear Inlet, the very square-rigged oak galleon that was bringing to that silvery schemer Sir Walter Raleigh's New World, the first American Hayes. Yes, right through these same choppy waters had come the gullible Obed — who by now knew just how nastily he'd been tricked into five years' indentured servitude on an indigo plantation. And so tenuously lasting are the styles of blood that Raleigh Hayes was not only in precisely the same foul mood as his ancestor Obed Hayes had been so many centuries ago, felt not only the same heartburning urge to haul God into court and sue Him, he made precisely the same defiant gesture against the Creator. He leaned over the boat rail and spat at the sea — not very far from where Obed had spat in 1660. And Raleigh's spittle, like Obed's, was swirled into the vast waters of the deep and joined itself to the unchanging, uncaring whole.

"How you doing, Raleigh? Okay?"

"Just great! . . . Gates! Exactly what is it you're delivering to Myrtle Beach? What is it and *where* is it?"

"Oh, that. We haven't got it yet. We're picking it up a little farther out! Great night, right!" yelled his brother, wind lifting his curls and flapping the long black scarf he wore like a pirate's flag.

No, Raleigh didn't at all enjoy drifting in a dark choppy cove on the tip of Smith Island at what Gates called "the drop-off point," drifting while his brother sipped Amaretto right out of the bottle between drags on a marijuana cigarette. He didn't enjoy having Gates "level" with him by explaining that he was not really in the drug-running business on a permanent basis, but merely substituting for the man with the broken arm and nose, because he, Gates, happened to have a little cash flow problem at the moment. Raleigh shouldn't think that this sort of thing was his line, because he'd soon be on to Something Big, the details of which he did not, thank God, disclose, since it was already horrific enough for Raleigh to learn that by "gangsters" Lovie must have been referring to certain "South Coast characters" engaged in organized crime, and specifically to someone actually allowing himself to be known as "Cupid Parisi Calhoun," who was "looking for" Gates in order to compel him to pay back the $15,000 he'd lost betting on greyhound dogs at a Florida track. It was horrific enough to find out that matters were "well, a little more complicated." That, in fact, Gates had received $15,000 from Mr. Calhoun in order to pay some *other* people back about the dogs, but he hadn't exactly gotten around to it yet.

"You borrowed the money from this Calhoun?"

"Not exactly." If Raleigh really wanted to know, Gates had sold Mr. Calhoun, for $15,000, Mrs. Jefferson Davis's Inaugural necklace, which would have been a remarkably good price had the jewels belonged to Mrs. Davis. But that hadn't been exactly true, and they weren't exactly worth $15,000, although their velvet case had cost "an arm and a leg." Despite the universally accepted business principle of *caveat emptor,* the "pissant proud" Mr. Calhoun had taken such umbrage at the duplicity practiced upon him (for he'd been laughed at by a young woman on whom he had grandly bestowed the necklace — she knew nothing of Confederate history, but was something of an expert on precious stones), so incensed had Calhoun grown that he had taken a public vow to do a number of unpleasant things to Gates Hayes (many of them with a knife).

Raleigh blew on his fingers, chilled to the bone by the handle of the searchlight he was sweeping over the dark foamy waves. "But how could you possibly lose *fifteen thousand dollars* on dogs in the first place!"

"Bad luck," Gates confessed. "Sorry."

In a while, Raleigh asked, "Well, goddammit, do these mobsters have any idea where you are?"

"Oh, them? I sure hope not. Know what I mean? I'm not exactly mailing out change-of-address cards."

Later on, Raleigh said, "Well, private gambling debts are certainly not legal obligations. And a . . . a gangster is hardly likely to take legal steps about that jewelry. I sincerely doubt either party will take you to court."

Gates laughed. "Right, sure, fine. Good old Raleigh. . . . Hey, here we go! Hear that? Off the port bow? Here're our boys."

"Please don't say 'our,' please."

No, it was not all the fun Aura had predicted, to be hanging over the gunnel of a rolling boat, while a scruffy adolescent shrieking Spanish held a rifle on him, as Raleigh helped his brother haul in a rubber raft packed with God knows what.

But there was no use pretending he didn't know what was in those two little white bags that Gates removed from the plastic bundle before sealing it up again. It was really hard to say which was worse — that his brother was being paid by men in the underworld with bags of cocaine, or that his brother was stealing bags of cocaine from men in the underworld. "Gates, I want to know what you're up to, and I pray it's not what it looks like."

"Sameo sameo Raleigh!"

Compared to the last three hours, motoring down the Intercoastal Waterway to North Myrtle Beach, South Carolina, and there mooring "Easy iving" in a pitch-black slip, was (comparatively speaking) not all that bad. At least it wasn't raining while they waited in the boat until a shadowy man drove up in a BMW, took the large plastic bundle from Gates without a word, and sped back into the night. At least at four A.M., there weren't too many tractor-trailers on the highway for Gates suddenly to decide to pass, so that wind suction seemed to be pulling the leaning motorcycle irresistibly under the big groaning wheels. At least they'd made it all the way to downtown Myrtle Beach, and Raleigh could see the Holiday Inn logo all lit up, and soon he could crawl into a warm bed and fall —

"What the fuck?" Sparks flew out of Gates's boots as he spun in a circle, while braking, throwing Raleigh off the motorcycle, onto the pavement under the motel sign that merrily announced to anyone in the world who could read, "WELCOME, RALEIGH & GATES HAYES!"

"Okay, we've got to blow this joint," snarled Gates, still spinning the cycle in a circle around Raleigh. "Thank your fat friend, okay! Let's go."

"Gates, calm down. We can leave in the morning."

"Maybe you can, but I don't exactly want my nose slit open and my ears and prick sliced off!"

This image stopped Hayes on his way to the door. "Damn you, Gates! What have you gotten me into?"

"Me? It's your bimbo pal that flashed our names all over the Grand Strand! Go get him, I'll wait right here."

Fortunately, Raleigh noticed the crafty look Gates had always gotten in his eyes as a child as soon as he'd stolen or lost or broken something that didn't belong to him. "I bet!" Raleigh said, and pulled his brother's soft leather suitcase off the back of the motorcycle. He carried it with him as insurance when he went to wake up the night clerk. Doing so wasn't easy, but it was easier than waking up Mingo Sheffield, who (even though his bed was vibrating, the lights were on, and the television was going) was dead to the world, under the covers at the foot of his bed, his arms locked around an enormous pink teddy bear.

Getting Mingo into the Cadillac wasn't easy either. Neither was following Gates, flying inland at almost ninety miles an hour (so that Raleigh had to listen to the smooth voice in the dashboard criticize his speeding every few minutes), until finally, in the gray dawn, Gates screeched into a Days Ease Motel in the middle of nowhere that was plaintively blinking "Vacancy" at any passing motorists. Not that the man who eventually stumbled to the door looked especially glad to see them, but he did admit he had one room with two double beds left, the key to which he threw on the counter. "Take it or leave it, soldier," he grumbled at Raleigh, who still wore his army fatigues.

"No TV," said Mingo sadly looking around. "Too bad."

Neither of the Hayeses answered the fat man. Nor did they do more than glare at him when he offered to share his bed with either one. In fact, a whole bed was scarcely wide enough for Mingo alone. He crawled in with his bear and was instantly snoring. And the Hayes brothers slept together in the same room for the first time in more than thirty years, in the same bed for the first time in their lives.

"I don't believe this," groaned Raleigh, lying there brushing away the smoke from Gates's marijuana cigarette. "Days Ease. Ha ha. Well, Aura, today was a lot of fun, okay. A real vacation." (Of course, our hero wasn't talking aloud, but soliloquizing in his customary way.) His brother Gates, however, did speak aloud, strangely, disturbingly close to Raleigh's ear.

"Right, yeah, great. I was in prison, you know, not so far from here. Man, I can *feel* it. Eight months! What a pisser! You came to see me, first Saturday of every month, never missed. Told me I deserved to be there and then never missed a visit." In the shadowy strange room the red light of Gates's pungent cigarette flared beside Raleigh; brighter, dimmer, brighter. "Right, Raleigh? Brought me some magazines and gave me a lecture. Every first Saturday. You always did the right thing. Good old Raleigh. Man oh man, what a world." Raleigh could hear the sound of Gates's breath blowing smoke, and he could hear the sound of his own heart in the hollow of his pillow.

Gray light had slatted higher lines across the thin motel wall when Gates said, "Didn't know the water was gonna be that rough. Sorry, Raleigh. Couldn't have done it without you." But the insurance salesman (despite his absolute certainty that he could never in a million years rest easily beside this familiar stranger) was sound asleep.

CHAPTER

20

The Great Adventure of the Bass Fiddle Case

MINGO SHEFFIELD, who'd gone to bed at midnight, was bursting with news. The Hayeses, who'd gone to bed at dawn, refused to wake up to hear it. They kept throwing him out of the room, until finally he wandered off to drive around the countryside. They also threw out the maid, and the motel manager, who charged them for another day. It was Raleigh, in fact, who was the last to awaken, startled to find himself embracing a pink stuffed animal, for he'd moved over into Mingo's bed as soon as it was vacant. Groggily, he showered, shaved, and dressed in his new white suit, blue shirt, and dotted tie. He looked in the mirror. He didn't look to himself much like Raleigh Hayes; he looked like somebody who would bet money on greyhound dogs. He felt like somebody who had bet on the wrong ones. As Hayes was transferring his envelopes of cash from the zipped pocket of his old army jacket, an impulse led him to take the money back out and count it. Sure enough, almost a thousand dollars was missing. "Okay," he snarled, and ran, blinking, out into the low sun, which was on the wrong side of the sky. God! It was 4:30 P.M!

"Raleigh! Raleigh! Look at me! Watch!" There at the motel pool, atop the curving slides, sat, in plaid trunks, Mingo Sheffield, looking like an albino sea walrus. Down he shot, heaving tidal waves over the deck chairs.

"Thanks to you, Raleigh! I love slides! Gollee, you look great! That suit looks really good on you!"

"Where's Gates? Is he gone?"

"He's over there." Sheffield pointed across the road at Kathy's Kountry Kitchen, and called after the racing Raleigh, "I'll be right over in a minute." He threw himself on an air mattress floating past; it promptly flipped over and sank with him.

"Aces! Check *you* out!" whistled Gates from his table in the corner of the overlit restaurant. "Why the outfit? Have some pancakes. Taking a cruise?"

"I took a cruise yesterday," snapped Raleigh. "Okay, Gates. Give me back the eight hundred dollars! Right now!"

Gates dumped sugar in his coffee. "What eight hundred dollars?"

"The eight hundred dollars you just took out of my army jacket." Raleigh had to pause to tell a pop-eyed waitress that he wanted eggs and bacon, and to answer her further inquiry by saying he didn't care *how* they were cooked. "Okay, Gates. I'm serious. I am sincerely not kidding. I will call the police."

"On your brother?" Gates sipped at his coffee.

"GIVE ME THAT MONEY BACK."

"Oh, that. All right, all right, no need to freak out. Fine, okay, here. Sorry." And Gates pulled the wad of hundred-dollar bills from the pocket of his beautiful tan leather jacket. "Can't blame a fellow for trying, can you? Just a temporary loan anyhow."

"Jesus Christ!" Raleigh took off his glasses and shoved hard at his eye sockets. "Gates . . . Gates . . . I'm completely speechless."

"Come on, I said I was sorry. What more can I say? I was going to tell you."

"I bet."

A plate of black curdled rubber slid into Raleigh's view. "You said you didn't care how they were cooked," drawled the vindictive waitress. Then Mingo Sheffield thundered in, knocking over a display of tiny souvenir cotton bales with the South Carolina flag on them. "Lord, he's back!" said the pop-eyed waitress. "He's already been in here three times today!"

Mingo was now wearing a green velour pullover with orange sleeve stripes. He certainly had packed a lot of clothes into that suitcase. "Hi, fellows. Excuse me, ma'am, can I please get a chocolate milkshake and some ham biscuits please?"

"How many is some? Two? Twenty?"

"Four, please. Boy, y'all sure do sleep late." Sheffield tried to slide into the booth next to Raleigh, but the table began to tilt and the plates to bounce, so he backed out and pulled over a chair. "How was y'all's boat trip? Fun?"

"Absolutely great," the older Hayes replied.

"It wasn't scary?"

"Not at all."

"Raleigh, well, you're never going to guess who I saw on the Ferris wheel last night."

"No? Miss, pardon me, may I have a touch more coffee?" The waitress poured a sixteenth of a teaspoon. "A little more than that, please. . . . Excuse me, miss. *Miss!* Just please fill the cup! Thank you."

Mingo's neatly combed hair dripped water on the paper mats. His round button eyes were dancing. "Well, listen to this! I was on the Ferris wheel, I rode a lot of the big rides last night, and there they were! The Hell's Angels! Except they don't want us to call them that. Right! The same ones!" He turned to Gates. "The ones I told you about, that threw us out at the convent? So I chased after them, but they got away from me in the House of Horrors, and beat me up a little bit. Too bad, hunh, Raleigh?"

"Sheffield, you kill me!" laughed Gates.

Mingo sucked away his milkshake. "And gosh, Gates, have I got some news for you! I went out driving today. Well, I got kind of lonesome when y'all wouldn't wake up, so in the next town over . . . could I have another milkshake, ma'am? . . . they're having a great big church revival meeting going on this weekend at the football stadium. A marathon, is what they call it. Today and Sunday. They said Reverend Joey Vachel isn't going to stop preaching the Word until a thousand souls come up and surrender themselves to Jesus."

"Damn, that is good news," grinned Gates.

"So, I went in and got saved again."

"That's great news!"

"Oh, for Pete's sake," said Raleigh.

"I've been born again six times," Mingo burbled on, wolfing down a ham biscuit in a single bite.

"Did you see that?" Gates asked his brother, opening his mouth as wide as he could.

"The thing is, I needed to get saved pretty badly, because I went to a whorehouse last night."

Raleigh spit coffee back into his cup.

"It was an accident, I swear. All I wanted was a massage, but I never got to get one. Seventy-five dollars was the bottom price, except Jackie said she'd do me for fifty because she liked me. She was nice. But, gosh, I was never so surprised in all my life. So I said, 'I better not,' so we played some double solitaire, Klondike rules, and I won a dollar seventy-five. They said things were slow because of the rain. Their friend was in bed with an old skinny man. . . ." Sheffield stopped short when he saw the way the two brothers were staring at him. "Anyhow, I'm kind of getting off the track. What I want to tell you, Gates, is," he stuffed in another biscuit, "I saw your old cellmate you were telling me about. The master criminal, you know, Simon 'Weeper' Berg."

"What are y'all talking about?" Raleigh inquired ominously.

"You're kidding!" said Gates. "You saw Weeper in this cathouse? He's not even up for parole till 'eighty-eight."

"No! At the revival meeting. I swear!" Mingo put his hand on his heart. "They called out his name and I remembered it. He's real real short and old and kind of scrawny and wears his hair in a ponytail, doesn't he?"

Gates rubbed at his mustache. "Weeper's a born-again Christian?! I can't believe it! He's a Jew. I mean he's a goddamn fucking atheist, but he's a Jew!"

"Well, I don't know," said Mingo, smug with the dramatic effect of his news, "if he's born-again or not, but he's playing the bass fiddle up on the stage with the choir. Reverend Joey Vachel's wife introduced all these members of the prison gospel band? They called them 'The Glory Bound Boys.' And she introduced them all and said they were all prisoners from the state prison, and how the warden had made special arrangements for them to come be at this marathon for Jesus. 'On bass fiddle, Simon "Weeper" Berg, ten years for burglary.' She told all their crimes one by one and then he'd play a few bars. The drummer killed his cousin with a kitchen knife by mistake. She said she was a sinner, too, and used to be an alcoholic and a call girl and write bad checks before she was saved by Reverend Joey Vachel and married him."

"I wonder if she was that cocktail waitress that almost married Daddy," mused Hayes aloud, but the other two weren't listening.

Gates kept rubbing his curls and his mustache and saying, "Weeper Berg!"

"Simon 'Weeper' Berg." Mingo nodded.

"Man, I didn't know Weeper played the bass."

"He didn't play it very well," admitted Mingo. "But the choir was great."

Gates wanted to go to the revival right then and there, and when Raleigh protested that they were supposed to be headed for Midway, he wheedled, "Oh, come on, Raleigh, this guy saved my ass in the pen. And, babe, that's no figure of speech, if you know what I mean. Come on, I just talked to Roxanne yesterday. She's doing okay. It's not like she's gonna skip to Canada. Okay? Great." He leaped up. "Look, catch the check, will yah? I'm busted. Some guy just cleaned out my pockets."

Mingo took the time to buy a souvenir cotton bale, plus a wide assortment of firecrackers, buzz bombs, Roman candles, and rockets. "You can't get these in North Carolina. They're illegal."

"That so?" said the pop-eyed waitress, who'd known it for years. "You want them in a bag or you gonna eat 'em here?"

While they waited for Mingo, Gates stood there at the counter flipping the skirt back and forth on a souvenir cloth doll. One half was a white antebellum girl and the other half was a black mammy; the head of each served as the feet of the other. "Look at this!"

"What a world of trash," Raleigh muttered.

"Y'all think I should get some of these pralines here, or wait till New Orleans?"

Raleigh grabbed the fat man's arm and pulled it back. "Mingo, I didn't give you all that money to waste on every damn piece of junk that catches your damn eye."

Gates tapped his shoulder. "Why, Raleigh, I didn't know you were giving away money. Don't forget," he rapped on the inside of his wrist, "we share the same blood."

"How can I?" Hayes growled.

The travelers packed, checked out, went to rent the smallest possible U-Haul trailer they could find that the motorcycle would fit inside. Then they attached it to Jimmy Clay's boat hitch.

"Thank God for Jimmy," said Hayes, and decided maybe he ought to give his cousin a call and find out if he'd married Tildy Harmon in the five or ten years since they'd left town.

"Red plush seats, Raleigh?" Gates strolled around the Cadillac. "Man, you have definitely had a change of life." He flicked one of the little black Buddhas and patted the plastic Christ on the head. "Definitely. And what's all that junk in the trunk?"

"Junk."

"Somebody rip off your radio?"

"Nuns."

By the time they reached the grass field beside the local high school's floodlit stadium, it was dark and almost eight, the time, according to

Mingo, when the Glory Bound Boys were scheduled to play again, for the next call to salvation. As Mingo had warned them, the forty-eight-hour marathon revival was "jam-packed." Raleigh wondered if every house in the county wouldn't have to be empty (and rife for robbery) this Saturday night, there were so many old cars and new cars and old trucks and new trucks crowded together in the rutted field, while their owners crowded into the bleachers to cheer and groan not for one football team against another, but for Reverend Joey Vachel against Lucifer and all his legions of devils. Some enterprising capitalist had parked a white food truck near the entranceway and was doing a brisk trade in fried pizza dough and soft drinks among those who presumably knew they couldn't live by bread alone. Families tugging children by the hand and calling to old people who fell behind, "Come on!," hurried toward the lights. A fat woman pushing a man in a wheelchair jumped in front of it and pulled it forward by the wheels when it stuck in the hard red rutted earth. Some people broke out for a few steps in a run, some people talked and laughed, some people stared straight ahead into the white starry floodlights, as they all were swept together through the gate of the little stone coliseum to surrender themselves to Jesus.

Our travelers had to park the Cadillac and trailer on the edge of a steep incline that dropped down into a big stretch of woods. Even from that far away, they could hear the Reverend Joey Vachel's tired, undulant voice calling out of the loudspeakers for more and more souls.

> And Jaezuz sahed. And uh Jaezuz sahed! Ah thank yew, Father, for hiding thaese thangs from thuh larn-ed and thuh wise, and uh reveeling thaem tuh thuh sample. Yaes! Yaes! Tuh thuh *sample!* Thuh *last* shall be first. Thuh last shall buhee first! It doesn't *matter* who you are. No sorrow is tuhoo daeep for thuh Man who walked on the water. It doesn't *matter* wut you've done. No sin in the *world* is too heavy for thuh Man who carried the Cross! Come on up, my friends, and take Lord Jaezuz by the hand. Take His hand! Yaes! Take His hand! Take His hand!

"That's Reverend Joey Vachel," said Mingo.

"No fooling," said Gates.

"I bet he's going to make his thousand souls. If his voice holds out. He had two hundred and ten at three this afternoon."

Raleigh saw a woman wearing a scarf stumble as she tried to move around two men who carried an ice chest between them. She was walking against the crowd, away from the coliseum, and he realized, when they passed each other, both that she was crying, and that she had a large ugly lump under her chin, half-hidden by the scarf. Was she crying because she'd already been saved? Not likely, thought Hayes, and angrily jammed his hands in his pockets. Far more likely, she'd simply turned around and left. There was nobody inside that football stadium, that huckster's tent, that circus of fools, who was going to hold out His hand and take away that lump in exchange for her soul. It *did* matter who you were, and the waters of some sorrows were too deep to walk over. And some sins were too heavy to strap to a cross, and raise.

Raleigh was so angry, he didn't notice at first the commotion storming toward him. It happened very quickly. Most momentous things do. People were already screaming when he heard loud sharp booms of noise, which he assumed were fireworks shot off to excite the congregation into salvation. He heard someone yell, "Wait, you lousy bastards!" He saw a half-dozen men dodging among the cars, throwing aside objects and running for the woods. He heard a scuffling behind their U-Haul. He heard more booms and saw more men racing toward him pointing things. He recognized the things as guns.

"DOWN!" yelled Gates, and dived under the trailer; and so did Raleigh, and Mingo tried to, but couldn't, so he screamed, "Don't shoot!" and flung up his arms. Men in uniforms ran to the fat man, looked him over, and kept going. One panted, "Which way they go?"

"Uh uh uh oh oh over there!" Mingo pointed blindly down into the woods almost a hundred yards east of where the first men had fled. The prison guards raced away and dropped below the incline.

Raleigh crawled out on the far side of the trailer and tripped over a bulky object. It made a hollow thrumming noise. It was a bass fiddle. Nearby was its huge black case. The lid, strangely, appeared to be trembling. Hayes crawled up, opened it, and found himself staring into a pair of tear-filled panic-stricken eyes. They belonged to a very small, very thin, very old man curled in a ball. He had long thick gray hair pulled back in a tight ponytail, and bony stick-thin white arms, and tiny praying hands. He wore green baggy prison pants and a T-shirt stenciled GLORY BOUND BOYS. He lay there, still as a corpse, and whispered, "For the love of God, will ya shut that s.o.b. lid?"

"Who's that?" whispered Mingo, squatting down.

"*Weeper!*" Gates leaned over his brother's shoulder. "What are you doing in there?"

"It's a crapulous miracle," the little man whispered. "Gates Hayes. Help me, ya beautiful bastard."

People were running all around, in and out of the gate, and from the noisy woods beams of light jumped like locusts. The loudspeakers boomed, "Friends! FUHRIENDS! Keep your SUHEATS! Let the Lord Jaezuz handle this! His *eye* is on the sparrow. PUHLEASE, GET BACK, FUHRIENDS! STAND ON BACK! Oh, shit! Number Five, *hit it!*" And the choir started singing, "Oh, put your hand in the hand of the Man who . . ."

Slamming the lid down, Gates locked the fiddle case. "Pick it up, Mingo!" He ran to open the U-Haul. "Can you carry it? In here. Get the bass, Raleigh!"

"Wait just a second," Raleigh hissed. "I don't know, are we sure we want to —"

But Mingo was already trotting with the big black case to the rear of the trailer. Gates was already hiding the fiddle under U-Haul mats, and kicking the case in beside the motorcycle. A groan came from within it. Scarcely had they slid the doors shut when a barrel-chested prison guard puffed back up the slope waving a flashlight. "Y'all see some men go by?"

"Yes sir," Mingo shouted. "I told you already, they all ran off down in the woods down there. Are they criminals or something?"

"Escaped convicts," the man gasped, mucus running from his nose. "How many? Six?"

"Or seven," said Gates, leaning on the trailer door. "Hard to say."

The guard flashed his light over Gates, then Raleigh, then brought it back to Gates. "I know you? You look familiar."

Gates smiled. "Well . . . You know much about baseball?"

"I sure do. Why?"

"No reason. You watch the soaps on TV?"

"My wife does."

Gates brushed his mustache. "Maybe you've seen me. I'm on *The Guiding Light.*"

"No kidding?"

"Right. Maybe that's why I look familiar. But I'm down here scouting locations for a baseball movie. This is my director." He pointed at Raleigh. "And this is my agent." He pointed at Mingo.

"No kidding?" The guard started patting his pockets. "What's your name? I wish I had some paper, I'd get your autograph. My wife'd bust a gut. Anybody got any paper?"

Raleigh had lockjaw; he just stood there and stared straight ahead.

A voice called from the woods, "Reuben, get back down here quick!"

"*The Guiding Light?* No kidding? What'd you say your name was?" The guard was trotting backward.

"Farley Granger!" shouted Gates. He added in a whisper, "Move ass." But as Raleigh didn't appear to be capable of moving so much as a toe, Sheffield took the wheel while Gates maneuvered his brother like a blind man into the backseat. Mingo shot the Cadillac into reverse and quickly backed its trailer half off the edge of the incline. The U-Haul dangled over the abyss for a few seconds, the length of a nightmare. Then the big car caught hold and hauled it forward.

"I'll drive!" Gates yelled, actually shoving his boot against Sheffield's bulk to push him out of the car.

When Mingo got back in on the passenger side, he had a clarinet in his hand. "Look what I found just lying there! Wait!"

Gates screeched off while Mingo still had one huge leg to haul inside. And then, despite the ruts in the field, the heavy weight of the laden Cadillac, the crush of parked cars, and a crowd now as excited by the prison break as they'd been by the call to salvation, Gates soared away from that revival meeting as if the Cadillac had grown the wings of a Pegasus. He was, as he said, a flyer. The male voice in the dashboard kept warning him, "You are exceeding the speed limit. Thank you." But Gates just laughed, "You're welcome!" and sped on.

So the miles rushed by, Mingo and Gates gleefully reliving the great rescue of Weeper Berg; Raleigh, silent as death, in the backseat. But he wasn't dead; he was taking inventory. Yes, the Cadillac was filling up; lucky he'd been forced to buy so large a car. It now held (or towed) his jailbird brother, a motorcycle, his great-grandmother's trunk (which he had not yet had the leisure to open), a trumpet and a clarinet, a giant pink teddy bear, the whoremonger Mingo Sheffield, Mingo's gun, Mingo's firecrackers, his souvenirs and bulging suitcase, an escaped convict in a fiddle case, the fiddle, Vera's cast-off clothes, a bust removed from a public library, stolen (?) bags of cocaine (?), a Bible, two Buddhas, and a plastic Christ. Yes, he was doing, as his aunt Reba had said, showing off her wooden legs, "just fine." All he needed now was Jubal Rogers, and he'd have everything his father had asked him so easily to bring him. "Daddy," said Hayes to himself, "I hope you don't think I am ever, ever, going to forget this."

Frantic banging seemed to be coming from the U-Haul.

"Pardon me." Raleigh leaned forward. "Oh, Gates. Pardon me. I think perhaps your friend is suffocating in that case."

"Nah, I unlocked it."

"Well, then, I think perhaps he's trying to attract your attention."

Safely hidden on a side road, they slid open the doors. The little man leaped down, holding his unzipped baggy pants, and hopped toward a tangle of bushes, wailing as he went, "My lousy bowels, they're letting go!" Indeed, they were, to judge from all the noise that erupted from the darkness. Finally the convict Berg reappeared. As he shuffled back to them, he lamented, "Awwgh. I can't take the crummy pace. I'm aching in every appurtenance. My guts can't stand much more. Listen, I'm too old for this. I'm an old man, what can I say? You get old, you gotta expect it." He tugged up his pants and zipped them. "The bastards left me in the dirt. When it was me was the animator of it all. Well, those puttyhead Crackers'll never make it without me, and serve 'em right. Oyyy. Tell me why, when Stubby O'Neill tried to snuff me in 'fifty-eight, I bothered to duck, anywise?" He wiped his teary eyes with a small veinous fist. "Gates, talk's cheap. I give you my benison."

Thus were the Thermopyleans introduced to the master criminal Simon "Weeper" Berg, who said that meeting them was a total cynosure. Raleigh was both impressed and confused by the man's peculiar vocabulary, but it was subsequently revealed that among the many self-improving projects (including the study of the bass fiddle) with which Mr. Berg had profitably spent his prison years, the most recent had been his plan to memorize the dictionary; an undertaking terminated by his escape, just as he'd finished with the *C*'s. It was obvious he had not by then had a chance to master all the pronunciations or orthodox usages, for he heaved his words like rocks into his sentences, sometimes sinking them into nonsense.

Mingo was pumping the little hand. "I've heard all about you, Mr. Berg. Gosh! What a life you've had! How'd you ever get into that sheikh's mansion?"

"Chopped liver," said Berg. "Dumb dogs."

The news that Gates was traveling to Midway to visit his sick mother was first greeted by the convict with some derision, but finally convinced — rather to his disappointment, it seemed to Raleigh — that there was no "scam" or "job" involved in the excursion, he accepted Gates's invitation to come along for the ride. The alternative, after all, was scrambling on foot through black wilds of cotton and peanut fields, with the police after him. He further admitted he had no other plans of an immediate nature, although "not to worry, I'll come up with something crystalline." A promise that filled Raleigh with horror.

It was decided that as the state police might already be setting up roadblocks, steps had to be taken. After some discussion, the step they agreed to take was to disguise Weeper Berg as their grandmother, since the only clothes they could find that would fit the five-foot-tall man, they found when they broke open Tiny Hackney's trunk. It proved to be stuffed full of turn-of-the-century outfits, some of which, Mingo claimed, were back in style. The trunk also contained a great many other oddities, thrilling to both Gates and Mingo, for they included a small Confederate uniform, a military sword, and, Raleigh was pleased to see, the engraved silver napkin rings he'd been looking for for the past twenty years. Mingo picked out a peach linen suit with a full-length skirt, because Weeper refused even to try to see if Mrs. Hackney's button-shoes would fit him or not. Nor did he want to take his hair out of its ponytail, nor did he want to wear the cloche hat, nor — in general — was he very cooperative at all. His mournful litany keened through the night as Mingo dressed him. "Oyyy awwgh. It's come to this. This is the end of the line. So anywise, why not? I could die from shame. Tell me why my mother didn't go to her grave a lousy virgin? Me that was the brains behind the Morgan heist and the Newport sting. Me that Polack Joe Saltis asked me for advice. Me that was complaisant with the biggest of the big. I could die abhorrent."

"Please stand still, Mr. Berg," said Mingo.

"So what should I expect? Nobody said, so Simon, go stand under the bird shit. Was I crazy? I'm a Jew. Jews aren't thieves. Jews don't go to prison. Jews own delicatessens. Jews sell clothes like my brother Nate."

"I sell clothes," said Mingo, fighting off Weeper's hands so he could stuff a little padding down his bodice. "What kind does your brother sell? Boy, I wish I had some lipstick or rouge or something."

"Don't tell me lipstick. I'm an old man. My prostate's kaput. I can't go on. Give me a break, will ya? Why do I ask?"

"There, Mr. Berg. Don't start crying now. Please. I think you look really nice." Mingo stepped back to admire his work. "Except you need to shave," he admitted.

Raleigh remained completely uninvolved in all this. He was sadly watching the air seep out of the rear tire, which had obviously sustained a puncture, doubtless when trying to claw its way back from the edge of that ravine.

Once unhappily dressed, his gray hair fluffed out, and his skirt hiding his prison boots, the convict was next confronted with the equally distressing news that he had to give up his bass fiddle, on the case of which was stenciled GLORY BOUND BOYS. He refused. In fact, he hugged the mammoth instrument to his bosom, his head scarcely reaching the neck, leading Raleigh to wonder if he'd had to stand on a box in order to play it. "Will ya wait," he pleaded. "From a crummy lousy paperback book, I learned! Sleeping with it in my bunk so as those tin-ear guards wouldn't chew it into toothpicks, the lousy anti-Semites. To buy this, I gave up cigarettes two years!"

"They aren't good for your health anyhow," Mingo said. "I mean, I wish I could quit."

"Look, you faggy Cyclops, I don't want to hear from your good health. I am in the grave with maggots up to my neck."

Mingo pouted. "Why do folks keep calling me a fag? You're the second one. I've never been a homosexual one single day in my whole life."

Berg wheezed, "They'd take care of that in a minute, the place I just left." Tenderly he placed his fiddle back in its case.

"Don't let him kid you, Mingo. Ease off, Weep." Gates tried to wrestle the fiddle case away from his former cellmate. But the old man fought back.

"Gates, Gates. If I wouldn't leave it with those goons blasting Winchesters at me, if I wouldn't leave it so as to catch up to those shit-kicking Crackers, am I now, you tell me, gonna leave it now?"

"Damn, okay, fine, fine. Just give me the case."

Gates ran with the case across the highway to a farmhouse, wiped off the fingerprints, and hid it behind a refrigerator in a pickup truck parked at the end of the driveway. The next morning, the truck's owner delivered the refrigerator to his sister outside Fayetteville, North Carolina. They had breakfast before he unloaded it. While they were inside, her two little boys pulled the case off the truck, dragged it into the backyard, and started filling it with dirt. They were spanked by their mother for lying when they claimed they'd found the fiddle case in their uncle's truck. Having heard on the radio about the prison break, the woman called the police, and, for the next week, deputies and hounds tromped the countryside around Fayetteville, searching for the notorious criminal Weeper Berg.

Meanwhile, more than a hundred miles to the south, Berg and his new friends were completely untroubled by the attentions of the law, either while they changed the tire, or ate supper in a Burger King parking lot, or drove to the outskirts of Midway. There (deciding it was too late to trouble Roxanne Digges at the hospital), they checked into a motel, or, rather, Raleigh checked in for them. He took the last two rooms on the second landing. One for himself and Mingo, one for his brother and companion. "I'm sure," said Raleigh, back at the car, handing Gates the key, "you two will want to be together to talk over old crimes."

"Your brother's a caustic and censorious s.o.b. In my humble opinion, anywise," said Berg to Gates.

"Right. Good old censorious Raleigh, we called him."

Now the little man in the peach dress ran his thumb and forefinger over Raleigh's dotted tie and white wide lapel. "But how your brother described you, you don't so much look."

The life insurance salesman told him sternly, "I *am* the way my brother described me. I am not the way I look. Is somebody going to help me unload this car?"

"Anybody want to go swimming?" shouted Mingo, running over to see the pool. Gates strolled after him.

A man with a big briefcase tried to offer his arm to Weeper Berg, who was tripping all over his long linen skirt as he climbed the metal stairs with his bass fiddle.

"Keep your lousy mitts off me," the convict growled.

"Ha ha," quickly laughed Hayes, behind them carrying Mingo's suitcase, the trumpet, the clarinet, and the teddy bear. "My ah grandmother gets a little crabby when she's tired. Excuse her, please."

The man looked affably down at him. "Mine's the same way. Y'all got a family band?"

"Right," said Hayes.

By the time Raleigh had added up his day's expenses in his notebook, and Mingo had cannonballed off the diving board until the manager shut off the pool lights on him, and Weeper and Gates had reminisced about prison life, by the time the four travelers had fallen asleep, the state police had recaptured all the rest of the Glory Bound Boys, and returned them to prison. All the prison guards had returned to their homes, including the one named Reuben, whose wife was so furious at him for either mishearing or misremembering the name of the soap opera celebrity (as she knew perfectly well Farley Granger was not, and never had been, the star of *The Guiding Light*), so furious at him for failing to have a piece of paper handy to get the actor's autograph, that she made her husband sleep on the couch.

Sunday morning, Gates in his silvery space clothes, Raleigh in his white suit, the two Hayeses left their companions playing five-card stud in the motel room. Weeper Berg, cheered by the morning news report of the recapture of the rest of the Glory Bound Boys, had condescended to teach Mingo how to palm an ace. The brothers drove through the spring-leafy streets out to the hospital to visit Roxanne. "I can't handle hospitals,"

Gates admitted, and said nothing else after that. They were sent by a receptionist up to Ward C. Raleigh, keeping Gates beside him, walked looking for Roxanne down white rows of sickbeds, in them women patients, some young, mostly old; some asleep, most in pain; some recovering, most of them not. Some of the women looked back at him, and while it had never been his habit to speak to strangers, he felt he could not pass their beds without mumbling, "Hello," to any whose eyes met his.

But he didn't see Roxanne. An intern sent them up to the intensive care unit. A nurse on duty there sent them to a little waiting room, where they waited and waited, until another, older, nurse slid silently through the door and nodded at them. "You're here to see Mrs. Fred Zane?" she finally said.

"Yes," Raleigh said. "Is there some problem?"

"Are you . . . are you friends of hers . . . or . . ."

Raleigh repeated, "Is there some problem?"

The nurse laced her fingers together as if she were going to offer them a prayer. "I'm terribly sorry. Mrs. Zane isn't here."

"What do you mean, isn't here? She went home?"

"Well, no. She passed away two days ago."

Raleigh just looked at her.

"On Friday," she was finally compelled to add.

"That's ridiculous," Raleigh told her. "He spoke to her on the phone two days ago, Friday morning." Hayes wheeled on Gates. "You *did*, didn't you, Gates? Did you lie to me?"

"No," mumbled Gates, whose lips had turned blue. "She was here. Right here. She was okay. She said, 'I'm okay.' "

Raleigh spun back to the nurse. "See? There must be some mistake."

"I'm terribly sorry. You can talk to the doctor if you like. But Mrs. Zane expired in O.R. Friday night."

"O.R.? Operating?" Raleigh stumbled. "She was having surgery Friday?"

"Emergency surgery," the nurse admitted. "She began hemorrhaging and was taken to O.R. at eleven P.M. I was on duty. Are you friends of the family? . . . Are you sure you don't want to talk to the doctor? . . . Well, is there anything else I can do for you?"

Raleigh couldn't think. He knew there were things he had to think of, but he couldn't find them in his brain. He said, "No thanks."

"Well, then, if you'll —"

"Wait. Where is she?"

The nurse offered to find out.

Raleigh turned back to his half-brother Gates, who was looking out the window with a queasy smile on his face. "Gates?"

". . . Yeah?"

"Gates."

"Right, fine."

"For God's sake, how awful."

"Yeah, well. Sorry, Raleigh. All your rush for nothing. Still . . ." Gates made a weak swipe at his brother's arm. "You did your best. Sorry."

Raleigh left Gates alone in the waiting room, while he went to tell the nurse that he would like to talk to the doctor. The nurse handed the doctor a chart, and the doctor translated the long and the short of it to Raleigh. The long of it was several paragraphs of thoroughly obscure Latin-rooted words, for which the doctor had paid so many thousands of dollars in tuition that naturally he wanted to use as many as possible. (And truly they were very valuable words, as valuable and powerful as any other priestly mumbo jumbo — for they meant the considerable difference between his income and that of the nurse — compelling the nurse to call him "sir," and obey his orders to hand him things that were six inches away.) So the doctor got his money's worth out of the long of it.

The short of it was that Roxanne Digges Zane had died in the operating room. When Raleigh returned to Gates, his brother had made a paper airplane out of a page of a magazine. He cocked his arm and threw it across the room; it landed in a philodendron plant on a shelf. Then Gates took a breath, rubbed his mustache, and laughed. "Well, let's face it, Roxanne and I didn't exactly have all that much more to shoot the breeze about anyhow."

In the car, Raleigh began oddly to shiver. "Gates, I don't know what to say. . . . At least you spoke to her on the phone."

"Yeah, we summed it up."

At the funeral home, when Raleigh asked to see Roxanne, a pink man who never spoke above a whisper sat them in a "Private Grief Room," and brought them a shiny brass cylinder, which he placed sacramentally on a coffee table between a Bible and an ashtray.

"Hi, Mom," said Gates. "Long time, no see."

"Gates, please!" Raleigh took the urn out of his brother's hand. It was cold and smooth and hard. How could it possibly be Roxanne Digges, with her heated temper that flamed out of nowhere and burned anybody in its path, with her rough bawdy laughter and her soft ample skin? How could all that yelling and laughing and dancing and drinking, all that noise and motion and flesh that thirty years ago he had stood watching with so much hatred, how could it all be sealed inside this little cylinder? When he'd stood there hating her as she danced in the bright noise — while his mother sat across town alone with her quiet glass flowers — hating her so much he'd wished her burned to cinders before his eyes; he'd never imagined this. How could anyone be reduced to this? And how could it ever happen, dear God Almighty, to someone he loved?

The pink man was whispering that he was surprised to see them there.

"So are we," Gates told him.

But the man was surprised because at this very moment they were missing Mrs. Zane's memorial service at a church across town.

"She went to church?" asked Gates.

"I couldn't say," the man whispered.

"For whom," Raleigh inquired, "are the ah the remains intended?"

"Miss Zane made the arrangements."

"Miss Zane? Gates, who's he talking about? Did Roxanne have a daughter?"

Gates turned his face into a parody of the funeral director's, and whispered piously, "I couldn't say."

The church to which they were directed was an eighteenth-century white clapboard building set in a grove of willows and oaks and worn, tilted tombstones. It was a very old church, comfortable with death, having hosted centuries of funerals. It was so old, it had in the back of its second floor, a slave gallery, installed in old times, so that black people could sit there and overhear the Good News that the last would be first. Into this gallery the two Hayes men slipped, so as not to disturb the service, for a small choir was singing "A Mighty Fortress Is Our God" (despite, thought Raleigh, the immediate evidence to the contrary). Apparently this hymn concluded Mrs. Zane's memorial service, for after "Amen" was hummed, the minister, who looked as old as the church, rambled in befuddlement a few more minutes, then gently told the few people gathered to go in peace. Except for a young woman in the front row, they stood and left, at the slow pace set by the dour organ.

At that moment, Gates started mumbling, "Oh shit, oh fuck, oh no," slid out of his seat, and crawled behind the pew. Raleigh had expected this. Even if the man hadn't known his mother from Adam and Eve, still, a breakdown of some sort was only human nature. But now Gates had slithered with his elbows to the back wall, where he was peering over the sill of a small round window. "How the fuck," he whispered, "did he find out I had a mother?"

"Gates." Raleigh cleared his throat. "Gosh. I wish there were something I could do."

"Get me out of here!"

"Yes, of course. Let's go back to the motel."

"Motel! Shit!" Gates jerked his brother down beside him. "Did you register under your own name?"

"What?"

"Did you use the name Hayes?"

"Of course I did." Yes, Gates was overcome; more so than Raleigh had anticipated. He had the eyes of a madman.

"Well, that's fantastic. He'll check them all out, you can count on that!"

"He? Gates, try to pull yourself together."

"Okay fine great fine. Think! All right, he walked past the car. So he doesn't know what we're driving. He'll be looking for my Harley."

Raleigh had realized by now that his brother was discussing someone real, someone presumably down in the churchyard. He looked out the window. Strolling among the tombstones was a fairly young, slender man wearing a white panama hat and a white suit (not dissimilar to the one Raleigh had on). With him was a blond, beetle-browed, fat-nosed man, easily as large as, if not larger than, Mingo Sheffield. This individual opened a big wicker basket, spread out a checked cloth on the grass, and began laying out a picnic, right there in the cemetery. Leaning against a little flowering dogwood tree, a few of its white petals floating down around him, the man in the panama hat began to point out tombstones to his immense companion. To do so he used a thin white bone cane. This object stabbed Raleigh's memory like a stiletto. At "Peace and Quiet," hadn't Gates been muttering in terror about a man with a white cane?

"Is that . . . Is that. . . ?" What was the ridiculous name? "Cupid Parisi Calhoun?"

"Right." Gates nodded. "What a run of luck, hunh? And he's got Big Nose Solinsky with him. Can you believe it? Sorry, Raleigh, I don't think this is my day. Definitely."

"Okay, well, well, slow down, don't worry, Gates. Don't worry. We'll just sit here, and together we'll, we'll think this thing through," said Raleigh Hayes.

CHAPTER

21

In Which Is Described the Famous Barbecue at "Wild Oaks"

AT FIRST Raleigh did not even recognize Weeper Berg, which was, said Mingo, good news. The convict, having refused to re-dress in Tiny Hackney's suit, now stood in pants, plucking a dirge on his giant bass fiddle. The pants he wore were very mildewed gray pants with yellow stripes up the sides. With them, he wore a gray moth-eaten military tunic. He now had very short flat white hair and very long sorrowful white mustaches. Mingo felt that he'd done a super-duper job of transforming Mr. Berg from a grandmother into a Civil War veteran; and all he'd needed were scissors, glue, and white shoe polish. But Hayes had time for only a passing skeptical glance, and the caveat that, however white Weeper's hair or decayed his bowels, he did not look the 140 years old he would necessarily have to be in order to have marched under the Stars and Bars.

"But listen," said Mingo.

"No." Hayes was too busy to listen. He was too busy loading the Cadillac, unloading the motorcycle, leaving the U-Haul with a note at a (closed) filling station that rented U-Hauls, telling the motel manager that if anyone dropped by looking for the Hayeses to tell them they were already on their way to Cleveland, Ohio. He was too busy trying to cope with the shock of the hospital; trying to scrub out of his mind the picture of the brass urn; trying to calm down Mingo, who'd never met Roxanne

Digges, but nevertheless went to pieces when informed that she was dead. Too busy trying to reason with Weeper, who was already complaining that he'd almost rather wear a dress than the uniform of the shit-kicking South, which he aspersed anywise, and who got tears in his eyes when told that they were now on the run from a crime syndicate as well as the police. Raleigh was too busy sliding down the sheer glass cliff of reason and flailing for a sliver of a fingerhold, to listen to a thing until the phone rang with word from Gates, hidden in the parish kitchen, that they could now return to the church, as the picnicking mobsters had gone.

Naturally, Weeper Berg could not ride Gates's motorcycle: His mustache would blow off, his legs were too short, he was from Manhattan and didn't know how to drive. Naturally, Mingo had to confess that he was too chicken to try. Naturally, it was left to Raleigh to straddle, in white pants much tighter than he was accustomed to wearing his trousers, the deadly chrome-crowded machine. Left to him to lurch it onto the street, down which, without stopping for lights, signs, or traffic, he swerved spasmodically, like a drunk escort for the big Cadillac behind him, Mingo at its wheel and the neck of Berg's fiddle sticking out its rear window.

At the church, under the peaceful willows, they found Gates in conversation with the young woman Raleigh had seen stay so quietly seated at the end of the memorial service. Mingo and Weeper rushed over to offer their condolences, and Gates disappeared for a moment inside Mingo's embrace. "She's gone to a better place," Mingo told him, and Berg added that he hoped she'd rest in peace. "I put it in the mental shredder," said Gates. "You know, what can you do?"

The young woman standing there was transparently a very beautiful young woman. Still, Raleigh was amazed that his brother would pick this time to start flirting with a stranger. But she was not, Gates explained, exactly a stranger, although until then unknown to them. This quiet, plainly dressed woman was Sara Zane, and she was, in fact, the niece of Roxanne's dead husband Fred. Raleigh was told that she was a local schoolteacher. He assumed she must be also a local martyr, for it appeared that, despite the remoteness of her family connection (and despite what Raleigh vividly recalled about Roxanne's horrendous temperament in the best of times), Miss Zane had visited her aunt-in-law all through the years of her alcoholic widowhood, and the further years of her slow cancer, and had sat beside her in the hospital, and had arranged this memorial service, and was now giving, without rancor, as her reason, "There was no one else."

In return, Roxanne Digges had bequeathed her niece-in-law her entire estate, which consisted of three items: the furniture in her rented house, the skeleton of Fred's long-distance truck, which since 1977 had sat up on blocks in the backyard and there been robbed by vandals of several of its parts; and, third, the hospital bills and funeral expenses not covered by her insurance.

This Sara Zane, her eyes grave blue, her hair dark wings, stood now apologizing to Gates, who was staring at her as if she were the mirage of an oasis. She was apologizing for not having been able to reach him, for having felt it necessary to proceed with the cremation, for the fact that Roxanne had not mentioned him in the will, which she certainly would have done, had she . . . had she . . . Had she thought about it, Raleigh silently finished. And, of course, Gates should have the ashes, and of course he should have anything else in Roxanne's house he wanted. She would be staying there for the next few days in order to pack and clean.

"Listen, really, thank you," said Gates. "I'll try to get over there tomorrow. Now, listen, okay? If those two guys come back, you know, the ones who were asking you about me, listen, I never showed, and, far as you know, I never even knew Roxanne was sick. And you never heard of me, okay?"

"All right," she said tranquilly, with what struck Raleigh as a remarkable lack of curiosity. Had she no questions for this stranger-son, wandering the churchyard, having missed his mother's funeral; mysteriously telling her to deny his existence to any who asked? Had she no questions about his companions, one of them an ancient minuscule man in a Civil War outfit; another, a behemoth shouting out information off gravestones: "Here's a general! Here's Oliver Wendell Holmes's father!"

Sara Zane was unsettling to Raleigh Hayes. It was, well, it was freakish, to meet in a cemetery on the day of Roxanne's memorial service a young woman with the same name as his own dead mother's. Miss Zane had clearly also upset Gates, for as soon as she left, he kicked a gravestone and said, "I don't need this now. I can't handle it."

"Handle what?" asked Raleigh. There was much to choose from.

But, "Her!" is what Gates replied, and pointed at Sara Zane driving away in a cheap little car. "That one."

"A chaste tomato," Weeper Berg acknowledged.

Now, as soon as he was told why and how Gates was being pursued for a $15,000 debt of honor, Berg wanted details. They didn't impress him. "Cupid who? Calhoun? Never heard of him, and if *I* never heard of him, not to worry."

"He's a Parisi," said Gates, hurriedly hiding his motorcycle behind broken pews in the back shadows of the rectory garage.

"Spare me my credence," Berg snorted. "Parisis! Parisis couldn't hit Faggy Sheffield over there with a bazooka! *Frank* Parisi, may he rest in peace, shot Simple Sammy Loretto six times in a crummy *men's room,* and following after which, he chucked him in the reservoir, and Simple Sammy swam to the other side, of about a mile away, and walked home. So, don't tell me Parisi. It cuts no ice with me. I am colloquial with Parisis, and I can inform you they are one big marshmallow."

"He's got Big Nose Solinsky with him."

This gave Weeper pause. "The Nose is out of the pen again? He was in for life."

"Well, he outlived it."

". . . Aghh, he's a cretin. He's a slab of concrete."

"Right. And I don't want to end up under it. I'm sorry, okay?" Gates found an old rug and threw it over his cycle.

"Yaaduda yaaduda. Listen to me, Gates. I'm an old man. My colon's let go. I got the jimjams. My pants are too long. My collar's too big."

"Weeper, not now, all right?"

"What pals I got left quit the business and are cohabitating in Miami playing lousy shuffleboard. I'm down to nickels and dimes in podunk towns. And, irregardless . . . you listen . . . irregardless, I could do a waltz around Big Nose Solinsky, *any day,* with my mitts cuffed! Any day! So. Not to worry."

"Thanks, Weep," said Gates and squeezed his shoulder. But despite these assurances, he proceeded to unscrew the (admittedly distinctive) North Carolina KISSY PU plate off the back of the Cadillac and to replace it with the innocuous South Carolina plate on the minister's old Ford, then parked in the garage. (As it happened, this switch was never noticed by the elderly clergyman, who very rarely drove and even more rarely paid any attention to what he was driving. A lady parishioner, on whom he paid a call the following week, did notice the scandalous license plate, but she was too embarrassed to mention it, so KISSY PU remained on the old Ford in the rectory garage until the day that decrepit vehicle received its annual safety inspection — long after the conclusion of this story.)

Weeper Berg shook his head sadly as he whispered to Mingo, "The boy's paranoiac. The boy's in a paranoiac crucible. He has talents, I give you, but he spooks when times get agonistic. Tell me they're gonna snuff him over a lousy bagatelle of fifteen lousy gees?"

"I guess I don't know what a bagatelle is," Sheffield confessed.

"An unimportant or insignificant thing; a trifle," Berg replied.

As hurrying Fortune would have it, the plan to hide out until Gates could recover his mother's remains (and see Sara Zane again) went into almost immediate effect, when, before they'd driven too far out of town, they found themselves at a red light side by side with a Saab, out of whose passenger seat window a gigantic nose, surrounded by a flat platter of a face, suddenly started to yell, "UHHHHHHHHH. QUUUEP! HIMMMM!!!" It was a voice like a flushing toilet.

Gates Hayes (of whom it had often been said that he had the reflexes of an Olympic athlete) took an immediate shortcut to the right, across somebody's lawn, mowing down, in the process, two little iron jockeys holding up lanterns.

"Jesus!" said Raleigh in the backseat.

"Jesus!" said Mingo, on the floor with the bass fiddle on top of him.

"Lose 'em!" said Berg, hanging out the window. "Attaboy!"

Gates swung into a residential road lined with new flowery fruit trees. The road climbed steeply; as did, clearly, the prices of the houses, for they grew taller and wider and farther away, and the grass grew brighter and the hedges higher, until finally Raleigh couldn't see anything but treetops — or rather the blur of treetops, for Gates was traveling at his typical speed, and usually on two wheels.

"Cut it left! . . . Cut it right!" Weeper was navigating. "You got him! Cut in, cut in!"

Gates slung the Cadillac off the street through what, thank God, proved to be an opening in a block-long high brick wall. They roared down a wide gravel road.

"Passed us!" Weeper gloated. "Rubes!" He climbed back inside the window as the Cadillac bucked to a stop. Miraculously, his white mustaches were still on his face.

"Gates, this can't go on," said Raleigh, an odd green. "It emphatically cannot continue."

"You're telling me," Berg agreed. "I'm a house of dry mud. I should live so long to die peaceful in bed like my brother Nate, may he rest in peace."

Mingo crawled up from the floorboard and peered around. "Gollee," he said. "This place looks just like *Gone With the Wind*."

The four travelers found themselves not on a public road, but halfway down a gravel drive lined with two rows of immense live oaks that twisted to join boughs overhead. Lawn rolled beautifully away on either side, and at its end, white as snow, was a wide, high Palladian house whose white Corinthian columns soared from its portico to its second-story balcony — on which someone appeared to be standing at an artist's easel. Between the travelers and the house, gaily fluttering on the rich lawn, were three large canvas canopy tents, red and white striped. Half-a-dozen black people in white clothes were running in and out of the tents carrying trays and chairs. On the other side of the lawn stood two little single-room brick houses.

"Awghh," said Weeper Berg, "there's peacocks on that porch! God, I hate these lousy Southern autocrats. Spare me the magnolias, please."

"Y'ALL THERE! HELLO? YOOHOO!" An oversized handsome middle-aged woman in a glittery copper pantsuit came running down the porch steps toward the car. She had crinkled tan skin like expensive leather, gold hair with silver tips, she wore two strands of big pearls, and carried a cut-glass punch bowl in one hand, a paper cup of whiskey in the other, and clamped a long cigarette between her oversized teeth. "Y'ALL THERE! HELLO? ARE Y'ALL THE BAND?"

"YES, MA'AM," yelled Gates, and drove forward to the crescent of gravel at the foot of the wide white porch.

"God damn you, Gates!" was all Raleigh had time to snarl before the woman was peering in one window after another, looking a little dubiously at the occupants, particularly Mingo's teddy bear, and Weeper Berg, who for some reason was pretending to be blind.

"But they said FIVE pieces! And a female singer!" The woman took a quick drink from her cup and dropped it in the punch bowl. "I swear I am losing whatever little rag of sanity I ever possessed and sincerely plan to hang myself before this day is through! Oh, what the hell! Y'all don't pay me any mind if I tell you you aren't a damn thing like what I was expecting the Dixie Troubadours to be! ETHAN, THAT IS THE *WRONG* CANDELABRA!" She was shouting at a large black man on the portico. "CARRY IT RIGHT ON BACK IN THE HOUSE, YOU HEAR! ETHAN, *PLEASE,* STOP KICKING THOSE FRENCH DOORS OPEN WITH YOUR FOOT! OH, GODDAMN, THERE IT GOES AGAIN!" Glass chinkled like loud chimes.

"Oyyyyy," groaned Weeper Berg, rolling his blank eyes up into their sockets.

Gates now climbed quickly out of the Cadillac, firing upon the woman at close range the sudden impact of his extreme good looks and trendy clothes. It was enough to silence her long enough for him to confess that he'd misunderstood her question about the band. Of course they weren't the Dixie Troubadours. How absurd.

"Uh oh," Raleigh whispered and mentally clutched his parachute straps. Gates was speaking with a French accent.

"Ah no no, absurd, *je m'excuse.* I am but of course you know Jean Claude Claudel. The director? You have perhaps seen my cinemas in your beautiful country?"

The woman, who had never heard of Jean Claude Claudel, nodded in a daze.

"I am so pleased," Gates bowed. "Permit me to make you acquainted with my colleagues.... Ah, but first *excusez moi* ... one moment only." For Raleigh, leaning out, had jerked Gates by the rear of his leather jacket back to the window, and muttered under his breath, "I'm not saying a word, you understand me, Gates, not a goddamn word!"

Gates continued smiling as he reached back to pry Raleigh's hand loose. "Permit me to introduce my American colleague, Mr. Mingo, my ... my ... how do you say ... designer."

Mingo gave his shy, furtive smile.

"... And here is my ... producer, Mr. ... Raleighkov of ... Czechoslovakia. I fear he does not speak one word of English. But he comprehends *un peu. N'est-ce pas,* Raleighkov?"

Raleigh growled.

"And," Gates looked into the car. "The older gentleman." Weeper Berg spasmed an unmistakable "No." "But, *pardonnez moi* ... I have not the liberty to tell you his name. He is a ... a writer. *Peut-être, un peu,* um," Gates searched for a word with his fingers. "... A little eccentric. It is his book you understand I am at the moment filming. A book about ..." Gates glanced around. "... About your *magnifique* American Civil War.... It is called ... um ... *Spare Me the Magnolias Please.*... You have perhaps read it?"

"Why, my, no, but ..." She lowered her voice. "Is the poor man blind?"

Gates peered into the car. *"Comme ci, comme ça,"* he said. "It comes and goes ... with the Muse. And your name, *chère* madame?"

"Why, aah ... oh my goodness!" Gates was kissing her hand, or more precisely the inside of her wrist, which no one had ever done before. "Lady Bug Wetherell," she stammered.

"And Lord Bug Wetherell is your most happy husband?"

"Oh my, no," she laughed hysterically. "Lady Bug's my nickname. Nickname? *Petty nomme?* Lettice is my real name. And that's my husband, Payne, up on the balcony up there."

Gates laughed with his fingers. "Ah, Payne the painter, no?"

"Yes. I mean, no. I mean he was in fertilizer and farm machinery and ranches and all. But that was in Texas. He's no longer actively engaged. He just paints for amusement."

"Ah, madame, it is for amusement that art was born," smiled wisely Jean Claude Claudel, offering his arm to lead her up the steps.

"Why, why YES," spluttered Mrs. Wetherell, thoroughly hypnotized.

"I'm going to throw up," Raleigh said.

"The boy's good," said Berg, still nothing showing but the whites of his eyes.

"You know," bubbled Mingo, "he could have said we were doing *The Optimist's Daughter*. That's set in the South."

Atop the wide curving steps, Gates had cupped one hand into a lens and with it was panning the house and grounds. "I am searching everywhere," he smiled, "for a location for my film."

An hour later, the four travelers were sipping piña coladas on a white wrought-iron table on the balcony. They had ostensibly joined Mr. Payne Wetherell for cocktails, but their host could not seem to stop painting long enough to enjoy a drink. His easel was looking directly out at his beautiful grounds. His canvas, however, reproduced in minute, if shaky, detail the postcard of Montmartre clipped to its edge.

Within minutes, the four were guests of the family, invited to make themselves at home for as long as they liked, but not to stand on ceremony, and not to mind the fact that on this particular day, "Wild Oaks," as they called their little place, was "a bodacious mess" and its inhabitants "stark raving maniacs" over "Crystal's coming out." Raleigh thought immediately of Holly's remark about Booger Blair's "coming out" as a homosexual, but it appeared that the Wetherells' daughter was coming out instead as a debutante. In honor of which auspicious occasion, they were "throwing a little shebang" this evening. To this "ittsy bittsy" celebration, the movie people would be welcome (indeed, exciting) additions. Indeed, the guests of honor. Indeed, Lady Bug admitted she could scarcely wait for her neighbors to hear that famous foreign celebrities were on her premises. "They're gonna pure and simple drop dead!" she prophesied. "Imagine, 'Wild Oaks' in the movies! Have you been in the producing business long, Mr. Raleighkov? Can he understand me?"

Raleigh shook his head as Gates said, "Oh, I think so," and gave him a Gallic kiss on the cheek. "We two, he and I, have been all our lifes longs like brothers. Have we not, Raleighkov?"

Hayes rubbed hard at his cheek. While doing so, he noticed a newspaper on the table near their drinks. This he quickly folded, as soon as he read,

"OLDEST GLORY BOY ESCAPES. HEADS NORTH." Below was a small picture captioned "Simon 'The Weeper' Berg," although it bore little resemblance to at least any of the versions of the convict that Raleigh had seen. He slipped it to Berg, slumped in a corner, who peeked at it out of one blind eye.

Mr. Wetherell (like his wife, florid and oversized) wore old blue jeans, a brand-new red velvet smoking jacket, and a beret. Mrs. Wetherell explained that now that her husband had the leisure, he was determined to be everything he'd ever wanted to be during the years he was instead making millions of dollars selling cow manure. And one of the things he'd wanted to be was a French painter.

"Parlez-vous français?" Gates asked in some apprehension.

"Lord, no," laughed Mrs. Wetherell, pouring herself a water glass full of bourbon and doffing it in a couple of swigs. "Lord, no! Payne doesn't even speak American, unless he has to, do you, sweetie? He's retired."

Payne took his brush from between his teeth, smiled, and put it back. It did seem that while thoroughly affable in his facial expressions, Mr. Wetherell was no longer actively engaged in speech, any more than in fertilizer. All he said on the balcony was, "Glad to have you," "Help yourself," "Want another?," "Crystal in the dog shed?," and, in a gush of prolixity, "Not so long back, not a pot to piss in. So damn many now, need a map."

His wife quickly put a stop to this outburst by singing over the balcony rail to the blacks below that they were setting the tables all wrong. Although professedly without a second to spare, the effusive Lady Wetherell more than compensated for her husband's muteness, and, for that matter, for the sulky silence of Raleighkov and the wide-eyed paralysis of Mr. Mingo, by chatting on and on at the pace and volume of a cattle stampede. "The broad can beat the gums," said Weeper Berg. "She can put the booze away likewise. Take a word of warning and don't light a match near her liver." It was later, of course, in the privacy of their guest cottage, that Berg made this comment. For now, he said nothing, but only sat in the corner on top of the newspaper, his blank eyes fixed on some inner Homeric vision. Or at least so Gates explained. "He writes, how does one say, inside his head. One sees a man *absolutement* engrossed."

"Is that why he wears that old Confederate uniform? For atmosphere?"

"Awwggh," moaned Berg.

"But, of course." Gates helped himself to crustless quarters of chicken salad sandwiches. "He is now deep deep within *Spare Me the Gardenias.*"

"You mean 'Magnolias,' " Mingo suddenly spoke up.

"The Muse is forever revising," explained the unflappable Jean Claude, his fingers dancing.

Because she was in "a complete flapdoodle" over her approaching buffet, Lady Bug (for "call me Lady Bug," she insisted) could now spare them only a few minutes for a quickie little tour of her eensie-weensie house, which was not, she had to warn them, even finished, for she still had eight rooms to go. Even so, and even at a brisk pace, the tour took, to Raleigh's swelling anxiety, a good half-hour; and not simply because the house was about the size of Monticello. Gates kept pausing to zoom with the lens of his hand down wide halls and through wide doors, murmuring, *"Magnifique!"* and *"Perfecto!"* Mingo kept pausing to ooh and gawk and dawdle and touch and say it all looked just like *Gone With the Wind.* Weeper Berg kept falling a room or two behind, ostensibly because of his blindness or visionary rapture, but more likely, Raleigh suspected — correctly, as it transpired — because he was, in his own parlance, casing the joint.

"Wild Oaks" was antebellum in every way but fact. It had been built two years ago. Payne had built it as a little ole present for Lady Bug. It was on the postbellum site of an antebellum farmhouse at which a division of Sherman's Fourteenth Army Corps had once spent the night. Cold, cranky, and bored with ripping up the ties on the Augusta-Charleston line, the Fourteenth had amused themselves by tearing this farmhouse down to build bonfires upon which to roast the edible livestock. They had sung as they swung axes at the siding, and chased pigs around the barn:

> *My boys can live on chicken and ham,*
> *For everything that we do find*
> *Belongs to Uncle Sam.*

All the Fourteenth had left intact were the two rows of oaks. They were the only antiques on the grounds. Even the two little slave cabins were replicas. They weren't really used as slave cabins anymore, of course. They were guest cottages. And, of course, the blacks running around among the tents weren't really slaves anymore. Except for Ethan and the cook, who worked there full time, and whom Lady Wetherell called "the house staff," all the blacks were members of the Holcomb family and owners of Holcomb's Homestyle Party Caterers.

But Mingo's filmic instincts were impeccable. "Wild Oaks" was modeled in minute if shaky detail on Twelve Oaks, Ashley Wilkes's plantation in *Gone With the Wind.* Apparently, another thing Payne Wetherell had always wanted to be was a Georgia slave owner. From its waxy parquet floors to its cantilevered stairway, from its gold damask dining room and

white satin canopy beds to its red brocade music room and its black overweight cook in the kitchen, "Wild Oaks" looked exactly like a movie set
of an antebellum mansion. And, like a set, the illusion gave way on the
backside to pure California. Behind the Wetherell house was a kidney-
shaped swimming pool, a Mercedes-Benz, a jeep, a Peugeot, a golf-cart, a
go cart, a bass boat, an electronic barbecue grill, and, in the dogshed,
Crystal.

Crystal was the only Wetherell child at home. (Their son, Boone, had
proved too much for the public schools to handle, and was locked up in
the Citadel, a South Carolina military academy.) Crystal was the debutante, but she was not at all antebellum. She in no way resembled Scarlett
O'Hara. Or anyone else in *Gone With the Wind,* except possibly one of the
muddy soldiers retreating from Atlanta. Crystal was quite a big, strapping
girl, as the travelers discovered when she'd stopped squatting in her gum
boots among the two dozen bassett hounds and Brittany spaniels who
were crawling all over her, and stood up to shake hands. She stood up to
about six feet, not counting her old slouch hat. It was difficult to tell what
else she was wearing, as it was all covered with mud (and dogs), but in
general she looked far readier to set out with Lewis and Clark than to trip
a Virginia reel at the cotillion ball.

Lady Wetherell laughed like a madwoman. "She is absolutely crazy
about those goddamn dogs! CRYSTAL! I thought I told you to go take
your bath hours ago! You are pure and simply NOT gonna be ready, and I
am planning to throw myself in front of the first car that shows up in the
driveway, you hear!"

"Mommy, come on. Just let me finish up here, will you?"

The young woman was tragically named. She was as far from crystal as it
was possible to get. She was as solid as brick, with long firm thighs and a
wide firm face. She was not fat, just big; not unattractive, just uninter-
ested. She did, however, politely shake hands with the visitors. She had a
grip of steel. "Nice to meet you. *Jumbo! Down! Get off them!"*

Despite her mother's continuing threats of suicide, the girl gave not the
slightest indication of being eager to "come out," even from the pen. All
she wanted to do, as she later confided to Mingo Sheffield, was to go to an
agricultural college to study veterinary medicine. She was clearly breaking
her mother's heart, as well as driving her to drink, for they left Mrs.
Wetherell in her oak-beamed kitchen, belting down a coffee mugful of
Wild Turkey.

Eventually, Raleigh was able to escape to the guest cottage he was to share with his brother, since (too depleted to argue) he'd allowed Gates to talk him into staying the night while "the coast cleared." Weeper Berg had obviously retired to the cabin next door, for Hayes could hear (though not identify) Saint-Saëns's "The Swan" squeakily bowed on the bass fiddle. Raleigh wanted to call Aura, but he didn't have the strength just yet. There was a phone by the bed, and a television and a few other modern improvements, but otherwise the cabin sustained the slave motif, with patchwork quilts and rough-hewn dressers with clay pitchers on top. Raleigh wrapped himself in his quilt and stared at the iron farm implements nailed to the pine wall. From across the lawn, he could hear the happy black laughter of the Holcomb family, who were charging Payne Wetherell four thousand dollars for their spare-rib buffet. He could also hear Mingo Sheffield (or should he say, Mr. Mingo?) joking a mile a minute under the tent with the increasingly voluble Lady Wetherell, as he advised her on arranging her orange rose centerpieces, her scalloped bunting, and her Dixie Troubadours, who must have finally arrived, for Raleigh now heard someone playing, "My Old Kentucky Home" on an electric guitar.

Yes, Mingo was laughing his head off out there. The indiscriminate fool could apparently get along with anybody. How odd that Sheffield had sat through twelve years of public school too terrified to open his mouth, and now should be incapable of shutting it in the presence of every total stranger who crossed his path. Well, thank God for small favors; he, Raleighkov?, was Hungarian, no, Czechoslovakian, and therefore not obliged to converse with a damn soul. Except Aura. He'd call Aura. At least she knew who he was. Surely, his hosts wouldn't mind if he made a collect phone call.

"Such a sob sister, I still can't believe yet. . . . Nah. . . . Trigger's wife was the skirt. Spilled her guts, that's what sent poor Trigger to the hot squat. . . . Yeah. . . . What can I tell you, she was a bag of cupidity, head to toe. The cross was on."

It seemed Weeper Berg was making a collect call of his own, for he was on the other guest phone in the cabin next door. (Actually, it had never occurred to Weeper to reverse the charges on the seven long distance calls he was making to Miami, Florida — as the Wetherells would have discovered had they ever glanced at their phone bills.) Having picked up the receiver, Raleigh shamefully sat on the painted iron bed, and listened in. (Despite the fact that he so highly disparaged eavesdropping, as he'd often said to Caroline.) He kept listening because he was fascinated by his inabil-

ity to understand a word Berg and his acquaintances were saying; it was
like listening to his cousin, Jimmy Clay, and therefore not really eavesdropping, since that vice implied comprehension. Berg did most of the
talking, and in the following vein:

"Nah. . . . Nah. . . . Stooley Norton never put the snatch on Trigger. . . .
Nah. . . . Don't tell me Heinie Hubler! The eyes of a mole, he's got! He
never saw such a thing! . . . So? . . . So? . . . Well, let me put you and the
Worm wise. Stoolie was in the can, 'forty-eight to 'fifty-one, so how *could*
he finger Trigger? . . . Yeah. Trigger was a beauty, an angel, we'll never
know another. Well, it's an amphibolous world. So, tell me, Patty, yah
crapehanger, yah'll get the word to the Cuban? So what's a measly fifteen
thou to him? . . . Yeah, so then is when you say, 'Where were you the
night of New Year's Day, 'seventy-nine, when Morris Brownstone took
the rap for detonating Willie Codder in his own garage?' The Cuban will
have a clue to my meaning."

Raleigh carefully slipped the receiver down. When he picked it back up,
Weeper was talking to a woman. "If Benny was alive, he'd drop dead to
hear it. Such a phonus bolonus. Art collector! So was Hitler. . . . Yeah, he
dumped the patootie. . . . Nah, a creep dive stripper. . . . Ha ha ha. . . . So,
you got a line on this Parisi squirt Calhoun? Who? Nah. She's a little old
lady in Bermuda shorts. She's a canasta player. We're not talking Ma
Barker. So, Rose, give me a cursory moment here. This is Who Parisi's
widow? Antony? Which one was Antony? . . . Even so, may he rest in
peace."

Raleigh hung up. He brushed his hair, his teeth, and his shoes. He tried
again.

"Listen, Mr. Johnny Carson you're so funny, you should try taking a
crap with *my* bowels!"

"EXCUSE ME! Mr. Berg, pardon me," said Raleigh. "Would you
mind? I've been waiting some time to use this phone."

". . . Nah, it's the kid's brother. So, I'll call you, Snooper, so, okay. . . . I
should know? See a pederast, podiatrist, whatever. . . ."

Past experience led Holly Hayes to accept the collect charges without
demur. She even confessed to missing her father, which he found so astonishingly comforting that he had not a critical word to say about her
news that Saturday night she and Booger Blair had brought the Triumph
in third, in an amateur road rally up Mosby Peak. "So, Dad, how's it
going?"

"It's going . . . okay. Where's Caroline?"

"Where else? Mall. You know Car and Kevin's crowd. Passive consumerism."

"But it's Sunday."

"Dad, you have to pull yourself out of the dark ages. Sorry Mom's not here. She went out to lunch with some guys."

"What do you mean, went out to lunch with some guys? What guys?"

"She said, 'Democrats.' The Democratic party, or something, I don't know. But Grandpa called! He left a message. You want to hear it? Mom wrote it down on a bag here. He wouldn't tell Mom where he was or anything. She told him he was driving you crazy and she was mad at him."

"Tell her thanks."

The message was that Earley Hayes now had reason to believe that Jubal Rogers might be living in Charleston — information that Raleigh, of course, already had, and a further, somewhat satisfying, suggestion that he was a few steps ahead of his father. The message was that if Raleigh could, he should go to Charleston, and if possible stay at the Ambrose Inn on the High Battery, where Earley would attempt to call him at 8 P.M. Tuesday and again on Wednesday. Earley had also asked whether or not Raleigh had found Gates, and whether he'd been able to persuade him to go visit Roxanne. This was upsetting, not only because it distressed Raleigh to think about Roxanne, and distressed him to remember that all his considerable labor to bring Gates to Midway had been in vain; it distressed him to realize that his father had no idea of the gravity of his third wife's illness, and certainly no idea of her sudden death. And even if that third marriage had been as unhappy as it had been brief (and costly), still, how was this news going to affect his father?

"Holly, please tell your mother that Roxanne, ah, died, ah, Friday."

"Died?"

"I'm afraid so."

"Gosh, who is this Roxanne anyhow?"

"She was . . . ah, in a sense, ah, your uncle Gates's mother."

"Boy, you never told me that! I never even got to meet her!"

"We weren't close."

"I'll say. Boy, your generation is weird. I wish you'd come home, Dad, things are popping around here."

How could things be popping around there, when things were popping around *here,* and around Myrtle Beach, and around "Peace and Quiet," and around all the other places Raleigh had recently found himself? How could things be popping everywhere? What about the law of compensation? Shouldn't somewhere in the universe be still?

Salvos of life did however seem to be shooting off back in Starry Haven. Aura had been invited by students at the university in Hillston to debate Congressman Lukes on campus Monday night. Mrs. Nemours Kettell had separated from her husband, and Mr. Kettell had stormed into the Hayes house and accused Aura of leading his wife astray. "Mom wiped him up," Holly summarized succinctly. And, last but certainly not least, Mrs. Sheffield had told Aura she was going into the porno business.

"Holly!"

Well, perhaps not really the porno business. But Vera was thinking of opening a small catalogue store in a Forbes Building office, one floor below Mothers for Peace. A sort of lingerie shop, or as Holly put it, "hot nightgowns. You know, Dad, like Frederick's of Hollywood. Maybe she'll call it Vera's of Thermopylae. Hunh?"

His daughter laughed. Raleigh laughed, too, and felt himself feeling, for the first time in a long while, how much Holly was *his,* how much they were alike, and liked being alike, in that pleasurable, comfortable way that somehow they'd lost since, since when? Since she'd started locking the bathroom door, and hanging up the phone whenever he entered a room, and crying at the dinner table for no earthly reason, and preferring the company of strangers to home, and, in general, not being any longer the small thin little girl in unraveling pigtails and unraveling sweater, who sat cross-legged on the rug beside him (her smooth bare knees showing through her jeans), and offered him, as they watched television together, her imitations of his ironic wisecracks on the programs they saw; offered them with his own raised eyebrow and flat sarcastic tone; always listening for his laughter, always proudly repeating her joke, again and again, trying to keep the laughter alive between them.

"Hey, Dad, I hear Mom. She's back. MOM, DAD! See yah, we miss you. Vera's of Thermopylae, hunh? Wild!"

Raleigh and Aura had only managed to talk long enough to "catch up," as they called it, with the facts (bizarre enough), but not the feelings of their respective last few days, when Hayes suddenly heard someone approaching the cottage door, someone rattling glass and yodeling "YOO-HOO!" He was just saying, "So I'll call you, Aura, from this Ambrose Inn —" when he heard this someone bang at the door, which, as it was not latched, flew noisily open. He made an abrupt decision and began to babble rapidly into the receiver, *"Bitte, ich müss Deutsch sprechen. Wo ist die Toiletten? Das Swine isst grosser als die Auto."*

"Raleigh, what's the matter with you? Why are you speaking German in that funny voice?"

"Wie lange haben Sie im München sind? Wieviel ist ein Zimmer mit Schlag?"

"Do I have a room with cream? Is that what you said? Honey, have you gone off the deep end again?"

Raleigh was making a valiant effort to smile at Mrs. Wetherell, who stood there in an evening gown of linked gold squares. She held a silver tray on which jiggled an ice bucket, a bottle of vodka, and a glass, and she smiled back triumphantly at the sound of sophisticated foreign language taking place in her guest cottage. Wait till those stuck-up old double D damn biddies, who had been so condescending about inviting Crystal to join the debutante list, tightening their nostrils as if they were smelling Payne's fertilizer, just *wait* till they met Monsieur Jean Claude Claudel and his associates. Wait . . . well, they didn't have to wait to hear that "Wild Oaks" was going to be in the movies, for Lady Bug had already called a fourth of the guest list to tell them so, and they'd already called the other three-fourths. But just wait till they heard Mr. Raleighkov talk!

"Da. Ja. Wo ist mein Vater? Aura, ich bin Czechoslavski." Raleigh faltered on, and deciding that he did not sound sufficiently East European, he recklessly added utter gibberish, *"Yosto Gragovitsch zintz Marksi, da, ja, da."* Yes, he'd sunk into Jimmy Clay's collapsed tower of Babel.

"Raleigh Hayes! Are you sure you don't have a drinking problem? I know I hear a glass."

"Nein! Ich müss gehen. Ich bin telephonen Tuestag vill. Ein Zwei Drei Vier Fünf. Ich liebe dich. Güten Nichtski."

My God, she laughed! "Well, Raleigh, I love you too. Sounds like you're having a lot of fun. 'Bye."

Sheepishly, Hayes hung up and faced his hostess. How was he to explain that he hadn't been calling Prague at her expense, if he couldn't speak English? But Mrs. Wetherell was beaming, wrinkling her rich leather face. "Would you like a teeny DRINK? Mr. Claudel said all Czechs love vodka. VODKA." She was shouting at him, presumably on the premise that to break the sound barrier was to break the language barrier as well. He nodded miserably and she nodded happily back and they nodded at each other for a while until she suddenly grabbed his jacket and yelled, "What SIZE do you wear? SIZE?" She pulled the collar away from his neck and attempted to look at the label. Raleigh twisted backward, spinning under her arm. He thought it safe to risk pretending he could follow some of this pantomime, so he held up four fingers on one hand and two on the other.

"Forty-two?" she beamed.

Nodding, he put his fingers together, then stretched his arms out.

"FORTY-TWO LONG? . . . That's one forty, one forty-two, and, Lord, one fifty-two, plus The Other One. . . . Oh my, Mr. Raleighkov, if I get through this night without slitting my wrists in the tub, I'll . . ." She didn't say what she would do, but poured herself a shot of vodka and tossed it down. Alcohol had astonishingly little effect on her; she should have been deep into delirium tremens by now. "I swear. I've got anywhere from nobody to two hundred and fifty people walking through the gates in an hour and a half, and Payne will NOT stop painting that goddamn outdoor café! My Dixie Troubadour singer is drugged up so bad she can't even hold her eyes open without using her hands, and if Mr. Mingo, bless his big ole heart, hadn't talked Crystal, and I don't know how, into putting on a dress, I swear I'd of canceled this whole thing and moved back to Houston!" Lady Wetherell, pacing the room in her gold gown, kicked the heavy train out of her way at each turn. She appeared not to mind (or perhaps to prefer) venting her troubles to someone who presumably could not offer a reply. She pulled a little gold cigarette case out from between her oversized breasts, and lit up. "Those damn caterers are telling me they are NOT gonna serve noodles almondine with the spare ribs the way I asked them to. They're gonna serve black-eyed peas and collard greens! Collard greens! Well, if it wasn't for you and Jean Claude and Mr. Mingo, I'd be in the garage right this minute looking for a rubber pipe. Well, hell, have a drink."

He had a drink. He agreed he needed one, especially when the woman flopped down on his bed and told him, "Jean Claude had the cutest idea you ever heard. He's setting up a little Monte Carlo kind of casino area so people can play games after dinner. I never would have thought of that! And Mr. Mingo! I have GOT to go see some of his movie designs after the way he fixed up my tents! Well, make yourself at home, Mr. Raleighkov. I wonder what size The Other One wears. I hate to bother him. I guess he's still in the bathroom, poor old blind man. The bowl keeps on flushing to beat the band."

The famous Wetherell Barbecue, as it proudly passed into the social memory of the county, was a thoroughly stunning success. Almost everyone who'd been invited came, and everyone who'd declined to come was sorry. Everyone was amazed to see two hundred place settings of real china and real silver — and it was real, for the old biddies had looked at the bottoms of the plates, and held the forks up to the candles.

Almost everybody drank himself silly. So many champagne corks shot off, the guests felt like gay, gallant revelers at the shelling of Fort Sumter.

The Dixie Troubadour had pulled herself together, and was wildly applauded for her spirited medley of "Carry Me Back to Ole Virginie" and "I Found My Thrill on Blueberry Hill."

Payne had put down his brushes and put on a tuxedo with a red velvet bow tie, and broadened his repertoire of phrases to include "Welcome to 'Wild Oaks'" and "Let me go get you some more champagne, how 'bout?"

Crystal had cleaned herself off to a surprisingly nice pinkness, and revealed, in the simple long white dress Mr. Mingo had picked out for her, a surprisingly nice figure. And if her walk still resembled John Wayne in drag, at least she walked among her guests, accompanied by only two of her smaller dogs. And if she had little more conversation than her father, at least she "mingled" the way her mother ordered her to, whenever they passed in the crush.

Everybody thought it was wonderfully witty to serve perfect reproductions of Negro food at this perfect reproduction of a plantation. Everybody thought Lady Bug Wetherell was wearing solid gold. Everybody loved the little Monte Carlo casino, set up on card tables on the portico, and nobody minded losing ten or twenty dollars while having so much fun, especially since all their winnings were to be donated to a fund for filmmakers struggling to sneak the horrible truth out of Communist countries like Mr. Raleighkov's.

Most of all, the whole crowd of drunk and stuffed smug provincial socialites who had "frozen" Mrs. Wetherell "double D damn long enough," were stunned with envy when introduced to the celebrity guests, whom Lady Bug moved around the grounds on touring exhibition, as if they were the Treasures of Tutankhamen. They bowed and nodded, and purred French and even mumbled a few Czechoslovakian "itzskis" and "itschs" if pressed to do so, and all looked as elegant as the Champs Elysées, for she had them displayed in tuxedos. Not that it had been easy to rent Mr. Mingo a fifty-two long on an hour's notice. But with limitless wealth, all things except health and happiness are possible. She'd even found a boy's tuxedo that would have fit The Other One, as she called Simon Berg, but he'd declined to join the fête, having been seized by another fit of inspiration and spirited off somewhere deep by the Muse. That story alone was sufficient to challenge the more literary of her guests (the local Library Club), but when Lady Bug threw into the kitty the suave, handsome, hand-kissing charm of Jean Claude Claudel, and the merry jitterbugging

Mr. Mingo, and that brooding Slavic silence of Mr. Raleighkov (so obviously hiding deep passion and dark wisdom), why then everybody folded their cards and declared Mrs. Wetherell, hands down, the victor.

Yes, the night of the Famous Barbecue at "Wild Oaks," Lettice Eulonia Lumpkin Wetherell had to admit that her cup had purely and simply run completely over, even though she never once stopped drinking every drop of 200-proof sour mash bourbon in it.

CHAPTER

22

Our Hero Succumbs to a Faded Beauty

DESPITE HIS SAVAGE HEADACHE and his dismay at being licked awake by a moil of bassett hounds, including the one called "Jumbo," Raleigh Hayes determined to press on to Charleston this Monday morning to look for Jubal Rogers. Frankly, he was relieved that Gates did not care to accompany him, after he learned that Cupid Calhoun *lived* in Charleston (which was where Gates had first met the young mobster, had first — fraudulently — traced his paternal lineage back to Senator John C. Calhoun the secessionist, and then sold him Varina Davis's Inaugural opals). Gates also wanted to help Sara Zane, who was closing his mother's house, to sort out those leftovers that even the sparest lives leave behind. And, although he didn't tell Raleigh, he also wanted to persuade Payne Wetherell that he (Payne) had always wanted to invest in the motion picture industry. As Raleigh had to come back by Midway anyhow, in order to drive to New Orleans, and as Gates swore that he was "sticking" until they found "the old man," Raleigh decided "to keep the faith" as his brother requested, while reserving the doubts of the past. "I promise I'll keep my promise. Just like you always taught me," Gates grinned, with a wink of his long-lashed hooded blue eyes, as he stuffed into his leather bag $435 to relieve filmmakers behind the Iron Curtain.

"You are beyond doubt . . ." Raleigh gave up.

"Mais, oui, mon frère," laughed Gates.

"I want you to know that last night was one of the most mortifying experiences of my entire life."

"Really? Sorry, Raleigh. I honestly thought you were having fun."

Why in God's name did everyone keep accusing him of having fun?

Frankly, Hayes was even relieved (if surprised) to learn that Mingo Sheffield was also planning to stay another day at "Wild Oaks," then to take the Trailways bus to Charleston on Tuesday. He'd promised Lady Bug to go fabric shopping with her in order to make a dent in those eight empty rooms, and he'd promised to take a jeep ride with Crystal, and, besides, he'd never had very many chances to travel on a long-distance bus, and wanted to add that experience to his Life on the Road. And, besides, he was too hung over to get out of his quilted bed, where he now wallowed, still in his tuxedo, with a bag of ice over his fat face.

Raleigh counseled him seriously. "Mingo, you can't keep up this charade. You're going to get yourself exposed and humiliated. You don't know a, excuse me, but goddamn thing about designing movie sets."

Sheffield groaned, "Oh, why do you always have to be so critical? I know *everything* about the movies. I've seen just about every movie ever made about a dozen times."

"Seeing is not making." Raleigh delivered this aphorism while neatly folding the formal wear Mrs. Wetherell had rented for him. "I absolutely cannot even fathom where you found the unmitigated nerve to go around last night telling all those people you designed the costumes for *The Sound of Music.* They're going to find out, don't you know that?"

"How?" Sheffield raised the ice bag from one eye. "And anyhow I did have the whole Trapp Family Singers in my window once. They were cross-country skiing in loden jackets and White Stag parkas."

"Good-bye, Mingo. I'll reserve you a room at the Ambrose Inn for Tuesday. Your own room. Because frankly I'd enjoy sleeping alone for a change. You snore."

"I do?"

"Frankly, yes. Like an elephant."

"Gollee, Vera never mentioned it."

"Perhaps she had her ears wired shut."

Early that afternoon, Raleigh (ostensibly off to scout battle locations for *Spare Me the Magnolias Please*) nodded his farewells at the steps of the "Wild Oaks" portico, where Lady Wetherell — the only person on the grounds not hung over — sat in a brass-colored caftan, knocking back Bloody Marys, yelling at Ethan to stop throwing the champagne glasses in the plastic bags with the empty bottles, and laughing richly over the discomfiture of Mrs. Gervais Lancaster, who'd claimed to have been to France three times, and then couldn't even understand half of what Monsieur Jean Claude Claudel was saying! Crystal was already back in the dogshed, and Payne was already up on the balcony trying to fix the dome of Sacre Coeur; but the mistress of "Wild Oaks" knew she could speak for them all in saying, "COME ON BACK, NOW," to Raleighkov and The Other One.

It was with some trepidation that Hayes found the blind writer ensconced with his fiddle in the backseat of the Cadillac, looking a bit bulkier in his old gray uniform than he had the day before (as well as a bit chillier — for he had a shawl over his head). Berg had privately confessed that he preferred to keep on the move, and not by means of public transportation, since the police had in all likelihood "plastered his mug all over Dixie." Mrs. Wetherell was worried for different reasons. "Jean Claude, I swear I feel funny letting Mr. Raleighkov and The Other One go off on their own like this, when he doesn't speak our lingo, and The Other One, you know, has those fits. I feel real funny. Maybe we ought to send Crystal with them. CRYSTAL! Where is she! Is she off in the woods with those goddamn dogs again? Let me get her. CRYSTAL!"

Raleigh drove away, spraying gravel over the beautiful lawn, before Gates could finish murmuring, *"Ce n'est pas necessaire, chère Laddeee."*

Lady Bug might have felt even funnier if she'd seen Weeper Berg twisting in the back seat to shuck off the shawl, revealing a head of slick black hair, to shuck off the Gray and the Gold, revealing beneath it the thirty-four short tuxedo that she'd rented for him; to shuck off his white mustache, applying in its place, with one of her eyebrow pencils, a tiny black one. She might have felt funnier still if she'd seen him (which Raleigh did not — for he was busy buying gasoline, checking tires, battery, radiator, and so on down his mental checklist) rip open the back of Mingo's giant pink teddy bear, disembowel it, and stuff into its cavity her new diamond watch, her antique Dresden milkmaid, six of her sterling place settings, and her tiny Frederick Remington drawing in a Tiffany frame.

As it was, Mrs. Wetherell didn't see Mr. Berg. And so, over the next week, she drew the following conclusions: The tuxedo had been misplaced in the madhouse of cleaning up, and, what the hell, she'd just pay for it. She must have lost her watch again, and what the hell, she'd just buy another one. Ethan must have broken her Dresden milkmaid, and there was no sense even asking him about it because he would naturally lie. As for that little bitty cowboy picture that had belonged to Payne's grandmother, she'd never liked it, which was why she'd put it in the guest cottage over on a corner wall, and why she never noticed it was gone, until years later, when she happened to see an article in a magazine about Tiffany collections, and that funny colored glass looked familiar. As for the silverware, some of the settings did seem to be gone, which suggested that the guests must have stolen them for souvenirs, and that only proved what a grand success Crystal's Coming Out had undoubtedly been. What the hell, they had so much money anyhow, they didn't know what to do with it. She'd just get some more sterling. Or better yet, gold-plate.

Nothing happened to our hero on the way to Charleston, except he had to listen to Weeper Berg complain about God, and how unjustly God had tortured his bowels, despite his (Berg's) hundred-percent lack of culpability for his own birth, and his subsequent hundred-percent abjuring of spicy food, whether Spic, Wop, or Caucasian. "God's had His teeth in me long enough. And I have personally in my life known the guy to be a welsher. As per example, when Tampa Freddie danced, after he never laid a mitt on the Pazzo brothers and was in Havana running hash at the specified time in question, which likewise he could have proved if he had ratted on certain parties, which he didn't. When they strung up Tampa Freddie, a man like an angel, may he rest in peace, I said to God, 'God, that was a lousy s.o.b. thing to do.' And I tell you, Hayes, I've been running to the john with these bowels from that day to this. So, okay, I say to God, God, the same to you, and contemporaneous with that . . ."

By the time they reached the Charleston peninsular, Raleigh had vowed never to complain of, or to, the Deity again; a vow he forgot within two days.

Mr. Berg appeared to know Charleston; at any rate, he led Raleigh into Old Town and down Church Street to the brick alley of boutiques still called Cabbage Row, where he wished to be let out. Here, he informed Raleigh, *Porgy and Bess* took place. His eyes moist, Berg added, as he ducked when a police car maundered past, "On the lam is not what Jews do. Jews write musical comedies. So I'll be in touch." Off he hurried, looking, in his tuxedo and trim black mustache, rather like Adolphe Menjou — if it were possible to imagine Adolphe Menjou playing bass fiddle in a nice nightclub, and wrestling a huge pink bear on the way to work.

The first thing Raleigh did was to hide everything in the Cadillac either under clothes or in the trunk, and then to entrust the locked car to a safe garage, whose attendant boasted that he guarded some of the best automobiles in Charleston, and that Raleigh's Cadillac was in the finest company it was likely to know. Then he checked with some misgivings into the Ambrose Inn. It proved to be one of the beautiful pale houses looking over the Charleston Harbor, now obliged (like many fallen aristocrats) to take in guests to keep up appearances. Raleigh was surprised by the grandeur of his balconied room, as well as by its cost. Either his father hadn't known much about the Ambrose Inn. Or he had. The son took out his notebook and jotted down the figures. He'd been embarrassed to have come into this mansion with no luggage, particularly as his white suit was by now looking a little the worse for a lot of wear; particularly as his host (for Hayes couldn't think of this elegant-voiced gentleman, inviting him to take a — Chippendale — seat, as the "night clerk") so charmingly pretended to believe him when he said his bags had been stolen earlier that afternoon. Nevertheless, Raleigh could not bring himself to ask this man for directions to a place called the Bayou Lounge (which for all he knew might be a topless bar), and, finding no such place listed in the phone directory, nor any such person as Jubal Rogers, Hayes took to the streets.

Raleigh did not know Charleston. He was surprised to find that it was the beautiful city he'd expected New Orleans to be. It was one of those rare cities that was vain enough to define itself, and fortunate enough to be worth defining. The city of Charleston was exactly what she claimed she was: a great beauty faded to an elegant charm; exquisitely hospitable, outrageously nostalgic, unabashedly parochial, as indolent and smug and perfectly beautiful as a cat. She was proud — proud even of the defeat she refused to acknowledge — but her pride was willowy, and swayed in a dance with her visitors. She was past her prime, sea-spoiled, assaulted by pirates, Redcoats, and Yankees, by hurricanes, by earthquake; long ago passed over by the skyscraping world; and she thought herself forever the belle of the cotillion ball, and she made Raleigh Hayes think so too. As he curved along the crescent seawall of the Battery, where old women threw lazy fishing lines into the soft waves; as he looked out over the slow-rocking crescents of harbor boats under the crescent moon; as he looked back, past palmetto fronds and Spanish moss stirred by Southern breeze, and saw the lights of the great shapely houses, with all their patched French windows opened on all their mended lace-iron balconies, and all their lace-white curtains billowing out like handkerchiefs waving to lovers bravely guarding the fort in the bay; when he stopped and looked at Charleston, Raleigh faltered, and then fell. He wandered in and out of the dark brick streets, breathing over the vine-laced garden walls the city's scent of azalea and camellia and rhododendron and the sea, and he fell to thinking that he had never before understood why they called cities "she," but that Charleston was, beyond doubt, a woman. And thinking of this, Raleigh began to think of Aura, and to think back to how he'd felt all those years ago, wandering with Aura the clean narrow gray streets of German villages, when falling in love was as physical and irresistible as any other great illness; when he'd walked around tingly and flushed and restive and dizzy and distractedly thinking every street as magically beautiful as the woman walking beside him. Maybe . . . Yes, maybe, this summer, he ought to take a trip with Aura. Maybe come here to Charleston. Maybe even go to other cities, like Paris and Venice, that he had never seen. Maybe they should *not* go once again for two weeks in August to the beach for the sake of the twins (whom, last summer he'd had to force, sulking, anyhow, into the station wagon). Maybe just he and Aura could fly to . . . maybe . . . maybe . . .

And so Charleston languidly waved her faded coquette's perfumed fan at Raleigh Hayes, and he fell dizzily in love again with his wife.

Of course, Raleigh did have a "real reason" for his evening stroll. He was, after all, still Raleigh. He was looking the whole time for the Bayou Lounge, the place where Flonnie Rogers had told him Jubal still played. The first few people he asked had never heard of the Bayou Lounge. He was beginning to suspect that he'd been led astray by Flonnie's strange, timeless anecdotage, but, then, at a restaurant, where he'd been eating as much she-crab soup as if he'd turned into Mingo Sheffield, his waitress, a middle-aged black woman, told him that there *had* been, not far from here, a jazz club called the Bayou Lounge. But it had been torn down in the 1960s, just a decade too soon to be saved by Historical Preservation. She then brought over an older waiter; he told Raleigh that he knew a man who had once played the saxophone at the Bayou. No, not a man named Jubal Rogers. Someone else, maybe Kingsley, who now sometimes played to pass the hat, right across the street there in the old open market. Hayes, a frugal man who calculated his fifteen-percent tips to the nickel, left this waitress a ten-dollar bill.

He walked the long cobbled blocks of the market arcade, down the rows of worn brick columns where once cotton and indigo and rice and tobacco and black people had gone to the highest bidder. Now the place was empty, except for a small crowd milling around, or perching on long trestle tables, to listen to a street musician perform "Won't You Come Home, Bill Bailey?" This performer was not the man Raleigh was looking for. He was young and white, and he was working in a cheerful sweaty frenzy to play musical instruments with every possible part of his body. He had a banjo in his arms, tambourines strapped to his knees, a cymbal foot pedal by his right toes, a bass drum pedal by his left toes, a harmonica wired in front of his mouth, and a cowbell around his neck, which he would shake whenever anyone sneaked forward to drop a quarter in the Greek fisherman's hat lying conspicuously beside a sign that said, "TRYING TO GET HOME. THANK YOU." For a dollar, the young man shook the tambourines with his legs. For five dollars, he told Raleigh where the saxophonist Toutant Kingstree could be reached tomorrow morning.

That night Raleigh slept not only in peace and quiet, but in a high, carved, canopied bed whose sheer curtains, stirred by the warm spring wind, fluttered against his face like an old kiss.

CHAPTER

23

The Very Extraordinary Adventures Which Ensued at the Inn

OUR HERO WOKE UP a new man. This was instantly proved by the fact that he immediately went on a spending spree. He, who according to Aura wore his clothes "to a nub" before he'd replace them, and then would only buy whatever Mingo had on sale that was "decent" and "not flashy," now purchased in less than an hour a pin-striped summer suit, a blue blazer, tan slacks, two dress shirts, two polo shirts, socks, boxer shorts (the bikini jockey shorts that Mingo had given him had been driving him crazy), pajamas, a robe, a sweater with two different colors in it, and a gleaming pair of brown tasseled loafers (which he'd always wanted, and always denied himself as too frivolous for good value). He bought a suitcase and put them all in it. He told himself, when he saw the total of his neatly added figures in his small notebook, "I can't keep traveling all over the country without a change of clothes, I can't bear to face that hotelkeeper without a change of clothes, I need new clothes, I didn't buy anything I didn't need; why, I only owned two lightweight suits, and my seersucker was ruined in the sewer pipe, and my gabardine destroyed by Hell's Angels, swamps, and Captain Nemo's. Aura always begged me to get some new clothes. These will last me for years."

Then, in the following hour, he, who gave presents only on Christmas and birthdays (and only then to his immediate family, and only to them because he kept a calendar with posted reminders), bought a jade bracelet for Aura, the color of her eyes. Bought Holly a crash helmet for her races, since if she was going to insist on risking her neck, she might as well try to protect her brains. Having made this purchase, he of course had to buy something for Caroline, and after a considerable argument with himself, he finally bought the bottle of cologne he'd twice told the pleading Caroline it was preposterous for a child her age to think of wearing, given its outlandish price, not to mention scent. Then, because Mingo Sheffield had given him the very clothes on his back (however inappropriate they were), he bought Mingo a giant picture book about the Civil War; having bought something for a neighbor, it seemed unjust to exclude his own kin, so he bought Gates a watch, with which Gates could, if he would, get control of his life.

Yes, there was no question about it, he was completely off the deep end. "Ha ha," said Raleigh. "Mama, what am I doing?" She didn't answer, doubtless too stunned to reply.

Soon looking like a new man as well, in his pale blue pin-striped suit, and dark blue silk tie, Raleigh walked back down the curved staircase from his room to the chandeliered foyer of the Ambrose Inn, where he had the satisfaction of seeing the proprietor silently decide that his guest now made sense. "Very good, Mr. Hayes. I see they were able to find your luggage for you."

Raleigh had a long delicious lunch, over which he searched a newspaper in vain for some mention of Aura's college debate with Congressman Lukes (surprised to find himself inconsistently both relieved and disappointed that her fame had not spread beyond the borders of North Carolina). Two other articles caught his attention. To one, he said, "That's ridiculous." It reported that Simon "Weeper" Berg, still missing, was armed and believed dangerous. To the other article, he said, "That's got to be a coincidence." It reported that a man had been found dead in a BMW parked in a drive-in theater outside North Myrtle Beach.

After lunch, Hayes took his white suit to be cleaned; he'd keep it for (as Mingo would say) a souvenir. When he went to pick up his white Cadillac, he found that it now had a green sticker on its rear bumper that said, "READY OR NOT, JESUS IS COMING." The garage attendant apologized, and wanted Raleigh to know he was thinking of calling the police. He waved his arm around the concrete landing. All the best cars in Charleston had green stickers warning, "READY OR NOT, JESUS IS

COMING." There was also one on the attendant's office door. "Some joker or Jehovah's Witness or some nut," the angry man said. "Must have sneaked in here last night. It's gonna take me hours to scrape those damn things off. No respect for private property. I mean, maybe somebody like you doesn't mind, I mean, you've got that Jesus statue on your dash and all, but some people have really strong negative feelings about this kind of stuff. I'm not kidding, I'm thinking of calling the police." Hayes told him not to worry about the Cadillac, then asked directions to the address that the one-man band had given him last night.

Toutant Kingstree either lived at the city dump or had created one of his own. It was the latter, as Raleigh quickly learned when, as soon as he parked, a tall long-muscled black man leaned a rifle out a milk truck window to say that if Raleigh were the Board of Adjustment, he'd "better put it in reverse and scat." After Raleigh earnestly denied the charge, Mr. Kingstree came out of the truck to explain his tone. His sleeveless T-shirt had blood down the front.

"My neighbors pick on me."

"Why's that?" asked Hayes, somewhat rhetorically, as he glanced nervously around the jammed lot at the four wrecked cars, the smashed milk truck, the old train caboose (from within which squeals and thuds could be heard), the tireless schoolbus, and the stack of gray warped planks as high as a house (if there were a house, which he couldn't tell). Just above their heads, electric wires crisscrossed like a cat's cradle to join all the vehicles. On the ground, chickens ran everywhere as if they'd just heard some disastrous news.

"My neighbors always siccing the Board on me, saying my place is an eyesore." The tall man asked Raleigh with a look to share his bafflement at this absurdity. "Saying I got commercial intent in a residential zone! How many times I have to tell them? Everything here is for my own personal use. I'm not selling this stuff. I'm not selling it."

Raleigh didn't think he would be.

"They think I'm selling these pigs and chickens. I'm not. I'm eating them."

Well, that explained all the red carcasses Raleigh could see hanging from hooks in the milk truck, as well as the blood all over Mr. Kingstree's undershirt and arms. The explanation was reassuring.

"People got to eat, don't they? Don't they?"

"Of course."

For such a lean man, Mr. Kingstree must have had an impressive appetite. There looked to be about two tons of dead pork in the milk truck, and there sounded as though there were a few more tons still alive in the caboose.

"Just plain picking on me. Just plain."

"Excuse me, are you Toutant Kingstree?"

"Depends."

"You play the saxophone?"

"I don't say no."

"I'm looking for Jubal Rogers. I think you used to play with him, at the Bayou Lounge? This would be a while back, but I've come a long way, and I wonder if—"

"You with RCA?"

"Pardon?"

"Atlantic! . . . Folkways?"

"Well, no, I'm —"

"Jubal was good, but I was really the one that had it, you know. It's all in the arrangements. I was the one." Toutant Kingstree wiped down his arms with a towel. A long-limbed, sinewy man, with balding gray hair, he had long elegant hands and very large lips that he kept in continual motion, as if he were exercising them for his saxophone. He shook hands, then asked, "Like a drink? I make it myself." He pointed at the schoolbus. Pipes stuck out of its roof. "Just for personal use."

"Thank you, but not really. I'm sorry, Mr. Kingstree, but I'm not with a record company. Jubal Rogers was a friend of my father's. This isn't business. I'm just looking for him for my father."

The saxophonist slowly spluttered his lower lip. "Not in the business?"

"No, sir, I'm sorry."

"Hmmmm." He sat down on a giant truck tire, licked his fingers, and rubbed a spot of blood off his long narrow white vinyl shoe. "I don't say Jubal wasn't real good. We didn't see eye to eye, him and me, but I don't criticize him. He was good, far as the clarinet goes. I always told him, we ought to have gone to New Orleans. Chicago. Something."

"Is Mr. Rogers still alive?"

"I don't know." He rubbed at the shoes with the towel. "He was yesterday."

"Here?! In Charleston?"

"Billie and him work most afternoons doing the circle. Nights, he plays here and there. Nothing much."

"Pardon? The 'circle'?"

"Tourists, you know, carriage rides. She and him do the circle round Old Town."

Raleigh thanked the man, then turned back. "Is Billie his wife?"

Kingstree laughed, showing a gold tooth. "Wife? She's his mule! I don't believe Jubal ever had a wife. Of his own."

They walked together through the scurrying chickens over to the Cadillac. The jazz man flicked at his lower lip. "I saw this car, your clothes, I was *sure* you was somebody big in the record business. It happens, you know. Right smack out of the blue. Happened to two or three different boys I knew. But they went to New Orleans. You play?"

"Oh, no." Raleigh shook his head. "Well, I used to study trumpet, but just in school. No, no."

Kingstree stuck his head through the window to look into the Cadillac. "I've been studying tenor sax more than fifty years now."

"You must be very good."

"I am."

The first time Hayes dropped by the Battery Carriage Co., he was told that Jubal Rogers (and the company's mule) were out on a ride. The second time he came, he was pointed toward a black-fringed red leather buggy in whose traces stood a white mule with a gardenia looped around the base of one tall ear. The animal's hindquarters were covered with the "horse diapers" that all the carriage companies were obliged by city law to provide in order to keep the beautiful cobbled streets of Charleston clean. There was no driver, so Raleigh climbed in back to wait. Finally he saw a man in a white dress shirt and black trousers unhurriedly approach, his hands in his pockets, a cigarette in his mouth. He stopped, looked hard at Raleigh as if he were appraising his clothes, then walked over to the buggy. He was not a large man, but perfectly proportioned, and a color between chestnut and cinnamon. His hair, cut close, almost shaved, was a silvered black, and he held his head with the chin slightly raised. Raleigh's first thought was that in his youth Jubal Rogers must have been amazingly, even alarmingly good-looking. (What had Kaiser Bill been rambling on about? The women thought he was Christmas candy?) Even now he had the most handsome face and the most extraordinary eyes Raleigh had ever seen. The eyes were shaped like almonds, and deep-set, and between the pupil and the dark rim was a circle of gold. Raleigh bizarrely found himself thinking that the man looked like something out of the Song of Songs. As soon as Rogers spoke, Raleigh's second thought was that this was the haughtiest, most arrogant, and most obnoxious man he'd ever met. He revealed so contemptuously hostile a disposition that the

Thermopylean was taken aback; how in the world could someone in the tourist business afford to take this attitude?

"Excuse me. Jubal Rogers?"

"Where's the rest of your party?" His acerbic voice had none of the languorously long vowels of the Charlestonians, whose *A*'s drawled endlessly out of their throats and who made the word *house* sound like the long slow whoosh of a wave. Rogers had a deep knife of a voice, and his questions were accusations. "How many in it?"

Raleigh said, "I'm not really interested in a tour. If you're Jubal Rogers, I have a message for you."

"I'm not interested in your message." Rogers leaned against the mule's flank and gazed straight ahead, past Raleigh's ear, as if there were no point in bothering to turn his head the extra inch it would have required to see him.

"Are you Jubal Rogers?"

The perfectly shaped head nodded once. "You want this ride? Twenty-five dollars."

Raleigh had already decided that he didn't like Jubal Rogers, but he hadn't decided yet what to do about it.

"All right, fine," he snapped, and leaned back into the dry leather seat. "But all I really wanted to tell you was my father would like to see you."

Rogers pushed the brake forward, and flicked the reins; the carriage lurched into motion. He didn't turn around to say, "Am I supposed to guess who he is? I don't like guessing games."

Raleigh's voice echoed the sarcasm. "My father's name is Earley Hayes. Does that sound familiar?"

Rogers not only still didn't turn around, he didn't even answer. Instead, he pointed with his stick whip at a beautiful brick house they were now rattling past. "Nathaniel Russell House. Eighteen-o-nine. Adams architecture. Rare example of a free-flying staircase. Rich New England slave trader."

Hayes, reddening, said, "Look. I've gone to a considerable amount of trouble as well as expense in order to find you. And make you a frankly advantageous offer. Are you the Jubal Rogers from Thermopylae, North Carolina, or not?"

With Raleigh fuming in the back, the carriage jostled for several more blocks over the cobbled streets before Rogers's head swung slowly around on his long handsome neck. The gold-flecked eyes were as cold as the metal they resembled. They were so cold that Raleigh's blush turned icy white while the two men stared at each other. Then Rogers slapped the reins to lead his mule Billie past a chartered bus of tourists gawking at Cabbage Row. He pointed his whip at the alley and said, "So-called Catfish Row. Setting of the novel *Porgy* by DuBose Heyward. Turned to music by George Gershwin." He then directed the whip at an eighteenth-century building next door. "Heyward-Washington House. Home of Thomas Heyward, signer of the Declaration of Independence. Original decor and furnishings built by slave craftsmen belonging to the estate. Survived the hurricane of eighteen eighty-six."

Despite Roger's inflectionless voice, every word he uttered sounded to Raleigh as if the man held him personally responsible for the American enslavement of Negroes. And after a few more silent blocks, Hayes said, "Look here. Just do me the courtesy of a simple answer, and I'll get out."

Rogers pulled Billie to a halt, lit a cigarette, and turned toward his passenger. "All right. How'd you find me? What does Earley want?" Having put these terse questions, the driver rested one beautiful hand on the dry leather seat back so that his smoke curled into Raleigh's eyes.

"Flonnie Rogers told me you worked in Charleston at the Bayou Lounge. A Mr. Kingstree told me where to find you." He swatted at smoke. "I'm Raleigh Hayes, and frankly I don't know what your problem is."

"What does Earley want?"

"He wants you to meet him in New Orleans on March thirty-first."

Rogers's laugh was not a warm sound. "Why?"

"I have no idea." Raleigh moved away from the cigarette. "I gather he has some news for you. Mr. Rogers, all I'm doing, trying to do, is convey a message. My father is not at all well and he's behaving a little erratically. Which, if you know him, is probably no surprise. I am forced myself to go to New Orleans in order to get him back into a hospital, and he'd like me to bring you." God, thought Hayes, what a hideous thought, to have to sit in a car with this hateful and contemptuous man. In comparison the company of gluttonizing Sheffield, of hypochondriacal Berg, of even Gates, would be a relief.

Rogers's smile was acidic. "Tell him, no," he said. "Tell him if he needs to see me, he can hire my carriage for twenty-five dollars. . . . To your right is the Old Slave Mart Museum, featuring arts and crafts and slave-trade artifacts. Closes at four-thirty. Tell your father, I said I'm not interested in going to New Orleans."

Now, perhaps Hayes should have been more sympathetic to Jubal Rogers's response to this invitation to travel to New Orleans, since it pre-

cisely echoed his own original reaction. Instead, however, he was so annoyed by the man's arrogant nastiness that he climbed out of the buggy,
took off his glasses, and glared defiantly at the strange supercilious eyes.
"I'm also instructed," he said, "to tell you that if you deign to appear at
the appointed time, he wants you to have some money." This remark
troubled Raleigh a little. First, he would have preferred not to mention
the money at all; surely his father could have no idea of what Jubal Rogers
clearly thought of him, and would not care to throw his kindness away on
such a man. Second, Raleigh (who was unlikely to forget until his dying
day one word of that tape recording which had played havoc with his own
life) knew perfectly well that Earley Hayes had said, "Give Jubal five
thousand dollars and bring him with you to New Orleans." Not, "Give
him five thousand dollars *if* he comes with you." But Raleigh, despite his
respect for the letter of the law, and his suspicion that the bequest had
been unconditional, simply could not bring himself to hand over all that
money (his own money) to a man who, by his withering refusal, was not
only going to stop him from succeeding at the final task left him on that
tape, stop him here (after his, yes, Herculean, efforts along the way), but
was possibly going to keep him from earning the inheritance he'd been
told *was* conditional upon his successfully carrying out *all* of these absurd
tasks, of which Jubal had been the first mentioned. For one thing was certain: Raleigh was not about to plead with Rogers to come along, not even
about to explain by a single further word why his father had to be found
and returned to the hospital. No, Hayes was certainly not going to give
this insufferable man the satisfaction of knowing that he needed him in
any way.

"How much money?" said Rogers.

"Five thousand dollars," said Hayes, for while he wished to name half
that amount, if not less, he couldn't make himself do so.

Rogers gave a flinty smile, looking at his hand where the cigarette had
burnt so low it was odd that the heat wasn't painful. "He doesn't owe me
five thousand dollars."

"I didn't assume this was a repayment of a loan."

"I don't give a fuck what you assume, mister."

"Now, just a minute!"

"He owes me five hundred dollars."

Raleigh was surprised, but recovered his sarcastic tone. "Maybe the rest
is interest."

"Two blocks down to your left is —"

Raleigh lost his temper. "All right. There's no sense in continuing with this, I assume you agree. Here's your five hundred." And he put five of the hundred-dollar bills down on the seat beside the driver. "I'm staying at the Ambrose Inn for a few more days if you care to reconsider. Frankly, five thousand, or even forty-five hundred dollars, strikes me as a rather generous fee for taking a short trip to New Orleans, and I should suspect it's considerably more than you can earn in a few days trotting this mule around town insulting your passengers. Now, I hope to hear from my father this evening. Is there anything you want me to say to him?"

Jubal Rogers flicked his burning cigarette straight at Raleigh so that it missed his ear by only inches. He said, one hand releasing the carriage brake, the other slapping the reins, "Tell him he can kiss my black ass."

Raleigh stood there, in a motionless rage, in front of the Slave Mart Museum so long that finally a young man took his arm and asked him if he were okay. Slowly nodding, Hayes said he was from out of town and needed a bank. The young man, who was black and wore a three-piece suit, said that as it was five o'clock, the banks were closed, otherwise he'd be at work, for he was the assistant manager of a bank just around the corner. Hayes arranged to meet this man there tomorrow to rent a safety deposit box, for he'd decided to leave Jubal the money at a bank, and to leave the key with a note at the carriage company. He certainly never expected, nor hoped, to lay eyes on the man again.

Was Rogers universally misanthropic, or was this hostility particular? If so, what could have ever happened between his father and Flonnie Rogers's nephew? For while Raleigh had his own serious reservations about his parent, to give Earley Hayes his due, he had never been a cold or cruel-hearted man, nor vengeful, nor wrathful, nor avaricious, nor unforgiving; he was not really, Raleigh had to admit, in any way, *evil.* His vices were not to be dismissed, of course, but they were rather the excesses of immoderation — improvidence, carnality, frivolity, disorder; they were the result of unreason, not hate. They were, come to think of it, the vices Sister Joe had so annoyingly (and wrongly) dismissed as "dog poop." Of course his father had behaved unforgivably to Raleigh himself, and to his mother, but to give the man his due, nobody else seemed to *hate* him — even those who disapproved; even Aunt Victoria, who clearly had very mixed feelings about her brother, had never hated him. And therefore it was difficult to see how an acquaintance like Rogers could feel, for heaven knows how many years, so deep a hatred, over what? An unpaid loan of five hundred dollars? How right Flonnie had been to advise him (falsely assuming he was Earley) to "leave it lie." How right, for that matter, had

Kaiser Bill Jenkins been to advise him to "keep away from Jubal Rogers's kind." Well, in future, he most assuredly would.

Muttering to himself in this way, our hero strode angrily back through the streets of Charleston, sidestepping a group of Japanese businessmen who for some reason had felt compelled to climb out of their touring carriage in order to take photographs of what their pleasantly drawling driver was describing as "Hibernian Hall, the lovely home of our St. Cecilia Society Ball, the most elite and exclusive and sought-after social event in the state of South Carolina, and I dare say the whole South." The Oriental businessmen bowed and snapped away.

It was not far from this hall that Raleigh had a terrible shock, jolting enough to erase Jubal Rogers from his mind. He saw something that he never expected to see, any more than he expected to see himself dance naked through the streets (the image by which he habitually conveyed the high improbability of his performing some action requested of him: "No, Aura, I will not wear a goddamn Greek tunic to this costume party; I'd as soon dance naked in the streets"). Glancing absentmindedly in the window of The Charlestonian, a women's dress shop so exclusive there was nothing in its window but a single silk blouse, Hayes saw, or thought he saw, standing by the counter, the Thermopylae merchant Pierce Jimson stroking a blue peignoir that was draped over his arm. As this visual signal made no sense, Raleigh walked on for twenty feet before deciding that he in fact had seen Pierce Jimson, whose twitching anteater lip was fairly unmistakable. He backed up. Yes, he was right. Raleigh had his hand on the doorknob and the words ready, "Why, what brings you down here, Pierce?," when his question was answered in the most unexpected way. A young woman appeared behind Jimson, kissed the back of his neck, then twirled around him in a white cocktail dress that had almost no back and scarcely much more front. It took no second look to prove that this woman was not Mrs. Jimson; she was half the size and half the age. This woman was Boyd Joyner's wife, Lizzie. Pierce Jimson was nodding enthusiastically at her, and she was twirling again and kissing his neck again. Hayes tried his best: Could the fifty-year-old merchant somehow have a daughter he'd somehow neglected ever to mention, and somehow she looked exactly like Lizzie Joyner? But there was no use in mental legerdemain. Hayes knew perfectly well there was only one conclusion to be drawn.

He drew it, ducked away from the door, and crossed the street, down which he hurried, swept along by the flooding memory of his recent con-

versation with Jimson in the Forbes Building. All that talk about Boyd
Joyner and his adulterous wife! Why, he'd been making a goddamn fool of
himself, while Jimson was probably smirking inside at his ignorance! And
all the time! Pierce Jimson, of all people! Leader of the town council,
leader of the church choir, leader of the chamber of commerce, and a dis-
solute, wife-stealing goat! The town tottered. My God, the hypocrisy of
that man, conducting an adult Bible class (attended by Raleigh himself,
and other innocent decent Thermopyleans) on "The Call to Christian
Marriage." Well, many are called, but obviously some are already off on a
party line! How the hell did Jimson let this happen to him? Oh, all right,
Lizzie Joyner *was* pretty. Always made you feel that if she had a problem,
you could fix it for her. Now that he recalled, he'd enjoyed getting her
stalled car started in the Forbes parking lot one cold evening, because she'd
been so grateful and so humorous about forgetting to turn off her lights.
All right, she did have a certain appealing . . . but for Pete's sake! And
what about Boyd Joyner? What a horrible humiliation for him if he ever
found out. And God knows, if Ned Ware ever once heard about it, he'd
blab the whole tale, with his commiserating sigh of gleeful sympathy, not
only to Boyd but to everybody else in town. Thus musing, Hayes set out
on a brisk jogging walk through the streets of Charleston; he really had
not been getting enough (at least of the right sort of) exercise. An hour
later, he entered a large elegant hotel to use the facilities. He heard "Summertime" being played on a piano, and as it was a favorite melody of his,
he wandered into the bar. There he eventually found himself seated at a
table, near a white baby grand piano, at which an attractive, freckled
woman with long auburn hair was singing — with little regard to
gender — "Bess, You Is My Woman, Now."

By the time Raleigh had finished his first scotch, he'd decided that never
in a million years would he do to Aura what Pierce was doing to Brenda
Jimson. After his second scotch, he became consumed with retroactive
jealousy about an incident that had occurred in 1972, when he'd flown
into a sulky rage at the Civitans' Christmas dance over what he'd
seethingly called "Aura's behavior." She'd spent most of her drunken evening giggling in the arms of Dr. Wilson Carmichael, a notorious satyr
from his youth, a high-school master of ballroom dance steps, including
the tango, which *nobody* knew how to do, including the then-popular
"spin." It had been enough to make you dizzy to watch Sonny Carmichael, like a red-headed top, zipping one poor breathless girl after another
in big blurred loops around the gym floor. It had been enough to make
you nauseated to hear this insufferable twinkle-toes brag of all the Ther-

mopylae High virgins (circa 1953–56) into whose panties he had spun, cha-cha'ed, and mash-potatoed his way (among them the cheerleader Raleigh had seriously dated for two tortured years of self-restraint). And as late as 1972, it had still been enough to make Raleigh Hayes too angry to breathe without pain to see Aura fly by, in a waltz, in a foxtrot, in the cursed tango, hour after hour, chirping things like, "Oh, Sonny, I haven't danced like this in ages!" While Carmichael burbled things like, "All righty, here comes the reverse, now, and *turn,* dip, left. Sweetcakes, you are good enough to eat!" While everybody else finally stopped their two-steps and just stood there and *applauded!* And most unforgivably of all, only four years earlier, Aura had actually allowed this cad (whose motives in becoming an obstetrician were doubtless too vile to be dwelt on) to deliver the twins! Raleigh had declined to speak to his wife for three days following the dance, and her response to his attempt, then, to bring her to trial over her behavior ("Well, dammit, Raleigh, why don't you go take dancing lessons if you're going to be so ridiculous, or just pee in a circle around me, and maybe nobody'll cross the territory") had added another whole week of silence.

It was in thinking of the Jimsons and the Joyners that Raleigh was led to this unhappy memory, and from there, via his second scotch, to reflections on what Aura might have meant by going out to lunch with "guys," whom she had claimed were "just a bunch of Democrats who want to talk politics," but had then confessed included their lawyer, Dan Andrews. Now, Dan (as Raleigh well knew from rooming with him in college, when Dan had befriended him in order to get into his fraternity, and then dropped him in order to befriend the inner circle — Raleigh was the fraternity's token grind), as Raleigh all too well knew, Dan Andrews was an aggressively competitive, invidiously ambitious, selfish rotten person. It was for these very qualities that Raleigh had engaged him as his lawyer. The man could not tolerate losing face, and by extension, cases. But he was a human consumer, trading wives in like cars for newer models. How dare he go out to lunch with Aura? How dare Aura be so stupid, so indiscreet, so *wanton,* as to accept this slimy invitation!

Raleigh, who by now had eaten all his cashews and shredded his napkins, ordered a third scotch. If the second drink had made him angry, the third had a very different effect. Halfway through this drink, he began to hear again the music from across the bar, and he remembered that he loved listening to music. Where in the world were all his mother's old classical records, where were all his old jazz records? Were they in the attic? No, that's right, he'd taken them to "Peace and Quiet." He remembered that he loved live music; despite Aunt Victoria's contempt, hadn't his father's informal little family combo actually been pretty good? Hadn't he himself actually shown a lot of promise on the trumpet? What a shame that here they were with a piano in their house, and neither of the twins had gotten past Thompson's first book of lessons, and nobody ever played it except Mingo, who invited himself over to play "Happy Birthday," or Christmas carols, or any other excuse he could find. But this piano in the bar now, this was really very pleasant, particularly these Gershwin tunes, particularly when so touchingly played by someone with so sensitive a face and such long long hair that fell over her eyes. Yes, Hayes would just slip a few dollars into her brandy snifter atop the piano; how sad it held only one bill.

It wasn't long after the Thermopylean had come over with an unsteady smile and made his contribution to music, that the pianist ended her stint at the keyboard with a sad run of scales to finish "The Man I Love." She was replaced on the white bench by a middle-aged man who immediately began singing, "Bess, You Is My Woman, Now." The woman, bringing her vodka collins along, joined Raleigh Hayes at his table and said, "I guess you like Gershwin."

"I love him," Hayes replied, and bit his mouth to discover if it was as numb as it seemed.

"Mind if I have a drink?"

"I'd love one," Raleigh replied. "Pardon me, please have a seat."

"I'm Rusty, what yours?"

"Mine? Scotch."

She laughed. "No, your name."

"Raleigh. Raleigh Hayes."

"Like the city? That's funny."

"No, actually I was named for Sir Walter Raleigh; you know, the Lost Colony?"

"That's funny. I guess you like my playing."

"I love it."

Now, because our hero lived, as we know, almost entirely inside his head, and tended to think of his body as an alien enemy to be subdued into longevity, he had only the most perfunctory notion of what he looked like. He certainly would never have described himself as a basically very good-looking man. But he was. He was not dazzlingly good-looking, like his brother Gates, nor affably good-looking, like his father Earley, but he resembled them both enough that, now, given his elegant new clothes, and the fact that he was too drunk to keep his mouth pinched and his eyes squinted, he looked (as Aura had told him not so long ago in their bath-room) "pretty good." It was not, however, this cause alone that brought the freckled pianist to his side. Raleigh, whose pockets were full of money destined for various parties, had, in the dimmed light and with his dimin-ished faculties, pushed not, as he supposed, two one-dollar bills, but two ten-dollar bills, into the brandy snifter, which meant to the piano player (a woman of some sophistication, as well as an apartment she couldn't afford, and an amorous disposition) more than our hero intended (or knew he intended) to say. Therefore, after much good-humored talk about music and several more rounds of drinks, and after Raleigh's odd announcement that he believed himself on the Atlantic Ocean in "Easy Living," this kind musician insisted on helping the Thermopylean find his way back to the Ambrose Inn, to which she was obliged to lead him by the arm. Along the way, he fell into a fit of humming. This was followed by a fit of terror when he became convinced that bugs were scurrying over his shoes.

"Hey, don't worry," Rusty laughed. "They really are. Palmetto bugs, they're all over at night around here. Creepy, isn't it?"

"Shurrtillyish," agreed Hayes. He got down on his hands and knees. She was absolutely right. Enormous black roachy creatures were crawling on the sidewalk, racing frantically from shadow to shadow. "Thash me, thas exactly me," said Hayes, and fell into a contemplative mood. Suddenly a dreadful bell began to bong. "STOP THAT!" He leaped to his feet and slapped his hands over his ears. "WHAT IS THAT?"

"Wow, take it easy, Raleigh. It's just a clock."

"A *clock?*"

"Church clock." She pointed above them. "See? Church. It's nine o'clock."

Hayes's hand flew from his ear and smacked him hard on the face. "Nine o'clock! Goddammit! Daddy!"

"Hey, what's with you?"

Raleigh abruptly realized that what was with him was someone he didn't know, and he began shaking Rusty's hand energetically, while bab-bling apologies. "Please shuuse me. Pardon me. Rushy? Rusty. I really preashate your going out of your way. I'm not like shis. Thank you. Got to run. Imporshant phone call. Familish 'mergency. Where am I? Which way . . . ah . . . I don't know how . . . musht have had . . . Feel strange . . . drink . . . excuse, please. Goosh-bye." Away ran Hayes backward, shouting apologies and crashing into a decorative horsehead hitching post. He turned the corner and left Rusty to conclude that it was all just as well, since the guy, while nice enough, was too far gone to know what he was doing, or else too odd for her to want to do anything with. And humming, "Our Love Is Here to Stay," she walked back to the hotel, where with a rueful wink she joined her replacement at the piano in a duet of "I Loves You, Porgy."

In this way was our hero saved literally by the bell from (possibly) jeopardizing the vow he'd taken fifty minutes earlier when he swore that never in a million years would he ever even give the appearance of doing what Pierce Jimson gave every appearance of having already done.

Hayes flung himself past two startled elderly women in rockers on the porch of the Ambrose Inn, and bounded into the hushed foyer. The proprietor, Mr. Vanderhost, was pinching back a trellis of fuchsia blossoms. Yes, said this soft-voiced Charlestonian, acknowledging by not so much as an eyebrow that his guest (despite his respectable clothes) was drunk as a skunk. Yes, he said, there had been a phone call at eight. Yes, from a Mr. Earley Hayes. No, no message; no, didn't say where he was, yes, said he'd try again tomorrow night. "Beg your pardon, sir, I couldn't catch what you said?" added this suave hotelier, who had perfectly clearly heard Mr. Hayes mumble, "Goddammit to hell son of a bitch," as he stood, or rather swayed, against a Duke of Marlborough desk, from which Mr. Vanderhost smoothly rescued a Chinese vase.

"A gentleman also called on you, Mr. Hayes."

"A genshman? What genshman?"

"He didn't care to leave his name, sir. A fairly elderly and a fairly . . . small . . . Northern gentleman . . . in formal wear. With a mustache?" Vanderhost held his hand out slightly above his waist, and used the other to draw a small line over his upper lip.

"Yesh yesh." Hayes recognized this brief description of Weeper Berg.

"He asked me to ask you to not . . . leave without him." Vanderhost tapped his paisley handkerchief down in the breast pocket of his navy blazer, then fluffed it out again. "He did not care to be more specific."

"Shank you." Raleigh now slid back along the edge of the desk, and caught himself by grabbing a brass standing lamp, with which he attempted a short lively dance.

"Mr. Hayes, could I be of some help?" The proprietor pressed his foot discreetly on the lamp base to steady it.

Hayes was utterly mortified, having come to suspect he was giving the impression that he'd been drinking. "Yes," he said, taking a great deal of care with each word. "I am not feeling very well. Do you happen to have any aspirin?"

"Of course. I'll have some brought up to your room."

So up to his room went the insurance man, and then down the hall to take a shower, for the Ambrose Inn, while luxurious, deliberately preserved its antique charm by declining to install private baths in its beautiful rooms. Raleigh, by his own testimony, almost never drank. Consequently, he believed all the false old wives' tales (for possibly the old wives didn't drink either) about methods to accelerate sobriety, which, as habitual inebriates know, cannot, and should not, be attempted. First he took the aspirin. Then he subjected himself to a long, hard, and entirely frigid shower. Having scantily escaped a heart attack there, he instantly courted another by jogging in his new tasseled loafers all the way around the Battery's White Park Gardens. After this, he hurried into the first restaurant he saw, ate two bowls of hot greasy soup, drank two glasses of thick warm tomato juice, rushed into the bathroom, threw up, sat back down, and swallowed three cups of scalding coffee. At the end of this ordeal, while he felt wretched, he did not seem to be as frighteningly remote from himself as he had felt a few hours earlier. He did not feel *hopelessly* drunk, and therefore he continued to believe those old wives' tales about sobering up.

One might think that poor Raleigh had endured enough for the day (particularly as he could not blame Mingo, Gates, or Weeper Berg for either the spending spree, the insults of Jubal Rogers, the shock of Pierce Jimson, or the enticements of Rusty's bar); one might think Fortune had exhausted even her capacity for derision, but obviously not, for she flew into a sudden ill temper as Raleigh was walking back to the inn, and began to pelt him not just with rain but with the very leaves and branches ripped from trees by squalling winds.

This time, sopping wet, he *ran* through the foyer and up the stairs before having to endure again Mr. Vanderhost's understanding face. He could hear the man calling, "Pardon me, Mr. Hayes? Did you know . . . ," but, cowardly, he ran even faster up the stairs, into his room, and flung himself down on the bed. He then reached out in the dark for the lamp he remembered seeing somewhere on a chintz-covered side table. The next assault on his heart came silently and suddenly. A soft, a warm, a naked, a female arm wound around his neck.

Oh Christ Almighty, thought Hayes in a flash, Rusty! She knew where he was staying, and while he was out, she'd told Vanderhost God knows what, and . . . "Listen," he burst out in a desperate whisper, "this is a terrible misunderstanding. You'll have to leave. I'm sorry, but I'm a happily married man."

Raleigh heard a carol of laughter. It was the laugh he knew best in the world.

"AURA!" he yelled, and leaped from the bed.

The lamp clicked on, and there indeed lay, hair tousled, rosy warm and apparently unclothed, Raleigh's wife, Aura Godwin Hayes. "You!" she laughed, "have certainly turned into some joker! You'll have to leave, I'm a happily married man! Oh, Raleigh! *Guten Nichtski!*"

"Aura, what the hell are you doing in my room?"

She laughed again, burying her head in the pillow, peeked out, looked at him, and laughed some more. "Raleigh, I am *so* glad to see you! And, honey," giggles swept over her again, "you haven't changed a bit! The last time I saw you, you came home soaking wet! Have you been jogging? Or drinking? . . . Oh, God!" She stuck her head back under the pillow to muffle a new outburst.

"Of course not," said Hayes, entirely forgetting that he had in fact been both jogging and drinking only a short while ago. "It's pouring down rain."

"I know! That's why I just fell in the bed. What a trip!" Aura sat up, tucking the laced sheet around her breasts. "Vera and I were driving blind as bats the last fifty miles. I thought we'd never get here. And you know Vera, she's so terrified of lightning, we had to pull over every ten minutes. Sweetheart, please get out of those wet clothes. And where'd you *get* them? *Très chic,* I must say. Well, were you surprised?"

Hayes took a deep breath. He was a quick-witted man, and it was clear to him by now that (a) his wife (rather than waiting for his call from the Ambrose Inn — which he realized he'd forgotten to make) had decided to pay him a surprise visit, (b) that Vera Sheffield had decided to play a similar surprise on Mingo, (c) that Aura assumed Mr. Vanderhost had told him that his wife had arrived, and that therefore (d) his insane blurting that she had to leave at once struck her as another instance of the madcap wit she'd found so amusing when he'd been forced to speak German gibberish back in the Wetherells' slave cabin. But just to make certain, Raleigh wiped the rain from his glasses, cleared his throat, and said, "Let me get this straight, you and Vera drove down here hoping to surprise us? Ha ha."

"Did Holly and Caroline *tell* you? Those finks! I told them to say I was at a meeting."

"I didn't speak to them at all."

"You didn't? They promised me they were going to stay home. Dam-

mit! I better call." She leaned out for the phone. Had she given up pajamas?

"Aura! You left our daughters at home alone?"

"Honey, they're sixteen! They could be married by now."

"By now, perhaps they are," growled Hayes. "Where is Vera? Do you
know Mingo and Gates are still in Midway?"

"She's in her room upstairs. Oh, she was so disappointed when Mr.
Vanderhost said you'd told him Mingo wouldn't be arriving till late tonight."

"Or tomorrow. Or never. Aura, honestly —"

"Shhh. Go take off your clothes . . . Holly?" Aura waved away her husband as if her hand were a whisk broom. "Holly, are you okay? . . . No, I'm
not checking up. I just want to know if you're alive. Is Caroline okay? . . .
Well, go *look*. Just because her record player's blasting, doesn't mean she
isn't dead."

"Oh, Aura!" Hayes muttered. "Stop worrying." With a useful economy,
Mr. and Mrs. Hayes had always taken turns at fearing the imminent de-
mise of their daughters. Whenever one had been leaning all night over a
crib with a finger held beneath a tiny nostril to feel any signs of breathing,
or racing a sleepy child into a lukewarm tub to bring down a fever, or
peering out the window at midnight for police lights in the driveway, the
other would scoff at the absurdity of such alarm. By alternating in this
way, they'd survived sixteen years of unrelieved anxiety. It was obviously
Aura's turn now, and so Raleigh left with his new pajamas and robe to
take another shower, a hot one this time. When he came back, his wife
was still on the phone.

"Okay, sweetheart, Daddy sends his love. Bye-bye kiss kiss." She hung
up. "They're fine," she said. "Come on to bed. By the way, I love your new
clothes. And," she waved her hand around the room, "your whole new
approach to life."

"Aura, I have to ask you a question."

She leaned an elbow in the down pillow and combed her hair with her
fingers. "Fire away."

"I don't want you going out with Dan Andrews."

"That's not a question, honey."

"Well, I mean, how do you feel about him? You do know he's pretty,
well, immoral, and a womanizer, don't you? I mean, you realize that?"

"Raleigh Hayes, I think you're pretty adorable."

Raleigh sighed as he took off his bathrobe. "Well, I'm just glad you're aware of that. I mean, about Dan. How was your debate with poor Charlie Lukes?"

"In the words of your daughter, Mr. Hayes, I wiped him up."

Raleigh laughed and crawled under the lace coverlet.

"Oh, Raleigh, honey. Now aren't you happy I came?"

"Aura. Aura. If you only knew . . ."

And it wasn't too long before Raleigh and Aura were doing exactly what his father had so outrageously advised them to do in his note of only one week ago today.

Had this Tuesday night ended here for our hero, it would have ended as pleasantly as any in his memory. Regrettably, he was awakened before dawn by violent crackles of thunder, gusts of wind, and banging shutters, and he found himself under the most urgent compulsion to use the facilities — a consequence of the inordinate quantity, and variety, of liquids he had imbibed during the evening. Slipping out of the room, he was surprised to see no light in the hall. Or indeed anywhere. A glance out a window showed not a single street lamp. The only light was what was bolting down from the black sky. Hayes, hearing sirens, concluded that the storm had knocked out a power line. He therefore felt his way in the dark to what he remembered to be the bathroom. The door was locked, and a female voice told him, "Just a moment, please." The moment dragged on longer than he could wait. He was truly in an urgent situation. Using his hands as guides, he worked his way up a flight of steps, and down a hall of doors, reading with his fingers until he reached one with a sign and not a number on it. It was, thank God, indeed a toilet.

But as Hayes started on his return journey, he made a fatal error. He did not realize that there were, as in most large old houses, two flights of steps between the floors, and he descended a different staircase than the one he'd climbed. Back on his own floor, he proceeded carefully, counting the doors — but approaching from the wrong end of the hall. It was his misfortune that what he took to be the right side of the hall was the left, and what he took to be the raised number 7 was in fact the number 1.

It was Raleigh's further misfortune that he had failed to recognize the voice of the lady in the restroom as that of Mrs. Boyd Joyner, and that she, in her hurry to return to bed, had failed to lock the door to Room 1, the grandest room in the inn, and the most old-fashioned, for it was romantically equipped with candle wall-sconces, which Mrs. Joyner had lit on this, the Thermopylean adulterers first real night together. (For all their previous assignations had taken place either in cramped automobiles or the crowded warehouse of Jimson's store.) These few precious nights, while

Pierce was attending a furniture convention in Charleston, and while Lizzie was presumably visiting her mother in Columbia, these few nights, they had schemed for, and waited for, all winter long. They intended to make the most of them, as who knew what the future might bring. Certainly not the poor illicit lovers, for suddenly, and accompanied as if in the climax of an opera, by a clap of thunder so loud it rattled the French windows, their door inched open, and there stood, in his bathrobe, Raleigh W. Hayes.

If Raleigh's horror may be imagined as he saw, by candlelight, on the bed, not his wife Aura, and not even, as he next thought, two strangers, and not even simply Pierce Jimson and Lizzie Joyner, not even simply naked, but Pierce Jimson naked with Lizzie Joyner naked, and inverted, atop him, engaged in what Raleigh had often heard his porno-film-fan cousin Jimmy Clay refer to as "good ole sixty-nine." If Raleigh's horror may be imagined, it utterly paled, it was absolutely less than nothing, compared to the horror experienced by Pierce Jimson, once Lizzie, with a scream, lifted herself from his face so that he could raise it and therefore see Raleigh Hayes standing in his room.

Having screamed once, Lizzie crawled completely under the pink satin comforter and burrowed her way to the foot of the bed, where she stayed, shaking. On his knees, Pierce, his magnificent voice paralyzed by shock, contorted every muscle in his face and throat without producing a single sound other than the repeated syllable "YOU!"

Raleigh had managed to croak out only "Oh my God, please, pardon, no idea . . ." before Jimson bounded from the bed, and, as it were, leading with his penis, ran at Hayes, hit him in the mouth, grabbed him by the neck, and began to bang him into the wall.

It quickly occurred to Hayes, who couldn't breathe, that the snorting, wild-eyed Jimson was very seriously attempting to kill him. And as Raleigh was larger, younger, and fitter than his thin-shouldered, flabby, and at the moment vulnerably exposed assailant, Raleigh (for once not tempted to think things through) decided instantly not to allow himself to be choked to death. As he couldn't pry the man's fingers from his throat, he started hitting him in the stomach, and finally as a last resort even kicked him in the groin. At this low blow, Jimson's hands loosened. In fact, he sank groaning to the floor. Raleigh gasped enough air to pant, "Damn you. You almost killed me!" Then he looked down at the pale hairy body writhing at his feet. "Pierce, you were choking me! . . . Well, I'm sorry, but . . . Are you okay?"

Jimson was gagging, but he nevertheless managed to splutter out some words. "You, vile, dirty, evil, bastard. You'll rot in hell for the way you're torturing us!"

"For Pete's sake, Pierce! I assure you I had no idea this was your room. And, frankly, don't try to blame me for what you're up to in here!"

"Come on, what is it you're after?" groaned Jimson. "Is it because of my dad and your grandfather? Revenge? You're sick, Raleigh!"

"*I'm* sick?" Hayes rubbed his throat. "You're *psychotic!*" He pulled his robe closed, and glanced at the quivering lump under the satin coverlet. "Mrs. Joyner, I apologize for embarrassing you."

"YOU HEARTLESS FIEND!" squawked Jimson, crawling over and shoving Raleigh by the knees out the door, as another burst of thunder shook the house.

In the shuffle, Raleigh's feet had slid completely out of their new bedroom slippers. Finding himself barefoot in the hall, he banged with his shoulder against the door, determined to retrieve property which was not only new, but of which he could have little expectation of any voluntary return. His forcible reentry, for this blow flung the door aside and Jimson with it, so incensed the adulterous merchant that without regard to shame or modesty, he shoved and butted Hayes right out into the hall, and then down it a good ten yards as if they opposed each other on a line of scrimmage, until, with a final push, he knocked his opponent into the now-open bathroom, slammed the door, and wedged a hall chair under the knob. Then, suddenly realizing he was naked in a public (albeit dark) hallway, Jimson squatted and scurried like a crab back to Lizzie.

As for our hero, he was truly in a maddening dilemma, or as his fellow Thermopyleans would say, a real pickle. Here he was, the sane party, locked up in a black cage of a toilet, by the insane party, who was still at large. The door would not budge. Of course, he could have called for help, but the circumspect habits of a lifetime made him incapable of such an outcry. Or he could have waited until dawn (which *had* to be coming), or at least until the next incontinent insomniac arrived to use the facilities. But, as we know, the virtue of patience was in our hero often confused with the vice of sloth. Therefore, after a moment lost to futile muscular gyrations accompanied by curses that in no way alleviated his feelings, Hayes stood on the toilet lid, where he discovered, as he'd suspected, that the piazza which ran the width of the second floor extended to the bathroom. He shoved up the window, hoisted himself onto its sill, and by the most agonizing contortions of back and legs managed to shimmy his way through the opening — suffering in the process a raw scrape on the stomach, a charley horse in the calf, and the loss of his drawstring pajama bottoms, which caught on the window latch, came untied, and fell to the floor while the rest of Hayes, hanging outside head over heels, was in no position to retrieve them.

Finally on his feet on the balcony, he fought to gather together the robe that violent winds and rains had blown above his head. Then with a dignity even his enemies should admire, he walked, or splashed, around the corner, climbed the lattice ironwork that separated each room's private terrace, twisted open the French doors through whose gauze curtains he could see the naked gesturing silhouettes of Pierce Jimson and Mrs. Joyner, and walked (rather, was blown, his robe flying up) back into their room. "You can bet I won't forget this," he announced in a hushed, ominous voice, then strode straight for his slippers, still lying by the door.

Too far from the bed to dive for the covers again, Lizzie threw herself behind her lover, who nevertheless abandoned her in order to take a different courtly action. He snatched up the umbrella hooked over the closet doorknob, and, a champion without armor, charged at his lady's persecutor.

As Raleigh, his back to Jimson, was now bent over in the process of picking up his slippers, he might have been done a serious injury by this weapon, had not, fortunately, the umbrella been of the automatic sort, for when Jimson's fierce grip squeezed a button on its handle, it flew up, both retarding and blinding the charger, so that he narrowly missed his target, and, unable to stop his run, slammed into the wall beside it. Hayes wasted no time on his foe, now caught in the spokes of a black umbrella, but, without a word, unlocked the door, returned to the hall, stomped to the bathroom, and pulled on his pajama bottoms.

Traumatized, Hayes stumbled back down the hall, now realizing how he'd gone to the wrong end. He felt the number 7 twice before opening the door. Nevertheless, he was immediately greeted by a scream of "Oh my Jesus! Who's that?"

"Dammit!" he said, then added in a polite whisper. "Sorry. Wrong room."

"Raleigh? Did you hear all that noise? What's going on?"

"Aura? . . . Aura?"

Hayes reached out for the bed, but the body he felt did not belong to his wife. It screamed again.

"Raleigh! What are you doing?" The voice *was* his wife's. "You're scaring Vera. It's Raleigh, Vera. Raleigh, you're soaking wet again!"

"Oh Raleigh, it's you. You scared me." This voice was Vera Sheffield's.

They were all whispering.

"Aura, what is Vera . . . Vera, what are you doing in here?"

"She was nervous," Aura explained, and Vera confirmed it. "I was nervous. Listen to that storm, I can't stand lightning. Mingo hasn't come yet, and what did you do with him, Raleigh? *Eeeeeck!*" Another bang of thunder had startled her into a long shriek. "Vera!" Aura whispered, "Stick your head under the pillow if you have to scream."

By God, thought Hayes, what in the world did the Sheffields do during lightning storms at home? Hide in a closet with all their guns? How miraculous that they had never before now raced next door and flung themselves into bed with Aura and him. "What did I do with Mingo? Well, Vera, I left him hung over in a tuxedo at a Texas millionaire's. Before that he was designing costumes for French movies."

"Dammit, Raleigh, don't tease her, can't you see she's really worried?"

"No, I can't see a damn thing! Mingo's fine, Vera. He wanted to ride the bus here from Midway. He's there helping my brother."

"Oh, if something's happened to him . . . He's the sweetest man in the world, isn't he?"

Raleigh was spared an answer by a modest rap at the door. *"Don't answer it,"* he hissed. "It's Pierce Jimson! He's trying to kill me!"

Aura whispered, "Raleigh, your thing about Pierce is really getting a little too weird."

Vera whispered, "Maybe it's Mingo."

But a polite voice called, "Mr. Hayes, pardon me?" It was that cursedly considerate Vanderhost.

"Just a moment." Raleigh cracked open the door and blinked into two glass kerosene lamps, behind them, the owner of the Ambrose Inn in a green brocade bathrobe and a yellow ascot.

"I'm so sorry to be bothering you all but I thought I heard a . . . noise . . . sounded a little bit like . . . screams. I'm afraid our power's off."

"Yes, I realize that." Hayes nonchalantly brushed back his hair.

"Pardon me, is everything all right?"

"Absolutely. My, ah, wife, is just a little nervous about the lightning."

"Oh, tell her not to worry. We've been here a long long time. Your mouth seems to be . . . bleeding, sir."

"Yes, I realize that." Hayes licked at it. Dammit, it *was* bleeding. "I took a little stumble trying to find the bathroom."

"Oh dear me. I'm sorry. Can I get you some salve and a Band-Aid?"

"No, thank you, I carry them with me."

"I see. Well, why don't you keep this lamp here in case —"

"Yes, thank you, very kind, good night." Raleigh pushed the door shut on the man. He turned to see his wife (now in a pink nightgown) comfortably settled into bed beside Vera Sheffield (in a mass of red ruffled chiffon that was no doubt a sample piece of merchandise from her new mail-order business). "Ladies," sighed Hayes, "it's four thirty-eight in the morning."

"He loves to tell the time," Aura giggled, and Vera giggled back. They were clearly trying to recapture the old girlish pleasures of the slumber party. Thunder shook the room. Vera screamed. Aura clamped the pillow over her head, and then they both burst out laughing.

"Raleigh, would you mind terribly being a sweetheart and sleeping in the Sheffields' room? Vera is truly uncomfortable being in there by herself in this storm."

"Would you, Raleigh?" Mrs. Sheffield lifted the pillow from her glossy black curls. "Oh, that's so sweet of you."

Raleigh did not feel he could admit that he *did* mind terribly being a sweetheart; he minded returning to those halls more than anyone was ever going to have the slightest notion. But Vera actually had her creamy plump hands raised to him in prayer, and Aura was blowing him a kiss of farewell.

"Vera, where is your room? *Exactly* where?"

CHAPTER

24

*In Which Are Continued the Misfortunes That Befell
Our Hero at the Ambrose Inn*

WEDNESDAY'S OPENING was so like Tuesday's finale that the unwilling
actor Raleigh Hayes at first insisted he was still asleep and refused to open
his eyes. This ploy, however, did not stop the curtain from going up, for
he could not avoid hearing a voice with which he was all too familiar.

"Oh no, oh gollee, oh please, oh no, don't say it's true after all, after all!
Oh please, oh Raleigh, no, I believed you! We were all such good friends!
VERA!"

Hayes was obliged to lift one eyelid open. Not seeing Mingo, he was
obliged to lean over the edge of the bed, where he glimpsed the mammoth
madras buttocks wriggling. The rest of Sheffield was presumably searching
for his wife under the blue-violets bed skirt. As Hayes now saw, this entire
room was papered, hung, draped, painted, and upholstered with blue violets, which made it somewhat difficult for Mingo, upset as he was, to find
the closet doors and the armoire and the hope chest in which Vera might
be hiding. Raleigh watched him, with one eye.

"Raleigh, Raleigh, wake up, and please, oh please, tell me I'm wrong!"

"You're wrong." Hayes sat up among the ruffled violets, and rubbed
his eyes. "Vera is downstairs sleeping with Aura. Only in, to the best
of my knowledge, the literal sense." Yes, despite his strange hideous
headache, the insurance man felt himself to be in excellent form this

sunny morning. "You see, Mingo, I was a sweetheart and gave up my bed to your wife, who I gather shares your entirely irrational fear of electrical storms."

At this news, Sheffield expelled so huge a gust of air that Hayes actually felt a breeze. "I knew it!" the fat man happily nodded. "I just knew my best friend wouldn't betray me." He leaned over to crush Raleigh in a hug. "It's true. Vera's scared to death of lightning. I bet it's the only thing in the world she *is* scared of. I guess I'm afraid she got it from me. Whew. I'm ashamed of myself, that's for sure."

"Good."

"I ought to know God wouldn't let something like that happen."

"Right," growled Hayes. "He's too busy starting earthquakes and famines." He snatched his glasses off the table to look at his watch. "Mingo, it's six thirty-three A.M. Did you just get here? And where's Gates?"

"I took an early bus so I could see the sun come up. Boy, was it beautiful! Plus they gave us a danish. But, oh Raleigh." Sheffield flopped down on the bed. "We've had the worst troubles. You're lucky you were gone."

"That's what you think. Where is Gates?"

"Hiding at Sara's house."

"Sara?"

"You know, Zane. I think he loves her."

"I bet. Mingo, would you please move over, you're crushing the life out of me. Well, I told you you couldn't keep up that ridiculous charade about the movies. The Wetherells threw you out."

"Not exactly, but we had to leave in a hurry and didn't even get to really say good-bye. I guess I'll write Lady Bug a note. My mama always said, if you don't write your bread and butter notes, pretty soon you'll run out of bread and butter."

"Mingo, it's clear you've outdone Emily Post."

"Well, I just don't want to hurt anybody's feelings."

"That's nice. Now, just excuse me one second. I have to use the facilities. Lend me your robe. Mine got wet. No, don't ask. Then I want you to tell me what happened. There's no sense in trying to sleep in this damn place."

What had happened was this, and not all of it was known to Mingo Sheffield. Yesterday morning, while Payne Wetherell was up on the balcony trying to decide if it was fair to use a ruler to fix the steps of Sacre Coeur, and while Mr. Mingo and Lady Wetherell (bourbon in hand) were in the conservatory trying to decide if they should strip the red lacquer from the linen-fold oak paneling, and while Jean Claude Claudel was in the library putting the finishing touches to a gentleman's agreement bestowing upon Mr. Wetherell, for only $25,000, all the prerogatives of an associate producership in *Spare Me the Magnolias Please,* and while Crystal was in the dogshed, the butler (as Ethan preferred to be called, rather than "house servant") was in the front hall, up on a high ladder, dropping the Venetian glass shades from the chandelier he was dusting. It was consequently Ethan who opened the door to the two men, one with a bone cane, one with a squished face, who announced brusquely that they were with the FBI, and were looking for the criminal Gates Hayes, who'd recently been seen in that neighborhood in a late-model white Cadillac.

Despite Mrs. Wetherell's slur on his veracity, Ethan was no liar. He told the simple truth. There was no one visiting in the house but a French filmmaker named John Claude and a friend of his, Mr. Mingo. But it was a fact that these two had arrived there in a white Cadillac, which the day before a Mr. Rallycough had driven off to Charleston, taking with him a little old blind man. Asked to describe this John Claude, Ethan had proceeded no further than "great big blue eyes and lots of black curly hair," when the younger man with the cane insisted that this was the very criminal they were after, and that Ethan should produce him at once. "If you like wearing your ears," added the other man. Ethan, having in his youth suffered the entirely meretricious harassment of the local police, found nothing improbable in such threats from the law. He dropped the light bulb, and started slowly up the cantilevered stairs.

The library happened to be directly off the front hall. Gates Hayes happened to hear enough of this exchange to decide to leave business behind, slip out a side door, race through the kitchen, and bound up the rear stairs, where he hurriedly told his *chère madame* and Mr. Mingo that two secret agents of the KGB, one of them named Solinsky, were at the front door disguised as FBI men, and that they were there to eradicate him for having helped Mr. Raleighkov escape from behind the Iron Curtain, and that if Mrs. Wetherell loved America, she would stall these Russian pawns while he, Jean Claude, her most happy admirer, and Mr. Mingo escaped. He had only time to say he would never forget her, not that of course they wouldn't be back in June or July or possibly August to begin filming their epic on the "Wild Oaks" estate. Now, Lady Wetherell did love America. She had, moreover, grown double D damn fond of Monsieur Claudel, even to the point, it must be admitted, of visiting his slave cabin on Monday night. Accepting his kiss on the hands with a heartfelt *ciao,* and a big bear hug from Mr. Mingo, Lady Bug watched until her two guests had raced to the dogshed. Then, flouncing the jet-beaded fringe of her Neiman-Marcus leisure suit, she descended the front stairs as if she were playing the lead in *Spare Me the Magnolias Please.*

By the time her hysterical laughter at his every word convinced Cupid Calhoun that he'd been given the slip, the North Carolineans had already tossed their possessions out of their cabins and into the jeep, which Crystal (with a wisdom beyond her years, born perhaps of her constant concourse with the animal world) declined to lend Gates, but offered to chauffeur.

"And gollee, Raleigh, could she drive!" continued Mingo, who (having concluded his approving examination of every object in the room, and unpacked the contents of his immense suitcase) was now back on the blue-violets bed beside his friend. "So, well, those guys jumped in their Saab and chased us, but Crystal shot right into the woods, and you know how it is, Raleigh, you just can't drive a regular car over rocks and stumps and all in the woods."

"Or a swamp," agreed Hayes.

According to Sheffield, if Gates were a flyer, Crystal Wetherell was a charioteer worthy of an epic simile placing her in the company of Charlton Heston in *Ben Hur.* "Why, she knew those woods like the back of her hand, and Big Nose and Cupid crashed right into this split-rail fence! They weren't hurt, though, 'cause I saw them jump out of the Saab and curse at us."

The debutante pathfinder had then driven the two men to Sara Zane's apartment in Midway, where they'd slept on the couch, and where, bright and early, Mingo had risen to take the dawn bus to Charleston and a cab here to the Ambrose Inn, only to find his wife registered and his friend in her bed.

"Well," sighed Hayes. "I guess we can kiss Gates good-bye for another five years."

"Oh, no, he's coming. Here." Mingo squeezed his hands through all the pockets of his madras pants until he found a balled-up piece of elementary-school notebook paper.

> Dear Ace,
> Hang on, Don't split. Tell Weep I need truck plates and a good body man. Keep the faith, babe. P.S. I think this is It, I mean Her, the big picket fence. Move over. It's hit hard. Not sure I can handle it.
> > G.

"Ah," said Hayes.

"I didn't read it, he handed it to me just like that. He was kind of in a hurry to get to Roxanne's while it was still dark."

"Help yourself." Raleigh handed over the note.

"Where is Weeper, anyhow? You didn't let the police get him, did you, Raleigh?"

"Oh, no. He drops by now and again. I have no idea what he's up to, and don't plan to inquire. Let's assume he knows what 'a good body man' means. I wonder . . ." Hayes mused in his peaceful ironic style, "if it means a hired killer? We'll probably need one of those any day now."

At this moment Vera, followed by Aura, rushed into the room. Leaving the floor about a yard from the bed, and flying through air like a full-breasted dove cooing "Sweetie sweetie," Mrs. Sheffield landed upon her spouse, on whose moony face she pecked dozens of kisses. The giant fortress of a bed having withstood this aerial attack, Raleigh saw no reason not to say, "Don't be so standoffish, Aura, please join us."

But before she could decide to do so, or before Mingo could comment that it was just like *Bob and Carol and Ted and Alice* or perhaps *Cheaper by the Dozen,* doors on the floor below began to be pounded upon, shaken, and in some cases, flung open. This commotion had neither the sound nor the pace of a maid, nor was it the polite tap of Mr. Vanderhost inquiring of all his guests if there were anything he could do for them at seven in the morning. But someone was starting up the stairs toward the Sheffields' room, someone moving at a house-shaking clip.

There is nevertheless a moment remaining to sketch in the background to what was about to occur. Although it is improbable that Pierce Jimson could ever be compelled to admit this, he was soon to owe his infamous blackmailer Raleigh Hayes a debt of gratitude. For thanks to Raleigh, Room 1 was vacant. So understandably distressed had the fairly in-experienced adulterers felt after being violently interrupted at the very moment of bliss, that their already stimulated emotions discharged themselves in a horrible argument about whether or not it had been poli-tic of Pierce to assault rather than placate a prominent Thermopylean like Raleigh Hayes. This, the first of their affair, was such a serious argument that, without even waiting for dawn, they'd thrown their clothes into suitcases and driven in furious silence to take Lizzie to her mother's in Co-lumbia. Any desire to speak had been burned away by the feelings that consumed them. For his part, Pierce was enflamed with rage against Ra-leigh (whom he now believed to be diabolically fixated on a family ven-detta to destroy the last of the Jimsons). He was enflamed with fear of exposure, with guilt about his wife, with shame about his morals, and, torturously mixed with all these, he was still enflamed, despite their fight, with Lizzie. As for Mrs. Joyner, her emotions were more concentrated. She was, to the exclusion of any other sensation, terrified of her husband, Boyd, and of his response to any public discovery of her shame. She no longer loved Boyd (if, in fact, she ever had), but he had convinced her so long ago that everything she had, including her self, "belonged" to him that she could not conceive of openly escaping his authority. She could only circumvent it. In such duplicity, she could take (she had discovered) some pride, as she took pride in Pierce Jimson's insatiable infatuation with her. For while Lizzie Joyner did not love Pierce either . . . not in any heart-stopping way . . . he had assuredly awakened just enough of a self in her for vanity to flourish. And as vanity cannot see itself without a mirror, Mrs. Joyner had eventually been unable to resist telling her friend Fran Whitefield how much the town leader loved her, and how cleverly she'd kept their complicated maneuvers secret from Boyd, who thought her such a silly incompetent; nor resist showing Fran a few of her lover's beautiful presents, which, sadly, she had to keep hidden in the attic crawl space. Panic now convinced Mrs. Joyner that somebody (probably Raleigh Hayes) was going to tell Boyd, and that Boyd was going to (though she couldn't define what she meant by this) somehow eradicate her existence.

She was right to worry. Naturally, though sworn to die first, sooner or later, Fran Whitefield had told her friend Misty Boylan who'd told her sister-in-law Patricia Ware who'd told her husband, Ned, who sooner or later (as Raleigh had predicted) took Boyd Joyner aside to console him about his wife's having an affair with Pierce Jimson. In saying so (and in adding that it was a rotten thing to have to mention, but if Boyd didn't make his loan payment in sixty days, Carolina Bank and Trust would be forced against its will to take his house), Ned Ware had not a malign thought in his head; he was really just trying to help.

It had been not until last night at the Civitans' spaghetti dinner that Ned's candor had found an opportunity to enlighten the cuckolded Mr. Joyner, for Boyd had not been a Marine hero for nothing: He enjoyed killing things, and had spent a long weekend off shooting birds with Nemours Kettell (who'd fled to the wilderness to curse the female sex); Ned had therefore looked for Boyd in vain at the golf course and the coffee shop, and was a bit sorry he'd ever found him at the spaghetti dinner, since the volunteer judo instructor had squeezed all the blood out of the old halfback's biceps while telling Ned that he'd better know what he was talking about, or, conversely, he'd better hope they never met again; for if Ned was calling Lizzie a whore, and if it turned out that she wasn't, Ned should accept the fact that he was, already, dead.

When Boyd Joyner called Columbia, Lizzie's mother (quite puzzled) told him she hadn't expected Lizzie until Thursday; he didn't explain a thing; he simply hung up. And called Brenda Jimson. He said nothing to her either, except thank you for the information that her husband Pierce was in Charleston at a furniture convention. Joyner's construction company's pickup truck arrived at the convention hotel at 5:30 A.M. It took him until 6:30 to learn that any messages for Jimson were to be sent to the Ambrose Inn. He went up (some of) the steps to the inn at 6:50. He walked into the Sheffields' room, without bothering to knock, at 6:59, looked at Raleigh, Mingo, and Vera in the big bed, Aura standing laughing beside it, and his handsome dark face turned as black as a raisin.

"BOYD!" bellowed Mingo, amazed.

Joyner spit out his words as if he couldn't stand the taste of them. "What is this, you creeps, hunh? A sex club? Hunh, y'all all come down here together? Don't need to go to work, just take off and stay in places like this, hunh? Come out, you Christ-fucking motherfucker! Y'all make me sick!"

Now, of the stunned foursome, only Raleigh had the vaguest notion of what Boyd Joyner was ranting about. And Raleigh's notion was not at all vague. But he didn't speak up at once. It must be clear by now that our hero balanced his moral books with fastidious care. It was imperative not to make a mistake, but to think, to evaluate, to judge, as if he were God — that is, if God were as just as Raleigh Hayes, which He manifestly was not. Hayes needed a moment to choose the correct response. Should he tell Boyd, "Try Room One," which would be tattle-telling, or should he tell Boyd nothing, which would be harboring the guilty? But while he was thinking, Vera rose up in the bed like a fleshy Venus in a fluffy red sea, and shouted, "You have got one HELL of a nerve, Boyd Joyner, bursting into my room and taking the Lord's name in vain and accusing us of being in a sex club! You can just march your butt out of here!"

"Right," said Mingo. "All we're doing is *talking!*"

"Boyd, what on earth is wrong?" threw in Aura. But by then Raleigh had crawled over the Sheffields, pulled on Joyner's arm and led him twisting into the hall, where they were confronted by the ever-vigilant Mr. Vanderhost. This man appeared to be immune to the normal human need for sleep, and impervious to surprise at seeing Raleigh emerge from a room not his own, with a man who (in his messy black jeans and black Orlon shirt, with his black bloodshot eyes and rumpled slicked black hair — for Boyd had been driving all night with a pint of Seagram's to his lips, and wasn't at his best) did not look anything like a guest of the Ambrose Inn. Not a shade of surprise was reflected in the hotelier's apologetic voice as he said, "I'm sorry, Mr. Hayes, but we've had a little complaint about a . . . disturbance?"

Hayes glanced at the irate faces peeking from most of the rooms up and down the hall — at all of which Joyner had pounded or kicked, including the door from which glowered (one white hair-netted head atop the other) the two elderly ladies whose rockers Raleigh had tripped over on the porch; including the door from which Mingo, Aura, and Vera were watching.

Boyd Joyner now grabbed both of Mr. Vanderhost's brocaded lapels in one muscled, grimy hand, and raised him to his tiptoes. Never before had Raleigh encountered such imperturbable poise. Even on his toes, with Joyner's knuckles under his chin, the owner of the Ambrose Inn managed to sound polite as he explained that Mr. Jimson had checked out earlier, and as for who was with him, or not, he certainly couldn't, or wouldn't, say. All the tension left Joyner's muscles. If Jimson and Lizzie weren't here to kill, he had no idea what to do.

Hayes led Mr. Vanderhost a few feet down the hall, and apologized. "Please excuse this disturbance. I know this man . . . slightly. He's deeply distressed. I think I can take care of it. Really, my apologies."

Vanderhost straightened his yellow ascot. "Not at all, sir. It's just that . . ." And he waved a ringed hand slowly down the line of doors as if to introduce his other guests, whom he then began to lure back into their rooms.

Raleigh had by now reached a decision. He would attempt to save the Joyner marriage. In doing so, he might be forced to toss Pierce Jimson's reputation to the dogs, but (1) Jimson had already done that anyhow, and (2) Jimson had tried to choke him to death for absolutely no reason, and (3) Jimson's father, PeeWee, had been a fat-faced, false-hearted hog who'd stolen Clayton Hayes's furniture store. Therefore, back in Room 7, Hayes sat the catatonic Joyner down in a Sheraton chair (whose needlepoint seat had been stitched by Mr. Vanderhost himself).

"Boyd. Boyd? I don't mean to pry. But I have the impression you think Pierce Jimson was here in this inn with Lizzie."

"Never mind what I think, it's none of your crap-ass business."

Hayes gave this response some thought, but decided to sidestep it. "Now. Look. Does that really make any sense? I mean, look at you. And

look at Pierce. He's ... well, let's be honest, the man is very homely."
(And, God, was he ugly without his clothes!) "Yes, Pierce is downright ugly, Boyd, and he's a real prig too. Come on. A beautiful woman
like Lizzie? Let's give her a little credit here. Now, who told you this
story?"

Sheerly by the pressure of his back muscles, Boyd snapped a dowel out
of the Sheraton chair. "Ned Ware," he said.

"Ned Ware. Ah." Removing his glasses, Raleigh studied the stem
hinge. "Well, now. Now, come on. We all know Ned. Don't we? ... I'll
tell you something. Do you know that fathead is actually going around
town saying that my father ran off with a black teenager?! Now, really! Be
honest with me, Boyd. I bet you heard that from Ned Ware, didn't you?
Didn't Ned tell you that?"

The miserable Joyner was staring at his fist.

"Didn't he, Boyd?"

"... Yeah. Well, I heard him saying it to some other guys."

"Well, really! Ha ha. Told you my seventy-year-old father, an ordained
minister, ha ha ... Well, that should give us some idea of what to think of
anything Ned Ware chooses to spew out of his sewer of a fat mouth! Ha
ha. Right?"

Joyner cracked his knuckles. Eventually, he growled, "I know Jimson
was here. If there was somebody with him, I'll find it the cocksucking
out."

It was following this, indeed, clairvoyant remark that Raleigh tossed
Pierce Jimson like Jezebel down into the street of dogs. "Okay, Boyd, I'm
going to level with you, embarrassing as it is. I'd hoped not to have to say
this. Sit back down. SIT. SIT!"

Those formative years in the Marines had left Joyner vulnerable to direct
commands. He sat. And Hayes recklessly continued. "As a matter of fact, I
did see Jimson here in the inn. The Sheffields and Aura and I are here on,
ah, a business matter. And well — now, please keep this confidential, let
me have your word of honor, because even they don't know — I did happen to see, to accidentally run into Pierce. And I'm sorry to have to say, he
did have a woman with him. But I assure you, Boyd. I *assure* you. This
woman was just some little tramp."

Boyd Joyner stared at Raleigh Hayes, known to everybody in Thermopylae as good old, fair-and-square, honest, decent Raleigh, and good old
Raleigh stared back as long as he could bear to, at which point he began
polishing his glasses. "So, Boyd. There's some other explanation. Where *is*

Lizzie? Perhaps called away on an emergency? Perhaps her car stalled?"

Confused, Joyner scratched with both hands at his unshaved face. "She's supposed to be in Columbia at her mother's."

"Columbia, South Carolina?"

"Yeah. I'm going to call her."

"No, don't."

"Listen, don't worry. I'm not going to charge it to you. I've got a card."

"It's not that . . . Don't you think it's a little early? . . . It's only seven twenty-four. . . . ." But Joyner was already at the phone, and Raleigh was halfheartedly searching for something unbreakable to hit him with, when the cursed call went through.

"Ma Leviston? It's Boyd. I want the truth. Is Lizzie there?"

Hayes picked up an iron doorstop. "Now, even if she isn't . . . let's not jump to any false conclusion . . . Let's not exhaust other —"

". . . Lizzie? Yeah, it's Boyd. . . . Nah, I'm . . . at home. . . . Nah, I'm okay. . . . Yeah, I know what time it is, but you weren't there last night, and I like knowing where my wife is. . . . Well, she said she didn't expect you till Thursday. . . . Well, okay, I know she is, but you should have told me if the car . . . Well, but you could have called from the garage. . . . Well, okay, but . . . ."

Sweat was dripping down Raleigh's sides like ice water, as his mind burned. It must be a two-hour drive to Columbia. They must have left the inn within an hour after his encounter with them. Someone from Thermopylae must have warned them that Boyd was on his way. Probably Ned himself. Now he, Raleigh Hayes, was the accessory of an adulteress, God help him. And an adulteress with execrable taste, to boot.

"Well, what was that all about?" asked Aura, returning to their room soon after Joyner had left it to drive back to Thermopylae to kill Ned Ware. "What's Boyd doing here?"

Hayes, exhausted, had climbed into bed. "Don't ask. . . . What are the Sheffields up to?"

She waggled her eyebrows. "My guess would be S.E.X."

"I'm sick of sex!"

Halfway into the bed, she sprang back out. "You know, I think I ought to find that remark insulting, considering."

"Aura, I'm sorry." Raleigh reached for her. "I don't mean you. I mean that goddamn Pierce Jimson."

She turned his head toward her. "Honey, after you get Earley back home, I'd like you to seriously consider seeing a psychiatrist."

"Aura, dammit. I'm going to tell you something. Don't you dare breathe a word of it. I've told a terrible lie!"

"Sweetheart, I won't tell a soul."

"Listen to me. I just stood here and convinced Boyd Joyner that his wife is not sleeping with Pierce Jimson!"

"That was a *lie?*" Aura pounded her pillow into a back rest and sat straight up. "Holy shit!"

" 'Holy shit'? I shudder to think where you get these expressions."

"Raleigh Hayes, this is no time for linguistics. Is that *true?* PIERCE? Pierce the pure? Pierce the Puritan? God of our Fathers Pierce? Yowza!"

And so the Hayeses talked of their fellow Thermopyleans until sleep closed their lips. At noon they awakened and found that rest had cured Raleigh of his sickness with sex. At one, Raleigh went to the bank, located the young assistant manager who had befriended him, and arranged to open a safety deposit box in the name of Jubal Rogers. In this box he placed $4,500. He wrote a note, enclosed the key, and left both at the Battery Carriage Company. At two, the Hayeses began talking again, and they talked, and walked, hand in hand, Raleigh wearing his new jacket, Aura wearing her new jade bracelet, through Charleston, until the sun grew sleepy, too, and rested its head on the edge of the blue harbor bay. Together Mr. and Mrs. Hayes leaned on the old stone seawall to watch the eventide.

"So, honey," said Aura, "that's it. Betty has Bonnie Ellen well in hand. No one's heard from Eddie Dellwood. Aunt Vicky calls every other hour. Four of the Kettell girls are siding with Barbara on the divorce, and the fifth, Agnes, of course, has moved in with Nemours and is cooking the spoiled brat his breakfast. So, my news certainly isn't anywhere near as dramatic as what's been happening to you, you poor man."

Raleigh could see the thrashing silver fish gleam under the waves. "I guess it hasn't really been completely awful," he said. "It's just been consistently awful. And, listen, I don't call deciding to run for mayor of Thermopylae exactly undramatic, for Pete's sake."

"Now, Raleigh, I didn't say I'd 'decided.' I said I'd been approached. I said I was considering it. Naturally, I need to discuss it seriously with you and the girls."

"Naturally . . . Well, seriously, I'm not really ready to take it seriously. Aura, please don't take what I'm about to say wrong —"

"Oh, boy, here we go. If you're ready to say, 'Who's going to take care of the house?,' remember what happened to Nemours Kettell."

"The truth is, Aura, you don't have one iota of political experience."

She pulled indignantly away. "That simply isn't true. I was president of my high school, president of my college student council —"

"That isn't the real world."

"Secretary of the Young Democrats Convention, Southeast U.S. delegate to the International Nursing Congress, six-term president of the PTA, District Six Democratic party alternate, and Mothers for —"

"Honey, I don't need your vita."

"I'm a leader, dammit. I can't help but lead."

"Well, that much I know from trying to dance with you."

"Oh, Raleigh, you can't dance worth a fart."

"Aura!"

"And look at Mayor Poinsett anyhow! He's a joke! He was the fish and game warden! Really, I mean!"

Hayes brushed back the strand of hair that always fell over his wife's eyes when she became enthusiastic. "Well, you certainly are a lot prettier than Billy Poinsett."

"Oh, you are such a chauvinist pig!"

"How in the world can that remark possibly be construed as anti-female, would you mind telling me?"

Aura did not have the opportunity to explain, as she was doubtless prepared to do, for the Hayeses were interrupted by someone calling, *"Pssht! Pssht! Pssht!"* from across the street. Raleigh looked into Battery Park, where he finally spotted a small, elderly, cassocked and bespectacled Catholic priest standing beneath the palmetto trees in the shadow of an immense Confederate cannon.

"Raleigh, honey, there's a little priest over there beckoning to you. I wonder why."

"Yes, ah, yes, just a second. Wait right here. No, actually, why don't you just go back to the inn, see what the Sheffields want to do about dinner, okay? Okay. Thank you."

"Oh, Raleigh!" She squeezed his arm. "Is that Weeper Berg?!"

"Shhh. Yes. He doesn't want anybody to recognize him. Act like you don't see him."

"Oh, all right. But he sounds fascinating. Wish him good luck."

So Raleigh hurried over to the cannon. "What are you up to now, Mr. Berg. Born again?"

"I should laugh at your jokes? It's bathetic. My brother Nate is crying in his grave from shame. You spotted me, hah? Well, what can you do? Even with the peepers?"

"Those glasses must be two inches thick. How can you possibly see?"

"With you, Hayes, I won't cavil. I can't see shit from Shinola. But any-wise, where's Gates? Good news for him. Here's the deal, I took out the Cuban. The fifteen gees on the dogs, forget it. I called a marker."

"I'm sorry, Mr. Berg, I don't even know what you're talking about. But Gates is still in Midway." Raleigh then explained what had happened at "Wild Oaks" after their departure.

Oddly enough, Berg seemed less worried than annoyed by this encoun-ter. "Awwgh, I tell yah, the kid spooks. He's gonna mess me up. So as to this Parisi angle, I'm working on it. But this you should know. It's acri-monious." He hiked up the skirt of his black cassock, which was tangled around his feet, and then pointed with his thumb at Aura, now walking past, ostentatiously ignoring them. "Is that, excuse me sticking my nose in, your conjugal?"

"My wife? Yes, that's my wife, Aura. A surprise visit. She wanted to meet you but I wasn't sure —"

"A beauty, an angel."

"Ah, thank you. Mr. Berg . . ."

"Call me Simon."

"Simon. Gates sent you a message with Mingo. He needs, ah, truck plates and a good body man. Does that mean anything to you?"

"Not to worry." The priest had pulled his cassock up high enough to take some cigarettes out of his pants pocket. "So listen, Hayes. Mind if I call you Raleigh?"

"Of course. Not at all. Please do."

"A pleasure. Weed?"

"Pardon? Ah, no, I don't smoke anymore."

"A wise man." Berg lit his cigarette. "So, listen, we got problems of a serious nature with the lousy Parisi squirt."

"We?"

"Yeah. I am cognizant now of certain facts, and we've got a problem as to this guy's wanting satisfaction for damaged goods, and, I'm kidding you not, 'a stain' on his crummy honor. This Calhoun guy's a Bedlamite, which is no news, considering. He's a lousy Southern meshuggenah on the one side of the tree and a crazy Sicilian Wop screwball in a certain family business, if you catch my drift, on the other. His honor's got a stain, see?" Berg smacked the black cannon with his small veiny hand. "Spare me these gassy high-nose gloryhounds. So this is honor? They should all climb inside here and get shot over the moon."

Hayes adjusted his glasses, but it didn't help. "I guess I don't really catch your drift. I realize that this Calhoun is upset about that necklace . . ."

"Give me a cursory moment. This Cupid is such a nuthouse schmuck, a permanent resident of cuckooland, as per he thinks he's the fucking Scarlet Pimpernel, that the family gives him the brush, yah see?, with all regards to serious business. And keeps him on a leash, with, believe me, a large-size chunk of annuity, and hires Big Nose Solinsky as his keeper, which if you are familiar with the expression of the blind leading the likewise, what more can I say?"

"Let me see. You mean, Calhoun is not, ah, a, ah, serious gangster?"

"Nah. They send these yo-yos out on two-bit back-burner jobs which a cretinous cripple would take as a crummy insult, and otherwise, they let little Cupid play in his sandbox, which is mostly crawling with patooties, and making like he's the King of Dixie on a white horse. You follow?"

Hayes sat down on a bench. "I think so. But is he dangerous?"

Berg crossed himself. "Was Christ a Jew? This however is not our problem. Calhoun, we could handle. The problem is that irregardless that the guy's skull is one-hundred-percent full of air, our pal Cupid is the choice beloved of his grandmother down in Atlanta, G.A., who is, believe me, not an insignificant tomato in the family. Not to mince words with you, Raleigh, your brother's testicles are in this old broad's mitts."

"I see." Raleigh, observing Mr. Vanderhost out in the park with his poodle, bent down to tie his shoes. The man nevertheless called politely, "Good evening, Mr. Hayes," as he strolled past them. Hayes waited before whispering, "So what do we do, Simon? Call the police? . . . Ah, I'm sorry. I forgot. Excuse me."

Berg forgave him with a priestly hand. "A lady of my acquaintance is colloquial with this Parisi broad, and Rose has cut us a deal." He took off his thick glasses, which had brought tears to his eyes.

"Well, gosh, that's very nice of you to go to all this trouble for Gates. Not that he deserves any help after getting himself in this kind of a mess. Keep your back to me, the damn hotel man is staring at us."

"So who deserves help?" Berg pulled his spectacles back on, and shuffled sideways. "God forbid we should get what we deserve. Do I deserve these bowels, which I still can't believe yet the lousy state they're in."

The deal of which Simon Berg's friend Rose had apparently been the negotiator, and of which Berg was now the articulator, was not, the small priest admitted, a flawless deal. It did have its good points. One was that Gates was required to repay only fifty cents on the dollar for the fake necklace, which meant he only owed Cupid Parisi Calhoun $7,500. The second good point was that if the deal were accepted, Mrs. Antony Parisi would call off the hunt, and as there was considerable historical evidence that Big Nose Solinsky had personally sliced off as many ears as the great matador Manolete, this news was bound to be of comfort to anyone unpleasantly involved with him. That concluded the good points. On the contrariety, there were a few drawbacks. They had to go to Atlanta.

"We?" Raleigh kept saying, to no effect.

They had to be at the Peachtree Plaza Hotel on Sunday, where Gates was to apologize formally to Mrs. Parisi for making a fool of her favorite grandson.

Raleigh sighed. "Well, I guess that's not so bad. I don't have to be in New Orleans till Thursday. Atlanta's on the way. At least she doesn't live in San Francisco. At least she isn't going to put a horse head in our beds. At least —"

There was one other drawback. On Monday, at a mutually agreeable site, Cupid Parisi Calhoun, in order to satisfy the stain on his honor (spilled there when his girlfriend publicly called him a sap, a chump, a total flake, and — although this was truly irrelevant to his ignorance of paste jewelry — a premature ejaculator), Mr. Calhoun intended at this site on Monday to fight a duel with Gates Hayes, the choice of weapons to be decided by a cut of the cards.

Raleigh tried to assimilate this, but his brain rejected the data. "Simon, you simply have got to be making this up for some reason I can't at the moment figure out. A duel? Nobody's that crazy."

"So look around." Berg waved his black knobbed hat at all the cannon and stone monuments to glory in Battery Park; some had fresh flowers beside them. "Listen," he added, as Hayes slumped back on the bench. "I'm sorry. I'm an old man. I've got my limits. It's a lousy deal, I wouldn't deny to my own mother, may she rest in peace. But from what could I bargain? And, Raleigh, are you and I gonna say, 'Truth's not truth'? Nah. Truth's truth. Truth is, your brother's a real fuckup. Chuzpah? Yeah. Talent? We should all have such gifts to crap on. I love the kid. But truth's truth. Am I right?"

Raleigh Hayes shook Simon Berg's hand. "Simon," he said, "you're a wise man."

"Raleigh, from a man I spoke too soon calling a censorious s.o.b., this is a compliment."

The tiny convict advised Hayes that he would keep in touch, and as for Hayes's concern about his safety now that the police had announced he

was armed and dangerous, "Not to worry." And as for Hayes's insistence
that perhaps it might be risky for Berg to accompany them to Atlanta,
"Not to worry." Indeed, he was, if complaisant with Raleigh, intending to
accompany them all the way to New Orleans, from which port he planned
to exile himself temporarily to Caracas, where he had a pal yet, God willing, among the living. The alternatives, after all, were prison or shuffleboard, both of which he aspersed. Besides, it was the opinion of Weeper
Berg, with no offense intended, that traveling with the Thermopyleans
provided a perfect cover. "I ask you, are the cops gonna believe for one
lousy minute that a man such as myself — me that was in and out of the
Ingersoll estate vaults in Newport in twelve-o-five flat, using no explo-
sives; plus going solo, irregardless that Chinese ivory is no lightweight
business for a guy my size, with a crummy back, which has given me serious problems from that day to this — that a man such as Simon Jerome
Berg should be consorting with small-town characters such as yourselves?
Never. Believe me, never." As the old priest scuffled tripping off, he
walked right into a woman coming the other way; she must have been a
Catholic, for she bowed to him. He held up three fingers and told her, "I
give you my benison," then hurried on.

Raleigh Hayes sat for a while to think about Right and Wrong. They
had never given him any trouble before, but over the past week, they undeniably had begun, in Flonnie Rogers's phrase, to act up. Raleigh suddenly, and very oddly for so literal a man, started to think of these two
abstractions as circus jugglers who were tossing rings back and forth so
fast that he couldn't tell whose were whose. Here he was, trying to stand
by Right, and somehow ending up on Wrong's side over and over again.
Here he was, despite his fastidious moral balance: protecting an adulteress,
drinking to excess, abandoning his work, throwing away money, getting
in fights, lying, stealing, not to mention aiding and abetting the duping of innocent people while sheltering (indeed, worrying about) an escaped convict (and not even a falsely convicted one, but a confessed burglarizer of
sheikhs and Newport magnates). And yet on the other hand, Berg was trying to help Gates, and yet Gates was a crook himself, and yet Gates was his
blood relation, and yet . . . and so the circus rings flew spinning by. Finally
Hayes just threw up his arms, and knocked them all down together, and
said to himself, "Raleigh, slow down. One step at a time." And with a shrug
unconsciously copied from Simon Berg, he added, "So what can you do?"

He found the Sheffields happily jabbering together in the rockers on the
front porch of the Ambrose Inn. He found Aura in their room on the tele-

phone with his father. Had he forgotten again? No, it was only seven. Was his watch wrong? Was his father in a different time zone? The Azores?

"Just a second, Earley, Raleigh's here." Aura put her hand over the receiver. "He already knew about Roxanne; somebody in Midway told him. He won't come home. The stubborn idiot. I swear, he's exactly like you."

Before taking the receiver, Raleigh said, "That is the most preposterous remark that you have ever, ever made! I am not aware that I am either stubborn, or an idiot."

"Honey, I know you're not." She smiled. "I'll be out on the porch. Try to avoid the old fireworks."

Before any fireworks started, Raleigh and his father talked for half an hour, by far the longest phone conversation they'd ever had. They talked mostly about Roxanne's death and Gates's entanglements and Jubal Rogers's refusal.

"Little Fellow, nobody in the whole world could have done any better than you've done. It's a by-fuck-miracle, that's all."

"You don't know the half of it," Raleigh snarled.

"I bet! Coming up with Gates! And Jubal!"

"I told you, forget it, I can't do it."

"Son, I'm proud and I'm grateful. By God, listen, I'm not doing nearly so well myself. I've had some sad times, Raleigh. Real sad. I went all the way to Memphis looking for somebody. The poor soul'd been dead six years. Six years . . ."

"You did not lead me to believe you were going to Memphis."

"Plus! Transmission went on Big Ellie. Tell chucklehead Jimmy Clay I want my old Chevy back. He pulled a fast one on a helpless old man. I didn't think he had the brains." The thin merry voice was laughing, but it sounded tired, and it occurred to Raleigh that he had never heard his father's voice when it wasn't zestfully (aggravatingly) animated. "So, you're headed for Atlanta?"

Raleigh pressed the phone hard against his ear, which already hurt. "Daddy? Listen to me. Please, will you please, if you won't come home, will you just go see a doctor wherever you are? Will you just go do it?"

Laughter. "Oh, Specs, you've got more sense than that. I don't have time to mess with modern medicine. It's slow and it's sloppy and it's stuck-up and it's missing the point by a mile. Now look, I want you to go back and talk to Jubal again."

"No. Absolutely not. That man is not about to come to New Orleans, or even across the street. I already told you, he gave me the distinct impression he hates your guts."

"He does. So you go back over there tomorrow and tell him I'm not trying to repay some by-God-pissy loan. I know I can't; he doesn't have to point it out. Tell him the money's a damn Christmas present. And — now, can you remember this, Raleigh? — tell Jubal, tell him I've got Joshua's child with me. Tell him I know what happened to Leda Carpenter. And tell him that Josh named the girl Billie. Billie. Off an album. Can you remember?"

Raleigh changed the receiver to his other hand. His wrist ached. "Why don't you tell him? You know where he is now."

"He won't talk to me. Will you do this, will you tell him?"

". . . Oh, dammit, all right. What were the names again?" And writing them down in his notebook, Raleigh said, "I don't know what the hell is going on here, and I don't know why you expect me to keep running your ridiculous errands when you won't even tell me the reason."

"I don't 'expect' you to. No reason in the world why you should put up with any of this. I just want you to."

"Well, I'm sorry, you can't always have what you want."

More laughter. "Oh, sure you can, long as you want the right things."

And here, as usually happened at some point in discussions with his father, Raleigh lost his temper. "Do not start talking that old crap to me. That's your problem, Daddy, you have always done everything exactly as you pleased, and other people have had to pay the price."

"Well, no, son. You want to know something sad but so? I didn't do what I pleased, and other people had to pay the price. I made some dumb mistakes."

"Well, at least you admit it."

"You know the kind of smug uptight pisspot you can be, Raleigh? Well, I could, too. I was, too."

"Listen, I don't care to stand here and be insulted."

More laughter. "Oh, Specs. Hang on to Aura. Promise me that."

"I intend to. You can be sure that I don't intend . . ." Raleigh, who was on the verge of making a sarcastic remark about divorce, stopped himself, and instead said, "I thank my lucky stars for Aura." He was puzzled to hear himself say this, since it was one of his father's expressions, and not one he was in the habit of using. He could hear the weak loose-throated reedy laughter pulsing in and out of the static of long distance. "Daddy. Speak up, it's hard to hear. Will you at least tell me if you're already in New Orleans? . . . Well, will you tell me why you're going there?"

Fading chuckles. "I'm going there to do something I've always wanted to do."

"Fine. That's just great for you. It's just ruining my life, that's all."

"How? Aura said you looked better than you had in years."

"Sure. Right. I hope you know there're only two reasons I'm going to show up there the thirty-first. Two reasons!"

Faint laughter. "Well, I know one."

"One, is to put you in the goddamn hospital. And two, is because I fully expect you to keep your end of this bargain, and not give your estate away to strangers. I think you know that if I remain your executor, you can rely on me to deal with matters such as Gates, et cetera, equably. I don't see what's so funny."

"Oh, Raleigh, you can do what the hell you want with the estate. That's not why you're coming to New Orleans."

"It certainly is."

"Oh bullshit. You're coming to New Orleans because you love me. So long, Little Fellow, I'll call you in Atlanta; want to hear about this dumb-ass duel. Oh Gates!"

"I must say you don't sound very worried about the situation he's gotten himself into."

"Well, I'm not worried." Raleigh could barely hear the voice now. "I'm relying on you. Just like you said. Give that beautiful Aura a great big kiss. Bye-bye."

"Daddy. Daddy? . . . Dammit!" Hayes slammed down the phone and rubbed his ear. Then he walked out onto his balcony and took a deep breath of the sea-rich air. Then he lifted his head all the way back to look up at the stars. "Spit at a star and blind an angel," he said. Then he said, "Mama, you married a nut."

Aura sat alone on the porch rail of the Ambrose Inn, looking out over the park toward the sea. Raleigh watched her for a moment before he opened the screen door. And looking, he brought her, as if he were slowly turning the lens of a camera, into focus; for once unfiltered by the twins, by himself, by hurried conversations at the breakfast table or frantic searches for car keys. There she was, seated on the white-latticed rail of the long piazza, a slender woman in a soft white dress, wearing a jade bracelet the color of her eyes. The sea breeze moved through her hair. It was brown-gold hair, caught up with small combs, and at the nape of her neck wisps of brown gold curled. She wore a gold wedding ring and gold earrings shaped like shells, and to the left of her mouth was a little mole that she had always hated and he had always loved. She sat there, Aura, full of thought and humor and affection, full of life as strange as the thin fragile bone of her wrist. Behind her gleamed the dark sea and the moon-silver moss hanging from the oaks of Battery Park. Raleigh thought of how, among all the old clipper ships once in harbors like this one, laden with sugar and cloth and rice for the New World, how one, thank God, had carried here the family who, after wandering generations, had given birth to Aura Godwin at the right time, in the right place, for him to find her, and, now, stand, seeing her here.

"I was just thinking," she said. "It's so pretty and quiet over in those gardens, you forget what 'battery' means, don't you? That this is where they lined up all those big cannons and shot them at the forts. And those pretty little islands really are forts. And this park was a place for hanging pirates, and flogging slaves, and God knows what all. Raleigh, we've got to ball this world up, toss it in the wastebasket, and start all over again."

"Aura . . . You are, well: Aura . . . I guess I'm going to New Orleans."

"You okay?"

"My mother married a nut."

"Thank God." She held out her hand. "Aren't you going to ask me to call the girls and stay another night?"

"I'm considering it."

"I couldn't wait. I called them an hour ago."

He leaned against the rail beside her. "Are they alive?"

"Holly says, 'Everything's cool.' Caroline says, if we're going to abandon her without a thought to her well-being, the very least we can do, rilly, is give her the station wagon. I told her I was bringing her a present from you. The message is 'Kiss kiss kiss.' How's Earley? I don't like the way he sounds."

"Don't worry, I'm going to bring him back if I have to lock him in the trunk."

"He told you, didn't he, that his house has already been sold? . . . He didn't? Some young couple from Hillston bought it. It really is a cute little house. Sixty-eight thousand."

"Oh, for Pete's sake! That house is worth more than that!"

"Well, you know him. He didn't explain he was signing the money over to Holly and Caroline?"

Raleigh sat down in the nearest rocker. "No. He did not. I trust he fixed it so they can't get their hands on it."

"Nope." Aura looped her sweater over her bare shoulders. "Nope, he fixed it so they *can* get their hands on it."

Raleigh leaped back up. "I don't believe it. Are you trying to tell me that man gave two teenaged girls thirty-four thousand dollars apiece?"

"More or less."

"Now, listen to me, don't you dare say a word to them about it. We'll put it in a trust fund."

"He said he already wrote them a letter."

"That's great!"

"Oh, Raleigh, really, there're worse things than having your children inherit some money. Why don't you just try to trust them?"

"Why don't I trust them? Ha ha. Aura, the driveway's going to be full of cars. FULL."

"And we already have three. Why don't we give them the station wagon?"

"Give it to them?"

"Well, honey, I suppose you could try to sell it to them, but, frankly, they can afford something much nicer. Maybe you could sell them your new Cadillac, and we'll keep the old ones."

"Aura, don't try to make me laugh."

"But I love to hear you laugh. Now, let's go eat, then you can drive me someplace romantic in your fancy car." She hopped down from the porch rail. "I'm starving. It must be the sea air. Or all this sex. Let's go to . . ." And she named the hotel restaurant where the Sheffields were already dining, and where, as it happened, Raleigh had so much enjoyed listening to Gershwin last night.

He took her arm as they walked down the wide white steps banked by azaleas. "Actually, Aura, let's try someplace else. I was in that place last night, and to tell you the honest truth, I have to confess, I don't know how it happened, because you know I don't drink, but somehow, all of a sudden, I was, well, drunk as a skunk, and the piano player was trying to pick me up, and before I'd go back in there again, I'd as soon dance naked in the streets."

CHAPTER

25

Raleigh Leads His Followers South

GATES HAYES HAD STILL NOT ARRIVED in Charleston by Friday evening. His older brother had spent the two days waiting and worrying about him, and had even called the young teacher in Midway, Sara Zane, who insisted calmly that she'd never met anyone named Gates Hayes. She persisted in this denial even when Raleigh assured her that while he knew she'd been instructed to say that, he honestly *was* Gates's brother. Finally he gave up — what a spy the woman would make! — and said, "Miss Zane, if you *do* ever meet him, would you tell him it is imperative, *imperative,* that we be in Atlanta on Sunday. Arrangements have been made to settle a certain situation about which I know my brother's concerned. Would you please tell him I'm still waiting at the Ambrose Inn, and it's eighty dollars a night!"

More accurately, it was a hundred and sixty dollars a night, not including garage fees, restaurants (and drinks); for Raleigh was paying for Mingo Sheffield's room as well as his own. He had determined that this was only fair, since (presumably) the unemployed Sheffield never would have come to so expensive a place on his own. Sheffield was, in a way, a business expense, and as such was entered in the insurance man's meticulous notebook, where all costs connected to his father were accounted, and set against the $2,500 Raleigh had saved by buying Knoll Pond for half of what Earley Hayes had expected to pay. In his fees, he was, of course, very scrupulous; for example, he billed Earley for the carriage ride with Jubal Rogers, but not for the drinks in Rusty's bar. Nor was he even charging his father for his time, only his costs. And if Earley was going to insist he stay in places like the Ambrose Inn, that too was going into the little spiral notebook. Yet, despite the fact that he was not spending his own money (though, in truth, it was his, since his mother should have left it to him in the first place), Raleigh could not stop seeing dollar bills floating past on their way out the French doors and over the balcony. On the other hand, he had to admit that he very much liked his room, particularly because of its memories of Aura. He certainly preferred it to the motels, swamps, thug vans, and slave cabins he'd been in lately. He also liked staying in the same room for more than one night again. He also liked having clean clothes to wear again; not only his new clothes, but the suitcase of his own clothes that Aura had thoughtfully brought him. But, of course, Raleigh was nevertheless a little at a loss. He wasn't comfortable with leisure, and this room didn't even have the television with which he'd grown accustomed at home to escape the time between one working day and the next. (Not that he didn't still feel so guilty about his addiction to this nationally induced opiate that he always kept projects beside his Naugahyde rocker in the family room, so that while he seemed to be dozing off in front of a police chase or family intrigue or expedition to wild kingdoms — for in all honesty, he paid little attention to what he watched — what he was really doing was putting a new plug on the vacuum cleaner or ordering bulbs from a seed catalogue or repairing gears on Holly's bicycle or circling the nonchalantly scrawled incorrect answers on Caroline's algebra homework.)

It was because of this new uneasy leisure that, Friday evening, Raleigh Hayes found himself holding a trumpet he had left stored in the attic decades ago. Aura had brought this instrument with her to Charleston. Having replayed Earley's tape at home, she'd decided that, should Raleigh not be able to locate his father's own trumpet, he could substitute this one. "Just trying to help," she'd said. "What a strange list. I wonder if maybe Earley *has* gone round the bend?"

"Well, I'm glad you finally agree; I've told you that for years."

"I wonder why he wants all these weird things? Or maybe he doesn't want them. Particularly. He just made them up to give you something to do. He just wanted to help you get out of your old rut."

Raleigh had sighed. "Aura, that is too diabolical to contemplate."

Aura had turned her husband to look at himself in the beveled mirror of the tall antique armoire. "Well, it worked, didn't it?" She'd smiled.

Aura had left the trumpet case on the dresser, and two nights after she'd left, Raleigh had absentmindedly taken it out, shaken the silvered mouthpiece from its careful green velvet wrapping, and inserted it in the horn. He was not surprised that at first he could produce nothing but splattering squeaks and incredible pain in his jaws. His face in the mirror was an alarming purple, his neck so distended that he looked to himself like his last sight of Pierce Jimson. Embarrassed, he put the trumpet away, but in a while, he picked it back up, and in a while (pausing every few minutes to gasp for breath), he began to play "Cherry Pink and Apple Blossom White," because this was the last solo he'd practiced, just before he'd precipitately dropped out of the high-school band in order to play basketball (and to avoid any more wisecracks about his father's directing a Negro college band, cracks like "How's it feel, your dad jiving with jigaboos?"). It was typical of Raleigh's lifelong need to stretch lines of continuity between the posts of time, that thirty years after he put the trumpet down, when he picked it up, he began practicing the same piece again.

Finished with a weak splutter, Hayes bent over, dizzy, and held to the post of the carved canopy bed. Just then someone rapped on the door and, without waiting for an invitation, bounced into his room. Mingo, of course.

"Gregory says, could you turn down — Gollee, Raleigh, were you *playing* that?"

"Gregory?"

"Vanderhost. He says it's kind of loud. . . . But, boy, Raleigh, I didn't know you still played. I remember you used to, but I didn't know you still — "

Hayes sat down on the bed. "Where have you been?"

The fat man looked like a Kansas meadow in his yellow sports jacket and green dotted tie. "Downstairs," he said, happily. "Playing bridge with Gregory and Miss Bess and Miss Jenks." (These were apparently the names of the two white-haired ladies in the room across from Sheffield's.) "You know what? They've been together for *fifty-three* years, ever since college, isn't that something?" The wide face crumpled in thought. "You think they'd mind if I asked them if they were Lesbianic, you know, like Shirley MacLaine and Audrey Hepburn in *The Children's Hour,* except with a happy ending?"

"That's up to you," said Hayes. "*I* wouldn't."

"Maybe I won't. Maybe they're shy about it."

"Possibly."

"I wouldn't want to hurt their feelings."

"Naturally." Raleigh rubbed his eyes, and then his neck.

"Raleigh, are you still worrying about Gates? You look kind of sad."

Hayes returned his trumpet to its frayed case. "Mingo. Mingo. I am worried about Gates. I am worried about you. I am even worried about Simon Berg, from whom we haven't heard in three days, and who I strongly suspect is up to no good. I am worried about my father, my family, my self, my clients, and my future. I know this may all seem terribly puny to people like you and Aura who are concerned only about truly large matters like the nuclear apocalypse. But there you are. I'm a petty person who worries about everyday things every day."

Sheffield patted his friend. "You can't worry so much, Raleigh."

"Yes, I can."

"It's like I always say, the Lord will provide."

"I realize that's your opinion, Mingo, and if you want any further proof of what a great job He's doing, just look at these newspapers." Raleigh pointed at a stack of local papers on the foot of the bed. "On the other hand, at least there's nothing about Gates's getting murdered in here."

Sheffield assured Hayes once more that his brother was a man of such adventurous flair that the fat man's own favorite star, the great Burt Reynolds himself, was scarcely his equal. "So stop worrying, really. I've got to get back. Miss Jenks is playing five no-trump, and she's a little mad because I was only queen high in spades, but I figured with my diamond void —"

"Don't let me keep you."

"Well, maybe you can practice some more tomorrow. I sure wish I'd known you still played, Raleigh. The choir's always wanted to have somebody play the trumpet with them Easters and Christmas. Bye-bye," and Sheffield happily returned to the card table.

So cheered had Mingo been by his wife's surprise visit (throughout which they almost never left their blue-violets room except to eat four or five meals a day), that his effervescence had become practically unendurable. At least, unendurable to our hero. To several of the other residents of the Ambrose Inn — obviously including the elderly ladies and the proprietor himself — Sheffield had proved a welcome addition at evening cards and afternoon croquet and breakfast chitchat.

He couldn't even be torn away from the inn to drive with Raleigh to

visit the famous plantation gardens outside Charleston, whose blaze of
colors and maze of patterns had filled the Thermopylean horticulturist
with awe and envy and homesickness for his little Starry Haven greenhouse. Alone, Raleigh had strolled along the paths shadowed by the tu-
pelo trees and water ash and high old cypresses, their Spanish moss trailing
down terraced lawns into the dark lakes and tangling with the lilies there.
Bicyclists whirled past him, clattering over the white arched wooden
bridges and through tunnels of flowers. Two black swans nosed among the
bending lilies at the bank, then seeing Raleigh, glided away together. It
had taken ten dozen slaves ten years to make the bricks, to lay the original
oystershell paths and line them with azaleas, with lavender iris and narcissus by the thousands, to plant the herbs and cut the mazes. It had taken
ten hundred more slaves slogging in vast acres of rice and indigo to pay for
the gardens, for the stable, the house, the Paris sofa, the British clock. War
had burnt the house, death had buried together masters and slaves, time
had rotted the sofa and rusted the clock. Now all was renewed, nurtured
by the fees of tourists like Raleigh Hayes.

Nor when Hayes set out again this evening, could Mingo be persuaded
to break up his bridge set in order to go to the Cakewalk Club, the bar
where, Raleigh had learned from Toutant Kingstree, Jubal Rogers played
on Friday nights. And so at ten, our hero arrived alone at the parking garage to take out his Cadillac; for the bar was some distance away, and by
no means in the best part of town. He found that since his last visit to the
garage the middle-aged attendant there had developed a nervous twitch
that squeezed one whole side of his face shut. "I'm getting spooked," this
man confessed. Raleigh could see why. All the finest cars in Charleston
still had on their left bumpers, green "READY OR NOT, JESUS IS
COMING" stickers, and now, as well, on their right bumpers, red
"HONK IF YOU ♡ JESUS" stickers.

"I'm calling the police. This is a direct personal assault on private property. It could be the Mormons. I'm gonna get a shotgun and some coffee
and catch this guy. I don't care if it's a woman or what it is. I'm gonna
make them take a razor and scrape every one of these things off." The
man's frazzled, lumpish face sagged with distress. "Some of my clients
don't believe in this shit, and even if they did, they've got taste, you know.
This is tacky. I honestly think I oughta call the police."

Raleigh said, "What I don't understand is why you haven't already done
so."

The attendant kept picking at the word "HONK" on the back of a

Lincoln Continental. "I'm a little bit afraid," he groaned, "that it could be maybe my mother. She used to be a Latter-Day Saint and now she's a Second Adventist." He returned to his frenzied scraping.

Hayes had not sat for long in the Cakewalk Club when he was joined by the tall lanky saxophone player, Toutant Kingstree, who stressed at some length the handicaps under which he was performing tonight. As he talked, he stared hard and hopefully at Raleigh Hayes. "You wasn't joking me about the record business? I know sometimes you guys don't let on that you're scouting. Because that last set didn't really show what I can do. Most of these birds I'm playing with are nothing but weekend birds, and they throw me off. 'Sides, no need telling a man like you, this is a nowhere place and a no-pay place. But you stick around for the next number. You stay put."

"Mr. Kingstree, I assure you I have nothing to do with the record business. If I could, if you'd just excuse me so I could catch Jubal Rogers there on his break."

"Jubal's good on the stick, I don't say no. But it was mostly me did the arrangements."

Raleigh slid out from behind his rickety table, where Kingstree was leaning over him, his fingers thrumming the wood corner, and inched his way through the noisy drinkers of the Cakewalk Club, which was actually just a low-ceilinged basement cheaply turned into a bar, jammed with a motley assortment of different-colored chairs and tables. The clientele was just as various, and ranged this Friday from slap-happy teenaged couples, to serious drinking blue-collar men with bunched muscles and sad fretful eyes, to suburban sightseers who laughed too loudly.

Raleigh caught up with Jubal Rogers as the man (cigarette and beer in one hand, clarinet in the other) climbed back up on the small concrete platform in whose corner the drummer looked to be halfheartedly swatting flies on his snare drums. Rogers still wore his white shirt and black trousers, but now had added a red leather vest and thin black silk tie. On one of the beautiful long-fingered hands was a gold chain, thickly woven.

"Mr. Rogers? I've been unable to locate you at the carriage company for two days." As the man made no reply (in fact, without a look in Raleigh's direction, set his beer bottle down on top of the piano, and began changing the reed in the mouthpiece of his very old-looking ebony clarinet), Raleigh went on: "I spoke to my father . . . By the way, did you receive the envelope Wednesday? With the safety deposit box key in it?"

Rogers tested the reed, and (perhaps) nodded. He did not, however, indicate whether he'd gone to the bank and looked into the box, or, for that matter, whether he ever planned to do so. Raleigh could not bring himself to ask directly if he had or not, since, if Rogers could be indifferent to thousands of dollars, so could he; therefore, lips pinched and arms tightly crossed, he said, "I'm supposed to tell you, one, that money is not to repay a loan; my father wants you to know he had no intention of attempting to do that, and knows it can't be done. Two. He very much hopes you will change your mind about New Orleans. Three. Excuse me, Mr. Rogers, it is difficult enough to be put in my position of passing cryptic messages back and forth without a clue to their meaning, but you could at least do me the courtesy of not making me talk to your goddamn back!"

The clarinetist turned slowly around, his arrogant chin raised, smoke from his cigarette curling past the strange gold eyes. "Get the rod out of your ass, man."

"Me? You're the one making this hard!"

The icy smile lifted the cigarette to a tilt. "This was hard a long time before you were born."

"Yes," snapped Raleigh. "So I gather. Therefore, your attitude to me seems a little gratuitous. If you will just listen a minute. . . . Just a moment." Hayes took out the small spiral notebook, which, like his aunt Victoria, he always carried to keep his life neat. "I'm to remind you, he'll be waiting in Jackson Square, the thirty-first, noon to six, and . . ." Raleigh flipped pages, looking for the names. ". . . I'm to tell you he found, or, I'm not sure what he meant, perhaps, has information concerning, someone called Leda Carpenter."

A young glassy-eyed white man with dirty hair leaped up on the platform and started to sit on the piano stool. "How 'bout beating it, Wade," Rogers told him flatly, gesturing with his chin, and the pianist spun in a circle on the stool, mumbled, "Hey listen, no problem," and hurried off.

Rogers lit a new cigarette from the one he had in his mouth. "Yeah? What information? The bitch is dead. I got that news."

"Ah . . ." Raleigh was still watching the alacrity with which the young pianist was backing away from Jubal Rogers, whose capacity to inspire fear was no surprise. "I don't know what information. The other thing he wanted to tell you was he has someone called 'Billie' with him. Josh's child? I presume, in New Orleans, or going to New Orleans. Josh's daughter? My understanding is that the child's name is Billie because — my father wanted you to know — because the name was taken from, ah, a record album. The child . . ." Raleigh stopped. It was only as he said this that, with a rush of adrenaline, he realized the import of his father's statement (for, as usually happened in conversations with Earley Hayes, he'd been too angry to pay close attention to anything except his own indignation). His father had said that he had this young person *with* him, not that he'd located her, or heard news of her, but had her with him. It simultaneously struck Hayes that his original assumption that "Josh's daughter" was a small child might have been wrong. It struck him sharply in the chest that as this person was obviously somehow involved with Jubal Rogers, and as Jubal Rogers was black, and as his father had abducted from the hospital, or escaped with, a young black female, that this girl — merciless logic suggested — the girl in the yellow Cadillac at the bank window and "Josh's child" were the same person. And Raleigh could now see his father's blue eyes laughing at Ned Ware's nosy inquiries about his companion, and blithely saying he planned to marry the girl. Earley had never liked the slanderously candid Ware, and was no doubt teasing him. No doubt. At least, it was possible.

So caught up in these sudden reflections had Raleigh been that he hadn't observed Jubal Rogers's response to his message. Now, he noticed that the man had walked all the way to the other side of the platform and that he was breathing so deeply his whole upper torso lifted and fell. Finally, he turned around again and walked back, his hands tight in his pockets, his cigarette tight in his mouth. When he took it out to speak, it seemed to Raleigh that the gold-braceleted hand was trembling. But all he said was, "Repeat it."

So Raleigh told him again everything his father had said, adding that he knew no more than what he had already conveyed, except, and unless, a report that his father had abruptly and ill-advisedly left the Thermopylae hospital with a young woman meant that she was the person in question. "My aunt discovered that Daddy had left with a young female, ah, vagrant brought there for observation. And then the manager at my bank saw them together, but this fool, instead of having the sense and the decency to call me, allowed a man in my father's condition to withdraw huge sums of money and take off all over the country in a convertible. Which is why, Mr. Rogers, I agreed to try to locate you. Daddy is, frankly, a little bit deranged, and he's obsessed with the notion of going to New Orleans for some reason, and of your coming too."

It was apparent to Raleigh that his message had stabbed a crack in the ice that enveloped Jubal Rogers. The black man had lit still another cigarette from the one burning in his mouth. His face was curtained in smoke, but through it Raleigh could see thoughts hurry across the tense eyes; it made him eager to leave the man to his privacy. "Well," he cleared his throat, "Mr. Rogers, I regret it if I've unwittingly brought you bad news. I won't trouble you any further. Good-bye." But the gold-flecked eyes had not dismissed him, and he couldn't move.

Rogers removed the cigarette to rub one knuckle over his lips. "You said Flonnie told you. She still alive?" The voice, no less hostile, was slightly tentative, almost imperceptibly so, but Raleigh was now listening so intensely that he could hear the difference, and it confused him.

"Yes. She's, naturally, not very well. She's over a hundred now. She's in a nursing home near Goldsboro. I went there to ask about you."

"Who's your aunt?"

"Pardon? I have several aunts. You mean the one I mentioned? Aunt Victoria?"

Rogers picked up his clarinet. "She alive?"

"Yes."

"Back in the country?"

"Back? Oh. Oh, yes. Of course. In Thermopylae. Well, she's fairly elderly. She's retired. More or less . . . Did you —"

"You keep up with her?"

Raleigh leaned back from the smoke. "Aunt Vicky? Well, yes. She and I are . . . I gather you knew my family?"

". . . Yeah." Jubal Rogers's fingers were now moving rapidly over the stops of the clarinet. "Yeah, I knew your family. My aunt kept their house clean." Ice sealed the haughtiness of his face back into a handsome mask. "Tell Earley, it's the wrong time, and the wrong et cetera. Tell him I don't believe him. Tell him we've all been dead a long long time. Tell him anything you feel like, mister." He dropped the cigarette onto the concrete floor, put the clarinet to his lips, and, without preamble, blew a remarkably intricate run of notes, rolling up quickly from the soft mellow bass to sharp thin high triplets. This was apparently a signal, for the drummer slapped hard at his snare drum, and the pianist sneaked back onto the stool.

Turning away, Raleigh saw the elongated shadow of Toutant Kingstree rise against a corner wall. The musician leaned over to shake someone's hand, then strolled toward the band. He nodded as he stretched one long leg up on the platform, and whispered, "Okay, catch my riff now, you'll see what I mean."

But Raleigh was too preoccupied to do more than nod; preoccupied not merely by his disquietening conversation with Jubal Rogers, nor by his shock at having that amazing burst of melody thrust in his face. For the man with whom Kingstree had been huddled was none other than Weeper Berg (now back in Lady Wetherell's tuxedo). Hurrying over to the smoky corner, Hayes crossed his arms and said, "What are you doing in here, Simon? And where have you been?" Not only had he not heard from the convict since their talk in Battery Park, his concern had intensified after reading in the Charleston newspaper that a small oil painting of Saint Elizabeth greeting the Virgin Mary (long the property of an affluent Catholic church nearby) had miraculously disappeared during the dedication of the new parish hall.

"I'm a jazz lover." Berg sipped coffee and neatly tapped his cigarette in the ashtray.

"I'm here on business."

"Likewise myself."

As Raleigh pulled out the wobbly chair to sit, a woman, on the arm of a portly, overdressed man, paused at their table. She brushed aside enough of her long auburn hair to say, "Raleigh! Surprise, surprise. Guess you do love music, okay. How goes it? See you around. Take it easy."

Her hostile companion muttered, "Come on, Rusty, let's go," and pulled her past them.

"Not the conjugal," Berg said with a shake of his head. "Concubinal, in my opinion. But a tomato, I grant you."

"Oh, for Pete's sake." Raleigh sat down. "Look here, what were you talking to Toutant Kingstree about?"

"You're familiar with the man? Correct my apprehension, Raleigh. Didn't you say you'd never been in this town?"

"I just met him. And that woman was a piano player . . ."

"Like she said, you're a music lover."

"And, listen to me," Hayes lowered his voice. "Did you steal that goddamn painting in the newspaper, out of a *church,* for God's sake? Is that why you were in that cassock?!"

Berg straightened his slipping black mustache with finger and thumb. "You're an incredulous man, Hayes. A crummy agnostic is what you are."

Raleigh stared at him, then blushed. ". . . Well, all right, I'm sorry. I suppose I did jump to conclusions. But frankly —"

"So, you got the word? Our kid's in town."

"Gates? No! Where is he? When? No."

"I checked by the Ambrose. He'd just made the call and Faggy Sheffield gave him my message."

Eager as Hayes was to know what Berg was talking about, he was compelled to interject, "Simon, please stop calling Mingo, 'Faggy.' He is not, ah, gay. If you knew how extremely, in fact, nauseatingly, uxorious he is, you'd realize —"

"I don't know this 'uxorious.' "

"Wife-loving."

"Good word." Berg raised his tiny hands. "No offense intended. Just a tag. Anywise I left word with . . . Fatty Sheffield that Gates should take the truck out to this guy Kingstree's place." He gestured at the musician up on the platform. "If you'd clued me you had the acquaintance of the sax player, I coulda saved walking my dogs off, which, believe me, are none of the best. I'm an old man."

Gradually, Raleigh translated the convict's narration: Despite Toutant Kingstree's contention that everything on his property was intended for his own personal use, he somehow had acquired the reputation of a man of business — and not only the poultry and pork business, but the automotive junk business; his more specific reputation was that of a man of such civility and discretion, he never inquired too closely into the transformations of color, shape, and origins which vehicles underwent on his premises — as if there were, unknown to him, a modern Circe living there who had not only filled his milk truck with swine, but amused herself by changing red Mazdas from South Carolina into gray ones from Missouri. Kingstree's reputation (however undeserved) had this evening come to Weeper Berg's attention, and he had therefore left a message with Mingo at the Ambrose Inn that when Gates called, he should drive to Kingstree's place on the outskirts of town the tractor-trailer truck (once the livelihood of Fred Zane). For Berg (though not Raleigh) had assumed, as soon as he heard the request for truck plates and a good body man, that Gates would be bringing this truck to Charleston. And Gates had called, according to Mingo, an hour ago, and gotten Berg's message.

And so the travelers left the Cakewalk Club to go meet the former French filmmaker. That is, they stood up to leave, but Raleigh was stopped at the door by an incredible ululant wail of music. Up on the platform, and to the surprise of the rest of the band, desultorily strumming through "People Who Love People Are the Luckiest People in the World," Toutant Kingstree had bounded out of his chair, leaned almost over in a backbend, lifted the curved saxophone to the ceiling, and launched into a cantata of syncopated blues so astonishing that the white middle-aged singer (also a waitress, and not very professional at either occupation) slid off the note on which she had in any case not been too securely seated, and closed her mouth. So too, soon, did many of the noisily chatting patrons, as they couldn't hear what they were saying, much less — and perhaps less interestingly — what was being said to them. So, too, and not pleasantly, did the Cakewalk's owner, who paid this informal band less than he did his dishwasher, and expected from them the same unobtrusive service to his guests.

The deep loose-throated saxophone talked on alone for some time in a soliloquy of such emotional virtuosity that grief chased joy and pleasure pushed anger tumbling out of the horn's mouth. Now, Jubal Rogers shoved back his chair, moved over beside Kingstree, and somehow slid a melody into the saxophone's monologue, turning it into a conversation. It was a tune Raleigh vaguely recalled. The black glow of the clarinet and the glistening brass horn swayed and leaped and darted in and out of the song like moths at a light. Then Toutant slung the saxophone to his side, and in a graveled voice started singing, while Jubal Rogers's slender black clarinet sang with him.

> And if you were mine,
> I could do such wonderful things.

And they finished singing together as Raleigh and Weeper stood in the doorway listening. Some people clapped; some people looked annoyed. Rogers sat back down, and the waitress started singing, "Raindrops Keep Falling on My Head."

"With you," said Berg, as they got into the Cadillac, "I won't mince words. That was music. This much I'll tell you, if those shit-kicking Glory Bound Boys coulda played like that, I woulda had a serious problem as regards to skipping."

Raleigh tapped Jimmy Clay's little bowling ball key chain. "Yes. That was music . . . " He thought with a blush of his spluttering attempt back at the Ambrose Inn to push noise, much less notes, through his trumpet.

"So Gates always claimed how you guys come from yourself a serious musical family, am I right?"

"Well, I'm not sure I'd call them serious. But, yes, most of my father's family played some sort of instrument, or sang, or something." Back in time, he was again on the Hayes porch that wrapped around the huge white house. His father was on the swing again, between Little Em and Uncle Bassie (himself still a boy). The glistening trumpet leaned out to Raleigh, song without effort rolling from the circle of gold. Near him, Hackney's fat fingers leaped up and down the ukulele's neck. "My father, well, yes, he was musical. After he, ah, retired from the ministry, he taught in a small college and coached their, well, their band. But I guess he'd always played the trumpet informally."

"Likewise yourself?" asked Berg.

Hayes shook his head.

"No? Fatty Sheffield tells me otherwise tonight. Puts yah on the trumpet."

"Not really." Hayes kept tapping the little globe that spun from the key chain.

"Says meanwhile he plays the piano himself." Berg snorted. "So, listen, we got a lousy road show here."

"That's for certain." Raleigh turned on the ignition. "Listen, Simon, I apologize again for what I said about the church painting. But, you know, Newport's one thing, but a painting that's a part of a *church* . . ."

Berg wiped his eyes. "So the Vatican's a shack? So somebody *gave* them the Apollo Belvederes and the Pharaoh's gold coffins? Raleigh, Raleigh, my pal, yah wanna be such a cynic, yah gotta acclimate yourself to the crummy world, which, believe me, has screwed over bigger and sharper boys than you, not to mention the entirely innocent by the trainload. This particular painting to which you have reference was donated to this tax-free church, see, on an April fourteen years back by a bimbo who needed the write-off, and it was given to bimbos who woulda rather had more real estate any day, but they hundred-percent insure it for what they figure it is, and stick it on the wall and give it the go-by for two score. Which I figure, if the blind rubes didn't know what they had, then such is the price of bimbodom, if you catch my drift. A Clouet, I still can't believe yet!"

Raleigh turned off the motor, and buried his head in his arms on the steering wheel. "Simon, did you steal that painting?"

"I'm a Jew. What do I want with some old picture of the Virgin Mary kissing her cousin? Jews like Chagall. Jews like Picasso. Jews, read your Bible, like abstractions. But it's a beauty, Raleigh. Chagall should learn to paint like that when he got to Heaven, may he rest in peace."

It *was* a beauty, as Hayes had the opportunity to observe for himself when, jostled in the van of a huge truck on the road to Atlanta, he opened his great-grandmother Tiny Hackney's trunk and saw, swaddled in the old Confederate uniform, the pregnant mother of John the Baptist embracing the pregnant Mother of Christ, and both of them smiling up at Raleigh, happy as larks, innocent of their sons' futures, luckily unable to see the head on Herod's platter, the body on Pilate's cross.

It was not however until very late Saturday night that Hayes glimpsed the painting, for (while he'd seen his brother Friday evening, and again the next morning — when Gates had announced he was working on a little surprise before they "rolled out") it was not until eleven that night that Gates finally invited him back to Toutant Kingstree's domain, threw out his arm like a ringmaster at the giant truck gleaming with wet red paint, and said, "TA DA! Step right up, Ladies and Gents, and let's move ass!"

Our hero therefore had all day Saturday to prepare himself to assimilate Gates's insane traveling plans. It was not enough time. Particularly as Raleigh was so busy impatiently listening to Betty Hemans telling him in one word how his life insurance business was doing ("Fine"), and in several thousand more words, long distance, how she planned to send Lady Evelyn alone in a motor launch across the English Channel to rescue her first love off the beach at Dunkirk. Raleigh had no idea how much gas Lady Evelyn might need for two crossings, nor any idea why in the real world the janitor Kaiser Bill Jenkins might have run moaning from the office when Bonnie Ellen Dellwood walked into it, or locked himself in the supplies closet and refused to come out, despite Mrs. Hemans's assuring him there were no ghosts in the Forbes Building.

Raleigh was also busy checking by the carriage company to see if in fact Jubal Rogers had picked up the bank key. He had. On the other hand, he had still not come back to work. This, however, was nothing new; he periodically disappeared, and seemed to have little interest in whether they rehired him or not. "Tell him, if you see him," Raleigh said to the young cashier, "we're leaving tonight from Kingstree's place, and he's . . ." He cleared his throat to force out the words, "he's welcome to come along."

The cashier was puzzled. "Come along? Well, okay, but I wouldn't count on it. He's a funny guy."

"Not really," replied Hayes.

Most of all, Raleigh was busy trying to track down Mingo Sheffield to tell him to start packing; in his case, an elaborate undertaking. For Sheffield had suddenly decided he'd better go sightseeing before he missed out on everything and never got another chance. Consequently, he'd risen early to escort Miss Bess and Miss Jenks on the "General Beauregard" boat tour to Fort Sumter, then on the old-fashioned trolley tour, then through as much of the "Festival of Houses" — "the loveliest homes in Charleston" — that Miss Bess's arches could bear, then on a quick trip out to Magnolia Plantation, where the fat man had nobly declined a mini-stagecoach ride for fear of straining the miniature pony who pulled the coach around the lawn. Mingo lost all track of time, he was having such fun.

Meanwhile, unable to locate him, Raleigh had settled his bill with Gregory Vanderhost, who politely never glanced at his check. The hotelier, seated at a Hepplewhite inlaid tea table, was at that moment copying out on monogrammed cards for his friendly Thermopylean acquaintance, the recipes for his callico scallops and his crab purloo, apparently in exchange for Mingo's Carolina squab and his secret barbecue sauce. Vanderhost gave Raleigh several leads for tracing his friend, so our hero set forth again for Market Hall. The guide at this replica of the Temple of Wingless Victory, used by the Daughters of the Confederacy to house relics of the War of Northern Aggression, remembered the huge man in the green sports coat vividly, not only because he'd arrived with a grandmother on each arm, but because he'd burst into tears at the sight of Robert E. Lee's silver camp cup. Next, at the Old Alps Rathskellar, the waitress in Bavarian apron, white knee socks, and red cap remembered Sheffield very well as two Bratwurst, double Low Country oysters, three steins of beer, and a strudel. And finally, Raleigh found the fat man himself in front of the Old Slave Mart Museum and Gift Shop. He stood by a blue rack, painted to match the blue shutters on the building, where handwoven sweetgrass and pine-needle baskets hung. He was talking to a black woman who sat on a folding chair beside her finished work. In her hands twisted the long palmetto fronds she was weaving into a mat.

"Excuse me," said Hayes. "I've been looking all over for you, Mingo! We're going, you've got to pack! Where are your lady friends?"

"Poor things, their feet gave out." Sheffield held up to the black woman a shallow flower basket, then a square picnic box. "Nancy, I guess I can't make up my mind."

The woman, who'd assumed she'd lost another sale to a claim of indecision, nodded tolerantly, but then Sheffield announced that he was ready to take both if she would accept Visa or a check. As she would accept neither, Raleigh had to "lend" Mingo "a little more cash," which Mingo promised to repay as "soon as things picked up."

"What things?" Hayes raised an eyebrow. "Before you worry about the Lord providing for me, you better ask Him to start providing for you."

"I have a feeling Vera's lingerie business is going to just take right off."

"Really?"

"I can't decide. You think we should call it 'Naughty but Nice' or 'Sweet and Sassy'?"

"Neither," said Hayes, hurrying ahead to his parking garage. "I think you should call it 'Vera's of Thermopylae.' "

"Gollee, that's a *great* idea! You always did have great ideas. Hey, Raleigh, wait up."

The garage attendant's bloodshot eyes pleaded with Hayes for sympathy. Hand-painted green letters two feet high announced all the way along the concrete wall, "HE IS COMING!" "I'm about to the point where I wish

He would, and take me out of my misery," the attendant groaned, his cheek twitching. "I can't take too much more. I'm losing my best customers. I just nipped out for a sausage sub, that's all. Don't I have a right to eat? Don't I have a right to sleep once in a while?"

"Just call the police!" Raleigh said.

"Sure, sure, would you? On your mother? And your son? Eleven years old?" He threw a bucket of water at the wall.

By the time Mingo had finished hugging Miss Bess, Miss Jenks, and Gregory Vanderhost, Gates had called again to tell the Thermopyleans to shake a tail feather. "It's ten twenty-seven, Ace, so says this heavy metal watch my, awwwh!, big brother gave me. Oh, few changes in the game plan."

"Gates, frankly I'd like to see a *lot* of changes in the game plan. What now?"

"Catch you later, Big Bro."

And so it was nearly eleven when, by the light bulbs hanging from crisscrossed wires, Raleigh saw, among the wrecked cars and smashed buses, like a Renaissance cardinal surrounded by crippled beggars, the freshly painted, shiny bright red eighteen-wheel tractor-trailer truck. Beside it, smeared with red paint, proudly stood Toutant Kingstree, Weeper Berg, Wade (the thin, dirty-haired pianist from the Cakewalk Club), and (stripped to his black silky bikini jockey shorts) the gorgeous Gates Hayes, who kept shouting, "TA DA!" and flinging out both arms. Finally he stopped. "Well, shit, Raleigh, aren't you going to say something?"

"It's pretty," Mingo said.

"Listen, man," Gates put his hands indignantly on his bare hip bones. "We had to do a whole engine overhaul, new tires, you name it. Right, fine. I drove this babe here with bobby pins! And four fucking tires missing. So let's hear a few cheers for the kid. We've been working like madmen for twenty-four hours."

"Like madmen is right," Hayes muttered. "I just frankly can't make myself understand why we have to take this damn eighty-foot truck to Atlanta in the first place!"

The red-splotched Gates (who looked, according to Mingo, like Tyrone Power in a South Seas epic, after a fight with the natives) crossed his arms with remarkable ease for a man wearing in public only bikini underpants and a wristwatch. "Raleigh, don't hassle me now, I can't handle it. I already explained."

"You did not explain. You *announced*. There's a difference."

"Fine. Right. My bike won't fit in the Cadillac. Right? Right. I do not have seventy-five hundred dollars to pay back Calhoun. I do not even have seventy-five dollars. I am planning to trade the semi, which is worth, what, Toutant? Twenty?"

"I don't say no," nodded the black man. "Depends on the heat."

"Not to worry," Weeper Berg assured him, "It's strictly kosher. A bequest from the maternal."

Gates was rubbing with a rag at the chrome side mirror. "So, Raleigh, comprendo? I throw myself prostrate, right?, at this Mrs. Parisi's feet, and I say, *'Buon giorno, bella bella mamma mia, come sta?* You wanna you dough? I no gotta you dough. You takea dis truck instead, *si?'"* He turned and grinned. "See?"

Raleigh reminded himself to breathe. "What the hell does Calhoun's grandmother want with a tractor-trailer truck?"

"Shuffleboard court?... Morgue?... How should I know? Everybody can use a truck."

Berg poked at Mingo with a tiny red finger. "So, Sheffield, let us take a hike from these two; it's getting acrimonious. You can help Kingstree and his pal here lock up the pig farm. I'm adverse to associating with an acre of pork. My brother Nate is down in his coffin getting sick to his stomach."

"I eat those pigs. They're just for my personal use," Kingstree reminded them.

Berg said, "From Sheffield, this I would believe. From you? My uncle Saul walked with not one lousy kopek to his name out of crummy Russia, seven hundred miles on his own two dogs, carrying my cousin Tettie in his arms, and when he got off the boat at Ellis Island, he had more fat on his bones than you do, Kingstree. So don't tell me what you eat. I know what you eat. You eat nothing." The voices faded back to the cemetery of dead cars.

Raleigh had not calmed down. "All right, all right. Now if you'd just explain why you don't drive the truck and *I'll* drive the Cadillac by myself? If you'll just explain why I have to put the Cadillac *inside* the goddamn truck!"

"Save gas?" grinned Gates. He gave a brisk polish to the Rolls-Royce ornament now fixed to the front grille. "Awwwh, come on, one big happy family. Stick together, thick and thin. Besides" — he swatted a leaf off the grille with his rag — "besides, the Caddy's been spotted."

"So what? Simon has very, ah, considerately arranged it so you don't have to worry about that. All you have to worry about is not getting killed in your duel. Ha ha." Yes, what could he do but admit that within two weeks Life had shoved him on the stage of a play so preposterous he could actually say such lines with a straight face.

"*Che sera, sera,* Raleigh. But about the car, it's a little more complicated. Later for that. Just keep the faith." Gates stepped back, muscles glowing, to admire his vehicle. "I don't want Weep to worry. He's a worrier."

"*He's* a worrier? And what do you mean you don't have seventy-five dollars? You had more than four hundred that you cheated out of poor Mrs. Wetherell's guests."

"They were having fun. And 'poor Mrs. Wetherell'? The babe's got twelve mink coats, living damn near in a tropical zone, and one of them's *plaid.* A cool dozen, count them!"

"I hope she did, after you left."

"Wow, that hurts. And here when I've got this nice surprise for you." Gates took his brother's arm and led him around to the other side of the truck. Big gold-glittered letters spelled out across the glistening red side, "THE KNICK-KNACK GEM-CRACK HIGH-TIME CIRCUS."

"TA DA!"

Hayes nodded. "Well, it is a surprise. . . . But I don't get the point. If you're planning to trade this truck in, or give it to Mrs. Parisi, or whatever you think you're going to do, what's the point in painting it red and writing this circus nonsense on the side?"

"For fun!" Gates, to Raleigh's shock, stood on his hands. Then on one hand. Then flipped back upright, tossing the black curls from his eyes. "Oh shit, man, don't tell me you really don't remember? Daddy's circus? Every summer? Family reunion? Forbes Park? Hey, come on, Raleigh!" Gates grabbed his brother's head in both hands and shook it. "Think back. Damn, that's the very first memory of my whole fucking life, and it slipped your mind? Lovie in her clown suit? Old Roxanne the coochie dancer? Uncle Bassie and His Famous Dancing Dog, Alexander the Mutt?" Gates laughed. "Remember Daddy drunk on the tightrope a foot off the ground? You don't remember *any* of that? I mean, I know you didn't exactly join in with a big gung ho, but a couple of times I'm sure you played your trumpet for the Grand Finale. 'Now presenting, in the center ring, every blessed member of the Hayes Family we could corner, in the Grand Finale of the Great, Unique, Never Before and Never Again Till Next July KNICK-KNACK GEM-CRACK HIGH-TIME CIRCUS. Ta da'?" Gates looked at his brother with an odd sweet smile. "Hey? Raleigh?"

"Yes," Hayes said. "I remember."

"Whew!" Gates tapped him on the chin. "Auld lang syne. Family reunion. All that jazz. Now, let's roll. I've got a duel to fight! Off to the field of gauntlets flung. Foggy mist. Muffled cloaks." He lunged suddenly into a fencing position and twirled an imaginary foil. " 'Tis for thee, fair Lulu Belle, loved I not honor more or less." Forward he pranced, shouting, "Ha! Aha! Lay on, signore, and be pissed with thee!"

"Gates, Gates," sighed Hayes, and he thought of his daughter Holly's response to his demand that she be nicer to Caroline: "How'd you like to be her twin for the rest of *your* life?" "Gates, how in the world can we be brothers?"

"Beats me," grinned the naked swashbuckler.

"Would you mind telling me, one, why you don't have any clothes on?"

"Hey! My threads are hand-tailored, man, I don't work in them. I *work* in them, if you know what I mean. My life's a mess, but my clothes are clean! Speaking of sameo, Big Bro, where'd you pick up the pinstripe? Not bad. Little too Wall Street maybe, but not bad. 'Course, I really liked you in that white number Mingo got you in Kure Beach. It made a statement, you know. 'Stud coming.' "

Hayes ignored this. "Two. What did happen to that four hundred dollars?"

Gates slapped the side of the truck cab. "You think Toots *gave* me these parts? Paint? Tires? Well, he practically did. I got a new carburetor in here. You didn't see this babe before, Raleigh, up on ole Fred's blocks. She was Turd City, no kidding."

"Yes. And wasn't this vehicle left to Sara Zane, not to you? Do you think it was fair, talking her into giving it up?"

"Yeah, well, skip it. I can't handle talking about Sara. I'm a flyer, Raleigh. Can you see me waltzing down the aisle with a *kindergarten* teacher?"

"No, frankly." Raleigh was about to begin the lecture "The Costs of Irresponsibility," when his brother changed the subject with news that pushed Sara Zane's financial problems out of his head. Gates changed the subject because (as Raleigh didn't know, but the reader may recall) he had recently possessed more than four hundred dollars; ten times more. He had brought to Midway in his shaving kit $4,000 in cash, money he'd received for making not his first, as Raleigh thought, but his fourth, pickup run to Smith's Island in the motor launch "Easy Living." This money he had vaguely planned to use to buy time from his numerous creditors. Instead, he had given every penny of it to Sara Zane, so she could give every penny of it to Roxanne's hospital, pharmacy, and funeral home. In exchange, Gates had accepted Fred's old truck, which Miss Zane had been ready to sell for $500 to an importune junkman who'd told her it was useless except for a few spare parts. There were many reasons why Gates did not want to tell his older brother that he'd given Sara $4,000, and the least important was that he didn't want Raleigh to ask him where he'd gotten the money in the first place. The fact is, he didn't want Raleigh to think he cared about Sara Zane, or, for that matter, about Roxanne, or, for that matter, that he could feel any strings at all tugging him earthward. The fact is, he was embarrassed that what he'd done might be construed as a good deed, and he certainly didn't want anybody to know he'd committed one of those. He was, as he confessed to Mingo Sheffield, a funny dude. So he changed the subject. "By the way, this Toots Kingstree cat's coming along with us to New Orleans."

"What?!"

"He's fixed it with his buddy Wade back there to herd his livestock. Okay by you? I mean, this is your show, Raleigh. I'm along for the ride. Myself, I don't mind. Nice old guy. Plenty of room under the big top." He banged the truck's side.

"What? Kingstree's coming? Why?"

"Got me." Gates shrugged. "Weird guy. Seems to think you're going to get him a contract with RCA Victor or something. Look, hell, he'll pay his own way. More than I can do. Sorry, Raleigh. Lucky you're loaded."

"I am not loaded, I assure you!" Hayes crossed his arms tightly.

"Hey, don't con a conner. Remember, I've been in your pockets. Fatsville. Okay, as my big brother would say, it's 11:12:45 in the post meridian. Haul ass."

And it was 12:03:19 A.M. by the time the group had dressed (Berg reappearing in a fedora and a suit of bold checks), by the time they had hooked up the ramp so Gates could drive the white Cadillac up into the belly of the circus truck, by the time Raleigh, like a dyspeptic Jonah, had crawled inside to lash down the car with chains. Even with a Cadillac, a motorcycle, a ramp, a trunk, a bass fiddle, Toutant Kingstree's bundles (for the saxophonist seemed to anticipate a long stay in the city he called the Land of Dreams), even with Mingo's souvenirs and Mingo himself, the space inside the truck's trailer was immense. There was room for the mattress, canvas chair, battery lights, plastic water jug, quarts of whiskey, and twenty ham sandwiches Kingstree was donating in exchange for his passage. There were all the comforts of home; even a small window up near the cab, for air and for yelling at Gates to slow down.

"Mr. Kingstree," said Raleigh, as the tall black man shoved a giant cardboard box into the truck. "Are you sure it's wise for you to just get up and go like this? I mean, to leave your business so precipitously?"

Kingstree sucked on his lips hard. "I'm in the music business. Mr. Hayes. Fifty years. It's time I took my chance. I'm ready." He was dressed for travel in a suit of black and blue vertical stripes, a black satin shirt and three gold chains.

"Well, I'm a little worried. A man your age taking off—"

"My age? I'm sixty-four. You were talking to Jubal, weren't you? He's three, four years older than me, maybe more. Doesn't look it, but it's so. Listen, I won't let you down. When you got the talent, age just smooths it out."

Hayes gave a last look out over the junk-crowded yard where the young pianist stood waving farewell to Kingstree. "You didn't happen to see Rogers today, did you? He didn't come by here asking for me?"

Kingstree pulled the metal doors closed with a clang. "I keep telling you, man, you don't need Jubal. I'm the one you need."

Maybe, thought Hayes, facetiously, as the truck lurched forward, maybe Toutant Kingstree was right. Of course, he'd never really expected Rogers to show up to join, ha ha, the circus. Maybe it had been so long since his father had laid eyes on Jubal Rogers, maybe, ha ha, Raleigh could palm the saxophonist off on Earley Hayes as the lost clarinet player from Thermopylae. "Mama, why did you ever leave Philadelphia?" sighed our hero, as he opened his great-grandmother's trunk and saw the Virgin Mary smiling at him. "Very funny," he told the Mother of God, and slammed down the lid.

CHAPTER

26

In Which Our Hero Enters Atlanta with
More Passengers Than He Expected

THE SHINY RED KNICK-KNACK GEM-CRACK HIGH-TIME CIRCUS
stopped outside St. George because Mingo had forgotten to go to the
bathroom before they left Charleston. Stopped outside Midway so Gates
could call Sara. "At one-thirty in the morning," said Berg. "I should feel
so concupiscent again before I croak." Stopped in Montmorenci because
Berg's bowels were letting go. Stopped on the outskirts of Augusta because it was discovered that Toutant Kingstree had sneaked a baby pig
into the truck in a cardboard box — a runt that the sow wouldn't
suckle — and it had to be walked. "Pigs are smarter than dogs and cleaner
than cats," he promised the other passengers. "Pet her. Her name's
Peaches."

"Thanks but no thanks." Simon Berg pushed away the squirmy pink
rooting nose. "I am not complaisant with pigs. Hereditarily. Keep it in
the box. Awgh. Let me sleep, wll yah? I'm a lousy senior citizen. My guts
can't take this pace."

So Berg wrapped himself in blankets on the mattress, and Mingo took
his place in the cab. Mingo, in tribute to Burt Reynolds, had always
yearned for a chance, if not to take the wheel of a big semi (which Gates,
remembering how the fat man had backed the U-Haul over the incline at
Reverend Joey Vachel's marathon revival, vetoed), then at least to sit in

the buddy seat, where — if the truck had only been equipped with a CB radio — he could have listened in for warnings of smokies ahead. So happily up in the cab, beside the urn of Roxanne's ashes, Mingo smoked and chewed gum while he described to Gates the splendors of the Ambrose Inn (the cut flowers on the dresser, the mints on the pillow, the wine bottle in the mini-bar). "Gates, I just wish you and Weeper could have stayed there and met Gregory; instead of Weeper wandering around and losing my Myrtle Beach bear like he did."

"Bet you the pissers don't take Jews," said Gates, bouncing behind the giant steering wheel, a beer between the legs of soft tawny leather pants that perfectly matched his high boots and wide-shouldered jacket.

"That's not true!" Mingo protested. "Gregory's mother is Jewish. She goes to the synagogue. It's the oldest nonstop synagogue in the whole country, right there in Charleston. And, anyhow, Gregory's not prejudiced. Two of his best friends are Lesbianic."

"From what you tell me, doesn't sound like ole Greg's exactly Mr. Macho himself." Gates downshifted and roared around three cars and a Greyhound bus.

Sheffield's face sagged into seriousness. "You know, maybe some people aren't as macho as you are, Gates, but that doesn't mean they aren't nice."

The handsome driver laughed as he slapped Sheffield's knee. "Damn straight. We can't all go tearing into Marines, you know."

Back in the trailer, Weeper Berg was groaning that he might as well be lying on nails, his back was so agonized. "Feh! So what am I, Count Dracula, I should have to wait for the sun to come up before I get some sleep?" Not that it was comprehensible that he should slumber; not with Toutant Kingstree (who'd told no less than the truth when he'd protested that his homemade whiskey was for his own personal use) continually refreshing himself with bits of melody between swallows of pure-grain alcohol. Out of the dark would come the murmur of his saxophone or the growl of his voice. "I danced with a gal with a hole in her stocking." Then quietness, as he sat tilted back in his canvas chair. Then, "You can't raise cotton on sandy land. Rather be a nigger than a poor white man." Then, his long lanky legs stretched out, he'd softly finger the brass horn awhile. Then, "Yonder comes little Rosie. How the world do you know?" And so on down the highway south, while Raleigh sat bristling in the driver's seat of the white Cadillac, as if he still refused to give up his plan to drive himself to Atlanta.

Luckily Mingo saw no highway patrols, since Gates found instructions to limit his speed amusing, and as Interstate 20 was nearly deserted in these early hours of Palm Sunday morning, he had announced, thirty miles after they'd headed off the Augusta beltway onto the big road, "Now, my friend, hang on, you're gonna fly." But just then Mingo did see something, something that made him scream "STOP!" so loudly that Gates, instead of flying, pumped the brakes and rolled onto the shoulder. In the trailer, Weeper Berg tumbled off his mattress, Toutant Kingstree hit his tooth on his mouthpiece, Raleigh slammed his forehead on the Cadillac's steering wheel, and Peaches ran squealing out of her box.

When they shoved open the rear doors, they saw Mingo Sheffield up the road under a highway light at an exit ramp. He was deep in conversation with a young blond woman in a raincoat, who held a big suitcase in both hands.

Kingstree licked at his mouth. " 'Nother inch, I would have ruined my lip and missed my chance in New Orleans. What's he want to go try to pick somebody up this time of night for, anyhow?"

They watched the fat man hugging the girl, who seemed to be crying. Then he gestured back at the truck. She shook her head. Suddenly she crumpled against him and he caught her in his arms.

"Picking her up is what he did," Berg nodded. "Anywise, I think she's got one in the oven."

Carrying both the girl and her large suitcase, Sheffield staggered back to the van, his face lunatic with alarm. "Raleigh, it's Diane! We've got to help her! Get off the mattress, Weeper. Here, hurry, let her lie down!"

"Oh, God," said Hayes.

Gates hopped out of the cab. "What the fuck . . ." He looked at the teenager. "Shit a brick. It's the kid from the department store! Kure Beach, right?"

"It's Diane, Gates, you remember her. I helped her with her window display. That's right." Sheffield, gasping for breath, handed the terrified young woman up to Raleigh and Kingstree, who laid her down on the lumpy mattress. She clung tightly to her suitcase, as she stared from one to the other, her head moving in sudden jerks like a bird's. The dozens of tight blond pigtails were dark near her scalp with sweat, and sweat matted the front of her loose cotton dress. She was panting now in shallow breaths, as she whispered, "Mingo? Mingo?" up at the circle of strange male faces above her. Raleigh, Berg, and Kingstree looked down, speechless.

"I'm right here!" The fat man groaned as he heaved himself up into the truck and crawled over beside her to take her hands. "It's okay. It's okay."

Raleigh tugged her suitcase away. The girl's stomach was enormous. "Mingo, you know this young woman? What is she doing —?"

"Yes, yes, I told you." Sheffield kept his eyes on the teenager. "From Kure Beach. She was hitchhiking. She had a fight with her family, and she left. Diane, I said, take that fifty and ride the bus! But she had to save some money for when she got to Atlanta so she could look for her husband, so she got off in Columbia and started this damn hitchhiking. And some rotten rotten bastard tried to, you know, get fresh with her, and then she had to defend herself. Oh you poor thing, I'd just like to kill him, and then he just threw her out here on the highway, and she's been standing there a whole hour too scared to do anything! It's okay. Everything's okay. And we can count our blessings I saw her. Out here, the middle of the night, never know what, look at her poor shoes, high heels! Oh, Lord, Diane. Everything's fine." The whole while he was talking, Sheffield kept patting her hands and fanning her face with his palm.

"Thank you," she whispered, then sucked in her breath with surprise, and doubled over.

"Diane. Listen to me," said Raleigh. "Are you going into labor?"

She looked up at him, startled; her childish face with its heavy, smeared makeup was clammy white. "No. No, I'm not." She shook her head over and over. "I just got so scared."

"Excuse me, what, ah, month are you in?"

"I'm not too sure," she admitted in a gasp. "But it's not time. The doctor said, after Easter."

"Well, you aren't having contractions, are you?"

"No, sir. No. I'm just so *scared.*" She heaved over in tears.

"Mingo, let's take her back to Augusta. There's got to be a hospital there. And she can call her parents."

The girl sat up, clutching at Sheffield. "No! Please! I'm fine, really. I feel better now." She smiled at them, wiping her eyes quickly. "You said you were going to Atlanta. Please. Just let me go with you. I'll be okay. It's only a few more hours to Atlanta, isn't it?"

"It's three," said Raleigh, and looked at his watch.

"Her husband's in Atlanta," Mingo explained, his enormous arms wrapped around Diane's shoulders.

"Husband?" Hayes said skeptically.

"He works at the Omni," she told him. "He wrote me. He sells ice cream at the games."

"Wonderful," Raleigh muttered to himself.

After more discussion, Diane, now again in hiccupping tears, appealed so desperately to Mingo that he finally insisted they let her come with them to Atlanta. "I'll sit back here with her," he whispered. "I think she's falling asleep. Poor thing. She's all worn out."

"This we maybe don't need," whispered Weeper Berg to Raleigh, who agreed.

They drove on for two full hours, the Hayes brothers in the cab, the others watching over Diane. But before they reached Atlanta, they were stopped again. This time by a man rushing out at them from the shoulder, waving his arms and yelling.

Gates swerved away from him. "Should I stop? Shit."

"No, somebody else will. . . . Oh dammit, okay, yes, dammit, stop!" Raleigh cursed his conscience. If not his conscience, his opinion of himself.

"Whooaaa!" his brother whistled, as the headlights illuminated the person in the road. He was a young, thin, muscular man with thick blond hair. He was in a skintight black body suit with bones painted on it.

"Not again!" Hayes grumbled as Gates opened the door, but if he'd thought he'd fallen prey to another band of Hell's Angels — or whatever those Mount Olive thugs preferred to be called — he was mistaken. This young man, who appeared to be wearing rouge and mascara, was breathless from running, his teeth were chattering with fear, and panic raised his voice into a falsetto stammer as he called *"You've got to help us."* He pointed off the road past what looked like an orchard of peach trees, toward a red flickering light atop a hill of tall pines.

"What's the problem? Fire?" asked Gates.

The man (boy really) shook his head, wheezing, clasping his sides as he fought for breath. "Go for police. Come help. They've got my friends. Shoving them around. Making them dance. Kicking at them. Something awful is going to . . . I got away. Didn't see me." He was swallowing tears as he spoke. "It's the Klan. I know it." He pantomimed a pointed hood. "They're going to kill Albert, I know it. Please!"

Gates jumped down from the cab. "The Klan?"

"Wait a minute, Gates, oh hell!" Raleigh slid across the seat and climbed out of the truck. He could now see that the boy was wearing stage makeup. He grabbed his arm. "Try to calm down, young man. What happened?"

"Just please go get the police!"

"If it's the Klan around these boonies," Gates told him, "they *are* the police. Are they up there? How'd they get your friends? Shit! He's right!

It's a fucking burning cross up there!" He pointed at the red light pulsing smoke above the trees. "Quick, kid, tell me exactly what's going on. Have they got guns?"

The boy tried to talk so fast, his words stumbled together. He gestured across the highway, where the Hayeses now saw an old white bus with its hood up. Lettering on the back said "APPALACHIAN SCHOOL OF THE PERFORMING ARTS." "Bus broke down, we saw lights up there, we went up, see if anybody could help us. Whole circle of them, white hoods, around the cross. Grabbed us. Saw we were ballet, started, you know, 'Let's have some fun.' They came back down and got Laura and Shawn and Mr. Rosestein. Listen! Two guys in our company are black! They're black! If you can't stop them, you could go, get the police. I don't know what to do! Yes, yes, I saw a rifle."

Gates rubbed hard at his mustache. "How many?"

"Nine, three are girls and Mr. Rosestein's an old man!"

"How many of *them*, I mean."

"I don't know! I guess about a dozen."

"Right, fine." Gates opened the glove compartment and took out a white-handled revolver.

Raleigh jumped in front of him. "Jesus Christ, Gates, what are you doing? Did you get Mingo's gun out of his suitcase, dammit?"

"Mingo has a gun? Great!"

The little window in the trailer flew open. Simon Berg stuck his head out. "Kid? You found a hospital, I hope? Oh God. A skeleton? Okay, I've gone senile and I'm a basket case already."

Gates ran over to him. "Weep, Mingo's got a gun in his bag. Get it, and tell him I want all those fireworks he bought. Move ass. The fucking Ku Klux Klan's up there on that hill hassling a bunch of ballet kids."

"For your funny jokes, mister, the KKK is not a subject!" Berg slammed shut the window.

Gates raced to the rear doors, hauled them open, and leaped up into the truck, followed by Raleigh and the ballet student.

"Watch out!" Mingo shouted, hovering over Diane, who lay whimpering on the mattress.

"I am not kidding, Berg!" Gates yelled. "Look over at those pine trees. See it! It's the Klan."

"Aw, *shit!*" said Toutant Kingstree as he jumped to his feet. "What are you back here for? *Drive, you motherfucker!*"

But Gates was flinging the clothes out of Mingo's suitcase, where he soon found the pistol and the bag of firecrackers. Everybody stood staring at him. "Okay, guys," he announced. "Here's the plan. Mingo stays with the girl."

That much was agreeable. But the troops of Gates Hayes did not respond with much immediate esprit de corps to his other suggestions, despite his rousing ad hominem battle speech, exhorting them to valor in defense of women, blacks, and ballet dancers, against (and, in Berg's phrase, he minced no words) shit-eating, sheep-fucking, anti-Semite white-trash dumb honkie lynching Nazi chicken dong-diddling wife-beating moron assholes, whose routing would be not only a duty and a pleasure, but "a piece of cake."

Raleigh said, "You have got to be kidding."

Weeper said, "Why was I born?"

Toutant said, "I want to go to New Orleans, I don't want to sidestep it to Heaven. Y'all go. Y'all are white."

Weeper said, "I'm a Jew."

Toutant said, "Man, that's still the front of the bus."

Weeper said, "Look, I'm a midget, a pygmy, a crummy old man in lousy shape. You're seven feet for crying out loud tall, you Alpine Goliath! You go!"

Toutant said, "Seven *black* feet! You ever hear of lynching?"

"You ever heard of Dachau!"

The ballet student said, "Do something, PLEASE!"

Raleigh said, "I don't believe this."

Mingo jumped up, "Y'all shut up! You're scaring Diane. Raleigh, I think she's getting ready to have her baby."

"Dammit, Mingo. She ought to know if she's having a baby or not."

"I'm not!" The girl shook her head frantically.

"Give me your watch," Mingo told Raleigh. "I'm going to time these contractions."

Hayes wheeled around. "I thought . . . Diane! Have your contractions started?!"

"Just a few," she whispered. "It's nothing to worry about, I swear. Honest."

"Oh, great!"

While everyone yelled, Gates stuck a gun in Raleigh's hand, filled Berg's and Kingstree's and the student's hands with Mingo's cherry bombs, buzz bombs, rockets, and matches, and pushed them one by one out of the back of the truck as if he were the training sergeant of a paratrooper squad. He headed them single file up the dirt road that ran beside the peach orchard.

Quietly, but not happily, they went. Halfway up the hill they could hear the crackling of fire and barks of laughter.

Starting at this point in the road, new cars and old pickup trucks lined the shoulders. Two bumper stickers wanted four more years of the former minor film star who was at this time President of the United States. Another sticker wanted everyone to know that the occupant had visited the Magic Kingdom. Another wanted a particular baseball team to go all the way.

Taking a Swiss army knife from his pocket, Gates stabbed a hole in the right front tire of a Pontiac Firebird.

"What am I doing here?" Simon Berg asked no one in particular. "Jews travel through Georgia in the air on their way to Miami."

Toutant didn't let this pass. "Black people can't afford Miami. Here, give me that knife. I'll do it."

While Kingstree punctured tires, Gates removed the fanbelts from all the trucks, on the premise that someone named Shawn knew what he was talking about when he'd said to the blond boy that the bus's problem was a broken fanbelt. As Gates was stuffing these inside his jacket, they heard a shriek, then someone yelling, "You bastards!" Then more shrieks.

"Motherfuckers," growled Kingstree and ripped open a Mustang's new radial.

"Do something," the young student pleaded.

Gates gave them their battle positions. He and Raleigh would go in. The other three would surround the ridge from three sides. "Stay behind those trees, Weep. Don't let them see you."

"Not to worry," Berg assured him.

"All right, guys. Here we go." Then the former Vietnam commando grinned. "There's only five of us, but God's on our side, so that makes six."

His squad (in whose breasts, Gates — unlike Henry V — had not really stirred much joyful sense of "we happy few") crawled into the fray. For there was no arguing with their leader, who had already hurried ahead in a crouching weave, motioning them with a military wave to follow. Another fifty yards, and they could see the clearing through the pines. It looked to be on the site of an old house, long since burned or collapsed, for nothing was left but four tall brick crumbled chimneys and wide stone stairs that now led to nothing. Between the two middle chimneys, red flames licked noisily at a giant cross. Moving in the smoky light were white-robed figures in high pointed hoods. They circled around an equally oddly dressed group, all in painted leotards and tights with leg warmers bunched at their ankles. These people looked to be awkwardly dancing.

The Knights of the Ku Klux Klan upon whom our travelers were about to descend — for to this chivalric organization the hooded men undoubtedly belonged — had been delighted to have their first set of visitors stumble into their midst. Their ordinary monthly ceremony provided its own pleasures, to be sure: the darkness, the costumes, the secrecy; and fire is, of course, always a thrill to the violent. It was all a lot flashier than the church services most of them would yawn through later this morning. But unbroken routine had taken the edge from their excitement in these forbidden fraternal gatherings. Their Klavern chieftain gave the same speech month after month, and while this man possessed all the qualities (zenophobia, paranoia, a vile mind, and a frightened soul) that a demogogue needs to inflame other bigots, he lacked the oratory. His long-repeated speech — even the faithful admitted — had gotten boring as hell; nor could he offer them with any impunity those physical outlets for brutality by which herded hate is nourished. No, the Klan, they all lamented, had lost something since its golden days. Now, they were so harassed, even hounded into court, even by white people, that they had managed to accomplish nothing much in the last few years except burn up some dirty schoolbooks, break the windows in a Jew's store, whip a white woman known to be sleeping with a nigger, cheer and wave funny signs outside a prison during an execution, yell at voters at a Democratic polling booth, shoot a dog belonging to a Vietnamese family (in fact, a South Vietnamese, in whose defense one of the knights had been overseas fighting, not many years earlier), and attend those monotonous monthly meetings.

Consequently, they were surprised and delighted when they rounded up nine ballet school trespassers who were just asking for it; particularly thrilled when they saw that two of them were black, another (a man with waves painted all over him) was Chinese, the oldest was decidedly a Jewboy, all of them were wearing makeup and painted hose; particularly thrilled when all the white men looked to the knights like queers, the blacks looked like rapists; and the three women were obviously whores. Just the sort to relieve the boredom of the meetings they attended to relieve the boredom of their lives.

The student ballet company of the Appalachian School of the Performing Arts was more than surprised. They were on a college tour with their original ballet, "Orpheus in the Underworld" — the young blond man who'd begged our travelers for help was himself Hades, King of the Dead — and they'd left Atlanta immediately after a performance to drive to their next university town, where they were scheduled to dance the following night. On this tour they were accompanied by their teacher, Mr. Rosestein, a man of sixty-some, whose only knowledge of the old bus he had finally wheedled out of his dean was that it was better than nothing. Or so he'd assumed, until it broke down, and he was looking into the excited eyes of a white-hooded man who pushed a rifle into his stomach and said they were all going to have some fun, because he (the Klansman) and his buddies were ballet lovers and especially loved to see niggers and queers dance, and they wanted, right now, to see a good show. Mr. Rosestein, whose enormous courage can only be judged by the extremity of his fear, and who had no idea that one of his students had slipped unseen away in the dark and run for help, attempted to dissuade the Klan by reasoning with them. For this folly, he was laughingly knocked to the ground by a rifle butt in the hands of a shy plumber who was just showing off with the help of a half-dozen beers.

The students were told that if they did not quickly entertain their hosts, their old Jewboy queer teacher would get what he was asking for, and so would they. Further jabs, shoves, and threats to the three young women finally compelled all the dancers to begin randomly moving around the base of the burning cross in halfhearted steps of the ballet they'd performed earlier that night. Persephone (her leotard half painted with flowers) was crying in the arms of Eurydice, while the black Orpheus tried to comfort them until backhanded by one of the hooded spectators. This had provoked the shouts of "Bastards!" which the approaching rescuers had heard.

Nudged and poked, the students were faltering on, to the jeers of their audience, who looked in their eerie robes like a corps of supporting actors in this performance of the poet's visit to Hell. How long the Klansmen might have forced the dancers to continue, or what subsequent merriment they might have devised, will never be known, for their show was suddenly stopped by a single shot from a gun. This sound was immediately followed by the appearance of a remarkable-looking man dressed entirely in leather and holding a white-handled revolver, who leaped down from the detached stone stairs and landed in their midst. Behind him was a tall man in a suit and tie, who wore glasses and also carried a gun.

"FBI," announced the handsome man in leather. "Agent Simon." He jerked a wallet from his jacket, flipped it open, closed it. "Anybody with a gun, drop it right now, you're under arrest."

One of the Klansmen, holding a shotgun, did just that, but the plumber with the rifle shook his head. "What do you mean, FBI?"

Gates raised his pistol and cocked it. "What do I mean? I mean I'm going to blow your chickenshit pointed head off if you don't toss that dick-extender in the dirt and back the fuck up."

The Klansman glanced at his brother knights watching him, and decided he had to be brave. "You and who else?" he sneered.

Gates smiled, his teeth gleaming in the red light of the blazing cross. "Me and the agent" — he pointed randomly into the group — "who set you dumb hicks up. Me and the ten agents out in the woods." He pointed randomly into the night. "And let me tell you good ole boys the news. Half of my men are black and the other half are Jews, and they'd like nothing better than half a chance to waste you turkeys." He yelled, "Am I right, men?" and fired another shot in air. It was instantly answering by booming volleys from in front, in back, and to the side of the clearing. The explosions sounded more like cannon than bullets (cherry bombs do), and long before they ended, so had the bravado of the shy plumber. He tossed his rifle away as if it had been shot out of his hand.

The black Orpheus picked it up, and the Chinese Charon (for such was his role in the ballet) bent down on one leg to scoop up the shotgun. Hugging one another, the rest of the troop closed ranks around their teacher, whom they helped to his feet.

"Right, fine. Keep those guns on them," grinned Gates. "The rest of you go on back down to your bus. Is somebody named Shawn here?"

A hefty young man in a turtleneck, with hair nearly to his shoulders, raised his hand. Gates motioned him over, turned his back, and gave him the fanbelts. "Try one," he said.

Too shocked and relieved to speak, the ballet students led Mr. Rosestein out of the clearing and down the hill.

"Now, boys." Gates smiled. "Let's take off these cute hoods and see your pointed heads. Agent Whittier here wants to see what you look like." He gestured at Raleigh, whose gun arm was perfectly steady; in fact, his whole body was as still as one of those stones Orpheus was supposed to be able to move with the beauty of his verses.

Now the Klan chieftain himself stepped forward to justify his high position. "Just what is it we're supposed to have done, mister? This here is our land, you know."

Gates strolled up to the baggy-robed creature. "That's what the Indians said." He smiled.

"We got a perfect right —"

"No, you don't. Not for illegal assembly, conspiracy to commit violence . . . what else, Agent Whittier?"

Raleigh swallowed. Everyone looked at him. He opened his mouth, and to his amazement said, "Forcible constraint. Assault. Conspiracy to defraud others of their civil rights. . . ." He stopped and closed his mouth.

"Right!" grinned Gates. "Plus campfires without a permit. Plus, I don't much like your outfits."

The Klavern marshal crossed his arms over his red insignia. "You're full of shit," he shrewdly guessed. "Lenoir, you believe this guy's with the FBI?"

Lenoir shrugged. Of all the participants in this drama, he was probably the most bewildered. For — as was not infrequently the case with members of secret organizations in the United States — Lenoir actually was an FBI agent. He didn't know what to think. The firelight was obscuring, but he was fairly certain he did not recognize Agents Simon and Whittier, nor was the first man's style at all conformable to Bureau procedures, as Lenoir knew them. On the other hand, Simon seemed to realize there was an undercover agent in the group. He could be with one of those countless committee-sponsored special task forces, and naturally nobody had bothered to brief the field man about it. Lenoir was sick and tired of having things sprung on him this way; he'd be damned if he wasn't going to complain to his district chief. But meanwhile, his instructions were never to blow his cover, whatever the provocation. He obeyed orders. Therefore he shrugged.

Now the Klavern leader tried a new tack. "Look here, buddy, you got nothing on us, we were just having a little fun. We didn't hurt a soul. We just asked, polite as can be, those folks to do us one of their faggot dances. Right, boys?"

"Right," mumbled the boys.

"What did you say?!" shouted Agent Simon. *"What* kind of dance?"

"Faggot," the Klansman snickered uneasily. "Well, look at 'em. You know what I'm saying."

"Right." Gates cocked the pistol and held it between the man's eyes. "Take off that hood."

"You ain't about to shoot me," the Klansman predicted defiantly, but as he saw the finger squeeze the trigger, he struggled out of the big hood and clutched it in his hands.

"Shit, man, are you ugly!" Gates shook his head. The man had a few long strands of dark hair slicked across his bald dome, and his sunken cheeks were pitted with old acne scars. "You are putrefyingly ugly. And I was planning on kissing you, too! See," and Gates grinned, brushing his black mustache and tossing his curls in a flurry, "see, *I'm* a faggot myself.

Bet you didn't think of that. And I was going to give you a great big smacky kiss. But you are so goddamn pitifully miserably disgustingly ugly, I can't make myself do it." He grabbed the hood and threw it onto the bonfire at the base of the cross, then spun around to where the other eleven Klansmen stood flanked by the armed Orpheus and Charon. "Okay! Let's see what the rest of you guys look like! Anybody worth kissing?"

Lenoir had now decided that if this was the kind of nut the FBI was hiring these days, it was time for him to go back to his job at the highway patrol.

No one moved. Gates fired his pistol over their heads. Again, volleys of artillery shot through the darkness. The white hoods came off fast, were gathered by the two dancers, and flung into the fire. "Nope," Gates told the Klan, "You're all too bad-looking for me. In total sincerity, I think I ought to bring my men up here and let them kill you just for being so damn ugly."

At this point, Lenoir, who had inched his way to a clump of pine trees, slipped behind them. From there, he watched his Klan comrades forced to lie down on their stomachs while the two students tied the backs of the skirts of their white robes together. He couldn't understand why the other agent (the one in the suit, the one who *looked* like an agent) did nothing to control his partner's wild behavior. He wondered if this bespectacled man might be in shock; if maybe the Bureau had sprung this weirdo Simon on him as well. Paddy wagon?! Had that fruitcake just said the Klan better not move a muscle until they got back with the 'paddy wagon'? Okay, that's it. He'd figured it out now. This leather guy had to be with the CIA. He was one of those flamboyant, crazy Gordon Liddy types. *Nobody* in the Bureau was that bizarre; or, for that matter, could afford those kinds of clothes. Lenoir blinked. Where'd they go? While he was theorizing, all four of the invaders had disappeared. Then suddenly from every direction the air filled not only with shots but hissing bombs and the whistle of flying mortar. Lenoir crawled into a gully. Was that maniac's squad firing missiles?

The Klansmen obviously thought so, for despite their instructions not to move, they were desperately struggling to stand up, while tied together by the skirts like a string of paper dolls. They stumbled and yanked and fell on each other and tugged each other in opposite directions and staggered this way and that, and, in fact, performed an entire chorus line dance, watching which, from their hiding places, their small audience had as much fun as the Klan had claimed to have had watching "Orpheus in

the Underworld." The audience watched, however, only while Gates unloaded the rifles and hurled them into the woods. Then they hurried back
down to the highway, where they received the spoils of victory deserved by
conquerors; in this case, the delirious embraces of all members of the Appalachian School for the Performing Arts, male, female, black, white, Oriental, straight and gay.

"There's no way to thank you," Mr. Rosestein admitted, as the old bus,
with its borrowed fanbelt, rattled to a start.

Gates pointed at the side of the red truck across the highway, where
KNICK-KNACK GEM-CRACK HIGH-TIME CIRCUS glittered in
gold. "We artists," he said, "have to stick together."

"The testicles on the kid," Simon Berg whispered. "Chutzpah? Talent? I
love him."

"We could have all been shot," Raleigh replied, the gun still frozen in
his hand.

Toutant Kingstree said, "Y'all could of been shot. *I* could of got coated
in kerosene."

When the travelers opened the rear doors of the truck, they received
news which made Gates Hayes (who had just bounded almost gleefully
into a clearing of armed bullies) turn gray with fear. Weeper Berg was
saying, "Fatty, yah shouda been there," and Toutant Kingstree was singing, "Hit the road, Jack, and don'cha come back," when Mingo Sheffield
said, "Diane's having her baby."

They all craned around him to see the teenaged girl, shadowy in the
light of the battery lamp. She lay on the mattress on the truck floor. A
blanket was now spread under her, and another rolled under her head.
Sheffield's suitcase had been opened, and his clean shirts and underwear
placed around the girl's body. Also beside the mattress were Kingstree's
plastic waterjug and the quart bottle of clear grain alcohol. Mingo held a
white T-shirt and was carefully wiping sweat from Diane's face. She lay
there, eyes squeezed shut, head rocking against the pillow as pain seemed
to swell over her in waves.

Gates lit a cigarette, and stepped back. "I can't handle this."

The others climbed up into the trailer and knelt around the mattress.
"Is that true, Diane?" Hayes bent over her. "Are you in labor?"

As soon as she could breathe, she admitted, "I think so."

Mingo whispered, "She's already been in transition for about twenty
minutes. It could be quick now."

"I'm rolling," Gates yelled, already running. "I'll make Atlanta in under
an hour." Seconds later the truck had rumbled back onto the highway.

"How far apart are your contractions?" Raleigh asked her, bracing himself on the truck wall.

"I don't ... I don't ... know. Not very far." She held both hands squeezed on her enormous stomach, now shaken by the speeding truck. They were the hands of a child, the knuckles were dimpled, the cuticles bitten. "They, they, oh please, they got a little quicker a while ago. Could I, Mingo ..."

Sheffield seemed to know she wanted water and held the plastic jug to her lips. "They're ninety seconds apart now," he told Raleigh. "Here's your watch. Time them."

Raleigh took off his glasses to press at his eyes in order to bring back memories of Aura's delivery of the twins. Not that he had seen it, but she and the detestable Dr. Sonny Carmichael had told him about it. "Has your water broken? ... Has, you know, had there been any, ah, liquid discharge?"

"Yes, yes, it's broken; an hour ago," Mingo said. "Pant, Diane. Here. Like a little puppy again. Like I told you. See? Huhhuhhuhhuhhuh. See?"

Hayes took a deep gulp of air. Toutant and Weeper took one noisily with him. They'd all been holding their breaths while the girl panted. "Diane, do you mind if I ask you why you said you *weren't* in labor? When I said you should go to a hospital back in Augusta? Two hours ago?"

"Dammit, what's the sense in asking stupid questions?" incredibly whispered Sheffield to the man who'd been his protector since childhood. Raleigh was shocked into an apology. "At this juncture, Mingo, I suppose you're right."

"I think that bastard that picked her up scared her so bad, it brought it on."

Diane, purple-faced and exhausted in Mingo's arms, now was breathing in quick short gasps of air. "I think it's ... Please ... Please, stop the bouncing ... Plea ..." The last syllable was squeezed out through a pain that tightened her body, curling her with a moan against Mingo's chest.

"In my humble opinion," Weeper Berg said, "does anybody know how to deliver a baby?"

"I know animals," said Kingstree, shaking his head, "but they don't need any help to speak of."

Raleigh kept his eyes glued to his watch; but this contraction appeared to be continuous. How could you tell when one stopped and the next began?

Mingo yelled to Berg, "For Christ's sake, tell Gates to stop the truck! Just pull over. Right now. Just stop!"

As Berg ran to the window, Mingo added, "And, y'all get back, okay? How can she breathe?" He crawled along the metal truck floor to the foot of the mattress, pushed aside the blanket and the girl's dark stained dress, and began swabbing alcohol from Kingstree's whiskey bottle on her legs. "Like I said, don't mind me, Diane. Everything's just fine. Yell as loud as you feel like. And push! That's all you've got left to do now, honey. *Push.*"

"Oh my God," Hayes groaned and turned away. The girl's legs were red with blood, and they were shaking uncontrollably. The truck slowed to a stop. No one talked. Raleigh could hear everyone's breath keeping rhythm with Diane's hurried gasps. Her small fists had grabbed into the mattress.

Mingo's voice was a strange hoarse whisper. "Diane? Diane! It's the tip of the head! I can see the head now. Push, honey! Keep pushing! Toutant, will you go up there and help her keep her head and shoulders up, give her something to push on, and you count with us. Okay? Yes, yes, like that, let her lean on you, that's right. Okay, Diane, we're going to count? You push, and we're just going to count to eight. Bear down hard as you can, push on him. Then you take a big breath. Just eight." He poured Kingstree's whiskey all over his hands, and began mopping bright red blood away from the opening where a curve of black-haired scalp could now be seen. "All we've got to do, Diane . . . Diane? All we've got to do is just push this little head out. That's all. Raleigh, bring me that other light over here, and get me some more clean shirts." Sheffield's face was now as red as Diane's. He crouched over between her quivering legs, holding them. Beside her head, Toutant Kingstree's gravely voice began to count, as the girl, her eyes widening with the swell of the pain, pulled her head tightly toward the huge rise of her stomach.

"I'm too old for this," Berg muttered.

Raleigh gave Kingstree a cloth to pat Diane's face, but she pushed it away.

Mingo's head bobbed quickly as he counted with Kingstree. "Now, Diane, hold your breath, push, push, push, push, push, push, push, eight. Okay? You can. Yes, you can! Sure. It's just like taking a great big poop." He squinted his fat face tight.

"No it's not," she panted.

Kingstree kept quietly counting. "And one two three four five six and seven eight."

"Now breathe!" Mingo sucked in breath. "Big breath." She fell back panting in the crook of the long thin black arm, and everyone in the truck breathed loudly. Then she bore down again.

The saxophonist went on, long long minute after minute while Raleigh, his hands pressed to his mouth, felt his own breath hot against his fingers.

"And one push three four five push and seven eight. And breathe two three four. And push two three four. That's right. That's good. Here we go, push two three . . ."

Mingo reached up and brushed the sweaty hair and tears from her eyes. "Diane, honey, you're going to have to keep pushing. Push harder. One two —"

"*I can't!*" she cried.

"Yes you can. Don't you want to see your little baby? Sure you can. Here we go!"

"Mingo," whispered Raleigh, distraught. "Do you know what you're doing? What if something goes wrong?"

"Nothing's going to go wrong. That's right, Diane, that's right!"

"You can't deliver a baby from watching goddamn *Gone With the Wind* ten thousand times, listen to me, don't try to do anything that —"

But Sheffield's Gargantuan lungs swelled and swelled. "Push Diane push Diane push Diane push Diane!"

The teenaged girl had both hands, the knuckles white, gripped around Kingstree's lanky arm as her head pushed back hard against his breastbone. Veins pulsed dark blue in her neck and her temples. Suddenly she screamed, a piercing shriek that echoed off the sides of the metal truck.

"THAT'S IT! ONE MORE. ONE MORE. HERE IT COMES!"

Diane jerked forward, pulling Kingstree with her.

"I CAN SEE THE EAR!" Mingo's huge hands cradled the tiny head and tilted it gently to the side. "HERE'S THE CHIN."

There was a sound like the plop of a fish in water, then as fast and as slippery, the blood-covered baby slipped into Mingo's outstretched arms.

"DIANE, DIANE, IT'S A GIRL, IT'S A BABY GIRL!"

"Slap it!" Weeper Berg shouted in a high squeak above Diane's gasps. "Slap it to make it cry!"

But Sheffield, holding the baby's feet up in one hand, moved aside the thick hose of the umbilical cord, wiped a finger over its mouth, patted it once on the back, and then the lips opened, the arms jerked out with tight fists, and with a high wail, life announced itself.

At the sound, the fat man burst out crying as wholeheartedly as the newborn. Toutant Kingstree was either laughing or bawling. Weeper Berg, in a coughing fit, had run to the front window and yelled out, "It's a girl!" And Raleigh Hayes wasn't breathing at all.

The truck horn began to shriek like a steamboat.

Diane, propped up on Kingstree's damp breast, had her arms reached out. Mingo placed the baby, which was only half the length of his forearm, in the crook of the mother's neck. Together he and Diane, both still gasping, stared at each hand and foot. Then Sheffield wiped his eyes. "Honey, you did just beautifully, you did a wonderful job, and we've got just a little bit more to do. We've got to push that placenta out, okay?"

She shook her head weakly. "No, please."

"The hard part's finished, honey. It'll be easy as pie now." Then he turned around, tears running down his wide cheeks. "Raleigh, get me some scissors or a knife and something to tie with, okay?"

Weeper Berg blew his nose in the stack of Sheffield's boxer shorts he'd been holding to hand over if needed by anybody for anything. "So, who is this guy, Dr. Kildare?"

Kingstree carefully reached into his blue and black striped trousers for Gates's knife, the blade of which Raleigh dipped in the grain alcohol.

"I'm just going to tie this cord off, honey, because she doesn't need it anymore," Mingo told the mother, who wasn't paying any attention. Exhausted, wet with tears, her breath slowing and deepening, she was staring transfixed and smiling at the moving fingers of the minuscule human hand.

Thus, just before dawn on March 27, twelve days after the Ides that had brought his father's message, and one week before Easter, our hero entered Atlanta with two more members in his company than he had anticipated. Not that he had anticipated Toutant Kingstree and his pig Peaches, or, for that matter, Weeper Berg, or Gates Hayes, or even Mingo Sheffield. He had anticipated nothing, thank God; for by no means could he have borne the foreknowledge.

The KNICK-KNACK GEM-CRACK HIGH-TIME CIRCUS stopped at the emergency entrance of the first hospital on their Atlanta map. Even at four A.M. on Palm Sunday, the place was harried with alarm, and false alarms. The sleepy resident on call told them that while mother and infant were perfectly fine, they should not make a practice of delivering babies, as childbirth in the hands of unlicensed amateurs was a very dangerous business. Then he turned to Mingo Sheffield, who was still breathing oddly, and whose sweat-dried hair poked out on the sides of his enormous head.

"You've been in on your wife's deliveries, I guess."

Sheffield turned bright pink from the neck up. "Wu ... wu ... we haven't been bu ... blessed with any children," he stammered. "But we tu ... tu ... took two sets of Lamaze classes, ju ... just maybe, you know, in ku ... ku ... case."

Raleigh sighed, "Jesus, Mingo," and took off his glasses because he pretended to himself that he'd gotten something in his eye.

"How are they?" said Gates, who'd waited in the parking lot. He couldn't handle hospitals.

"Fine, they're okay."

"What a night! I almost tossed my cookies."

"I can imagine. You just about got shot."

"Oh that," Gates shrugged. "Piece of cake. What a night, wow. Better to light a few little candles, toss a few little cherry bombs, than curse the darkness, *n'est-ce pas,* hombre? Where's Mingo?"

Raleigh explained that Mingo Sheffield had insisted on spending what little was left of the night at the hospital with Diane, whose parents he was already trying to telephone. In turn, Gates explained that Weeper Berg had taken off, but would be in touch.

"All right," said his brother. "That means we only need rooms at the Peachtree Plaza for you, me, Toutant and Peaches."

"Nah. Toots took off too." Gates tossed his cigarette out into air. "Said he had a sister on Auburn Avenue. I do believe he meant in the sense that ..." and the black mustache crinkled while the voice became baritone and evangelical. "We are ALL brothers and sisters under the skin, brothers and sisters. And let us get on UNDER that skin and FuHEEL the Power of LUVE. ... I told him to show up in the lobby nine sharp Monday or we'd be going way down yonder in New Orleans without him. So, it's just you and me, babe." He kicked out a long-leathered leg at the sky. "Here's the plan."

"No more plans, Gates, please."

"We park the circus wagon at a truck stop, unload the Caddy. And arrive in style!" Gates shook his curls, arched his head, threw out his arms and howled, "Ladies and Gents, the one and only, the unique, the never before HAYES BROTHERS! Home delivery and Klan-busting our specialty. Famous stars of yesteryear's Hayes Family KNICK-KNACK ET CETERA CIRCUS. Now appearing in the Big Peach of the Hustling Bustling Fast Track Quick Buck Integrated Amalgamated Incorporated New South. Man, I mean, Atlanta. G.A.!"

"Gates, you're crazy. Please stop yelling! It's five in the morning."

Gates's wrist shot out of the tawny leather. "No, it's not. It's five-o-four thirty-two. Must be something wrong with your watch, Big Bro." He flung his arm around Raleigh and led him back to the bright red truck.

CHAPTER

27

Why Raleigh Took His First Communion

LIKE EVERYONE ELSE, Raleigh Hayes saw the world, and the people with whom he was obliged to share it, through the kaleidoscope of his own colored designs. As the years turned the viewer round and round, the bits of glass fell into new patterns, but the perspective remained limited to Raleigh's eye.

That there was a world that was not merely an elongation of his own limbs, that there were people in it who were not merely extensions of his own will, he had accepted, in frustration, before the age of two. He had learned by then that he did not make himself bounce merrily in air, nor was the woman's voice saying, "This is the way the ladies ride. Trot trot trot," his own. The fingers that made the church and steeple, made the white bear jump out of no place into view, tucked the shiny blanket around his shoulders, were not his own fingers, nor was the man's voice his that said, "Goodnight, sleep tight, don't let the bedbugs bite, Little Fellow."

But if this knowledge gradually shrank him, so that he no longer painted pictures in which he towered not only over his stick-legged parents, but over the square house and the round spoked yellow sun; still, to the boy, the world beyond his ken stayed shadowy, and he as indifferent to it as it was to him. Outside Thermopylae there was nothing mapped on the globe but Cowstream to the east, the state capital to the west, the beach, beyond the beach a vague ocean, and, indistinctly, a shape called North Carolina surrounded by an incalculable shape called America, surrounded by, in the first seven years of his life, that "Overseas" where "We" were trying to win against "Them" before they took over the world and killed everyone in it.

Thermopylae itself consisted of the Crossways and the length of Main Street from his parents' home beside St. Thomas Church to his grandparents' big white house beside a Baptist Church; with a few other buildings placed here and there around the town like Monopoly pieces. Thermopylae existed for him to live in, as food was there on tables for him to eat it, and clothes were there in his dresser drawers for him to wear them. St. Thomas Church existed from nine until noon on Sundays when he was inside it; otherwise it vanished, as the school and the teachers vanished in summer. The sidewalks of Thermopylae were there for him to walk on to school, for him to ride his bike or pull his wagon with empty Coke bottles to the store, for the postman to deliver mail to his house. Girls on the sidewalk, their dresses tied with straggly bows in back, their white socks fallen around their thin ankles, were there to chant silly rhymes as they hopped into swinging ropes, "I love coffee, I love tea, how many boys are stuck on me? One, two, three.... I asked my mother for fifty cents to see the elephant jump the fence ... forty-five, forty-six, forty-seven...." Girls were there so that they could giggle as he walked off the curb to move around them, so that he could ignore their giggles and sock his cousin Jimmy Clay for stopping to chant back, "First comes love, then comes marriage, then comes Raleigh with a baby carriage, haw haw haw, do you like jelly?, punch in the belly," and sock Raleigh back.

Like everyone else, age did not entirely enlarge the young Raleigh's point of view. He realized there were a great many other people, up to their vague other business, but he assumed that the world around him was, simultaneously, unremittingly engrossed in Raleigh Hayes, while remaining utterly incapable of penetrating his secrets or understanding his unique personality. He believed both that his teachers noticed no other pupils but him, and that they never saw him down the row of yellow desks, reading "Joe Palooka" comics behind his math book, or nodding off to sleep in warm study periods, or staring heartsick at one of those girls whose rope-jumping usurpation of the sidewalk had once so annoyed him. Believed both that the whole fourth grade stared at him in the halls, and that none of them knew that his parents had divorced. Believed both that his mother had no life distinct from his, and that she had no inkling that he ever hid the evidence of his wet dreams at the bottom of the laundry hamper. Believed both that the entire town of Thermopylae was talking about the fact that he had bought a package of Trojan condoms at the drugstore, and that not a single person suspected what he might want to do with them. Like everyone else, Raleigh Hayes did not realize that most other people heard more and cared less than he imagined, just as he cared less about their secrets than they believed.

In his preoccupation with himself, Raleigh was certainly not unusual. Our hero was, however (particularly for a citizen of a small southern Piedmont town, out of which, or into which — as his aunt Victoria said — almost nobody had budged for two hundred years), rarer in the thoroughness of his indifference to what did not concern him, and even to what did. As the edges of his world moved back and the shadowy figures in it took on color and form, it was his habit to map and neatly label the typography, then explore no further. This disinterest he came to perceive as a virtue: He never gossisped, and would not willingly listen to the gossip of others. Nothing was more distasteful to him, whether at eight, at eighteen, or now, than to be cornered by Ned Ware and sadly told that Stevie Richardson, whose mother drank, had been kept back in third grade, that Bobby Perry hadn't made the team, that Mandy Dilleton had gotten knocked up and Roy Barnwell refused to marry her, wasn't it awful? Neither was Hayes interested, at any age, in Mingo Sheffield's benign babbling about the lives of schoolmates, sisters, teachers, neighbors, puppies, customers, movie stars, movie *characters,* and strangers in the newspapers. All his life, Raleigh was scrupulously disinterested. He did not ask his parents to explain their divorce. He did not ask his clients for more particulars than were absolutely necessary to warrant their policies and insure his own politeness. As long as his daughters did not violate the Rules (did not endanger their safety and their health, let their grades slip, consort with undesirables, drive without permission, get home after curfew, borrow or lend money, smoke, drink, have intercourse, or fail to keep their rooms clean), he did not require them to detail their days.

All his life, Raleigh congratulated himself that it was not in his character to open mail not addressed to him, to open doors without knocking, to pry when it was none of his business. When his Hayes relatives began chortling together through long evenings of garbled gossip about each other or anecdotes about whatever they had managed to remember or make up about the Family Past ("Tell the one about when Papa went up with the barnstormer and the wing fell off. Tell the one about Aunt Mab and that jibber-jabber bigamist from Chicago"), Raleigh picked up an erector set or a stereo kit or a book. He, frankly, wasn't interested.

And, therefore, his grandparents, his uncles and aunts, even to a degree his parents (all the adults that had peopled the child's world), stayed, in some sense, the flat distant figures (however fleshy and noisy) they had seemed to that child: a composite picture of a few poses, a few phrases, a few stories, without precedence or consequence, or connections. His great-grandmother Tiny Hackney, by her own boast just knee-high to a grass-hopper, was always to Raleigh the floppy doll sunk in white goosedown pillows in a white brass bed, set up, for reasons no one explained, in the corner of the immense dining room. A thin ancient doll always brushing her long troublesome white hair, always begging for peppermints or for her old tonic (a bottled stimulant called Elixir Vitae, long since taken off the market, as it contained laudanum, kola nuts, Indian hemp, and a dash of belladonna); always shouting her own reminiscences (most of them scurrilous and presumably fabricated) into the midst of the general conversation; always calling, "What? What?" when laughter danced around the dining-room table.

Raleigh's grandfather Clayton Hayes was always a bald, long-armed man with sky-blue eyes, with distorted speech and a strange uncontrollable laugh. A legless man in a wheelchair listening to Jack Benny on the radio and slapping his armrests with startling glee. A man who, despite the advantages of inherited property and education, had had so little get up and go that he'd never asked people to repay their loans, and had allowed his business to be stolen from him by PeeWee Jimson. He was always the man who'd chosen his wife at the railroad tracks, filled the big white house with thirteen children, and died listening to the Song of Songs.

Ida Hayes, Raleigh's grandmother, was always the frowning woman who watched for her flowers to bloom, who didn't know how to read, who had worked from age eight in a factory winding cotton from six in the morning until six in the evening, who called her husband "Mr. Hayes," even when she had to feed him from a tray and change diapers on his legless trunk; who said of her husband, "He was just a good man," with the sighing cluck that made the remark both homage and rebuke, just as his phrase about his wife, "She's a proud woman; she knows her own mind and God and the devil in cahoots couldn't change it," was both praise and lament.

Neither in childhood, nor as a man, had Raleigh any knowledge, any thought, of this couple as they might have seemed to themselves, or each other. He knew nothing of Clayton Hayes, the lanky town dandy — pockets full of money from an indulgent mother — driving the first car East Main Street could claim, pitching baseball in straw hat and striped tie; nothing of the diffident, uncertain college student, the shy lover, the haphazard businessman, the cardplayer who loved the games at which he was continually beaten by better gamblers, and gulled by less innocent — losing money so cheerfully that his wife finally sent Flonnie Rogers to a poker party with his suitcase and the ultimatum that he choose between cards and her; Raleigh knew nothing of the man and father so gentle that his wife despaired of him or his children (despite their skills at sports and music, despite the looks of some, the brains of some, the literacy of all) ever amounting to anything. Our hero had no sense of the pride that made Ada Hackney call her husband "Mr. Hayes," no sense of her fear that the thirteen children to whom she'd given birth in her bedroom, helped only by Flonnie Rogers and a neighbor, might slide back into the numbing labor and bitter poverty from which at fifteen she'd rescued herself and what little of her kin she had surviving, by marrying Clayton Hayes as soon as he asked her, learning only years later that it was safe to love someone. These two people, Raleigh had never imagined.

Nor were Clayton and Ada Hayes's children any realer to him, although he'd lived his life surrounded, in fact, hemmed in, by the close community they called The Family. He thought of his aunts and uncles, and his many cousins, primarily in the aggregate, as his "relatives." Had he ever been asked to let his mind picture them, he would have heard, first, music on the long front porch, then laughter around the dining-room table, then the noisy circus that shared with baseball, eating, talking, swimming, drinking, poker, gossip, tears, and jokes, the two-day carnival called the July Family Reunion. That fumbling, laughing, unrehearsed horseplay that Earley Hayes had named the KNICK-KNACK GEM-CRACK HIGH-TIME CIRCUS. If asked to describe his relatives in a phrase, Raleigh would have quoted Flonnie Rogers. "Pack of fools."

His individual impressions of his aunts and uncles were only those same few family tags, traditional as epitaphs, those summaries almost unchanged since his childhood, amended only to add wives, husbands, children, grandchildren, to subtract limbs, to conclude with death. The baby twins Thaddeus and Gayle were to him the photograph of toddlers in sailor suits. They were the horrible thought of small coffins in the parlor, and the fear that he too might suddenly die while a child. His godfather Whittier was the photograph of the thin, smiling soldier on the dresser, with the jelly jar of flowers in front of it, the Purple Heart and Bronze Star on either side. Was the elaborately curled inscription ("1938. Welcome, Raleigh Whittier Hayes. Beauty is Truth, Truth Beauty, That's all you need to know. Yours, Uncle Whit") in the yellowed book *The Poetry of John Keats* that was still somewhere up on the shelves by the Naugahyde rocker in Starry Haven. Was the horrible image of his grandmother in tears beside the gold star flag in the front parlor window. Was the fear that he too might be shot flaming from the sky when only twenty-three.

Raleigh's uncle A.A. was the frowning bookworm who'd had "ants in his pants," and "Gone North," as if this phrase were synonymous with "gone to the moon," or "gone insane." His aunt Serene was a gentle deaf woman who'd died of cancer at forty because she was "too good for this world." His aunt Big Em was "brokenhearted" since her husband's death in Germany, but always chuckling. Was the woman who weighed almost two hundred pounds, never came into a house without a lemon meringue pie in each hand and a new dirty joke to share, who astonishingly possessed a cabinet full of old track-meet trophies, who let her children "run wild as Indians," who inherited her father's wheelchair when she lost her leg to diabetes, from which unregulated disorder she died at fifty-two. A warning to Raleigh to control his diet.

His uncle Furbus, a radio announcer, long-shanked, wire-thin, blue-eyed, was "the best fun in the world," and could match Big Em's obscenity, joke for joke. For Raleigh, he was always hunched over the baby grand piano in the front parlor, Lucky Strike dangling from his full, loose lips, his eyes squinted shut by the smoke, the heel of his white buck shoe shaking the floorboard. The one who would sing to Raleigh and his cousins jingles like "Marezleetoats Dozeleetoats and little itchy heinies," like "Trickle trickle. Trickle trickle. Nickel nickel. Nickel nickel. Pepsi-Cola hits the spot. Makes you vomit in the pot." Furbus was the one who died of lung cancer at thirty-nine, a warning to Raleigh to quit smoking.

Furbus's younger brother Hackney was "another Clark Gable," who "could have been another Babe Ruth." Instead, he sailed through life smiling on a sea of beer and Coca-Colas, ate away his looks with mountains of spare ribs and fried chicken wings, smoked when he wasn't eating, strummed his ukulele and hummed love songs, got his lung punctured in a poker game at the beach, chased married women he didn't plan to catch, and died of a heart attack at forty-two in a semiprofessional baseball game, chasing a fly ball he didn't catch either. He was another warning.

The rest of the Hayes children were still (if barely) alive, but Raleigh had already summed them up as well. Bassie the baby, the "sweet as pie, give you the shirt off his back" golf pro, only ten years older than Raleigh

himself (and in whose room in the old house Raleigh had often slept —
with its pictures of Bobby Jones and Joe DiMaggio on the walls, and its
Esquire Petty girl pinup in the closet — Bassie was now a paralyzed, inarticulate replica of Raleigh's grandfather.

Hackney's twin sister Reba, legless in her wheelchair, had once had "the
voice of an angel," had once been "the best-looking gal in Thermopylae,"
had once (Raleigh had seen the photograph) sat on the porch steps in an
oversize white shirt with the tail out, her jeans rolled to her knees, her
saddle oxfords raised on their toes as if life were an irresistible dance. Clustered around her, half-a-dozen boys, their jeans rolled at white-socked
ankles above loafers or army boots, their wallets in their hip pockets, their
long awkward arms a blur of energy, waited to be chosen to take her to the
roller rink, the record store, the gym dance, the reservoir where jalopies of
lovers parked. Reba was the one who'd sung the solo at her high-school
graduation, and the next day married one of the boys in the photograph — the one with the sailor hat. In Raleigh's memory she was eter-
nally hung with children, in her arms, around her neck, hidden in her
skirt, or crawling up her back. "The more the merrier," she claimed.

Her little sister Lovie had not even waited for high-school graduation to
marry Senior Clay, who'd said for the next forty-five years that he never
knew what hit him. She gave birth to Jimmy Clay at sixteen, Gayle at seventeen, Thaddeus at twenty-one, and Whittier at twenty-five, at which
point Senior wryly and wanly begged his wife's surviving brothers please
not to die until Lovie had reached menopause, as he couldn't afford any
more sons to carry on the names of her dead siblings. This request Furbus
ignored, and at thirty-nine, Lovie gave birth to Furbus II. The duplication
of all these Hayes names might have made family storytelling confusing,
except that Lovie never called anyone by their given names (although,
strangely enough, her name really was "Lovie"). She called her husband
"Senior" because she called Gayle "Junior." Thaddeus was Butch, Whittier was Chips, and Jimmy Clay's name was actually John. She rechristened
as well the motherless nephews whom she hauled, for months, for years, at
a time, into the loud, clothes-strewn house in Cowstream. Five-year-old
Gates Hayes became her Buddy and her Little Lady-Killer and her Sugar
Pot.

God, said Lovie, had given her only boys because He knew she loved
them to pieces, loved everything about boys from their cute little penises
to every hair on their head. Everyone thought Lovie was a riot when she'd
climb up on the piano, unwind her cheap chiffon scarf from her neck,
wring it through her hands, and wail the torch song, "Oh my boys, I love

them so, They'll never know, All my life is just despair, But I don't care!"

Aunt Victoria would snort, "I don't know about despair, Lovie, but it certainly is a slipshod mess."

Dramatically Lovie would sniff under each armpit, then announce as if she were on television, "My life's a mess, but my clothes are clean. Try Lye. It does the job." And leaping down from the piano, she'd begin to tap, shake her hands and sing, " 'Well las' Monday mornin', Lawd Lawd Lawd. I did the laundry. Lawd Lawd Lawd.' Stand back, boys, here comes the showstopper!" High in the air she'd kick the long tan leg that had once worn the majorette tassel, the Talent Show tap shoe, the carhop's boot, until her shoe flew off and broke a lamp, or she slipped and fell into the piano, or a boy ran into the room, blood pouring from his nose.

Yes, Lovie was "the Family Clown," with "more talent than you could shake a stick at," which Raleigh always assumed meant this abrupt dancing and singing, or her odd tendency to speak in strange dialects, to imitate the way people talked (he was continually anxious that she would single him out for mimicry), to converse loudly and at length with the dead, as well as the imaginary — including a French maid named Fifi, to whom she was always yelling to come clear the table or pour lye down the laundry hamper. "Damn that girl! Fifi! Fifi! Bonejur! Lord, she's run off again, and forgot to take me with her! She was going to get me a job in the Folies Bergère and out of this boot camp. Oo la la, kick! Oo la la, kick! Watch the leg, boys! Stand back. Well, leave Furbie's truck alone, Buddy-Gates, and he'll *stop* crying!"

Lovie the clown, the star of the Knick-Knack Circus, who for a laugh would pull strings of sausages out of her baggy sleeves, trip over her long rubber shoes, pour a bucket of water over her head, smack herself with a fly swatter, and allow Bassie's mongrel sheepdog Alexander the Mutt to chase her around the Big Top, that ring of rocks and pebbles roofed by red streamers stretched from tree boughs. Lovie was the one who always led the singalong with which July Family Reunions drew to their ceremonial close, as dozens of hot, salty-sweaty, sunburnt, stuffed, inebriated, sleepy Hayeses swayed against one another while they sang the medley that made up the credo of their impossible church: the ones they called "happy songs." Always songs like "Life Is Just a Bowl of Cherries," "I've Got the World on a String," "I Can't Give You Anything but Love, Baby," and other such rollicking rose-colored lies about the sunny side of the street. How, thought the adult Raleigh, could a woman like Lovie, who had lost both her parents, half her siblings, random parts of others, both her own breasts, who'd lived through a heart attack, her husband's bankruptcy, the deafness of one son, the two divorces of another, the refusal of her eldest, Jimmy, to give up, at forty-five, his pathetic fantasy of wedded bliss with his nymphomaniacal cousin Tildy Harmon; who'd lived through the Depression and World War II, not to mention the world since then, not to mention what the people in it were doing to each other and what God was doing to them; how could Lovie think Life was a bowl of anything except ashes? Unless, as Aunt Victoria told him, Hayeses never looked up from the card table long enough to notice disaster crashing through the wall; never closed their mouths long enough to notice that they'd thrown their lives away like the wasted food Lovie called on the imaginary Fifi to throw out, when there was a world out there ready to kill for the leftovers. Never noticed that their easy profligate love was not enough, and never had been.

Raleigh had always thought Victoria was right in her appraisal of The Family; she was the sanest of his relatives, the only one who made any sense. But what of this first-born Hayes, with whom our hero so identified? The truth was that just as he accepted her dismissive synopsis of her siblings (including her annoyance with his father Earley for being a stubborn, irresponsible, improvident, irrational ne'er-do-well), so, in a sense, Raleigh had for many years reduced his favorite aunt to her siblings' tags about her: Their big sister Victoria Anna had devoted her life to carrying God's supplies out to the darkest corners of the third world; she had done so at the complete sacrifice of "a real life" — which to them meant a husband and children in a house in Thermopylae — done so out of motives in which (depending on the speaker) Christian fervor, Communist leanings, celibate feminism, and an inexplicable dissatisfaction with "home" were mixed. They talked about her without judgment or comprehension. "Well, she's not the marrying kind." "Likes to keep to herself, never did like sharing our room, put a *lock* on her closet, oh Lord, I couldn't even believe it, 'member that?" "She's gone to do the Savior's work." "She's got this notion about advancing the races or something, I don't know." "She lets men see her brains and that scares them off." "She can't stop speaking her mind, I guess." "She can chew up your face all right, but she doesn't mean what she says." "She's a lot like Mama." "Remember the time when Vicky Anna just blew up out of nowhere at the table and kind of went crazy; heaven sakes, we all just sat there with our mouths open; it's a wonder they didn't fill up with flies." "She's just kind of a mystery, I guess, don't you?" They saw but did not grasp her ambition, they heard but did not feel her irony and anger. They infuriated her by loving her without understanding, by giving her, upon her forced semiretirement from World

Missions, all their shares in the house on East Main, as long as she promised never to sell it. They offered it as "a little surprise" on the benighted theory that she was the only one in the family without "a home," the insulting assumption that now it was time for her "to start to have a real life" — she who had been more places than they had ever heard of! She told them, "Thank you, but I suggest we sell the house and divide the profits equally."

"Sell Mama and Papa's house? Oh, Vicky Anna, you know you don't mean that! Besides, what would Flonnie do if you sold the house? Heaven sakes!"

What Flonnie did was move out the day Victoria took possession of the property. Flonnie Rogers understood more about Victoria Anna Hayes than did any of her siblings except the one closest in age, Earley, the first-born son. Possibly, Flonnie understood more than Earley did. Certainly she knew more than Earley's son ever was to imagine. Despite the fact that from the first day he met her, Raleigh began to build a bond with his world-traveling godmother, forged of their shared impatience with the happiness of their blind relations, our hero at forty-five knew little more about Victoria Hayes than he had learned the day they met. But that particular day had been, for other reasons, a momentous one for Raleigh, and he was far too preoccupied with his own secrets to sense any secrets his aunt might be hiding behind her clear level ice-blue eyes.

In the fall of 1945, in the presence of his relations and from the episcopal hands of the bishop (who by the laying on of those hands that day had confirmed the boy's membership in the church), Raleigh Whittier Hayes, his eight-year-old knees shaking, received his first taste of the dry wafer and warm sherry known as the body and blood of Christ. "Yeeuck!" said his cousin Jimmy Clay. "I sure wouldn't want to drink Jesus's blood. You ought to come to our church. It's a lot lot bigger than this one. A *lot!* Hopabobalopalong Cassidy! And we don't drink blood like VAMPIRES. Whhooooooo!"

Two decades were to pass before Raleigh Hayes took his cousin's advice to join the popular Baptists. At the time, he pulled primly on his new bow tie and replied with a precocious grasp of the Elizabethan compromise, "You don't have to believe it's really blood, dopehead, it's supposed to help you remember Jesus died for other people. You don't know anything."

"Yaga Yaga minka linka chinka to you!"

Having dutifully memorized the lessons of faith for this occasion, Raleigh was prepared to be catechized, and was disappointed that no one but Jimmy Clay bothered to challenge his knowledge. He had really expected something a little more momentous, something along the lines of the boy Jesus's stunning the rabbis in the temple. At the noisy reception, his father brought the bishop over, but this beautifully robed elderly Yankee only shook his hand, and failed to make any queries about the Ten Commandments or to demand the Lord's Prayer. Instead, the man wisely puffed on a slim expensive pipe, sipped wine, and told stories about Earley Hayes.

"Your father here has given me a considerable amount of trouble, young man. Did you know that? But he's very special to me. I ordained him as soon as he got out of college, 'thirty-two, I believe it was, Earley, or 'thirty-three, wasn't it? Most attractive candidate I'd seen in ages, certainly down here." The bishop dismissed the South as an Anglican wilderness with a wave of his wineglass. "Then, before I can place him, he drives up in the middle of the night and tells me he's in a 'crisis of faith'! Has decided to be a trumpet player!"

Earley Hayes leaned down to tie one of his son's brightly polished black oxfords. "Come on, George. That was the summer Grace Louise died. I went off my rocker."

The bishop's puffs on his pipe acknowledged the cost of bereavement, then he leaped ahead. "So, Raleigh, *four* years later, in comes this father of yours again, as if he'd just stepped out in the hall. He tells me Father Farell here at St. Thomas wants him as his curate, and he'd like my blessing." He took the pipe away from his lips and put the glass in its place. "Horrible wine, Earley. By 'blessing,' you know, he meant the job. He'd had the good sense to marry your mother. You, young man, were soon to appear, and it was time to put away childish things." He smiled at his pipe. "And so, Raleigh, this is a very pleasant occasion for me. My faith was rewarded, my judgment — I should say, my gamble — paid off. An indulgence of pride to boast, but I trust forgivable on this happy day. Because your father was a fine curate, a fine chaplain overseas, and now that the war, we must thank God, is over, he's making a good start as rector. I only wish," the bishop glanced around the small, sparsely furnished lounge, "there were some way we could build up the membership down here."

Earley Hayes grinned, his thumbs stuck in the belt of his black cassock. "We could, George. All we have to do is consolidate with the Negro Episcopals. Poor Chester Haroldson at Holy Advent can't even pay his fuel bills. Invite them in. Right?" He winked a sky-blue eye down at his son, who studiously buttoned his new jacket and wondered if they were going to ask him to recite the Creed.

The bishop handed his rector his empty wineglass as he said, "For everything under heaven, there's a time and a season, Earley," and he turned to chat with Mrs. PeeWee Jimson, having already ascertained that hers was the largest pledge in the parish.

This poor bishop had, of course, publicly indulged his pride in Earley Hayes just a year too soon. Already, if he'd paid closer attention, he would have noticed that Sarah Ainsworth Hayes pulled slightly back whenever her husband took her arm to bring her into a conversation. By the following summer, she'd asked Earley to leave their house. Earley, living in sin with the pregnant Roxanne, had asked the Reverend Chester Haroldson not only to preach but to say mass, and asked Haroldson's entire and entirely black congregation to attend St. Thomas's Easter Sunday services, the most important social event on the church calendar. By the following summer, the vestry of St. Thomas had asked the bishop to tell Earley Hayes he was not the sort of shepherd they had in mind, and the bishop had done so. "'This shabby situation,'" he'd said, with a sad puff on his pipe, "I take as my personal mistake, my personal shame, and, I say this, Earley, with sorrow, my personal loss. But I will not reassign you in this diocese nor recommend your transfer to another. You're still, of course, an ordained priest. Only you can renounce those vows; but as you've seen fit to renounce every other —"

"Oh, George," said (ex) Reverend Earley Hayes. "You're such a by fuck pompous ass."

But none of this had been predicted the day of Raleigh's confirmation. All the Hayeses were happily gathered that day, not only because they loved coming together for any festive or ceremonial occasion — particularly if it involved one of their own — but because Raleigh's godmother, Victoria Anna Hayes, had just flown in from Hawaii, back from the Far East for the first time since 1933, a twelve-year absence from Thermopylae which her siblings blamed completely on the Japanese, since it was impossible for them to imagine anyone's not coming home sooner unless physically constrained by world catastrophe. Victoria, still wearing her trim blue WAC uniform, was the last of the Hayeses to return from the war (of those who were returning — Whittier and Big Em's husband had both died overseas for their country), and everybody was showing Vicky their spouses and children and whispering about the little surprise party for her that evening at "Papa's house."

The first thing Victoria Anna Hayes said to her godson was, "It's not going to be much of a surprise if they keep talking about it, is it, little boy? How do you do, I'm your aunt Victoria Hayes." She held out a white-gloved hand and briskly shook his small one.

"I'm Raleigh Whittier Hayes," he solemnly replied. "I'm named for my godfather Whittier. The Nazis blew up his plane. You're my godmother." He was staring at the ribbons over the breast pocket of her jacket. "I didn't know they let women fight in wars, but Paschal says you killed a million Japs."

"You can tell Paschal, he's confusing me with Harry Truman," she said. "Did you get those stamps?"

"Yes, ma'am. . . . Thank you."

"You look like your grandfather. My papa."

"No, I don't." Raleigh was horrified to hear himself compared to a speech-garbled spastic legless man in a wheelchair. "I look like my daddy."

She gave her nose an angry pinch. "Your daddy looks like my papa. He'll look more like him too, if he keeps on smoking and drinking. But try to tell a Hayes to use their head. Do you like stamps?"

"Yes, ma'am. I'd like to see all those places you saw."

"Then do it, little boy."

Raleigh could think of nothing to reply to this command, and was beginning to tug at his bow tie under the scrutiny of steel-blue eyes intensified by the startling dark tan of her face. It was a very handsome, but not a very comfortable face; the nose was too sharp, the chin was too strong. Her hair, sun-bleached the color of bronze, was trimly cut, and she wore no makeup or jewelry. Like her hair, her figure was trim and orderly. In the silence, Raleigh was driven to say, "I'm almost eight."

"I'm almost thirty-five. . . . When you're that age, you won't think it's so old. Besides, then you won't have to do what people tell you anymore, when they don't know what they're talking about."

This psychic reading of his thoughts was the first inkling Raleigh had of a shared sensibility with this brisk, tanned woman. It prompted him to confide, "I got confirmed today. I had to study all summer, and now I get to take communion."

She crossed her arms, her wrists brown between the white gloves and the gold buttons of her sleeves. "Why?"

"What?"

"Why do you want to take communion? If you're going to do a thing, you've got to have a reason. Unless, of course, you're a Hayes."

Raleigh crossed his arms; his blue jacket also had gold buttons. "You're a Hayes."

"No, I'm not."

"How come?" he challenged her. "Did you change your name or something?"

She stared back down at him. "Or something," she said, adding, "I brought you a present in my steamer trunk. From a place called New Guinea."

"What is it?" Then, "Thank you," he remembered to say.

"Wait and see."

Raleigh put his hands into the pockets of his new blue suit pants. "I do have a reason. Why I took communion. But I don't want to say it."

"Fine." Victoria was whisking her hand to brush away the smoke of her brother Furbus's cigarette, as he came over and stretched his thin arm around her shoulder. She finished her sentence. "You don't have to say a reason, little boy, but you ought to know it."

Furbus grinned. "Vicky Anna, oh oh oh you beautiful doll, listen to this one. There were these two Catholic bricklayers working on the sidewalk outside this whorehouse. So a Protestant minister comes along and goes right inside, so the first bricklayer says . . ."

Raleigh did have a reason for deciding to join the church, and he knew very well what it was. He had drawn up a private contract with God in which he was prepared to offer dutiful faith in exchange for two favors: (1) that the Almighty stop his mother from being sad, and (2) that He invest Raleigh himself with superhuman physical strength, just as He had earlier done for Samson (and Raleigh had no worries about doing anything so ridiculous as allowing a silly girl to get near enough to cut his hair). In offering this exchange, the eight-year-old cast aside a skepticism already disposed to doubt Superman and Santa Claus. He would take a chance: If adults honestly believed that faith could move mountains, then Raleigh was willing to see if it could enable him to pull an automobile. For this was the test he'd devised to verify whether or not that wafer was the magic pill it was reputed to be. He would pull a car down the street, just as Samson had pulled down the temple.

The desire for strength was not a new one; Raleigh had always hated being thin and frail, particularly when he was powerless to stop his father from flinging him happily in the air, or his hefty cousin Paschal from sitting on his chest and tickling him. So drawn was the boy to feats of brawn that despite his shy dislike of public display, he'd asked to be his uncle Hackney's assistant in performances of the Knick-Knack Circus, where the barrel-chested baseball player starred as "Hercules Hackney the Man of Steel," whose easy lifting of barbells, picnic tables, and even of Big Em, awed the small child. It was Raleigh's job to hand Hackney the bike chains to snap, the old golf clubs to twist into hearts, the tin cans to crush atop his head. For this privilege, he even allowed Lovie to pin a tablecloth around his neck as a cloak.

It was not surprising that Raleigh should worry about his frailty during these war years, when all the male grown-ups vanished, leaving a house of women (half of whom themselves disappeared during the day, in overalls and hair nets; returning at night to listen with frowns to the radio talking about "Yanks pushed back," and "Corregidor fell," and "Allied forces bombed Hamburg yesterday," and other cryptic statements whose meaninglessness made them scarier). It was not surprising, when his father (gone for more than a year, not to fight, but to help fighters say prayers) had told the four-year-old to take good care of his mother and be a strong little fellow on the homefront. On the homefront, Raleigh did what he could: He kept his light out after dark, he helped his mother count her ration coupons at the grocery store, he pulled his wagon behind Lovie as she marched down Main Street pounding on doors and demanding nylon hose, toothpaste tubes, rubber tires, and anything metal that wasn't nailed down. But Raleigh worried. Even after his father returned and grown-ups started cheering by the radio at night, he brooded on his weakness. He lay on his back waiting for airplanes to roar out of the big slow clouds, fearful that if the planes came, he would not be quick and strong enough to grab the bombs before they fell, and hurl them back at the sky. Certainly not big enough to stop the "20,000 TONS OF T.N.T. DROPPED ON JAPS," that he'd read about in the *Thermopylae Sun* that summer of 1945. He certainly wasn't big enough to catch an A-bomb and throw it away.

In the autumn of that year, Raleigh's anxiety was not alleviated by Emperor Hirohito's surrender. In fact, it grew. His mother was going away for a short while because "sometimes grown-ups need to be alone to think about their problems, and sometimes they can't solve those problems, and sometimes lives have to change, and we have to be strong." And she'd begun to cry, a sight so rare and dreadful that her son began to cry as well. That night, he offered God his proposal: Solve his mother's problems, make him as strong as Samson, and he would believe.

Therefore, the evening after his first communion, at the surprise party for his aunt Victoria, while all the Hayeses, singing, "Rye whiskey rye whiskey rye whiskey I cry, If I don't get rye whiskey, I swear I will die," lounged in the green rockers and swings and along the white rails and wood steps of his grandfather's porch; while his cousins were screaming, "Red Rover," off in the dusky side yard; Raleigh slipped away. He went to the cavernous basement, walled with all the vegetables Flonnie Rogers had "put up" in her war against the trashy modern world. There he removed his confirmation suit with ritualistic precision. He wrapped about his loins a large white pillowcase, modeling the folds on biblical movies. Then, with a long clothesline tied at one end to the front bumper of his uncle Hackney's new blue Nash, and the other end tied tightly around his waist, Raleigh Hayes brought to trial the power of God. He was scrupulously fair. He picked the Nash, not only because it was half a block away from the porch, but because it was on absolutely level ground. He wouldn't require that God enable him to pull the car uphill. He even finally found and managed to release the emergency brake. He gave God every chance. While Raleigh strained against the rope, his bare feet stinging as they pushed into the gravely asphalt, he chanted aloud the Lord's Prayer. He said it ten times while he jerked and pulled and leaned and panted. He squatted on his haunches, waited for breath to return, then — scrupulously fair — he tried again; this time, Christ's two commandments, which, like the Pledge of Allegiance (with which he sometimes started by mistake), he could race through with only three gulps of air. "Thou shall love the Lord thy God with all thy heart, with all thy mind, and with all thy strength. This is the first and great commandment. And the second is like unto it: Thou shalt love thy neighbor as thyself."

Nothing happened.

"All right," warned Raleigh, and gave God a final, third chance. He started to sing the Creed he had struggled so proudly to memorize. "I believe in one God, the Father Almighty, Maker of Heaven and Earth. . . ."

He felt something! A tiny lessening of the tension in the rope! "Heaven and earth . . . Heaven and earth . . ." Frantically, he tried to remember what came next in the Creed. then skipped rushing ahead, guessing at words he didn't know. "And of all things visional and invisible and in one Lord Jesus Christ, forgotten not made, being of one supper with the Father by whom all things were made." He felt it again! The slack in the rope. He could take a step. Another step. *The car was moving.* Raleigh strained until his neck ached and blood ran from the corner of his lip. He had pulled the blue Nash ten feet forward when he heard the hideous sound whose remembrance, even thirty years later, sweated his hands and face.

It was the sound of half a dozen of his cousins kicking leaves as they ran up the deep-shadowed sidewalk. It was the sound of laughter. They crowded around him, knocking into each other with mirth. Then Butch Clay and Tildy Leacock both shouted in his face, "It's Uncle Hackney! It's

Uncle Hackney!" Sickened, Raleigh rushed, tripping over his rope, to the sidewalk. And there, rising from the rear of the Nash like a giant, stood his twenty-year-old uncle Hackney, cigarette glowing in his wide handsome face, Coca-Cola bottle in his hand, painted tie with a palm tree billowing out from his stupendous chest. "You little shits!" Hackney thundered at the skipping circle of Raleigh's tormentors, and they scattered in a flurry of leaves. Then he leaned down to the boy. "Hey, Raleigh, hey little buddy, I'm sorry. I just wanted to give you a hand."

His nephew, enraged at the knotted rope he was desperately yanking free, said nothing until he could fling it to the sidewalk. Then he snarled, "I'm not your buddy. And I won't ever be!"

"Listen, hold up. Hold up. You just needed just a little bit of help, that's all. You had it going, little buddy."

Already at the corner, already in tears, Raleigh shrieked, "I don't need *any* help!" And by the time he had run the long way around the block to the basement, Raleigh Hayes had become the cynical agnostic he was to remain for the next thirty-seven years; his atheism tempered only by the necessity to posit a God in order to despise Him. Slamming the cellar door twice, he stood beating on it until a voice came out of the dank musty shadows.

"You, Bassie! You stop banging on that door! Miz Hayes trying to nap!"

"I'M NOT BASSIE."

Flonnie Rogers, her round gold-framed glasses glinting, moved into the light of the bare bulb that swing from the beam where strings of gourds and peppers also hung. "You the boy left his good clothes on that barrel over there where spiders fixing to lay their eggs in them and eat you alive?"

Silent and sullen, Raleigh rubbed his arm over his eyes, then he picked up his trousers from his neat stack.

"What you doing with that good pillowcase? You think nobody had to bend over with sciatica so bad they can't do nothing, and wash and iron that pillowcase?"

"I HATE EVERYBODY." Raleigh flung off the loincloth and pulled on his blue pants. "They're all fat stupid dopeheads!"

Flonnie yanked him into the shirt. "How come your stomach all scratched up and blood spotted? You gonna mess up this new shirt. Stand still." She spat on the edge of her apron and blotted the raw rope burn that circled his waist, then brusquely started buttoning.

"Ouch. I wish the A-Bomb would blow them up. I wish they'd all drop dead a million million times."

"You better not let the Lord hear you talking like that."

"I hate Him too!"

Stuffing the shirt into the pants, the wiry black arms spun him in a circle. "You think He cares? Hunh? He's not studying some puny little skinny white boy's sass."

Raleigh shouted, "Shut up!" and instantly felt the hot slap of her hand through his trousers.

"Don't you *never* tell me shut up again, you hear me!" Her small hand squeezed around his wrist and the glasses glittered close to his face. "I had about all I can take of fool Hayeses for one day."

Raleigh pulled his hand away from her to wipe his nose.

"That's right. Act like trash, wiping buggers on yourself and talking ugly to old people. Use this handkerchief like you was raised." She yanked the neatly folded triangle from his jacket pocket. "Now. Help me carry this kindling to the kitchen. I got to bake my biscuits for tomorrow. None of them going home tonight, the way it sounds. Hold your arms out. You can carry more'n that, big as you are. All right. Go on."

Raleigh stuck his chin out over the top hickory branch. "If you'd just use the gas stove, Flonnie, Grandma says, then you wouldn't have to tote this wood so much."

"Open that door so I can shut off this light. That's right," she continued, behind him on the steps, "and if everybody just ate potato chips and trash like they do, we wouldn't need to grow no vegetables neither."

After three trips up and down the back porch stairs to stack the wood pile, Raleigh left Flonnie viciously jabbing with a poker at the bowels of her immense black stove. As she stabbed it, she sang, "I'm going down the road feeling bad. Yes Lord. And I ain't gonna be treated this way," adding, "Pack of fools!" at the end of each verse.

Unable to face the detestable crowd on the porch, who were, Raleigh was certain, all making jokes about him, he stayed in the house. Tiptoeing past his grandmother's room, he climbed the dark mahogany stairs, and stopped at the turn of each landing to lean on the crudely carved newel post and listen to the clear sharp notes of his father's trumpet below, piercing through the familiar voices harmonizing, "And love can come to anyone. Bee-cause the best things in life aaare freeeee."

"Fat old stupid dumbheads."

On the third floor, he saw a light under one of the long row of rooms, and he thought he heard the sound of crying, but when his aunt Victoria came out into the hall and said, "Who is it?," there were no tears in the vivid blue eyes.

Raleigh was kept speechless by fears that this strange uniformed woman suspected he was spying on her. However, all she said was, "Would you like your present now?"

Relieved, he nodded and followed her back into the room. Very much like the other, now usually empty, third-floor bedrooms, this one had a wide bed with a white fringed bedspread, a tall dresser with a white doily hanging over the edges of the top, a plain table with a cane-bottomed chair, and pale rugs on the floor. But it was a room that Raleigh had never wanted to sleep in because on the wall was a framed print of a wolf in a snow blizzard, standing all alone on the edge of a jagged bluff. He was afraid to sleep with that wolf's remorseless eyes on him.

"I brought this a long way," Aunt Victoria said. In the middle of the floor was a large scarred steamer trunk covered with fraying stickers and tags. It stood on its end, taller than Raleigh, and opened in the middle. Everything inside was folded or rolled precisely. "There's my whole life," she told him. "I got chased with this from Singapore to New Guinea to Samoa and Fiji. Then I decided to turn around and fight back." She unsnapped a canvas section and pulled out a large flat package wrapped in burlap. "Here."

"Thank you. Were you scared?"

She redid the compartment's snaps and belts. "Unless you've been washing your hair in a helmet and had it blown out of your hands by pieces of a building that was right in back of you a second ago, Raleigh, you don't know what scared is. But the thing is, when the really scary things happen, you don't have time to get scared."

By now, Raleigh had unwrapped the burlap from what he realized at once, from pictures and movies, was a small oblong shield, its handhold carved out of the single hollowed piece of ebony wood. The raised design on the face of the shield was a serpentine pattern of twisted lines. He put his fingers through the handle and raised it.

"Little boys," she said, "get these when they have their confirmations. When they're old enough to take spears and hunt wild pigs."

"They do? Why?"

"To eat."

Raleigh moved his arm back and forth. "Thank you."

"You're welcome."

Resting his shield on his lap, the boy ran both his hands over its mysterious design. Finally, he spoke again without looking up. "I don't think I'd be strong enough to hunt wild pigs."

"Have you ever been on a train?"

Raleigh looked up. "One time."

"Were you scared?"

He shook his head.

"Well, those little boys in New Guinea would run like crazy from a train."

Raleigh sat quietly on the bed as his aunt Victoria arranged a few objects from her trunk onto the dresser top. A brush, a comb, a bronze plaque with, as she showed him, her name engraved on it. When she removed her jacket and hung it neatly over the chair-back, he was surprised to see she had breasts like other women. Winding her watch, she said, "Have you ever been to Richmond?"

Raleigh had never even heard of Richmond. "Not really," he replied.

"Tomorrow, would you like to go with me?"

Adrenaline raced up his chest. "I have to go to school."

"You can learn more going places. I'll ask your mother." She rolled her sleeves up her brown arms. "Now, excuse me. I need to wash up."

Raleigh stood, but at the door he turned back. "Do you think . . . Can I ask you something . . . Aunt Victoria?"

She crossed her arms and waited.

"Do you think, if you made a deal with God and He broke it and you didn't get what you wanted, then do you think you should still have to believe in Him?"

"I think you don't always get what you want."

"My daddy says you can't make deals with God.'

"He ought to know."

"But if God doesn't keep His promise, do you think that's fair?"

"No." She closed her trunk and locked it.

So Raleigh went to Richmond. At Thanksgiving he went with his aunt to Asheville. Right after Christmas, when his father and mother were separating, Victoria took him all the way to the top of the Empire State Building in New York City, where she said, "I don't believe a Hayes would climb these stairs unless they heard somebody was playing baseball or canasta on the roof." By spring, she was gone again, and the first packet of stamps to arrive for him in Thermopylae was postmarked Rangoon.

On their trips together, Raleigh never told his godmother how all that winter he'd slept with his shield on the floor by his bed, and that it had proved a more powerful talisman against fear than the weekly communion

wafer that was now dust in his mouth. No, he didn't share his secrets with
his aunt Victoria, and she didn't share hers with him, not then, and not in
the following decades when she would return to Thermopylae for the long
succession of funerals. Nor was anything said between them in all the evenings the adult Raleigh spent with her, after World Missions finally
coerced the traveler into semiretirement, and she moved into the big
empty house on East Main Street.

No one but Victoria's brother Earley and her mother's maid Flonnie
Rogers knew why she had first left home, gone to the other side of the
world, and not come back for twelve years. And she had never forgiven
Earley for persuading her to leave, and Flonnie Rogers had never forgiven
her for going.

As it happened, our hero had been given in these past two wandering
weeks of trying to carry out his father's quest all the clues to Victoria
Anna Hayes's past. But, like everyone else, he saw and heard only what had
been filtered and funneled into the narrow frame of his preoccupations.
There was another reason, too, why he had made no connections. He was
white. Now, Raleigh Hayes would have vehemently protested any suggestion that he was to the slightest degree blinkered by racial prejudice.
Hadn't he, upon reaching his teens, taken some retroactive pride in his father's failed effort to integrate St. Thomas? Hadn't he been embarrassed
not by *where* his father taught, but by that frivolous marching in the
streets, whatever the color of the band behind him? Hadn't Raleigh himself (leading his aunts Reba and Big Em to accuse him of Communism)
joined three sit-down strikes in college, and hadn't he severely repri-
manded a soldier in his unit for racial slurs about a black bunkmate?
Hadn't he and Aura fallen in love in a bus half-filled with blacks on the
way to John Kennedy's funeral? Hadn't he thrown down his napkin and
left the Civitans luncheon at the Lotus House when Nemours Kettell
proposed a toast celebrating the assassination of Martin Luther King, Jr.?
Hadn't he encouraged Holly and Caroline to make the little Miller children up on Strawberry Court feel at home at the Starry Haven pool? No,
he was not a bigot. Nonetheless, it never once occurred to Raleigh Hayes
that there could possibly be connections between his family and the family
of Flonnie Rogers other than those of service and compensation, by which
he meant the obligations and, yes, the affections that long service earns.
He had never, for example, considered that he had been far more deeply
formed by Flonnie's tutelage than by that of his grandmother. He had

never thought, when instructed to "find Jubal Rogers," that Flonnie's nephew was more than such an obligation.

Had our hero's view not been so filtered, so constricted, all the bits of glass that seemed to him meaningless would have fallen into their pattern. He would have noticed sooner that foremost in his father's mind was an effort to make some kind of restitution to Jubal Rogers, with whom he'd obviously shared a past so profoundly intimate that even now the wounds weren't healed. He would have heard Flonnie say at the nursing home that the two men had once been musicians together, and he would have realized that the trumpet and the trip to New Orleans (news that had not surprised but only angered Rogers) were tied to that shared musical past. Had he not been deafened, Raleigh would have listened to the fact that no one — his father, Flonnie, Lovie — wanted Jubal Rogers's name mentioned to Victoria Anna. And having heard that fact, Raleigh would have paid attention to Jubal's and Victoria's faces when each was talking to him about the other. Then perhaps his own childhood memory of Flonnie's furious anger the day she'd taken him with her to visit Jubal's mother's house would have made sense. Because he would have agreed with what Flonnie had said in 1944: It was as true now as it had been then that nobody in Thermopylae was going to "put up with a black boy messing with a white woman," so it was just as well that "She'd" gone halfway around the world, and "He" was in a German prison camp, where he would be better off staying, until he came to his senses.

Now, there were some things about Jubal Rogers that either Lovie or Reba could have told Raleigh, and probably would have, if he'd asked them directly. This much they thought they knew:

Jubal Rogers had been coming to the East Main house for years, to help his aunt Flonnie in her garden. In that way, he'd earned the money to buy a clarinet. People said he was a smart, handsome boy, but not a comfortable one to have around, for he was conceited, and suspiciously sarcastic-sounding, and argumentative, and, well, not really respectful. Still, Earley had befriended him, and was always going on about how talented Jubal was, and soon had him joining the nightly music on the Hayes porch. When Jubal was sixteen and Earley was eighteen (the eldest son, already in college, just married to Grace Louise, but still living at home), the two young men had started playing over in Darktown for a few dollars or a few drinks, playing and consorting with people Flonnie condemned as trash jugband niggers.

When Jubal was eighteen, he began visiting the house even when Earley wasn't there. He began sitting at night on the porch with Victoria Anna, who was then twenty-two, unmarried and still living at home. She drove her own car to her own job (a very good job, everybody said, considering her age and sex and the Depression) as the secretary to Zebulon Forbes, Jr. Her job was to try to sort out the mess that Zeb Jr.'s father had left when he'd jumped out the window of the Forbes Building. And Zeb Jr.'s job was trying to get Victoria to marry him. Instead, she started to sit on the porch with Jubal Rogers. She started to bring home from the library stacks of political books and to sit in the parlor reading them with an eighteen-year-old black man, and she continued to do so for a year, and no one noticed what was really happening. In Big Em's opinion, thirty years later (she was fifteen at the time): "You know how Vicky was, fired up over all these Communist-type ideas, and I don't think black people could use the library back then, could they?, and you know how she was about doing the Lord's work all the way to China and back; well, she was that way with Jubal, too, when she saw he liked to talk talk talk those same nutty ideas of hers. And he *was* Flonnie's kin, even if he was awful full of himself." In Lovie's opinion (she was nine at the time): "Oh, Vicky Anna, she always wanted people to *do* things if they had some talent, you know, like asking me why I didn't go to *New York,* Lord love us, instead of marrying Senior; and she and Earley just thought Jubal was the cat's pajamas. He was always hanging around the house, and I don't care if he was purple or green, he sure could play that clarinet. I guess she sort of adopted him, you know how these things happen."

By these things, she certainly did not mean love. In the house of love and laughter, everyone saw the young black man and young white woman bent over the books, the newspapers, the record player, time after time, and no one thought of love.

Then, and in the same horrible month when suddenly the little twins, Thaddeus and Gayle, and Earley's young wife, Grace Louise, all died of diphtheria within days of each other, whatever relationship there was between Victoria Anna and Jubal Rogers also died. Earley, stricken with his own griefs, put Jubal on a train to New Orleans, where he intended to join him, where they would find jobs together in a band. As for God, Earley renounced Him for murdering his wife and baby brothers. He planned to start over.

But Earley never went to New Orleans. He did instead what he thought he ought to do.

When Victoria came one night into her brother's bedroom to tell him she wanted to go with him to New Orleans because she was carrying

Jubal's child, Earley, twenty years old, the family's eldest son, the bishop's choice, made a number of decisions. He felt he had to. His parents, devastated by the loss of their youngest children, were not at all aware of what was happening to their oldest daughter. Earley thought he knew not only the world better, he thought he knew his sister better than she knew herself. He'd seen Jubal with girls, he'd heard him talk about the kind of jazzed nighttime life he wanted to live, the life he'd already started on Bourbon Street. He didn't believe Jubal knew what he was saying when he sent the letter to Earley with five hundred dollars to bring Victoria to New Orleans, when he enclosed the letter to Victoria that Earley never gave her. The young widower was in, as he'd told the bishop, a crisis of faith. He didn't believe Victoria and Jubal could do anything but destroy themselves over what he knew, if they didn't, could not possibly be love; not what he had shared with Grace Louise.

And so he did the right thing. Earley took his sister Victoria not to New Orleans but to Richmond. He told everybody that she was going there to start those college courses she'd always wanted to take. He told nobody that she was pregnant. He told Victoria that Jubal's life didn't and couldn't ever include her, and finally he convinced her that the only sensible thing to do, given their ages, given their races, given their hometown, given the world, was to let the baby be put up for adoption as soon as it was born.

And that was what Victoria thought her brother had done. She was not allowed by the clinic's policy to look at her son. As soon as they released her, she went to a Richmond employment agency, accepted a job with World Missions Supplies, and left from Newport News three weeks later for Hong Kong. It was 1933. She never heard from Jubal Rogers and he never heard from her. She didn't come back to America until 1945, the night before her godson Raleigh's confirmation.

The name Earley wrote on the birth certificate, when he realized that he couldn't give the baby away forever to strangers, was Joshua Rogers. But the woman to whom he brought the infant, Carra Rogers in Thermopylae's Darktown, always called the boy Josh. And when Jubal came through town with his new wife, Leda Carpenter, and took the boy away with him, north to New York City, Joshua would not let this stranger-father change his name.

THE RETURN

CHAPTER

28

Of a Discovery Made by Raleigh

ATLANTA WAS THE "TERMINUS" of the Old South; her original name pragmatically bestowed by men looking only for a place to load their freight and change their trains. A terminus was all they needed. But, of the New South, she was the young Atalanta, racer after golden apples. She was Atlantis, newfound city of gold, as she burst up from the sea of Sherman's whirlwind, reborn on geysers of millions upon millions of gallons of Coca-Cola. And now all underpasses and overpasses, all beltways and throughways, all cloverleafs, all trains, planes, buses, trucks, all roads led to Atlanta. On them half-a-million new people a year homed like wasps in their Audis and Peugeots to her hive of money. She was a new home. Home of the new Braves, new Hawks, new Falcons, new industry, new symphony, new art, and new cuisine. The new California calling the hi-tech, hi-rise, hi-fi, high-energy, lo-cal, lo mein and tortellini primavera lifestyle people. She was the new Liberty, lifting the light of her revolving skyscraper tops to all those Northeasterners tired of being mugged, poor from being taxed, wretched from being cold huddled masses on dirty snowy streets. She was a place to start over, and at her center soared a high bronze statue of a bare-breasted woman raising aloft a phoenix. She was a place to think big. Bulldozers scooping red clay day and night couldn't keep up with her appetite for malls and condominiums and subdivisions and more, more roads. She manufactured a million products, the best known of which were Scarlett O'Hara and Coca-Cola, the Real Thing, the Pause That Refreshes. But Atlanta herself never paused; she picked up the golden apples on the run, and faster coke came not in bottles but in packets.

"It's Sunday and this town is hopping!" said Gates Hayes. "Wake up, Raleigh, let's hit it!"

But our hero rolled over in his new sheets on his new bed on the forty-seventh floor of the new seventy-story-high cylinder of glass and blue steel called the Peachtree Plaza Hotel; he slept on, girded above the clouds, for eight hours, even if the wrong eight. When he did awaken, his new pin-striped suit was gone, and his new sports jacket hung in the dazzlingly bright bathroom, soaking wet and smelling like the wreck of Caroline's perfume collection. Raleigh had to wear the white suit Mingo had given him. At least the new zipped pouch with his cash had been left behind; at least if Gates had stolen fifty dollars from it, he'd left a note on hotel sta-tionery:

> Stole $50. I.O.U.
> XXX, G

Raleigh spotted his pinstripe as he was plummeting in the glass bubble of one of the outside elevators down to the free-form landing that was sus-pended over the enormous lobby's enormous free-form reflection pool known as "Half-Acre Lake." His suit was draped on a beautiful modern armchair beside the pool. In the suit was Gates Hayes. Across from Gates, an elderly woman in black leaned forward from the fur stole draped over her chair; her face was bent down to one of Gates's hands, which she held in both of hers. Was she going to bite him? No. She was taking his other hand and turning it backward and forward. Was this Mrs. Parisi? She cer-tainly didn't look like the character from *The Asphalt Jungle* whom Hayes had imagined. She looked more like Rose Kennedy than a friend of any Rose who might be colloquial with Weeper Berg. Was she instead the newest Daughter of the Confederacy soon to fall prey to a fabricated gene-alogy and a forged letter of condolence from Robert E. Lee? Carefully de-scending a curving space-age ramp, Raleigh moved in for a closer look. At two of the tables nearby, business-suited black men studied folders from their open briefcases.

"Sir? Hi, I'm Timothy. Would you like to be seated in the peninsular lounge area?"

A young man in a short red jacket with a tray of drinks balanced on his fingers circled in front of Raleigh to ask this question.

But Hayes shook his head. If his brother were in the midst of his penitential apology to the grandmother of Cupid Parisi Calhoun, Raleigh wouldn't intrude. From here at any rate, the woman did not look ready to pull a machine gun out of the potted gingko tree behind her. Besides, the man apparently known as Big Nose Solinsky was nowhere in sight — and would be hard to hide in this wide-open atrium of reflected lights and water. Leaving Gates to his own experienced devices, the elder Hayes went to the desk where he learned that a telephone message had just arrived from Mingo Sheffield: He was at the Omni looking for Pete and they should not expect him until eight or nine.

"Thank you," said Hayes. "Excuse me, miss? What's the Omni?"

The sleek and chic young black woman ("Carole," according to her jacket), one of the many "hotel personnel" on duty at one of the many lobby desks, looked at the Thermopylean very much as a Parisian might look at an American who asked, not even, *"Ou se trouve le Louvre?"* but "What is the Louvre?" Then she caught herself, smiled helpfully, and said that the Omni was just about anything you could ask for. It was shops, restaurants, discos, a hotel, and the coliseum home of the Atlanta Hawks.

"Thank you," said Hayes, no further enlightened about his neighbor's message; for he had paid little attention to Diane Yonge's comment, in the middle of her labor, that her boyfriend Pete ("husband" was a legality only in Mingo's mind) sold ice cream at the Omni. Our hero then went into one of the dining areas where "Byron" said he'd like to tell Raleigh some of their specials today and proceeded to describe most of the ingredients of five complex dishes. Hayes chose a delicate pastry stuffed with crab and sole in a lightly flavored white sauce called "Gustav's Favorite." Afterward, he chose American coffee over cappuchino, espresso, Viennese, mocha, Irish, and Gustav's Special Blend. Afterward, he decided to call his wife while the rates were low, and before the Mafia rubbed him out.

Amazingly, even on a Sunday afternoon, the future mayor was home, although (according to Caroline) bombed to the max with Mrs. Sheffield.

"I beg your pardon," the father sternly said to his daughter.

"Oh, you know, Daddy, like gassed. Listen, I *love* my perfume. It's the absolute platinum. Kevin just goes, you know, freaksville. Thank you thank you, hug hug, kiss kiss. Daddy, guess what! Grandpa left Holly and I a zillion dollars!"

"Holly and *me*. And," Hayes sighed, "it wasn't a 'zillion' dollars, Caroline, and Grandpa is still alive, I assume, and therefore didn't *leave* it to you. He . . . gave it to you."

"Oh, you always twist my words around." He heard a loud pop. Doubtless the receiver was covered in pink gum again. "Daddy, rilly, are you ever ever ever coming home? I have to talk to you, I mean seriously. I need to."

"Honey, I'll be home as soon as I can find Grandpa. Is there a problem?"

"I don't want to talk about it now."

Was Caroline getting married, dropping out of school, buying her own apartment? "I want to talk to you too." He spoke earnestly. "You and Holly and I have to sit down and discuss the best thing to do with that money. It's a real responsibility. When the time comes when you two decide to get married —"

"For shurr! Daddy, you know Holly's never going to get married, and I'm going to marry for money first and then for love the next time."

Both were appalling projections, but Hayes let them go. "Well, you need to save that money for the future, for college."

"Oh, gross."

"Well, we'll discuss it later." He rubbed his eyes. The discussion wasn't going to be easy.

"Couldn't I *puhlease* just at least buy a secondhand car? Nobody, I mean nobody, has to ride the schoolbus but us. With kids! It is *so dorfus!*"

"As you know, I had to walk to school, and no one considered it an injustice."

"Daddy, the world has changed. You can't keep going back to the Old Days. You just don't trust me, you never did, and I might as well be dead."

"That's not true. Caroline, listen to me, I'm going to give you and your sister the station wagon." Good Lord, what had he said?! Was he crazy?

"OHMIGOD! You are? You ARE? Oh Daddy, I love you I love you I love you kiss kiss." A loud clank hurt Raleigh's ears, then he heard a shriek, "HOLLY! HOLLY! MOM, *YO,* PHONE! *HOLLY!*" Caroline had obviously simply thrown the phone away and raced off with the news.

Well, all right, but he'd certainly have to set some ground rules about the car: no week nights, no out of town . . .

"Hello, hot stuff." It was his wife; as ever, determined to talk like a cable television film.

"Hello, Aura. I just gave the twins our station wagon."

"Hey hey! So that's why they're jumping up and down on the couch."

"Tell them to get off that couch!"

Peculiar laughter.

"What's the matter with you, Aura?"

"Raleigh, honey, I am, as Caroline informs me, bombed to the max."

Giggles.

"Are you serious?"

"Nope, I'm loaded. Why should you be the only one? Vera and Barbara and I have polished off the last year's anniversary champagne, a bottle of Cold Duck, and let's see, now we're on a Lancer's Rosé."

"It's Sunday afternoon!"

"More precisely, it's Palm Sunday afternoon, and when Nemours took up the collection at church this morning, he skipped right past our row as if we weren't sitting there, so we all went to lunch with the money!" Hilarious laughter from his wife, and in the background, the cackle of her drinking buddies. "We are celebrating, Raleigh. There is a serious celebration going on here."

Hayes closed the glass door of his telephone booth. Outside it, eight young women in brand-new designer blue jeans were excitedly talking in German either about selling their brothers to a pencil factory or meeting their mothers there.

"I'm sorry, Aura, what did you say? What are you celebrating?"

Their celebration, she explained, was to congratulate Barbara Kettell on her formal separation from the world's worst repressive patriarchal pig (presumably Nemours), and also to congratulate Vera Sheffield on suddenly becoming an honorary grandmother. It was the first Raleigh had heard of it, but apparently, unable to restrain himself, Mingo had called his wife at six in the morning to describe the delivery of Diane Yonge's baby girl, and to announce that Diane (with no names of her own in mind — not surprisingly, since she had persisted in denying she was having the baby at all until thirty seconds before it arrived), that Diane had asked Mingo himself to suggest a name, and he, of course, had suggested "Vera."

"Isn't that the most wonderful thing? Vera's been crying all day!"

"Where *is* Mingo? Yes, that's wonderful."

"Why are you asking me? Aren't y'all in Atlanta?"

"He's at the Omni."

She laughed. "Honey, you're strange."

"I mean, what's he up to? He should be back here now. Did he tell Vera?"

Finally Vera came to the phone herself to say that Mingo was looking for Diane's husband. "Isn't he the sweetest man that ever lived? And, Raleigh, the Lord will bless you forever for all you've done for him."

Hayes rubbed his hair hard. "What?" Had Mingo told her that he'd found him a job? "Vera, I assure you . . . What do you think I've done for him?"

"Here's your sweetie pie," was the only answer he got. The phone clanged to the floor again.

"And what are *you* celebrating, Aura? Decided to run for President? Ha ha."

"I am celebrating, oh, I don't know . . . Life," she airily replied. "Oh, Raleigh, I forgot, I have some sort of bad news."

"Wait." Hayes sat down on the bronzed stool. "All right. What is it?" Surely she wouldn't say "sort of" bad news if the house had burned down, if his father had just telephoned from Bangkok, if . . .

"I was at my office yesterday evening."

Her office? Oh, Mothers for Peace.

"And I went up to yours, to see how things were going . . ."

"Oh God, what is it?"

"Betty Hemans and Bill Jenkins went down to the basement and threw her whole manuscript in the incinerator."

Raleigh took his knuckle out of his mouth. "Is that all?"

"All?! Honey, she was just in pieces. She hates you and your whole family."

"Me? How is it my fault if her stupid novel's no good?"

"What? No, it's not that. . . . Oh, I like that one, Vera, especially the straps."

"Aura . . ."

"Sorry. Just a sec. We're all trying on Vera's samples, you know, her lingerie. You should see us."

"No doubt."

"She's taking your advice about 'Vera's of Thermopylae.' By the way, Raleigh, Holly said you stole that idea from her."

"I did." Out in the airport of a lobby he could see Gates and Mrs. Parisi (?), standing to look at the spouting water fountains gushing out of the pool. Now Gates was holding *her* hand. "Aura, I've got to go. Tell me. Is Betty quitting? She's not leaving Bonnie Ellen alone in my office again, is she?"

"No, don't worry. She says she honors her commitments even if some people named Hayes don't."

"Oh, for Pete's sake, I've explained to her about those retirement benefits a thousand times!"

"Raleigh, you're not listening. Betty gave her novel to Sue Ann Swain to read, and then Friday Mrs. Swain came over in an absolute tizzie because she thought Betty had stolen all her old love poems and letters from your uncle Whittier and stuck them in her novel. Then it turns out Betty had stuck her *own* love poems from your uncle Whittier in her novel. Then late yesterday they both pull out all their old letters, and they're all exactly the same. Including marriage proposals! Word for word! 'Remember Me!' I'll say. I don't want to speak ill of the dead, but, honey, your godfather sure didn't mind taking risks. What if he *had* come home?"

"Excuse me, Aura, I can't assimilate this just now, and your voice sounds funny anyhow."

"Funny ha ha, or funny bombed to the max?"

"Gates is over on the other side of the pool here talking to a woman in the Mafia about this idiotic duel."

"Oh, Raleigh, your family! And you think *I* sound funny?"

"But I'll call Betty tomorrow."

"I wouldn't. She said she'd like to spit right in your eye. In fact, she said I ought to go through your dresser drawers and your checkbook because you were probably a bigamist. Come on, Buster, spill it. Have you got a wife in New Orleans?" Laughter and screams. "Oh, don't worry about the rug, Barbara! I've been needing to get a new one for ages."

"Aura, good-bye. I love you. I wish you were here. No, I wish I were there."

"Wait a minute, Raleigh, wait a minute. Oh, damn, I've got to pee!"

"You want me to wait here long distance while you go to *pee!?*"

"No, no, I'm crossing my legs. I just wanted to tell you Aunt Vicky may call. She was over here last night, asking me what was going on, and I told her everything I knew, but she's all upset. You know how she likes to be in control."

Raleigh stood up to open the phone booth door. The young German tourists (glittery Styrofoam stars and hearts bobbing on wires atop their heads) were following the girl with a map out the door. "I wouldn't mind being in control myself. Well, okay, I'll talk to you soon. If I'm not at the bottom of a river. Anything else I need to know?"

"Well, I'm wearing a black see-through nightie."

"Aura, really, is that all you can say?"

"Well, I have absolutely *got* to pee! Bye-bye. Remember, you're a happily married man. *Güten Nichtski.*"

The glass elevator floated up and down with guests. The escalators glided, the fountains rose and fell, the bellboys strolled racks of luggage. The waiters sped trays of food. People hurried along the ramps and walks from entertainment areas to bar areas to shopping areas. High at the very top of the skyscraper, a restaurant revolved in circles so diners could see the new skyline from every angle. Atlanta did not sit still, even for Sunday supper.

Neither did Gates Hayes, who skipped three moving steps of the escalator at a time and caught his brother near the elevator. "Back to the sack, Ace? You just rolled out."

"Why are you wearing my new suit, Gates? How many times have I told you I don't like your wearing my clothes?"

"Lots. Sorry about that. It was the best I could do. Little long in the cuffs, but not impossible. By the way, never never put things in your pockets. It bags the fabric and spoils the lines."

"Yes, I noticed you removed my money pouch. And what were you doing to my new blazer, for Pete's sake? Soaking it in Old Spice?"

"Please! Giorgio Armani. I said I was sorry. Okay? My hand slipped. Listen, Raleigh, I'm under a lot of pressure here." He leaned over the curving rail to point down to where Mrs. Parisi, flanked by a praetorian guard of dark-haired men, was being escorted through the lobby.

Raleigh made a short speech in which he proved that Gates would always be under a lot of pressure until he reformed his life and rechose his career.

"Right sure fine. But come on, let's go chow. I heard about a place with great risotto, across town. We'll grab a subway."

Beside them, a potbellied man in a salmon Lacoste shirt had been staring at Gates. Now he said he wanted to offer some outsiders some friendly advice: it was, to steer clear of MARTA (Atlanta's downtown subway system) at night. "You know what we call MARTA, don't you? M.A.R.T.A. Moving Africans Rapidly Through Atlanta. Awwkah awwkah awwkah," he snuffled. His joke fell flat, and so did his face when Gates grinned evenly about six inches from his nose.

Gates said, "Hey, honkey, take a closer look. My mother happened to be from Africa, and I happen to have a switchblade in the pockets of my pants right now, right next to my long thick dick, and if you don't want the former stuck up your fat ass, take a hike."

"Jesus," hissed Raleigh, as the man strode indignantly away. "I don't believe you! Why do you make these things up! He's going to go straight to the manager!"

"Nah. Probably go jerk off in the men's room."

The Hayes brothers rode the handsome new subway, untroubled, to their restaurant, where Raleigh sipped wine while his brother ate artichokes, risotto, and calf's liver with sage, and where Raleigh learned that Mrs. Parisi (softened by Gates's heart line and his fleshy pads of Venus — for while a good Catholic, she always took a second opinion from palmistry) had been persuaded that the anxieties of a dying mother's hospital bills might have driven a good son to the desperate measure of selling her Cupid that flea-market jewelry as an historical heirloom. "See, Raleigh, that was the thing," explained Gates as he raked an artichoke leaf through his beautiful teeth. "Soon as I saw the missal in her hands, I didn't try to con her, and feed her a line how I didn't know the necklace was fake."

"Didn't try to con her?"

" 'Mother Parisi,' I said, 'I came here ready to lie to you. But you are too good and too wise a woman for me to think of that.' So I said, 'I have just lost my own mother.' "

Raleigh, neatly arranging the artichoke leaves flung onto his empty plate, sighed. "How could you say that? That's disgusting."

"Hey. It's true, right? Sop some bread in this sauce. *Delizioso.*"

"Well, good, I'm glad she accepted your apology. We have enough problems without your having to go ahead with this stupid 'duel.' "

"Oh that." Gates wiped his mustache with the red-checked napkin. "That's still on. Oh yeah. In a macho society, *caro mio,* the power of the matriarch is influential but not executive; know what I mean, jelly bean? Nine tonight, I meet Calhoun to discuss terms." He glanced at his watch. Nor had Gates "exactly" talked Mrs. Parisi into accepting a circus truck in lieu of $7,500, a proposal that had not proved as irresistible as the financial exigency of a grieving son.

"I tried to tell you," Raleigh nodded. "Didn't I?"

"Big Bro, you're always right and I'm always wrong. You're morally, mentally, and personally *perfecto.*"

"Oh shut up."

On the return subway ride, Gates swung by an arm from the handrail while speculating on their father, the former Episcopal minister, Earley Hayes, and his peculiar relationship with the Charlestonian Jubal Rogers. One of his theories left Raleigh aghast: "Man, from what you say, there was something really heavy between those guys. Hey, maybe they were lovers. See? Daddy gets the heave from the church because he's gay, plus his lover's black and they're moonlighting at these Darktown jazz joints."

Raleigh diverted his eyes from the crocheting woman across from him, eavesdropping. He lowered his voice. "Daddy got the 'heave' because of your mother."

"Well, Specs, let's not get personal. Okay, so you don't like my boys in the band theory. I guess you're right. If there's one thing we know about the old man, it's he couldn't keep from blowing his trumpet up any skirt that slowed down walking by."

Turning his back on the pinched-mouthed woman, Raleigh pretended to stare out the subway window, but all he could see was his own embarrassed face.

"Besides," his brother went merrily on, oblivious to the accelerating crochet needles below him. "It doesn't jive with what ole long tall Toots tells me about your pal Rogers. Sounds like far as chicks go, Jubal couldn't keep his dick zipped either. Toots says he went through them like a bag of peanuts. Says they couldn't keep their hands off him. Some guys are born lucky."

Raleigh did not think Jubal Rogers considered himself a particularly lucky man. When he said so, Gates had a theory about this as well. "You're right. I sure wouldn't thank my lucky stars either. Would you? Let's face it, would you want to grow up black in Thermopylae? In the Depression? Man, that's pre–Jackie Robinson days. That's *Strange Fruit* days. *Especially* if I came on like Malcom X, before it was exactly fashionable."

"What do you mean?"

"Toots says this guy talked a real hard line. I mean, 'Shoot the fuckers.' Anyhow, it sounds like he'd had enough bad breaks to make Coretta King wanna line 'em up against the wall. The Germans shove him in a POW camp for two years, and when he finally crawls back to the States, he gets to New York, and his wife's split and taken his kid, his little boy, and no forwarding address. He looks all over hell and back."

"Toutant told you all this?"

"Yeah, right." The subway slowed. Holding her crochet needles like a weapon, the woman shoved past them. Gates raised his voice. "Well, if Daddy wasn't buggering black guys, I don't see why his congregation had to go and lynch him and leave us orphans." The subway doors slid shut with the woman outside them staring in at Gates, who blew her a kiss. As they lurched forward, he laughed. "Aces! I really had that old dragon going, didn't I? WATCH IT, RALEIGH!"

"What? What?" Hayes ducked, expecting an Underworld grenade tossed down the aisle.

"Don't lean on a dirty window in a white suit, babe."

Back in the circling lobby of the Peachtree Plaza, the two brothers sat talking about the past in armchairs beside the pool.

"Hello, I'm Timothy," said the red-jacketed waiter.

"Bloody cheek, never met the bugger in muh life," rumbled Gates Hayes, chin tucked in, jowls sagging, his mustache suddenly very British.

"I'm your waiter for tonight," Timothy persisted.

"Howchewdo. I'm Colonel Diggeson-Hayes, not that it's rally any of your bloody business, I must say."

"Could I bring you gentlemen something from the bar?"

"Rather! The bosomy lass behind it! Har har. Righto, Sir Raleigh, old chap? I say! Her tits *are* splendid!"

Timothy did his best to smile. "Could I get you a drink?"

"Glenlivet. No ice. Barbarous custom. Utter rot. Harumph, harumph."

Raleigh looked at his brother, the cold merriment of the blue eyes, the strange sweetness of the mouth. "Gates?" he asked quietly. "Why are you always pretending to be somebody else, why don't you just be yourself?"

The man shrugged, Raleigh's pin-striped suit snug across his shoulders. "Who wants to be a fuck-up like me?"

Hayes didn't know how to answer that. Hadn't Gates, in fact, accurately described his life? Juvenile courts for shoplifting and joyriding. Biannual expulsion from high school for back talk and wildness. Terminal expulsion from college, for getting F's in the courses in which he wasn't getting A's — which proved to the dean that he could do the work, if he would, but he wouldn't. Detention in Vietnam for going AWOL, and demotion for backtalk and wildness. Inability to stay with a job or a girl or a town or the truth. Almost a year in prison for false business practices. Lies, debts, scams, risks, speed, and gambles — and what did he have to show for it? A motorcycle and leather bag of outlandish clothes. Raleigh rubbed his eyes. "Gates, that makes me sad."

"Awwh, Big Bro's sad."

Raleigh blushed, and then Gates blushed, and then at the same moment they looked away toward the pool; and upon the hapless waiter's return, Gates told him that if his man in India had taken this long, he'd by Jove see him flogged. More of this followed and Hayes was actually relieved to catch sight of Mingo wandering through the lobby in awed open-mouthed circles, a huge shopping bag in either hand. Hayes stood up to call his neighbor over.

At first Mingo could say nothing but "Gollee, this place is big!" But soon enough, he sufficiently overcame his wonder to drink two strawberry daiquiris and eat a bowl of smoked almonds while he recounted, in a narrative of excessive high relief (for it included even the search for a public toilet and a subway trip in the wrong direction) the many events of his busy day. First and foremost, Diane couldn't be better. Little Vera (for Sheffield confirmed Aura's news) couldn't be better, nor could she possibly be more beautiful, more angelic in her nature, more amazing in her intelligence, more satisfactory in her height, weight, eyes, ears, fingers, and toes. These few little things in the bags were for her, and while Little Vera might have no immediate use for an engraved silver brush, a Cabbage Patch doll, and a musical mobile of white teddy bears, she probably could use all the pink nightshirts, blankets, and booties. No, Mingo was not tired, for he had caught some sleep on the couch in the maternity lounge while waiting for Mrs. Yonge to drive from Kure Beach to Wilmington and fly from there to Atlanta. It had taken her until four this afternoon, ten hours after Mingo had telephoned her with the good news. News which, unfortunately, *Mr.* Yonge had taken so ill that, far from praising the Lord that his missing daughter was alive and well and mother of the most perfect baby every born, he had refused to come to Atlanta, and even claimed to be sorry that Diane had ever been born herself, much less given birth to his grandchild. Mingo, however, had no doubt that as soon as Mr. Yonge saw Little Vera, all would be forgiven. Parenthetically, it had to be confessed that Raleigh was right: Diane and Pete had taken her father at his word when he forbade them to get married so young. It could also be admitted that Pete had not behaved as gallantly as Mingo might have hoped when he ran off to Atlanta, leaving Diane behind to cope as she could. Nor had Mingo liked the way Pete had tried to run off down the aisles of the Omni coliseum as soon as he'd asked him if he were the father of Diane's baby. Nevertheless, after a long talk, some hot dogs and beers, Pete had returned with Mingo to the hospital, where he was now walking the halls, proud as punch, and even though it couldn't be said that Mrs. Yonge had treated Pete really warmly, nor had yet stopped periodically asking Diane to agree that she'd broken her mother's heart; still, when all was said and done, time heals all wounds, and there's no limit to what love can do, as the good Book says in Corinthians I or II.

"You done good, mountain man," announced Gates Hayes with a Western slap on the Gargantuan back. "What you need now's some vittles and a tall brew. Follow me." He headed up a ramp to the glass bubble elevators.

"I am pretty starved, okay; I walked a million miles. Boy, Atlanta sure is bigger than Thermopylae. I guess you never could get to know everybody here if you lived forever. Not like home. Oh, Raleigh, guess what? I was reading this newspaper in the maternity lounge, and there was nothing in it about Weeper, so that's lucky. But guess what I read? Your secretary's husband held up four liquor stores in Jacksonville, Florida, and he's going to jail."

Raleigh said, "That's ridiculous! Betty Hemans's husband died fifteen years ago. He fell off his roof!" With a double-indemnity policy! And Betty had the gall to complain about retirement benefits!

"No, not her. The pretty one. Bonnie Ellen." Mingo called to Gates, bounding ahead, "You know, the one the police thought we'd murdered, when Raleigh threw my guns in the hole where she was lying."

"Tell the world about it," hissed Hayes, as people turned to stare.

"Bonnie's husband. That's what it said: 'Charged were somebody somebody from someplace else and Edward Dellwood, twenty-four, of Thermopylae, North Carolina.' He must not have gone to California like you thought. Uhhho*OOOO*, RALEIGH, RALEIGH, RALEIGH! *NO, I CAN'T! I CAN'T!* Let me out, LET ME OUT!"

Now, Mingo had been babbling away and automatically following Gates into a cluster of hotel guests; with his shopping bags raised high, he'd walked right inside the all-glass outdoor elevator without noticing, until the doors shut, that he was trapped inside a crowded transparent cubicle that was shooting straight up the side of a skyscraper. Around, below, and above him was *space*. Empty space. Far, far below were lots of little midgets running around a lake. When he realized this, Mingo turned a very dead waxy white and shrieked the above remarks, to the consternation of the other passengers, two of whom he had flattened by backing up against the inside wall. He stayed there, eyes shut, breath sucked in, until Raleigh and Gates pried his stiff outstretched arms away from the man and woman crushed behind him.

"He's, ah, a little afraid of heights, I'm afraid," Raleigh somewhat superfluously suggested to the spluttering couple who'd just been squished. But Gates took the offensive.

"Hey, give my buddy a break. He was shot out of a helicopter in 'Nam and spent the next two years getting tortured by filthy V.C. Commies." The elevator slid to a stop, and the couple fled. "We were fighting for *your* freedom!" Gates yelled after them.

"The poor man," a woman beside Raleigh murmured with a sympathetic glance at Mingo's wide paralyzed face and clenched fists.

"Yes, ma'am," Gates nodded. "He paid a high price, but he paid it gladly and he paid it proudly. Because he's an American. And that's what America is all about."

Everybody still left in the elevator nodded solemnly as they rode to the top of the giant gleaming skyscraper, where the glass cage opened to let them out at the glass restaurant that slowly turned to see how far in every direction Atlanta lit up the night.

"Man," Gates chuckled. "You see their faces? 'Nam is in! I'd tried that a few years back, I'd have been frosted. 'Nam is cool, now. What a pisser."

"Yes? Do you have a reservation?"

Gates looked at his watch, and with a smile turned the pretty hostess's check-in book toward him. "Yes, ma'am, howdy. Round 'bout eight-thirty? We certainly do. Right here it is. Daniel Austin, party of three? By the window? That's us. Me and my partners. We've been looking at nothin' but oil figures and A-rabs so long, we just had to come on up and see if y'all git a sky full of stars like we do back home. I guess we're a little bit early, but that's right, Rawley, y'all follow on all behind this young lady. She's giving us one of those nice tables looking right out on that gold dome. Thank you, ma'am. I 'preshate it." He handed the mesmerized hostess the "Reserved" sign from the elegant table for three. "Why look here, this little ole restaurant's *movin'*. Reminds me of my living room, dudden't it you, Rawley? 'Mind you of my living room back in Houston? 'Course they don't have a Jacuzzi up here. Ma'am? Y'all carry Dom Perignon?"

"Gates," said Mingo as the champagne was poured, "you sure are funny."

"Ha ha," Raleigh agreed. His concern that he and his brother had already eaten was solved when Mingo ordered enough for three. His concern that they shouldn't take up a table reserved for someone else was solved when a short, loud, truculent man, who claimed to be Daniel Austin (and was accompanied by two blondes young enough to be his daughters but bearing no family resemblance), caused such an unseemly disturbance when he was seated at a cramped inside table that the bartender asked him to leave.

"What a ruckus," Gates sympathized with the hostess.

"I'm sorry, sir, but he insisted he was you. And a guest here in Suite C."

Gates gave his hotel key a quick shake. "If that dudden't beat all. That's our suite, idden't it, Rawley? That feller tried to mosey up to me in the bar a while back. Now it looks like he's trying to rustle up some mischief with those little ladies. I call that lowdown, don't you, Mingo?"

Raleigh stared at the stars; they winked at him, as if, like Mingo, the universe above him was amused by his younger brother. Okay. Serves him right. Now, what's he going to do?, thought Hayes, as a waiter solicitously strolled the aisles calling, "Gates Hayes? It there a Mr. Hayes here?"

"Fuck a duck," whispered the party in question. He pointed a surreptitious finger at the two men who stood looking around at the top of the stairs leading down to the tables. One was slim and foppishly dressed, with alabaster skin, straight black hair, a narrow face above bee-stung lips. Spinning in his pale thin hands was a bone cane. The other was three times the size and strained the seams of his garish suit. He had red skin, a flat face with an enormous nose, and blond hair. He was cracking his knuckles, which were already as big as a wrist.

"Is there a Mr. Gates Hayes here?"

"Stand up, Mingo."

"Gates, are you crazy?"

"Raleigh, cool it. Mingo, stand up, go over there, and say I'll be right over."

Mingo gulped, but so deep was his admiration of the adventurer that he went and stood head to head with Big Nose Solinsky, who recognized him immediately — to judge from his flaring nostrils. In a moment, Mingo came back in a huff. "They want you," he told Gates. "Boy, I don't like that Big Nose guy. He said he was going to tear my ears off, for no reason."

Gates was rubbing his mustache as if it were a rabbit's foot. "Raleigh, do me a favor. You and Mingo go down to the room. There's a package under the bed. Bring it to that bar where we had the drinks. Wait for me there." He laughed. "If I don't show, give my love to Daddy. And, oh, I borrowed fifty bucks from you to send Sara a few flowers. Right. Fine. Roll out. You leave the tip. I'll grab the check."

Distraught, Hayes threw five dollar bills on the table. "Gates, for God's sake, don't go anywhere with those two."

"Worried about your suit?" Gates bounced out of the chair. "Listen, go on. Everything's jake, folks."

So, with his stomach muscles spasming, Raleigh led Mingo out of the revolving restaurant; too soon to see his brother scrawl "Daniel Austin, Suite C" across the foot of the bill. Too soon, also, to see the well-dressed man at the bar, who'd been watching them since the waiter had paged Gates Hayes. This man nodded at another well-dressed man, who quietly followed the Thermopyleans out. Gates didn't see these men either, and even if he had, he wouldn't have recognized them, because in arranging his trips on "Easy Living," he had dealt only with the lowliest and most dispensable members of a large, discreet organization.

As it took Raleigh some little while to persuade Mingo of the absurdity of *walking* down thirty flights of stairs to their room, ten minutes passed before he opened the door and heard the telephone ringing. He crawled quickly across the wide bed to answer it. "Hello? Yes?"

"Raleigh? This is your aunt Victoria Anna Hayes." She always introduced herself as if he'd never heard of her, nor suspected a relationship. Her voice was furious. "I've been calling you for hours!"

"I'm sorry, Aunt Vicky. I've been in and out all evening with Gates. I'm sorry you didn't call person-to-person. Excuse me a second. . . ."

Sheffield, having given the room his customary ooh-and-ah inspection, was pantomiming his desire for his luggage by hoisting and shaking an invisible suitcase. As Raleigh pointed at the closet, he thought he heard his aunt say she was in Atlanta, but of course he must have been mistaken. "Pardon, Aunt Vicky?"

"I said, I'm at the airport. Can you hear me?"

"At the Atlanta airport?"

"My plane leaves in twenty minutes."

"Plane leaves?"

"Stop repeating me, Raleigh. I've got to go. Now, listen, Aura explained a little of what's been going on. I'm flying to New Orleans to find Earley. I'm not about to sit on that porch and wait till Thursday just because he's decided to play games with you and everybody else."

Shock rolled Hayes off the bed and stood him upright. "What? What are you talking about? You're going to New Orleans?"

Exasperation blew into the phone. "Raleigh, would you mind not making me miss my plane. Just answer me. One, do you know where Earley's staying? Two, last time you talked to him was this . . . this . . ." He heard her pull in her breath. ". . . was this young person from the hospital still with him?"

Hayes was now pacing the thick carpeting, dodging Mingo who was trying to hop out of his pants while reading the room service menu. "Aunt Victoria, honestly, really, I can handle this alone. This is too much for you —"

"If I can get out of Singapore after the Japanese took over, and find my way to New Guinea, I hope you'll have the sense to admit I can find my way around New Orleans, Louisiana."

"Of course, that's not what I . . . But there's no need for —"

"Raleigh, dammit, answer me!"

Stunned by this unprecedented profanity, Hayes blurted into speech. "I don't know where Daddy's staying, but probably the French Quarter, somewhere near Jackson Square, don't you think? All I know is that's where I'm supposed to meet him Thursday. And I don't know if that black girl's still with him, but I bet she is. He gave me some crazy message I had to go pass on to Flonnie's nephew, you know, this man called Jubal?"

"Yes, yes, Aura told me. And?"

"The message about a girl named Billie, somebody who's called 'Josh's child'? I think she's got to be the girl from the hospital and that's why Daddy wants Jubal Rogers in New Orleans. The first time I could get Rogers — and Aunt Vicky, you wouldn't believe what a horrible experience I had trying to talk to that man — the first time he would even do me the courtesy of *looking* at me, was when I gave him Daddy's message about somebody called Billie. I cannot tell you what I went through with —"

"Is he with you?"

"Who? Rogers?"

". . . Yes."

"Are you kidding? I won't even repeat to you what he said I could tell Daddy from him! Absolutely no, thank God, he isn't with me, and he is *not* coming to New Orleans because —"

"Raleigh, listen to me, they're calling my plane. When you told him 'Josh's child'? Did he know, did he say he knew where Josh was?"

"If he did, he certainly didn't tell me. You don't understand. This man wanted nothing to do with me or Daddy, or, I assume, whoever this Billie is. He hates Daddy. What the *hell* is going on? What's Daddy doing? Do *you* know?"

She snapped, "He's not doing what he should have done about this, which was *tell me,* instead of running away from the hospital. And he's not going to do it to me again. Raleigh, it's last call. I'll be at the St. Ann's Hotel on Ursulines Street. Write it down."

". . . Aunt Vicky?" Hayes clicked the phone repeatedly. "Aunt Vicky?" But he knew he was talking to a dead line. Well, there was no sense in rushing out to the Atlanta airport. If Victoria were going, she would have gone long before he could reach her. And if a seventy-two-year-old woman wanted to wander the streets of a strange city looking for her seventy-year-old idiot of a brother, well, how could Raleigh stop her? But it was disturbing, very disturbing, to think that not only was his father endangering his life, now, here was his aunt crazily taking off as well. What if something should happen to her? What was the matter with all these old people? This isn't the way they were supposed to act. They were supposed to sit still quietly while their lives drew to a close. They weren't supposed to rush around in an emotional maelstrom like Caroline and Holly, for God's sake. And then Raleigh thought, "Who *are* these people? Earley? Victoria? Jubal?" And he had to admit, "I haven't the foggiest idea."

"Raleigh, did you get the package?" Sheffield had changed into his madras jacket, with a green cravat tucked into his open shirt. "Gates is waiting."

"What?" Hayes still had his hand on the phone. Flopping to the floor, Mingo swept his arm under the bed and pulled out an oblong brown-wrapped parcel. "Gollee, this weighs a ton," the fat man said. "It feels like a bomb."

When the Thermopyleans (on an ordinary elevator) reached the lobby, Gates was not waiting. They ordered drinks from a waiter who resembled Timothy, but announced that his name was Russ. "It's nine forty," said Raleigh. The next thing he said was, "It's ten-o-five."

"Don't worry," Mingo said at 10:15, when he returned from phoning the hospital to tell Mrs. Yonge he'd be back over in the morning to give Little Vera a few little things before they checked out.

"Have another drink," Mingo said at 10:35.

"This may surprise you," said Hayes, "but I wish Simon Berg were here."

It didn't surprise Mingo. "Weeper'll be here tomorrow. But Gates doesn't need any help, Raleigh, he can do anything."

"Where is he?" said Raleigh. He walked to the edge of the pool. He walked down the ramp to the lobby desk and back. He walked to the elevators and back. "He's dead," decided Raleigh at 10:45.

Meanwhile, among the drinkers chatting together in the handsome modern lounge chairs, sat one well-dressed man who was neither drinking nor talking. He was just watching Mingo Sheffield (or, as he thought, from the paging in the restaurant atop the Plaza, he was just watching "Gates Hayes").

Raleigh threw himself back in the chair. He stared at the blinking digital numbers on his watch; second by second, time vanished and was replaced. The sound of his heart throbbed in his ears. His pulse was racing. Checking it, he was amazed to find it was 125. He might as well be jogging! Raleigh Hayes sat there, shaking his crossed leg, and suddenly realized how he felt. The discovery surprised him. He felt exactly as he had the hideous afternoon when he'd sat in the emergency waiting room at the pediatrics ward and waited for the doctor to come back to tell him whether or not the eight-year-old Caroline had spinal meningitis. He'd sat there with his stomach tight, his mouth bitten, his pulse racing — just as he was sitting now — until the doctor came out to admit he'd been wrong: all Caroline had was a severe abdominal flu (and a very theatrical personality). Hearing this, Raleigh's muscles had untensed so quickly, his legs had given way and Aura had caught him when he stumbled.

"Wait here, Mingo." Raleigh stood up. "I'm going to look for Gates." Now there was another sound in Raleigh's ears. A sound twenty-eight years old: the squeal of tires skidding and the deadened thunk of the car hitting the bike. And the shrieks of his cousins leaping in the sprinkler on the flat lawn in Cowstream changing to Lovie's endless scream. And everyone running to the corner of the block where the seven-year-old Gates lay unconscious under the twisted bicycle, his black curls red with blood. Raleigh felt now that he could still smell the strong odor of the Toni permanent Lovie had been in the middle of giving herself before she ran out of the house. He felt he could still hear the terrified voice of the young male driver, "I didn't see him! He just flew right out in front of me!"

Mingo pulled on Hayes's arm. "Gollee, Raleigh. Just calm down." He patted him. "But, I guess if it was my baby brother, I'd go completely to pieces too."

"For Pete's sake, I have not gone . . ." But at that moment, across the pool, an elevator opened, and the giant man known as Big Nose Solinsky pushed Gates out into the lobby. The bodyguard, in his ill-fitting tan suit, carried a small leather box. He looked carefully around for some time; finally, he waved his hand. Then Cupid Parisi Calhoun came out of the elevator, his arm linked through that of a striking young woman taller than he was. She was very new-fashioned in skintight leather pants, high-heeled boots, a quilted jacket with pointed shoulders, and short hair coated with gelatin. She was sucking on a plastic swizzle stick in an extremely nervous way.

By the time this group reached the bar, a composed Raleigh Hayes was quietly seated behind the glass coffee table, scotch in hand. He stood, and remained standing after the introductions, for the — what should he call them? plaintiffs? — declined to sit with them. In fact, Cupid Calhoun declined even to focus his eyes on the Thermopyleans, or on anything else except the knob of the bone cane, where he rested both slender pale hands. Calhoun's coal-black eyes were such glazed, dreamy eyes, his skin was so deathly white, his mouth so dainty, his black velvet tie and ruffled shirt so nineteenth century, that Raleigh was oddly reminded of a schoolbook picture of the poet Edgar Allan Poe.

And in fact, Calhoun did share a habit of Poe's, for he was (as Gates

later explained, but Raleigh already suspected) "stoned out of his gourd"
on opium. He was even more stoned than usually, because hotel lobbies
made him nervous. His grandfather, Antony Parisi, had been shot to death
in the lobby of a seaside resort many years ago, just after his new young
wife had placed in his buttonhole the yellow rosebud he always wore. He'd
been seventy-nine at the time (quite an advanced age for a bootleg czar),
but still it was a startling way to die, and his grandson, who'd often been
told the story by his long-widowed grandmother, never entered a lobby
until his bodyguard Solinsky had walked through it first to draw any gun-
fire. Cupid had been raised on fanciful stories about Antony Parisi: how
he'd dined with Valentino, fought with Dion O'Banion, danced with
Fanny Brice; how he'd kept D.A.s and judges in one pocket, and raw diamonds like worry beads in the other, and how at a party once he'd thrown
a handful of these diamonds into his swimming pool to watch women in
evening gowns dive for them; how hundreds of mourners, all wearing yellow rosebud boutonnieres, had walked behind his armored hearse. It was
this life that Cupid longed for. He was a hopeless romantic, and therefore
fairly dangerous. But, fortunately, the glamour of bygone crimes and the
bygone South that mingled in him kept him too busy at bookstores and
movies and antique shops to do much damage. In Atlanta, he had a 1930s
Warner Brothers apartment (all Art Deco whites and blacks); in Charleston, he had an 1860s antebellum apartment (all bronzed claw-feet and
brocade sash-pulls). What he couldn't alter into the past with his grandmother's generous allowance, he blurred with heroin, unable to tolerate
modernity anywhere but in his girlfriends. Stories about the past had
spoiled any interest the young (and — even Mrs. Parisi admitted — not
very intelligent) Calhoun might have taken in current business. Organized crime today was too organized; it was all lawyers, accountants, and
laundered cash flows. For example, the association of cocaine importers,
whom he knew to be meeting in this same hotel this very weekend, were a
drab, merciless group who might as well be running General Motors as far
as Cupid was concerned. He'd much rather kill or be killed in a duel any
day.

Calhoun leaned on the girl. The rest stood in a circle around the coffee
table. "These are my associates." Gates grinned, his arms around Raleigh
and Mingo. "Mr. Hayes. Mr. Sheffield. Let me introduce C. P. Calhoun of
Charleston, and Mr. Big Nose Solinsky of the Black Lagoon."

"You want your face, you watch your mouth," rumbled the huge blond
man, his neck stretching open his shirt collar beneath the fat orange knot
of his tie.

"Sorry," Gates shrugged.

"You watch it."

"Fine, fine." Gates rolled his eyes. "Okay, here's the plan."

Solinsky poked him in the shoulder with a sausage-thick finger. "That pretty face could end up not so pretty, you know that?"

"All right, all right, I hear you! C.P., will you call off this goon?"

Solinsky's horrible toilet-flush of a gurgle was stopped by the bone cane's flicking across his ankle. Until then, Raleigh had thought, from the otherworldly look in Calhoun's eyes, that the man was in a coma and secretly held upright by the girl who was luridly sucking the plastic stick. But apparently some of the young mobster's faculties were functional.

Gates now instructed Mingo to put the oblong wrapped package on the table. "There's that," he said succinctly. The bodyguard started to rip at the tape, but the cane flicked his hand away. Calhoun languidly removed the brown paper, revealing a shiny brass urn, at the sight of which Raleigh gasped so loudly that everyone looked up. He yanked his brother aside, and hissed at him in a whisper, "For God's sake, Gates! Is that Roxanne?"

"Sort of."

Behind him, Calhoun was unscrewing the metal lid. He stuck his finger inside, then licked off the white powder clinging to the tip, then nodded, then closed the urn.

Staggered, Raleigh swayed against his brother. "I . . . I . . . I don't believe you did that! You mixed cocaine with your dead mother's ashes?"

Gates shrugged, and whispered back, "The one thing everybody said about old Roxanne was, she was a party girl, right? I figured maybe she'd like to go out that way, one last high."

"I have to sit down."

Gates looked at his brother's greenish face. "Aw, Big Bro, I was just kidding you. Sorry. Roxanne told Sara she wanted her ashes sprinkled over this lake right outside Midway. We did it the day before I left for Charleston. Okay? The urn was just a safe place to stash the goods. Sorry."

"Gates, I'm going to kill you."

"Hang on. Let me fight this duel first." He sauntered back to the group. "C.P. chosen a meeting place for tomorrow?"

The slim man in formal wear fluttered his black eyes half open, then prodded Solinsky in the ribs with the tip of his cane, as if he were pushing a button in a mechanical doll.

"He wants you," the big bodyguard growled, "on the island in the riverboat lake at Stone Mountain Park, noon sharp. That's twelve o'clock."

"It is?" Gates smiled. "Oh, thank you."

The plaid sleeves covering Solinsky's biceps jumped. "I'm not gonna tell you again, wise guy."

Gates cocked his finger and tapped his temple. "You don't have to. I think I've got it. Noon is twelve o'clock. Is that it?"

Calhoun held the cane in front of his heaving bodyguard like a tollgate. The huge man growled, but finally swallowed down his rage in gulps, and said, "So be there. Or your ears are in the trash, and that goes for you too, Blob."

Mingo began to bristle. Raleigh, somewhat recovered, cleared his throat. "May I inquire? Pardon me? What is this 'duel' being fought with?"

Solinsky's thick fingers struggled to undo the silver clasp on the leather box. Inside on velvet padding were two engraved long-barreled pistols.

"Wheeww! Beautiful," Gates admitted, after a long look. "But you've got to win the cut first." Pulling a new deck of red Bicycle cards out of his jacket (or, rather, Raleigh's jacket), the duelist explained with a wink to his brother that, as prearranged, they would now open a new deck of cards. Each party would shuffle, then each party would draw a card. The highest draw would choose the weapons for tomorrow's duel at twelve, that's noon, at Stone Mountain Park, where General Lee, Jeff Davis, and Stonewall Jackson, carved in granite bigger than Mount Rushmore, would act as silent seconds above the field of honor.

Calhoun leaned his black velvet sleeves over the coffee table. He slit the seal on the deck with a buffed fingernail. Languidly he shuffled the cards while gazing elsewhere, presumably into a more interesting world. When he finished, he handed the cards not to Gates, at whom he shook his head, but to Raleigh Hayes, who shook *his* head and handed them to Mingo Sheffield, who sat down and laboriously began to shuffle the cards as if he'd never done it before; some splattered out on the table and he stuck them back.

The girl suddenly crunched her swizzle stick in two, spit out the pieces, rubbed at her nose and her eyes, and spoke. "C.P. No fooling. I need to get to, you know, the can." Her high-heeled boot was tapping as if her foot had gone to sleep.

Her remark sufficiently penetrated the fog to cause Calhoun not only to wince, but to speak, disproving Raleigh's theory that he could do so only through the throat of Big Nose Solinsky, which was certainly large enough to store an extra set of vocal cords. Calhoun's voice was a soft, hazy slur. "You don't mean the 'can,' a can is a container; you mean the ladies room. Arnold will escort you to the ladies room when I say so."

"Arnold?!" grinned Gates. "Is it Big Nose Arnold? Or Arnold Big Nose?"

Solinsky bared his lower teeth, which were in serious need of dentistry. "You're in the ground, buddy."

"How'd he know *my* name?" Gates winked at the girl, who was now tapping her fingers on her arms as if they'd gone numb too. "Okay, Arnold. Cut the cards. That means pick up some of the little square things on the table. Cut deep and weep. Cut thin and win."

Solinsky grabbed away half the deck in his meaty first. "Jack!" he crowed, and held it up.

Gates nodded. "Good guess. You're right. Raleigh, you want to cut for our side?"

'No," said his brother. "I don't gamble." He crossed his arms.

Solinsky growled. "Not you, Pretty Face, I don't trust you."

"Awww."

"Let the Blob do it."

Mingo's chest swelled. "Don't call me a blob again, Mister Fat Nose."

"That's 'Big Nose,' Mingo," Gates explained. "If you'll notice, that nose surpasses simple fatness. It's more like a, like a, codfish covered with barnacles. You know, Solinsky, you ever heard of Cyrano de Bergerac? You ought to get somebody to read it to you someday."

This time, to stop the bodyguard, Calhoun had to whack him twice in the stomach with the cane.

"No fooling, C.P.," the fidgety girl repeated. "I need it."

Gates rubbed Mingo's shoulder. "Go ahead, Killer. Too bad Weep isn't here, know what I mean?" He winked. "Cut me an ace."

Sheffield took a deep breath, held it, shut his eyes, moved the deck from one hand to the other, then took away about half-a-dozen cards. He held his choice up without looking at it, and whispered, "What is it?"

Gates slapped his hands. "Mountain man, it's the fucking ace of hearts!"

"It is?!" Sheffield looked. "Oh gollee!" and he sighed so deeply, a card on the table trembled.

"Okay, right, fine, sorry about that, C.P., but you're going to have to put your derringers away for your next duel. I don't like noise." Gates lunged forward and whisked the cane out of the man's hand; he twirled it, and poked Solinsky in the stomach. "I choose — aha! — the first, the original, the strictly classical, *rapier!* Two fencing foils. Capped. First nick, that's the winner. One hit. Let's not go the hari-kari route, okay? And . . ." Jabbing air with the cane, Gates began sliding across the floor. "And, to add a little fillip . . . roller skates."

"You want your ears?" Big Nose rumbled.

Calhoun's dreamy eyes blinked. "No skates," he said. "I don't skate."

Gates shrugged. "So, don't. I'll skate." He held out the cane, and bowed. "The rules, C.P., are the rules. Am I right?"

Calhoun's girlfriend was now plucking at his sleeve. "Come on, Cupe, no fooling. You promised."

Signaled by a flick of the cane at his shinbone, Solinsky led the young woman away, and Calhoun floated back to the elevator.

"Boy, she sure did need to go to the bathroom bad," Mingo whispered to Raleigh.

"I don't think it had anything to do with her bladder." And Hayes was right.

In fact, such an appetite for heroin was shared by Calhoun and his new fiancée (and so reluctant was he to have his grandmother learn of this drain on his allowance), that the young man was always looking for items to sell. Not awkward items like tractor-trailer trucks, of course, but two small packets of cocaine were just the thing to trade for that much more peaceful if less modern drug made not from coca but poppies. In fact, nothing could be more convenient than that Gates Hayes should settle his outstanding debt by providing Calhoun with so salable a commodity just when the perfect buyers were right here in the hotel.

The first thing these buyers asked Mrs. Parisi's grandson was where he'd gotten his merchandise. He didn't like these men; still, he didn't mind telling them he'd gotten it from a guy called Gates Hayes.

CHAPTER

29

How the Glorious Battle of Stone Mountain Was Won

BACK IN 1909, Mrs. Helen Plane of Atlanta, charter member of the United
Daughters of the Confederacy, had one of those grandiose, futile ideas of
which Southerners are so fond (such as winning the War Between the
States without factories): Wouldn't it be a nice tribute to the Lost Cause
if somebody carved the world's largest sculpture right into the side of the
world's largest exposed mass of granite — which just happened to be right
outside town, and the property of a local family whom she personally
knew?

Of course, Stone Mountain had not always been the property of that
Venable family; or even always the property of the United States, although
the government had been obliged to purchase it a half-dozen times from
different Indian chiefs, including one Chief McGillivray, a Scots half-
breed, whom Gates Hayes would have admired, for the chief was simultaneously a salaried colonel in the British army under orders to incite his
tribe against the colonists, a salaried agent of the Spanish imperialists with
the title Emperor of the Creeks, and a salaried general appointed by
George Washington to betray the Spanish and the British on behalf of the
Americans.

Even the Indians hadn't been on Stone Mountain first. It was, after all,
over two hundred million years old. Somebody had to have left those

Stone Age bowls for anthropologists to poke at, and that mysterious ring of boulders at the top for tourists to shove over the sides a century before the anthropologists heard about them. Nor had the huge molten rock always been called Stone Mountain; Captain Juan Pardo had christened it Crystal Mountain, thinking it might be the lost El Dorado. But he could never get anyone to go back with him to kill the Indians and pick up the diamonds and rubies he claimed to have seen lying all over the ground. Four hundred years later, when our travelers reached the mountain, the ground at its base was still covered with the crystals of quartz that the Renaissance Spaniard, dodging spears and arrows, had mistaken for precious stones. And growing up the barren slopes were still muscadine and blackberry vines, and the red carpet of diamorpha leaves, and the rust-colored slippery lichen that had cost so many climbers so many broken limbs. Hawks and vultures still circled the highest gnarled pines. Tiny yellow daisies and white milkweed still forced their way through the smallest slivers of granite. Tinier fairy shrimp still bred in the shallowest puddle of rainwater.

But by 1909, the Spanish, British, and the Indians, not as durable as moss or shrimp, had all gone. By then, Sherman's Yankees had long since burned the town of Stone Mountain and surrounded Atlanta with one hundred thousand soldiers. Too many men even for gallant Rebels like Goodrich Hale Hayes to defeat; even when he so distinguished himself at the long hot furious battle of Peachtree Creek (by shooting until his gun melted, and then stabbing or bashing everything around him that moved and appeared, in the haze of rifle smoke, to be wearing blue), so covered himself with glory that he was promoted on the spot, and given an important assignment: to evacuate north to the Carolinas with a wagonload of gold bullion from the Dahlonega mines, and get that gold to Richmond as quickly as possible, and not to get caught by Sherman's pursuing army. An assignment Lieutenant General Hayes might have carried out had he not left the wagon at his home on Knoll Pond Road in Thermopylae, North Carolina, while he galloped off a few miles to fight the Battle of Bentonville, where he died a hero's death, several weeks after Lee had surrendered and only a few days before the last remnants of his good gray troops lay down their arms as well.

By 1909, it was high time, thought Mrs. Helen Plane, to pay some sort of tribute to all those dead heroes. Sixty years later (long after Mrs. Plane had gone to her reward — and hundreds of sightseers falling down, and suicides jumping off, the side of the mountain had gone to theirs), her dream was finally finished. And it was one of the seven wonders of the modern world. In fact, Atlanteans would be pressed to imagine any six others that could compete with it. In the end, of course, they didn't have the entire Confederate Army trotting around the face of the mountain as they'd originally planned. They just had Lee, Jefferson Davis, and Stonewall Jackson on their horses, and the horses didn't have legs. Still, right there, cut into the sheer north slope of Atlanta's Stone Mountain, was the world's largest piece of sculpture. Three acres of sculpture, ninety feet high and four hundred feet above the ground. Why, Lee's ear was as big as a man's body!

"Bigger, maybe," gasped Mingo Sheffield, staring through the coin-slotted telescope. "Gosh, what a great place!"

And Sheffield didn't mean just the mountain. For, not content with nature and art, man had added dozens of other amusements. Putt-putt golf, tennis, water slides, a carillon, a Mississippi riverboat, a steam-engine train that circled the mountain and was attacked by cowboy actors, pedal boats, rowboats, helicopters, bicycles, roller skates, ice skates, and even a musical laser light show. There were nature paths to walk up the gentle south slope, and skylifts to fly up the sheer north slope. There was a scale model of the entire Civil War in Georgia; and a full-scale ten-building "genuine reproduction" of a Georgia plantation, from Out House to Smoke House to Big House, that would have left Payne and Lady Bug Wetherell pea-green with envy. There was so much, that Mingo had been begging Gates to stop the truck as soon as the travelers (or as Gates had just baptized them, the Knick-Knack Gang) drove at ten in the morning through the entrance to Jefferson Davis Drive. They'd come early, on Simon Berg's advice, to "case the joint."

"We could stay here for days and days," burbled Sheffield, holding the park map and passing out the "Seven Attraction Tickets" he'd charged for all four of his friends on his Visa. For they were, he was happy to say, all together again. "We could stay a week, I bet!"

"No, we couldn't," said Raleigh, hauling out of the back of the truck the two secondhand fencing foils he couldn't believe he'd had to purchase as soon as a pawnshop had opened. Hayes was wearing his new sweater and slacks (having been assured by his brother that one needn't wear a tie to a duel), and the rest of his clothes were in the Cadillac, which was back in the truck. "We're going straight to New Orleans."

"That's right," Toutant Kingstree nodded.

The saxophonist had appeared promptly at nine that morning in the

Plaza lobby. And without Peaches — whom he'd given to his niece. (Despite Gates's theory, Mr. Kingstree actually had paid a surprise call on his actual — and very surprised — sister.)

Weeper Berg had appeared even earlier. And without his Clouet oil painting, which he'd sold to a certain party of his acquaintance in the transatlantic liaison business; this particular liaison being with a certain Dutch broker whose weakness for owning art from the past was supported by his talent for guessing currency futures. "So already it came from Europe. So let it go home to Europe," Berg moralized. Most of the convict's payment for this sale was now sewn inside the lining of his green-checked suit (with the proceeds from Mrs. Wetherell's geegaws), and while he had been compelled by circumstance to part with the little canvas for fifty times less than it was worth, still, Raleigh Hayes would have been stunned to know that that fiftieth came to $10,000.

Three of the Knick-Knackers were having coffee now in Memorial Plaza by the glass wall looking out at the mammoth gray sheet of mountainside, and at the big cable cars hoisting tourists to the Plaza of Flags on the peak. Gates was off at the Sports Complex renting roller skates, against Raleigh's wishes. Mingo was off in the souvenir shop, buying Vivien Leigh dolls for Vera and Little Vera. He'd already had to tour the Antique Auto Museum and the Plantation alone.

Or so he thought. As a matter of fact, he had two escorts. These escorts had been following him since six A.M., all the way from the hotel, to Diane's hospital, to Martin Luther King's grave, to the old Fox Theatre, back to the hotel, and here to Stone Mountain Park, where the two men had been forced to stand in line twice at the Skylift, then back away at the last minute when the fat man confessed to the attendant that he'd "chickened out." The escorts hadn't seen him making any more drug deliveries yet. These men, Mingo never noticed. It was their job not to be noticed while they were doing whatever their employer (a cocaine-trafficker named John G. Neill) wanted done. Things often needed to be done to protect all the apartment complexes, restaurants, and yachts that needed to be purchased to legitimize the $250,000,000 street value of five tons of refined Colombian merchandise. These escorts were careful men: they had not been noticed when they'd machine-gunned to death the wife of a federal witness prepared to testify against Mr. Neill, and they would be certain that no one noticed when they persuaded "Gates Hayes" that he'd made an irretrievable error when he'd become even a short-term delivery boy for a double-crossing subordinate of Neill's organization. This subordinate had been doing a little skimming and a little peddling on the side. He wasn't doing it anymore. He'd been gassed to death in his BMW near Myrtle Beach. And this fat "Hayes" guy wouldn't be doing it any longer either as soon as they got him alone. So far, he'd kept in constant conversation with any tourists nearby. Very shrewd of him, his escorts thought. But being careful meant being patient, too.

Meanwhile, in the snack bar, a philosophical discussion was in progress. Toutant Kingstree sighed. "I can't believe all these black people standing out there gooping and gawking up Robert E. Lee's ten-foot nose! Standing in line to peek into some old slave cabin!" He dropped his cigarette into his Styrofoam cup. "I swear, it just plain gives me the blues."

"Listen, you wanna understand?" Simon Berg, across from Raleigh, leaned over the Formica table. "What do you think I did anywise, after the war, day one I got leave from Berlin? I'll tell you what I did, Kingstree. I went to lousy Auschwitz and stood in line and peeked in. Hah? How're you gonna know if you don't look? Hah? Who'd remember if nobody says a word?" His small forefinger pounded the tabletop. "For the truth, a big confluence should see and talk, all together. So who's autonomous, you tell me, in this crummy world? Am I right, Raleigh?"

Our hero stared out at the mountain and thought about Berg's question. "You're right, Simon," he decided.

"We talk, we learn, maybe we change; likewise, maybe not. Yecch, such a lousy danish I can't believe yet. You look, you learn. An ostrich, mankind shouldn't be."

Kingstree ran his hands through his balding gray hair. "White people think they can dodge and shift, and trouble'll get everybody else and leave them alone. That's why white people can't sing blues. They sing off to the side and skip around. But man was born to trouble, sure as the birds fly up."

"So Jews don't know this? It's conceivable you're Jewish, Kingstree?"

The saxophonist smiled. "I don't know of but one black Jew and that's Sammy Davis, Jr., and he's rich. Anyhow," he shook his head, "I don't need to pay five dollars to look at a outhouse. My folks had one of their own."

"Their *own* already," said Berg. "You should share a john on the East Side with twenty other people, which is — I wouldn't be surprised — why my bowels are in their current state; in three lousy freezing rooms and no hot water."

"We didn't have *cold* water unless it rained hard."

Toutant Kingstree and Simon Berg had formed a friendship whose meeting ground was an exchange of familial and historical disasters. Raleigh listened. What could he offer? Once his basement had flooded, shorted out his freezer, and spoiled six hundred dollars' worth of frozen meat? He sat and listened.

"Back in Mississippi, my mama and papa hired out, burning stubble, beating it down, you know, with pine branch. Dawn to dusk for a dollar a week when they could get it. The Man came up, told her her baby brother George had fallen under a freight at the depot and he was gone. But he was a union man and she found out how'd they'd shoved him under the train and then poured white mule all over his body to make out he'd been drinking. She found that out, she just let go. We carried her to the doctor. But after that, she never really came back. Early on, she was always singing, had a voice like a dove."

"Irene Balashovich, my grandmother's sister, God rest her, stood in her yard the day the lousy Cossacks rode through the shtetl and with her own two eyes she saw her husband Malachi at the gate, a simple hoe in his hand; so the bastards come by with their swords out, and then there he lies in the road with his head gone. So tell me what this world is like?"

"You from Russia, Berg?" Kingstree accepted an offered cigarette.

"Hereditarily. . . . So from where is your family, Raleigh? Weed?"

"Thank you, no. North Carolina. I guess they've always been in North Carolina. I mean, ah, I suppose they were originally from England or someplace like that." Raleigh was distracted by a noisy group of men walking into the snack bar. One carried a mock-up of a check, the size of a door. It announced he was the winner of the Big Peach Barbecue Pig-Out. A T-shirt and a cap with plastic pig ears also celebrated this event.

Kingstree spluttered his lower lip. "They ought not to make fun of pigs like that. . . . What business your folks in, Raleigh? They in the record business, too?"

"I'm not in . . . Well, my father was a minister and a band director."

Berg said, "My uncle Vassily was a rabbi in Warsaw. Not a good place for such a job at such a time, however."

"My grandfather," Raleigh said suddenly, "lost his furniture business and meat store. He could never make himself ask people to pay their bills."

The two other men stared at Hayes after this unprecedented personal disclosure. He blushed, and went on. "He lost his legs to gangrene from diabetes, and then he had a stroke. . . . He was a very sweet man. His eyes were very . . . kind."

Kingstree and Berg nodded.

"Ida Hayes, my grandmother, started work at the Hillston Mills when she was eight. She never got to learn to read or write."

"Mine neither," nodded Kingstree.

"Likewise mine," Berg said, "never spoke English in America."

They all nodded.

Outside the window, Gates Hayes held up his skates and banged on the glass. Beside him, Mingo Sheffield was straddling a bicycle.

Only Gates and Raleigh were going to the little picnic island at noon. By Cupid Calhoun's stipulation, there were to be no outside observers at the field of honor.

"Not to worry," Weeper Berg shrugged. "Two meshuggeneh goyim fighting a cockamamie duel? This I can live without."

Kingstree agreed. "I don't say no to that. Berg, let's you and me go see the outhouse."

Mingo planned to accompany the Hayeses on the bicycle he'd rented near the parking lot where they'd been asked to leave the red truck. He'd never been very good at bike-riding, and now he wanted to see if Life on the Road had given him the courage to speed up (which is what his friend Raleigh had told him countless times — thirty-five years ago — was all he needed to do to keep the bike from wobbling over on its side). "Here I go," he gasped. Then down the road he flew, careening from curb to curb, but gritting his teeth and clamping his hands on the grips to keep them from grabbing the brakes.

Gates laughed. "Look at him go! Man, you can't help but love that guy, right?"

Raleigh watched the voluminous Hawaiian shirt fluttering in zigzags down the shaded road. A trio of fishermen scattered, holding their rods high. Finally Raleigh said, "Right," and nodded.

Now the brothers could have simply walked down the road and crossed the covered bridge to the island, but Gates wanted to arrive in style; a phrase that always appeared to mean arrival by some peculiar method of transportation. They went therefore to the Small Craft Marina, where they found Mingo consoling himself for having just missed his chance to take the big steamboat, by renting instead a little pedal boat. He was already in the water, paddling alone near the shore.

"Jesus, Gates," Raleigh said, when told to jump in the front of a canoe. He hadn't been in a canoe since the last time he'd gone fishing at Knoll Pond, and using one there had been — as his father admitted — just for fun, because anyone with half an arm could throw a rock across Knoll Pond and hit the tin roof of the little cabin beside it.

But here Hayes was now, gliding along past red cedars and Georgia pines, in the shadow of Stone Mountain. It was actually, come to think of it, a very peaceful feeling.

"Damn straight," agreed Gates. "*Lot* more peaceful than the Mekong."

When Hayes pulled the bow of the canoe ashore on the north side of the island, he saw a little boy sitting up on a cedar branch, watching him. The boy held a plastic tomahawk in one hand and a hot dog in the other.

"How, Kemo Sabe," Gates called, his palm raised. "Me look for paleface with white stick. And Ugly Big Man with eyes of a buffalo and snout of a possum."

The boy stared down at them. Then he pointed the tomahawk toward a grove of trees.

"May your spirit soar like an eagle, Little Brother," Gates told him by way of thanks.

Under the trees near the cul-de-sac of the road, and hidden from the picnic grounds, they found C. P. Calhoun and his bodyguard seated in a golf cart. Calhoun, his eyes slightly less glazed today, was reading a book entitled *The Art of Fencing,* and Solinsky was crushing peanuts and spitting the shells out.

"Hey, Arnold, it's twelve o'clock. That's noon to you."

"You wanna be dead, buddy?"

"Only my mommy calls me Buddy, Arnold. You can call me . . . Scaramouche! And I'll call you . . . Scare-ah-yourself-in-the-mirror."

Solinsky lunged. Calhoun swatted him back, and Raleigh hissed at his brother, "Will you please not make this any worse than it already is?"

The two parties met. The two principals shook hands. A great many bells began to peal, as if to commemorate the moment: actually, they were the seven hundred bells in the carillon spire, and they always played at noon.

While Gates laced up his skates, Raleigh told him, "Okay, I'll do it, but I just hope you realize I've never been more mortified in my life."

"Oh, Specs, you say that every day."

And so Hayes, feeling like an idiot, offered both fencing foils to Calhoun, accompanied by the following speech in his best polysyllabic style. "I trust we are agreed on the rules, Mr. Calhoun. This engagement satisfies all grievances between you and my, between you and Mr. Hayes; serving as full and sufficient apology and restitution for any previous loss or, or, offense committed by my principal." He waited. Calhoun bowed. "Second. The first to draw blood is the victor. On both parts, all proper care will be taken to avoid any serious injury. I presume you wish to proceed."

Calhoun bowed, tossed Solinsky his book, whisked both foils at his sides, picked one, returned the other, then offered Raleigh his hand. "Understood," he purred in his hushed silky voice. "I like your style," he added.

The duelists made quite a couple. The romantic gangland heir was dressed in loose white trousers with a black sash, a ruffled shirt and a white vest with a silk handkerchief in its pocket. (He bought most of his outfits at antique clothing stores.) Gates was wearing his soft white textured Japanese-looking apparel. (He bought most of his outfits at high-fashion discount stores.) The thin fabric fluttered now as he suddenly shot past them on one skate, swooped the fencing foil out of Raleigh's hand, swirled back in a figure-eight, and, with the foil's tip, flicked Solinsky's orange tie out of his jacket. *"En garde!"* he grinned, skating backward, just out of reach of the purple-faced giant's balled fists.

"Mr. Hayes," Calhoun murmured. "No skates."

Raleigh had to agree, and told his principal so. Gates then tied his laces together, crouched to his knees, and rolled toward them. "Like this?" he asked. "Fair?"

Calhoun shook his head. "No skates."

"Oh, all right fine okay. Just trying to add a little color." Gates put back on his white leather shoes, while Arnold Solinsky (held back by his employer's foil) growled and shuddered.

"Come, sir, your *passado!*" Gates tossed the foil from hand to hand.

And so at the signal of Raleigh Whittier Hayes (namesake of a great Elizabethan swordsman, but never himself much of a fan of the sport), the duel over Mrs. Jefferson Davis's (sic) opals began in earnest. Hopping and whacking and circling and shoving, the two combatants had at it for ten hot noisy minutes, to the awed excitement of the little boy with the tomahawk who was hiding behind a trashcan. Neither man had ever fenced before in his life, and was relying for instruction primarily upon Errol Flynn movies seen on television. But Gates Hayes was not only — as everyone said — a natural athlete, he had also (1) played Mercutio in the Thermopylae High production of *Romeo and Juliet,* and (2) chopped his way with a machete through the thick jungle foliage of Vietnam; and while he'd endeavored to put the latter experience in the old mental shredder, he nonetheless had the advantage of some experience over Cupid Calhoun, whose only steady exercise took place on a bed. Gates therefore was soon clearly ahead on points. He'd whisked Calhoun's handkerchief out of his vest pocket, slashed his sash, and torn open his sleeve, when all at once Solinsky bounded forward, grabbed Gates from behind with a thick arm around his neck, and yelled, "Now! Stick him!"

Calhoun had been already lunging forward, and the foil bent as it stabbed into Gates's shoulder. Shocked, Calhoun jerked it out. A wet red circle instantly widened over the white fabric.

"Gates!" Raleigh cried.

His brother wrestled free of the bodyguard's arm, and looked down at his own. He grinned. " 'No, 'tis not so deep as a well.' " Then he wagged his finger at Calhoun. "But bad show, C.P."

The slender man's alabaster face was now splotched with pink. He strode furiously over to Solinsky and slapped the side of the foil across his wide face. It left a red streak. "You're fired," he shouted.

Solinsky's response was truculent. "You can't fire me. Mrs. Parisi fires me."

"That's good to hear." Gates kept on grinning, but did so now through gritted teeth, for his brother was ripping his shirt off. "Hey, man, what are you doing to my threads? That's a Ron Chereskin!"

Raleigh tore the cloth into strips. One piece he wadded and pressed into the wound. It turned red. He put another one over it. "Hold that!" He looped a strip around his brother's shoulder and tied it in place.

Gates laughed. "It's nothing. It's nothing. A scratch. Two out of three, C.P.?"

His face livid, Calhoun stuck the foil in the dirt, where it stood quivering. "I forfeit," he announced. "You were winning. The debt's settled."

At this moment Raleigh Hayes, running down to the lake edge to wet some cloth, had no idea that he was about to become a hero. But he was. The opportunity was coming in a broadside from Fate, who had been merely playing games when she set up the dueling accident: Gates's wound, in fact, was only a scratch, albeit a very bloody one. Perhaps it was the sight of that red stain that quickened Fortune's perennial bloodlust; at any rate, her next trick on the Thermopyleans was very deadly indeed.

It had upset Mingo Sheffield to hear he wasn't allowed to attend the duel. The more he thought about it, the more it worried him to think how his help might be needed there. He particularly didn't trust the bully called Big Nose. Consequently, all the while the combatants were negotiating terms, Mingo Sheffield was pedaling as hard and as fast as his fat legs could maneuver in the tiny pedal boat, down the lake toward the wooded island. He was almost there when to his terrified astonishment a motorboat suddenly buzzed by, inches away, splashing water all over his clothes; then the boat spun around, pounded back, and shut off right in front of him! Two burly men in windbreakers grabbed hold of his little boat. One of them said, "Out, Hayes," and the other one showed him a gun.

Sheffield flung his arms up in the air. Tourists leaning along the rails of the big gaily painted steamboat merrily waved as they churned past. But Raleigh Hayes, on his knees at the lake edge dipping a shirt in water, was closer, more knowledgeable, and more paranoiac. He assumed that associates of Calhoun's were taking Mingo hostage. While it was conceivable that his neighbor might crawl, as he was doing, voluntarily into a stranger's motorboat, there could be no affable reason for one of those strangers to fist Mingo in the stomach as soon as he sat down, while the other one held a gun to his temple. Their boat spat into motion — slow motion, with its stern almost underwater, weighed down by the new passenger. It was passing very close to the island; so close that behind him Raleigh heard Big Nose Solinsky shout to his employer, "Hey look, C.P.! Couple of Neill's men. They got that blob guy! He's dead, huh, huh!" Raleigh heard Gates shout, "Neill? Neill! *John G. Neill??*" He heard Gates and Calhoun shout at each other. "Coke . . . Why? . . . Kill . . . Hotel . . . You? . . . Ripoff . . . Told them what?! . . . Me? Me? I'm nobody! . . . What! . . . Outside Myrtle Beach . . . Hit . . . What! Sheffield?! . . . Oh, no! . . . Here? . . . Dead. . . ."

Raleigh started running.

He saw glimpses of Gates's bare back leaping ahead of him.

A family of picnickers was standing open-mouthed at their table when Raleigh streaked around them. Simultaneously, he and they heard a motor on the water splutter, then roar off. *"That's my boat!"* squawked a man in a Georgia Tech sweatshirt, and squirted so much lighter fluid on his charcoal that flames whooshed over his head. An aluminum fishing boat bucked into view, with Gates standing at the helm, steering south with his good arm. Raleigh spun around and ran back to the cul-de-sac without slowing down or arguing with the Georgia Tech man who leaped around the fire screaming at his family, as if they didn't know, *"That's my boat!"*

Raleigh didn't wait to argue with Solinsky either, when the giant yelled, "Hey, that's our cart! You don't steal that!" The Thermopylean leaped into the golf cart and whizzed toward the bridge. The big guard considered stopping the cart with his body, but when the machine accelerated as it headed straight for him, and when the driver kicked him in the chest, he changed his mind.

Clattering through the covered bridge and heading south, Raleigh tried both to steer and read the park map taped to the little dashboard. Robert

E. Lee Boulevard ran between the narrow-gauge railroad tracks and the lake, and all three curved to follow the southern slope of the mountain. At one point, the road abutted a small inlet. That's where he was headed. But the golf cart, despite his attempt to press the pedal through the floorboard, wasn't fast enough. He thought he heard a shot, but he couldn't be sure. There was too much noise: his motor, boat motors, the paddle-wheeler's hoot, the chug of the steam locomotive coming up quickly behind him, and the seven hundred bells of the carillon pealing "Maryland, My Maryland."

He was too late. By the time he reached the bend from which he could see the lake bank, the empty motorboat was banging against a rock. A quarter-mile ahead, two men in windbreakers were running across the road, pushing Mingo in front of them. They scrabbled up the incline to the tracks just as the tourist train slowed at the curve. Leaping on the back steps of the bright caboose, they hauled the fat man up onto the moving platform with them. A whistling blast of smoke puffed from the engine, and away the train sped, with Raleigh in torment scooting down the road beside it.

Part of his torment was the infuriating slowness of the golf cart; no amount of yanking, pounding, or kicking would hurry it closer to Mingo. Part of his torment was an inability to convince himself that somewhere out on the lake, "everything was jake, folks," with his brother Gates.

But actually Gates was doing, in the Hayes phrase, "just fine." Surprisingly fine, considering that one of Neill's hired guns had taken a shot at him, and instead put a very large jagged hole in the aluminum hull of his borrowed boat. Without a thought to his captaincy, Gates abandoned ship, dived over the side and started swimming underwater. Despite his bad shoulder, he'd made it to shore by the time his boat, bubbling protests, sank.

Like his brother, Gates Hayes was in torment. He knew (vaguely) that the guy who'd paid him to make those pickups in "Easy Living" had had some (vague) falling-out with a powerful drug dealer named John G. Neill. Calhoun had quickly made it clear to him just now that the cocaine syndicate thought Gates Hayes was this dead man's partner, that the syndicate planned on Gates Hayes's being a dead man, too, and that they seemed to think Mingo Sheffield was Gates Hayes. All Gates could hear as he kicked under that water was "I fucked up, I fucked up, he's going to get killed, he's going to get killed!"

When Gates staggered from the weedy bank up to the road, far far off to his left he saw Sheffield being yanked inside the caboose door of a moving train. On the parallel road, his brother Raleigh was flying after the train in a golf cart. "Oh fuck!" gasped Gates. Across the road, a young bicyclist sat under a tree beside his helmet; he was reading *Walden Two* and eating a banana and alfalfa sprouts sandwich. The alfalfa hung out of this young man's open mouth like moss as he watched a wet, half-naked savage covered with blood and lake slime steal his thousand-dollar Italian racing bike.

At the same moment that Gates was stealing the bike, his brother was passing one of the park campgrounds beside a baseball field. Parked right next to the road was a black van; the motor was running, the radio was blasting, the door was open. Hayes looked ahead. The train seemed to be making a stop. Yes. According to the map, there was a trading post up there. He thought he could catch it if . . . No, he didn't think: there was nothing in his head but the image of a trembling Mingo Sheffield with his arms raised. Grabbing the fencing foil, Hayes jumped off the cart and jumped in the van and threw it into drive and drove! Just as he did so, a big young man covered with black hair and wearing nothing on his chest but a black leather vest with a red devil painted on it trotted out of the woods zipping his fly. "WHOOOA! BIG JOKE. OKAY, ASSHOLES, VERY FUNNY!" The van was a hundred yards away before this individual decided enough was enough, and started running after it. Inside the van, the girl named Wendy, the sumo wrestler, the girl with a crew cut, and the tattooed longhair rolled all over the black fur floor and walls. They thought the werewolf was playing a joke on them by leaving the road and bumping the van right up onto the railroad tracks. They laughed like crazy.

"Ride 'em, Bradley!" yelled the wrestler.

But when the crew-cut girl stuck her head between the curtains that separated the front from the back of the van they called "Sympathy With The Devil," she didn't see a man who looked like a werewolf. Instead, she saw a man who looked vaguely familiar. "Space-out," she said. "Who are you?"

Raleigh, flying up and down in his seat, and desperately struggling to steer the bucking van over the train rails, had time for only the quickest glance; it was enough to recognize the girl who had, that hideous night in the rain, helped pull down his pants. "You're under arrest," he told her. "Go sit down."

Her head disappeared. He could hear her in the back. "Oh man, oh man, too much. Those fairies we rolled in North Carolina? One of them's busting us. No shit."

Other heads popped out behind Hayes's. He paid no attention. He was closing on the caboose, fifty more feet, twenty more. Was he going to hit it? He slammed on the brakes. Damn, the train was moving again! In one motion, he cut the ignition, rolled out of the seat, and sprinted down the tracks.

Back in the van, the devil sympathizers somersaulted into a heap. "What's happening? Easy, easy," said a voice from the corner, a young man with a spoonful of cocaine.

"Wow, wow, wow," said Wendy, looking through the curtain. "He's jumping a train now! He's got a fucking sword in his teeth."

"No way. You're stoned. Oh, shit. She's right!"

Yes, Wendy was quite right. Raleigh W. Hayes, middle-aged and middle class, had just chased down a train, had just leaped on it, and finding the caboose door locked, had just crawled up the ladder to the roof, with a fencing foil clamped between his teeth. He didn't even know it was there; it was simply the habit of a lifetime not to throw things away.

Meanwhile, Gates Hayes, pedaling hard and pressing his palm into his bleeding shoulder, couldn't see the steam engine until he rounded the bend at the trading post. What he saw then was a black van sitting right in the middle of the tracks. Ahead of that, he saw four yelping cowboys rush out of the woods and start firing guns at the train's passengers, who stuck their faces out the windows and waved happily at the show. Suddenly the cowboys all stopped. They pointed up, and began to applaud. "Oh, Jesus!" Gates panted. Leaping from the roof of the caboose to the roof of the last passenger car was a man in a blue-and-white sweater. Something silvery glistened in his hand.

"GO BIG BRO!" Gates shouted, and pedaled faster, dodging a big hair-covered fellow who looked like a Hell's Angel and who was trotting painfully down the road in bare hairy feet.

Now, John Neill's two hired guns were confused. They weren't confused because their hostage kept babbling that his name was Mingo Sheffield and that he didn't even know what cocaine looked like and that he'd never double-crossed a single soul once in his entire life. Naturally, that's what anybody would say in his situation. They thought he was doing a very fine imitation of a mental defect, but they didn't believe him for an instant: after all, he had enough sense to sit still with his mouth shut, once they told him they'd blow a hole through his head if he didn't.

No, they were confused because they were being so hotly pursued in such bizarre ways. This Gates Hayes appeared to have a fairly good-sized organization, but an odd one. His men called attention to themselves, and that was bad for business. The hired guns didn't like attention; when they wanted information out of somebody, they wanted to get it in private; when they wanted somebody dead, they wanted him privately dead. They didn't want some maniac leaning off the roof of a train, staring at them upside down through the window. These men couldn't afford to be noticed; they were wanted in too many states for too many unpleasant reasons.

Their plan was quietly to leave the train with the rest of the tourists, quietly walk the hostage to their car, drive off someplace very secluded and quietly dispose of Gates Hayes, after he'd told them the names of every person even remotely connected with the boat "Easy Living." Naturally, they hadn't told the fat man their plans, but even a colossal optimist like Mingo was beginning to suspect the worst.

Mingo Sheffield knew a great deal about guns. He recognized a Magnum .45 and a silencer when he saw them. He and Vera had both taken Beginning, Intermediate, and Advanced Target Practice evening classes at the Thermopylae VFW Post — just in case they ever needed to defend themselves. But these courses had never explained what you were supposed to do if you didn't *have* a gun, and if some other people had two that could very easily blow your head off, and if these somebodies' eyes looked as if it didn't upset them at all to think about doing just that. Wedged in the railway car seat, facing away from the other passengers, Mingo was not making a move or a sound; he was so panic-stricken, he couldn't have done so, even if he'd known what to do or say. He tried to think: What would Raleigh do? But Raleigh was too smart ever to get caught in such a dilemma. And Gates would just whirl in a blur of karate kicks, knocking the guns right out of their pockets. It was too bad, sighed Sheffield, that when Weeper Berg had taught him how to palm an ace (which had certainly come in handy when he'd cut the cards for Gates's duel), the master criminal hadn't added lessons on how to escape from killers.

Or maybe if he could think of a movie escape . . . But Mingo's mind was blank. His whole body had wilted with fear, and his vocal cords were unstrung; he couldn't even cough. Besides, he was all talked out. These men just wouldn't believe he wasn't Gates Hayes, and he couldn't tell them where Gates was, because then they might go straight back to that island and kill Raleigh and his brother both.

So Mingo kept his hands, which were shaking, tucked inside his thighs, and he prayed. And he wondered if people still had eyes when they went to Heaven, so they could see what it looked like and could find their dead parents and special friends already up there. Or if maybe people in Heaven had even better eyes, sort of like God's, so they could look all the way down on Earth and watch over their living loved ones, the way Clarence the angel watched over Jimmy Stewart in *It's a Wonderful Life.* Mingo prayed that if he did die, Vera wouldn't go all to pieces. But the thought of not seeing Vera again was so unbearable, he immediately changed the prayer to a request that God either change these horrible men's minds, or drop a tree on their heads. Or *something!*

The something arrived as Sheffield was shoved out of the train door at the railroad station. Suddenly there was a man with a spear on top of the roof of the rail car yelling in a loud strange voice, "MINGO! RUN!" It was Raleigh! A fencing foil hurled down and stabbed a gash in the back of the neck of one of the hired guns. He let go of Mingo's arm, fell to his knees, and grabbed frantically at the pain. At the same instant Raleigh flew off the train roof, landing on top of the second man, knocking them both into the gravel track bed. The crowd began to shriek and jostle. Mingo ran.

Kicking, desperately hanging onto his opponent's hair and windbreaker, Raleigh rolled back and forth in the gravel, but was flung off and punched hideously hard in the kidney. This man then knocked a path through families of tourists to chase after Mingo, whom Raleigh could see racing away across the wide green slope where picnickers lounged and stared up at the Confederate Memorial. Now the thug at whom he'd thrown the fencing foil was stumbling to his feet. Hayes picked up a wood sign ("Steam Engine Ticket Holders Only") and smashed its round steel base down on the man's head; he fell back to his knees, then to his face. Staggering away, Raleigh chased after the one following Mingo.

Remarkably quick for his size anyhow, the fat man, spurred by terror, kept ahead of his kidnapper as he galloped past the Memorial Plaza. He ran blindly toward the next building he saw, skidded inside, and rushed into a tightly knotted crowd. It was the last place in the world Mingo Sheffield would have gone on purpose. For he was caught in an inexorable tide of shoving flesh pushing its way into the Skylift to ride up Stone Mountain. The crowd was already anxious and belligerent because those who didn't make it inside had to wait twenty-five minutes in the crush for their next chance. As a result, everything from seething stares to nudges to efforts at physical constraint resulted when first a huge flailing man hopping up and down to look behind him, then a stocky cursing man in a windbreaker, elbowed their way past everybody else and snatched the last spaces in the big Swiss cable car just as the door was closing. Even more outrageous, here came a third man, a tall, thin one in a sweater, whose eyes behind his glasses were completely insane, who simply crawled on top of them and dived over them. Then (to the appalled, thrilled astonishment of both those jammed in the waiting line and those jammed in the now-moving glassed-in funicular), the man in the sweater *chased* the car as it swung upward, tilting beneath its enormous blue steel arm that hooked it to its cables. This man not only chased it, he *jumped* onto its guard bumper just as it jerked free of earth, he grabbed hold of the door rails, and he clung there to the *outside* of the Skylift while it swooped away toward the top of Stone Mountain. Some mouths just fell open, some screamed.

Three voices cried, "Oh shit!" simultaneously. One belonged to the Skylift attendant, who turned to telephone the control booth at the summit. One belonged to Gates Hayes, who skidded in a circle on the Italian bicycle fifty yards from the ride's entrance when he saw, high above the tips of a forest of pines, the blue-and-white sweater stretched across the side of the blue and glass cable car. Gates didn't stop; he bounced down the hill toward the main parking lot, with the pedals spinning so fast his feet flew out to the sides.

The third "Oh shit" came from Raleigh Hayes. Now, if our hero had taken the advice he so often gave others ("Use your head"), he probably would not have found himself plastered, spread-eagled, against the side of an airborne trolley. Never before had fear so sickened him. Not at four, when he fell into a pile of burning leaves; not at fourteen, when he was caught by three local hoods in an alley behind the Rialto Movie Theatre; not at twenty-four in Germany, when he knew the car that had just spun over the median strip was going to hit his jeep head-on; not at thirty-four, when he and Aura had had such an awful fight, he'd thought they might separate. And not even at any point in the past two weeks had Raleigh Hayes ever felt so nauseated with terror. Perhaps his predicament could have been worse; at least he had a solid rail to stand on and steel bars to loop his arms through, and the wind wasn't bad, and the Skylift didn't move very quickly. At least he was so high up that if he fell, he'd die instantly rather than end up mangled in a wheelchair. As an expert on actuarial charts, Raleigh knew that he was now in such a high-risk category that the probabilities were not all in his favor. But at least he had a $200,000 double-indemnity life insurance policy, which surely ought to pay for Aura's mayoral campaign.

Ironies like these had none of their old soothing effect. He hadn't used his head, and his present critical situation was the result. Not that when warning his daughters against the perils of not thinking had he ever thought that by their failure to do so, they might end up looking *down*,

from the outside of a Skylift, on the largest sculpture in the world. For
Generals Lee and Jackson and President Davis were now behind and below
our hero. All three held their stone hats over their stone hearts, as if they
were already paying their respects at Raleigh's funeral. Or honoring a bravado they hadn't seen since Jeb Stuart died. Or perhaps simply yielding the
spotlight. For a closer view of the Confederates was usually the main attraction on the Skylift ride. But this trip, no one was paying them the
slightest bit of attention. Only inches away from the crowd lucky enough
to be on the right side of the car, and sturdy enough to protect their positions, was a much more interesting statue attached to the glass door. A
man in a sweater who looked as if he were being electrocuted: His hair
stood on end, tears were running out of his eyes, and he was spasmodically
shaking his head, no. Some people in the car shrieked, some people beat on
the glass and laughed, and the fat man wearing a Hawaiian shirt keeled
over in a faint and had to be jerked back to his feet by a man in a windbreaker.

While the tourists were watching Raleigh, and Raleigh was trying to
signal Mingo (once he came to again) not to notice him, and while all the
Skylift personnel were trying to decide whether a suicide was more likely
to jump if they stopped the car or if they kept going, Gates Hayes had already sped to the parking lot. There, Simon Berg and Toutant Kingstree
were lying on a grassy incline beside the back of the red circus truck. They
were deep in competitive reminiscences; Berg's father was peddling junk
in a handcart through the snowy streets of the East Village, and Kingstree's mother was sucking copperhead venon out of her own leg, when the
two older men saw Gates, bare-chested and bleeding, hop off the bicycle,
jerk open the truck's front door, and leap back out with his white-handled
pistol.

"I never did like that dueling shit," said Kingstree as they hurried over.

"Kid, kid, you're hurt!" Berg shouted. "Enough already!"

Gates had flung back the rear doors and was climbing into the van. He
yelled as fast as he could, "Listen, Weep! I fucked up bad. Big mess with
John G. Neill's operation, okay? Two of his goons got Mingo! Think he's
me! Taking him up the Skylift! Raleigh's hanging off the fucking outside!
I'm going up the trail on the south slope, okay? Get back! Get back!"

An immense roar bounced off the metal walls of the truck; gray smoke
fumed up; then through the thick cloud flew in air straight out of the
opened doors the big black motorcycle with Gates floating on top of it.
He landed bouncing down the grassy incline and sped away.

"Motherfuck!" Kingstree gasped.

Berg was already trotting toward the Ticket Center at the end of the lot. "John G. Neill, I don't believe! Dumb, dumb, dumb! He's never gonna make it!"

"I don't know, Weeper, he looked good on that bike."

"Will yah listen? There's got to be some security guards down there in that building. Here's what I want you to do. . . ." Berg pulled a carefully folded newspaper clipping from his pocket.

The security guards at Stone Mountain Park were already so frazzled they were cursing at each other. The guides and attendants and vendors and administrators of the park were all in an uproar too. Phones were ringing, people were running all over the place as if the Russians had just surrounded the mountain. Every few minutes brought another peculiar report: A private boat had been stolen and sunk. Picnickers on Covered Bridge Island had set a dead pine tree on fire. A golf cart had been abandoned on a softball field. A missing pedal boat was floating on the lake with no passenger. An empty motorboat had been found smashed on some rocks. An expensive bicycle had been snatched, and its hysterical owner described the thief as "a naked man covered with blood and mud." Doped-up Hell's Angels had parked their van right on the railroad tracks by the trading post and, after a loud exchange of vulgarities, had challenged the troupe of cowboy actors to a free-for-all. People were coming into the main office claiming to have heard shots, to have seen a swordsman on top of the train, to have seen another swordsman in a white ruffled shirt forcing a huge blond-haired man to crawl down the road on his hands and knees. People claimed to have seen a man get stabbed in the back of the neck, then get bashed with a sign, then get run over by two senior citizens on a tandem bike. Now here came all these calls that there was a suicidal maniac clinging to the outside of the Skylift. The security guards were really hard-pressed to be civil to the tall elderly black man who barged in on them to insist that they phone for the police and the highway patrol because he'd just spotted the notorious escaped criminal Simon "Weeper" Berg sitting in the snack bar on top of Stone Mountain.

"Look here, grandpa," snapped the young guard, "don't bug me with this Simon Weeper whatever foolishness now. I don't know diddly-squat about any such person. I got a possible suicide and all hell's broken loose around here, so move on, okay. So long."

Blocking his path, Toutant Kingstree unfolded a yellow piece of newspaper. "Well, I want this reward." He pointed at the clipping. "I'm the one saw him. I'm the one with the information leading to his arrest."

"Reward?!" The guard grabbed away the paper, furiously reading. "You sure this is the guy? You saw him up there?"

The black man nodded. "I sure am sure. But you ought not to go up after him by yourself. I believe he's got some of his gang up on top the mountain with him. See where it says, 'armed and believed dangerous.' You better get the police fast. Now, you going to fix it so I get my thousand-dollar reward?"

"Yeah yeah, I'll fix it. Leave your name." The young guard rushed to a phone.

The Skylift ride was not very long, but it was long enough for Raleigh Hayes, fluttering in the wind, to consider in sequence most of the Great Philosophies of the Western World, as they'd been synopsized in the college course he'd taken a quarter of a century ago. At that time, he'd leaned toward a nihilistic angst flavored with a dash of French absurdist existentialism. But now, on reflection, he found he'd changed. Now, his ultimate conclusion was that while the world might well be a transitory vale of tears, or the pale reflection of an Idea, or a causeless, purposeless hodgepodge of matter, or the world might not even exist at all — still, he didn't want to leave it behind. Now, while life might well be environmentally determined, or fatalistically predestined, or nasty and short, or a fool's dream, or a Freudian nightmare, or life might be just a joke — still, he didn't want to lose his. Now, on reflection, Raleigh Hayes's ultimate conclusion about life in the world was, "I'll take it." And he clung to the steel bar of that Swiss cable car so tightly that his arms hadn't stopped aching three days later when he put them around his father in New Orleans.

But contrary to Raleigh's impression, the Skylift ride was really not very long at all. By the time the staff had decided that as the psycho hadn't jumped yet, there was no sense in stopping the cable car — which might encourage him to do so — by that time, the car was already approaching the summit. A small assembly of guards and tourists (one waving a Confederate flag) was waiting there for Raleigh's arrival. When he saw them, he jumped from the car as soon as there was a platform to jump onto. Then using the shoulder of a sightseer as leverage, he pole-vaulted the entrance gate, and squeezed into the crowd, spinning and shifting in moves his body hadn't made since high-school basketball games. As he bounded down the steps, he pulled off the distinctive blue-and-white-striped sweater and shoved it down in a trashcan.

The peak of Stone Mountain was not a peak. It was an immense rounded wide smooth gray stone dome, matted in spots with bristly lichen, and sparsely dotted with clusters of tough little pine trees. There weren't very many people walking around on the peak; there were too many newer attractions down below. Still, it took a while before Raleigh caught sight of Sheffield's bright flowered shirt, far off on the other side of the Plaza of Flags. The man in the brown windbreaker was jabbing Mingo in the back, pushing him behind some trees, toward a steel-mesh safety fence that circled the edge of the dome. There was no one else in sight.

The flags bordered a long, shallow, rectangular pool; Raleigh did not take the time to go around it. Instead, he ran right across the middle, fording the water in a splashing sprint. Then, "STOP," he cried, and stepped between his neighbor and the hired gunman. The man did stop, and stared at the intruder, who was panting for breath and shaking water from his shoes. Wind, hissing through the pine needles, made Raleigh shiver as he pushed Mingo behind him, and said, "I don't know what you think you're up to, but this man is an innocent bystander. His name is Mingo Sheffield."

The gunman had an empty face and dead eyes. His mouth didn't appear to open when he finally spoke. "You made a bad mistake, butting into this, fucking with my partner down there." He put his hand inside his jacket. "Who are you?"

"My name is Hayes." Raleigh held Mingo back with his arm.

For the first time John G. Neill's hired gun considered the possibility that he'd made a mistake about the fat man. This crazy thin guy was a much more likely candidate. "Gates Hayes?" he asked, with a slight twitch of the lip.

Raleigh swallowed, crossed his arms, and then he nodded. "Right."

"Raleigh!" said Mingo. "Don't! Listen, mister, he's —"

"Mingo, will you shut up!"

The gunman might or might not have been saying something; his mouth didn't move, and a loud roaring noise drowned out any possible words. They all looked up. A helicopter was buzzing over their heads. It was one of the sightseeing helicopters, but the second gunman had not hired it for the regular tour; he'd hired it very precipitously in exchange for a look at his Magnum .45.

The helicopter was making so much racket that none of the three men standing at the edge of the ridge heard the sound of another kind of motor approaching. And this second noise had come up the south slope so fast, swooping off the road to pass a jeep full of policemen, and it now sped over the ledge so fast that the man in the brown windbreaker didn't have time to turn around before the big motorcycle struck him in the back. He pitched forward; his head hit a rock, his gun skittered under the mesh fence.

"Get the gun, Mingo," shouted Gates Hayes, as he sprang down from his Harley and shoved his foot against the thug's neck. But the man didn't flinch; he was out cold.

Mingo Sheffield had already scrambled over the fence, already scooped up the gun, already slipped on a wet piece of lichen moss, and already slid five feet down toward the sheer drop-off, below which there was nothing to hold on to until Robert E. Lee's ear, hundreds of feet below; Mingo had already fought down panic, pawed up fistfuls of moss until his hands caught on the root of a cedar sapling and his feet wedged themselves in a crevice, when he saw the helicopter whirring back, dropping closer, so close his wind-flapped Hawaiian shirt stung his skin like a wasp. Mingo saw his other kidnapper leaning out the side of the helicopter. He saw the gun in the man's hand jerk twice as it shot at Raleigh and Gates. Clutching at the sapling with one hand, Mingo raised the pistol with the other. He held his breath, squinted one round eye, and fired. The man disappeared, and the helicopter lifted and zoomed away.

Then Mingo breathed. Then he screamed, "RALEIGH! RALEIGH, ARE YOU OKAY?" Sheffield looked straight up. He stopped breathing again, until the Hayes brothers both leaned over the fence. "Help!" said the fat man, and dropped the gun as the tree root started pulling loose.

The first thing Raleigh Hayes said after they hauled Sheffield back over the fence was, "Mingo, dammit, you've killed a man! Jesus Christ, oh God, we've got to get you out of here! Let go of me!"

Sheffield stopped hugging his friend to say, "I didn't kill him at all. I just shot the gun out of his hand. Maybe I got his wrist a little bit."

"*I love this guy!*" Gates shouted, wiping blood from his hair. "Hey, man, don't sit down." His older brother had actually not so much sat, as collapsed on a boulder.

"Did they get you, Gates?!" Mingo gasped.

"Nah, I hit a tree. Let's haul ass!"

"How?!" Raleigh pointed first at the motorcycle, whose front tire had been blown to bits by the first bullet from the helicopter (the second had barely missed Gates's head); he pointed then at a jeep about a hundred yards away and moving slowly, as it was filled with policemen and surrounded by excited tourists, Skylift attendants, and security guards.

"Follow me," Gates suggested, while lifting the body of the still-unconscious thug, removing the brown windbreaker and pulling it on over his still-naked chest, and over the gun still stuck in his pants belt. "Come on." He trotted into the cluster of pine trees.

"Gates! What about your motorcycle?"

Raleigh's brother turned and shrugged. "Easy come, easy go?" He led them quickly to the south trail, then over a ridge to a flat ledge of rock where they saw a high firetower. At its base was a jeep on whose side was painted the logo of the national forest service.

"You're kidding," said Raleigh.

Thirty seconds later, the jeep was bouncing its way down the trail to the foot of the mountain. The whole time Gates kept saying he was sorry. Mingo kept thanking God they were all alive. Raleigh, suddenly realizing what he'd been through, went catatonic. The trio abandoned the forest ranger's jeep near the trading post, where they saw a tow truck hauling a black van off the railroad tracks.

"We walk to the truck, and we hit the road," Gates said. "Man, I'm sorry. I really am. What a pisser."

They did walk to the truck, but they didn't hit the road right away. There was a note on the windshield from Toutant Kingstree. On the off chance that they made it back there without getting killed or arrested, he wanted them to know that Simon Berg, in order to force the park security to send police to the summit (where their presence, Berg hoped, would dissuade Neill's hired killers from murdering the Kid and/or Fatty, i.e., Gates and/or Mingo), that Simon Berg had personally surrendered himself to a security guard, and forced this man to acknowledge a resemblance between Berg's present face and Berg's newspaper image. They were holding the master criminal at the Ticket Center until the police returned from the mountaintop, where Berg claimed to have been parlaying with drug traffickers. Kingstree was at the center too, under the pretext of waiting for his reward.

"Okay fine right," said Gates, then suddenly sagged at the knees and leaned against the side of the truck. Blood had soaked through the shoulder of the brown windbreaker from the stab wound, and blood was dripping down out of his hair from a glancing blow against a low tree bough during his motorcycle race up the south trail. "I'm fine, I'm fine, I'm going after Weep." Slowly he slid down the red metal to the asphalt. "This is all my fault. Man, I'm sorry."

Raleigh Hayes took only a moment to press on his eyes, bite his forefinger, and jerk on his hair. Then he said, "Mingo, clean out that wound. Gates, can you drive? Gates?"

The curls tilted up, the beautiful teeth flashed the old grin. "Hey, I'm a flyer, Big Bro."

Raleigh changed into his pin-striped suit so fast, he was already back out of the truck van and running across the lot before Mingo had finished easing the jacket off Gates.

At the information desk, Raleigh walked past Toutant Kingstree with only a slight shake of his head. Outside the door labeled Park Security, he said gruffly to the young guard seated there, "You the guy who thinks he's got Simon Berg? You better be right. Is he in there?"

The guard stood up. "Sir? You're the police detective, right? They said a detective was coming."

Hayes crossed his arms. "I'm Whittier. FBI. Open that door."

"There's a reward." The guard waved an old piece of newspaper at Raleigh. "He's in my custody. It was me that called the police."

"Then it better be you that knows what he's talking about." Hayes grabbed the clipping. "Open that door."

In a plastic chair with his hands cuffed together sat the notorious convict Simon "Weeper" Berg, in his green-checked suit. He had his joined hands raised, rather like Gandhi, except that from one tiny hand curled smoke from an unfiltered cigarette. He didn't speak as Raleigh looked him over.

Quickly, Raleigh turned to the guard with an icy frown. "Are you kidding? You think this pitiful old geezer is Simon 'Weeper' Berg?" He pointed a derisive finger at Berg. "You brought me all the way from Atlanta for *this?!* I ought to have you sacked. Where's your boss?"

The guard backed away fidgeting. "But but . . ."

"Have you ever seen Simon Berg?"

"No, but but . . ."

"Well, I have. And he would think this was very funny."

"But the picture in the paper . . ."

Raleigh waved the clipping at the guard's red face. "Right. Right. Look at it! Does it remotely resemble this little jerk? Remotely?" And in fact, the photograph (which was ten years old) looked not at all like the man in the chair. "Did he tell you he was Berg?"

"YES. And a black guy came in here, and he swore —"

"Uncuff him. He's a nutcase. You get them all the time. Nobodies that want to be somebody. I'll have to take him in for questioning now. And waste some more time, thanks to you."

The guard wheeled on his prisoner. "Aren't you Simon 'The Weeper' Berg?"

The little man's eyes widened, then they floated up beneath the lids. "I'm the one that really killed the President. It wasn't Oswald. I'm tired of running. I want to pay for my crime."

"Goddamn you dumb little asshole midget!" the young guard now shouted, spraying spit.

As Raleigh led Berg out of the building, the guard shifted between apologies to the FBI, castigation of the imposter, and lament over his lost reward. In this last, he was joined by Toutant Kingstree, who hurried over and kept up a refrain of "Where're you taking him? I'm the one that saw him first. I'm supposed to get a thousand dollars. Y'all aren't going to cheat me 'cause I'm black, are you?," and continued protesting until Hayes shut the door behind them.

The back door of the truck was already open; the motor was already running.

"So, listen. Raleigh, my friend," said Simon "The Weeper" Berg from the mattress of the circus van, as the victorious Knick-Knack Gang flew down Robert E. Lee Boulevard and out of Stone Mountain Park. "You're an admirable and benevolent man. But 'pitiful old geezer' already was not strictly necessary. 'Little jerk' you coulda skipped. Oyyy. I should live so long, me that Bugsy Siegal said was the best in the business, to be called an asshole and midget to my face by a cretinous shit-kicking Cracker. So, you didn't lose my clipping, did yah?"

"Move over, Simon," Raleigh sighed, and lay down on the mattress beside him. "In the words of a famous criminal, 'Let me sleep. My guts can't take the pace.' "

And our hero fell fast asleep and didn't awaken until he heard Mingo Sheffield say, "Gollee, Montgomery, Alabama is really pretty. Do y'all think we could just take a minute and go see the White House of the Confederacy?" Hayes then opened one eye. He saw Toutant Kingstree put the saxophone to his lips, and start a sprightly jazz rendition of "Dixie," as he winked at Simon Berg.

CHAPTER

30

The Consequences of a Remarkable Scene

LOVELY AS MONTGOMERY WAS with its pink cherry and white dogwood blossoms, with its wide avenues and soaring capitol, our travelers had no time to drink in its beauty or soak up its history; at least not on Monday night. The only Montgomery they saw on Monday was a hospital.

Gates had made the trip from Atlanta in less than four hours; then he pulled into a truck stop and more or less fell out of the cab. He looked, Mingo told him, pretty awful. His hair was stiff with dried blood, and so was his jacket (or rather the hired gun's jacket); his eyes were glassy as blue marbles, and his speech sounded as if his lips had been shot full of Novocain. He kept insisting there was something the matter with the truck, but not with him. With him, everything was jake, all systems go, A-okay, and a piece of cake. Finally, however, he admitted that he was only guessing at the number of fingers Raleigh was holding up (which Raleigh already suspected, since Gates was consistently guessing wrong), and further admitted he'd been only guessing at the number of other cars on the highway. Toutant Kingstree took the wheel, and kept the truck more or less on the right side of the road. Persuading Gates Hayes to go to a hospital was rather like persuading Mingo Sheffield to walk a tightrope over Niagara Falls, and finally Raleigh and Toutant pretty much had to slide him through the doors with their hands under his arms.

The two interns on duty there didn't like Gates's story about getting accidentally stabbed during a rehearsal of *Romeo and Juliet* and so falling off her balcony. "Why were you fighting on Juliet's balcony?" asked the first intern, a former English major.

"Sexual jealousy. Modern interpretation," mumbled Gates while his brother tried to hold him down in a wheelchair. "Way we did it, they're *all* sleeping with her. Mercutio, Paris, Tybalt, Friar Lawrence. Not the Nurse, nothing kinky. Great show. Want two free tickets?"

The other intern pointed at Raleigh's swollen eye and Mingo's scratched arms. "Is that where you two got all these contusions and lacerations? From this show?"

"No," Mingo said. "I slid off a mountain, and he —"

"Great show. French production. Jean Claude Claudel. You know his work?"

"Please, Gates," Raleigh groaned. "My brother's a little delirious. Look at him."

The interns didn't like Gates's bloodless color, his fumbled reflexes, his blurry focus, his odd remarks, and his total lack of any medical insurance. But after Raleigh promised to pay, they wheeled the wounded swashbuckler off for an examination. Raleigh came with them, and when Gates didn't know what type blood he had, his older brother (who carried life insurance on him as well as on most other living Hayeses) said, "Type B, the same as mine."

"Well, hey, Big Bro, can I borrow a quart? I'll pay you back, I promise."

And so Raleigh Hayes lay down beside Gates and watched the bright red healthy result of his careful diet, his diligent exercise, and his moderate habits flowing through a tube to mingle with the reckless, thoughtless blood of his half-sibling.

Gates winked, mumbled, "Blood brothers, Kemo Sabe, let us live in peace, sharing the buffalo forever," and fell asleep.

The interns didn't like the loss of blood, the chance of infection, the possibility of a concussion from which, they cheerfully predicted, Gates might drop dead at any moment. They wanted to keep him for at least twenty-four hours.

Before returning to the hospital, Raleigh drove with the other three travelers to the nearby Dogwood Motel, a perfectly fine old place with a pool and a bar and swing sets and even a lobby, but with no customers, for it had been built before it realized it needed to be near an Interstate exit ramp. That night, Mingo was too tired and bruised even to try the Dogwood's TV set, much less its pool. He was too worn out to do anything

except call Vera, and call Diane Yonge at the Atlanta hospital, where he
learned that she and Little Vera were doing so well, they were leaving the
next day for Kure Beach. He promised to write and to bring Vera for a
visit soon. Then he said a prayer for Gates, then he fell asleep, while in the
next bed Toutant Kingstree softly played "Mood Indigo" on his saxophone.

But by Tuesday morning, after they heard that Gates was much better,
Mingo sufficiently recovered his spirits to persuade Kingstree to come
sightseeing with him. Berg declined, having business of his own. The day
manager of the Dogwood was a little alarmed when a six-and-a-half-foot
gray-haired black man, wearing gold chains and a peach-pink pleated suit
over a black shirt, and accompanied by an enormously fat white man in
madras checks, asked directions to the White House of the Confederacy,
and explained that he was interested in it because his friend's guidebook
said it had been built by the grandfather of the wife of the guy who wrote
The Great Gatsby, which was an old favorite movie of his because of the
jazz.

"Y'all arrive last night? Together?" asked the manager, as a tiny Jewish
man joined them and asked directions to a beauty salon, a book store, a
delicatessen, and a travel agency.

"That's right," smiled Mingo. "There're two more of us, but they're in
the hospital."

Sheffield and Kingstree walked around Montgomery most of the day. At
lunch they read about themselves in the Atlanta newspaper. They weren't
of course mentioned by name. The article, "Drug Gangs War at Stone
Mountain," emphasized police optimism that a break was coming their
way soon on the cocaine-trafficking racket. There was clear evidence of in-
ternecine battling between rival rings in the Atlanta area. On Monday afternoon at Stone Mountain Park, factions had apparently crossed paths,
and violence had erupted. The police had captured two men — one on top
of the mountain, the second in a helicopter; both unconscious, the second
wounded in the hand — who had presumably fired on one another after a
chase involving stolen park vehicles. Both men had known connections to
local financier John G. Neill, long-suspected head of a big Colombia-based
cocaine refinery. Moreover, on the scene was an abandoned motorcycle registered to a man recently found murdered in Myrtle Beach, North Carolina; a man who also had connections to John G. Neill. Other men
appeared to have been participants in the gang war episode at Stone
Mountain Park, including, possibly, an escaped convict named Simon
"The Weeper" Berg, who'd been rescued, after his capture by park secu-

rity, by a man impersonating an FBI agent known as Whitmore. There followed a very unflattering description of Raleigh given by the young security guard.

"I thought Gates owned that motorcycle," pondered Mingo.

"I thought we were going straight to New Orleans to cut some records," Kingstree sighed.

After lunch, the two men visited the brass star embedded on the spot outside the capitol where Jefferson Davis was inaugurated (and where Varina was *not* wearing the necklace Gates had sold C. P. Calhoun); afterward, they visited the Baptist church on Dexter Avenue where Martin Luther King, Jr. had organized the Montgomery bus boycott. They were on a bus themselves, returning to the Dogwood Motel, when Mingo said, "I couldn't believe it when I heard they'd shot Reverend King. Could you?"

"I didn't have a bit of trouble," Kingstree replied.

"Well, we know a guy named Kettell, Raleigh and I do, and he was *celebrating* it. The assassination. Raleigh got right up and walked out of the restaurant! I was always sorry I didn't do it, too." Sheffield turned pink. "I was too shy to stand up. I just sat there and said, 'I hate you, Mingo Sheffield, you fat stupid chicken.'" He squeezed over closer to the window to give his companion a little more room on the seat. "Because, Toutant, I'll tell you a secret. I sometimes used to think, well, maybe Martin Luther King was really Jesus come back, you know, to see if he couldn't fix things." The fat face crumpled. "And here I was, just sitting there at the Lotus House letting Nemours Kettell make fun of him and laugh at his getting murdered, just like the Romans did. I went in the bathroom and cried. Did you ever think that?"

"Think what?"

"That he was Jesus."

"Nope." The black man stretched his long legs out in the aisle and rubbed the toe of his beige shoe against the back of a peach pants leg. Then he pointed up and down the bus. "I think King fixed it so blacks could sit anywhere we wanted to on this bus. . . . Soon as we did, white people quit riding buses." He leaned down and brushed a speck of dirt from his shoe. "That's my own personal opinion. Soon as we could live anywhere in town we wanted to, white people picked up and moved to the suburbs. Soon as we could get in the booths to vote Democrat, white people signed up with the Republicans. There's no catching white people. But King was good. I don't deny it. Ring that bell cord; here's our stop."

Mingo was thoughtful as they ambled slowly down the block toward the Dogwood Motel. Finally, he said, "In Thermopylae, my home town? A rich girl in junior high with me had a dance at the hotel. We have this old hotel that's got a ballroom. Anyhow, she didn't ask me. I guess I wasn't very popular, I guess. I was, you know, fu … fu … fat, and I got teased and sort of laughed at, except Raleigh never did. But I just wanted to see what this dance looked like, so I went to the hotel anyhow. And they had a black band? And this band had to come in from the back through the kitchen. They couldn't even walk through the lobby. So well, what I mean is, I was telling my momma, and she said, 'Baby, if you feel left out and all hurt inside, 'magine how colored folks feel.' "

"Like fat white people?"

"I guess you mean I could have lost weight?"

"Maybe." Kingstree rumbled into song. " 'Them that's got shall get, them that's not shall lose. So the Bible says, and it sure ain't news.' … You know that song?"

Sheffield had begun humming. He stopped and shook his head. "No. But the thing is, if I hear something, somehow I can always sing it back, I guess. Or, you know, play it on the piano. I mean, not like *you*. I just mostly sing and play for my church. You're professional."

"I sure am." Kingstree nodded at the door, and told Sheffield to meet him back in the bar.

It was Happy Hour in the Alabama Room at the motel, but there was no one in the room to be happy except the bartender. As long as his guests drank, this man had no objection at all to their using the piano or even playing their own saxophones. His theory was that even bad live music was bound to be more interesting than watching a *Little House on the Prairie* episode for the fifth time.

Fastening the brass horn over his pleated peach jacket, Toutant Kingstree said to Sheffield, "Sit down. Okay, now listen." He played quietly, bent over by the piano bench.

"Oh, 'Stormy Weather'! I know that." Mingo's fat pink fingers stretched over the keys and began moving.

"Well. Okay. That's okay." The black man rubbed his hair, then his nose, then his mouthpiece. Then he nodded. "Now listen." He played the melody of "St. James Infirmary." "You know it?"

Mingo shook his head. Kingstree played it again, slowly. Mingo played it back. "That's a sad tune." Mingo sighed.

"Right." The saxophonist reached over the fat man's shoulder; his long fingers jumped from single notes to chords in the bass. "Do that." Mingo did it. "Listen up. Da BUM puh da da BUM. Hear the skip? Don't push it, lean behind it. Lean back. Lean back. Good. All right. Now listen." He raised the saxophone.

Mingo slapped his hands. " 'Honeysuckle Rose'! I always thought it was a fast song."

"Let's us go slow." Kingstree nodded the beat at him with the horn, and soon Sheffield joined in with his skipping chords, stopping for corrections and instructions along the way. Then they played "Just a Closer Walk with Thee." Then they played "See See Rider." Sheffield, his face flushed, his arms glistening, leaped up from the bench to try to hug the other man. "Boy boy boy! You are *so* good!"

Toutant Kingstree smiled. His gold tooth sparkled. "You're not as bad as I figured on. Now, pay attention. We'll do a local tune. 'Alabama Bound.' You know it? Right, that's right. You keep playing that melody. That's good. Now, listen to what I'm gonna do. I'm gonna play around, you stick on that tune, okay? Okay. Here we go." His fingers floated over the stops.

As soon as Kingstree signaled Mingo to a final chord, they were both startled by people clapping: the bartender, two couples who'd wandered in from the lobby, and, near the door, Simon Berg. Beside Berg were shopping bags and he was dressed in a new black overcoat with a black homburg. He walked over. "So, Sheffield, you said you were a piano player." He tapped the fat man's back. "You're a piano player. Anywise, I'm impressed. I'm talking human beings, of course. Toutant here is . . ." Weeper thought a moment. "Toots is chthonic."

"Whatever grabs you, Berg. Where've you been, anyhow?" asked Kingstree as the three gathered chairs around a table. "You steal your new rags off an undertaker?"

Mingo squatted down to stare in Berg's face. "Weeper! You didn't used to have brown eyes! And you didn't used to be so tan either. I swear you used to have green eyes, didn't you? Gollee. You look like an Indian."

"Brazilian, maybe?" Berg replied.

"You seen the brothers?" Kingstree asked. "They still at the hospital?"

"Nah, I just called. They let the kid go. With him already, who could know if his skull was cracked or not? And where I've been is walking my lousy dogs off looking for a kosher deli in this town." The little man pulled off his homburg, revealing further radical changes in his appearance. His formerly gray straight hair was now black and curly, and atop it was a yarmulke.

Mingo pointed at the black skullcap. "And I didn't know you were religious! I wish you'd told me you were going to a synagogue; I've never been to one."

Berg began pulling groceries, paper cartons, and paper plates from his shopping bags. "With friends such as yourselves, let me be honest. I stepped in, a few measly minutes, for my brother Nate who personally never missed a Shabbat himself once in his life." Unwrapping his packages, the convict gave a long sad sigh, then blinked his watering eyes. "Nate always used to say to me, 'Simon, Simon, it would kill you to come to synagogue? Frogs and lice and locusts, et cetera, et cetera, would land on your rotten head if once in a blue moon for Pesach you should come sit down at a Seder with your own family? You can't be bothered to read a few lousy pages of the Haggadah before our mother dies?'" Berg set a jar of horseradish on the table. "He always said, 'So, every Passover the Bergs have to sit with two empty chairs? One for Elijah the Prophet, one for Simon the criminal bum?' He did not mince words, my brother Nate." Next Berg shook out two short white candles from a box with a Star of David on it. "Twenty years ago today Nate dies from overwork selling women's lousy underwear. So may they all rest in peace." He lit the candles and stuck each one in an ashtray. Then he ordered glasses and a bottle of red wine from the intrigued bartender, who was unabashedly staring at the group.

As Berg's small, freshly tanned hands arranged five paper plates around the circular table, his sad voice kept talking. "From overwork and virtue, Nate dies, and Simon the bum walks free as air. I said to God, 'So what is this? Last week you hang Tampa Freddie. This week you snuff my brother Nate. This is Passover? This is when the angel of crummy death's supposed to pass over the houses of the good Jews? So instead he nips in and snatches my brother Nate, a better Jew you'll never meet since Abraham?'"

Mingo picked up a box of matzo crackers. "Oh, it's Passover! Is that when you smeared the blood of the lamb on the door?"

Berg shrugged. "This we forgot to do. So God had to grab Nate, He's such a stickler for details?"

"I mean, in the old days." Sheffield patted his friend's arm. "I'm sorry about your brother. I didn't know today was Passover. You know, Jesus went to Jerusalem on Passover. For His Last Supper."

"Not a wise decision, I hear," Berg said, as he carefully arranged a piece of parsley and a hard-boiled egg on each paper plate.

"No, really, His Last Supper was actually a Passover meal. Remember? When He breaks the bread and says, 'This is my body.'"

Berg poured red wine in the glasses. "You're telling me Christ turned himself into a matzo ball?"

Kingstree's laughter crackled like foil. "Berg. What the hell are you doing, man? What is all this stuff?"

The convict sighed again, then looked across the table at them. "Spare me a minute. For Pesach, a man should be in the presence of pals. Do me the civility, will yah?" He raised his glass, and so they raised theirs. "So, Nate," said Berg to the cork ceiling, *"Hag Sameath,* a good Yom Tov. Next year in Jerusalem, right? *Olov hashalom."*

When Raleigh and Gates Hayes finally located their friends in the Dogwood Room, they found the three men, the bartender, and a young house-hunting couple from Birmingham, all crowded together at a round candlelit table near the piano. They were all drinking red wine, and eating big crackers with sardines on them.

"No," Mingo happily explained. "It's gefilte fish. And this is parsley for spring." He bit off a sprig. "And this is the bitter horseradish of slavery. Sit down, Raleigh. Boy, Gates, do you look a lot better! And these eggs are for, you know, new hope. And the matzo crackers are the bread of the poor, because the Jews didn't have a chance to put in any leaven when they were in a hurry to escape from the pharaohs, and we're all supposed to remember what it's like to be in bondage, and hope that everybody can get set free."

"Right on," said Toutant Kingstree, and poured the bartender another glass of wine. There were three empty bottles on the table.

"And the wine, well, the first glass you call *maror* . . . no, that's wrong. It's *kiddush,* and it's the day of deliverance. Is that right, Weeper? Gosh, you should tell the story."

"Why me? You're a regular rabbi, you're a *tsadik* with your *midrash* yet. A bona fide Solomon in the temple."

Gates, wearing his own skullcap of white bandages, pulled over a chair. "You're looking good, Weep. Snappy outfit. You tan quick, too. Hey, is this a party?"

"It's a Passover party," Mingo explained, and popped an entire hard-boiled egg in his mouth. "How 'bout another bottle, Bobby?" The bartender headed toward the counter at a tilt.

"Well," rumbled Kingstree, "long as where we're passing over to is New Orleans."

"I couldn't agree with you more," said Raleigh Hayes, and squeezed his chair into the circle.

Simon Berg, pouring out wine for the Hayes brothers, surprisingly said, *"Baruch Atah Adonai Eloheinu Melech haolam borei p'ri ha-gafen."*

"That's real Hebrew," Mingo Sheffield informed them. "It means, 'Thank God for the wine.' "

"Hey hey," Gates raised his glass. *"L'chaim!"*

By midnight, the Passover party was, in Toutant Kingstree's phrase, "socking and rocking." He and Mingo played one request after another for the customers who kept drifting into the Dogwood Room, drawn by the music. The young house-hunting woman from Birmingham said she could still play the clarinet a little, and it was too bad she didn't still have one. "I've got one in my suitcase," Mingo exclaimed, and galloped off to get it. The three then played "Bye Bye Blackbird" and "Sweet Georgia Brown" and, for Gates, "Hey, Mr. Tambourine Man." Then Mingo sang "Wichita Lineman" for Bobby the bartender, and Mingo and Toutant harmonized especially for Weeper Berg, "Go down Moses, way down in Egypt land. Tell old Pharaoh to let my people go" — which was not exactly an orthodox *Hallel* song, but did tell the same story. At any rate, either the gospel tune or his new brown contact lenses brought on such an attack of tears that Berg had to leave the bar. When he returned, he was struggling with his enormous bass fiddle. He dragged it over to the piano, stood on the edge of the dais, rested the bottom of the bass on the floor, and joined the trio, then in the middle of Otis Redding's "Sitting on the Dock of the Bay." His enthusiasm dragged them pretty quickly to a flat halt.

"Ummm." Kingstree shook his head. "I like you, Simon. I like you a lot. I don't mean to heavy up on you, but . . . you're not so good."

The now-swarthy convict leaned on his fiddle's neck and scratched his new black curls. "Will yah give me a break? From a lousy paperback I had twelve lessons."

Mingo said, "I think that's wonderful."

"With the Glory Bound baboons, all we played was 'Amazing Grace' except when we played 'Rock of Ages,' you know what I mean?"

Ten minutes later, Kingstree had reduced Berg's contribution to a simple, repetitive picking pattern, and stationed the convict beside Mingo so the fat man could call out his chord changes. Then they played "I'm Always Chasing Rainbows," with Simon weeping from start to finish, either from pleasure or eye irritation, or both.

"Dammit," sighed Gates back at the table. "You know, Lovie kept telling me I was going to be sorry I skipped out of those piano lessons. What a loser. Listen, Raleigh, let me go get Daddy's trumpet, and you play with them. You were good, remember?"

But Hayes shook his head, and crossed his arms, and said, "No. I'm not going to make a fool of myself voluntarily. I've had too many compulsory opportunities in the last couple of weeks."

"Aww, give it a shot."

"Gates, I'd as soon dance naked in the streets." Raleigh stood up. "Look, let's get going early in the morning, okay?"

"Stop worrying about Daddy. He's fine."

"That's what you said about Roxanne." Raleigh told his brother not to stay up late, not to drink any more, and not to fiddle with his bandage. He left the bar as the now fairly sizable crowd applauded Toutant Kingstree's theme song, "Way Down Yonder in New Orleans."

Raleigh was worried, and worrying more the closer he drew in space and time to Jackson Square, noon, March 31. The date had seemed, when he'd opened that infuriating note in Starry Haven, so far away, so long to wait, so ridiculous to propose. Now he was in Alabama, and it was Tuesday the twenty-ninth; no, it was already Wednesday. Back in his motel room, he tried for the third time that day to call his aunt Victoria. Yes, the St. Ann's Hotel was still certain that she'd checked in late Sunday night. They were still certain she was not in her room. Raleigh left his number. He took a shower, checked his bruises and cuts in the mirror. Then in his bathrobe he sat on the bed, pulled over Gates's leather bag, and took their father's trumpet out. For a long time he held it, fingering the stops without looking. Finally he took his towel, spit on it, and rubbed at the tarnish. Then he started to play.

After a while, he put the horn back, and called Aura and apologized for waking her up.

"Isn't that funny?" she said. "I was just lying here thinking about you."

"What were you thinking?" Raleigh lay down on the bed, another strange bed, another unexpected ceiling.

"That you must be so worried something may have happened to Earley, that he may not be where he said he would." She laughed. "Or that he will be there, chuckling his head off, and you'll kill him."

Raleigh closed his eyes. "You know what, Aura? I miss you."

". . . Then I'm glad about this whole crazy thing, because, honey, I've missed you for a long time."

The Hayeses were still talking half an hour later when Gates came in the room and stood there juggling three hard-boiled eggs. Raleigh was telling

Aura that with or without his father, he'd definitely get back to Thermopylae by Sunday in time to hear Caroline sing the solo at the Easter service.

"It means a lot to her, Raleigh, not that she wouldn't die if she thought anybody thought so."

"I know. . . . Aura, just a second, say hello to Gates, okay? Hold on." He held the phone out, but his brother caught the eggs in air, and stepped back.

"Nah, man, too much water under the bridge. She doesn't want to talk to me. Tell her, hi."

"Come on," Raleigh whispered. "Come on. Listen, Gates, if you can make me take on the KKK and the goddamn Mafia, I can make you take on saying hello to somebody that cares about you." He shook the receiver.

Gates rubbed his thighs, his arms, his ears, and his mustache. Finally, he reached for the phone. ". . . Hi, babe. Long time, no see. How's it going? . . . Uh huh. . . . Uh huh. . . . Right. . . . With us?" He cocked his head at Raleigh. "She wants to know how it's going with us."

"Tell her, 'just fine.' " Raleigh took an egg out of his brother's hand and bit into it. "Tell her we'll call her tomorrow from New Orleans. Unless we go to jail or the truck breaks down."

The truck broke down in Biloxi. "At least it picked a pretty place," said Mingo as he climbed out of the back and pointed at the Gulf of Mexico. "Why don't we go get some hamburgers and have a picnic on the beach? Want to come with me, Weeper? I saw a Denny's about half a mile back."

"A mile on my dogs? You should live so long to agonize with my bunions. Bring me a pastrami sandwich. And some Alka-Seltzer. My guts are killing me." Berg walked across the shoulder and kicked his foot in the sand. "Who knew already there was so much lousy nature in the sticks outside New York? Crummy forests, crummy mountains, crummy sky, likewise look at this ocean, look at this beach, wasted real estate, who needs it? I could die from so much nature."

Toutant and Gates struggled with the engine for an hour before they agreed to give up. "Think maybe we could float it to New Orleans?" Gates grinned. He unwrapped his head bandage and wiped his hands.

"That old wreck ought not to have even got this far," Kingstree sadly admitted, as he sat down with the others on the beach. "Man, I tell you this. New Orleans sure is a hard place to get to. I see why Jubal was against it. I been trying thirty years."

"You're only three hours away. Don't give up now. Here, have some more onion rings." Mingo opened another large sack. "Gollee, Raleigh, it's not the end of the world. We've still got the Cadillac. Right?"

"Right."

Back on the shoulder, they found a tan, sinewy young woman in khaki shorts and a Mickey Mouse T-shirt, taking Polaroid pictures of their truck. Her immense knapsack leaned against a tire. In a thick Polish accent, she told them that she was a painter in exile from her native Warsaw, where she'd spent a year in prison for exhibiting dissident canvases. Now, she was getting ready to paint the meaning of America, as soon as she figured it out by walking across the country.

The young woman took their picture against the background of blue sky and green sea. The five men leaned against the side of the red truck in front of the letters "HIGH-TIME CIRCUS." Gates in leather. Raleigh in a blue blazer. Mingo in his orange-striped velour sweater. Toutant in his peach-pink suit. And Simon Berg in black homburg, black overcoat, and round black sunglasses.

Mingo asked the painter if she would take another picture so they could have one to keep for a souvenir. "With the most pleasure," she replied. Mingo then asked if she would join them for lunch. "I have a big hunger," she admitted. Mingo then asked her what the meaning of America was. The young painter held up her can of Coca-Cola. "And also freedom," she added with a grin. "I am learning this. Freedom is here so much, nobody is even noticing how much they are free. I am amazing with it. It is very wonderful."

"Nothing like it," nodded Gates, and Kingstree brushed sand from his shoe.

While the travelers quizzed their visitor about her life under Communism, Gates drove the Cadillac out of the truck (delighting the painter, who snapped more pictures), and went in search of a garage.

Mingo, checking his guidebook, discovered that only two blocks ahead, overlooking the Gulf, was the pillared plantation "Beauvoir," where Sarah Anne Ellis Dorsey (best-selling authoress of the romance *Athalie: or, a Southern Villeggiatura*) had invited Jefferson Davis to come retire (an invitation he'd happily accepted, for "Beauvoir" was considerably more pleasant than the woods where he'd been hiding from Federal troops, and the dank fortress where they'd chained him after they caught him). Mrs. Dorsey had offered her services to the former president as ghost writer of *The Rise and Fall of the Confederate Government,* until his poor wife Varina — worn out by the general ups and downs of fortune and by jealousy of the Davis-Dorsey collaboration — packed and left for Memphis.

"She any kin to Tommy Dorsey?" Kingstree asked.

Mingo didn't think so.

"Then I'll sit this one out."

In fact, despite their close ties to Varina's "opals," no one would accompany Mingo to see "Beauvoir" except the Polish painter, who erroneously believed they were going to President Jefferson's Monticello. "Life, lebberty, and also the pursuit of the happiness," she reminded the Americans with a farewell wave of her white Pittsburgh Paints cap. "You are the most luckiest pepples of the world."

Her knapsack, stacked with bed roll, pup tent, cookstove, flashlights, Sony Walkman, plastic umbrella, Baltimore Orioles pennant, and a six-pack of blue toilet paper, stretched high above her head and reached almost to Mingo's shoulder as the two trotted together up the sidewalk under the moss-hung oaks.

While they waited for Gates to return, Raleigh sat with his friends on the beach and watched the sun slip down into the sea. Simon Berg read the books he'd bought in Montgomery. *Let's Go: South America* and *Spanish for Beginners*. Kingstree played Duke Ellington melodies on his saxophone. And Raleigh Hayes sat under the orange-ribboned sky and practiced what he might say first to his father, testing ironies and accusations: "Oh, hi, Daddy, what a coincidence." "Don't think this hasn't been just a bowl of cherries." "Where do you want Jimson's bust? Sorry, but Knoll Pond wouldn't fit in the trunk." "The Reverend Hayes, I presume? Jubal Rogers says you can kiss his black ass." "You owe me $1,997.35, including tax. Gas, $92.40. Hotels, $883.26. Food . . ." None of these openings felt sufficiently satisfying. But even worse was the image of standing in Jackson Square and *not* seeing his father; of discovering that Aunt Victoria hadn't been able to find him; of discovering that she had vanished as well. Raleigh returned to his calculations: replacement clothes, oil filter, dry cleaning, Flonnie's radio, donation to the Sisters of Mercy (well, perhaps, as that was a tax deduction, he shouldn't put it on the bill), ten dollars stolen by Hell's Angels (well, perhaps his father should absorb Mingo's $280 loss as well), fifty dollars stolen by Gates to purchase flowers for Roxanne's niece-in-law, two secondhand fencing foils . . .

At nightfall, Gates returned with a tow truck. By ten P.M., he had sold the tractor-trailer for six thousand dollars. By midnight, he'd had a luggage rack installed on top of the Cadillac. "Let's roll," he said. "Last lap, last tango, last picture show, and all that jazz."

The white car had lost some of the luster of which Jimmy Clay had been so proud. After all, in the past two weeks it had been rolled into a pecan grove that was seared by lightning. It had been stripped by nuns, shoved by Marines through a swamp of cypress stumps, raced by Gates Hayes over rutted fields and residential lawns, banged in and out of a metal truck, and strewn with the debris of Mingo Sheffield's insatiable snacking. The Cadillac was dented, scratched, dirty, and plastered with religious bumper stickers. And now it had an old trunk, cardboard boxes, and a bass fiddle lashed to its roof; it had suitcases, instrument cases, and souvenirs roped into its trunk. It looked more like the Grapes of Wrath than Jimmy's "Stars and Stripes on Wheels."

"Hey, man, don't knock it. It runs," said Gates, who sat with Weeper and Toutant in the back seat.

With Mingo beside him, Raleigh drove. He insisted on taking the wheel. He told the others that if there were anything they wanted to do, do it now, because he was not stopping again until he parked in Jackson Square. These last miles of the idiotic marathon, this last task of the whole insane scavenger hunt, he wanted to finish himself. He had run the race, and it was almost over, and he was going to enjoy each highway marker that told him he was drawing nearer and nearer to his goal.

It was a still, cloudless night, the sky extravagant with a million stars, blazing as if all the dead Hayeses were celebrating a Fourth of July Family Reunion, running around heaven with sparklers in both hands.

Shrimp boats had already hurried home, chased by pelicans and gulls. The lights of the offshore oil rigs flickered like stars.

Past Gulfport, past Bay St. Louis, over the bridge above Lake Pontchartrain, Raleigh drove in silence inland along the coast toward where the Mississippi met the sea. He glanced at Sheffield beside him, sleeping with his huge head tilted back, a bubble of saliva on his lips. He glanced in the rearview mirror at the others, asleep too, except for Toutant Kingstree, who looked out his side window and quietly hummed. Simon Berg's chin bounced gently against his small chest. Gates's cheek pressed against the window, his long lashes uneasily flickering.

"It's over," Raleigh Hayes said to himself. And then he laughed softly and whispered, "I'll be goddamned."

The most remarkable thought had struck him. He didn't feel any of the ways he'd waited two weeks to feel. He didn't feel triumphant or relieved or righteous. He felt almost sad, almost lonely, almost sorry. What an incredible joke. Here he was with four men, not one of whom he'd originally wanted to bring along, all of whom had caused him endless trouble and worry; none of whom bore the vaguest resemblance to his own "type of person." And now, when he could already see the lights of the city where all their travels together would end, and their separate lives begin, all he could think was that he was going to *miss* them.

"Ha, ha," said Raleigh to the sky of stars. "I've gone completely to pieces. Daddy did it. He drove me crazy. You know what I've been doing? I've been almost, almost . . ." He laughed. ". . . having fun."

Toutant Kingstree leaned forward from the backseat. "You say something, Raleigh?"

Hayes kept on chuckling. "No. No. I'm sorry. I was just talking to my dead mother."

"Oh. You do that, too?"

CHAPTER

31

What Passed between Our Hero and His Father

IN NEW ORLEANS THE LAND OF DREAMS, not everyone slept at two in the morning. On Bourbon Street and Royal Street, on Rampart and Toulouse, neon winked behind lace-iron fans as the merchants of dreams for night people peddled their old attractions, wine, women, and all kinds of songs. They peddled inflatable lovers in store windows, and roses in the cobbled streets. Tired waiters swept the evening out of restaurants. Tired strippers walked, invisible in clothes, past the drunks who had hooted and snatched at them an hour earlier.

Near the French Market, a block from Jackson Square, Raleigh Hayes sat alone in the parked Cadillac. Berg and Kingstree had disappeared down the narrow brick streets, Berg with his fiddle, Kingstree with his saxophone, toward the sound of jazz. Gates and Mingo had gone to find a hotel. When they returned, they begged Raleigh to come back with them to the place they'd chosen near Pirates Alley. Mingo's moon-pie face bobbed in the car window. "It's pretty old. It's got inside balconies and fans and banana trees and a patio with a parrot. I bet you like it."

"I'm staying here awhile. Go on," Hayes insisted.

Finally, Gates gave up. "Specs, you're one crazy bastard." He grinned at Mingo. "But I love the guy. He's just a little embarrassing, you know, to take out in public."

"I just want a moment to sit here and think. I just want to get some closure on this trip."

"Some what?" Gates spun his forefinger beside his temple.

"Never mind."

"He needs to think, he's always thinking, that's the thing about Raleigh," Mingo said, and Gates said, "Right, old Raleigh the Thinker," and reached through the window to rub his brother's hair.

Hayes combed his hair back in place as he watched the two stroll away with more suitcases. Then he stared at his hands on the steering wheel. The thumbs looked like his father's; the palms looked like his mother's; the gold ring had been put on his finger twenty years ago by Aura; the gold cuff links had been his last Christmas present from Holly and Caroline. Turning on the overhead light, he took out his wallet and carefully studied all the photographs he'd kept there so long that the crowded plastic cases were cracked and yellow. His mother cutting irises along the back fence. Aura graduating from nursing school; Aura reading under a beach umbrella at "Peace and Quiet." Holly's third- and eleventh-grade school portraits; Caroline's third- and tenth-grade portraits. (She'd torn up all copies of this year's pictures, claiming they were "super awesomely gruesome.") A little black-and-white snapshot of his aunt Victoria in her WAC uniform was stuck to the back of a picture Reba had taken in 1963 of Raleigh and Victoria at Raleigh's wedding party. The two were seated at a table in the ballroom of Thermopylae's Delaware Hotel. Blurred in the background at other tables, other Hayeses were frozen in the act of laughing, shouting, pointing, raising glasses or cigarettes or cake or coffee cups to their mouths. With their arms crossed, Raleigh and his aunt sat looking past the camera at something happening behind it. That something, Raleigh now remembered, was his father and Lovie Clay "entertaining" the guests with a drunken, dancing, burlesqued performance of "Making Whoopee," "The Girl That I Marry," and "Indian Love Call." He remembered that for the last number Lovie wore napkins woven into green braids, and his father had taken off his shirt, painted his chest with lipstick, wrapped his tie around his head, and stuck in it feathered fern leaves from the flower arrangements. It was Victoria and Raleigh's unexpected response to this folly that the camera had saved from the past. Caught off guard, they were both, in fact, laughing.

Sliding the snapshot out of its plastic case, Hayes held it up to the overhead light to peer at that thin twenty-five-year-old just-married man in his white dinner jacket, a rosebud in his lapel. How new and clean and unfinished he looked; his hair close cropped, his face unlined, his neck so straight and slender above the crisp black tie, his eyes so candidly certain that the world was going to make sense for him, because he was never going to make senseless demands on it. Because his requests would be modest and reasonable: a wife he loved, unblemished children, good health, a house, an income to pay for it, leisure to care for it, the authority to serve his community, and their respect for having done so well.

My God, thought Hayes now, what outrageous demands he'd made on Fortune. When at her indiscriminate whim, she could, and did, sweep away houses, love, children, position, health, and life, he'd asked for immunity. And he'd gotten it. Some rare, fragile, lucky — unparalleled lucky — fluke or grace had *given* him, for no earthly reason, like surprise presents, everything, absolutely everything, he'd thought he earned, and sustained by his own will, and deserved, and deserved *more*. Whereas, in fact, the world, or its creator, had not the slightest obligation to him at all. The world or its creator, thought Raleigh Hayes, was under no injunction to do a thing. It was not obliged to put the much-remarked petals on the lilies, nor keep its famous eye on the sparrow, nor reward Raleigh W. Hayes for his virtue, nor punish sinners for their vice, nor protect the innocent, nor judge the guilty. It created for creation's sake alone — for no cause but infinitely that one, striping the zebra, spotting the leopard, making the eel glow and the deer leap — and it was not obliged to nourish or even preserve at all any of its creatures, species, planets, or galaxies. Given that this was so, thought Hayes, the truth was, it's possible, one might say, assuming creation owed him no more debt than it owed the dinosaur, than an artist owed a doodle, then, all things considered, he, Raleigh Hayes, with his wife and children and health and house, had been an extremely lucky man. And he turned off the Cadillac's overhead light to analyze this hypothesis.

The next thing Raleigh knew, he was jolted awake by a loud honking. He jerked upright, and his knees smashed against the steering wheel. By the time he'd figured out that he was in a car, and why, and where, and that he must have fallen asleep because it was now almost nine in the morning, and that it was miraculous he hadn't been towed or mugged or arrested, another car had passed and honked. Was he parked obstructively? Illegally? Hayes found his wallet and his glasses beside him on the plush red seat. In a while, a third car honked; this one, a Volvo, slowed down beside him, the woman in the passenger seat waving and grinning enthusiastically as she appeared for five seconds in and out of his life. On the rear bumper of her car he saw two stickers: One said, "READ THE BOOK." One said, strangely enough, "FESTINA LENTE." Hayes got out, walked to the back of the Cadillac, and stood there scratching at his unshaved cheek. Yes, that had to be it. The "HONK IF YOU ♡ JESUS" sticker from Charleston. Well, at least it was just slap-happy Christians, and not the police.

Across the street at the outdoor French Market, Raleigh had a cup of coffee so he could use the facilities. Then he had two more cups because it was the best coffee he'd ever tasted. Then he ordered breakfast, and sat for more than an hour watching people go by. New Orleans, wide awake, was a slow-strolling, easygoing, quick-laughing, soft-spoken — and to Raleigh, very foreign — place. He liked it. Finally, he climbed the steps to Jackson Square, where the warrior Old Hickory proudly sat his bronze rearing horse, and urged everybody on to victory. No one seemed in a hurry to follow him. Under palms and magnolias, people sat reading papers, as if they'd been headed for work, but decided to take a break on the way. Children stalked pigeons. A derelict rummaged through trashcans for empty drink cans and bottles. "Two cents," Raleigh heard his uncle Hackney call, holding out the green Coca-Cola bottle. These days, Raleigh's garage was stacked with bags of empties. Caroline and Holly couldn't be bothered to return them for the deposits.

At the far end of the square, there rose like hats on medieval ladies the three cone spires of St. Louis Cathedral. Facing it, Raleigh sat down on a bench beside a woman who looked at him sympathetically, then returned to her paperback. For a long time, he watched people pass in and out of the ornate Spanish portal. Twelve o'clock, his father had said, twelve o'clock, March 31, St. Louis Cathedral. Not that time meant a thing to the man. There was no sense in waiting there for him an hour, or for that matter, a day, maybe a week. Raleigh was grimy, wrinkled, unkempt, and unshaven. The sensible thing would be to go to the hotel. Instead, he walked over to the church, and then went inside. A flyer on the pew rack invited him to a Maundy Thursday potluck supper tonight. He sat in the cool hush among the kerchiefed women, the sleeping vagrant, the whispering tourists, the unhappy businessman who rolled his forehead back and forth over his folded arms. He watched the skirted priests glide silently by in front of the altar, bowing at the crucifix when they passed, as if nodding to an acquaintance on the street. Raleigh heard the eight-year-old voice of his cousin Jimmy Clay: "Hey, Raleigh the Robot, how come your daddy wears that funny skirt like a girl?"

One rainy winter Sunday long long ago, in the little Thermopylae church, Raleigh saw his father seated alone in shadows on the floor of the nave, leaning back against the altar, his arms wrapped around the knees of his black skirt. The nine-year-old had been sent to find him for supper, but the man looked so worried, his eyes so bright and wet, that the boy was afraid to bother him. Finally, Earley Hayes looked up and said hoarsely, "Hello, Little Fellow."

"Hi, Daddy."

"Come on and sit down here with me. Mind if I give you a hug? I'm feeling pretty sad. It's kind of a sad rainy day, isn't it? Doesn't it look like everybody up in Heaven has got the blues today and can't stop crying?"

"I guess." Raleigh scooted over beside his father. He could feel the chill of the floor through his corduroy pants, but Earley's arm was warm around his neck and shoulder. His father smelled like the fall, like trees and smoke and apples.

". . . Are you sad because Grandpa died?"

"Yes, Specs."

"Mama's sad too. She says she has to go away and think again."

"I know. . . . It's my fault she's sad, Raleigh. You know how if you hurt somebody you love, your heart feels all squeezed in a knot?"

They sat silently a long time in the darkening stillness. Then Raleigh pushed on his new glasses. "Is Grandpa's body really in the ground back there?"

"Yes."

"But I thought we were supposed to believe people can rise from the dead. Like Jesus. Do you think Jesus really did? Rise up? It's hard to believe."

Earley rubbed his eyes. "Well, Specs, His disciples sure didn't believe it either at first. They ran like crazy when the women told them. And then, you know, He joined them and had a fish fry on the beach, and those morons still didn't know Him from Adam. It was the women who had the guts to go in the tomb. It was the women that kept the faith. The best luck in life, Specs, is to keep a woman's love."

Raleigh wasn't at all interested in women's love. "But do you think Grandpa can rise from the dead? Flonnie says, no grave can hold him down. But I don't see how he's going to be able to get the coffin open when there's so much dirt on top, and he couldn't even move his arms anyhow, I mean, you know how they kind of flopped? So how can he get out?"

Raleigh felt himself pulled closer into the warm black scratchy wool, as his father said, "Well . . . well, I don't know the answer."

"You don't?"

"But my *guess* is, maybe you don't need your arms to climb out of the grave. You just need enough people to have loved you. And I figure Grandpa has enough of those...." The priest leaned forward to tie his son's shoelace.

Raleigh shook his head. "But he'll still be dead. I don't understand."

"Neither do I, Specs. It's one of God's dumber-ass roundabout notions, everybody's dying so then maybe they can go to Heaven. This dying is a crappy plan."

Excited by the profanity, Raleigh wriggled his cold back and buttocks. "In Sunday school, Mrs. Jimson told us we had to die because Eve ate this apple that the Devil told her if she ate it, she'd be as smart as God."

Earley nodded. "Well, actually he said, if you eat it, you'll know the difference between good and evil, which is what God knows. And so, what Satan told her was really true. Here, come over here." He took the boy's hand and led him up into the carved wood pulpit, where he switched on a light and opened a large Bible at the beginning. "Can you read that?"

Raleigh nodded; he liked to display his reading skill. His father lifted him and set him down on the lectern itself. "Start right there. That word's 'behold.' "

"I know, I know. 'God said, Behold, the man is become as one of us, to know good and evil, and now, lest. . .'?"

" 'On the chance that . . .' "

" '. . . He put forth his hand and take also of the tree of life, and eat, and live forever: Therefore the Lord God sent him forth from the Garden . . .' "

"Boy, you're some reader."

"Well, I think God stinks. His rules aren't fair. Mrs. Jimson wrote all these sins on the blackboard? And she says if we do any of them, we have to go to Hell, even if we aren't even grown-ups."

"Mrs. Jimson is a horse's ass."

"Cursing's one of the sins."

"Bullshit."

Raleigh flushed with excitement. He looked at his father's face, only inches away. Tiny blond hairs bristled out of holes in the skin. He could see his own face in the dark center of the blue eye.

"Specs, remember when Christ said there were really only two commandments . . . Love . . ."

"I already know. Love God with all your heart, and love your neighbor as yourself."

"Right." Earley rubbed the boy's corduroy knee. "Well, there's only one sin. . . . What do you think it is?"

Raleigh looked in the eyes for a clue to the answer. He didn't like to be wrong. ". . . Not loving them?"

"Right."

Raleigh thought. "Well, I don't love everybody. Do you? Do you love Mrs. Jimson even if she's a . . . she's a bullshit?"

"Nope."

"Me neither."

Earley Hayes flicked off the light, and the two stayed there in the pulpit as darkness moved along the church wall. Then Earley laughed. "Nope. I don't have the guts. Christ was a tough little bastard, Raleigh. . . . 'Course, He never said it'd be easy to take His two bits of advice. All He said was, you'd be in Heaven if you did. . . ." The priest picked up his son in his arms and carried him down the aisle. "Come on, let's go walk to the drugstore and get some ice cream for after supper."

"What kind? Mama likes strawberry, but I like chocolate."

"Well, hell, let's get both."

As they walked down East Main's sidewalk, under one umbrella, clumsily knocking into each other, Earley Hayes took from the pocket of his black cassock his silver trumpet mouthpiece, and began whistling through it, "Pennies from Heaven."

Outside St. Louis Cathedral, the morning brightness blinded Raleigh. He shielded his eyes with the back of his hand. His arm raised, he started down the steps. It was then that he heard the music, the whisk slapping the snare drum and cymbal, the sharp clean trumpet melody floating around a woman's voice as she sang, "So wrap your troubles in dreams, and dream your troubles away." Raleigh listened some more, his arm raised. The trumpet was playing alone; it swooped down and came back with a new melody. The voice joined it. "If I should take a notion to jump into the ocean . . . Ain't nobody's business if I do."

Raleigh lowered his arm and slowly turned his head to the square. In the middle, in front of a small fountain, he saw a black man seated on a stool surrounded by glittering drums. He saw a young black girl in a white dress. Sunlight was so dazzling on the gold trumpet raised to the sky that he had to cup his hands around his eyes to see his father.

"Hi, Daddy," said Raleigh when the song ended, and the few bystanders clapped.

"You're early." His father grinned.

Raleigh took a deep breath, and then he said, "No, I'm Raleigh. You're Earley." This had been his first joke, planned at age five and delivered on the first suitable occasion — for which he had eagerly watched and waited. It was a great success and had gone into the family story as "Raleigh's joke."

"Right." His father held out his arms, and Raleigh, despite all his intentions, walked into them.

Fear turned his hands cold when he felt the sharp shoulder blades. Earley Hayes was smaller than Holly or Caroline. His head scarcely reached his son's shoulder, and the back Raleigh remembered as so sturdily fleshed was bone-thin, frail as a child's. How could the man have shrunk and faded so in only two weeks? Or had Raleigh just not noticed before how insubstantial he had become? His white hair was dry and flat. His dirty blue seersucker pants bagged beneath the tightly belted waist. The blue short sleeves of his shirt gaped flapping around his arms. Only the eyes were the same, blue as the sky.

Raleigh stepped back. "Well, here I am."

"Here you are." The old man nodded up at his tall, wrinkled, unshaved son. "You did just fine, Specs."

"I couldn't make Jubal come. I brought Gates."

"You did fine."

Raleigh held up his fingers. "I brought your trumpet, your Bible, Pee-Wee's stupid bust, the deed to his crummy cabin, and Grandma Tiny's goddamn trunk."

"I figured you would. Give me another hug, Specs. You're a beautiful sight."

"I bet." Raleigh crossed his arms. "I'm a wreck. I've lost six pounds. I've been through royal hell and back."

Earley shook saliva from his trumpet. "Well, that's some trip. Least you had a lot of fun, Aura said."

"Ha ha. Where's Aunt Vicky? Did you know she's down here looking for you?"

"She's shopping. Come on over here. . . ."

"Shopping? What do you mean, shopping?" Raleigh kept talking as his father pulled him along. "I presume you're now going to explain what this is all about."

"Music, sort of," said Earley with a curiously shy smile.

"Daddy, I'm serious. Aunt Vicky calls me in Atlanta; she doesn't sound like herself at all. She asks all about Jubal Rogers and then she takes off down here after you —"

"She told me to let her talk to you herself first. She thought you'd get here a couple of days ago."

"Well, sorry. Gates had to go to the hospital to get his, ha ha, head examined, okay? Dammit, Daddy!"

"Where is Gates? And you really got him to come!"

"He's back at the hotel. He's supposed to check by here at twelve. Three, ah, friends of mine . . . Mingo Sheffield and two, ah, people I sort of met on the way are down here with us."

"Brought your friends with you? Well, that's wonderful. I'm just sorry about Jubal. I don't blame him, but I'm just sorry. I want you to meet some folks now." He looped his arm through Raleigh's and walked back to the middle of the square. ". . . This is Allen Thornhill. Allen, this is my oldest boy, Raleigh." The drummer, a bald pudgy black man about forty years old, leaned across the cymbals to shake hands. He wore a striped tie and a button-down shirt with its sleeves rolled.

"Allen played in the band back in Hillston College when I was teaching, we won't say how long ago."

"Let's don't," nodded Thornhill. "But I seem to recall I had a head of hair."

"And now he teaches theory at the university here, so he just came in to do an old geezer a favor. Right? Excuse us a second, Allen?"

Thornhill slapped the cymbal with his whisk by way of reply.

Earley then walked Raleigh over to the fountain on whose concrete rim the young black girl had seated herself with a book of sheet music. She did not have a blond wig or purple eyeshadow or an overnight case full of money. She was a dark, small-boned, slender teenager in a soiled plain white dress that looked like a Mexican shirt. Her cloth sandals laced around her ankles, and she wore several bright bracelets on each wrist. Her crimped black hair was dramatically long and electric, but her eyes were soft, tentative, like a deer's eyes. She stood up and Earley put his arm around her; they were the same height. "This is Raleigh," he told her.

"Hi." She looked as if she might be going to ask something, but instead she turned to Earley.

"This is Billie Rogers, Raleigh. She and I have come a long way together. Haven't we, Billie? Long, tough way?" He hugged her shoulder, then took his arm away. "Been looking for some folks we couldn't find, and finding some folks we weren't looking for, and generally trying to get our act together. Right?"

She smiled in just the tolerant bemused way with which Holly and Caroline responded to adult efforts to speak their language.

"Billie's *some* singer."

Raleigh was confused. "... Ah, yes, I heard you. Yes. ..." He didn't know whether to speak in front of the girl or not. "Billie *Rogers?*"

"That's right," Earley nodded. "Jubal's granddaughter."

"Jubal's granddaughter? Did you ...? Was she ...? Did you two meet in the hospital in Thermopylae?"

"Meet?! I tell you, Raleigh, it knocked me over, too. This child has got more guts than ... than ..." He pointed at the giant statue behind them. "Than General Andrew Jackson ever dreamed of. Well, Billie, yes, you do, too. This child." He squeezed her hand. "There she is, Fullerton, California, nineteen years old, she loses her mother. Poor Josh died when she was a baby."

So, Raleigh had been right: This whole wild goose chase had started over the strange angry man in Charleston. "Jubal's son was Joshua Rogers?"

"Yes. Billie's dad. She loses her mother, and she thinks there's nobody else. Well, she thought there was maybe an aunt in Memphis, but it turned out she'd passed away. I want you to know, Billie here ..." Earley Hayes kept nodding at the girl and patting her shoulder and shaking his head to convey amazement to Raleigh, who stood there, looking from one to the other.

Billie Rogers just stood there, too, with a look half indulgent, half embarrassed. Back in the middle of the square, Allen Thornhill busied himself adjusting his drums.

"I want you to know, Raleigh, Billie here, nineteen years old, gets on a Trailways bus all the way from California to Thermopylae." Earley took a cigarette from his shirt pocket. "Some shithead steals her bag and her purse, but she just keeps on, and she by fuck gets to Thermopylae. And hasn't eaten in about two days, and faints in the bus station, right, Billie?"

"I guess so. I was pretty weirded out. It was no big deal."

"No big deal!? Honey, don't call my miracle no big deal!" Earley bent over, coughing.

"Daddy, are you okay?" Raleigh pulled the cigarette from his father's fingers.

Straightening up, the old man wiped his eyes and mouth. "Fine. I'm fine. ... Billie passes out in the bus station, and that asshole police chief of ours hauls her in on *vagrancy,* and whips her over to the hospital like she's a mental case! So in she comes to that hospital, I swear on the wings of a dove, and saves my goddamn life."

The girl smiled. "Listen, okay?, stop saying that. That's pretty heavy."

She rubbed the front of the music book. "This whole thing has been pretty heavy. I sure didn't expect —"

Raleigh said, "I can imagine. So, Daddy, you took Billie out of the hospital?"

"I'm sneaking down the hall to Reba's room — see how she's doing — and I hear Billie at the nurses' station trying to explain to those fucks she knew who she was. They're acting like the dumb shits they are. *Five minutes,* Raleigh, five minutes sooner or later, and I would have missed her. That's the kind of squeeze-play chance that joker God gives you. If I'd stopped to pee, I would have missed her."

The girl turned to Raleigh. "Earley says, you found Jubal in Charleston. My grandfather? Listen, thanks, okay? I don't know, I guess maybe he's not gonna show, right? But you talked to him? Jubal Rogers?"

Raleigh stared from one to the other. "Ah . . . I'm not sure. Ah, I don't know if he's coming here or not. I asked him to."

Billie nodded. "Well, thanks anyhow, okay?" She sat down by the fountain again, and ran her hand through the water. "Anyhow, I guess he'd never heard of me, had he? . . . Is he, like, you know, a, you know, a real musician? I mean, good? But you probably just talked to him on the phone or something, hunh?"

Sitting down beside the girl, Earley rested his trumpet on his knees; there was a hole worn in one pants leg. He looked up at his son.

Raleigh cleared his throat. "Yes, I did hear him. He plays the clarinet in a very nice nightclub there in Charleston. Yes, he's very good."

She nodded slowly. "I thought he had to be. . . . Well, thanks again, okay? For going to all that trouble. Now I can, you know, write him. When he wasn't in Thermopylae, and then he wasn't in New Orleans, I figured that was, you know — it. . . . We going to rehearse some more?" She held up the music book.

"She's some singer," Earley said again, and went on to explain that in the year since finishing high school, Billie had been trying to find work around Los Angeles, but had decided after her mother's death to come East to find her grandfather. "She just had this *feeling,* goddamnedest thing, this *feeling* he could help her."

She knew nothing about her grandfather except the penned words "Jubal Rogers, Thermopylae, N.C." on a few old 78 rpm record albums, one of them by Billie Holiday. And her mother's story that Josh Rogers had kept the records and wanted his child named Billie because his father had been a great jazz musician. Earley Hayes pointed at the drummer. "Allen here's had Billie over at the university music school, interviewing, and they're going to take her in, this fall. We have a deal. She'll try going. See how she likes it. Right, Billie?"

"I'll try it," she agreed. "But all I want to do is sing. Victoria says I ought to do what *I* want to do. Oh, look, there's a guy selling Popsicles; I'm going to go get one. Anybody else? Okay, be right back." She took off in an easy run after the white pushcart.

"Isn't she something?" Earley asked his son.

So many questions jumbled together in Raleigh he couldn't even think through to an order in which to ask them; it was as if someone had poured a jigsaw puzzle of the ocean in front of him with all the pieces of the borders missing, so there were no square edges to start with. Finally, he said, "Daddy, can I talk to you a second? I'm not really sure what you're up to. Not that that's any news. But I came down here to put you in the hospital. You *need* to be in a hospital. You promised me.... What do you mean, rehearsing? Rehearsing what?"

The old man lit another cigarette as he told his son that Allen Thornhill had arranged with a friend who owned a small club called The Cave for them to play there the next few nights, after the scheduled performers. He told Raleigh that he'd tried to find some other musicians he'd once known, to join them, but the men had died. At any rate, he couldn't go to the hospital just yet, because he knew they'd try to stop him from playing.

Raleigh rubbed hard at his scratchy cheeks. "You run off and come down here to play in a nightclub?! At seventy years old, you suddenly decide to be a trumpet player?!"

Earley Hayes outrageously replied, "That's right."

"After Aunt Vicky and I came all this way to try to get you to save your goddamn life!"

"I am saving my goddamn life, Specs."

"What did she say about this when she found you?"

"Vicky?" Earley grinned. "Well, the first thing she did when she found me was she hauled off and *slapped* me. Right in the hotel lobby. She'd been saving it up for fifty years, and, man, it knocked me back into my chair."

"Aunt Victoria *hit* you?"

Earley was pointing at a faded scratch on his cheek when they heard a voice call, "Raleigh, Raleigh! There he is! Raleigh!"

Hayes turned around. Mingo Sheffield, wearing his green sports jacket and carrying two large shopping bags, was trotting across the square toward them. Behind him, sun flashing on his peach suit and on the metal clasps of his saxophone case, came Toutant Kingstree.

"Well, *hi,* Mr. Hayes! Boy, are we glad to see you! You remember me, Mingo Sheffield? Raleigh's best friend? You just about drove him crazy, you know. What in the world made you run away like that? You ought to be ashamed of yourself!" The fat man hugged Raleigh's father. "But here you are, and we made it, and boy it's just wonderful to see you! What a beautiful day! And gollee, New Orleans! This is our friend, Toutant Kingstree? He knows your old friend Jubal, and wait till you hear him play! This is Raleigh's daddy, Toutant. *Right* where he said he'd be. After all that!"

Everyone was introduced, and Toutant Kingstree said, "Y'all playing here? This a good spot? Good tips?"

Mingo jabbered on to Raleigh, "Guess who I saw this morning?"

"Gates, I hope. Why didn't he come with you?"

"What do you play?" Earley asked Kingstree, who knelt on the pavement and took his saxophone out of its case.

Raleigh pulled Mingo aside. He watched his father and Allen Thornhill talking with Kingstree as Mingo whispered to him, "Gates said he was asleep, but I think he's kind of scared to come. You know, he's kind of shy. But I told Weeper to make him come, and we'd just wait for him here with your dad. Raleigh, you must be so happy. But did you get any sleep? You sure don't look like it. And your daddy looks *awful.* I didn't want to tell him so. No, I saw your aunt Victoria! She was in a store right next to her hotel. St. Ann's Hotel. Well, I got up early and I thought I'd just check by there for her before I met Toutant. And so we had some coffee. These are hers." He held up the shopping bags.

"Hers? Where is she?"

"She's coming in a minute. She just ducked into that little shop right over there." He pointed through the row of magnolia trees. "Oh, there's Billie! *Billie!"* Sheffield called to Billie Rogers, strolling back with an Eskimo Pie.

"You met her already?" Raleigh asked.

"Billie? Oh, yeah. This morning. With Vicky. Hey, Billie. Vicky says she'll be here in a second. Then she wants you to come back to the hotel and try this stuff on." He shook the shopping bags.

"Oh, hi, Mingo. Hey, great, let me see." The girl ran up to them, took the bags, and ran back to the fountain, where she sat down and began pulling dresses out of tissue paper.

Mingo pointed at her. "Isn't it just amazing, Raleigh! It makes me want to give God a great big hug, I swear it does. Everybody all together, and it all working out this way? I mean your aunt Vicky and Billie finding each other, after so many broken hearts, and your dad, and now, oh look at that." His moony face bobbed at the three musicians. Toutant Kingstree had assembled his saxophone; now he strapped it on and began playing scales.

Raleigh squeezed his friend's wrist. "Broken hearts? What the hell is everybody talking about?"

"Why, finding Billie!" Sheffield looked hard at Raleigh. "Oh, gollee, your daddy didn't tell you yet? . . . Uh oh. Maybe I wasn't supposed to say anything, but I mean, gosh, Vicky told me when we had our coffee. She's so happy, Raleigh, when I started in crying, she just started in crying too. . . . Oh, Billie, I like that dress! Hold it up! Can I see?"

At that moment Raleigh saw his favorite aunt hurrying briskly down the wide stone steps into the square. She wore her blue traveling suit and carried two more shopping bags. He had started toward her, he had seen her notice him, when behind him he heard Mingo saying, "Billie, I just have to tell you this. I mean maybe you don't believe Vicky yet. Maybe you don't even *want* to believe her. But I sure hope you're going to give her a chance. You know what? You and your grandmother are about the two bravest people I ever met. I mean that, as God is my witness."

Raleigh Hayes heard these words, and like a man who's been shot, he walked on for ten more feet before his knee buckled. Even then, he simply kept moving straight ahead until he reached his aunt Victoria.

"Well, Raleigh, you finally got here. Why in the world didn't you get a decent night's sleep, why didn't you shower and shave? Look at yourself. There's no reason to look like a slovenly mess no matter how crazy the world's gotten."

Hayes stared furiously at the square-jawed woman. "Aunt Victoria. You owe me an apology and an explanation."

The spectacles were pulled slowly down the sharp nose, and the ice-blue eyes looked at him calmly. "I don't owe you any such thing."

"You used me."

"Used you?" She pinched her earlobe. "I see. You think I knew what Earley was up to all along? Well, I certainly didn't. You think that idiot bothered to tell me he'd found Billie? Or even that he was looking for Jubal? Of course he didn't. He just took off like a sneak thief in a Hong Kong alley. And you didn't bother to call and tell me either. *Aura* told me you found Jubal. *Aura.* Sit down on that bench. You've got the shakes."

She nudged her nephew with her elbow to the black wrought-iron bench, pushed him back onto it, and, placing her shopping bags beside him, stood facing him. "I swear I'm going to kill Earley. I told him not to just drop this on you like he does everything."

Raleigh stared at her. "Did I just hear, *overhear,* Mingo Sheffield imply that that girl, that Billie Rogers is, is . . . related to you?"

She stared back at him for a while. Then she nodded. "She's my granddaughter."

"I thought she was Jubal Rogers's granddaughter."

"She is."

Raleigh kept shaking his head. "I don't believe this. I goddamn don't believe it. It can't be true."

Victoria's white watch-spring curls stirred in the soft breeze. She patted them back in place. "Why's that, Raleigh?"

"Why?! First of all, for God's sake, she's black! I mean, frankly, Aunt Victoria, how can you say, 'Why?' Like I should just say, 'Oh, that's nice.' When I've known you all my life, and I thought we were, well, kind of close, and well, understood each other pretty well. And you never bothered to mention once, not once, that you had a child!? Much less a grandchild!? Much less, excuse me, please, but really! A black teenaged grandchild! You never told me, *nobody* every told me, you were even *married,* much less —"

"I never *was* married. . . . This happened a long time before you were born, Raleigh. And I didn't talk about it to anybody. Then or later. It was nobody's business but mine."

"I don't understand. How could you have a child, and nobody know?"

"By being a coward, and listening to your father. When he was an even worse coward. I gave the baby up for adoption. And that's the short and simple of it. I didn't know anything about Billie until Aura told me what Earley was up to, sending you to give Jubal that message."

"I just, I, I, I'm . . ." Raleigh took off his glasses. "I'm speechless. You might as well tell me the sky was green." Elbows on knees, Hayes put his head in his hands.

"Well, Raleigh . . ." He felt her hand briefly touch his hair. "Sometimes it is. If you'd been with me in Fiji when that hurricane hit and a tree landed right on top of my bus, you'd have seen the whole sky look as green as grass. The sky can turn green, Raleigh. Now listen to me. I know you're shocked, but I want you to calm down before Billie notices. We've already upset her enough as it is."

Raleigh looked over at the small group of musicians in the sunlit square. His father was nodding as Toutant Kingstree played his saxophone while the girl sang, "I'll Get By."

After a while, Raleigh said, "What does she think of all this? Does she know?"

"Yes. I don't know if she believes it. I'm not sure I would have thought I had the right to tell her. Earley did. . . . And I'm glad." Victoria pinched hard at her nose, then sat down beside her nephew on the bench; her back in the blue tailored jacket as straight as it had been in the WAC uniform forty years earlier. "Raleigh, I'm an old woman. I've been angry most of my life. Mad at the world for being so damn full of sloth and cruelty. So mad at Earley I thought I'd lose my mind. Mad at myself. Fifty years ago I said no to something. Maybe I was wrong. Maybe I was right. That's all dead now. You can't change the past. For a long time I couldn't forgive it either, and I couldn't forget it. But now, look. Here comes the past again." She rested her hand on Raleigh's knee. "And I can say yes. At least I can buy her some decent clothes. That idiot Earley's been dragging her all over the country dressed like a wild Indian. Just look at her."

Raleigh raised his head and watched his aunt looking at Billie Rogers. The two sat quietly together on the bench, listening to the girl's voice and the saxophone singing. Then Raleigh put his hand on top of his aunt's and left it there.

Passersby stopped to hear "Weeping Willow Blues" or "Don't Blame Me" or "It Had to Be You." A few dropped bills or coins in the open saxophone case. From other parts of the square, other kinds of music faintly floated toward the bench — two middle-aged female guitarists harmonizing folk ballads, a group of young boys break-dancing to taped rock-and-roll. Birds and cars and vendors and dogs joined in, too.

Raleigh had just asked his aunt how ill she thought his father was, and she had just answered, "Very. . . . But I'm not going to try to beat some sense into that man's head. Earley's stubborn. He's spoiled." She took an ironed handkerchief from her purse and gave her nose a sharp twist. "And he's a sweet man, Raleigh, with the thinking capacity of a cocker spaniel. He never had more than about one-tenth of my brains, and I just wish I hadn't been such a damn idiot, it took me seventy years to figure that out."

They both had just laughed at this remark, when, in that peculiarly sudden way he had of appearing without anyone seeing him arrive, Simon Berg walked around from the back of their bench.

With a tip of his homburg, the old criminal said, "So, Raleigh, forgive me butting in. And I betcha this is Aunt Victoria, about which I have heard a bundle, all of it, believe me, inclusively compliments." He thrust his small hand at the startled Miss Hayes. "They tell me you're a world first-class traveler. Likewise myself."

Raleigh stammered, "Aunt Vicky, I'd like you to meet, this is a friend, old friend of Gates, and, ah, friend of mine. He's been traveling with us, doing some, ah, ah, art collecting. Sim —"

Berg cut him off. "The tag's of no consequence. Call me Syme's fine."

"How do you do?" Victoria murmured, extracting her hand as soon as possible from the one vigorously shaking it. The man did not look healthy to her. He was wearing a black overcoat on a balmy spring day. His skin was very splotchy: in some places, bluish-white; in others, burnt umber. Moreover, his eyes — the left one brown, the right one pale green — gave the impression of an unbalanced personality.

"So, Raleigh, your paternal over there with Toots, he's a regular bucolic Louis Armstrong. Also, I like the chanteuse; a voice strictly from the angels direct. You know what I mean? . . . I brought the kid. Look. Back behind the fountain. Nah, to the left, under that fat waxy tree."

Standing up, Hayes followed the direction of Weeper's arm. Yes, there beneath a large magnolia tree stood — or rather, swung, his hands looped over a low twisting bough — his brother, Gates, dressed in an apparently new white linen suit.

"Is that Gates?" Victoria asked, shading her eyes. "Behaving like a chimpanzee?"

"The kid spooks." Berg sadly shook his head. "I leave him there twenty, thirty minutes ago, he's heading to say hi to his dad. I do a little business. I come back. Cheesh, he's still casing the joint. He's a lousy statue. He's comatose with anxiety: How they had this big blowout way back when; how your dad's got no use for him; how this is your show, and he oughta just take a powder, et cetera, et cetera. Go, Raleigh, will yah? Drag him out."

Hayes started forward, but then he stopped. "No." He rubbed his cheek. "I don't think so. No. Let him take his own time."

"Maybe a wise decision," Berg nodded. "Likewise, from Time we could all drop dead. So, then, I'll rest my dogs here a sec and shoot the breeze with your aunt — if congenial, of course — then I gotta scram." He sat down on the bench beside Victoria, crossed a leg, pulled off a shoe, and rubbed at his foot through a black sock so large it hung off his toes and bunched around his tiny white ankle. "Getting to know these guys has been an automatic pleasure, miss. But for even the best of friends, like the poet says, the days dwindle down to a precious few. I'm shipping out at midnight. Caracas."

So Raleigh Hayes waited, watching his brother across the square, hidden in the sun-shadowed trees; while on the bench Simon Berg and Victoria Hayes (looking at first somewhat pinched in the mouth) shot the breeze.

"You know Venezuela, Victoria? Mind if I call you Victoria? A beautiful name, and fits you like a glove, you'll pardon the familiarity."

"No, South America's about the only place I don't know. I covered the Far East for thirty years. Are you traveling with Mingo Sheffield? He was going to South America, too. Tell me why, and we'll both know."

"Fatty? Nah. He's pulling your leg."

"I wouldn't be surprised. Why are *you* going?"

Simon Berg sighed, holding open his hands. "Why not? I got no home. No family, unlike yourself. So, I travel. That's what Jews do. They wander. You travel, maybe you learn. Weed?"

"I don't smoke, Mr. Syme, and at your age, you certainly shouldn't either."

He shrugged. "At my age, I might as well. Thirty years on the road, hunh? A beautiful lady like yourself. . . . Homesick a lot?"

"No. Thermopylae, North Carolina, never felt like home."

"You're right. Anywise, what's a home? You nail your planks. They burn them down. You lay your bricks. They blow them up." Berg waved away the smoke from his cigarette. "You bury your dead. Sand covers the names. Such is the crummy world we live in, Victoria. Am I right?"

She turned to him on the bench, pulled her glasses down on her nose, and looked at him a moment. "Nine times out of ten," she replied.

"True." He nodded. They sat awhile, watching Raleigh watch Gates. Then Berg said, "So, the Far East, hunh? Singapore?"

"At the start of the war, yes."

"Not a good time."

"No."

"Perchance you ever frequented a bar in Singapore, very classy joint called the Gold Dragon? I had the close personal acquaintance of the owner at a later date. Name of Duke Songkhla, also called Sing-Sing?"

"I don't drink," she replied.

"With my guts in their condition, I also abstain. So, how'd you like this town, Singapore?"

"If you'd spent the night with a rat crawling over your legs on the floor of a jail there, you wouldn't bother to ask, Mr. Syme."

He nodded sympathetically. "What'd they pull you in for?"

Raleigh turned to stare at his aunt as she straightened the crisp white collar of her blouse. "Trading smuggled cigarettes on the black market for penicillin."

"Good God, Aunt Vicky!"

Victoria glanced from her nephew to Berg. "I guess that shocks you, Mr. Syme, but people were dying like flies then, up in the missions, and somebody had to get up and do something about it."

"Call me Simon." Bert tapped her shoulder. "You were a missionary, this I didn't know."

"I'm a salesman. I've got no use for missionaries." She folded her arms tightly. "I wasn't about to stand around while they handed out crossed sticks and hymnbooks, when women were sitting right there in the dirt outside the doors holding dead children in their laps."

Berg breathed a long sigh. ". . . This you saw? . . . This you saw. . . . The world, Victoria my friend, is to weep. . . . Anywise, as you say, nine times out of ten."

Raleigh had listened without taking his eyes off Gates, and Gates had not taken his hands off the tree bough. Sun luminous on the black curls and beautiful suit, the man swayed back and forth as if he were a swing tied to the branch. "Oh Gates, Gates," said Raleigh to himself, and then to Victoria and Simon, he said, "See you later."

Hayes walked back to the middle of the square, where his father now waited beside Billie, his trumpet raised, for Toutant Kingstree to finish an extravagant set of variations on "St. Louis Woman." A fairly large-sized crowd had collected to listen.

Raleigh put his hands quietly on his father's shoulders.

"Hi, Specs. Vicky okay? You okay?"

"We're just fine." The old man's shirt was wet, his skin cold, his arms shaky. Turning him around, Raleigh took the trumpet and pointed it past the fountain at the gleaming figure beneath the magnolia. "Daddy, don't y'all ever take a break? Look over there. My baby brother's been waiting a long time to say hello."

CHAPTER

32

How Raleigh Was Ordained in The Cave

OF THE THERMOPYLEANS AND THEIR FRIENDS, our hero was the last to leave Jackson Square. He stayed there with his father until long after dark.

Jubal Rogers did not come between noon and six — the hours Earley had promised to wait. No one was surprised.

Allen Thornhill left to teach a class. Before he went, Toutant Kingstree handed him $2.75, a fourth of the donations dropped in the case on the pavement. Simon Berg took Gates to the docks to look at the freighter he was boarding for South America at midnight. Kingstree wanted to check out, just for his own personal satisfaction, The Cave, where Allen had invited them to play, and he asked Mingo to come along. They arranged to meet Billie there before supper, to work out a list of numbers. In the meantime, Victoria was taking Billie back to the hotel to rest.

While the girl was packing her sheet music together, Kingstree said he had some advice about singing he wanted her to think about before tonight, some advice about originality: "Listen here, don't get me wrong. Billie Holiday was the best there ever was, but sooner or later you got to cut yourself loose from the Lady. All right? Learning from her, that's fine. Stealing from her, that's fine too. I have ripped off Lester Young, child, for all he was worth. Jubal now, your grandpa, he turned guys like Benny

Goodman inside out. Turned them mad and mean, took the top off their heads when he wanted to. But that's my point: You just take what *you* can use. You got to go down in and take a good look around yourself and pull that you on out and see what it has to say. Earley here understands how I mean, don't you, Earley?"

Earley Hayes was lying on the grass beside Raleigh; his shirt was damp and his white hair was stuck with perspiration to his forehead. He said to the sky, "Mister Kingstree, it didn't take me anywhere near three hours to know you and I are not in the same league."

"Well, that's true," the tall saxophonist agreed solemnly. "You got no wind left. No sustain to speak of. And it's a pig in a poke what you're going to do on that high D every time." Kingstree thrust his long arms into his peach pleated jacket and brushed off the sleeves. "But, Earley, listen here, you got a *style*. And that's the bottom line. That's God's doing."

Earley raised up on his elbows; his blue eyes brightened with tears. He stared at the black man. "Thank you," he finally said. "You wouldn't shit me, would you?"

"Man, I don't ever shit with music."

Earley grinned. "Goddamn, I wish we were sitting right here, twenty years old!"

Kingstree nodded. "You and me both. I waited too long. Forty years old! I'd take forty."

"I'd take sixty," Earley laughed.

Victoria Hayes snatched up two shopping bags. "Well, if I were you two fools, I'd go take a nap, instead of dawdling around here, crying for the moon. Raleigh, don't let him lie there on that grass until the dew falls. Are you ready to go, Billie?"

The girl turned slowly in a circle, looking toward the cathedral and toward the French Market. "You don't think Jubal's coming, do you, Victoria?"

The old woman straightened her back. "No. . . . I'll put you on the plane Monday. You fly to Charleston and go see him there. If Earley'd had a lick of sense, that's what he would have done in the first place, as soon as he found out he wasn't in New Orleans."

Earley sat up, hugging his thin knees. "I know. I'm sorry. You're probably right, Vicky."

She glared at her brother. "I am absolutely right. Earley Hayes, I tell you this, ever since I was a little girl I have wondered what in the world God had on *His* mind when he made *yours!*"

Laughing, Earley shouted after the square straight shoulders. "Me too! Hey, Vicky! VICKY ANNA! I LOVE YOU."

The two women turned around. "Tell the world about it," Victoria said.

Raleigh and his father sat on the grass side by side. The sky turned orange, then pink, then indigo blue. For a while, the sun and moon were in the sky together with the first evening stars.

Earley talked in his soft reedy whisper to his son as they waited.

". . . I'd seen Jubal with women, even at nineteen. And Vicky, well, you know the kind of person she is, and, Christ, she was almost engaged to Zeb Forbes, and . . . well, I almost killed Jubal. . . . I don't think she ever forgave me. I know he didn't.

". . . I never thought Flonnie would tell Vicky about Josh when she came home after the war . . . I was in a bad way then myself, and no help to anybody. I'd screwed up my marriage with your mom past forgiveness. My church was kicking me out on my ass for the sins of fornication and, quote, 'nigger sympathies.' Jubal would have loved that.

". . . No, Jubal never found Joshua. During the war, his wife Leda just left New York with another guy, went out West and took Josh with her. Maybe she honestly thought Jubal was never coming back, or maybe she thought he'd been killed in Germany, maybe they told her that. God knows. Jubal spent a lot of years looking for them. I only know because he kept up with Flonnie, thinking maybe Josh would come back to Thermopylae, I guess. . . . Josh was only thirty-one when he died, Raleigh. . . . Thirty-one years old. . . . I don't even know if Jubal knows or not.

". . . Oh, Specs, who knows what a calling means. I felt like God had picked me out to shepherd one of His flocks. I was going to bring everybody together. I was going to integrate the world. Christ Almighty, what an asshole I was! Drove the whole herd off in a by fuck stampede. Ran the ones I loved the most over a cliff. Vicky. Jubal. Your mother. Gates. What I didn't manage to screw up with my vices, I put my virtues to work on. They did even worse. Lend me your jacket. I'm freezing my ass off."

Raleigh draped his sports coat over his father's shoulders. The sleeves trailed down onto the grass.

Earley shook the last cigarette out of his pack and lit it. "That's what scared me about you, Raleigh. I lay in that damn hospital and said, shit, that pompous ass is just *shriveling* with virtue, evaporating to where Aura won't even be able to find him, and he won't even know he's disappeared.

I said, that lucky bastard is going to blow it. See, I hadn't worried about you, Specs. I *knew* Gates was fucking up. He made sure we all knew, didn't he? I knew *I'd* fucked up. But I didn't see, till you and Vicky stuck me in that hospital like that, how far gone *you* were, son."

In the blue moonlight, Raleigh Hayes looked a long time at the small, thin old man seated on the grass beside him, hugging his knees. Finally he spoke. "Listen to me. Mama never stopped loving you. Vicky never stopped loving you. Gates never stopped loving you. And, Daddy — despite the fact that you couldn't figure out any better plan to keep me from being a pompous ass than the insanity you put me through the last few weeks — I never stopped loving you."

Earley's warm, reedy laugh sang out over the square. "When Joshua's child walked into the hospital the way she did, it all came smack together. I'll tell you this, I leaped off that bed like Lazarus. God was saying to me, 'Okay, you little fuck, I'm gonna hold the curtain for you; get your ass down to New Orleans. Do something for this girl, do something for yourself, do something for your sons.' It was a beautiful plan!"

Raleigh smiled. "Let's get up off this wet grass and you come show me what you want out of Tiny's goddamn trunk."

"'Ready or not, Jesus is coming'? That doesn't sound like you, Specs."

"Daddy, for Pete's sake, you don't think *I* put that sticker there, do you? Here. Here's Lovie's Bible. And here's your trumpet. No, wait a minute. That's my trumpet. Yours is in Gates's bag." Raleigh put the book and the horn down on the hood. "Look at this car! It's a wreck, and I haven't even made the first payment!"

Earley Hayes walked around the white Cadillac. "Jimmy sold you this, hunh? Hell, I'd hate to see the clunkers he sells people he's *not* related to, because, I tell you, that Big Ellie convertible he unloaded on me wasn't lemon yellow by accident."

"Well, let's take it back. It's bound to be on at least a thirty-day warranty." Raleigh had hauled out the steamer trunk, and was now lugging the plaster bust of PeeWee Jimson over to the sidewalk.

"I gave it to Billie. Vicky Anna wouldn't let me do anything else for her, because she wanted to hog it, you know, paying her tuition and all. You know how she likes to be in charge."

It occurred to Raleigh Hayes that he had possibly just lost to Billie Rogers his inheritance from his aunt Victoria, possibly including the house on East Main Street, in which a dental clinic and a Seven-Eleven chain had already expressed interest. "Daddy, you've got to stop giving things away!"

"Why? You want to bury me in a fucking Cadillac?" Earley knelt beside the old steamer trunk and pushed up its rusty latch.

"And stop talking about burying you here and not burying you there. In the first place, you're not going to die."

"I'm not? That'll be a first. Even God's only Son died, and I don't have anywhere near His connections."

"In the second place, I can't bury you at Knoll Pond! People have to be buried in the proper places."

"Oh, bullshit. Hey, what's my cassock doing on top here? I stuck it down at the bottom."

Raleigh grabbed at the small rumpled black vestment as his father felt through its pockets. "Damn! So, there's where Simon got it. I'm sorry, Daddy, Simon Berg must have borrowed this. We had to, ah, use a lot of the clothes in there. For, well, one reason or another. . . . Are you telling me I brought that trunk all the way down here so you could get your old cassock out of it!"

"Well, sounds like it came in handy." Earley pulled a letter from the cassock's inside pocket, and handed it to his son. "Give this to Vicky, okay?" Raleigh moved closer to the streetlamp. It was a plain opened envelope with a three-cent stamp, addressed to "Earley Hayes, 5 East Main, Thermopylae, N.C.," The postmark was not, as Raleigh originally thought, 1983, but 1933. The return address was "Rogers, P.O. Box 373, New Orleans, La." Inside was a sealed envelope, addressed in the same careful handwriting with the single word, "Victoria."

When Hayes looked back around, his father had taken the military sword that Weeper Berg had also once borrowed, and with it was slitting open the brittle lining of the trunk's lid. He stuck his arm down inside and pulled out a square of paper, which he carefully unfolded; then taking the large frayed Bible from the car hood, he opened it and showed Raleigh that the edge of the piece of paper fit the rip where the first page of the book of Job had been torn out. At the top of the page, fastidiously written in small pale brown script around the margins, were the words, "Gen. G. H. Hayes. Gen. Goodrich H. Hayes. Lt. Gen. Hayes. Hayes. Hayes. He saith among the trumpets Ha, ha, & he smelleth the battle afar off. The thunder of the captains & the shouting. 39:25. Jess's hearth, Apr. 15, 1865."

"Daddy, what in hell is going on here?"

"Did you bring a gun? . . . Here, thanks for the jacket. Nice jacket. New?" Earley pulled on the black cassock and started buttoning it.

"What do you want a gun for?"

The old man patted the fat white plaster face of PeeWee Jimson. "Shoot this shit between the eyes."

Raleigh threw his arms up in the air. "You *are* crazy. I am not about to let you shoot a gun off in a public place. We'd be arrested in two seconds." He pointed at the passing cars and strolling pedestrians and at the French Market café across the street where people sat drinking coffee. "Listen. Where do you want to be at ten o'clock? Do you want to be playing your trumpet at The Cave, or do you want to be down at the police station? It's as simple as that."

"Well, I was looking forward to plugging PeeWee, but maybe you're right, Specs."

"Maybe?! *Daddy, what are you doing?!* Put that thing down! Jesus!"

With a groan Earley Hayes had lifted the plaster bust as high as he could, and then hurled it down on the edge of the sidewalk pavement. The head snapped off and rolled over the curb. "How about a lug wrench then?" the old man said.

What was inside the head of PeeWee Jimson, as rendered by his widow Gladys, was a piece of paper the Reverend Earley Hayes had stuck there one December afternoon in 1947, as soon as Mrs. Jimson left the dining room, where she was applying plaster to her husband's bust. She left the room after telling Reverend Earley Hayes that the vestry would very much appreciate his immediate resignation from St. Thomas Church. She left the room in a hurry because Earley Hayes, declining her invitation to resign, had just called her "a by fuck racist bitch." As the former priest now told his son, almost forty years later, the idea had come to him in a flash to embed a certain piece of paper he had with him in PeeWee's memorial as a poetic irony, or in his phrase, a practical joke. He thought it would be a wonderful joke if hidden right behind the hoggish eyes of the man who'd ruined his father, Clayton, was the coded key to even more Hayes-begotten wealth. For, by then, just after Clayton Hayes's death, the Jimsons owned the Knoll Pond property, and by then, Earley had figured out the meaning of the piece of paper, scribbled with numbers and, like the Bible page, dated 1865, that years earlier he'd found buried on that property. He'd found it under a hearth brick in the little cabin that was all Federal troops had left standing of the Goodrich Hale Hayes home once called Knoll Pond House.

Bewildered, Raleigh examined the yellow sheet, cracked along its folds.

There was nothing on it but a peculiar arrangement of numbers and symbols, written in the same faint brown ink.

    3.15(6) 1.7 (22-24) 1.5 (31-34)
    1.7 (17) 1.10 (11-12) 38.6 (11-12) 9.9 (12) 1.7 (18-19) 1.10
        (5-6) 9.17 (9) 1.2 (7,9-10)
    41.32 (4) 1.7 (18-19) 41.24 (18)
    9.9 (12) 42.16 (5-8) 40.17 (7)
    38.24 (1-7) 2.11 (4) 3.6 (25-30)
    40.21 40.22
    40.14 (9-12) 20.25 (11-13) 38.31 (14)

They didn't look like any system of mathematics or measurement with which Raleigh was familiar. "Is this some kind of code?" he asked his father, who was tossing pieces of Jimson's bust into a trashcan chained to a palm tree. "Are you trying to tell me you think this is some kind of stupid treasure map that this man Goodrich Hayes left behind during the Civil War?"

"That's right. See if you can figure it out. You've got the key in your hand. Now, I dug up that chart one day when I was a teenager, out there at the cabin sneaking some liquor. But it wasn't till just after Papa died, when I was so down, I was spending a lot of time with Job, that I saw how General Hayes had devised his system. Wish I could have met him; sounds like he was a real weirdo." Earley looked at the broken plaster face. "God, PeeWee was a pig. Gladys got his eyes just right." He dropped the head in the basket. "And now, Specs, the wheel turns, by holy fuck, and you've brought that land back to your family." He chuckled. "And dirt cheap too! That knocked my socks off, the way you bargained with Pierce." Brushing white dust from his arms, the old man belted his cassock tighter to keep the hem off the ground. "So, Raleigh, my son, that's my legacy to you." He smiled, raising his hand in benediction. "That and this great vacation you've been on. Because, listen, give whatever's left in the damn bank to Gates. Throw my will out. I don't remember what it says exactly, but seems like I left everything to you."

"That's exactly what it says." Raleigh jerked off his glasses. "What do you mean, you don't remember?"

"I mean, the damn details. But that's awful, isn't it? I must have been really pissed at Gates that day. I didn't leave him anything?"

Raleigh took a deep breath. "You asked me to settle a yearly allowance on him."

"Oh, well, that's more like it. Okay, why don't you do that? Except give it *all* to him. Well, you don't need it, do you? Hell, everybody in Thermopylae tells me you're loaded."

"I am not loaded. I am . . . comfortable."

"Well, talking to Gates, I get the feeling he's *un*comfortable."

"For Christ's sake, Daddy, he'll throw it away! You have no idea the sort of things he . . . well, shit. . . . Okay, I'll set up a trust fund, and he can have the interest. Then, if he settles down, I'll sign over the principal. If he *tries* to settle down. If he says he *wants* to try. How's that? Is that fair?"

Earley grinned. "I never knew you when you weren't fair. You're about the fairest soul I know. In fact, right this minute you look all light and shimmery."

Hayes crossed his arms. "That's because you're probably going blind on top of everything else. . . . Let me get this straight. You want me to settle whatever's left in your estate after these latest escapades on Gates. And all I get is a bunch of stupid buried silver spoons. . . ."

"How do you know it's spoons? Maybe it's a million dollars."

"Okay, whatever it is you found buried somewhere in two boggy overgrown acres of sumac, thorn bushes, and poison ivy!"

"Raleigh, you crack me up!" Earley was now looking through the trunk, pushing clothes aside.

"What *did* you find?"

"I never found anything. I never looked."

"You mean, because we didn't own the property? But you used to sneak us out there fishing all the time. We used to shoot B.B.s at the No Trespassing sign. You had us picking boysenberries for Grandma and Flonnie. Cutting Christmas trees. God, what held you back from digging a simple hole?"

"I was already screwed up enough, without getting my hands on a wagonload of Confederate gold bullion."

Blood raced down Raleigh's arms. "What did you say?"

Earley shook out a pale satin dress. "Look at that. Mama's wedding dress. Reba got married in it; why don't you take it back to her. . . . Well, that was the family story. Oh, you heard about it. How this Goodrich Hayes had a wagonload of Confederate bullion that General Hood sent him off to Richmond with after Atlanta fell. But he never got any farther than Themopylae with it, or never intended to get any farther, and how he buried it at Knoll Pond House. My aunt Hattie swore her grandma saw the wagon with her own eyes. . . . Oh my, was this Papa's harmonica? I think it was. Yep. . . ." Earley cupped his hands around the silver rectangle and blew into it.

"A wagonload of *gold?*"

Slipping the harmonica in his pocket, the old man picked up a crushed stationery box with a rubber band around it. It was junked full of cheap broken jewelry, tarnished medals, and old photographs of all different sizes. "So they say. They say that's why the Yankees burned the house down, looking for the gold. . . . Well, time. Time, time, time. . . . Look here, Raleigh." He opened the car door so the light would shine on a photograph. It was a very old brown-and-white group portrait taken on the porch of the East Main house. Rows of sunlit Hayeses stood on each step. Clayton and Ada, his straw bowler at a tilt, her face frowning, each holding a twin baby boy in a laced smock. Around them all their beautiful daughters in cotton summer dresses, all their handsome sons in white shirts and ties, except the youngest, Hackney, whose middy blouse rode up over his round stomach. Victoria, slender-armed, bright-haired, hugged on her lap a little girl who was sticking out her tongue.

"That must be Lovie," Raleigh said.

"That's right. Look at those balloon-sized knickerbockers on Furbie. God, he loved those pants."

Raleigh picked up a handful of the medals. One had a female racer on it, one, a male golfer. One was for debating, one revealed no clue at all to what it honored, one said "Camp Cherokee." "Daddy, Uncle Whittier's Bronze Star's in here, just thrown in here with all this junk."

"Oh my word, Reba and Big Em in toe shoes, now there's a sight!" Earley had poured all the pictures out on the car seat. ". . . Okay. Here it is." He held up an old bent snapshot, one corner torn off. Two teenaged boys leaned with a swaggering nonchalance against the front of a dilapidated stucco building; in its open door a black woman sat holding a cardboard fan; on its dirty window were painted the words "BEER, 10¢." The black young man had a cigarette cocked in his mouth and a clarinet held by his side like a sword. The white young man was shorter, and cradled his trumpet across his chest.

Earley shook his head, softly saying, " 'You two keep away from that jugband trash, you hear me. Y'all headed straight for Hell.' Well, Flonnie . . . pack of fools." He put the photograph in his shirt pocket to take to Billie Rogers.

"I said, I'd like to say grace," yelled Earley Hayes. "Hey, everybody." He rapped his wineglass. "Can y'all hear me down there?"

"No," said Victoria. "And between the smoke and the noise and that loud music, I am losing my faculties."

Resting the elbows of his cassock on the table, Earley folded his hands. "Dear Lord, thank you for this day and this meal and these people and this chance. Raleigh did a beautiful job getting us all here together, and thank you for helping him. It's a wonderful. . . . Oh hell, they're not listening. See you later. Amen." He put his fingers in his mouth and whistled. Everybody turned. *"There.* How 'bout a toast then?" He raised his glass. "To my sons Raleigh and Gates. I'm proud of you both. Long life and happiness."

"Hip hip hooray," said Mingo and Billie. *"L'chaim,"* said Simon. "Hey hey," said Gates. "Right," said Toutant, and Vicky and Allen Thornhill nodded. Earley put his hands around Raleigh's head, pulled him off balance, and kissed him. Raleigh grabbed hold of Mingo's arm, Mingo sloshed his strawberry margarita into his shrimp gumbo, everybody laughed and then went back to talking and eating.

"This is my own personal opinion, man, but the way I hear it going is, Billie leads in the verse on 'Stardust,' solo — da de da da deedee, like that — and *then* I come slap in with the sax on the refrain, and then, just like we practiced this afternoon, Earley goes straight into 'Wrap Your Troubles in Dreams.' What do you think, Billie?"

"Gollee, Vicky, that is really delicious. I sure never had rabbit jumbalaya before. I would have been too scared to try it on my own, I bet. Taste some of this, Weeper."

"Awggh. Get it away. Rabbits I should inflict on my guts yet? . . . So, Sheffield, you're ever in Caracas, you look me up. Likewise yourself, Victoria. South America, you never covered, am I right? Try it."

"I might just get up and do that one of these days. Mr. Kingstree, you are not doing Earley any favors giving him cigarettes. Gates, go ask that waiter what happened to Billie's hamburger. I could have walked to a farm, shot a cow, and made one myself by now."

"Man, what are you talking about, Gershwin invented the Charleston!? *Blacks* invented the Charleston. It was stevedores that took it up to Harlem, and Gershwin went over there and stole it."

"So, Toots, tell me already he never wrote *Porgy and Bess?"*

"He was good, I don't deny it. Besides, 'Charleston' isn't even what these birds are playing. They're playing 'Varsity Drag.' Trying to. Now, Weep, I'm not heavying up on you, but except on 'I'm Always Chasing Rainbows,' just the way we worked on it in Montgomery, I don't want you to lay a finger on those frets. You just stand there and give that bass a slap every now and then. And don't you change any chords 'less Mingo here gives you the nod."

"Oh, Weeper, gollee, I'm going to miss you to pieces. Why do you have to go to South America anyhow?"

"Mingo, my friend, with you I won't mince words. Certain parties in the U.S. are too colloquial with my, with my . . . dactylographics."

"Oh. Well, I don't know what that means, but I wish you'd come back to Thermopylae with us and meet Vera. And we're all going to go to Kure Beach this summer, and even if it rains, it's still fun because we can play cards and sing."

"If I hadn't met your mother, Mingo Sheffield, I'd swear you were born a Hayes. Raleigh, will you please go see if that waiter flew to Alaska and took your brother with him? Well, I can certainly see why they named this place The Cave. I want y'all to know I've been down in volcanos in Sumbawa that were better lit."

The Cave did, in fact, look like a cave, and in the nineteenth century had been a wine merchant's cellar. In a bright, noisy alley off Bourbon Street, not far from Jackson Square, black iron stairs led down to the massive door with the brass plaque that still said "Le Cave," although nobody had called it Le Cave for decades. Behind the door (the sliding peephole of the old speakeasy now painted shut), food and music had been fighting it out since the 1920s. Heavy black wood tables thickened with years of shellac circled a round dais in the middle of the room. The low ceiling curved down to white plastered walls hung with newspaper clippings and album covers and photographs of New Orleans musicians. On this Maundy Thursday, the place was not jammed, but according to Allen Thornhill, the real music people didn't show up until the dinner trade had cleared out. It was nearly ten o'clock now, and a jazz quartet was just finishing its final set.

Squeezing his way between the tables, Raleigh Hayes looked first for a waiter, and then for Gates. He found his brother in a narrow side room at a corner bar table. Nearby, an attractive woman ignored her escort (angrily insisting that he deserved a full-time secretary) and sat openly staring at the handsome man in the elegant white linen suit. Gates was folding cocktail napkins into wings, tossing them at the ashtray.

"Gates, what are you doing hiding in here? Why didn't you come back to the table?"

"Hey, Big Bro, the old man's act on yet? I want to catch it. He's a crazy bastard, you know that? Listen, talk to me a second, okay?" Looking up at Raleigh, he rubbed the black mustache, then the black curls. "Right, fine. Here's the deal. . . . I'm going to split. Let this John Neill thing blow over.

I'm heading out with Weep tonight." He tapped his breast pocket. "They had a berth free, and I've got this truck money, and well, it was one of those things, why not, right? So, anyhow, I'm just going to slip out of here in a while, and you kind of explain to Dad and the gang later on. Will you do that? I'm not exactly big on farewell scenes, know what I mean? Not sure I can handle it."

Raleigh sat down. "Gates, is this a joke?"

Gates showed him the ticket.

"You can't just decide to go to South America in one day. Do you even have a passport?"

"I'm a flyer, Raleigh. I'm always ready for take-off." From a wallet in his breast pocket, he took out a blue passport and then a fifty-dollar bill. "Here. Pay your debts, that's what you taught me. And thanks, listen. I don't mean the money, you know. . . . Do me a couple of little favors, okay? Here's two hundred dollars." He tapped a roll of money bound with a rubber band. "When you get back home, would you go to a bakery and have them do a really *big* cake, five or six tiers, and I want it to have the Eiffel Tower on top, and I want it to say, *'Folies Bergère.'* And then I want a magnum of champagne, and order a huge, I mean *huge,* horseshoe of roses, and have them write 'HAPPY BIRTHDAY, LOVIE,' on it, and then April sixteenth, have it all sent out to Lovie for me? Could you do that?"

He rolled the money toward Raleigh, who caught it and said, "Lovie's birthday was March sixteenth, not April sixteenth."

Gates grinned. "So tell them to write, *'Sorry I'm Late.' "*

"Why don't you come back with me, and go see Lovie yourself? And what about Sara Zane?"

"Oh, her. I don't know, Raleigh. Fences, all that jazz. I'm not sure I can handle it."

"Gates, are you sure you want to do this? Did you seriously think it through? Let's just calm down, and analyze this. . . . What's so funny?"

Gates leaned over the table and rubbed his brother's hair. "Old Raleigh-kov. . . . Grab the check, willyah? Let's go hear our cousin Billie sing the blues." He stood up, shaking his black curls at the well-dressed woman still staring at him from the next table. Her escort was still talking about why he shouldn't have to share his secretary with Joel, but he stopped in midsentence when a man who looked like a movie star suddenly bent down, kissed his wife on the inside of the wrist, murmured to her, *"Buenas noches, señora,"* and said to him, "Here seets your wouman, beauteefool like *las flores,* and in your head ees only beeznis, beeznis. Thees is not good, *amigo. Adios.*"

"Who the hell was that?" spluttered the businessman at his wife, who just kept staring as the man in white turned back at the door and, with a wink, kissed his hand to her.

CHAPTER

33

What Raleigh Decided about Death

AT TWENTY PAST TEN, when he slid into his seat behind his drums, Allen Thornhill was wearing one of the beautiful Chinese red silk short-sleeved shirts that Gates had presented to each of the musicians after dinner. Now, as they all started for the dais, Gates rubbed each on the back. "Hey, show time. You look good, you sound good. Billie, that's a dynamite dress. Matches your voice. Hey, Daddy, hold up. Your shirt's buttoned wrong."

"Give me a hug for luck, gorgeous," Earley Hayes said to Gates. "God, I'm glad you came to see me."

"Knick-knack gem-crack high-times, right? Break a leg."

Raleigh didn't say anything. His heart was pounding too hard, and besides, his aunt Victoria was squeezing all the blood out of his hand. "Well," she whispered, "thank God Gates had the sense to buy those shirts, so Earley didn't go up there in that fool cassock and embarrass Billie to death."

Thornhill stepped over to the microphone. "Good to be back again. Thank you. I brought some people with me tonight I want everybody to welcome. . . . On trumpet, the Reverend Earley Hayes, an old marching friend, and a good teacher, and the man who told me a long long time ago, 'Drums are louder than hate.' . . . At the piano, Mr. Mingo Shef-

field. . . . Joining us for a little while on bass, Mr. Sy Berger. . . . On tenor
sax, the astonishing Mr. Toutant Kingstree. . . . And The Cave's special
guest, a young lady I have a feeling we're all going to be hearing about
one of these days. A young lady with a wonderful new feeling for some old
traditions. Let's give her a warm welcome to New Orleans — Miss Billie
Rogers!" He lowered the microphone, and Billie walked up to it. Her
black sleeveless dress flowed loosely down from her shoulders, and she
wore no jewelry. Her black hair flared out glittering in the smoky light.

Toutant's long shiny narrow shoe began to tap. Lifting the saxophone,
he looked at Billie as she took a deep breath, let it slowly out, and nodded.
Then he said, "And one. And two. One two three four."

> *Way down yonder in New Orleans . . . in the land of dreamy dreams,*
> *There's a garden of Eden . . . that's what I mean . . .*

"Breathe, Aunt Vicky, she's fine. Listen, they like her. They're clapping.
Look."

"Of course they like her, Raleigh, don't be an idiot. What time is it?"

"Why do you keep asking me the time? It's ten forty-one." He pointed
at the round watch pinned to her lapel. "Is there something the matter
with your watch?"

"My watch works perfectly. This light's so bad and smoky, I can't see
it."

> *. . . The way he's treating me . . . he'll do the very same to you.*
> *That's the reason . . . got these weeping willow blues.*

"Does Daddy look funny to you, Aunt Vicky? He doesn't look right."
Raleigh watched his father slip backward when he pushed himself out of
the chair to stand beside Billie. The man's red shirt was now a dark shiny
crimson, and his eyes were closed as he waited, swaying, the trumpet
raised.

> *Now he's gone, and we're through.*
> *Am I blue.*

Victoria folded her napkin into an exact square and placed it back beside
her coffee cup. "Raleigh, I said I wouldn't tell you but . . . I took Earley to
a good doctor Wednesday, and he admitted there was nothing they could
do, except try one of those artificial hearts, and then he'd probably die on
the operating table." She tapped her nephew's hand. "Earley's got two
choices. He can sit in a hospital and wait. Or he can keep on the way he is.

Which do you think a Hayes is going to pick? Let him alone, Raleigh. I've known him a long time. I honestly think this is the happiest I've ever seen him."

I hope that he . . . turns out to be
Someone to watch . . . over me. . . .

Gates came back from the cloak room with his leather bag, a leather trench coat over his arm. "Hey, okay, Big Bro, she *is* good! And look at old Mingo hanging off that bench, thumping away, beating the shit out of that piano! Damn, they sound like a fucking *band!*"

"Gates Hayes, the only reason for that kind of language, young man, is sloth pure and simple."

"Sorry, Aunt Vicky." Gates unzipped the bag and set the gold trumpet on the table. "Raleigh, go on up there, go on. Oh shit, man, why not? I wish *I* could."

But Raleigh shook his head.

Go down sunshine . . . see what tomorrow brings.
Well, it may bring sunshine . . . then again it may bring rain.

"What time is it?"

"Eleven-o-three. Aunt Vicky? Where're you going?"

"To take a walk. I need a breath of air. It's thick as a Malay monsoon in here. Sit down. I don't want you dawdling along, slowing me up."

"But you can't just wander around the French Quarter by yourself at night. Let me or Gates walk you —"

"Women are not puppies, Raleigh. They don't need to be walked. I swear I'm going to go out and campaign for Aura. I've put up with enough male foolishness to last me a lifetime."

"I just meant in case —"

"Nobody's going to bother me. And if they do, they're in for a surprise." She picked up her purse, and patted it. "I'll be back in thirty minutes."

"Tough broad," said Gates. "What'd she have in that purse, a forty-five?"

When skies are cloudy and gray . . . they're only gray for a day.
So wrap your troubles in dreams . . . and dream your troubles away.

There were no empty tables in The Cave now, and the hurrying, jostling waiters carried only drinks on their trays, bending their heads down close to the customers to hear new orders over the music. Occasionally, they'd make a halfhearted effort to shoo away the small boys passing among the crowd trying to sell single long-stem roses.

A suntanned man in a blue blazer stopped at Raleigh's table, and whispered to him, "Pardon me, the maître d' said you were associated with this group? What did they say their name was?"

"... Ah, they're not actually a, ah, formally, a group. They're just backing up Miss Rogers tonight. Billie Rogers."

So keep on looking for a bluebird ... and listening for his song.

"I see.... She has a very exciting voice."

Raleigh nodded.

The man looked at the stage awhile, then bent back down. "Excuse me. Who's the saxophonist?"

Raleigh looked at the man's manicured fingernails and gold watch bracelet. Then he smiled. "Ah, you recognized him? Yes, that's Toutant Kingstree."

"Pardon? Kingstree? Where does he usually play? He's not local, is he? I'm fairly familiar with New Orleans jazz."

"Well, just lately he's been touring through the Southeast, but, ah, he was away quite a long time. Paris, Stockholm, Berlin. You know."

"I see. Do you represent him?"

"No."

"Thank you. Sorry to interrupt."

"Shhh," said Gates, as Raleigh tried to theorize about this encounter. "Quiet. Weep's going for the gold."

With his dyed curled hair and open red shirt, the former convict looked, as he pulled his bass fiddle closer to Mingo Sheffield at the piano, like an aging Puerto Rican street musician. As soon as Kingstree ended an introductory slow, high, bird call of notes, Mingo struck a chord with his right hand, and with his left, held two fingers up toward Berg, then one, then four, then two again. Simon Berg leaned his cheek against the fiddle's neck, and—as he told Gates Hayes later that night when they walked along the wharf to their freighter, past the towering crates of rubber and sugar and coffee and rice—he played "direct from heaven."

Believe me. I'm always chasing rainbows.
Waiting to find a little bluebird in vain.

Raleigh moved quickly through the applause to the edge of the dais when he saw his father beckon. "You okay, Daddy?"

"Just fine." Earley wiped his forehead with his arm. "How about Billie, hunh? And *look* at her. Oh my. 'A young hart upon the mountains of spices,' isn't she though?"

Raleigh smiled at the girl. Yes, she had the strange beauty still so startling in her grandfather. She swept the hair off the back of her neck and shook it, cooling herself, the sheen of her raised slender arms like the color of almonds. "How do you feel?" he asked her.

"I *love* it!" she said.

"Hi, Raleigh!" Mingo shouted from the piano bench. "What do we sound like out there?"

"Like a million dollars."

"Sheffield, listen up." The saxophonist turned to the piano. "She decided to skip 'Body and Soul,' go to 'Blackbird.' You wanna come in on the vocal, like we tried? Second verse. Take it a third down."

Raleigh said, "Just a second, Daddy. I've got your old trumpet, you want it?"

"No, but tell you what you could do. Downstairs in the office where we changed? Look in my cassock, there's a little bottle of pills. You want to bring them up for me? And some water? Oops, here he goes. Toutant doesn't mess around. I'm just hanging on to his coattails, catching a great ride!"

> *Could make me be true . . . could make me feel blue,*
> *And even be glad . . . just to be sad . . .*

It took Raleigh a while to find someone to show him where the office was, then let him into it. Finally he found the cassock thrown over a chair beneath Mingo's green sports jacket. The pills must have fallen out of the pocket because he eventually felt the bottle on the floor under the desk.

While Raleigh worked his way back toward the dais, Mingo's voice soared happily toward him, in harmony with Billie's.

> *Make my bed and light the light. I'll arrive late tonight*
> *Blackbird, bye bye.*

Raleigh placed the pills and water glass on the piano top. He noticed that Simon Berg's bass fiddle was leaning against his chair, but that the old criminal was no longer on the stage. Turning quickly, he looked back at their table. It was empty. At Gates's place, the yellow trumpet stood on its end, a long-stem red rose stuck in its mouthpiece.

> *If I had Aladdin's lamp for only a day,*
> *I'd make a wish and here's what I'd say . . .*

At the end of the second set, Raleigh asked his father to sit the next one out. "You did it, Daddy. Now, just call it a night. It's after midnight."

"It is? Well then, you know what today is?" Earley sat on the dais floor, propped against the back of the piano, hugging his arms to his chest.

"April first," said Raleigh, whose watch told him so.

"It is? April Fool's? Well, I'll be damned. Now, there's a Jesus joke for you. What I meant was, it's Good Friday. Now, that's funny, Raleigh. Old Jesus is hanging there, they're jabbing swords in Him and shoving vinegar at Him, and He flops over dead, then He winks open one eye, see, and says, 'April Fool's.'"

"Ha ha," said Raleigh. "If you went around in your church saying things like that, it's no wonder they fired you. You know, a lot of people don't find the Crucifixion a comic matter."

"Well, the joke's on them." Holding onto Raleigh's arm, the old man pulled himself up.

> *I'd say to the stars, stop where you are.*
> *Light up my lover's way.*

When Raleigh's aunt returned to her seat, she folded her hands tightly together on top of her purse, and stared at them without speaking. The strong jaw was as firm as ever, but her nose sharpened as she sought silently to slow her breathing. Raleigh leaned forward, looking into her lowered eyes, and then, suddenly, instantaneously, leaping over words, he *felt* what she was feeling. Down the back of his neck he felt it, and he twisted around in his chair, saying, "Where is he?" But he saw him at once, before she could have answered. Standing apart from the press of people near the door, in one hand a small old tan suitcase, in the other the black clarinet case, Jubal Rogers leaned against the far wall, listening. His rumpled suit was the same silvered black as his hair, and his thin black tie shimmered against the white shirt. Rogers's head was turned toward the music, his chin lifted, his arms motionless, as if he'd forgotten they carried luggage. On the dais, Billie stood between Toutant and Earley, the two horns and her voice talking to each other, following and leading one another down through the melody into the song.

> *Cried last night, and the night before,*
> *Gonna cry tonight, and then I'll cry no more.*

"Don't you want me to ask him to join us, Aunt Vicky? He's just standing there."

"No."

"When did you know he was coming?"

"When I saw him."

"Well, Daddy and Billie have no idea he's here. Did you ever tell them that Toutant had called him in Charleston for you?"

"No."

"All right. I'm sorry. I don't mean to pry." Raleigh picked up the trumpet. "I'm going back up there and just sit with Daddy for a while, all right?"

"Yes. . . . Just excuse me, Raleigh, I'm . . ."

"It's okay. Don't worry." He brushed his hand quickly over hers.

> *They sparkle, they bubble,*
> *They're gonna getcha in a whole lot of trouble.*

Hands were waving at several tables in response to Allen Thornhill's call for requests for the last set. On the dais, Raleigh saw Jubal Rogers suddenly push forward from the wall, and start toward them.

"Hey, man!" Toutant called to him. "You made it! Get up here, we're rolling!"

"Yeah." Rogers's impenetrable gold-flecked eyes stayed on Billie. "You're Billie Rogers," he said. "Well, my name is Jubal Rogers."

The girl nodded solemnly back. "I know. I saw you over there listening. I could tell it was you." Suddenly she smiled. "Hi."

Raleigh was sitting beside his father. He felt the small body tense, then let go, the breath leaving like a low soft wind.

Billie said, "We figured you weren't coming. We waited in the square all day."

"I couldn't make it then." Jubal's head now tilted down toward Earley. "I'm too old to play hide and seek." He pulled a worn thick wrinkled bank envelope from inside his jacket. As soon as Raleigh saw it, he knew the $4,500 was inside. "This belongs to you," Rogers said, and dropped the envelope on the floor in front of Earley's chair.

Earley nodded, staring up at the still eyes. "Okay." Then he said, "I'm real glad to see you. God, you look just the same."

"Yeah. I am just the same."

Earley nodded again. "Thanks for coming. I appreciate it."

"This doesn't have a thing to do with you, Earley."

"I know."

"And it doesn't change a thing."

"Thanks for coming, Jubal."

"Hi, Mr. Rogers, my name's Mingo Sheffield. I've heard so much about you, and boy, this is just great. You don't know what this means to Billie!

Well, that's stupid. Of course you do, or you wouldn't be here, would
you? Did you have a good trip?"

Allen Thornhill played a roll on his drums, and Toutant swung the saxophone forward, saying, "Y'all gonna talk, or y'all gonna play? Let's go.
'Honeysuckle Rose.' Same way we did it before, Mingo, laid back. That's
okay, Earley, listen, sit it out. Catch your breath. Jubal, we could use you,
if you feel up to it. All right. F's the key, just follow me." The tall man
grinned. "Anyhow, try to."

Flowers droop and sigh, when you wander by . . .

Billie Rogers twisted the mike stand closer and raised her arms to the
applause. "Thank you. Wow. Thank you very much. And thank you,
Thomas Fats Waller." A man in the back of the room whistled. "Hey!
Right! . . . You people sure have made this a lot of fun. Listen, I want to,
you know, introduce somebody now, and see if we can't get him to play
something with us." She walked to the edge of the dais, and put her hand
through the arm of the crumpled black suit. "This is my grandfather, Mr.
Jubal Rogers from Charleston." Smiling, people clapped, as she drew the
man forward up onto the stage.

Fastening on the old ebony mouthpiece, Rogers said, "Okay, girl . . .
what can you sing?"

"What can you play?"

His chin jerked up. "Anything that's got music."

Billie nodded. "Well, I can sing anything that's got words." Toutant
Kingstree laughed.

"That so?" said Rogers, testing his reed.

". . . Yeah. It is."

"Okay . . . You know 'Mother's Son-in-Law'?"

"Sure."

"Kingstree and I'll do the first sixteen. I'm going to take it fast. You be
ready."

She raised an eyebrow, then smiled. "Ready and waiting," she said.

You don't have to have a hanker . . . to be a broker or a banker.
No-sir-re, just simply be . . . my mother's son-in-law.

Allen Thornhill was standing behind his drums, applauding too, so that
Raleigh couldn't hear at first what his father was saying. "Sorry, Daddy?
Help you what?" He bent over the chair, putting his ear beside the man's
tightened lips. All color had faded from the lips and the cheeks, so that the
eyes looked even bluer.

Earley's voice was a thin cool whisper. "Help me out."

"You want to leave? Want me to get a doctor? Let's go."

Earley shook his head. "No, I want you to do me a favor. Will you?"

Raleigh's pulse jumped in his neck. "Of course. What is it?"

"We were planning on doing one of my favorites at the end. Howsoever." Earley shifted in the metal chair, and smiled. "It appears I don't have the heart for it."

"Daddy, don't joke around."

"Stand in for me. Time to bring on the bench, right? Oh, sure you can! 'I Can't Give You Anything But Love.' Just the melody line, that's all. Nothing to worry about. Jubal and Toutant will cover you . . . like a rainbow."

"I'm sorry, but —"

"Quit saying no, Raleigh. I know you know the tune. Remember the first time we did it?"

Raleigh didn't think he remembered, but then he saw himself standing in the makeshift circus-ring with his father, the two trumpets side by side.

Earley pushed his fist against his breastbone. "It was the reunion Hackney hit that homer right up into the park lights. Remember that?"

> *I can be lonely out in a crowd.*
> *I can be humble. I can be proud.*

Earley asked Raleigh to lend him back his jacket because he was cold. But he wouldn't go down to the office to lie down, and he wouldn't go back to the table where Victoria still sat, her hands folded on her purse. "It's because that damn chair's freezing. That's all. I'm just going to sit on the floor here and lean on your friend's piano. I like the way the music feels."

"Daddy, you aren't making any sense."

"Well, haven't you been telling me that for years?" He handed his son the old trumpet, then leaned his head around the corner of the piano. "Hey, Toutant, man, you think this is what Heaven sounds like?"

"Depends on who they got up there now," laughed the saxophonist.

"Listen, y'all, this has all been a little much for an old man. Mind if I send in a substitute? He's got a sweet style, I've heard him play." Earley patted Raleigh's knee. "I swear, Specs, it's the last crazy thing I'll ever ask you to do."

Raleigh rubbed the trumpet against his leg. "Honestly, it's not that I won't. I just couldn't . . . I'm, I'm . . . not like you people. I can't play by ear. I have to have things written down."

"Got a piece of paper?"

"Oh Daddy." Raleigh felt down into the breast pocket of the jacket now wrapped around his father, and found the small account book. "Here. Dammit, I don't believe I'm doing this."

Maybe Tuesday will be my good news day. . . .

Propped against the back of the upright piano, his small legs hugged to his chest. Earley Hayes reached his hand up to put it around Raleigh's over the trumpet. The hand was cold. The blue eyes closed, and, smiling, he said, "Play me on out, son."

Raleigh knelt down close to him. "Don't say that. You aren't going anywhere."

The chest rose and fell. Then a blue eye blinked open. "By fuck, I hope I am."

And Raleigh swallowed a taste like vinegar, and said something he never would have expected to say. ". . . Let me know. I'll be listening."

"Listen up," said Toutant Kingstree. "Y'all ready?" His foot began its slow steady tap. Raleigh Hayes, his tie precisely knotted, his cuff links glittering, pushed on his glasses, and checked again the piece of paper carefully stuck to the top of Berg's fiddle. He watched Kingstree's shoe, then his own began to move with it. "And one. And two. And . . ."

I can't give you anything but love, baby.
That's the only thing I've plenty of, baby.

Raleigh, staring hard at the shaky block-printed letters — G, F♯, E, G — could still see in the corner of his eye Kingstree turn around and nod at him, then step back beside Billie and Jubal Rogers. Mingo swiveled on his stool and raised one fat pink thumb, the other hand bouncing over the keys. Down at the edge of the upright piano, Raleigh could see the shoulder of his father's red shirt, and his bare thin white arm, and his small hand clasped around the neck of the golden horn.

Dream awhile, scheme awhile, you're sure to find
Happiness, and I guess . . .

Above the music, Raleigh heard the sharp sound the trumpet made falling over. He turned his head and saw the horn's gold fluted bell rock once back and forth on the hollow floor. Then the gold blurred, glistening brighter, and Raleigh couldn't blink his eyes clear enough to read the piece of paper.

And it was strange to him, a man who had rested his life on his reason, that while he couldn't see the notes at all, he nevertheless kept on playing, because he could hear them.

CHAPTER

34

Showing Our Hero's Return Home

"RALEIGH, I GUESS WE HAVE TO LOOK ON THE BRIGHT SIDE. He died happy, and that's more than a lot of people do. I mean, just think how he would have felt if you hadn't gotten there, and Gates, and everybody having such a nice dinner together, and the band being such a big hit, and all. Gosh, I wish my daddy had died like that, instead of all by himself in the bathroom after he'd just finished yelling at us for leaving too many lights on. Uh oh, are we moving? It's not supposed to sound like that, is it, Raleigh? Is it? Is it supposed to shake like that? Raleigh, Raleigh!" Mingo Sheffield's eyes were squeezed shut and his fat hands gripped the orange armrests of his seat, as the jet roared up over rice fields now sown by planes, and sugar plantations now cultivated by machines, up into the black sky of stars, over the sparkle of New Orleans.

It was a first-class seat, because two stewardesses had finally agreed that it was simply physically impossible to mash, wad, or otherwise compress Mingo into a coach seat, and that leaving him on top of the armrests was bound to be against safety regulations. On this night-owl flight to Atlanta and then Raleigh-Durham, the "Business Club" section was in any case nearly empty; Victoria Hayes could have sat comfortably in the front of the plane with the two Thermopyleans, but she preferred to stay back in coach by herself. Like her nephew, it was her long habit to think alone.

* * *

Raleigh was taking his father's body home. He had not slept in the more than twenty-four hours that had passed since the ambulance screamed down the alley to The Cave, since doctors pronounced Earley Hayes dead on arrival at the hospital. "Massive coronary thrombosis. Doubt he ever knew what hit him," the doctors pronounced, but Raleigh knew better than that. Then came more than twenty-four of those busy hours with which the world kindly anesthetizes grief and numbs shock, by paperwork and phone calls and the placebo of hundreds of preposterous necessary details. This was the busy world where Raleigh felt at home, and gratefully he hurled himself at its frustrations, knocking over the inert pillars of bureaucracies with ruthless demands for a speedy death certificate, autopsy, embalmment, flight arrangements. Loss had not stunned him into the bewildered passivity on which funeral industries thrive. Instead he'd grown cunning and aggressive and stubborn. He'd demanded forms, argued costs, jumped lines, grabbed telephones, insisted on priorities, and cut his way with lies through the yards of tape that shroud modern death. He told a doctor named Farbstein that he had to hurry the burial because his father was Jewish. He told a mortician named O'Bannion that his "uncle's" body had to reach North Carolina Saturday because a Catholic archbishop was flying there to say the funeral mass. As for burying his "uncle" in an old cassock with a trumpet in his hands, he said the vestment had been worn at the priest's first mass, and the horn had been played at the Vatican. He told the chauffeur driving the hired hearse that he'd give him a twenty-dollar tip if he made it to the airport by three A.M., and he told the highway patrolman who pulled them over for speeding that he was fighting to get his father's body on a plane in time for a ceremony at Arlington National Cemetery. Only on three occasions, from Thursday night (or rather one A.M. Good Friday morning), when, running to the piano, he'd pressed his fingers to his father's neck, until four in the morning on Saturday, when a forklift raised the casket into the belly of the plane, had Raleigh faltered. Once was in the first of his many long-distance calls to Aura; then, her sudden terrible sobs unloosed his own, until finally Victoria had to pry the receiver from the clenched hand holding it against his chest.

The second time was when he found inside a Prayer Book in his father's scruffy suitcase — open on the floor of his small hotel room, and filled mostly with sheet music, mismatched socks and soiled shirts — a picture taken by one of those itinerant photographers who'd once combed neighborhoods with their Shetland ponies looking for children to pose. In it, Gates and Raleigh both sat on the back of the sturdy dappled pony. At the pommel sat Gates, no more than two, his dark curls like a cluster of grapes, his bare toes pointed with delight. Holding him from behind, frowned a thin, stiff-backed boy of eleven, his eyes a glitter of glass.

The third time was when Toutant Kingstree, arriving at the funeral home with a potted Easter lily wrapped in pink tinfoil, solemnly shook Raleigh's hand and said, "Earley was good on the trumpet. I enjoyed playing with him." He added, "Man, turns out I was right, didn't it? You being in the music business after all. I appreciate that ride to New Orleans."

Kingstree was returning to Charleston only long enough to dispose of his private personal property and livestock; then he was coming straight back to the French Quarter. He was convinced, and had convinced Jubal Rogers, that they could find work there as musicians. "Maybe I'm too old for the big time, but I was too good for the small town. Now, I'm home."

While our hero rushed through New Orleans from place to place, his aunt Victoria took care not to rob him, by offering assistance, of any of his time-consuming tasks. She had her own busy work to do to deal with sorrow. And not just new sorrow, but old. And old anger, as well. For in the hospital waiting room, Raleigh had handed her a letter that he said was from Earley. It was, in fact, *to* Earley; sent to him in 1933 from New Orleans, and enclosing an unopened message for "Victoria." A message from Jubal Rogers, asking her — no, telling her — to come to New Orleans and join her life to his. A message from the dead to the dead, written whole lost lives ago, and saved by a man who'd died today, foolishly trying to tear half a century from the past's calendar as if the years had never happened. It was just like Earley to have saved the letter, not to have opened it. To have thought, at twenty, that it was his God-demanded responsibility to run her life for her own good. And to have preserved the evidence of his maddening usurpation of her choice, and, at seventy, to have confessed it. Just like his repenting the decision into which he'd browbeaten her — to put the baby up for adoption — and then, without telling her, bringing Joshua home to Thermopylae. Just like his losing the affection of a wife whom he loved when she'd objected to his decision that the "right" thing for him to do was marry a woman whom, in a casual affair, he'd impregnated. The man was, had been, a fool. And everything he'd done, he'd done for love. So thinking, in that too-bright emergency room lobby, Victoria Hayes had placed the letter in her purse, taken out her notebook, and begun to list the busy necessary details that would keep out of her mind the love, and fury, she felt toward her dead brother.

She comforted Billie, telling her it was as much nonsense to blame herself for Earley's leaving the hospital and racing around the country, as to blame herself for his bad habits, bad diet, and lack of sense.

She broke the news to her siblings in North Carolina. She packed. She opened a savings account for Billie in New Orleans with the money Jubal had returned to Earley. She took a sizable order from the New Orleans–based coordinator of a Central American missions council. She persuaded Billie to sell the smoke-sputtering yellow Cadillac convertible, and then herself bargained with half-a-dozen car dealers until she finally drove one to such exasperation that he paid her almost what she asked. She persuaded Raleigh that it wasn't necessary to hire a driver to bring his Cadillac back to Thermopylae, since Billie had offered to drive it up a few weeks from now, when she came to visit. She talked to Allen Thornhill about college costs. She advised Billie to start familiarizing herself right away with university buildings and the locations of apartment possibilities near grocers and dry cleaners, so that when she returned to New Orleans she'd already know her territory.

She listened to a man to whom Toutant Kingstree introduced her — a man in a blue blazer who said he owned two nightclubs and a radio station — tell her that Billie had a great future in music. She told the man, "Billie's future is Billie's business." She said the same thing to Jubal Rogers the only time she saw him in those twenty-four hours, which was when he appeared Friday morning in the lobby of the St. Ann's Hotel. Victoria said the same thing to Billie herself when the girl asked her how she'd feel if — instead of returning to Thermopylae as they'd arranged — she stayed in New Orleans for a while with her grandfather.

On the airplane, when Raleigh walked back down the aisle to ask his aunt if there were anything he could do for her, she'd been thinking of having said just that to Billie: "If there is ever anything you want me to do for you, that I *can* do, you ask me. But don't ever ask me, or anybody else, permission. Your future is your own business, Billie, where you go, what you do, whom you love. If you never want to set foot in Thermopylae, don't you hesitate to say so. If you don't want Mr. Thornhill's help, tell him no. If you want to move to Timbuctoo, get up and go. That's my advice, take it or leave it. But I hope you will come visit me, whenever you want to. You're a gift to me I never earned."

"You don't have any right to her," Jubal Rogers had said, standing by the doors of the small, spare lobby; his first words. "She came to Thermopylae looking for me. Not you, not Earley. Her name is Rogers, it isn't Hayes. You've got nothing to do with her."

"I know that. I don't claim any right. I didn't claim any right to Joshua. I know that." She'd looked at the man, fully, for the first time in almost fifty years; angry at her cheeks for reddening, at her heart for knocking so fast at her breast. He had changed less than she, but he was still a stranger, and there was nothing familiar in his eyes but their strange gold. Then all at once, someone she'd once known appeared in the eyes, someone no less angry, and she felt she needed to say something to that person, although he might not even remember what she was talking about. She waited until she knew her breath would carry her through, then said, "I never answered your letter because I never got it. Earley thought he was keeping me from making a mistake."

Rogers's chin went up, and stayed cocked, while he searched for a cigarette. Finally he said, "Yeah. Well, you did what you did. I didn't expect anything different."

Her cheeks flamed. "You could have sent the letter straight to me. Not through him. You could have written more than one."

"I could have done a lot of things." His smoke curled toward her. "But would you have done different?"

Her arms tightened around the blue suit jacket. "Yes. I think I would have. I'll go see if Billie's ready."

Up in the front of the plane, Mingo was still ordering drinks of all varieties, in order to save the little bottles for souvenirs, when Raleigh returned from checking again on his aunt. He sat back down and tried urgently to think of something else to do. He couldn't afford to stare out the window at the night. He couldn't afford to close his eyes. He looked at his account book, the superfluous expenses of this trip, never totaled; the scribbled musical staff crossed out when Earley decided it would be easier for Raleigh if he wrote the letters of the notes instead. Feeling through his pockets, Raleigh found the pieces of paper that were either his legacy or another one of his father's moronic jokes. The torn page of the Bible, with its brown marginalia inscribed by a man clearly proud of his name and title: "Gen. G. H. Hayes. General Goodrich H. Hayes. . . . He saith among the trumpets, Ha, ha." No wonder the words had caught Earley's eye. And then, the paper taken from Jimson's bust, with all its odd columns of numbers. Well, here was something to do. Raleigh pulled out his tray, took a pencil, and set to work. He tried adding, subtracting, he tried inches, miles, alphabet substitutions. None of it made sense.

Finally Mingo returned from his long visit to the bathroom. He'd asked Raleigh to accompany him on the trip. "I heard about a lady that opened

the wrong door and fell right out of the plane, and nobody even knew she
was gone till they landed."

"That's impossible, Mingo. Things like that just don't happen." Of
course, maybe, on the other hand, things like that did. "Well, wait till
somebody else comes *out* before you go in."

Now Mingo bounced back into his seat with a souvenir bar of soup.
"Boy, that toilet was a tight squeeze. You know, it looks like it just flies
out a hole in the bottom, right out into the sky!... What's that, Raleigh?"

"I don't know what it is. It's a list of numbers. I'm trying to figure it
out.... Here, what do you think it is?"

Sheffield stared at the yellowed fraying paper.

> 3.15 (6) 1.7 (22-24) 1.5 (31-34)
> 1.7 (17) 1.10 (11-12) 38.6 (11-12) 9.9 (12) 1.7 (18-19) 1.10
>   (5-6) 9.17 (9) 1.2 (7,9-10)
> 41.32 (4) 1.7 (18-19) 41.24 (18)
> 9.9 (12) 42.16 (5-8) 40.17 (7)
> 38.24 (1-7) 2.11 (4) 3.6 (25-30)
> 40.21 40.22
> 40.14 (9-12) 20.25 (11-13) 38.31 (14)

"It's a real old piece of paper," Mingo decided.

"Yes, thank you. But what do you think the numbers mean? When you
look at these numbers, do they say anything to you?"

"Oh." Sheffield's wide face tightened with thought. "Well, gosh, Raleigh, I guess they just look like the Bible to me."

"The Bible?"

"You know, chapter three, verse fifteen. But I don't know about that
extra six. What is this anyhow, is it trigonometry or something? I wasn't
very good at that."

Hayes stared at his friend, then grabbed up the torn opening page of the
Book of Job. All it had on it was Chapter One and part of Chapter Two.
And the Bible itself was packed away in his suitcase. "Mingo, you don't by
any chance have a Bible in your carry-on bag?"

"Gosh, no."

"Well, could you go get the stewardess to find me one? I need a Bible."

Sheffield patted his arm. "I know. I think that's wonderful, Raleigh. It'll
do you a lot of good. When the dark times come over me, I just open the
Savior's book and let Him —"

"Mingo, please, just go find me a goddamn Bible, will you?"

The numbers in parentheses couldn't be whole lines; they were too high. They had to be, yes, individual words in the text. So, he should try Chapter 1, Verse 7, the twenty-second through twenty-fourth words. That meant that 1.7 (22-24) was, let's see . . . "And the Lord said unto Satan, Whence comest thou? Then Satan answered the Lord, and said, From going to and fro *in the earth.*" So, "in the earth." Blank . . . in the earth. And, so, 1.10 (11-12) was "Hast not Thou made an hedge about him, and about *his house. . . ?*" His house. Soon Raleigh had deciphered:

blank   in the earth   according to the number
from   his house   blank blank   going to an hedge

It was possible, it was just possible. . . .

"I got it," said Mingo happily. "A real nice lady back in coach had one in her purse. I hope you don't mind. I told her your daddy died, and a little bit about him, and she wants you to try Psalm Ninety-eight."

"Give it here." Hayes grabbed the Book.

He was so preoccupied he didn't notice until Mingo cut off the circulation in his left arm by grabbing it that they were descending to Atlanta.

"You mean we have to go down and come back up?! Oh God, Raleigh, don't forget my insurance for Vera."

"Mingo, if the plane crashes, I'm not any more likely to be in a position to remember your insurance than you are."

"Oh, why'd you say that? You think it's going to crash?"

"Calm down. We've already landed."

"Then why aren't we *stopping?*"

But after the second successful takeoff, Sheffield decided that maybe airplanes weren't so bad, and maybe he'd been too much of a chicken in avoiding them. Because the stewardesses were really nice, and it was wonderful the way they'd bring you magazines and little snacks whenever you asked them. "That's one thing I've learned on the road with you, Raleigh." Sheffield raised his swizzle stick in a pontificating way: "If you have to, you can do a lot of things."

"Well, yes, that's good, Mingo, but just let me concentrate here, all right? Thank you."

By the time the No Smoking light went off, and Mingo waved his lighter under the cigarette he'd held clamped in his teeth for ten minutes, Raleigh had extracted the message from Job. In so doing, he parenthetically read the miserable man's story, struck by echoes of his own indignation, his own refusals to deny his righteousness, his own realization that his righteousness was, like this tiny aluminum container now shooting through the measureless night, neither here nor there.

Decoded, the instructions, if such they were, left much to be desired, as treasure maps go. The message appeared to say, "Gold in the earth according to the numbers/ From his house corner stone south going to an hedge multiplieth seven-and-three/ Path going to millstone/ South an hundred and forty cedar/ By what way is the light parted? Three into the number of the months./ He lieth under the shady trees, in the covert of the reed, and fens. The shady trees cover him with their shadow; the willows of the brook compass him about/ Thy own right hand the glittering sword. Orion."

Raleigh ordered himself a scotch. Hadn't he always been good at logic problems, at cartography, at thinking things through? All right. What did he have? There was gold in the earth according to the [following] numbers [measurements]. From [Goodrich Hayes's] house['s] cornerstone, [proceed] south going to an hedge. Multiplieth seven and three? [Twenty-one feet, yards?] Path going to millstone. . . . He tried to imagine walking in the tangled underbrush at Knoll Pond. The stone foundations of the old house were still there, moss covered, a home for spiders, slugs, and ants. If he started there, and walked south, yes, he'd be headed toward the pond. Say he found the path to the millstone. Then south again, "an hundred and forty" — it must be feet — to a cedar. Well, why shouldn't the cedar still be there? "By what way is the light parted?"

"What did you say, Raleigh?"

"By what way is the light parted?"

"You mean, where does the sun go down? Is this like a crossword puzzle?"

"God bless you, Mingo."

All right. West. Three into the number of months was four. Four feet. Then all this stuff about shady trees and willows and fens and reeds. Ah, okay, he was down by the cabin [Jess's hearth?] near the pond now. He could remember the two willows, and the catspaws in the muddy water. Thine own right hand the glittering sword? Orion? Obviously, the constellation, the Hunter, wasn't it? Wasn't it near the Big Dipper? But what did it mean? Had there really been gold bullion lying buried there, all those years, all those days of lazy peaceful fishing and dreaming stories in the clouds?

"Aunt Vicky," said Raleigh, crawling into the empty seat beside her place at the window. Across the aisle, a man stared glazed at his briefcase. "I thought maybe you'd be asleep. I don't see how you've borne up under all this."

The old traveler was mending rips and unraveled edges in a lapful of white handkerchiefs. "I am a little tired," she said — an astonishing admission from her.

"Well, you'll be home soon, and you can get some rest. . . . What are you going to tell the family? I mean, about Billie?"

She looked at her nephew. "The truth. What else would I tell them? If they bother to ask me. And if they don't, I won't tell them anything."

"Can I tell you something, Aunt Vicky? It's just that I think that was very brave of you, getting Toutant to call Jubal about Billie. It can't have been easy to see him, now."

"He never was an easy man." Her needle moved briskly in and out of the white linen. "Why should he be? *How* could he? Compared to him, I never did anything that wasn't easy. So, listen to me, Raleigh, don't call me brave. It makes me want to spit." She turned her head to look out the thick beveled window as the airplane tilted its wings to circle back to earth. Bright lines of rose-red light now streamed through the darkness, like the pennants of an army marching across the sky.

"The sun's coming up," Victoria said. "I've traveled far and wide for fifty years, and it always surprises me."

CHAPTER

35

In Which Raleigh Inherits a Fortune

"Morning, Mr. Hayes. You okay? Kaiser Bill's right here, just like he told you on the phone. Don't fret your mind." The large black man stood, just inside the flight arrivals gate, puffing on the pipe that hung below his white Teutonic mustache. Dressed in a blue work shirt with a red tie that must have been a Christmas present — for it had "ho ho ho" in small letters all over it — the Forbes Building janitor towered above the bleary passengers who filed past him into the overlit echoing corridor.

Raleigh let his aunt and Mingo walk ahead. Then he took Mr. Jenkins's arm in order to speak to him; the arm was a heavy, helpless weight, and, embarrassed, he couldn't make himself let go of it. So arm in arm, the two walked into the airport lobby.

"Thank you, Bill, I really appreciate this. And I appreciate your brother-in-law's letting us hire his hearse. I hadn't remembered you had relatives in the funeral business. I was simply planning to ask if I could rent your station wagon. But this will work out much better, because frankly I've been a little worried about the airline officials."

"Un hunh. . . . So how are you, you doing all right? I tried passing the word to you, how you could of come on home sooner. Those old troubles we had? 'Spect you know, it all got fixed. She's back, good as new."

Once again, Raleigh had no idea what Kaiser Bill Jenkins was talking about. This time he said so. "Bill, what are you talking about? Who's back?"

"Your secretary."

"Betty Hemans?"

"Naw, she's gone. Least, she's going, soon's you show up, is what she says. Looks like you messed up bad with that lady. She took a hate to you. Naw, I'm talking 'bout the other one. She's back. The one you thought you'd, you know. . . ." Jenkins suddenly went limp, flopping his head to the side and sticking his tongue out.

"Ah, Bill, excuse me. Let me just put my aunt in a cab, then we'll go to the baggage room."

Mingo didn't really see why they couldn't have let Vera and Aura know when their plane was arriving, instead of Raleigh's hiring Kaiser Bill Jenkins to pick them up. And although Vicky Anna had claimed that if she hadn't minded riding around the world alone in oxcarts, rickshaws, junks, mail planes, and donkey wagons, she certainly wouldn't mind taking a cab alone to Thermopylae — still, Mingo hated to see an elderly single woman go off by herself with a strange taxi driver at 5:30 in the morning.

However, Raleigh said he had his reasons. And even if his friend hadn't had his reasons, Mingo's philosophy was, as he reminded himself, "If you're going to stick with a person, then stick with a person," and if that person didn't want his father taken to Baggett Mortuary, where all the other dead white Thermopyleans went; if that person preferred the services of the Negro funeral parlor, Thomason & Jenkins, well, that person undoubtedly had his reasons for that too, and ought to be stuck by. Of course, probably Ernie Baggett would have sent more people than one single, handicapped, elderly relative to collect the remains, so that the mourners would not have been obliged to load the casket into the hearse themselves. On the other hand, Ernie Baggett might not have wanted his hearse packed with suitcases, a steamer trunk, and a bass fiddle, on top of the coffin. Further on the other hand, Thomason & Jenkins did have a very handsome white Cadillac hearse, lined with white tufted satin (much grander than the Baggett model), and its stereo radio speakers were of a very high quality, which Earley Hayes certainly would have appreciated, loving music as he did. Further still on the other hand, Ernie Baggett had always been sort of fussbudgety about his funerals, always handing you special pens with his name on them, and making you sign forms he took one by one out of vinyl folders with his name on them; always rearranging the flowers in their sponge bases; even measuring the distance between the folding chairs with a snap-out yardstick. So maybe Ernie would have come

up with some finicky objections to Raleigh's burial plans. Maybe he
wouldn't have wanted to drive his hearse off Hillston Road up onto a dirt
lane that wasn't as wide as the tires, causing shrub branches to whack the
sides like those brushes at an automatic car wash; causing the casket to
bounce around as if Earley Hayes had changed his mind and was trying to
get out. Ernie Baggett might have simply declined to associate his mortuary with what apparently (despite Mingo's advice) was going to be a funeral in the woods, with no guests to speak of, and therefore nobody to
appreciate what Ernie was always calling "that little something extra, the
Baggett touch."

While Mingo, wedged in the back, between the old trunk and the
gleaming new coffin, was mentally sticking by Raleigh, in the front of the
hearse, Kaiser Bill was analysing the risks of doing the same. It was not
the fifty dollars the insurance agent had offered him by phone from New
Orleans that had brought the Kaiser to Raleigh Durham airport at five in
the morning on Holy Saturday, a vacation day when he might have been
sleeping late. It was rather his continuing conviction that the Man Upstairs had assigned him Raleigh Hayes to watch over; just as He'd assigned
Gabriel to help out Joshua, and other angels to help out Daniel. The Kaiser therefore needed to know precisely how hot a fiery furnace Hayes had
walked into this time — after God had already saved him once by bringing
his young secretary back to life.

Holding tight to the steering wheel with his one good hand, as the long
white car lurched over ruts and around trees up the hill, to Knoll Pond,
Bill pushed his chewing gum to the side of his teeth, and said to Raleigh,
"You catch up with Jubal Rogers?"

"Yes. Yes, I did."

"He in the coffin?"

"Good God, no! I told you, Bill, my father passed away."

"Un hunh. . . . Who's in the trunk?"

"What? The trunk?" Raleigh put on his prescription sunglasses in order
to look at the driver. The pink sky had now caught fire, and the rising sun
blazed through thick-grown pines and oaks atop the knoll. "You mean in
the back? Mingo Sheffield, a friend of mine."

Politesse was not only the Kaiser's natural inclination, it was a safety
screen against actionable knowledge. He rephrased his question. "We fixing to bury that old black trunk too?"

"Why in the world should we do that? We're just going to bury my
father. Wait. I think this is where the house was. Can you stop here?"

"Sure can."

Hayes jumped out of the hearse and began beating with a stick at the high weeds.

"He's pretty upset," said Mingo Sheffield to Jenkins. The two men stood beside the car door, watching the insurance agent, his arms extended as if he were walking a tightrope, put one foot carefully in front of the other — counting his steps aloud as he tramped toward a bramble hedge. Then he pulled pieces of paper from his pocket and stood there studying them.

Now, however far the Kaiser believed Hayes to have gone in his obviously persistent messing with trouble, he did not believe him capable of murdering his own father. Consequently, he'd concluded as soon as he saw it, that there was somebody *else*'s body in the gleaming rosewood casket; and if not more bodies in the steamer trunk, then more stolen money — all of which Hayes planned to bury out here in the middle of nowhere. It was therefore a shock to hear the unmistakable sincerity in the fat white man's sigh as he repeated, "Boy, Raleigh's so upset about his daddy's dying, I'm not sure he hasn't lost his mind a little bit. Listen, Kaiser Bill, maybe we ought to try to stop him. I mean, gosh, why is he burying Earley out here in the woods, when they've got such a nice family plot just waiting right there at the cemetery in Thermopylae?"

"What's he doing now?" asked Bill, squinting his large brown eyes into the sun to follow Hayes as he suddenly spun to the left, ran forward, then dropped to his hands and knees in the underbrush.

"Well, I guess he thinks he's looking for some buried treasure from the Civil War. That's what he was talking about on the plane."

"That so? Un hunh." Jenkins stood still, thoughtfully stroking his white mustache, while he watched the insurance man march in one direction, then wheel about and march in another, then stride over the knoll toward the little ramshackle cabin that was sheltered in willow trees beside the red muddy fishing pond. A new message was coming down to the custodian from the Man Above. Or a new interpretation: Hayes was still obviously a lost soul; but maybe not willfully lost; maybe not a shrewd criminal leading a double life. Maybe Hayes was simply touched in the head. Like that old white fellow that had died years back, the one that used to rob women's clotheslines, that Elwood Bragg. Maybe all those things he'd heard that the police were so confused about — like pouring paint on the store clothes and robbing cannonballs off the monument — maybe Hayes had done them all for no more reason than Elwood Bragg had stolen girdles. What after all would any sane person want with that big ugly statue belonging to the library that he'd seen Hayes hiding in his office?

This new interpretation in no way mitigated the Kaiser's responsibility. Quite the reverse. He now looked in Sheffield's eyes for the first time. "You a friend of his?"

"I'm his best friend," the fat man replied, breaking into a trot as Raleigh stumbled back over the top of the knoll and yelled, "Mingo, would you mind bringing me that sword out of the trunk?"

"We don't want to let him mess with swords," Bill called after the fat man. "But les' don't rile him either. Best thing to do is coax him on home easy like."

It was not the fact that Raleigh was looking for treasure, but the fact that he was looking for treasure and burying his father at the same time and in the same place that was bothering Mingo Sheffield. Mingo would not have been as wholly Southern as he was had he discounted out of hand (despite Victoria's opinion that he and Raleigh were idiots to believe rubbish like the Goodrich Hayes gold story) the possibility of Confederate treasure being buried at Knoll Pond, or, indeed, under any and every old tree below the Mason-Dixon Line. Like a great many people in Thermopylae — all of whose ancestors had been dirt-poor scratch farmers without a single silver candlestick to their names — Mingo had from time to time lamented the fortune his family had lost in the War, and had wondered if some brave Sheffield woman might not have slipped out in the moonlight to save her sterling from Sherman's whirlwind. He had no idea who such a courageous, small-waisted, fiery-eyed creature might have been — and it appeared that Gates Hayes would not be tracing his genealogy to find out for him anytime soon — but Mingo imagined her as a perfect wife to that gallant officer, St. Hilary George Stonewall Phillippe Sheffield — or something like that — who was always curling his upper lip as he said, "Sirs, we shall never surrender," and was always gracefully expiring without dropping the banner of the Stars and Bars. Where St. Hilary and his beloved might have lived, and hidden their fortune, Mingo had no idea. He didn't even know where all of his grandparents had lived. Raleigh was much luckier; at least he knew where to look, for the Hayeses must have somehow managed to keep the old homestead right in the family all these generations.

Mingo had no idea that there actually had been a Sheffield who had fought for the South, a Private Zachery Sheffield — Zinc to his friends — who had, one June evening in 1864 on Kennesaw Mountain in Georgia, actually had a conversation with a Colonel Goodrich Hale Hayes. But their talk hadn't been about gold. And Zinc had borne not the slightest resemblance to the imaginary chevalier, St. Hilary George.

Goodrich Hale Hayes, a longhaired, full-bearded, thin-nosed dandy, and a glory-crazed suicidal maniac, had stopped that hot evening to scrape his knee-high boot against the log on which Zinc Sheffield was sitting, bare-footed, in a homemade coat (dyed a butternut yellow with walnut hulls) and a patched pair of pants pulled off a dead gunner from Tennessee. Zinc was eating a cup of watery cornmeal, and with his finger he was following the words in a *Phunny Fellow* comic book that he'd pasted inside *Satan's Bait* — a tract the chaplain had handed out.

"I like to see a man preparing his soul for battle," said Hayes on this occasion. "Sadly, soldier, most of your companions are not so inclined." And he pointed at the collection of thin rags lying about the camp. He was right. Not a one looked to be preparing his soul. Some were playing chuck-a-luck with homemade dice; some were betting on a louse race; some were toasting grains of corn picked up off roads where Yankees had been carelessly feeding their horses. One was singing "Annie Laurie." One was writing a letter with blackberry juice. One was standing in tears hold-ing a twenty-pound cannonball attached to a leg chain, and wearing a sign that said, "I STOLE A PIG." (Colonel Hayes was a strict enforcer of the rules.) And others of the Rebels were only scratching fleas or swatting flies or shaking with malaria or lamenting feet lost to frostbite or arms lost to gangrene.

"Where are you from, private?" asked Colonel Hayes, and when he learned that Sheffield came from a North Carolina town not many miles from Thermopylae, and had served in Tennessee as well as Georgia, he condescended to ask him how he liked the adventuring life of a soldier.

"I cain't to-reckly say, sir. I seen a rite smart of the world since I left home," replied Zinc, licking with his finger the last grains of meal from the tin cup. "I guess that's all right. But this army vittles of yourn is woss than horse pittle. Dyerear turned loose on me with the Georgia Shits well nigh going on a week now."

". . . I see. Well, good luck to you tomorrow, private. The Cause is in God's hands." And Hayes strode away, his long curls brushing his shoul-ders, the filigreed sword he called Orion, the Hunter, brushing his thigh.

After Atlanta, Private Zachery Sheffield left the Cause in God's hands, and walked home to North Carolina to harvest his tobacco. He got there long before (now General) G. H. Hayes's hard-pressed party arrived in Thermopylae with the wagonload of Dahlonega bullion. Despite subsequent rumors to that effect, it had never occurred to General Hayes to embezzle the gold which he secretly (and he assumed, temporarily) buried near the cabin of his wife's cook, Jess. He simply wanted to keep it safe while he went to do something important before proceeding to Virginia. And so he spent his last afternoon at home with his wife and children, off by himself devising his biblical code, and hiding it under a brick in Jess's hearth. Then he galloped away with his high boots and his sword Orion to beat the hell out of Sherman at the Battle of Bentonville. It certainly never occurred to Goodrich Hayes that a minié ball could blow a hole through his handsome head in the very first minutes of that engagement. If he'd been the kind of man capable of conceiving such a possibility, he probably never would have been wealthy enough to build Knoll Pond House by the time he was twenty-five, or promoted enough to become a general by the time he was twenty-eight, or crazy enough to have high-jumped his horse over a gully full of Yankees by the time he was twenty-nine.

It also never occurred to him to tell his wife there were four dozen three-pound bars of gold planted in a wooden crate six feet under a patch of sumac near her willow trees. Consequently, when Kilpatrick's Federal cavalry questioned her on the matter, she honestly had nothing to tell them. Nor could anything they did (killing her last prize chickens, stealing her jewelry, smashing her piano and pulling out its wires to cook their coffee on), not even vandalizing her house and then burning it down, persuade Mrs. Hayes to confess what she didn't know. Finally, they decided that the local gold story was just another false rumor, and off they rode, kitchen matches in their saddle bags to set fire to Thermopylae. Mrs. Hayes and her children moved into what was left of the town, and with the money she made by selling to Carolina Crockery the clay pits where her husband's hot springs had once flowed, she built a big house on East Main Street.

But for the next hundred years the gold story was passed down, mangled this way or that — Hayes had robbed the entire Confederate Treasury, slaves had murdered Hayes and stolen the gold, Mrs. Hayes had murdered Hayes and stolen the gold, Mrs. Hayes had murdered the slaves, Yankees had stolen the gold — and occasionally someone would even go out to Knoll Pond and poke around with a stick. Occasionally, while he was fishing or reading on the pond bank, Earley Hayes would hear the gold seekers wandering about, snapping branches and raking aside leaves back up in the woods near the ruins of his ancestor's house.

* * *

"All right, rest a minute, Mingo. Climb out. I'll take another turn." Raleigh Hayes jumped waist-deep into the hole, and began immediately to shovel out the dark red clay. Sheffield scrambled over the side and lay down panting beside Bill Jenkins, who leaned against the willow tree with his pipe and his pint bottle of cherry brandy. "You want a sip?" he asked the fat man.

"Oh boy, thank you, yes," Mingo gasped, accepting the bottle. "I just wish I had a Coca-Cola. I'm hot as fire, and it's not even eight o'clock."

"Digging's warm work," the Kaiser commiserated. Because of his withered arm, he'd been able to help only by sympathizing with Sheffield, whose loyal devotion to a crazy person like Hayes — carried even to the extent of helping the poor soul dig a big hole in the ground — he found worthy of admiration.

Raleigh Hayes was certain the message was real. He was certain as soon as he'd found the dead cedar tree exactly 140 feet from the half-buried gray millstone, as soon as he'd suddenly remembered having seen (engraved in Italianate script on the scrolled hilt of the sword his father had used to slit open the trunk), the word *Orion,* as soon as he'd walked four feet west from the middle of the willow trees, held out the sword in his extended right arm, looked down and seen that not only was the ground there noticeably lower than its surroundings, but a large stone was sticking out of the earth, into which an "H" had been so deeply scratched that it was still visible. He was certain he was in the right place. He was certain the gold was there.

Mingo was not quite so certain; plus he wanted to go home and see Vera, and get some sleep, and get ready to sing in the choir on Easter Sunday, his favorite church day; plus he wanted to get Raleigh home to Aura so that she could persuade him to give his father a decent funeral even if he hadn't wanted one.

Bill Jenkins was certain that the gold wasn't there, that Raleigh Hayes was as mad as a hatter, and that Mingo Sheffield was a garrulous paradigm of the Good Book's enjoinder to love your neighbor as yourself, even if he were a killer or a lunatic.

So Mingo and Kaiser Bill sat with the brandy bottle under the shady willow tree, while Mingo recounted to the janitor what he described as his Adventures on the Road (which Jenkins later described to his wife as "A Bunch of Whoppers"): the Battle of Stone Mountain, the Rescue of Weeper Berg, the Barbecue at "Wild Oaks," the Kidnapping by Hell's Angels, the Routing of the Ku Klux Klan, the Triumph in The Cave, the duel, the nuns, Diane's baby, Earley's death — tale after tale, until Jenkins received word from the Man Upstairs that the fat one beside him was just as off his rocker as the thin one down in the hole, and no wonder they were such good friends.

Eventually, warmed by the sun and the brandy, the Kaiser dozed off. Mingo took another turn at the shovel, after which Raleigh suggested that he take a break and stroll down to the pond, and maybe look at the old cabin, too, and see what kind of condition it was in. Sheffield decided his friend just wanted to be alone with his thoughts for a while, so off he ambled through the woods alone.

What a nice spot, Mingo decided, this gentle slope leading to the water's edge. Then he had a wonderful idea. Wouldn't this be a perfect place for the outdoor drama Vera had once talked about organizing? The outdoor show that would put Thermopylae on the map, the way "The Lost Colony" had done for Manteo, and "Unto These Hills" had done for Boone. And Vera's idea was even bigger and better than a history pageant about Sir Walter Raleigh's poor lost colonists, or a pageant about the rotten way America had treated the poor Cherokee Indians. For Vera's idea was to do the Greatest Story Ever Told, using the townspeople to play Jesus and the disciples and the Romans and Jerusalemites and all — just the way they did it in that little German town Raleigh had told them about — Obeydamnarung, or something like that. Mingo had always thought it was one of Vera's very best ideas, and it was really a shame they'd never had the venture capital to get it started. He could see the billboards at the town limits right now: "THERMOPYLAE, NORTH CAROLINA. HOME OF THE GREATEST STORY EVER TOLD." And they wouldn't do it in a gloomy way either; they'd concentrate on the happy times — with lots of blind people getting their sight back, and cripples leaping around, and water turned into wine, and then at the end Mary Magdalene (Vera would be wonderful playing that part) rushing to tell Peter that the tomb was empty. Why, this pond would make a perfect Sea of Galilee. They could put in a long ramp just under the surface, so Jesus could walk on the water out to talk to the fishermen in their boat. The Savior could do the Sermon on the Mount from that little hill right over there, and the cabin could be both the stable at Bethlehem and Pilate's palace, and if they cleared out all that poison ivy . . . Well, maybe after the lingerie business got on its feet, and put Vera and him back on theirs, he could talk to Raleigh about renting this Knoll Pond property; maybe Raleigh would even like to be partners. It always helped to have a good thinker in your organization, to help iron out the details.

* * *

While Bill Jenkins was napping, and as soon as Mingo Sheffield left to take his stroll, Raleigh Hayes quit digging. He'd come to a decision, having carefully weighed his responsibility to carry out his father's burial wishes against his responsibility not to involve his companions in an illegality, against his responsibility to the living Hayeses, who (he well knew) would want to share in Earley's death, would want to see him laid to rest among the family. And having made his decision, Raleigh grabbed the hammer and screwdriver out of the janitor's tool kit, and raced with them back to the hearse.

When Sheffield returned from surveying his future amphitheater, he didn't see his friend under the willows, and horrified that the dark times might have swept over Raleigh and put terrible thoughts in his head, the fat man trotted as fast as he could back up to the hearse. But all Hayes was doing was trying to pull the old black trunk out of the back.

"Gosh, Raleigh. Why are you taking that out? In case we find the gold?"

Hayes, red-faced and sweaty, sat down on top of the steamer trunk. "Listen to me, Mingo. I thought about everything you said on the plane, and I've decided you were right. Even if it was Daddy's last wish to be buried out here at Knoll Pond, I've decided you're absolutely right."

"I am?"

"Yes. So I've changed my mind. We'll take the casket back to Thermopylae. It's not fair to the family. Daddy ought to have a proper funeral, and he ought to be in the cemetery with the people he loved, just like you said."

Mingo, pleased and honored, squeezed his friend's shoulder. "Gosh, I know it wasn't easy, but I think you're doing the right thing, Raleigh, I really do. And I bet Earley would understand too."

"I'm sure he would. And I appreciate your advice. . . . Now, listen, Mingo. Daddy also wanted me to bury this old trunk out here."

"He did? Why?"

"Ah, Mingo, it has a sentimental aspect that he associated with Knoll Pond, and, ah, he felt, well, maybe it's hard to explain, and maybe he wasn't all that rational, but what difference does it make, and let's just do this one little thing for him, okay?"

"Well, sure. . . . But aren't we going to keep digging for the gold since we started?"

"Of course we are. Here, grab that handle, will you? That's right. Be careful. Stay on the path."

"Hey, Raleigh, maybe we could bury the trunk in the gold hole, and not, you know, have to dig another one."

Hayes called back over his shoulder as they struggled down the hill with the heavy trunk. "Mingo, that's a great idea."

"Well, it just sort of occurred to me."

"Good thinking."

At nine o'clock, Kaiser Bill awakened, took a few contemplative sips of brandy, gave his mustache a few meditative strokes, and started to wonder if he shouldn't sneak away and telephone Mrs. Hayes to come collect her husband. She seemed like a nice woman, with a good head on her shoulders, and always with a friendly hello whenever they passed each other in the Forbes Building, even though she was always in a bustle. Maybe she'd been too busy to notice how her man had pretty well lost his mind. Maybe the Kaiser ought to drive her out here to take a look at him, bare-chested and bare-footed, up to his shoulders now in the hole.

"It's too bad Gates isn't here, isn't it, Raleigh?" said Mingo, leaning over the side of the deep pit, and keeping out of the way of the flying dirt. "He was so interested in the Civil War. It's hard to believe he just left without even saying good-bye, but I guess he was too shy. I sure hope he'll come back for Christmas, and bring Weeper, so I can give him back his bass fiddle. Gosh, we could start our own band here in Thermopylae. You've got these trumpets, and I've still got that clarinet.... Boy, I sure hope they come back someday."

"Me too," Raleigh panted, and at that moment the handle of Jenkins's shovel quivered in his hand as the blade struck something harder than clay. Holding his breath, Raleigh stabbed all around the area. "Mingo? Mingo? *Mingo!*"

Sheffield jumped down beside him, and together on their hands and knees, they flung away earth from what was undeniably, indisputably, and soon enough, absolutely visibly, the rotted, caved-in lid of a long wood chest. Raleigh spit on his hands and rubbed hard at the oak boards. He could see a black *A,* then in front of that a black *S,* then in front of that a black *C.*

"C.S.A.," he whispered. "I'll be goddamned."

"Dear Jesus," Mingo whispered. "C.S.A. Confederate States of America. Raleigh, Raleigh, it's true!"

And peering down on them, Kaiser Bill received still another interpretation from Above. This man Raleigh Hayes was the *special* kind of crazy. He had the Power. Like that mean old spinster woman he kept asking about, Flonnie Rogers, who used to come around and charge you a dollar to scare off ghosts, or tell you where to dig your well. When Hayes had started beating through the weeds with that stick earlier on, he'd been divining for the treasure, and he'd felt his way right to it. Right to it!

After pulling and digging and scraping for ten minutes, the Thermopyleans gave up trying to raise the rotted box out of the hole. Instead, they pried the planks off the lid, one by one, shoving away the falling dirt.

They knelt back so the sun could shine in on all the gold.

It didn't.

"Oh, Raleigh, Raleigh, it's empty!"

No one spoke for a full minute, then, "Ha ha," said Raleigh Hayes, and knelt there, hearing very distinctly the gloat of a blue jay behind him in the willow tree.

But Mingo was prying off another plank. Then another. "No, wait," he cried, "What's that?"

Light flickered over a dull gleam at the very bottom of the deep chest. Reaching his arm in through the ripped wood, Hayes pulled out a small, square, dented metal container that appeared to have once been covered with canvas or leather. Clots of decayed fabric fell off in his hands when he held it up to the light.

They had to chisel the top off the little box. Inside there were two relicts of the War Between the States. One was a personal letter written on the back of an official military document regarding the transport of forty-eight bars of Confederate bullion from the Dahlonega mint to the Richmond treasury.

The other relict was a very real and still very yellow and still brightly glowing small rectangle of solid gold.

The personal letter was written in smudged lead. It was not easy to read, not easy to comprehend, and not easy to accept.

This is what it said:

> I wisht i could see yor Face you G.D. son of a bitch Hays when you no yor goal is misen and I taken it. i gess this puts you in the shithouse, dont it? wen they dont beleave you aint got it.
>
> i'm writing caus i *waunt* you to no. Whoo follered you closter than Flees all the way form Attlanta? Whoo wawtched and wated untell you buryed it? And whoo come back and TOK IT?

CAVIN BUNCOMB

You had no call to Speake slack about me and call me wurthless afore my friends and Put a brand on a white man like he wus a Mule, and drum me out ans sutch.

Now yore paed. it'll Bee a coal day in Hell when sumboddy throws a stigmey on Cavin Buncomb and i don't take cear of him Good. I hope the hole G.D. Yankey armey tromples you bludy.

You ken ceep 1 bar so as evryday you dont never for get CAVIN BUNCOMB who were as good a rebbil and jest as white as you, Hays.

Yrs, Serg. Cavin BUNCOMB

Unseen in the sun sparkle of the willow tree, the blue jay laughed on and on. And before long, Raleigh Hayes joined him, and the insurance man laughed and laughed until tears rolled plinking down his cheeks onto the metal box. He said, *"Cavin Buncomb?"* and laughed. He pointed at the "HO HO HO" on Bill Jenkins's tie, and laughed some more. He danced bare-chested up and down in his bare feet on the shoveled mound of clay, and laughed some more. He laughed until Kaiser Bill, tapping his temple with his pipe stem, whispered to the speechless Sheffield, "Poor soul. He's gone now. Bill told him not to mess with trouble the way he kept on doing, and now it's took him off for certain."

Mingo Sheffield hated to concur, but he was shaken. Even Mingo had to wonder if his friend hadn't been felled by this latest blow from Fortune — who'd cruelly tantalized him with a genuine buried treasure, after she'd already let some spiteful rotten bastard, like whoever that Cavin Buncomb was, rob it all (or practically all) a hundred years before Raleigh even got there — even Mingo had to wonder if Raleigh hadn't right in front of his eyes suffered a permanent nervous breakdown. Because laughing and dancing when you'd just lost a fortune (and your father) was strange enough. And burying a steamer trunk was strange enough (even if your father had begged you to do it). But asking people to bow their heads while you read Psalm 98 over a buried steamer trunk — that just wasn't like the old Raleigh at all.

Praise the Lord upon the harp; sing to the harp with a psalm of thanksgiving. With trumpets also and cornets.

Let the sea make a noise, and all that therein is; the round world, and they that dwell therein.

Let the floods clap their hands, and let the hills be joyful together.

"Amen," said Raleigh, closed his father's Prayer Book, and shoveled the first dirt clattering down onto the metal lid.

"Amen," said Mingo, for company's sake.

"Amen," said Bill Jenkins, who didn't for a moment believe that the fat man knew what he was talking about when he said the trunk was full of old souvenirs. No doubt that's what Hayes had told his friend. But the Kaiser was certain that the trunk contained some poor soul's body.

"I'm really sorry somebody stole all your gold, Raleigh," sighed Mingo as they drove around the curve of the beltway at noon on Holy Saturday, and saw again the Forbes Building looking down on the little skyline of Thermopylae. "Gollee, just think, if that nasty guy hadn't hated your ancestor so much, you would have been a rich man!"

Raleigh Hayes patted the shiny rosewood casket that was stuffed with old clothes, old pictures, old trinkets, and a few large stones for ballast. He started laughing again. "Mingo, I *am* a rich man. And when I say that, I'm not just yanking your wank."

And the insurance agent kept on laughing so wholeheartedly that, despite themselves, Bill Jenkins and Mingo Sheffield finally started laughing, too.

CHAPTER

36

Wherein the Story of Raleigh W. Hayes
Draws to a Close

BRIGHTNESS OF THE MORNING gleamed through the rose-stained window glass. Flowers garlanded every pew rail. In baskets before the altar, lilies lifted their white-petaled horns. New dresses rustled and new hats tilted up when all together the congregation of Thermopylae's Baptist church stood to welcome Easter. In the back row of the choir stall, Mingo Sheffield, his robe yards and yards of robin's egg blue, sang out beaming as if he'd just heard the news, "Jesus Christ is risen today! Alleluia!" Beside him, Pierce Jimson's pious baritone boomed its moral certainty. "Sinners to redeem and save. Alleluia!" Two rows down, next to Mrs. Ned Ware, and the only soprano with a green streak painted across her blond hair and a pink feather hanging from her creamy ear, Caroline Victoria Hayes sang, "Where the angels ever sing. Alleluia!"

And next to the organist, at his own request, by special arrangement with the choir, to the delight of his family (some of whom cried as they sang), to the astonishment of his neighbors (some of whom lost their places in their hymnals), stiffly stood Raleigh W. Hayes, deacon, Civitan, and Mutual Life insurance agent. Wearing a three-piece suit and frowning behind his glasses, Mr. Hayes was accompanying the organ and choir on a trumpet so highly polished that it glistened like gold.

"The strife is o'er, the battle done. The victory of life is won. The song of triumph has begun. Alleluia!"

From where he stood playing, Raleigh could see the congregation, books in hand, sing back to him. He saw, in the first pew, Nemours Kettell beside his only faithful daughter, Agnes. He saw, behind them, the old halfback banker Ned Ware, juggling to turn the page of his hymnal, because for some reason Ned's arm was in a cast, held out from his side by a metal brace. He saw, across the aisle, a large group (mostly women) all wearing on their jackets or hats distinctive round green-and-white buttons. Mr. and Mrs. Wayne Sparks wore them; Holly Hayes and Chief Hood's daughter wore them; Barbara Kettell wore one; Vera Sheffield wore three; all the Millers (the first black family to move to Starry Haven) wore them; most of the Thermopylae PTA and the Thermopylae Friends of the Library wore them. Some of these buttons said, "WHERE THERE'S HAYES, THERE'S HOPE," some said, "NO MORE NUKES, NO MORE LUKES," the one pinned to Wayne Sparks's tie said, "PEACE POWER," and the rest said simply, "HAYES FOR MAYOR."

In the midst of these people, singing on as she wiped her eyes with the tissues Vera kept handing her, was the woman Raleigh knew best in the world; the back of whose neck, the shape of whose ear, the bone of whose wrist he could have chosen from a thousand indifferent pictures, and said, "This is Aura." He caught her eye, and bobbed hello with the trumpet, and she waved up at him, the jade bracelet sliding on her arm, while, alone, their daughter's high sweet soprano sang, "Now the queen of seasons, bright with the day of spendor, With the royal feast of feasts, comes its joy to render."

"*Alleluia!*" shouted Mingo, out on the church steps after the service ended. He had one huge arm around his wife, Vera, who squeezed his hand in both of hers, and one arm around Raleigh Hayes, who resigned himself to the embrace with an embarrassed smile.

Everyone paused under the portal to wish each other a Happy Easter, to swap greetings and gossip until next Sunday. It surprised Raleigh that very few of his fellow Thermopyleans appeared to have even noticed his two-week absence, so almost no one welcomed him back. Some, however, had heard rumors of his father's death, and, accepting their condolences, he explained that the funeral would be tomorrow at St. Thomas Church, and that the casket would be closed. Some of his fellow Civitans asked him when he'd suddenly decided to run for mayor, and some poked him in the ribs or arms and asked him why he was allowing his wife to run for mayor.

"Boy, Raleigh," said Tommy Whitefield, "How does it feel? Don't ask me to open a paper or turn on the tube and there's *my* wife. What are you going to do if she really goes ahead and runs?"

"Vote for her," said Raleigh.

"Oh gollee, what a happy morning!" Mingo threw his arm back around Raleigh. "Look at everybody's new clothes! Look at those daffodils!"

"Jonquils," said Hayes, smiling at Aura. He looked around the steps and lawn at his fellow townspeople. "I'm surprised Betty Hemans didn't come to church. I mean, it's Easter. I was going to try to see if I couldn't get her to listen to reason."

"She's home rewriting her novel," Aura said. "She told me she'd be working all weekend."

"I thought she threw it in the furnace."

"Oh, not the original. But she said she's changing everything. It's not *Remember Me!* anymore. It's *Betrayal!* Lady Evelen finds out her American pilot is a two-timer, and she takes her revenge on every American she meets at the canteen. I don't think I'd try to patch things up with Betty just yet if I were you. Your uncle Whittier! Yowza! I can't wait to read this book."

"Look at those jonquils! Gosh, gosh, the whole world's new," Sheffield bubbled, and then soared irresistibly back into song. " 'Tis the spring of souls today! Christ hath burst his prison!'"

"Sweetie!" Vera shook her enormous spouse. "Stop it! Everybody's staring at us."

"That's probably because they think you're Dolly Parton." Raleigh winked at her, with an eyebrow ostentatiously raised at her lavish blond wig and tight, scallop-necked, white and gold dress.

Vera's sooty lashes fluttered. "Why, Raleigh Hayes, that's one of the sweetest things you ever said to me. . . . Now, tell the truth. Are you excited about Aura's running for mayor, or are you going to be an old chauvinist pig about it?"

"Both," he said.

"Hi ya, Dad," called his daughter Holly.

"Say hey, Mr. Hayes, how's it going?" With Holly was Booger Blair, her seven-foot friend and racing companion. "Hey, I heard something wild. I heard you scored twenty-eight points for the Tomahawks in the state finals way back when. That true?"

"Come on, Booger!" Aura grinned. " 'Way back when'?! We're just heading for our prime."

"Twenty-nine," said Hayes. "Twenty-nine points." He held out his hand to the boy.

Holly tugged on his arm. "Dad, listen, okay if I split? I gotta get out of this straitjacket." She yanked at the lovely leaf-green dress, rolling her eyes.

"Where are you going?" said Hayes.

"Just be at Aunt Vicky's by six," said Aura.

"Don't speed," said Hayes. "There's no reason to exceed the speed limit."

"Welcome back, Dad," smiled Holly Ainsworth Hayes.

Nemours Kettell, clutching his captive daughter Agnes, and shooting his hand angrily over his gray flattop as if he were firing a rocket at Aura, walked past them without a word, but Ned Ware stopped to sigh at Hayes sadly, and to say, "Raleigh, when I heard, I swear my heart went out to you. It's just a tragedy. Your poor daddy. Was *he* driving, or was it her? The, you know, colored girl."

"What? What do you mean, driving?"

"Didn't Earley die in a car crash?" The thick-shouldered banker let go of Raleigh's arm.

"Who told you that? That's not true."

"It's not?"

"No, he died in a nightclub."

Ware tried to keep the grief in his eyes, but excitement pushed it out. "God! In a nightclub! Was, was *she* with him?"

"A lot of his family was with him." Raleigh tapped the man's cast. "Ned, what happened to your arm?"

"Can you believe this?" Ware looked reproachfully at the cumbersome brace. "Unbelievable. Boyd's lucky he's not in jail. I don't know if you heard, but we had to foreclose on Joyner. Anyhow, the guy's a maniac! This is somebody I put in time trying to help, personal and business-wise, you know? So I was standing in the bank last week, and in he comes spewing crazy filth right in front of the tellers."

"He broke your arm?"

"Well, Raleigh, I tell you, even if he did, I still feel real sorry for Boyd. I mean, losing his business, and they say his marriage is pretty damn shaky. But turn the other cheek, that's my kind of philosophy. Lizzie Joyner moved in with her mother, is what I hear. Well, Raleigh, 'course, you know I'll be there for poor Earley's funeral. Tomorrow, right? Is there a viewing at Baggett?"

Raleigh pressed on his glasses. "No, no viewing. The casket's at Thomason and Jenkins."

Ware stepped back amazed, swinging his raised arm into Mrs. Pierce Jimson, who was trying to squeeze past him on the crowded church steps. The old football player whispered, "Raleigh, that's a colored establishment. I mean. I'm no racist but . . . did *she* make the arrangements?"

"I made them. Pardon me, Ned, sorry about your arm. . . . Caroline! *Caroline!* Come back here please!"

Out of her choir robe, Raleigh's beautiful rose and cream daughter was wearing rags. Ripped, tied, straggling pastel rags. "Yo? Oh, Daddy, you were toedully *fab!* Everybody, I mean, everybody was wasted!"

"Ah, that's . . . thank you. And your solo was beautiful, Caroline. Just beautiful. I'm sorry Grandpa wasn't around to hear it."

"I know. . . ." The girl hugged him tightly. "Listen, okay? Mommy says I can still go eat at Kevin's, 'cause it's all, you know, fixed, so I'll see you later at Aunt Vicky's."

"Kevin's? Who's Kevin?"

"Oh, Daddy, you know, Kevin, rilly, Kevin! Holly's off greasing with Booger, so I've got the wagon. Bye. Kiss kiss."

"Greasing? Come back, Caroline, come back here! I'd like to speak to you. I'm not even going to discuss the fact that your hair seems to be turning green. But . . ."

She ran her hand down the lime green stripe. "Jeez! I told you yesterday, like you never ever listen, this is *punk.*"

"No doubt. What happened to your clothes? You can't go to anyone's home on Easter looking like this. Your blouse is ripped right off your shoulders. Did you have an accident? Or is this more of your 'punk'? I'm just trying to understand. You tear up your clothes on purpose?"

"For shurr! They *come* this way, Daddy. Oh hi, Mom. He says fine."

"I do?" Raleigh asked Aura, who'd slipped her arm through his. "What do I say fine to?"

A very tall, slender young black man dressed in a khaki suit was calling up from the foot of the church steps. "CAR! CAR! Let's go! We'll follow my folks. Hey, hi there, Mrs. Hayes, Mr. Hayes. Happy Easter. See you later. Come on, Caroline!"

"Caroline, wait a . . . Aura, where is she going?"

"What do you mean, where is she going? Kevin's. But they'll come over to East Main after supper. Do you think I dare smoke out here, honey? I suppose I have to watch my public image now."

Raleigh stared at his wife, tilting his head to look under the brim of her wide white hat. "Was that Kevin? That young *black* man is Kevin?"

"Oh, Raleigh, you know Kevin. *Kevin.* Kevin Miller."

"That's the *Miller* boy? The Starry Haven Millers?"

Aura waved at a friend. "Of course. How many Millers do we know? Oh God, here comes Pierce Jimson." She nudged her husband in the ribs. "I've got to leave. I'll crack up."

"But, but the Millers' son was only about nine or ten!"

Aura laughed. "About seven or eight years ago! Bye-bye. Yep, the Voice of the Patriarch is headed our way. Yuck, look at that man! Pretending we don't have the goods on him, the slimy creep. Here's poor Boyd Joyner going bankrupt and leaving town, and here's old Pierce buying Knox-Bury's and opening a second branch, and his wife and everybody else still thinks he's Mister Truth and Light."

Pierce Jimson, deep circles under his eyes and his long upper lip twitching with a nervous tic, asked Raleigh Hayes for a moment's privacy. They stepped inside the church foyer, colored light dappling through the windows. "Raleigh, you've destroyed my life," the businessmen began without preamble.

Hayes thoughtfully considered this possibility, then shook his head. "I don't think so, Pierce. You look like you're doing okay to me. Lizzie and Boyd seem to be the ones having the real trouble."

The deep voice cracked in Jimson's tight throat. "I have a position in this town to uphold. I have responsibilities, I have a reputation."

"Oh bullshit."

"I loved Lizzie, you don't understand, but I couldn't allow . . ." Jimson put his hand on his lip to stop it from twitching, and Raleigh oddly thought to himself, And God so loved the world, He really made a mess of things. The burden would have been so much easier on a God who didn't care. . . . Jimson was struggling on to justify himself and blame others. "It's over, Raleigh, and mercifully — despite you and Ned Ware — my wife's been spared any knowledge, and you'd be a fiend to try any more of your vile blackmail schemes. You've got Knoll Pond, now leave me alone."

The furniture merchant started to push past our astonished hero, but Raleigh, as we know, was a very fast thinker. He turned Jimson back, hand on his shoulder. "Hold up, Pierce." And Raleigh smiled. "I understand you're opening a new branch."

Jimson's flesh shriveled away from Hayes's touch. "That's right."

". . . Well, Mingo Sheffield needs a job. He's an excellent interior deco-
rator. And I think he'd make a wonderful manager at your Knox-Bury
store."

The two Better Businessmen stared solemnly at one another for a while.
Then Pierce Jimson bit down on his fidgeting lip, then he nodded yes,
then he slouched back out through the big doors and into the community
of his admirers.

For the first time in anyone in the family's remembrance, Victoria Anna
Hayes had invited her relatives to Easter dinner at the old East Main Street
house of turreted bays and square columns they annoyed her by still calling "Papa's House." They all came, canceling what other plans they might
have made or still hadn't quite made or thought they ought to get around
to making soon. They came because they were touched by Vicky's "little
surprise invitation," and because it seemed right that they should mourn
Earley at the home of the sister who had always been closest to him. They
came to sorrow at Earley's loss and to wish him well. "Wherever he's
gone," said Raleigh's youngest uncle Bassie, propped up at a tilt on the
couch. Or at least they thought that's what Bassie had meant by "Webber
gug-gug-geez on."

"We shall meet, but we shall miss him, there will be an empty chair,"
Lovie Clay sang; and pulling a Kleenex from her bosom of tissues, she
bent down by the wheelchair and wiped tears from her sister Reba's
cheeks. "Oh Lord, honey, I bet they're playing up there in Heaven to beat
the band. Furbie and Hackney and Earley. *Hey, Earley up there!*" she called
to the ceiling, then began to tap in her white plastic heels. "When I get to
Heaven, gonna put on my shoes. Gonna dance all over God's Heaven,
Heaven. . . ."

"Oh, Lovie, don't cry," said Reba, crying. "This is so sweet of Vicky
Anna, fixing everybody dinner right when she just got back. And she says
she's having us all over again in two weeks' time. She said, 'I want y'all to
meet somebody.' 'Somebody special,' is what she said. Do you think
maybe Vicky's going to get married at last? Wouldn't that be wonderful?
Somebody to take care of her."

"Good golly, Miss Molly," Jimmy Clay whispered to his cousin Tildy
Harmon. "Hand me another one of those frozen dacs, darling. We got to
fill up now. You catch a winkadinkalinka at what ole Vicky Anna's serving on *Easter!* Well, I sure wouldn't want to call it ham and potato
salad!"

The counters of the old kitchen where Ada Hayes and Flonnie Rogers had baked and argued together for so many years were now stacked with dozens of white cartons, delivered to the house by Butch Shiono, who was out on the porch talking to Holly Hayes and Booger Blair about dual carburetors. Inside the cartons were each and every one of the Lotus House specialties, not the ordinary chow mein and sweet-and-sour pork that most Thermopyleans asked the Shionos to make, but the dishes the Japanese restaurateurs made for themselves and for a few favorite customers like Victoria Hayes.

At the long, crowded dining table, all the Hayeses fell silent and stared as Aura and Victoria placed platter after platter of Blue Willow china heaped with strange meats and fish and vegetables in front of them.

Victoria sat down, straightening her blue jacket. "Would anyone care to say Grace?"

"Grace," yelled Jimmy Clay. "Hotcha hotcha hotcha."

Then Lovie folded her hands. "For whatever we are about to receive, Lord help us be thankful," she said. "Pass the one that's pink and green." And they all began talking and laughing at once.

Two hours later, when the fortune cookies were passed around the table, Aura read hers aloud. It said, "This is your lucky day."

Jimmy read his aloud. " 'This is your lucky day.' That true, Tildy? Just say the word."

Reba read hers aloud. " 'This is your lucky day.' Why, they're all the same! Isn't that funny?"

And Raleigh Hayes, strolling out with Aura onto the wide front porch, read his aloud. " 'This is your lucky day.' "

As Orion brightened in the Easter sky, Raleigh sat with Aura in the green wood swing, while all around them his relations told each other stories about his father. "Remember the day Earley let the calf run down the street and Vicky had to chase it?" "Remember the day when . . ." "Remember the day . . ."

Raleigh blinked. Out in the middle of the quiet street, under the glow of light, he saw a small man dancing. "Aura," he said, "do you see anything over there?"

"Where, honey?"

"Over there in the street? You don't happen to see Daddy standing over there doing something that looks like a jig, do you?"

"No." She took her husband's hand, and rubbed the old gold ring. "But I'm glad you do."

CHAPTER

37

Why Raleigh Married Aura

"HONEY, WHAT IN THE WORLD are you doing!?" whispered Aura to her husband.

"In my Father's house are many mansions: if it were not so, I would have told you. I go to prepare a place for you."

"Doodling," he whispered back, and chuckled. He was doodling in his Prayer Book the design for the gold medallions, embossed with trumpets, which he planned to have made out of the bar of Dahlonega bullion. A medallion for each of the travelers on the journey to New Orleans. A souvenir, a little surprise.

"Shhh," whispered Aura. "Stop giggling."

"I can't help it," he whispered back, and burst into tears.

In St. Thomas Church, on Easter Monday, Raleigh Hayes sat laughing and crying through his father's funeral. Surrounded by all his relations, he sat in the front pew, where he had once sat Sunday after Sunday beside his mother. He sat beneath the pulpit from which long ago Earley Hayes had preached the sermons that had so outraged Mrs. PeeWee Jimson. What would she think now, to see the color of the young curate saying mass? Raleigh chuckled out loud, and was hushed again by Aura. Across the